Envoy: The Kharakian War

By

Daniel Adler

For information on upcoming works, follow me on Facebook!

Daniel Adler

@ArloweArtaven

To be updated, send questions or simply chat, tweet me on Twitter!

@ArloweArtaven

Text copyright © 2020 by Daniel Adler.
All rights reserved.

ISBN: 9798856520902
Imprint: Independently Published

Edited by Stephanie Kirk

Cover Art by Arcane Book Covers

V2

Acknowledgements:

I'd like to give my thanks to my wife, Hollie. Without your support and your love, alongside the occasional cup of tea, the realms of Äkin and beyond may never have come into existence. The book lives and breathes because of you.

-

I would also like to give thanks to my boy, Gabriel. I may not be the best father in the world, far from it perhaps. However, you make me strive to improve myself every day, to be a father worthy of you. Daddy loves you very much.

-

To Charlotte Horobin and Stephanie Kirk, thank you for spending so much of your time beta-reading my book to its entirety, picking up the pieces where my writing had faltered. Your criticisms have made the book far more than it could have ever been on its own.

-

Last but not least, I want to give the biggest thank you of all to Jack Gill, my (unofficial) writing tutor. You were there during some of my darkest days, aided my family back onto its feet more times than I can count and gave me the motivation to make this book a reality.
A truer friend, this world has never known. A friend in me, you shall always have.

Contents

Chapter One:

"If my God is fallible, so too are their creations."

"This is it. A tale I remember well. Remember fondly.

"Don't fret, I'll be with you every step of the way.

"Savour it as I have. A new perspective has much to teach.

"When you're ready, you may begin. Good luck."

*

"Though their origins are unknown, the celestial being known as Arn travelled into this plane of existence, living just beyond its border, yet close enough to shape it with their immense vision. While the entity created the landmasses that would come to be known as Argestra, Tyreiin, Shikith, Logritrias and Imikuin, Arn had also created a new being: a child called Aros. Aros, though weaker than their creator, was designed to follow in Arn's footsteps. Aros quickly understood the responsibility in creating the new world, and proceeded to assist in building it piece by piece. Together, they decided to name their new plane Äkin.

"As time passed, and the world began to bring itself together, Arn had begun to fall apart. At first, Aros believed it to be overexertion, but as Arn's form deteriorated, so too did the spirit's personality. At numerous points, Arn did not seem to be the same, sending plagues and tragedies upon their world, each more morbid than the last.

"This all came to a head with Arn rending apart, looking at a dark interpretation of oneself; two halves of a whole, one light, the other much darker. The being titled their form as Nra, and embodied all the darker traits that lived within Arn. While Arn tried to reason with Nra, claiming that the two of them could create a balanced world, Nra instead chose to claim the world of Katosus as their own. They saw Äkin as a plane

1

corrupted by Arn's vision that needed to be reworked.

"Arn and Nra fought, gauntlet and trident clashing respectively, shaking the foundations of Äkin. In an attempt to remove Nra's destructive outlook, Arn begrudgingly forced Nra's traits into their creations on Katosus, weakening the demon to strike it down. While Arn and Aros, the latter of whom hid from the fighting, considered Nra destroyed, this was not true. Nra had barely pulled their form back together, creating a separate plane known as Erethys to secretly reside in whilst recovering.

"As the eons rolled by following the colossal battle, there was peace. Arn and Aros continued to shape Katosus until it was truly complete. Arn's people, free of the power and difficulties of their creators, roamed the lands in search of their purpose, and the spirit looked forward to how the created would develop the world that was crafted for them. Their future was bright, or so the spirit thought. The created wouldn't have to face the darkness they once had. It wasn't long, however, until this belief was proven wrong.

"Upon the face of Arn's creation hid a terrible blemish. A gate, alien at the time, appeared upon Katosus releasing waves of unknown forces to strike at the created. Another gate appeared, followed by more blazing upon the horizon. Though Arn's creations could hold their own initially, the constant summoning of gates led to them being overwhelmed. To make matters worse, the graikhurst and Nra-devout orcs had joined forces with the invaders, turning traitor on their world. Nra had appeared nearby, watching Arn's world crumble beneath its creator. Arn in turn was aware of Nra's presence, though even the creator couldn't foresee what would soon follow.

"Arn had to make a decision. When the spirit had initially set Äkin into motion, a barrier had been placed around it to keep it safe from any that meant to interfere. Any

2

that made their way through the barrier would have their strength sapped and immortality briefly snatched away. The gods were not an exception to this rule.

"While Nra was unable to enter without invoking the barrier's wrath, the demons created in Erethys could, moving in for a full victory. Arn was unable to intervene without being attacked by its own barrier and had to either let their world fall or interrupt the assault on Katosus, weakening them.

"Arn chose to make the ultimate sacrifice, stunting their form to close the demon gates and, in turn, cripple the forces that had already arrived. As Arn passed through the barrier, Nra took the opportunity to let loose their trident, pinning the spirit to their beloved world. Arn was wounded and on the edge of life.

"As all seemed lost, Aros emerged from their hiding place amongst the stars, willing to expose their own identity to Nra to save what was left of Katosus. With Aros' support, Arn made one last attempt to stop Nra's conquest, and with a final push of energy, all were bathed in holy light. Blessed were the created that stood by their creator, and cursed were the ones that stood against the spirit.

"Arn's most recent creations, the humans, were now truly complete, able to wield magic and think for themselves. They became a true race like the others that had come before, freeing themselves of the chains that had been forced upon their incomplete forms. The elves and the dwarves, though cruel to the humans, remained loyal to their God, gifted as the humans were. The elves were now able to commune with nature due to their gentle tending of it and the dwarves would be able to craft life from cold stone, accompanied always by their familiar surroundings.

"The orcs and graikhurst, however, felt the force of Arn's anger at their betrayal. The orcs, known for their love of community and allies, were cursed with a natural lack of trust and agreement from the other races, and the graikhurst, known for their vanity and well-kept appearances, were corrupted into the small, hideous creatures they had created in their fictional writings: goblins.

"Nra was not forgotten by Arn's curse, making the creature unable to create the demon gates at their will. Though Arn did not have the power to remove Nra's demon-creating powers entirely, they did have enough power to limit it, forcing the being to one gate every few centuries.

"As their last breaths were drawn, Arn sadly divided Aros into all of their separate traits, scattering their child as Fragments to walk the world so that Nra could not abuse what remained of their power. The curse that had been placed upon them would not be reversed. In the end, the spirit became surrounded in a protective tomb, laying to rest at last. With both father and son departed and the demon armies decimated, Nra punished the demons and sealed them away, choosing to leave Äkin and its traitors behind."

*

A round of applause livened up the silent classroom, with the speaker sheepishly taking their seat as the applause died down.

Arlowe rose to his feet, impressed with the child's work. "There's no need to look so nervous, Imogen. I could feel the passion coming from you with every word you spoke. The only recommendation I can make would possibly be to touch on the various religions that were born from this event."

He looked to his sleeping tutor for confirmation, unsure of what had already been studied. "Though I'm sure there will be a lesson dedicated to that at some point."

Eased by his words, the weight had been lifted from the student's shoulders, evident by the relaxed slump she had taken.

Before Arlowe could pick any more students to present their work, the rhythmic clanging of metal began to fill the air. The students jerked up, aware that school had ended for the day, though their grizzled tutor had other plans. The stocky elder was awoken by the school bell; a grey-haired Cael raised an arm for his students to remain seated, understanding that they were eager to move.

"Nice try runts, but I had your guest here as a student too. Good luck gettin' outta my sight before I've closed the session." Arlowe played along, acting shocked that Cael could remember all the different ways he found to escape the clutches of his classroom.

Cael shot Arlowe a look, confirming that his memory was not disappearing with old age.

The tutor began scrawling onto the chalkboard, adding in a few crudely drawn stick figures to keep his students interested. Though the contents of the board looked like one big mess, Cael seemed proud of his art, throwing in a few artistic swishes to make it appear fancier.

"Right, with the First Demon Invasion out of the way, I want you all ta' look at the others, from the Second with the sirens all the way up ta' the Sixth with the titans. This stuff's important kiddos. Not only is each one an important mark in history since, you know, we're still alive, but also 'cause figuring this stuff out will help ta' understand the layout of our calendar. Got all that?"

The students nodded vigorously, eager to leave the confines of the room. Arlowe noticed a concealed sigh from his tutor, aware that he could keep them no longer.

"Fine, lemme be the jailer and say you're free to go. Just, please study for this. I'm not taking the blame if ya' fail!" he called out, hoping to get through to the children as they collected up their belongings, rallying for the door.

The students had already vanished, reminding Cael that his ranting was futile. The man planted himself in his trusty wooden chair, slamming his feet onto his desk before lighting up his pipe.

Though the tutor gestured for Arlowe to take a seat, he waved away the offer, leaning against one of the student's desks instead. Once Cael had taken a few puffs from his pipe, the old man felt ready to strike up a new conversation.

"Hey, thanks again for comin' down for the day and teaching them. Most of the subjects they eat up, but history? Nah."

Arlowe chuckled, reminding himself that Cael's history lessons weren't his strong suit either. "It's no problem, Cael. Besides, I know how much you like to kick back and take a nap while I'm doing your work. I picked up on a few of your tricks too. I hope your throne's comfortable."

"Ey!" Cael chuckled whilst choking on the smoke from his pipe. "After students like

6

you, a nap is strongly recommended ta' get through the day. Besides, the students are… educated."

He took one more puff from his pipe before giving it a few firm taps onto the desk, the old man wiping the ash down his front to compliment the ragged beard draping over his collar.

Arlowe watched and became aware of his tutor's shift in expression. Cael's playful eyes had been replaced with an inquisitive look, piercing straight through him. "Speakin' of thrones Arlowe; when will you be claimin' yours?"

Arlowe flinched. Cael had been posing this same question for the last few years and Arlowe had always found a way to dodge his bombardments of curiosity. Now though, he had nowhere to hide, and as his tutor had expected, his response came out the same as it always had. "I… don't think I'm ready."

The tutor stood; Arlowe was conscious of his repeated excuses. "Arlowe, you can't keep doin' this. The people need a leader, and you've been preparin' for the last six years. It was understandable when you were younger, but not now. We can't keep postponin'."

"There are so many things I haven't learned yet. I don't feel ready to guide them. Can you blame me?"

Cael placed his hand on Arlowe's shoulder. "I don't blame you kid; I couldn't do it. But if I can give you a little tough love? This is bigger than you. Between the Administration becomin' irate with the lack of a monarch and the increase in kharakian attacks, the people need someone ta' look up to, and if anyone in this city could fill that role, it'd be you."

Arlowe nodded, agreeing with his tutor's points. Cael returned a reassuring smile, trying to relight a portion of self-confidence in his student. His arms were held out, extending an invitation to a hug. The prince gladly accepted.

As the embrace was released, Arlowe began to make a move for the door, carrying himself with a sense of renewed purpose. Grasping the handle, he turned back to face Cael. "Thanks for the pep talk."

Cael looked up from an empty bottle of port that had miraculously appeared from nowhere, beaming with pride, though Arlowe was unsure at whether he was proud of his advice, or because of his alcoholism. "Don't mention it, kid. I just want what's best for you," he stated.

The prince smiled to himself, before leaving the classroom.

Arlowe made his way to the western side of Eyenridge. The last kharakian attack on the city had been especially brutal, with the molten beasts making enough of a push to heavily damage the outer wall.

One of the exploding kharakians had sent debris hurtling towards one of the taverns, and while there were only minor casualties, the tavern couldn't withstand the onslaught and toppled. Even now, Arlowe could remember pulling Cael from the carnage, with the man so drunk that he was more upset that his local watering hole had been destroyed than at his potential death.

Arriving at the site, Arlowe was welcomed by the workers and volunteers that had arrived earlier in the day, getting straight to work on rebuilding the tavern. Only the foundations of the ancient building remained, the ruined building one of Eyenridge's earliest works.

"That the prince?" one of the workers queried. "What's he doing here? Don't think I've ever had a royal on the work site."

"You must be new here," another called, working on the upper floor of the tavern. "Arlowe's one of us. Actually gives a damn about his people. Far back as I can remember he was pickin' up tools and earnin' his keep."

The prince was warmed by the praise, though he kept himself busy, not wanting to make a scene.

As the sun slowly traversed across the sky, Arlowe wiped the sweat from his brow, sweltering under its immense heat. Exhausted, he planted himself on a piece of nearby debris, drinking his body weight in water and rubbing the ache from his muscles. He stared up to the sky, watching the few clouds roll by in the deep blue above him.

For a moment, he felt as light as they did, drifting off into a world of his own. *How had the world become so complicated?* It only felt like yesterday that he sat by his parents, watching the sunset from the castle's balcony without a care in the world, with their hands in his, hoping that time would never march forward again.

Arlowe's hand tightened into a fist, trying desperately not to let go of the memory. *I wish you were here. I could really use your guidance.*

The memory was cut short by the feeling of eyes upon him. As he opened his own, Arlowe spotted a woman he didn't recognise staring at him a short distance away. Her golden-brown hair was tied back into a small ponytail with pointed ears peeking through.

As Arlowe had fully awoken from his daydream, a surge of anxiety hit him; his hand was instinctually raised to wave at the stranger. "H-hello?"

Seemingly amused by the response she received, the elf made her way over to him. "Hey! Sorry if ya' caught me staring. I wanted ta' make sure it was you!" the elf exclaimed, her accent catching the prince off-guard.

Arlowe, trying to keep his composure, gave himself a moment before responding. "I'm sorry, who did you think I was?"

"Aw jeez, ma' apologies stranger," murmured the elf, excusing herself. "I thought *you* were Arlowe Artaven. I'm a wanderer ya' see, and I heard through tha' grapevine that he was here. Sorry fer' wasting yer' time."

A few of the workers began to chuckle to themselves, causing the elf to cross her arms in frustration. "What's so funny, fellers? It was an easy mistake to make." Her twangy accent betrayed how flustered she had become.

Arlowe himself laughed a little, though he waved his amusement away to set things straight. "They're not laughing because you got it wrong. They're laughing because you got it right and then doubted yourself. Pleased to meet you." Arlowe extended a hand to the elf, noticing the excitement in her eyes.

"Yer' kiddin' me! I've spent many years travellin', but I've never met a monarch before. It's an honour," voiced the elf, shaking Arlowe's hand with a great deal of enthusiasm, bowing her head in respect. The elf's grip was strong, a trait that didn't match the friendliness of its owner.

"There's no need to be so formal. It's kind of embarrassing getting a reaction like that. I'm not even the ruling monarch yet," answered Arlowe, evidently taken aback by the elf's intrigue. "What brings you to Eyenridge, Miss…?"

The elf took notice of Arlowe's shy personality, taking her energy levels down a notch for his sake. "There's no need ta' be so formal," mimicked the elf. "Tha' name's Schukara. Schukara Parle. I was passing through yesterday and saw these folks havin' a spot of trouble, so I thought I'd lend a hand."

A guild emblem on her breastplate caught the prince's eye. "You're a part of the Warforged Guild?" he posed, shrouding his distrust with a smile.

"I was, but that was a long time ago."

What stood out most about Schukara was the suit of steel armour wrapped around her, catching the light of the warm midday sun and clear skies, making it even more impressive to Arlowe that she was working so hard in such blistering conditions. The suit had its share of scars, sending the prince's imagination wild as to where each and every one of the markings had come from, each one a story of its own.

His amazement brought his question to light, curious at how she was barely phased by the searing weather. "How are you working with your armour on? I'm only in my casual clothes and I'm struggling."

Schukara snorted, waving her hand in the air. "Ya' call this hot? I hail from tha' southern reaches of Ryvineon. We huddle 'round our fires in this weather."

Arlowe shrugged. He had read about the climates of the other countries, though unlike his father, he had never travelled outside of his own borders.

The two continued to work on the tavern as the day moved on, blue skies moving to crimson as the two teamed up to cut down on the number of tasks they had left to do.

As Arlowe dropped tools and hammered his thumb preoccupied by his thoughts, an occasional glance from his new friend became more apparent after every incident.

"S'cuse me fer' pryin', but is somethin' on yer' mind?" Schukara queried. "Arlowe?"

The elf's words brought his mind back to the tavern, his fingers barely avoiding another beating from the offending hammer. "If yer' not feelin' too good, I'm sure no-one would mind ya' headin' out. You've done plenty."

Arlowe finished repairing one of the walls, placing the worn tool by one of the workbenches. He gave the nearby pillar a shove to make sure it was stable before leaning on it, while Schukara spun one of the chairs around, sitting on it with her arms resting on its sturdy back.

"I mentioned earlier that I'm not a ruling monarch yet. Truth is, I don't know what to do. I don't know what it means to be a king. I'm worried that I'll make the wrong decisions and that people will suffer for my mistakes. Ever since my father passed, I've tried to educate myself as much as possible for the role, but it's been years, and I can't keep the people of Eyenridge waiting forever. The kharakians certainly won't." Arlowe took a moment to collect his thoughts. "Forgive the request, but if you found yourself in my boots, what would you do?"

Schukara spent a good portion of time mulling over the question. The elf's bright and cheery persona had been replaced by a deep concentration; faces pulled at her internal thoughts.

After a while, Schukara made eye contact with Arlowe once more, looking like her mind was made up. "If it were me, I wouldn't worry about makin' mistakes."

The prince cocked his head. "I... don't understand. I don't think it's that simple."

"Look at it like this, Arlowe. These people respect ya' fer' tha' things you've done fer' them, not yer' money nor yer' title. You've already been makin' decisions, ya' just didn't have tha' title while ya' were doin' them," she stated. "Tha' way I see it, treat yer' title like just that: a title. If ya' put tha' people ya' care about first, then what're ya' worrying about? I think ya' know what I mean."

Arlowe remained silent for a moment, processing what Schukara had told him. As he moved away from the comfort of the pillar, a smile beamed across his face, confirming to Schukara that he had found the answer he was desperately seeking. "You're right."

Arlowe began to brim with energy, ecstatic that he had solved the puzzle in his mind. "All this time, I've been so worried about making mistakes that I haven't allowed myself to make any. I spent so much time trying to learn how to be a leader, that I never tried *being* one," he pronounced, confident in his appearance. "I know what I have to do."

The mercenary lifted herself from her seat, pushing it aside with her boot before clasping Arlowe's hand in response.

"May your travels treat you well, Schukara Parle," the prince thanked. "You've allowed me to see things clearly."

Schukara rolled her eyes, placing her hand on Arlowe's back to push him towards the broken doorway. "Stop it, you'll make me blush. It was an honour ta' make yer' acquaintance, sir."

Arlowe turned to bow for Schukara before making haste towards the castle, eager to reveal his plan to Cael.

*

Climbing staircase after staircase looking for him, the tutor was nowhere to be found. The guards he questioned were sure that they had seen him within the castle, though none were sure where he currently was, his quarters empty.

Deciding to give up the search, Arlowe returned to his room; the prince half-expecting to find the tutor in a drunken mess in one of the guest rooms again.

Allowing not a creak from his door, the familiarity of his room drew the prince like a moth to a flame. His tensions were eased, free of watching eyes.

Shedding the clothes from his body, Arlowe approached the mirror; a bowl of fresh water was prepared beneath it. With the sweat washed from his weary body, chestnut hair slicked away from his eyes, the prince turned his attention to the scar branded on the right of his face. He delicately dabbed at the burns as they travelled down his arm and torso, ending just above his ankle.

Returning his blade to its display, Arlowe looked over the books on his nightstand, curious of which adventure his mind would depart on tonight. *The Persecution of Necromancy*? Only a handful of years into his adulthood, his interest in history had only grown stronger, though his mind sought comfort, not knowledge. *The Spectral Cat*? A tale born of superstition and overactive imaginations; Arlowe was uninterested in either.

The final book piqued his interest: *The Pursuits of an Argestran Knight.* "I've read this too many times," he commented, though he picked it up with glee, flicking to his favourite passages. "One more time couldn't hurt."

His gaze soon rested over the bed to his side, the silk sheets glistening from the candlelight. Arlowe cleared his throat, sheepishly advancing upon the lavish piece of furniture.

"Oh, hello. I didn't see you there. Do you come here often?" The bed didn't respond, though the prince reacted to an unseen admission. "You've had your eye on me for this long? Well, you may have my attention for the rest of the night."

As he sunk into the doughy pillows, the prince's door slammed open. Arlowe jumped out of his skin.

Cael stood in the doorway, breathing heavily. "I don't know what you were doin', and right now, I don't care. You need to come with me. Now."

Arlowe put his trousers and boots back on, confused at Cael's request. "C-Cael? Where've you been? I was looking for you. I've made up my mind!"

Cael entered the room, picking up Arlowe's blade before pushing him towards the door. "That's swell kid, but there's somethin' that you need ta' see."

The prince pulled himself away from his old mentor, concerned by his fearful expression. "I don't understand. What could be more important than—"

Cael swiftly cut Arlowe off with two simple words. "Look. Outside."

He hesitated, still expecting one of Cael's hilarious pranks to come to light, though the tutor kept a serious expression. The prince moved towards the balcony, ready to see what the view had in store for him.

He froze. Fear anchored his feet in place, forcing him to take in the horrific sight.

14

In the distance, the city of Kharaki could be seen hovering in the sky, expelling molten lava to the crater beneath. The sight of the floating mass didn't frighten Arlowe. On the contrary, the city was quite a common view; the cursed city that was born of Eyenridge's hostility.

What shook Arlowe was the stream of light heading straight towards them. Each light was a single kharakian marching to their city. "There are hundreds ready to strike with hundreds more at their rear to replace the fallen," Cael noted.

"That's impossible. They've never come in such numbers." Arlowe turned to Cael, feeling the fusion of fear and adrenaline flowing through him. "Sound the alarm. They'll be here any—"

An explosion sounded, signalling the forced entry of enemy forces. Their strike was sudden, and Eyenridge had already run out of time.

Chapter Two:

"If I was burdened with eternal life, what could I do to stay so innocent of the world?"

13ᵗʰ Thuvalos

Land's Legacy

2084∞ (Current Age)

Arlowe and Cael charged down to the castle's entry hall to close the portcullis as a means to temporarily keep out the invaders. They entered to find that the castle's guardsmen had already begun shepherding people inside to keep them safe, though from assault after assault, they were already beginning to tire.

The prince rushed to the guard operating at the castle's entrance. "Gonald, bring down the portcullis," he ordered, grasping the guard's shoulder. "Things are going to get a whole lot worse if we let those things into the castle and—"

It wasn't hard for Arlowe to notice Gonald's hands securely wrapped around his hammer, preparing to strike at the release latch whilst trying his best to hold his shaky composure.

"I can't, sir. My partner, Gregory, is still out there," the guard whimpered. "We were ushering people in when a spear struck him. I last saw him hidden behind that pillar over there. I don't want to leave him to those things, but I…"

"I'll go out there and grab him," he blurted, quick to find a compromise as the guilt weighed down on him; no one left behind. "If another wave of kharakians gets too close, I want you to close off the castle."

"Sir? I can't leave you out there."

Arlowe drew his blade from its sheath, preparing to enter the hellish cityscape. "We need to protect as many lives as possible. If we're going to stick to that, we need to take risks. Are you ready, soldier?"

The guard nodded, visibly swallowing as he moved to one side.

Arlowe took a deep breath, sprinting in between the pillars to find the unfortunate soul, keeping himself hidden from the enemies' line of sight. *Where are you hiding, Gregory?*

Upon reaching the farthest pillars, the prince found a uniformed guard grasping a wound on his leg, desperately trying to stop the bleeding. Gregory was eager to send him away, frantically waving his arm, though Arlowe had no intention of heeding it.

"What are you doing out here, sir?" the guard questioned, frustrated in his tone. "It's too dangerous. Head back and save yourself. I'd rather die on the battlefield than in my sleep! Don't try to change my—"

Arlowe moved a finger to his mouth to hush the honourable speech, hoping to reawaken some sense in him with his own words. "You deserve better than bleeding out in the corner out of our view. I'm getting you on your feet and back to the castle. Do you understand?"

Though the guard motioned to argue, the stern gaze from a member of the royal family gambling their life for his own had set his perspective straight. Defeated, Gregory held out his arm in a huff.

Arlowe took the offered arm across his back, lifting the trembling guard up and back to safety.

Pillar after pillar, the two crept back to the safety of the castle. The roars of the kharakians charged by them, put down like animals by the archers holding the line within the castle and atop the walls.

One of the archer's arrows had not fully disposed of a stray kharakian, with the beast taking its threat to new heights. Knowing of its likely death, the creature ignited itself, blowing down the pillar that Arlowe and Gregory neared.

The prince stood before his guardsman with a raised shield, taking the brunt of the blast for himself as they were both blown back.

"Argh, fuck!" yelled Gregory as they collapsed, clutching his leg in agony.

Arlowe had attempted to cover his mouth, though their presence had been revealed to the growing horde. The prince had no choice but to carry Gregory down the most direct path, making haste through the open to the castle portcullis.

Stealth mattered not. The glowing eyes of the beasts were upon them now.

A spear hurtled by their heads, flying with enough force to hit the portcullis guard directly in the chest, sending his body further into the hall. Cael took Gonald's hammer into his grasp, repositioning to bring the metal gate down himself.

The bellows of the kharakians grew ever closer; Arlowe's attention was brought to his flank. Ascending the stairs to the castle, the kharakians stood front and centre.

Their skin comprised of an igneous substance, their form humanoid; the stature of the beasts was far taller than the most mountainous of men. An unholy fire surrounded them, which the beasts could utilise as projectiles just as effectively as the spears that they could call from the smoke that billowed from their bodies.

Arlowe pushed the injured Gregory towards Cael in time to put up his blade, parrying the impact of a kharakian's spear.

Face to face with its prey, the molten beast uttered only a single word: "Doomed."

The prince moved his blade away, dodging to one side to avoid a spear brought down upon him. Arlowe's sword had found its mark shortly after, piercing the kharakian before a swift kick sent it reeling back.

The kharakian fell to the floor with a tremendous thud, convulsing upon impact. Arlowe was well aware at what this meant, swiftly retreating back to the castle.

As the prince dived under the lowering portcullis, a volatile explosion rocked those nearby. The fallen kharakian was now nothing more than a scorch mark upon the stone floor.

Arlowe returned to a room rife with panic. Civilians from the various sectors of the city were gathered within the entry hall, looking for lost ones or tending to their wounded.

A handful of the guardsmen began sliding a beam under the portcullis, preventing the remaining kharakians outside from raising it; their frenzied fists made their presence known loud and clear.

Gregory was slumped near the castle's eastern stairwell alongside Cael, too preoccupied with Gonald's chest wound to be of any assistance to another.

With the old man preoccupied and the healers overwhelmed by the city's casualties, Arlowe knelt to Gregory, resting his hand over the spear that remained fixed within his leg.

"That spear needs to come out. Its fire will continue to turn you to ash until there's nothing left," the prince voiced in concern, examining the wound. "It's now or never, Gregory. The sanamancers that survived won't make it to you in time."

"S-sanamancer?"

"Sanamancy. Healing magic. You'll make it through this."

"No, I-I can't," protested the guard, his face burning up. "I'm not strong enough."

"This encounter with the beasts wasn't your first, right? It won't be your last."

"My liege, I—"

Distracting him, Arlowe snapped one side of the spear, ripping out the other half to Gregory's displeasure. The suffering guard cried out to Arn, screaming in agony as he watched the open wound seal itself, leaving only a bloodied hole behind.

"Their weapons will slowly tear you apart if left embedded, though once removed, their heat cauterises the wound." Arlowe explained, showing the guard the broken spear within his hands falling to ash. "I've been around their destruction long enough to know."

The tutor had already noted his pupil's arrival, glad that his compromise came to fruition. "Good thing you didn't get stuck out there, ya' fool," voiced Cael, leaving an unconscious but stable Gonald to his rest.

"I had a plan. I know what I'm doing," Arlowe replied, catching a glimpse of a smile upon his tutor's face. "Besides, if things went wrong, I know I can count on you."

Cael chuckled to himself. "I may keep an attractive physique, but don't ask me ta' lift that portcullis for you, kid. It'd take Arn's big toe just to budge that thing now that we've got it locked down."

The old man took in his surroundings, extinguishing his jovial tone. "From what I've heard, the northern sector of the city is pretty much a dead zone. Only beasties in there. The eastern wall isn't looking too good either. Our troops on the internal walls have been doing a solid job of keepin' them away, but there's just too many. I don't know how we're gettin' out of here. Any suggestions?"

Arlowe made his way to the grand dining table without so much as a word, with Cael simply following in tow. The prince removed the cloth that adorned it before holding out his hand to the tutor. "I may have something. Could I borrow your knife?"

Cael patted down his jacket before reaching into his boot to reveal an ornate dagger. "We've been over this. When you ask for the knife, you ask for her by name. But sure, Mavis would be happy to help."

Arlowe took Mavis from Cael, shaking his head. The prince began to carve shapes into the wood, forming a crude view of Eyenridge. His finger was placed upon what

20

appeared to be the north of the city.

"As you mentioned, the northern sector of the city is overrun. From what we saw up top, the guards are still fighting back the enemy along the eastern sector, but it's a losing battle," Arlowe clarified. "My plan is to extract any survivors from the east and lead them to the top of the wall and across the bridge that connects it to the castle. Once we have everyone housed inside, we can destroy the bridges to keep the kharakians from us."

Cael shook his head in disapproval. "Getting everyone ta' the castle's great, Arlowe, but what then? We have no way to evacuate the survivors you'll have saved. The northern and eastern gates are too dangerous, kharakians are beginnin' to appear from the south and the western gate is blocked. It hasn't been repaired yet."

"It's not the western gate we need, it's the western wall," Arlowe noted, taking Mavis once more to slice through his carving of the wall. "We can use the cannons around the western side of the castle to punch a hole through, giving us an opening for our evacuation. The old ballistae can be fitted with cables to form a stable line, sliding the survivors down them once we know they're secure."

The old man had his hands firmly placed upon the table, eyeing up his student's plan to the tiniest detail. A nod of his head indicated to Arlowe that it was the best chance of survival they had.

"Those ballistae were meant to be ornamental. When needs must," he growled. "Come on. We don't have time ta' stand here and plan while our boys are out there getting slaughtered. Head ta' the east. I'll keep you covered from above."

Cael was able to grab Arlowe's wrist before he ran off, getting his attention once more. "Hurry. The kharakians are floodin' in as it is, but give them enough time, and they'll be in here too. What they lack in intelligence, they make up for in numbers."

The prince sprinted into the eastern sector, exiting the tower to see the carnage first-hand. The eastern portion of Eyenridge was home to the training camps for its armies, though while the troops had always been prepared to fight, a battle between them and the seemingly limitless hordes of kharakians was always fated to go one way. Their corpses had been unceremoniously tossed to one side, left in a smouldering heap.

Arlowe passed through the destroyed barracks and training areas to encounter his soldiers working alongside members of the Warforged Guild still holding the line, with many of their casualties simply hiding behind those that could still fight.

Among them, he could easily make out a helmeted Schukara, assisting and giving out orders, flowing through the battlefield like a heavily armoured typhoon. The prince moved up, slicing his way through a kharakian that meant to strike at their flank.

Schukara could see Arlowe entering into the fray, the breaks in the continuous onslaught making it possible. Taking cover inside of a kharakian crater, the elf hailed for him to join her, raising her visor to give clear sight.

Arlowe leapt in, avoiding the collection of spears aiming to take his head before dusting himself off.

Despite their situation, Schukara couldn't help but smirk at the prince's lack of armour, or clothes. "I'm not one ta' judge, but don'cha think ya' should be wearin' somethin' a lil' more... protective?" she mocked. "Are the common people allowed to see their prince in all his glory?"

Arlowe noted her response and ignored it, peeking over the crater to get a better look at his surroundings. "How are things here? Are you doing okay?"

Schukara shrugged. "We're doin' as well as we can. I've been leadin' whatever members of tha' Warforged I could find, and we hooked up with yer' guardsmen a lil' while ago. Quite a few of us have been injured, and a few more are down fer' good. I hope you've got a plan, cus' we could sure use one."

"I want you to go with anyone who is willing, and travel through the city, from here to the south sector and onto the western, collecting any survivors along the way. I'll take your injured, and any who can't go that far with me to the top of the wall where we'll cross the bridge and destroy it," Arlowe reasoned. "Sound good?"

Schukara looked back at the kharakians, fearing for those still fighting. "That's good 'n' all, but how're ya' gonna grab their attention?" Schukara argued. "We can't leave if we're fightin'. We need an openin'."

"Everyone, fall back!" Arlowe ordered, drawing his blade. The sword was pointed to the sky, before being aimed at the enemy.

Out of nowhere, explosions rained down upon the kharakians, decimating those in the immediate area. Schukara looked up to see Cael and more of the guardsmen manning the eastern line of internal cannons, waving from above. Arlowe sheathed his blade once more, nudging her. "There's your opening."

"Those willin', on me!" Schukara bellowed as she slammed down her visor, charging off armed with her dual blades. Arlowe moved over to the injured, lifting one up with each arm, escaping back the way he had arrived.

Just as the survivors were rushed into the tower, the next wave of kharakians had already reinforced the eastern sector, replacing their cannonball-riddled comrades in no time.

One of the guards dropped a barricade as another knocked over a barrel of dirt to block the reinforced door, though none of them were convinced that it would hold.

Ascending the stone stairs to the wall above, the prince urged those beside him forward; their stomachs sank as the sound of splintering wood echoed from the bottom of the wall.

As they reached its peak, Arlowe rushed over to the walls edge, swinging his blade to acquire the attention of those at the castle. "Fire! Fire at the supports under the bridge!"

Cael grabbed one of the cannons in frustration, moving it into position. "If you're not careful, I'll end up killing you! Get your ass over here!" he yelled, holding fire as the survivors made it over to the safety of the castle.

The prince stood his ground, allowing all who followed him the time to make it across as his steel struck down the first of those who intended to follow him. The cannons, however, had already begun to fire, pressed to service faster by the sight of the kharakians standing upon the bridge, now in conflict with their prince.

Though the survivors had made it back alive, Arlowe's own fate was not yet decided. The bridge shook to pieces before his eyes, the cracks of the rumbling bridge growing larger by the second. He had to wait for the right time to move, making sure that none could follow him back to the city's last bastion of safety.

The pressure of the horde was becoming too much to bear. For every kharakian he defeated, two more took its place. The young prince stood valiantly against the beasts until he felt the bridge fully surrender to his forces, throwing himself at what remained stable.

Predicting it so, the bridge collapsed from under his feet, his body feeling the sudden lurch of gravity's pull. To his tutor's held breath, Arlowe had managed to grab the edge, lifting himself to safety. The old man lent over the cannon taking a deep sigh of relief, calling for a flask from one of his men.

"If I'm not careful, he'll end up killin' me. My heart can only take so much."

As Cael moved the guards on the cannons to new firing positions, Arlowe passed by. The prince gestured for his tutor to follow once more.

24

The two moved through the bustling crowd, ending up by the ballista on the western side of the castle. Arlowe began loading a round into the machine. "Have the other bridges been dealt with?"

Cael stepped to the same ballista, attaching a thin cable to the giant javelin. "The southern bridge was brought down by an explosion, but it wasn't us. I'm assumin' that the other group you were with down there were responsible. As for the western bridge, I had a separate team bring down the western bridge as we took down the eastern one, just in case," Cael explained. "Are we ready to evacuate?"

"Carry on sorting the ballistae. I'll be right back," Arlowe replied, leaving briskly. He returned a short while later with a handful of men, dragging boxes filled with a collection of items to the ballista his tutor was currently preparing.

Cael looked through Arlowe's gatherings, finding things such as prison shackles, linens, flag hooks and horse saddles, evidently concerned. "Fill me in. What's with all this junk? Is your head on straight?"

The prince dragged over a second container, ripping open the lid to reveal similar items to his last haul. "They were the only things suitable for sliding down on that were in the castle's storage. They'll have to do."

"Are we ready to land the final blow on the western wall, sir?" one of the guardsmen at the cannons yelled; his voice could barely be heard over the castle's panicked inhabitants.

Arlowe looked to Cael, who nodded in approval. Cael moved to one of the cannons himself, aiming it directly at the western wall. "Ready yourselves, men!" Cael ordered, signalling for the row of cannons to fire at the weakened wall. "Light the fuses!"

The barrage of cannonballs filled the sky, erupting upon their contact with the western wall. As more were fired, bombarding their target, the weakened wall tired of the assault. Accepting its demise, the weakened stone crumbled away, allowing those it had originally guarded to escape its protective embrace.

With an opening made, Arlowe called to the guards on the ballistae to fire, sending their javelins to the western sector below. The cables attached sailed through the air, digging into the ground to form a stable line.

It hadn't taken long for those within the castle to take notice of Arlowe's plan, overwhelming the Fertren Guard to escape the doomed city. In response, Cael rallied the remainder of the guards to take control of the situation and intervene between the citizens and the ballistae, aiding their escape via the line down as quickly and safely as they could manage.

Arlowe left with what few guards could be spared to run back and forth between the castle's stores, replenishing the items that were rapidly being depleted to descend to safety.

Though the number of survivors within the castle were lowering, this had not stopped the kharakians from wanting to enter where they had been previously been denied.

While the evacuation had been going at full steam, the beast's numbers had continued to swell, now creating dead zones in the eastern and southern sectors of the city. The castle's portcullis adamantly stood its ground, though it was only a matter of time before it too would fall.

After the fall of the final civilian, what remained of the Fertren Guard took to the lines to reach the lower levels of Eyenridge, leaving those within to watch helplessly as the kharakians poured all of their effort into entering the castle, eager to strike at the guards left behind.

Cael's voice bellowed over the sound of the monstrous roars from outside, calling to the guards to quicken their pace. "Come on! We don't have all day. I don't want to be

26

in here when the beasts break through!"

Pummelled by the projectiles and explosions of the molten creatures, the walls surrounding the portcullis had been peeled back like a fine fruit, revealing what was left of the chains connected to the grating blocking their way.

Working as a collective, the kharakians changed their approach, using a portion of their horde to pull on the chains within the walls while others near the portcullis began trying to lift it. With their immense numbers, the steel portcullis began to screech as it rose, the metal twisting as the beam beneath shattered.

Three of the guards approached the portcullis to hold off the monsters. The kharakians made sure to use them as an example.

Two of the guards were pulled under to their deaths, pleading for Arn to save them, with the third taking a spear through his skull whilst trying to put his weight down upon the rising metal.

Cael took hold of a necklace from his shirt, originally concealed beneath it. "Not sure how well this is gonna work, but I'd suggest movin' back," he stated, pushing his free hand forward towards the first kharakian to squeeze under the defunct portcullis. "Sorry in advance about the castle!"

The kharakian began to light up, convulsing in a similar fashion to the one Arlowe had stabbed earlier. With an ear-piercing scream, the kharakian detonated, bringing the floor above down on top of the intruders.

Cael swung his hand in pain, hardly an expert with the spell he had cast. "I learned how ta' cast enrage spells purely for these blighters. Not sure how it works, don't care either. It's bought us a few more seconds." He turned to Arlowe. "Stray spears took out the ballistae we set up, but there's still one left. Let's go."

With most of the castle's resources used, Cael pulled out his sword, placing it on top of the line ready to slide down with Arlowe towards the evacuees.

As Arlowe drew his own blade, another explosion rocked what remained of the castle, sending Cael down the line prematurely.

"Arlowe, we're out of time. Get down the line!" Cael yelled, unable to prevent his descent.

As the prince regained his footing, a kharakian had charged onto the platform, launching a spear in his direction. Though the spear missed its mark, some of the kharakians had already circled him, cutting him off from the last functional ballista.

Unable to use the line to escape, Arlowe braced himself, engaging the horde in the hopes that he could find another way out in time.

The prince clashed with the nearest kharakian, disarming its spear before lopping off its arm. However, as the beast started to regenerate its lost limb, another kharakian lunged forward, eager to take one more life from Eyenridge.

Arlowe continued to fight the horde, aware of the futility. With every second, the ballista grew further from his reach. His body shook from exhaustion. His anger was matched only by his sadness upon the sight of those that had not made it, both atop the castle and upon the cobbles of the streets far below.

"To my last breath," he muttered to himself, struggling to hold his defensive stance. His throat was sore, choked on the sickly scent of the kharakian's victims. "They'll start again. Without me."

The kharakians from below had been clever, cutting free the last cable that granted the prince his escape. Though his life was now forfeit, the tiring prince continued to hold the monsters at bay upon the harrowing edge, buying the survivors precious seconds to flee from the city.

From the molten masses, another spear was thrown, piercing through Arlowe's arm, pinning him to the ballista at his back. One of the kharakians ran forward, ripping the spear out of the prince before swinging it into his chest, knocking him to the ground.

Using what little strength his body would still allow, Arlowe took his blade, thrusting it forward towards the offending beast with all his might, hoping to at least even the score.

Alas, as the blade was removed, the kharakian began to convulse. Even with a weakened shove from his shield to push it away, the resulting shockwave sent Arlowe over the edge.

The few remaining evacuees within the city below could only watch in horror as their monarch fell from the castle. In his descent, Arlowe could make out Cael and Schukara attempting to force their way back into the city, only to be denied entry by the mages using their magic to seal the breach; their manipulation of the earth replacing the opening they had made.

Time froze for Arlowe, who felt at peace with the world. He had done all he could to aid his people, which eased his conscience. He found it amusing that only a few hours ago, he had asked for the guidance of his mother and father, only for Arn to reunite them so soon.

With a tired smile still on his face, Arlowe closed his eyes, preparing to meet the face of the creator he had been taught so much about.

Time stood still no longer, and he was ready.

Chapter Three:

"If a wise man is always ready to perish, what is said of the man who returns?"

Unknown Date

Unknown Season

2084∞ (Unknown)

"Another visitor enters our humble abode. I do hope he's friendlier than the last!"

"Not now, my love. This human has multiple lacerations and broken bones. Our healers are doing their best, but it will be some time before he can even move. I don't envy him."

"Silver lining; the longer he sleeps, the more time we have to prepare the festivities! Ooh, I can't wait!"

*

Arlowe awoke in shock, unaware of his current location. Hampered, grunting in pain, the prince regretted bolting up so quickly. His arm grasped his searing wound. Oddly, the discomfort quickly vanished, drawing his eyes to an alarming discovery.

The hole left by the spear was gone, leaving only a scorched scar behind. Furthermore, most of the injuries he had sustained fighting the kharakians back had gone too, though a dull pain still remained.

Arlowe took a closer look at his surroundings. Someone had laid him upon a stone slab with what appeared to be medical tools lining the walls around him. Most of the ornaments adorning the room were shaped from stone, the walls decorated with intricate carvings.

As the aching prince slid across the slab to place his feet on the ground, he spotted a set of bright green eyes watching him from the corner of the room.

Arlowe sat in silence, unsure of how to react; his body was as still as the eyes that watched him. The two exchanged blinks before the owner of the eyes, still concealed within the shadows, made their escape through the nearest doorway.

Still unsettled by the recent events, Arlowe scanned the rest of the room for any more curious eyes. Content that he was alone; he slowly got to his feet, stretching out the stiffness. "I really hope that was Aros, or a Fragment, or an Angel. Erethys, I'll take anything over finding that I'm actually in Erethys…"

What he assumed to be a medical room was left in favour of what appeared to be a labyrinth. Green crystals hung from the walls, lighting up both the halls and signs above each of the doors Arlowe came across. The language looked like Dwarvish, though Arlowe had no idea of what the language deciphered into.

"Dwarvish? In the afterlife? They couldn't have used a more universal language?" he commented, proceeding with his exploration. "Typical."

The prince began peering into room after room, looking for any signs of life; his mind was eager to make sense of his place in this world or the beyond.

Though he found no-one, he had noticed that he was treading the same ground, passing the same rooms despite making no turns. The curious green flames flickering from the torches offering him no aid.

Arlowe drew a circle into the sand before continuing in a straight line. As he predicted, the circle came across his path again, confusing him all the more.

Deciding to take a different approach, Arlowe took a turn, which placed him on a path away from the familiar. As he travelled far enough, he spotted a man and a woman ahead of him talking. He prayed that they weren't figments of his hopeful imagination.

"Hey, excuse me. I'm looking for someone to help show me the way?" he called.

Like the eyes earlier, the two perked up at being noticed, running further into the hallway. Arlowe decided to follow, his stomach uneasy at the lack of communication.

As he pushed onwards, the sound of hushes and whispers began to fill the hallways, becoming progressively louder as Arlowe delved further. The young prince used these whispers to guide him, craving the answers to the myriad of questions that plagued him.

His search came to an end upon finding a large stone archway granting entry into a pitch-black room. Though he believed it unwise to walk in blind, Arlowe grasped the hilt of his blade, reluctantly entering against his better judgment.

"Hello? Is anyone there?" he asked, expecting contact at any moment. "I need to know where I—" Caught off-guard, an unknown force swiped at his hip to steal his scabbard, leaving him defenceless against whatever was in the room with him.

The room flooded suddenly with light, both from the hundreds of crystals lamps lighting in unison and a giant emerald-like structure hanging from the ceiling. Not only was Arlowe blinded, but also deafened by the sudden sound of applause.

His senses overwhelmed, the prince fell backwards.

As the heavy approach of boots marched towards him, all Arlowe could do was try to adjust to the intensity of the light as soon as he could. His fatigue left him exposed, his adrenaline unable to push his body any further.

As the light became bearable, a large man stood above him. His eyes shone green like the others that stood within the halls, though they did not pull attention away from his bushy, ginger mutton chops, proudly decorating his cheeks.

With a giant grin across his face, the man took the hand Arlowe had been using to wipe his eyes, shaking it with the greatest of pleasure. "It is very nice to finally meet your acquaintance stranger! I would like to welcome you personally to our home! I hope the party we planned is to your liking?"

32

Arlowe was stunned. In his search for answers, he had found only more questions. He picked himself up, examining the hall in more detail.

With the lights on, he was able to identify giant stone dining tables which travelled the length of the room, ending at the other end only to give space for four separate thrones, each with a pillar towering behind them. To each side of the room, crowds of green-eyed people stood patiently waiting for his reaction; their clothes were torn and ragged.

What are all these people doing here, the prince thought. *Have they shared the same fate as I?*

Arlowe figured that saying anything would be better than nothing at all, hoping to gain any kind of understanding. His mind was baffled by this 'party'.

"Sorry to spoil the mood," he mumbled, "but what afterlife is this? Where am I?"

Laughter was the only response Arlowe received, which only confused him further.

"Your statement is *dead* wrong, young one! The only thing that's *expired* is whatever fell from your arse when we scared you!" the giant bellowed, tearing up at his jokes.

The prince was unimpressed by the jests being made at his expense. As his patience dwindled, a red-haired woman clad in iron armour approached, nudging the man out of her way.

"I apologise for having no-one meet you in the medical room." She punched the man's arm, bringing his enthusiasm to order. "Apologies are also to be made for my husband's abysmal sense of humour."

The mountain of a man loudly clapped his hands, sending his people to begin feasting and dancing. The woman gestured for Arlowe to join her further into the room, to which he followed behind warily.

"So, where am I? This can't be Erethys. You're no demons. The people's obedience indicates that you're someone of rank." The prince paused. "Could you be Arn?"

"Don't give him a title like that. I won't be able to fit his head through any doors for the next week," the woman mocked, wearing a smirk upon her face. "Why do you believe you are deceased, child?"

Arlowe was astounded. "My last memory was being flung to my death. The next thing I know, I wake up somewhere completely alien to me. How does that not sound like the afterlife?"

The husband chuckled to himself. "Interesting predicament. He has you there, my sweet."

As they approached the thrones, the armoured woman pointed to a staircase; the steps led to a portal covered in green markings.

"I'm unaware of what happened prior, but you came from there," she voiced. "There was another, a woman that came through, injured like you. Battered, bruised and in need of medical assistance. She believed that she had died too. Sounds similar."

The man sat in his throne, perplexed by the situation. "Maybe the gate chooses those worthy to be gifted to us? To restore them and return them to whence they came?" Sipping at his wine, the man refreshed his parched throat. "The gods love to torture the pterravun, it seems."

The pterravun? The prince knew not of this race of people. He knew of many names: Human and demon, elf and dwarf, goblin and orc, aautgal and dragon, but pterravun? *How long had they existed in their world?*

"So you're, what? Underground people?" Arlowe queried. "Who get sent those on the edge of life?"

The husband shrugged his shoulders. "We know little more than you do, but yes, that about sums it up."

34

Arlowe turned his attention back to the portal, barely able to make out a destroyed Eyenridge through it. "And I can leave this place? If that's true, then I can't be dead. This isn't an afterlife."

The two remained silent, unable to comprehend Arlowe's situation. Arlowe on the other hand, had begun to scale the stairs, devising strategies to reclaim his city.

"This must be fate," he muttered to himself, turning his attention to the inhabitants of the cave. "Will you join me? I don't mean to impose, as you've done so much for me already, but with your numbers here we could take back my city."

The woman shook her head. "You may be able to see through that portal, but we can't. To us, it's just cold stone. The woman before you claimed she could see another world, and we've seen her pass through it multiple times, but for some reason it refuses to work for us."

The man coughed, acquiring Arlowe's attention. His large smile returned once more, eager to dispel the current mood. "There's no need to think on it, my boy. We're content living as we are. You can't miss what you never had, am I right? Ignore our plight and rest with us a while longer, if you can."

The red-haired lady spoke up once more. "We may not be able to help you out there, but the least we can do is offer you a port in the storm."

Beginning to feel at ease, the prince held out his hand to the woman. "I'll take you up on that. My name is Arlowe Artaven. May I have yours?"

The woman had a much softer grip to her husband, grasping Arlowe's hand with a touch reminiscent of silk. "My full name is Queen Be'Ail'La, though to friends, I am simply known as Bela. Pleased to meet you." Bela placed her arm across her stomach before bowing; her stance was reminiscent of the Fertren soldiers back home.

Arlowe turned to the man who extended his arm, before returning it to his side. "I've already shaken your hand once, and from the looks of you, I almost took your arm off. Just call me Conquest!" he bellowed, slapping the top of his head. "I took a knock to the head a little while back. Now this dome of mine can't seem to remember my name, so I've gone with what the people have called me. I kinda like it! Makes me sound like a king!"

Conquest began to laugh, bellowing loudly enough to be easily heard over the commotion of the party.

"You *are* a king, dear," uttered his wife. The jolly man raised his tankard to a toast.

At once, Arlowe remembered that his trusty blade was not by his side, and spotted it resting in Bela's throne. The queen, in turn, noticed the prince's eagerness to retrieve his scabbard, and returned it to him.

Arlowe sighed in relief, though he was curious at how he was separated from it so easily. "How did you take this from my side? I couldn't see anything, and it all happened so fast."

Before any more could be said, Arlowe felt a slight tug on his belt, noticing that his sword he had only just re-equipped had been taken again. Bela pulled it from behind her back, amused at Arlowe's confusion.

"We can all see in the dark, but it wasn't I who stole your sword," she stated, looking towards the thrones. "Come on out, my cheeky cherub."

A young girl emerged from behind one of the thrones, running to clasp onto Bela's leg, giggling. Bela stroked her face, before tightening up one of the girl's many dark ponytails. "This is our mischievous little daughter, Ka'Orl'At, though if she prefers, you may call her Kaat."

The girl nodded her head, offering the scabbard to her mother to pass to Arlowe. "It's nice to meet you mister," Kaat said with a severe lisp.

36

As Arlowe retrieved his weapon from the girl, her small stature reminded him of his earlier encounter, still slightly shaken by it. "When I woke up, I had a pair of green eyes watching me. They seemed to belong to a small child. I know it's not very specific, but do you know anyone like that?"

Kaat rolled her eyes, re-joining the party. Conquest chuckled, his eyes revealing to Arlowe that he was already aware of the answer. "That sounds like our boy, though I'm surprised you saw anything of him. We rarely do," he blurted out.

Bela returned a look of disapproval at Conquest's choice of words, his hand raised as a sign of apology. "Xanth is incredibly shy, even with us, and he was the one that agreed to be adopted by us," she explained. "I imagine he was just checking up on you to make sure you were okay."

Arlowe scanned the hall, unable to spot him alongside the rest of his kind. "Is it okay if I go and look for him? I'd like to thank him for taking care of me."

Both parents smiled at Arlowe's words, shrugging at each other. "If he's willing, I'm sure Xanth would love a new friend! Don't worry about the party, it isn't going anywhere. Not while I'm in charge anyway!" Conquest called, chugging the remainder of his wine.

The crowd cheered for him. Bela put her face to her palm, though she could still be seen smiling under her disapproval.

Arlowe returned to the never-ending hallways, keen to meet the illusive son. His search took him all though the maze-like corridors, struggling to keep track of where he had visited and where he had left to explore.

Alas, it soon became evident that Xanth had no interest in being found. Though scratching and footsteps could be heard, Arlowe felt as though he was getting nowhere with his search, even with the constant feeling of those same eyes watching him.

Trying a new approach, Arlowe took his scabbard and threw it a good distance away, planting himself on the ground where he began to whistle. At first, nothing happened. The whistling echoed, riding along the smooth breeze that flowed through the underground.

However, after a small while, Arlowe noticed that his sword was slowly being dragged into one of the adjacent rooms to his right, though he made no effort to confront the thief.

"Be careful with that, okay?" he asked gently. "It's sharp."

The blade stopped for a moment, before continuing its disappearance into the room. Arlowe rotated to face the doorway, crossing his legs with his head rested in his hands.

He couldn't see who was taking his sword, though the prince began to speak towards the room, uninterested in whether he would be heard or not.

"I don't know if you're going to come out of there, but I just wanted to say thank you, for watching over me while I was asleep. You didn't have to, but you did. I imagine the people back home would've loved having someone like you around."

He paused for a moment, picking up a fist full of sand, letting it slide out of his hand. "Fun fact for you: my home? Eyenridge? It was the smallest capital city in the whole of Argestra, but it was still a gem. We had new faces coming and going, some really interesting types, but even then, I knew most of them. I saw them all as family, not subjects or whatever else you'd name them.

"It's gone now. The monsters showed mercy to no-one. I hope the others got away before the kharakians caught up to them. I don't even know how long I was out for."

"I'll be heading back out there soon, and I don't know what I'll find. I don't care how perilous it is, or how long it takes me. I will fix this. I owe it to the family I lost to make the world a better place for those they were forced to leave behind."

The prince turned his body, leaning his back against the wall. Giving in to his emotions, he began to cry, soaking the sand between his legs with tears. "I know they wouldn't want me to blame myself, but I couldn't forgive myself if I didn't mourn them, for a few moments. Just for a few moments, I want to be selfish."

"You're not being selfish if you're doing it for the right reasons," a voice murmured, filling the sorrowful prince with a sense of reassurance.

Peering to his left, Arlowe noticed a young boy sat cross-legged like him, fidgeting with his fingers. The boy peeked at Arlowe with his big green eyes, though this was only temporary, with the boy quickly returning his gaze to his fingers. Arlowe couldn't help but smile, knowing that he had been heard.

The two sat in silence for a good while, though there was no tension between them. Both felt comforted sharing each other's company.

"You're Xanth, right? Conquest and Bela's son?" Arlowe queried.

The boy nodded. "Xan'El'Th."

The prince could still hear the commotion of the party, with Conquest's voice being heard clearly over the music and cheering. He tried to make conversation. "Did you know there's a party in there? I'm sure your parents would love to see you."

The boy shook his head. "I-I don't like parties."

His comment made Arlowe grin with nostalgia. "I can understand that. I was never around for my parents' parties."

The boy's eyes were focused on the prince. "What's wrong with your face?"

Arlowe placed his fingers upon his right cheek, feeling the familiar ridges of his scars. "Oh, you mean these?" He turned his head for Xanth to see. "Those monsters attacked my home. I was with my mother when one—"

Arlowe turned his body to face the boy, causing him to flinch.

"Sorry, I just…" muttered Xanth, playing with the sand by his feet. The prince shuffled a few metres back, not wanting to make the boy uncomfortable.

"So, what do you do for fun?" Arlowe asked, looking around at the barren halls. "It looks… entertaining down here." He had tried to make that sentence sound genuine, hoping not to hurt the boy's feelings.

"It's fine, I guess. Most days I'm just hiding from my sister, though. She thinks we're playing hide and seek, but I never really want to play. I try to explore, but it's just the same places every day," he said, dejectedly. "Speaking of; Kaat, I know you're there. Mother and father sent you."

Upon the boy's statement, a shuffle came from their left; the quiet footsteps of a child returned back to the central chamber.

Arlowe moved onto his knees, shifting his finger through the sand. Xanth watched from where he was sat, though he stretched up to get a better look when he thought he wasn't being watching.

Once finished, Arlowe moved back to the wall, urging Xanth to take a proper look. His new friend had made him a simplified map of Argestra in the sand, leaving dots where the capital cities stood.

"I don't know where we are now, but this is where I was," Arlowe said as he pointed to the dot symbolizing Eyenridge. Xanth began pointing out other places for Arlowe to describe, eager to learn more. "That's Templen, capital of Ryvineon to the north-east, there's Stelgaren, capital of Quazin in the south-east and up to the north is Wicilil, the capital city of Calaveil. Pretty cool, huh?"

Xanth became extremely excited at all of this new information, taking hold of Arlowe's wrist to pull him closer, using his hand to point at more locations.

"What are these two?" he queried, getting as close as he could without ruining the drawing.

"That one to the west is Thaedlon. It's the capital city of Hietruce," the prince

answered. "And up here is—" He paused for a moment before continuing. "Up here is

Haaroith, the capital city of Vexinth."

Xanth could see right through him, calling out his hesitation. "Why did you stop?"

Arlowe decided it was better not to lie to the boy. "My father died there. To the west

of the capital are the Lifesight Mountains. That's where he was taken from me."

The young pterravun sat back, staring at the north-western part of the map intensely.

"I'm sorry. I didn't know."

To his surprise, Arlowe still had a smile on his face. The prince moved towards his

drawing, placing a cross next to the mountains. "You don't have to apologise so much.

You did nothing wrong. My father died a hero. He and a few others sacrificed

themselves during the last Demon Invasion. Without his sacrifice, my world would

probably be dominated by titans."

The prince placed his hand in the sand, leaving his handprint. "I miss them, but even

so, I'm proud to be their son. I hope they know that, wherever they are."

Arlowe could see Xanth looking to him in awe. The pterravun seemed stunned by his

composure on the subject considering how he was just a few moments ago.

The prince rose to his feet, dusting the sand off his trousers. "If it's okay with you, I'd

like my scabbard back, please. I think it's been stolen enough for today," he jested.

Xanth slowly rose to his feet, using the wall as support. While Arlowe expected him

to run into the room to the right, the boy instead walked over to a pile of sand a few

feet to the left, digging out his sword. The prince would have been more surprised, had

he not been witness to so many peculiar things already.

Arlowe returned to the main hall where the party was still going strong. The king and his daughter were in the centre of a large crowd dancing together, whilst the queen sat in her throne speaking to one of her people.

As soon as he was noticed, the crowd let out a huge cheer for him, panicking Xanth who followed closely behind. Arlowe looked to him, offering support. "You're doing great. Just take a deep breath."

Xanth took the advice, remaining in his proximity.

Bela gave a warm smile to the both of them as they reached the thrones, holding her hand out to her child. He took it, though his eyes were glued to the floor.

"How are you feeling, my munchkin?" she asked. Xanth only responded with a nod, though it looked as though Bela was used to this kind of communication. The young pterravun climbed into the smallest throne, fidgeting with his fingers once more.

"I'm ready to leave," Arlowe stated. Bela was thrown off by Arlowe's sudden declaration, calling her husband to join them. Arlowe continued. "You've done a lot for me, and I am eternally grateful, but I have a duty to uphold. The longer I stay here, the harder it will be to bring balance back to my world."

Conquest nodded his head, clapping his hands to organise the underground populace.

The people lined themselves up, with the monarchs standing side by side to face Arlowe. The king stepped forward, placing his hands on the prince's shoulders.

"We must all fulfil our purpose, and I applaud you for staying on the path fate has set you on. We, as pterravun, wish you the best in your future endeavours, and we, as pterravun, shall accept you back with open arms should you return to us. You are always welcome in our halls."

"Kaldaren ordein!" he yelled, with both the monarchs and the people repeating this phrase, placing an arm over their chest and stomach respectively as they repeated the phrase. "Kaldaren ordein, young Artaven! Kaldaren ordein!"

42

Arlowe felt the raw energy in Conquest's words, reciprocating the bow to show his respect. "How do I come back?" he posed to them, rising from his bow.

Bela placed a hand to her chin, figuring out how best to word her answer. "The woman who came before you mentioned that when she returns to us, she closes her eyes and thinks of this place. When she opens her eyes, she has arrived. Hopefully, the same holds true for you."

Arlowe nodded in response. He turned to face Xanth, who had remained perched on his throne, facing away. The prince knelt, addressing him. "Xanth? Back where I'm from, we don't say goodbye, we wish safe travels. Goodbyes feel too long. Think you could do that for me?"

Xanth didn't budge. Arlowe understood, getting back to his feet, climbing the staircase to the portal. As he neared the top, the sound of footsteps drew his attention, bringing the sight of Xanth climbing up after him.

"I want to come with you!" he called, confusing Arlowe.

"You can't, Xanth. Your parents told me that your kind can't use the portal."

"I have a solution. Come closer! I have a surprise for you!"

Arlowe was lost for words. Humouring Xanth, he crouched down enough for him to reach. Xanth took his index finger, placing it directly in the centre of Arlowe's forehead.

As he did, the prince's vision was swallowed in green, forcing him to grip onto the bannister of the staircase.

With his vision cleared, Arlowe regained his footing. "What did you do?" he asked. "I don't see a difference."

The eyes of the young pterravun were glowing brighter than usual, unnerving Arlowe. "Turn around and pick random numbers with your fingers, uh, please?" he asked. "I don't want you to show me."

The prince did as such, creating four different numbers on his hands without showing anyone. "Six, eight, one and six," Xanth answered, needing no prompt.

Arlowe spun around in amazement. "How did you do that?"

"The pterravun can connect to the minds of others, being able to see what they see, though it has to be done willingly. I've done it with people down here, but it gets dull when it's people in the same place doing the same thing. You could show me all those places that you drew!" Xanth soon retreated, becoming quiet. "I-if you don't want to, I understand. I-I acted without thinking. I'm sorry."

Arlowe thought hard over Xanth's request. "Can you read my mind? I don't like the idea of anyone doing that."

The boy perked up, defending his skill. "I can communicate with you, but I can't read your mind!"

The prince continued to ascend the staircase, moving towards the portal without saying a word. Xanth kept his eyes on his friend, keen for a response.

Arlowe placed his hand on the portal, feeling it pull him through. He closed his eyes, focusing his mind to speak. "Xanth, are you ready? There's a whole world out there to explore."

Ecstatic, Xanth ran up the stairs to see Arlowe as he faded from view. "Thank you! Thank you so much! M-may you have safe travels!" he called, waving to the prince.

With his eyes still closed, Arlowe could no longer feel the warm breeze of the underground, instead feeling the cold winds he was accustomed to, accompanied by the scent of charred wood.

"Arlowe, I can't see anything. Open your eyes!"

Chapter Four:

"What truly is a monster when you take away its title?"

21ˢᵗ Thuvalos

Land's Legacy

2084∞ (Current Age)

Arlowe opened his eyes, confirming that Xanth was speaking in his head and was not stood beside him. "Are you back, Arlowe? It's really dark where you are."

The prince moved around, taking in the familiar architecture of a Fertren home. Slate tiles laid shattered around him, the interior gutted and scorched. Glass rested at his side, with the roof above containing a royal-shaped hole.

Arlowe checked himself, finding no injuries beyond what had already been tended to. *The pterravun portal must have snatched me from my fall? How peculiar.*

Drawing back a curtain, the familiar sight of the sealed western wall greeted him alongside a full moon. Arlowe spoke softly. "I'm back in Eyenridge, Xanth." He then focused his mind. "Can you hear me? Vocally and mentally?"

"I can hear both."

Arlowe inched the front door open, hoping that none had been drawn by its creaks. "It may be a good idea to keep it that way, not just to minimise my noise, but also because I'll look weird talking to myself."

Xanth giggled at the thought.

The prince listened to his inner voice. *Xanth?* He heard nothing back. *At least he was being honest about the mind reading. I hope.*

The western sector of the city was mainly residential, housing a large amount of Eyenridge's civilians within it. While it was unintentionally a good spot to evacuate

45

the populace, Arlowe knew he would struggle to collect any supplies of note.

Upon peering out of what he now found to be one of the city's community centres, he glanced up to discover that the castle had been ripped to pieces by the beasts, leaving only a ravaged corpse behind; the prince drew an odd parallel between himself and his home. "Of us both, I assume fate deems *me* important," he muttered under his breath.

Arlowe left the building cautiously, hoping not to draw the ire of any kharakians left behind after their assault. Though he was surprised to find the nearby area empty, that didn't stop him from raising his guard, expecting their presence around every corner.

The prince reached the large street that would have connected to the western exit, had it not been sealed off. Here, he turned his head. "Xanth, avert your gaze."

"What was that?"

"It's not appropriate. I'll let you know when you can look again, okay?"

Arlowe had hoped that many of the people had escaped Eyenridge, though the sight in front of him spoke otherwise. Mangled bodies of those who had fallen from the ballista cables lined the street alongside shackles and linens, limbs and torsos scattered as far as the eye could see.

The metallic tang of dried blood invaded his nose. Craters and collapsed buildings made up the rest of the scenery, with Arlowe refusing to imagine how many were unfortunate enough to be caught underneath them.

He turned in the opposite direction, lightly retching as he looked for a new way to escape the fallen city. His stomach settled, Arlowe's eyes rested upon the tunnels beneath the castle that hadn't collapsed entirely. They would be the quickest way to the southern sector, a merchant's district of sorts.

Navigating them would be a treacherous task, though in Arlowe's mind, the risk was worth the reward. Not only would the tunnel conceal him from any lingering threats

46

outside and grant him direct access to the sector, but the sooner he could equip himself, the better. The cold Fertren nights were in full swing; his trousers and boots were ill fit to warm him.

"Can I look now?" asked Xanth, sounding bored.

"Go ahead, but next time, don't question me when I ask you to look away," Arlowe instructed. "When I ask you to do something, I'm doing it for a reason."

A few moments went by without any response from Xanth, though it didn't take long for his curious mind to urge more questions from him. "You keep talking about these… kharockans? Is that right? What are they?"

Arlowe thought about the question for a moment. "Do you want the short answer or the long one?"

"Short?"

Weaving through the broken buildings to the tunnel entrance, Arlowe carefully climbed to the top of a large pile of debris, peeking over the top. "That's one."

Directly ahead was the groaning of a lone kharakian, its footsteps alerting the prince and the boy. Of note was the beast's calm appearance; its body was unignited, in clear contrast to those that had stormed the city.

Sliding down the mound, the prince took cover behind a large crate. Upon closer inspection, he found that the beast was breaking open the crates and supplies left behind on the chance of finding any lingering survivors. Using its destructive nature to his advantage; Arlowe repositioned himself as the creature tore the remnants of his city apart, closing in with every broken item.

With only a set of stacked barrels between his target and himself, the prince drew his blade, manoeuvring around the barrels to slice down the creature's torso. As the kharakian began to materialise a spear, Arlowe spun, slicing the monster's head off with one clean stroke. The kill was quick and silent.

"They are called kharakians, and that was one of them," he stated, sheathing his sword.

"So you didn't want me to see what was in the street," Xanth debated. "but you were comfortable cutting up the monster with me watching?"

Arlowe climbed atop another mound of the collapsed city, reaching the crossroads connecting the four sectors. "There's a difference between staring at long deceased bodies and surviving threats like that."

He slid down to the other side, keeping an eye out for more of the invaders. "Besides, I'm not promising anything, but if we can ever find a way for you to be here, picking up a few tricks from me might be useful."

Arlowe crept into the tunnel leading towards the southern sector. Unlike the western tunnel that had mainly been filled with debris, the southern tunnel contained a mass of bodies, unceremoniously dumped by the careless brutes.

Kharakian scorch marks littered the tunnel floor, though amongst them there were also bodies that Arlowe identified as Arcane Guild members.

The mages must have travelled into the tunnel to try and seal it off, though their end goal was never achieved. Arlowe muttered a prayer to the deceased before pressing onwards, their sacrifice admirable.

"Xanth, look away," requested Arlowe, weaving through the corpses to avoid disturbing them.

"Okay," Xanth replied. "But can we still talk? You never told me about the kharikans. I want to know more."

Seeing no threats in his immediate vicinity, Arlowe decided it would make sense to sate the boy's curiosity. *Besides, wasn't that the reason he allowed Xanth to join his*

48

quest in the first place?

"Back in Three-Hundred-and-Four Siren's Age, a large detachment of soldiers and civilians were sent to the country of Fertral. Their task was to locate an appropriate location and begin construction of a settlement so that they had closer contacts in the new region, and more options and opportunities for trade.

"The man in charge was one General Evret Rainerus, a man with… questionable beliefs. Like many of his time, Evret believed that once the humans were 'completed' by Arn at the end of the First Invasion, they should have taken over as the superior race and should have demonstrated this. His feelings on the matter never publicly came to light until after his arrest. His position within the military wouldn't have allowed it."

Arlowe reached the tunnel exit, detecting a pack of kharakians aimlessly searching the sector. Spotting a general store to his left, the prince took a piece of rubble to toss at the butcher's shop on the opposite side of the street, buying himself time to enter.

The kharakians picked up on the noise immediately, tearing the butcher's shop to pieces as Arlowe fumbled with the store's latch. With a little finesse, the door was unlocked and just as quickly locked behind him.

"Sorry for the pause," Arlowe apologised, keeping an eye on the beasts through a window as the pack moved on. "The people looked forward to a new life in the new country under the watchful eye of the general, though Evret craved the chance to abuse his newly obtained power, aiming to gain the adoration of his family and the uninformed populace.

"As the civilians began the construction of Eyenridge, Evret had already begun weaving lies and deceit into his men, claiming that nearby farms had threatened their party with an attack, presenting them with forged letters as evidence.

"While the walls of his cities were being built, Evret was far from them, butchering innocent townsfolk to slowly gain the country for himself. Any who caught on to the general's plan were butchered alongside the townsfolk to keep the men fighting on his side, another cruel fact that wasn't revealed until much later."

"What does this have to do with the… monsters?" Xanth questioned. "Evret sounds like a terrible person, but I don't understand how he was behind their creation."

"I'm getting there." Arlowe kept his pace slow, slinking by each of the shop windows. "Evret's plan would have succeeded, allowing him to appear as a great hero standing proudly atop the corpses of his aggressors, if not for the meddling of the Tsaraithi Coven.

"During Evret's conquests, the general stumbled across the coven to the east of Fertral, near the border into Quazin. As his army approached, a magical barrier was formed, blocking their way into their village. These witches, through their magic, had seen the destruction that followed the general and denied him access, adamant that he was only interested in more violence.

"After days of repeated attacks on the barrier, with no scratches upon it, Evret altered his strategy to setting up camp and waiting, confident that the barrier could not hold forever. The witches were stunned at the general's altered tactics, the pain of their cast magic growing with its continual use. Though for as long as the opposing army waited, the coven held its barrier, refusing to let another die by Evret's hand.

"Their messages failed to bypass the general's forces; their winged messengers were slaughtered by Evret and his men for target practice. With no other option, the witches sent two of their own beyond the barrier to create a distraction. Their last crow taking flight, the witches could do nothing more but watch as their barrier faded, their family executed just out of their reach."

While he had been telling his tale, Arlowe had been searching for anything of use.

The wares of the shop did not line the shelves, but the floor, leading Arlowe to believe that some of his people had claimed the items for the long journey ahead.

Upon his inspection, a cluster of collapsed chests had blocked the door to the cellar. Managing to pry the debris from the door, the prince was met with an unsavoury smell. "Put a bookmark on where we were, Xanth. I need to check something."

As Arlowe descended further into the cellar, the putrid smell became more pungent. Following his nose, the prince found the source: Levanim, the owner of the shop and an old friend. The elf had started to rot, clasping onto a small wedding band. His eyes were glazed, though still focused on the ring.

"Damn it," Arlowe mumbled, averting his own gaze for a moment. "You deserved better than this. I pray that Arn treats you better than this world has."

From what he could deduce, Levanim must have been hiding in the cellar when the kharakians attacked, becoming trapped when an explosion knocked the chests in front of the door. Schukara's rescue band must not have heard his cries as he tried to force his way out, evident by the state of his fingers and the blood on the inside of the door.

As Arlowe scanned the cellar, he caught sight of Levanim's remaining wares, including flax garments and a worn leather backpack. Hung up around the corner, the prince also came into contact with a padded jacket, which he immediately recognised as one of the shopkeeper's handmade gambesons.

Considering his current attire, Arlowe jumped at the chance to fortify himself and keep himself warm, tightly equipping the green jacket to his person.

Taking the backpack from its hanger, the prince looked inside, surprised to find a single gold piece alongside a flask filled with water. *An old family tradition,* Arlowe remembered, returning the gold piece to the pack. *You were good to me in life, my friend. Maybe you could help me one last time.*

The prince took a cloth, wetting it with the flask of water. He swabbed Levanim's eyes, closing them shut.

"So, what happened to the witches?" asked Xanth, urging for the story to continue, the boy unaware of Arlowe's mourning.

The prince climbed the stairs, freezing as the breathing of the monsters could be heard on the opposite side of the wall. "You do realise that I'm trying to stay alive here?"

The breathing moved on, allowing Arlowe to ascend to the main floor.

Upon his return, Arlowe could see one of the kharakians outside the door. He ducked, hidden himself behind the shop counter.

"Are you ready to continue with the story? I can rattle off the rest of it while I wait for the monsters outside to clear," posed Arlowe, readjusting his new threads.

"Mm-hm, the witches. Two left the barrier."

Arlowe cleared his throat, before realising that he was still speaking with his mind.

"Though the two witches had lost their lives to Evret, beheaded as punishment for their 'assault' on the king's army, their sacrifice was not in vain. The letter had not only reached Thaedlon, but it was the king himself that looked upon the contents.

"The letter made reference to several villages around the general's expressed destination, alongside strong accusations of treason. Upon reading it, the king brought his finest men together and set off for the locations mentioned in the letter.

"On arrival to the first few settlements, it didn't take an expert to tell that something was wrong. While the king was hesitant to place the title of traitor on one of his most trusted men, he felt uneasy at the sight of hundreds of elven corpses strewn across every inch of their villages, their homes looted and sacked.

The king was familiar with the equipment that was sent with his general, and from this, noticed that the wounds on some of the elven corpses were matches to the weaponry of his own troops.

"The king arrived at the location outlined, watching the assault on the barrier from the nearby hill. Sounding their horn, the king called out for Evret's soldiers to cease their attack at once. Every soldier, including Evret, stood to attention, surprised at the king's appearance. Upon seeing him, the witches slowly lowered the barrier. Some echoed sighs of relief as others fell from exhaustion.

"While Evret attempted to lie his way out of his predicament, the King of Thaedlon had no more patience for his general. The many deaths he had seen heading to the camp had turned his stomach, and the evidence he had collected on the way argued against much of Evret's explanations.

"The corpses of the witches near him did not help Evret, and upon being restrained on the king's orders, pieces of gold fell from his pocket. On closer inspection, the gold was not of the regular print that the soldiers were paid in. Instead, this had a much older appearance; the witches identified them as old elven coins.

"Evret was arrested, charged with theft, mass murder and treason. The bodies of the dead witches were returned to the village and the Hietruen forces were pulled back, with apologies given to the witches for all that had been done to them.

"It was only once it was too late that they realised the witches had no interest in Thaedlon's apologies. They had damned the men, king and country, and through their words, Kharaki was born."

"It sounds like they were born from a curse," Xanth deduced. "Could your people have tracked down the witches and asked for the curse to be removed?"

Arlowe perked up, hearing the grunts of the monsters returning once more. "They tried, but it didn't work. Apparently, when a creature is born of magic, you can erase them just as easily as when you summon them. However, if you leave them in the world for too long, they bind to it," he clarified. "The descendants of the witches tried to remove the kharakians, but by that point they had integrated too much."

At once, the groans of the kharakians ceased. An unwelcome silence filled the air, broken only by the occasional creaks of the shop. As Arlowe peered up from the counter, a crossbow was aimed at his head. A finger gently clutched the trigger.

The prince glanced around the room, finding himself surrounded by five rag-clad figures. The wielder of the crossbow stepped forward, gesturing for Arlowe to stand, while the remaining four remained in formation.

The crossbow wielder gestured to Arlowe's scabbard, forcing the prince to unhook it from his waist and place it on the counter.

In response, the figure took his finger away from the trigger, placing the crossbow alongside Arlowe's sword. With a wave of his hand, the rest of the group dropped their guard, dispersing to different parts of the room.

The figure removed their hood and mask, revealing a dark-haired man underneath; a large nose stood out above all else.

"Thought you were dead, Your Majesty," the man queried, with Arlowe noticing the sarcastic tone in his voice. "We've combed through this city a couple of times, and haven't seen hide nor hair of *you*. Where'd you come from?"

Arlowe focused on that word. *Combed.* He was surrounded by vultures.

"I could ask the same. I don't recall offering my city to scavengers, mister...?"

The group kept themselves quiet, though they couldn't help but snigger at the prince's statement. The unmasked man waved his hand again, muting the group.

"The name's Vernard. When Eyenridge fell, and Fertral couldn't support itself, the surrounding countries placed their armies at the borders to keep the monsters out, quarantining your country. While the Mad Queen of Quazin hired a bunch of men and women to watch her border, she also hired a collection of us to enter Fertral and lend a hand snuffing out these cretins. We're *combing* for survivors."

"That all happened in a few hours? I don't believe you."

"A few hours? You think the fall of Eyenridge happened a few hours ago?"

The prince's breath was caught. "What do you mean?"

Vernard snorted, raising his hands for his big reveal. "You and the city have been declared dead for over a week." The mercenary captain leant forward. "We're the rescue team. You're welcome."

Arlowe forced the panic of his late awakening to the back of his mind, making himself focus on the here and now. "You don't look like a rescue team to me."

Vernard shrugged his shoulders. "If we're rescuing, does it matter what we look like? Now, back to our original topic. You didn't answer my question: Where were you?"

The prince looked towards the door leading to the cellar, which Vernard picked up on instantly.

"Something in the cellar of note, my liege?" he asked, again with a note of mockery.

Feeling apprehensive at his prying, Arlowe crafted a tale from what he had seen outside, hoping to keep the mercenaries off his back.

"I was one of the last to head for the evacuation point. As I got close, the exit was swarmed by the kharakians, forcing me to retreat. I fought alongside members of the Arcane Guild in the tunnels, though in the end, only one other survived with me. He was wounded badly. He didn't make it, which meant that I had the supplies necessary to sustain myself while I shunted the door."

One of the man's group pulled the door to the cellar open, only to recoil back from the rancid odour spilling out.

Vernard smirked at his friend's misfortune, taking his crossbow and placing it in the sling on his back. "I'll trust my associate's judgment," he said, patting the back of the disgruntled mercenary; the man near-retching. "So, what do you plan to do now? I'm assuming since you're out here, you've ran out of supplies."

Arlowe returned his scabbard to his side, moving from around the counter. "I want to head north. My father was good friends with the current King of Thaedlon, and I'm hoping to use that old bond to gain his aid. I'll need a large force to wipe Kharaki off the map, and Thaedlon's army would be a good start."

Vernard wagged his finger, stopping Arlowe in his tracks. "You'll be on your own then. We're going east, back towards our camp. We *were* set up in the north, but a gaggle of goblins took it upon themselves to take our old camp from us. Between them and the kharakians, it'd make more sense to go east and travel the borders where it's most safe."

It wasn't hard for Arlowe to be aware of the group's equipment, making them much more effective in the field than standard soldiers. "I'll help you take back the camp *if* you assist me in travelling north. The longer it takes me to get there, the harder it'll be to purge the kharakians from Fertral," responded Arlowe. "I have no interest in being overly proud. I need help."

Vernard stayed quiet, weighing up his options. A member of his squad stepped forward, taking hold of his boss' shoulder. "With the kid, this could work. There's nothing more we can do here, and there're more towns to the north that could use our help. Re-establishing our camp up there would be a good move."

Another of Vernard's squad stood by the window made their way towards the back of the shop. "Whatever our plan is, we need to get out of here first. I don't know what's drawing them, but those things are getting mighty suspicious."

Vernard turned to the team member tasked with examining the cellar. "Arkle, ready to put on a show?"

The masked mercenary simply nodded in response. The twitching man placed his hands together, disappearing from sight. Vernard lifted the latch from the door, ushering everyone through. "Stick close and watch each other's backs. We need to return to our horses in the northern sector. They'll get us out of this."

Arlowe entered back into the tunnel alongside the mercenaries, looking back to see Arkle running towards the southern gate. "What about him? He's going to get himself killed!"

Vernard ran alongside Arlowe, keeping track of his men. "Arkle? Nah, the bastard's too slippery!"

Arlowe glanced back once more, watching the kharakians pounce at their prey. Screams pierced the air, putting the pressure on Arlowe's conscience.

Vernard tapped his arm. "Don't worry about it. It's probably just a flesh wound."

The prince scowled in response.

As the group reached the crossroads, another horde of kharakians had appeared from the north, blocking their way. One of the kharakians raised its arms, releasing a bright light that blinded the party.

Vernard tackled one of his allies to the floor, calling out to the others. "Everybody, get down!"

As their vision returned, the group spotted no injuries amongst them, nor any structural damage around them.

To their front, the kharakians began to drop to the floor one by one, turning to dust as they slammed to the ground. This continued until only the centre kharakian remained, visibly different to any other kharakian Arlowe had seen before.

The kharakian took a step forward, holding an orb of light in its hand. It looked directly at Arlowe, crushing the orb within its palm. "We are a blight, weaponised by those beyond us. Can you feel their presence?"

The group froze where they were, horrified at what stood before them. A kharakian, surging with far more energy than they had seen before, was trying to communicate with them.

Arlowe raised his hands as a sign of peace, approaching the beast. Vernard kept his feet planted, though he was heavily opposed to the idea. "You're gonna get us killed, jackass!"

The prince ignored the squad leader, trying his best to communicate with the kharakian. "You... can talk? Why are you doing this? Why are you annihilating everything in your path? Eyenridge is gone, our curse should be fulfilled!"

The beast kept its eyes on Arlowe. Its fist grew brighter, shaking as if struggling to contain something within. "Our power grows, and we cannot control it. We are beyond our purpose. Plead to your gods."

Opening its hand, the kharakian fired a continuous beam of energy, which the group barely avoided. As the creature began to readjust its aim, the arm was severed by none other than Arkle.

Vernard picked himself up, rallying the others. "Now's our chance! We'll cut through the eastern sector! Thanks Ark!"

Arlowe looked back, watching the alpha kharakian not only regenerate his lost arm in no time, but also materialise a wave of spears to fill its prey like a pin cushion.

Arlowe caught up to Vernard, visibly distressed. "You're disgusting! That man saved us twice, and we're just leaving him?"

"Quit your whining!" he yelled back. "Your royal arse looks no worse for wear!"

The group reached the eastern sector; all ran through the destroyed barracks as quickly as they could. The prince was starting to flag behind, though with the kharakians following so closely behind, stopping was hardly an option.

Though the north-eastern gate sat a stable with five horses peering out. As they got closer, a familiar figure appeared, opening the stable doors.

Arlowe was bewildered. "Is that Arkle? How? I don't understand…"

Vernard passed him by, nudging the masked man's chest; his silence persisted.

"Good job once more, Ark," he blurted proudly, "though we're not out of this yet. We can outrun the beasts on horseback, but we're gonna have to take out their ace." He turned to another of his team. "Lyra, move the horses closer to the north gate. Make sure we're ready to move on my mark."

Lyra agreed, taking the reins of the horses to lead them out of the imminent war zone.

Vernard was giving out last-minute orders, still calm and collected despite the circumstances. "Arkle, keep the thing busy. Exploit any weaknesses you can find. Corla, keep the kharakians out of my sight. I've got an idea. Wern, you're with me."

Before anyone could object to Vernard's plan, the leader and his chosen had already vanished amongst the demolished buildings.

The alpha moved into the northern sector, followed by a small mass of its brethren. While the standard kharakians charged at full speed, vaulting over fallen beams and toppled walls, the alpha kharakian flickered from place to place, transporting itself great distances over a short amount of time.

Arkle had jumped into the fray almost immediately, moving through the kharakians at unnatural speeds to strike at the anomaly. Unable to match his blazing evasion, Arlowe instead held the line with Corla, her hand prepared with a spell.

Though the horde had begun to thin, the noise of combat had drawn more kharakians from the rest of the city, raising the pressure. Arlowe cut down two more kharakians, kicking them away to avoid any potential detonations. "Where's Vernard?" he questioned. "If enough of them rush us, we won't stand a chance!"

"Keep your worries to yourself." Arlowe's attention was drawn to the returning Lyra, her black hair nearly masking her stern expression. "His survival is his own concern."

Corla downed a kharakian aiming to strike at their flank; the spectral animals summoned by her hand bolstering their numbers aided in turning the tide just enough. "You worry too much. We'll be fine!"

As if to counter her positive nature and prove her wrong, fate took a turn. The alpha kharakian swiped at Arkle, taking his throat into its grasp. Letting out a burst of energy, the creature disintegrated the mercenary, though the blast oddly left no ill effects on its surrounding allies.

Xanth suddenly piped up, keen to inform Arlowe of his observation. "Arlowe, that creature didn't die by exerting all that energy, but it's not moving. I think it needs time to recharge!"

As if on cue, Arkle had reappeared by Arlowe's side, assisting with the onslaught of kharakians striking at them.

Wern stumbled around the corner, passing on a message from Vernard. "Arkle, one more time! The boss's plan is ready. Keep it still!"

Arkle took a deep breath, disappearing once more. In his place, another Arkle took shape, charging towards the alpha. Uninterested in playing more games, the alpha kharakian immediately discharged its energy, disintegrating Arkle's clone again.

Like before, the alpha had been left paralysed, exactly where his boss had wanted it.

A large explosion sounded by the nearby water tower, with Vernard rushing around the corner to meet them. "Unless you're extremely thirsty, I'd suggest moving!" he warned, dashing to the north.

60

The water tower had already begun tilting to one side, trying to keep itself upright, yet the wounds inflicted upon it were too much to bear. Unable to hold up its bulk, the tower let out a crack of pain, diving straight towards the three.

Arkle's invisibility had expired, revealing him by their side unconscious. Arlowe took the initiative, clearing away any obstacles as Lyra and Corla lifted their ally to safety.

Unable to move, the alpha kharakian could only watch as the tower came down upon it, crushing the being with its weight and dousing its flames with the water inside.

The party regrouped by the horses in the northern sector, meeting minimal resistance. Most of the kharakians from the eastern tunnel had been washed away by the flood of water, leaving few to continue fighting.

Arkle had come to, though he was in no position to mount his steed, instead riding as a passenger on Lyra's horse. Vernard, Corla and Wern had already mounted up. Putting the remaining horse to good use, Arlowe mounted himself upon Arkle's horse, eager to leave his home behind.

The prince took a sigh of relief as the kharakians faded from view, though his heart sank as he looked forward, seeing the alpha kharakian flicker into his sight. Standing in his path unflinching, his horse reared in fear, throwing Arlowe from the saddle.

Reacting in time, Arlowe rolled out of the way of the alpha's stomp, stunned at the creature's strength and speed despite its hampered state.

The prince got back to his feet, ready to strike, only to find that the alpha could no longer stand. Its brittle leg had shattered, toppling the savage beast.

"The fight is over," remarked Xanth. "The water must have damaged it when it was trying to recover. It can't regenerate."

Not backing down, the alpha lunged at Arlowe, only to be shot in its other leg by Vernard, returning it to the floor.

"This is just sad," he commented. "I almost feel bad for it. Put it out of its misery."

Arlowe approached, readying his sword. The creature raised itself up with one arm, looking directly at him. "Fight us, and pray you do not become us. That was our folly."

The prince plunged his sword into the alpha kharakians head, looking away from his deed. The being dropped and turned to dust. As it came close to fading entirely, it uttered one more word. "Arlowe…"

The group remained quiet, allowing the prince a moment to comprehend his situation. He turned, climbing back onto his horse. He looked around, offering a smile to his allies. "Come on everyone, it's not safe here. The sooner we move, the quicker we'll get there."

Vernard nodded at the recommendation, leading his band north.

While the group had their own conversations, Arlowe was stuck in his own mind, hearing the voice of the alpha kharakian over and over again.

"That kharakian sounded weird," Xanth questioned. "Are you having second thoughts about killing them?"

"I've had second thoughts about anything I've had to kill Xanth, but after today, my mind is really struggling with the definition of what a monster is."

Chapter Five:

"Hear me, oh Father who resteth within the great tower, for I have sinned."

24th Thuvalos

Land's Legacy

2084∞ (Current Age)

The journey from Eyenridge was arduous, unforgiving to Arlowe and his companions. The mercenary captain and his men had only intended to travel within their group, not accounting for the prince's company. Though their rations were already tight, what they had was split further, forcing them all to go hungry.

Rest was another issue. For one, with Arkle so badly wounded, multiple stops had to be made to check up on him, halting their progress. As they were still within Fertral territory, kharakian ambushes were frequent, especially when they stopped to make camp at night. With the monsters hunting in packs, the party had no choice but to take what rest they could before swiftly moving on.

Regardless, morale had not dropped. Arkle had been slowly recovering with no complications, and Vernard's old camp was getting closer with each day. After days of travelling, the group set up one more camp, using it as a final stop before their arrival.

Arlowe didn't have much preparation to do, unlike the others. They had plenty of equipment to maintain and spells to practice. By comparison, he simply needed to properly button up his gambeson and make sure that his scabbard wouldn't get stolen again; the prince had lost count at how often it had already slipped from his grasp.

While the group made sure all their equipment was up to snuff, Arlowe sharpened his blade against a whetstone, using his spare time to inform Xanth about the different races on Katosus.

"Well, you know what a human is. That's what I am. Do you know what an elf is? A dwarf?" he asked. "No pressure or anything. It's not like I'm testing you."

Xanth enthusiastically responded, making it evident that he had an answer. "I used to know lots of dwarves! Wern is one too! They usually live underground, and they're kind of short and stocky, like someone took a human and then smushed them! I only know one elf though. At least, I think she's an elf? When she visits, she only meets with Kaat. She clearly doesn't have taste."

Arlowe laughed at the comment. It was nice to hear Xanth able to express himself, a far cry from the boy he met in the labyrinths a few days ago.

"I don't know any others," said Xanth. "Wait, you said something about gobins?"

"They're called goblins, though you may hear people refer to them as graikhurst. From what I've read, they used to look like very tall elves, with the physiques of orcs. Their kind sided with Nra during the First Invasion, which invoked Arn's wrath in the form of a curse, transforming them into what we know today."

"Which is…?"

"Tiny, green or brown-skinned creatures, weak and warted. Their vanity stricken, they're a corruption of what they once were."

Xanth paused for a moment, processing the information. "You said orcs. What is that? That sounds like a made-up word."

"No, I'm serious. Orcs are a large, green-skinned race who hail from the mountains." The prince began counting on his fingers. "There are also the kharakians, who I'm sure by this point don't need an explanation, the stone giants known as aautgal, the various forms of demon and the dragon beings known as soreiku and sorvanc. That's not even counting half-breeds and possible extinct races."

Arlowe placed the stone into his backpack, admiring his newly sharpened blade.

"Are you going to kill the goblins, Arlowe?" Xanth asked bluntly.

Arlowe sheathed his sword, unpacking his glass to fill it at the stream.

"I hope not. I don't keep a weapon on my person in the hopes of stabbing something. I'm not a psychopath. I only use it as a last resort to defend myself," he replied, corking the filled glass. "Words can cut much deeper than any weapon I'll wield."

Off in the distance, Vernard could be seen bringing his team together to discuss something. Arlowe wasn't fazed about being left out of their plans. After all, he was the outsider that forced them to go tired and hungry to travel north rather than take the shorter and easier trip east.

Lyra approached Arlowe's little camp, wearing the strong face of disapproval. "Have you sorted everything?" she asked, looking down her nose at him. "You dragged us into this mess, so I hope you're ready to support us."

Arlowe bit his tongue at her statement, uninterested in making enemies before such an important task. "Yeah, I'm good. What's the plan?"

Lyra moved towards their camp, gesturing for him to follow her. As her allies departed, Lyra took a nearby stick to point out the plan they had devised in the mud.

"Here's what we're doing. For lack of a better word, *we're* bait. We walk up to the front gate and see if they'll leave peacefully. We're not expecting them to give up the camp so easily, so we've got Corla hiding behind us with her conjurmancy spells."

"Conjurmancy?" Xanth asked.

"Summoning magic," Arlowe answered.

"Focus," Lyra snarled, snapping her fingers. "Corla will break down the front gate with her spells while Vernard and Wern, on the east and west respectively, stand ready with crossbows to take out any goblins that become hostile. We'll be out in the open, so I expect you to give me a hand when everything goes to Erethys."

Arlowe looked around, confused. "Where's Arkle? I didn't see him in your little gathering. I thought he recovered?"

Lyra shrugged. "Pass. He's Vernard's right-hand man. I imagine he's been given something oh-so important to do."

The irate woman slung her backpack across her back, making sure her short sword was firmly strapped to her hip. "Everyone's already in position. They're waiting for our signal. Don't drag your feet."

Arlowe and Lyra began their trek up the hill towards the camp, passing Corla hiding in the bushes. The prince waved to her, though Lyra slapped his hand away. "They're only supposed to think there's two of us, you dolt. Make mistakes in your own time."

As the two got closer, a mass of goblins left their cover, revealing themselves upon the walls with bowstrings drawn. With eyes upon them, both Arlowe and Lyra ceased all movement with hands raised, awaiting any communication from the opposing force.

The front gate creaked open, with a robed goblin leaving its protection. The goblin inched closer, visibly trembling. "What're ya' doin' 'ere, travellers? I'd advise ya' ta' be on yer' way. Those molten fiends are everywhere these days."

Lyra took a confident step forward; the goblin flinched closer to the gate. "Don't tell us what to do, goblin. We want what you stole from us."

"I'm... not understandin' what yer' gettin' at," he replied. "We've lived here fer' years. Not even tha' kharakians have been able to pry us from our homes. We're not lookin' fer' violence."

Arlowe was more than happy to aid Vernard's squad, especially since they were doing him a favour, but something felt wrong. He was expecting the goblins to be highly aggressive, and while they were pointing arrows his way, he could tell that they were just as frightened as the one forced to act as their communicator.

66

Lyra got down on one knee, getting much closer to the goblin.

"We won't ask again," she snarled. "We need our camp back."

The goblin began to breath heavily, struggling with the immense pressure. "If we stay, we have to deal with you. If we allow ourselves to be ousted, we'll have nowhere to go from those innumerable animals. We're not going anywhere."

Lyra gritted her teeth, understanding that she was getting nowhere. From beyond the walls of the camp, an arrow flew through the air, skilfully wedging itself within her leg. Lyra fell to the ground, calling out in pain.

The goblin intermediary was shocked by the arrow coming from the side of his people. He quickly turned to flee back to safety, though Lyra had other plans.

Though the arrow had forced her to remain stationary, she had enough reach to grab the goblin's collar, sinking her blade deep through his chest. The goblin screamed as the sword emerged through his torso, alerting the forces along the wall.

Vernard and Wern could see where this series of events was leading and tried to take out as many as they could, but the goblins along the walls were too numerous. The goblin forces launched a volley of arrows towards Arlowe and Lyra.

In the nick of time, a large bear leapt before the arrows and their targets. The outline of the beast glistened like the night sky; its fur was reminiscent of shooting stars. The bear kept its side facing the arrows, acting as a wall against the goblin assault.

Corla took cover beside her companions, patting the bear she had summoned. "Good job, Ambjörn! Get ready to move up on my signal!" She turned to Lyra, who had already ripped the arrow from her leg. "Aros' mercy, Lyra. Your healing magic will only go so far, you know!"

Lyra pressed her hand against the wound, causing it to glow. She moved it away to show that the wound had been sealed, though heavy bruising still surrounded it.

"You'll know how far my magic will go when I'm dead," she retorted, standing. "This was how I was expecting the plan to go. What's our next move?"

Corla peeked around her summoned pet, making sure not to catch an arrow with her face. "Vernard and Wern are almost done clearing the walls. Once that's done, Ambjörn here is going to charge ahead and bring down their main gate. From there, we converge within the camp and clear the remaining goblins out."

Arlowe stuck out like a sore thumb, being the only member of the party without their weapon drawn. For some reason, he felt uncomfortable every time he went to draw it, though this only pushed Lyra's temper further.

"May I remind Your Highness that that stabby stick by your side is called a sword? Point it in the direction of a threat and it dies." Without a response, her condescension was swiftly replaced by fury. "We helped you get this far, so return the damn favour!"

Corla peeked around her bear once more, now able to see Vernard out of his hiding spot. The captain pointed to the camp, moving his thumb across his neck. She jumped for joy, eager to please her leader.

Blowing the whistle around her neck, Corla sent the bear charging towards the front gate. "Go, my fuzzy friend! Show that gate no remorse!"

As expected, the gate stood no chance against Corla's summoned bear, smashing it into a thousand pieces under its immense weight. The summoner charged after it, eager to enter the fray.

Arlowe offered Lyra his shoulder to lean on, though she slapped him away in disgust. "You want to show me kindness? Then help us clear that camp," she spat. "Though I can see it in your eyes. You won't kill. You don't have the spine."

Nearing the gate, one of the camp's inhabitants came into view. Though they had avoided Corla and her pet, the goblin was caught in the gaze of yet another invader.

"Leave us alone!" the goblin screeched, charging with a dagger in each hand, forcing Arlowe to draw his weapon at last.

The goblin lacked a defensive strategy, instead trying to keep his target off-guard and away from the camp, though this only sealed his fate.

Leaping at the wrong moment, the prince raised his blade in self-defence only for the goblin to catch his neck on the sword, slicing an artery.

Lying in a pool of its own blood, the creature looked up at the prince with a pained expression. "Help... me..." sputtered the goblin, its eyes rolling.

The prince stood in horror of what he had done.

"I didn't want this," Arlowe muttered, bending down to its level. "I'm so sorry that this happened to you. May Arn retract his curse and take you in."

With one swift movement, he snapped its neck, ending its suffering. Behind him, Lyra watched without a word, though he could tell that her impression of him hadn't changed.

Arlowe entered the camp to find that most of the work had already been done. Goblin corpses hung from the walls and were cut up within their homes, reminding him of what the kharakians did to his own people. Arkle exited a hut covered in blood as Vernard and Wern entered the centre of the town dragging goblin corpses behind them.

"I'm sure there's a few more," Vernard called out. "When you kill 'em, bring 'em here. I don't want rotten corpses stinking up the camp, and I don't need their pestilence making us ill."

Shuffling footsteps moved behind Arlowe, though they were close enough that only he could hear them. The only way they could have gone was behind the hut closest to him, leading him to examine it.

Surely enough, hiding among the waste at the back of the house was a young goblin, shaking with tears in her eyes.

Arlowe kept his distance, showing his hands as a sign of trust. "Look, I don't want to hurt you, but we need to get you out of here. Your people stole. They were bad."

The goblin looked confused, unsure at what the stranger had said to her. "Mama said this was always *our* home. We've never hurt nobody, but ya' hurt them anyway. Now they won't wake up."

The goblin child began to cry. Arlowe moved closer to the goblin, though the girl pressed her back up against the wall. "Yer' tha' bad person! You made 'em sleep! Yer' a bad person!"

The prince took the goblin's hands, pleading for her to shush, though this only made the goblin shout louder, resisting Arlowe's grip with every fibre of her being.

A blade passed by his face, piercing through the goblin's chest. Arlowe was frozen on the spot, with only the child's tearful gaze in his view. The blade was removed as quickly as it entered, leaving the body to slump to the floor, lifeless.

The prince turned to see Lyra wiping away the blood from her short sword on the nearest tent, looking down at him in disgust.

"So, you were supposed to be Fertral's next king? Now I understand why the kharakians burned your city to the ground," she hissed. "If those beasts wouldn't stand to have you as king, why would anyone else?"

Arlowe drew his blade, pointing it directly at Lyra. In response, the woman moved her fingers across the weapon's edge, taking a step closer so that the tip was tickling her throat.

"Do it," she goaded. "I know you're bluffing, Arlowe. You were happy to kill the kharakians because you view them as animals, but if you won't kill goblins, at least on purpose anyway, I know you won't kill me either."

The prince kept his stance, keeping eye contact with the woman. After a few moments, Lyra slapped his sword away, punching him in the face, knocking him into the mud.

"I guess while you were up in your ivory tower, the world was so beautiful," she mocked, shaking the pain from her fist. "It isn't. If you're buckling after a few days of being in the real world, do your country a favour and stay dead."

Lyra went for the goblin's body, only to be stopped by Arlowe. He picked himself up and moved over to the goblin before delicately cradled the body in his arms.

"Wow, so noble. Make sure to bring it to the centre of the camp," she sneered, leaving Arlowe's presence. The prince took a nearby piece of cloth, covering the goblin's face before following Lyra back to the others.

Arlowe soon reached the mound of corpses. He placed the tiny body amongst the rest of her kind. He looked around, believing that his companions would have been respectful at a time like this, though it was apparent that he was expecting too much.

Arkle was nonchalantly slinging the corpses onto the pile, kicking over any bits that were separated from their owners. Wern was cracking jokes with Corla. To one side, Lyra was whispering to Vernard who was leaned against one of the huts with a torch in his hand.

Emotionally drained, Arlowe took a seat on a nearby bench, awaiting the inevitable.

Corla gave a thumbs-up to Vernard, who looked around for any objections before throwing the flame onto the bodies. To assist the fire, Arkle took out a sachet containing some kind of powder, spreading it over the flames to strengthen them.

The stench of burning flesh filled the camp, with only the prince raising his hand to cover his nose; Vernard's men took in a breath of accomplishment. They were proud of what they had done here today.

Vernard sat by Arlowe, holding a pouch of gold within his hands.

"Here, for your troubles," he offered, passing it over.

The prince looked at the bag, before moving his gaze back to the pyre. Vernard returned the pouch to his satchel, rising to his feet.

"What, too good for our money now? You'll need it to fill your stomach if you're gonna carry on north."

Arlowe remained seated, unsure of how he was containing the anger within. "I don't want your blood money. I was the reason we came here, and you butchered these people."

"They turned hostile. What did you expect us to—"

"Some. Some of them turned hostile. Most of them ran or hid, and you murdered them all. I hope the people you relocate to this camp are grateful. Many lives were lost here to enable that."

Arlowe stood, walking towards the destroyed front gate.

Vernard called after him. "Good luck. I hope you find what you're looking for."

The prince stopped by the gate, his back turned. "Yeah, same to you."

*

As the corpses continued to burn, Vernard rounded up his team, eager for their attention.

"Everyone, gather 'round!" he announced. "I had no doubt in my mind that we'd make it here, but I want you all to soak in the view. Not only is there plenty of food and drink in the main hall, but there's plenty of stuff here for us to sell on for a profit. For now? Dine and be merry. I think we've earned it. Kaxrax Village is ours!"

Wern and Corla ran straight to the hall, arguing over who was going to grab the first pint, laughing all the way.

Arkle followed, stopping by Vernard to hand him a bow, dropping a collection of the goblin's arrows by his feet.

"Nice shot on Lyra," Vernard praised, kicking the ammunition aside. "We really had the kid fooled. Go let those two know you're the man of the hour, and that you get first dibs on the grub."

The silent mercenary pumped his fist, joining his friends in the hall.

Lyra still remained outside, waiting to be the prime recipient of Vernard's attention. "Speaking of, what *about* the boy? How do you know he won't rat us out to the authorities?"

Vernard laughed to himself, piquing Lyra's interest. "You may want to use that healing magic on your eyes, Lyra. Maybe use it on mine too! The authorities? They're surrounding us as we speak!"

"Hilarious. So funny, in fact, that it makes me want to climb to the top of your wit and kill myself by dropping to your intelligence. You know what I mean."

Lyra's insult knocked the wind out of Vernard's sails, wiping away his smile. "It's a good job I like you Lyra, and that you're our only medic," he threatened, a smile returning to his face. "If by some miracle we're caught doing what we're doing, they'll have the elevenths hunt us and use their stupid magical abilities to see what was going on. They'll see that the prince was helping us. Why do you think I brought him along? We were gonna raid this place anyway, may as well have an ace up our sleeve to get out of trouble."

Lyra seemed satisfied with her answer, barging past Vernard towards the smell of food. Vernard raised an eyebrow, following her in.

*

As the party moved into full swing, a single goblin rushed into the camp, only to stop dead at the sight of the flaming pyre. "W-what's goin' on 'ere?"

Shaking himself out of his shock, the goblin rushed around the camp, looking for any survivors.

"No. No, no, no, no. W-what 'appened? T-this can't be everyone. I can't be... alone."

Though he searched extensively, the goblin had to stop, realising that his search was futile. Everyone in the camp had perished at the hands of these invaders.

The goblin climbed to the top of the hall looking down upon the intruders. He recognised all of them. Hunters that prowled the walls, taking lives for sport.

The goblin climbed back down, careful not to alert the hunters. As much as he wanted his vengeance, he wasn't a fighter. He wasn't skilled in anything but foraging for supplies; the goblin cursed his inadequacies under his breath.

Slinking in to the remains of his home, the goblin picked up a stick and a piece of fabric, fashioning it into a bindle to carry the last of his possessions.

"No one'll hire a goblin with no skills 'n' no friends," he muttered. "The best I can hope for is ta' beg fer' enough money 'fore tha' cold days reach tha' lands."

Placing the bindle stick across his shoulder, the goblin proceeded to leave his home, trying his best to look away from the pyre highlighting the destruction of his home.

As he began to close what was left of the gate, a purple light began to glow from one of the corpses. As the goblin inspected it, another began to glow, and another, and before the goblin could figure out what was happening, the bodies had dragged themselves away, absorbing into the central mass. The goblin watched in horror as the bodies twisted and cracked, pulled into the ever-growing corpse fire.

As the transformation ended, a colossal being stripped of its flesh, shaking off the embers of the fire, knelt towards him. The hands made of sharpened bone dug into the earth as the creature released a cold breath, wilting the grass beneath it. The skulls fused into its body lit up; every socket was inhabited by lights, all taking in their surroundings.

Brought to its feet, the being uttered a singular, ominous word: "Arlowe."

The goblin recognised the voice to be that of the village's elder. "Baxka?"

As the being examined itself, its attention turned to the pitiful goblin, gripping him inside of its palm, bringing him to its face.

"Arrsk?" the being asked. "Is that you?" The voice was different this time. Arrsk recognised the voice as Kweez, the village's mystic. "Of course it's only you left. Who else could it have been?"

A headache began in Arrsk's mind, unable to track all of these voices. "Baxka? Kweez? Was that Rilit? What happened ta' you all?"

The creature looked over their free hand, moving the immense vessel over to a ditch; a hulking monstrosity of melded goblin carcasses stared back. The voices all spoke at once, struggling to answer the question.

Baxka spoke once more, silencing the masses. "We're all here, Arrsk, though only a few of us seem to be vocal. Those are the voices you can hear."

The goblin pondered for a moment, thinking about the monster's first word.

The voice of the terminally ill beggar, Kivyx, came through. "Arlowe. Arlowe was the one who killed us. Those hunters had been trying to take our home from us for so long, scouting and picking us off for weeks. Then *he* came and they felt confident enough to attack us, like savage dogs. We just wanted to protect our home, our loved ones. But *he* took that away, and once those hunters have been dealt with, we will find him and rip him limb from limb."

Arrsk began to smile, then laugh, climbing onto the monster's shoulder, drawing his daggers. "W-we can't lose! They'll all pay! Especially that lousy prick!"

The creature took Arrsk by the neck of his clothes and placed him back on the ground. They then came close, with the voice of Amizi, Arrsk's lover. "You can't come. I couldn't bear to see you get hurt."

The monster then pulled back at what they said, with Rilit speaking in her place. "You're joking," he scoffed. "He left us all to die! If you'd just let me, I'd kill him right here."

Arrsk's confusion turned into rage, which he aimed directly at the monster with enough force to move the form back.

"I'm not stayin' 'ere, and I'm not leavin' any of ya' behind! I never did! I can't do this on ma' own, b-but neither can you. Who's gonna carry important items? Who's gonna search fer' trails? Who's gonna sneak around so that we can ambush? Set traps? Climb through holes? Talk to people? We need each other 'cause we're all we've got! Leave if ya' want, but I will follow you through everythin' 'cause it's our duty, not yours! Ya' hear me?"

The behemoth stood speechless as Arrsk swiped the tears away from his eyes.

Baxka's voice emerged to end the silence. "Well, three hundred and nineteen minds are better than three hundred and eighteen, isn't that right, Arrsk?"

The goblin's eyes lit up, beginning his ascent of the creature's arm, hearing a commotion coming from the village's hall.

Arrsk dropped to the floor, pulling on the monster's arm. "Come on, Kaxrax, let's give our new neighbours tha' tour of tha' village!"

The behemoth cocked their head. "Kaxrax? Why?"

Arrsk turned with a smile. "Don'cha get it, ya' big lug? You *are* tha' village!"

Chapter Six:

"A new day brings new obstacles and new people.
A liar brings both."

26th Thuvalos

Land's Legacy

2084∞ (Current Age)

"Arlowe, please rest. You've been walking for hours."

Xanth wasn't wrong. Since departing from Kaxrax Village, he had spent the last day travelling towards Hietruce without rest to ease his aching body. With no supplies, his stomach had remained empty, and a lack of sleep had not helped his condition.

Arlowe continued following the path onwards. "We're not far now. Besides, we need to find someone."

"Someone? Like who?"

"A guide of some sort. I've read plenty of books about the world beyond my city, but I need someone more experienced *within* it to show me the way. I thought Vernard's men would be up for it, but I guess I was—"

Xanth cut him off. "Be careful. I can hear footsteps behind you."

The prince turned his vision to his flank. Sure enough, Arlowe could see a hooded figure treading the same path. In calmer times, many would travel along the roads, keeping them lively. However, with the raised hostilities of the kharakians, the roads had become near-barren.

"Did you hear their footsteps earlier, Xanth?" the prince queried; his tiring mind was unable to recall. "I didn't."

"I only heard them recently," the boy responded. "Be. Careful. You're in no state to fight."

As Arlowe pressed onwards, a bridge came in to view with another hooded figure sat upon the guardrail. Seeing him approach the bridge, the hooded figure at the prince's back whistled, calling for a stone giant to emerge from the waters, climbing out of the depths to join them.

The towering aautgal stepped forward, gesturing with its hand for Arlowe to halt. The prince was confident in his skill as a fighter, but between the ten-foot aautgal, its two allies and his own exhaustion, he refrained from drawing his weapon, certain that he wouldn't last more than a few moments.

The hooded male on the bridge moved to the side of their stone partner, looking Arlowe up and down. "Lookie 'ere. The beasts missed anotha' meal!"

The aautgal hadn't moved since raising its arm, though the two figures moved closer, grinning from ear to ear as they inspected their prey.

Arlowe kept still as the two circled him. "Look, I don't have time for this. I need to reach Thaedlon. It's urgent. The kharakians are—"

The two hooded figures came together. "Oh no!" the partner whined, her voice and stance melodramatic, mocking him. "How could we do such a thing? To stop you on your way to such an immense task. Go, be on your way, and let us bother you no longer! Boulder, let him through!"

Arlowe turned his focus to the aautgal, who moved its arm at the order, now gesturing for him to pass. As the prince sceptically made his move, however, the aautgal snapped into place. Striking the prince in the gut, the prince was sent crashing into the dirt, reeling from the blow.

The hooded male from the bridge grabbed the back of Arlowe's collar, raising him to his knees. While suspended, the female figure moved to her captive's front, getting close enough to touch noses with him. "I can't believe you actually fell for that. Are

78

you for real?"

Aching and injured, Arlowe couldn't compose himself to answer.

The woman took a dagger from her belt, resting it over his throat. "I know we're not on the best of terms, darling," she said with a devious smile adorning her face. "But we were wondering if you'd seen someone. Dark skin, hooded, metal mask covering his eyes. Ring any bells?"

Arlowe shook his head, still unable to move his words from his mind to the air.

The woman moved her blade away from his throat, skilfully rolling it between her fingers. "Well, if you don't know anything, there's no point in keeping you around. Sorry champ," she uttered, clasping his throat tightly. "I would make it quick, but I'm a sucker for pain."

As the dagger neared his eye, the grip around Arlowe's collar lessened, dropping him back down to the ground. The hooded man fell on top of him, foaming at the mouth.

The woman took a step back to survey her surroundings. "Boulder, use your head. Calidius was hit by a dart that came from somewhere over there. Go check it out." Her attention returned to Arlowe. "I'll deal with our friend."

Arlowe pushed Calidius off his back, looking up to see a large rock hurtling down the nearby hill. The rolling stone struck the aautgal's legs, shattering them with ease.

Using the tree to its side as support, Boulder lifted itself up, only to be met by the same masked figure the bandits had been describing.

"No leg to stand on, giant?" the stranger taunted. "I got a hit in for free. Want a turn?"

Boulder wound up its arm and swung at its target with great force. Predicting its movements, the stranger moved his fingers into the shape of a square, opening them up to create a small portal that absorbed the aautgal's fist.

Within moments, another portal opened, connecting the giant's fist to its torso. The aautgal was knocked back down with an aperture in its chest.

Giving it no time to recover, the masked man drew a small blade in each hand, digging them into the giant's chest to excavate a larger opening, unearthing the giant's life crystal buried within. A spherical object was then jammed inside, the stranger leaping out of the way of the orb's detonation.

As the dust cleared, the assailant stood proud, surrounded by the bits of rubble left from his kill. The stranger approached the last standing member of the bandits, stepping over the aautgal's head as he closed in on her.

The bandit stood her ground. "You fool. You can't stand against the Katosian Hunters. You think that you've crippled me because you took out my allies, when in actuality all you've done is made it so that I have a better chance of joining their ranks once I kill you! I do have to give you props though, you make a good hero, but all that means is that you were braver for a few moments longer." The woman chuckled to herself. "We're not so different, you and—"

With a resounding thwack, the woman fell to the floor with a crossbow bolt between her eyes. The stranger loaded up a new bolt, before placing the crossbow back under his cape.

"Why do they *always* monologue? They make such easy targets." The man twisted the bolt from her skull, making sure not to damage it. "And I swear, if I hear the 'we're not so different' spiel one more time, my next shot will be going somewhere *very*—"

The stranger turned to face Arlowe, raising his hands above his head as a sign of peace. "I know this doesn't mean much since you know I'm well equipped, but *I* have no intention of harming you." The prince remained motionless. "In fact, I overheard you saying that you needed someone. I'm sure you can pay well, if you're picking up what I'm putting down?"

The man jogged over to Arlowe's position, offering his hand to raise him to his feet. Arlowe cautiously accepted his saviour's hand, though he only rose to be knelt, taking a moment to regain his breath.

Trying to use his current stance to his advantage, Arlowe peered at the various pieces of equipment strapped to the stranger, piquing Xanth's interest too.

"Woah, that's a lot of stuff! I wonder what it all does," the boy pondered.

"Well, I know he's carrying weapons for long and close-range combat, as well as some kind of explosive, so I'll keep my distance," Arlowe replied telepathically. "He also caused that aautgal to hit itself. He must be using some kind of illumancy."

"Illumancy?"

"A user of illusion magic. Another of his unseen weapons."

The stranger coughed, regaining Arlowe's attention. "My eyes are up here, my friend," he stated, sniggering to himself. "Don't get me wrong, I'm honoured, but you're not my type."

Arlowe backed away, unnerved at how someone could be so cheery after murdering a group of people. "You sound like you know who I am based on your comment about being paid."

"Well, money does make the world go 'round."

"That's not what I meant."

"I know who you are. Most people are blind because you're not dressed the way they expect you to be. That, and I saw you all the time back in Eyenridge, when you weren't secluding yourself." A devious expression filling his face, the stranger moved himself over to the bridge. "Must've been some good books in that personal library."

The prince's personal hideaway was a secret known only by a select number of people, unnerving Arlowe that someone so well-armed knew something so private about him. *It's becoming abundantly clear that I was saved only to return a favour.*

Arlowe followed the man to the bridge, fully aware that this stranger was the only thing between him and another deadly encounter.

"That wasn't just a casual fact. How do you know something like that about me?" he demanded, tired and agitated. "Are you a thief? An assassin? Or are you just some kind of well-armed royalophile?"

"None of the above," the man responded. "I'm a guardian, hired specifically for the royal families and government leaders. I'm young, but I've travelled to all of the capitals, though I'm utilised more often in some places than others. Since your parents passed and you decided to give the people the choice to vote as opposed to ruling it yourself, I found myself in Fertral often. My condolences, by the way."

"But I never saw you."

"That's my shtick. Potential assailants wouldn't make themselves known if I was stood by your side. They'd know when to strike and when to keep to themselves."

Xanth's voice echoed in Arlowe's mind. "Does he fit your requirements? He could be who you were looking for. I like him."

"He's holding enough red flags to start a parade, Xanth. Let's not get hasty."

Arlowe approached the stranger, who had stopped to watch the stream. "It's convenient for you to show up now. How do I know I can I trust you?"

"You'd rather trust the bandits lining the roads? It's not safe."

"You don't seem safe either."

"And commit regicide? No thank you."

"And if I choose to go on without you?"

The masked man shrugged. "I'll sleep soundly."

The prince knew when he had been beaten. As sceptical as he was, he couldn't turn down the aid of another. He couldn't handle the rest of his journey with Xanth alone.

Xanth has taken a liking to him. Maybe it's an omen.

"If you're interested, I need a guide," Arlowe stated, begrudgingly at that.

The masked man kept his eyes trained over the water. "Hm?"

"You sound like you're well-travelled and you can definitely handle yourself. Plus, it would be nice to have some company on the road. I can't promise you that we'll be safe though. What do you—"

In his peripheral, Arlowe spotted an outstretched hand, balled into a fist. The man was smiling, urging it forward for Arlowe to accept it. "You had me at, 'I need.' You seem like the interesting sort, and the danger is no worry. My line of work isn't exactly safe anyway. The name's Onyx."

Oddly relieved at his words, Arlowe took the fist, shaking it to seal the deal.

As the awkward handshake ended, Onyx's hand swapped from one of offering to one of asking, with his palm facing the sky. "Not meaning to be rude my friend, but talent doesn't come cheap."

The prince removed his backpack, rummaging around for anything of value. Finding what he sought, Arlowe fished out the single gold coin that Levanim had left him.

"The coin!" exclaimed the pterravun.

Arlowe placed the coin into his saviour's hand. "This is all I have to give you."

Onyx thought for a moment, turning the gold back and forth. Nodding, the man rolled the coin between his fingers before flicking it into the air; the coin landed perfectly into one of his pockets.

"I guess it'll do for now. It's not like I'm making any money around here anyway," Onyx remarked, shrugging. "I'll put it down as an I owe you."

The man departed; a finger signalled for the prince to follow. "Come on, we're burning daylight."

Arlowe caught up to Onyx, walking by his side. "So, you're leading me to Thaedlon, right? That's where I need to go."

Onyx gave his new employer a light shove, knocking him off-balance. "We're taking a little detour. There's a tavern not far past the refugee checkpoint. I'm going to do you a solid and pay for you to have a meal. If we run into trouble, it'll be a lot harder to protect you if you can't protect yourself."

Arlowe opened his mind to speak to Xanth. "Still like him?"

"I do," he replied. "He's willing to help, and even if things don't work out, he wants you to be a full strength for the journey ahead. That has to mean something."

*

It didn't take long for the two to reach the tavern. Arlowe immediately sat at the closest vacant table, while Onyx slid up to the counter, conversing with the woman behind the bar.

Though he couldn't hear what they were talking about, due to the commotion of the tavern, the slap that connected with Onyx's face was loud and clear for not just Arlowe, but the whole tavern to laugh over.

Onyx came over a few moments later, carrying a bowl filled with broth, placing it down in front of the prince alongside a few slices of bread. The meal looked revolting, though Arlowe proceeded to inhale his meal, savouring every mouthful.

"You sure you're not missing the cuisine from your castle? I doubt that's what they served you," Onyx posed, keeping his voice low to avoid outing his ally. One of the serving staff handed him a tankard, with the assassin bowing to her. "Thank you."

The prince looked up from his meal with food all over his face. Taking a moment to swallow, he gave a sigh of relief before responding. "You'd be surprised. I didn't join

84

the banquets in the castle very often. Too showy. Usually, I'd just eat in my library."

Onyx was taken aback, though his mind drifted onto other questions. "I don't get why you're worrying about how your people see you."

"I'm easily identifiable for one," Arlowe muffled through his food, pointing to the burns on his face. "I'm avoiding your question. I apologise." The prince stopped eating, now smirking at Onyx's comment. "Wait, coming from the man who snuck through the checkpoint to get here?"

"You pulled up the hood I loaned you as we passed through the checkpoint and didn't take it down again until we were through the tavern door," noted the assassin, taking a sip from his tankard. "What have *you* got to be so worried about? *You're* a hero."

Arlowe shook his head. "I failed. Even if I made my escape, that doesn't change what happened. Eyenridge is gone." His hand tightened into a fist. "I'm no hero."

Onyx leaned forward, his drink to one side. "If what you told me on the way here is to be believed, I'd be proud to be under your banner.

"You fought off hordes of those monsters, survived the fall and still managed to make your way over here. Sure, you had a little help getting out of the city, but I wouldn't underestimate your determination. Most people I know wouldn't have even stayed to protect the city, let alone emerge from it.

"Don't sell yourself short."

A gracious smile warmed Arlowe's face. "Thanks, Onyx. I appreciate it."

Onyx moved out of his chair, evidently uncomfortable at the praise he was receiving. "Yeah, sure. Don't mention—"

At that moment, the door to the tavern slammed open, with a plethora of Hietruen guards filling the entryway. The men and women stood to each side of the entrance, allowing their heavily armoured captain to enter the establishment; his cape was decorated with the Hietruen royal crest, his breastplate lined with medals.

"Word has reached the Hietruen Guard that the assassin known as Onyx came this way, presumably through the refugee checkpoint!" the guard captain declared. "This man is a threat to all and is highly sought after for crimes both in this country, and others. If he is taking refuge in this tavern, any who bring him forward will be generously rewarded for their actions! Any takers?"

Arlowe looked at Onyx, who gave him a wink. "Don't worry, I gave a fake name at the bar," he whispered.

"Looks like I didn't speak loud enough, men!" the captain bellowed. "Since no-one complied, this tavern is now on lockdown while we search the premises. Any actions against us will be swiftly dealt with!"

Arlowe went to raise his hand, only for Onyx and Xanth to shut him down, physically and mentally respectively.

"Are you crazy? Do you want me to get arrested?"

"Arlowe, no! He's our friend. He's helping us."

The prince fell back into his chair, snatching back his hand. "Look, we made a deal, but I didn't know you were an assassin at the time. If I'd have known, we would've gone our separate ways at the bridge!"

Onyx moved his thumb over his throat repeatedly, signalling for Arlowe to keep quiet. "First off," he uttered through his teeth. "I'm not just your average assassin, I'm a member of the Defiant. I've got rules. I'm not freelance."

A guard moved past their table, the assassin readjusting his hood. Arlowe attempted to get her attention, though Onyx was quick to grab his hand again. "And I really didn't want to use this, but since you're not aware, you're sat with the criminal. They'll count you as an accomplice of some sort. How do you think it'll look to the people that the *deceased* Prince of Eyenridge was dabbling with assassins?"

Their private argument had drawn unwanted attention. A hand slammed into the table to silence them. The guard from earlier had returned, interested in what the commotion was about.

"What seems to be the problem, you two? Anything I can help with?" Her eyes turned to Onyx. "Maybe you could both drop the hoods, talk face-to-face."

Onyx peered at Arlowe before looking back at the guard. "Oh, fuck this," he muttered, drawing a dagger from its sheath, plunging it into the guard's hand.

While the guard was still pinned to the table, the assassin grabbed the tankard from their table, launching it at an orc patron being interrogated by another guard.

Believing that the blow came from the guard, the drunken orc retaliated with a headbutt, knocking down the guard before turning his attention to another. Incited by their orcish comrade, the pressed patrons took swings of their own, initiating an all-out bar fight.

Though his mind was set on bringing his 'partner' to justice, Arlowe found a new problem within the chaos. While most of the patrons were set on fighting back against the Hietruen Guard, one of the customers had prowled around the bar.

"Out of my way, wench!" a dwarf slurred, trying to shove her back. "You've been watering down the drinks for months! I want what's mine!"

As the barmaid drew her mace from behind the counter, the sound of glass smashing arose, resulting in the dwarf dropping to the ground unconscious. Behind him stood Arlowe, equipped with a broken bottle in his hand, his hood still raised.

"Are you okay? I know the guards have their hands full," he asked, gently placing the shattered bottle back on to the shelf. "I had to pick top shelf…"

The woman rested the mace over her shoulder, looking upon the ongoing brawling.

"I'd be more annoyed if this didn't happen at least once a week. Part and parcel of being in this business. Go on. Get. You ain't doin' me any favours by standing here."

The prince slid over the bar, looking out for the assassin. Though the tavern was thick with fighting, Xanth was able to spot Onyx in the crowd. "He's over there! To your right!"

Though Arlowe knew where he was, he couldn't stop Onyx from adding another kill to his name. Weaving around the guard captain's attacks with ease, the assassin had been planting his blades within the exposed points of his armour to bleed his target dry.

As the fight carried on, the guard captain had become sluggish, unable to keep up with Onyx's speed and his own pain. As he attempted one last strike, Onyx sliced open his throat, pushing him over with a light tap.

Arlowe charged through the brawl, bringing his sword down upon the assassin. Moving out of the way, Onyx raised his dagger, parrying another of Arlowe's strikes.

"Hey moron," Onyx spat. "Don't know if you're aware, but I'm not wearing a Hietruen Guard uniform. Mind swinging your blade in a different direction?"

"I know where I'm swinging!" Arlowe roared. "Don't know if you're aware, but murder is against the law."

"Funny, I don't remember *Your Highness* cutting me to pieces when those bandits attacked, or do you just pick and choose when to follow the law?"

"Those bandits were breaking the law. I'm pretty sure it's not legal to be a bandit!"

Arlowe tackled into his target, causing Onyx to drop his dagger. In response, Onyx struck Arlowe's wrist, stealing his blade before throwing it to one side.

Onyx nimbly dodged Arlowe's newest advance, though he was surprised at how nimble the prince was, being just as adept with his fists as he was with his sword.

As the two continued to swing at each other, another wave of guards entered the

88

tavern, with their eyes set on both the hooded men.

With all his force, Onyx knocked Arlowe back before throwing another spherical object at the door. This time however, the object began producing billows of smoke, adding to the mayhem within the tavern.

Arlowe found himself by his blade, rearming himself to strike at Onyx once more. The assassin was ready for the prince, drawing his crossbow. Arlowe's blade neared Onyx's throat as the assassin's finger hovered over the trigger of the crossbow, readied to fire.

"Be straight with me," Onyx argued. "You know what I am. Why not leave me? It's not like *you'll* be arrested once they figure out that you're alive."

The prince held his gaze. "I don't want them to *know* I'm alive. Not until I have a plan to fix this mess."

"Don't be so emotional. They need you—"

"Not until I have a plan in place. I refuse to come back from the dead to fail them a second time."

The prince pulled back his sword slightly, giving the assassin space to breath. In return, Onyx lowered his weapon, placing it back on his back.

A firm click came from behind Onyx. With closer inspection, the two found that a trap door had been opened, presumably used for escape. Arlowe looked around, spotting the bartender from earlier waving at them.

"Look, I owe you for helping me with the dwarf, and since you two are the troublemakers, the sooner I can get rid of you, the better," she stated, keeping her eyes out for the guard. "Though, if anyone asks, you got out through a window. That door is an unauthorised alteration, if you get what I mean?"

The prince nodded, bowing to the woman, mouthing his words. "Thank you."

Arlowe rushed to the hatch, though Onyx stayed behind. "So, uh, no hard feelings, right?"

The barmaid raised her mace into his view, motivating him to leave her sight, shutting the trap door behind them.

*

Taking refuge in a cave north of the tavern, the prince and the assassin sat on opposite sides, catching their breaths after their ordeal.

Onyx was busy adjusting his equipment, replacing any items used from a pouch connected to the top of his back, while Arlowe sat in silence, weighing up his options.

The assassin rose from his stony seat, flicking Arlowe's coin back at him. "I'm heading out soon. If you have questions, it might be a good idea to ask them."

Arlowe caught the coin, remaining silent for a moment, thinking of the best questions to ask given his now-limited time.

"Why did you kill the guard captain?" he posed. "What did he do that was so bad that you thought murder was the best course of action?"

"He attacked me?" Arlowe's stern gaze quickly drew out the answer he sought. "I had a contract recently. The guard captain's wife was a priestess at the nearby Arythol chapel. She was secretly of a radical mind, believing that those other than humans deserved to die, and that she would be Arn's hand in that religious undertaking. Someone must've caught on to what she was doing, as the Defiant were hired to find proof of her deeds and eliminate her."

Onyx pulled out a note from a pocket on his right leg, handing it to the prince. "This is one of her letters to her husband, outlining what she was doing. Seeing as how she wasn't arrested, he must have been in on it."

Arlowe read through the note, shocked at its contents. The note mentioned how; *many had risen to be judged* and that *together they could wipe Argestra of this filth to please their lord.*

He handed the note back, with Onyx returning it back to his pocket. "I tracked her to the chapel basement. I wish it could've been anywhere else," he uttered, shivering at his own comment. "The basement was filled with the corpses of those she had poisoned, dragging them down to be buried. I could still hear some of her victims, meaning that whatever poison she was using must've been slow-acting. I killed her right there, but there was nothing I could do for her victims. That was when her husband walked in."

Onyx pulled another item from his pocket, though this time, it was a warrant for his arrest. The word *Onyx* filled the top of the sheet, with the hood and metal mask drawn on the bottom half to identify him to others.

"He knew my name, and he knew that I'd killed his wife. That's where you and I crossed paths. The guard captain had hired bandits to scour the roads searching for me. They'd find travellers, and ask them if they had seen me. Regardless of their answer, the bandits would kill them, stripping their bodies of valuables.

"In return for their service, the guard captain would turn a blind eye to all bandit activity in the area, and pulled what men he had from the roads to avoid attacking his allies. I tried to save as many as I could, but he was pulling a lot of strings.

"You're lucky I found you."

Arlowe remained silent, trying to imagine Onyx's tale. "I'm not looking for a morality contest, nor do I have anything to prove to *you*," Onyx asserted. "If you don't want me by your side, I'll understand your decision."

Arlowe stood at last, moving towards the assassin. He held out his hand, offering back the coin he had offered in the first place.

"I need to be more realistic," Arlowe spoke, looking to Onyx smiling. "I'm trying to prevent as much death as possible, but you can't always avoid it. You did spare the other guards after all."

Onyx tried to take back the coin, only to meet resistance, with Arlowe not letting go. "But," he continued. "I need you to communicate with me. Even if you're killing for a reason, we have to work together. I imagine that the barmaid could've handled herself, but during your little stunt, she was attacked. We need to minimise casualties. I don't want innocents getting caught up in our conflicts."

Arlowe let go of the coin, allowing Onyx to take it. The assassin rolled it between his fingers once more before returning it to his pocket. "We still partners?"

"You saved me. That means something."

Arlowe held out his hand for a new handshake. Onyx took his hand, though he balled it into a fist before doing the same with his own. The prince knew where this was going, moving his fist forward to bump his partner's.

Picking up his backpack, the prince left the cave, continuing north with Thaedlon in his sights and his partner by his side.

"Besides, everyone around here has seen me with you. It may be a while before I can approach anyone else for help," Arlowe noted. "Looks like I'm stuck with you."

"Oh ha ha. Very funny," Onyx said, trying to call Arlowe's bluff. "That was a joke, right?"

Chapter Seven:

"The elves had claimed that the most powerful weapon was the mind. The dwarves accepted their challenge."

30th Thuvalos

Land's Legacy

2084∞ (Current Age)

With many miles behind him, Arlowe was amazed at how far out he had travelled. The familiar surroundings of densely packed forests had been replaced with rich open plains, stretching as far as the eye could see. The weather had also been kind to them, if a tad warmer than Arlowe was used to. Taking in the view, it only pushed him harder to secure Fertral, craving this kind of peace for his own people.

During their trek, Onyx's mind had exploded with questions, firing them all at the prince with barely enough time for an answer before moving to the next.

Arlowe didn't mind. It didn't feel as though the assassin was prying, and Xanth would have only asked the same questions, so it made sense to sate both curiosities.

"So, why did you give up your birth right of control to strangers? I don't understand," Onyx queried, quenching his thirst for knowledge. "Surely it would've made more sense to take the reins yourself. Keep everything under control."

Arlowe stopped, resting himself atop the stone wall that followed the path. "My father didn't leave as soon as the Sixth Invasion started, but even when he did leave, I was only thirteen. Would you want a child leading you? Making decisions for you? Erethys, you've seen me out here. I still have a lot to learn. I'm not ready to lead."

Onyx rested on the wall opposite. "You saying that genuinely, or are you using that as an excuse to hide that you're scared of ruling?"

"I *was* scared. Honestly, I still am. But whatever set me on this path, be it by the divines, fate or simply my need to right this wrong, now is the time to face my fears. I'm ready to be proven wrong, and I'm ready to be beaten down. Only through failure can we truly succeed."

The assassin had already left the wall, ascending the hill ahead of them. "Unless you die. Can't learn from that," he shouted down. "Though I guess you came as close as you can. Feel any different?"

Arlowe ignored Onyx's playful jabs, departing the wall to re-join his partner.

"Your feet made of lead?" His new partner was waving for him to hurry. "You're gonna want to see this!"

The prince reached the top of the hill, understanding why Onyx was so eager for his company. From the top of the hill, Arlowe could make out the bustling jewel of Hietruce: Thaedlon.

His father had told him all about the city, from the giant walls scarred by countless battles to the bronze statues that had stood through them all, the Hietruen Grand Bazaar featuring traders from across the continent to the glorious Castle of Aalkeitirei Tuupaank.

"According to my history books, the Thaedlon line has existed since Thaedlon itself first came into being," the prince silently passed on to Xanth. "Existing as nothing more than interconnected refugee camps and the castle, Thaedlon now stands as a beacon to any escaping their lives as slaves."

"The humans built over the dark legacy of the dwarfs," Xanth added.

The prince nodded. "Once slavery had been abolished, Frederick Thaedlon returned here, aiding his people in building a city that they could all be proud of. You'll see a monument as we enter, to show that not only were the humans as important as the other races, but that my ancestors were willing to forgive; they invited those that

94

enslaved to live among them."

"It looks incredible, wouldn't you agree?" Arlowe posed to Onyx.

While the prince had stood in awe of the city, the assassin had already made his way down the hill towards its front gates. Arlowe sighed, understanding that most were not as sheltered as him. The view ahead would be normal to anyone else.

"Could we stay a little longer? I've never seen a city like this—" Xanth choked up at his own words. "I'm... so sorry. I didn't mean it like that. Eyenridge was..."

Arlowe laughed, patting himself on the head. "Don't worry about it. We could stand here and look from afar, or we could go inside? How about it?"

Excitable noises came from Xanth, indicating a resounding yes. Arlowe couldn't help but get excited with him, travelling down the path with glee.

It wasn't until he took a hold of himself that he realised two things: Onyx was not as far down the path as he thought, and that he was watching the whole time.

"Heatstroke?" he asked.

Arlowe froze. Improvisation was not one of his strengths. "H-heatstroke?"

"Yeah. You're acting weird. Laughing and patting your head. Are you too warm?"

Xanth spoke up. "Tell him you have porphyria."

"I have porphyria."

An awkward silence arose, with Onyx taking a few steps back. "Well, so long as you don't infect me, we're good." He shook his head. "We're almost there. Come on."

Onyx moved ahead, leaving Arlowe behind once more.

"Xanth, what is porphyria?" Arlowe asked.

"I don't know. I read it in a book."

"Then why did you recommend *that* illness? I don't even know what porphyria is!"

"By the looks of it, neither does Onyx. You're welcome."

Arlowe went to continue arguing, only to realise that Xanth had a point. With his backpack adjusted and his fake illness in check, the prince followed his partner's lead towards Thaedlon's front gates.

*

The entrance to the city was crowded with people, animals and wagons all rushing to complete their daily routines. Onyx moved through the crowds like a petal in the winds, while Arlowe moved through with the etiquette of a hurricane, apologising with every knock and bump.

Passing the front gates, the two partners were able to reconvene at the bronze statue centrepiece known as The Liberation of Arn's Last. The statue depicted humanity rising above both the conqueror demons of the First Invasion, and their past enslavement to the elves and dwarves. The metal hands of the slavers and the damned were clasped around the chains of the enslaved.

The scent of spices and perfumes filled the air as cargo was transported through the claustrophobic streets. Various races and animals passed by in mere moments, rushing to move their shipments on time. Each piece of clothing signified their affiliation, from performer to guild worker, beggar to Hietruen guardsman.

"I need to meet with the king as soon as I can," Arlowe stated. "Are you with me?"

Onyx chuckled to himself. "Do you want me to draw a target on my chest too?" He placed a hand over his torso. "I'm lucky that Thaedlon draws such large crowds for me to blend in with. Going to the castle seems like the opposite of a good idea."

"Then what are you going to do?"

"Since you owe me and I have some free time, I was gonna go and see if anyone needs…" Onyx began jabbing the prince in the chest, pretending to stab him repeatedly. "Well, it rhymes with harassin'. I'll meet you back here later."

"Onyx, wait—" All it took was a blink for the assassin to blend into the crowd, disappearing from Arlowe's view entirely. "Arn give me strength."

Lost for words, the prince turned his attention to the castle standing proudly in the distance. Though the base was of dwarven origin, stone shaped into a simple bed house, the human inheritors used the structure as a foundation. It was the prominence of the human's own stone that guided Arlowe to it. It was there that he could attempt to regain his home.

Thaedlon was laid out differently to Eyenridge, throwing Arlowe's sense of direction. Where Eyenridge was split into four districts with the castle at its centre, able to block off any one district in the event of an attack, Thaedlon had all of its entrances at one side, with the castle on the other.

One long walkway connected the two, with everything from the housing, stations, guilds and places of worship either side of the stretch. Arlowe trod upon metal grates lining the walkway, concealing walls that could be raised to provide cover should any threat not be contained outside of the city.

Walking up the continuous hill, Arlowe eventually found himself nearing the castle, seeing a mass of different races protesting against the guards. A town crier in particular grabbed Arlowe's attention, with a length of wood strapped to his back. A sign was raised above his head that read, *Please collect your number!*

The prince approached the crier, only to be handed a slip of paper with a number on.

"That is your number," the crier muttered, almost falling asleep from his monotonous routine. "You may either stand and wait or return later to gain an audience with the King Demetrius. Late returns will not be accepted. Thank you for your understanding."

Turning to leave, Arlowe nudged the town crier, partially waking him from his slump.

"Excuse me sir, but what's going on?" he queried, glancing around. "Why are there so many people here, and why do they look like they're on the verge of rioting?"

"It's the kharakians, kid," the crier responded, removing his hat to wipe the sweat from his brow. "People don't feel safe. They're saying that we're next, even with troops from the neighbouring countries on the border. A lot of people want a word with the King of Thaedlon, but he's already busy as it is. We're trying to deal with people as quickly as we can to move them along, but with both citizens and visitors wanting an audience, that's not easy—"

A handful of citizens charged up to the crier, snatching the tickets from his belt only to be herded back by the castle guards.

The man dusted himself off, readying another ticket as he returned to his rehearsed dialogue. "Ugh, hopefully that answered your question?"

Another crier came into view, stood upon a central stage. "Forty-six thousand, eight hundred and one! I repeat, forty-six thousand, eight hundred and one!"

The prince looked at his own sheet of paper, only to bring it closer to confirm what he saw. "You're kidding."

*

"Eighty-three thousand, two hundred and seventy-seven. That's not too bad," Xanth encouraged, hoping to ease Arlowe's mind.

Arlowe had taken the crier's advice, leaving the protesters to wander the city. "I can't imagine this being easy on the king. He has all of these meetings to keep everyone calm, and still has to lead the country? I can see why my father looked up to him."

Descending the hill, Arlowe spotted a signpost containing a map of the city.

"So, what now?" Xanth pondered.

"Well, since we won't be seeing the king anytime soon, the Warforged Guild seems like the next best option. I can maintain my equipment and throw in some training too.

Arn knows I need it," The prince moved his finger down the map. "And if you're up for it, we can take the long way there. Do a little sightseeing, if you want to?"

Arlowe's detour allowed them both to take in Thaedlon's many wondrous sights, including the Thaedlon Crossroad that separated the city's churches. The two saw the beauty of the carved sandstone and flying buttresses that made up the Housing District and visited the Hietruen Cemetery, famed for being the burial site of Umisdaec, the first recorded dwarven leader and inventor of dwarven politics.

The Grand Bazaar was Arlowe and Xanth's final stop before the Guild District. Eyenridge's market was a sight to see, but it had nothing on Thaedlon's bazaar. While he was used to seeing smiths, grocers and alchemists, the prince was surprised to see musicians with unique instruments, chefs with ingredients from lands far and wide and even mages selling small comedic spells and cute little trinkets.

Of all the stalls though, Arlowe fell in love with the book stall, which even had a small pile of discarded books free to the public. With a stroke of luck, Arlowe found a spare copy of The Pursuits of the Argestran Knight, placing it in his bag with the gentlest of care. *A good story for Xanth, though I imagine I'll be reading it first. I won't be losing it again.*

Upon reaching the Guild District, Arlowe came to find it reasonably quiet, much more so than the rest of the city. This was to be expected, as many of the various guild members would be hard at work studying, training, or out in the field completing their contracts for the day.

As the prince reached the entrance of the Warforged Guild, his eyes caught a notice board filled with contracts. These contracts were highly varied, with some simply being; *get insert item for insert person*, to quests that would last months in other countries. It impressed him that some could be so dedicated to their work. The thought of a slight income enticed him; his fingers sifted through what was available.

"Are ma' eyes deceiving me?" The prince recognised the accent. "Arlowe, is that you?"

Arlowe turned to see Schukara stood before him, looking as though she had seen a ghost. The elf placed a finger on his chest, confirming that he was not the spectre she believed him to be.

"Hey Schukara, it's good to—"

The prince was cut off, tackled by the mercenary into a tight hug that crushed him into her steel armour. Schukara let go, wiping her eyes with a massive smile on her face, while he took a deep breath upon being released from her vice-like grip.

"I'm sorry, I get a lil' emotional over tha' silliest things." The elf composed herself. "But how? I saw ya' fall from tha' castle. There were explosions and everythin'."

Like Onyx before, Arlowe kept the part with the pterravun to himself, swapping it for his established lie.

"You're right, I wouldn't have survived, if not for the pond that I fell into. It broke my fall and kept me alive, though getting here was a nightmare," he expressed. "I've had to deal with bandits, goblins and kharakians. I'm lucky I found Onyx when I did."

Schukara looked confused. "Onyx? Who's that?"

Arlowe lowered his voice. "Believe it or not, he's an assassin. A member of the Defiant. I would've died before reaching the refugee checkpoint if not for him."

"A prince workin' with an assassin? Is that wise?"

"Probably not, but I didn't really have a choice. Besides, he's grown on me."

Schukara's expression made it evident that she didn't feel comfortable with his choice of companions, though she kept her thoughts to herself, quickly changing the course of the conversation.

100

"So, what brings ya' ta' Thaedlon?" the elf questioned, still smiling. "You could'a gone ta' any of tha' other neighbourin' countries. What made ya' choose Hietruce?"

"My father was good friends with the king. They had a better connection than any of the other monarchs. If I can secure his aid, the other countries may be more willing to throw their lot in with us," Arlowe voiced, looking towards the castle. "Though that may take a while."

Arlowe handed Schukara the slip of paper. Her brow furrowed. "I got handed one a' these too. I would say ta' tell 'em who ya' are ta' get in, but tha' guards don't seem ta' care who ya' are. Morons," she huffed, passing back the slip.

"It's fine," Arlowe noted, shrugging. "Whether I do it before or after, I need to get my hands on some new equipment, so I may as well do it while I'm forced to wait. Any strings you could pull here?"

Schukara frowned. "My, I'd do what I can if I could, but as I said back in Eyenridge, I haven't been a part of tha' Warforged fer' tha' longest time. Sorry friend."

However, as her energy began to fade, the mercenary's eyes caught a specific contract hanging from the board behind Arlowe, barging past him to collect the sheet.

"It can't be. He's here?" Schukara murmured, clenching her fist as she read it.

A smile warmed the elf's face once more, though her energy felt different. The Schukara from a few moments ago felt calm and friendly, whereas the Schukara that stood in front of him now was brimming with determination and restraint.

"Arlowe, if a' may be so bold," she stated. "I need yer' help. Follow me."

Schukara left the Guild District at an immense pace, stopping only once she reached the centre of the city. Arlowe caught up to her a few moments later, only to find his companion trying to pull a sewer grate out of the ground.

"Schu, hold on. I'm more than happy to help out a friend, but you're leaving me in the dark," he uttered in an attempt to be the voice of reason. "What's this about?"

Schukara released the grate, raising the now-crumpled contract for him to take, though she remained crouched with her back turned.

Arlowe took a closer look at the contract. A dwarf's face graced the sheet, naming him as Reitgrar Omasis, a criminal known for dabbling in the likes of murder and theft. His main claim to fame was the production of morbidthorn, a dangerous and addictive drug granting incredible highs at the cost of the user's senses.

The prince shifted his attention back to Schukara, who had taken the hilt of her blade to the edges of the grate, hoping to loosen it. "What did he do?"

Schukara turned her head, though she didn't speak back.

"Forgive me if I'm wrong," Arlowe continued, "but you don't seem like the type to go after drug lords for fun; not with this level of intensity anyway. What did he do?"

Schukara stood turning to face him, though her eyes refused to meet his. "I tried ta' save as many lives as I could that day. We got as many as we could outta that city before the mages sealed it off. Thought we'd be home free after that.

"Gettin' through the countryside wasn't easy, but we made it ta' tha' checkpoint. I led a bunch of 'em towards Thaedlon, leaving 'em in the safe hands of tha' guards. While I was gone, Reitgrar must've caught word of refugees in tha' city, and using their desperation, got 'em hooked on morbidthorn. He bled 'em of everythin' they had.

"His gang didn't just steal money 'n' valuables from 'em neither. They took children and killed who stood up ta' their sick enterprise."

"You couldn't have predicted what Reitgrar was going to do."

"I left my cosy town ta' protect those that can't protect themselves. I abandoned yer' people when they needed me most," Schukara growled. "I killed those survivors."

"*Reitgrar* killed the survivors. *You* did what you could for them. You could have run from Eyenridge, but *you* stayed to save them. *You* guided them here," the prince disputed. "From what you've told me, Reitgrar isn't going to stop there. If *you* give up, he wins."

Arlowe moved into the elf's sight, placing his hand on her shoulder. "You can make a difference, and this time, you're not alone."

Schukara finally raised her head, looking the prince directly in the eyes as she took his hand. A kind smile returned to her face, showing Arlowe that the fire within her had been relit.

"Thanks, I needed that." With a newfound zest, the mercenary removed the sewer grate, dropping it to the side. Taking hold of the ladder down, her attention returned to her newfound ally. "It's funny, I remember givin' ya' a good talkin' to a lil' while ago. Nice ta' know yer' good at returnin' favours."

The two descended into the sewers below. Arlowe dragged the metal grate back into place, joining the elf at the bottom.

While the sewers weren't exactly held to a high standard, it was clear that they were being used, as the outline of footsteps disturbed the grime that covered the tunnel floors. Old tents could also be seen lining the sewers, giving refuge to the disillusioned beggars currently pleading for spare change above them.

"So, which way?" Arlowe enquired. "I doubt Thaedlon has a small sewer system."

"Wanna flip a coin?" Schukara asked, leaving the prince confused. "So long as we head fer' tha' centre, it doesn't really matter." Her voice lowered. "I heard through tha' grapevine that a certain someone had tha' central cistern done up a lil' while ago, using it as a hive fer' illegal activities. The guards leave it well alone 'n he keeps everythin' flowin'. We can use tha' sewers as a back exit; try 'n' get in unnoticed."

Taking the initiative, Arlowe took the lead, travelling down the tunnel to his right. At his flank, Schukara had taken a torch from the wall, lighting their way onwards.

"Is Cael okay?" the prince questioned, asking as soon as a free moment was available.

Schukara giggled to herself. "Oh, he's doin' just fine," she confirmed. "He doesn't look it, but tha' old man knows how ta' fight. Handled every threat that crossed our path with an axe in his hand an' a pipe in his mouth."

"That sounds like Cael. Where is he now?"

"We parted ways at tha' checkpoint. I went through 'n' he went back. Nothin' I said could change his mind."

Though he had faith in his tutor's abilities, his thoughts turned to Eyenridge, praying that Cael had resisted the urge to go looking for him there. Even as a seasoned fighter, the kharakians were not to be trifled with.

As the two traversed further in, Arlowe felt a tap on his shoulder. Schukara had a finger over her lips, handing him their torch. As he took it, the elf spun around, swinging her fist at a figure behind them.

A cry of pain echoed through the sewers, with the prince peeking around his companion to see another elf, lightly armoured with a blade in his hand.

Schukara knelt, patting the would-be assailant down for anything she deemed dangerous before throwing it into the nearby water.

"Tch, 'ow in Arn's arsehole did you know I was there? I've been keepin' tabs on tha' both of ya' since ya' dropped down 'ere!" the elf yelled.

Taking him by his collar, Schukara lifted the elf to his feet, throwing his lean body into the nearest wall. "I didn't see anyone in tha' crowds outside, but my hearin' didn't fail me. I heard the grate move, so I knew someone was behind us. Just needed ya' ta' get close enough," she answered, moving into his personal space. "I'm seekin' an audience with yer' boss. Lend a lady a hand?"

"Why would I 'elp you?" the elf sneered, looking her up and down; his hand moved towards Schukara's waist. "Unless…"

His hand stopped inches away, feeling a sharp point on his groin. Looking down, Schukara's own blade was drawn, pointed directly into it. "I suggest ya' keep yer' hands to yerself. It's flatterin', but try that again, and yer' lil' partner there'll be joinin' tha' rest of tha' waste downstream."

The would-be assailant had gone white, pressing his back against the wall. Her lips were to his ear. "I wasn't requestin'. Take us ta' Reitgrar."

The elf nodded his head violently, almost falling over as Schukara's grip was loosened, leading them further into the sewer's darkness.

"Don't get on the wrong side of her," Xanth commented. "Though, I doubt you needed me to tell you that."

"I'm starting to wonder who I should be more worried about. Should it be the kharakians, or my own allies?" Arlowe replied, half-joking.

The deeper they delved into the sewer tunnels, the clearer it became that using this back exit was an option none preferred. Rats dominated this sector, feeding on the crumbs of those living above, as well as the corpses of those that had been disposed of by society.

"I'm glad I can't smell what you're smelling," Xanth spoke, noting the hand tightly clasped upon Arlowe's face.

Though the sewers continued to twist and wind, the group eventually found themselves confronted by a large metal door, with an equally large wheel to the right of it. The elf tried to turn it by himself, though his strength alone was not enough to move it, requiring Arlowe's help just to make it budge.

With their strength combined, the two managed to activate the mechanism, lifting the door that was blocking their path.

The elf leaned on the wheel, resting his arms. "I can 'old it in place 'ere, but I need you two ta' 'old the wheel on tha' otha' side. We travel tha' sewers in groups. We redesigned these sewers to fit *our* needs."

Arlowe and Schukara begrudgingly accepted the rogue's explanation, moving through the doorway to find the wheel. However, upon seeing no wheel and realising the deception, the door had already begun to drop. By the time they returned to the doorway, it had already been sealed, trapping them behind it.

The elf could be heard through the door, with a mocking tone added to his voice. "Hey, miss? Bet you wish ya' sliced off me' tackle now, eh? Go straight ahead 'n' have fun. Yer' fucked now!"

Schukara unclipped the helmet from her waist, placing it on her head before continuing down the tunnel. "Jokes on him, Arlowe. Reitgrar wanted us ta' find him, 'n' if he thinks this plan of his is gonna stop us, he's sorely mistaken."

As the two progressed further down the tunnel, the light at the end of it grew ever stronger, accompanied by the sound of chanting. A surge of concern shot through Arlowe's mind; a wave of excitement shot through Schukara's.

Entering the light, the prince and the elf were introduced to Reitgrar's headquarters: an arena built underneath the noses of the Thaedlon citizens. A lively crowd sat behind a sturdy cage, chanting out Reitgrar's name with unmatched adoration.

The chanting turned to cheering as a large dwarf graced their presence on the observation deck directly ahead of them, clutching some kind of gadget in his hand.

With a few taps of the machine, the crowd fell silent at once, allowing the dwarf to speak through it.

"Welcome one and all to the Thaedlon Arena. Today I, Reitgrar Omasis, bring you a

106

fight I've very much been lookin' forward to. In the prey corner, I give you Schukara Parle, a precious little soul who's been mucking up the plans of my predecessors and I every time she's set foot in our city. However, let this be the day that we remove her from Äkin once and for all!"

The dwarf cocked his head, noticing Arlowe at her side. "Ladies and gentlemen, it looks like the elf brought a friend! No 'ard feelings, tuupaan, but if you're with 'er, you're against us!"

Schukara rolled her eyes, stepping forward with her blades drawn. "Any reason why you're yelling into a microphone, Omasis? Overcompensatin' for yer' height?"

"Ya' know, my bosses weren't fond of your humour, Miss Parle," commented the crime lord, leaning over the balcony. "Don't know why, I always found you quite charming. I'll remember to ask for a joke before I stitch your mouth shut."

The dwarf returned to his previous volume, hyping up his audience. "Let's get this show on the road, everyone! In the predator corner, we have a very special guest: Me!"

Yanking a nearby lever, Reitgrar opened a hatch beneath him, revealing a dwarven ironsoul suit from its depths. The suit towered over the combatants, making even the greatest of aautgal seem puny by comparison.

Jumping from his perch, the dwarf landed in the machine's cockpit, moving it in the direction of Arlowe and Schukara. "I don't often see to matters personally, elf, but you've earned my respect!" the suit called, leaping at its target. "And my wrath!"

*

The assassin was nearby, though he was safe behind the cage, unaware of his partner's situation. Instead, he had been relaxing in a familiar space, playing a few rounds of sacred law with the locals. His time had been well spent, winning the card game with a trick commonly referred to as 'cheating'.

After fleecing a few more pieces of gold from his latest victim, his opponent kicked her chair to one side in protest. "You're a cheat! There's no way you could be this lucky!" A battle axe was drawn from underneath the table. "Keep the gold! I'll have your head!"

Onyx was unfazed, counting his money with his feet on the table. As the axe came down upon him, the assassin fell to the side; the axe wedged itself into his chair.

Upon the ground, Onyx kicked the chair over, shoving the table forward to wind his opponent. As the woman let go of her axe to support her weight, Onyx slammed her throat onto the table's side before throwing her over the table, face-first into her own weapon.

Leaving her body to twitch, the assassin had noticed that the arena match was drawing a much larger crowd than usual. The brutal murder meant nothing to those around him. To his surprise, the monstrous ironsoul suit had been unleashed, though to his horror, his partner stood in the arena against it.

"I leave him for a few moments, and he manages to get into an underground arena fight with an ironsoul suit? I'm envious of how fast he works," Onyx mused, preparing to drop into the arena.

However, as his foot touched the bar, the sound of clanking machinery hit his ears. Some of Reitgrar's men were fiddling with a cannon above their master's balcony. The assassin concocted a safer strategy. "Hmm, that'll leave a dent."

*

Back in the arena, Arlowe and Schukara continued their struggle against the dwarf. The suit's immense durability and bulk proved to be more than they could handle. Their blows bounced from the suit's thick armour, their attempts at sabotage met with the machine's stomping tantrums. Their only advantage was their size, allowing them

108

to dodge the lofty swings of the suit.

Without warning, a deafening horn sounded from the suit; the crime lord retreated backwards. With a point of its finger, the suit gave out a dangerous order. "Support cannon, fire!"

Though the explosion did sound, Arlowe was surprised to see Reitgrar's suit fall forward, propelled by the force of the cannons assault upon it. Looking up, he could make out the assassin waving, hastily reloading the cannon.

The prince pointed his blade forward. "Schukara, that's Onyx! He's helping us!"

Arlowe spun to face her, only to find the mercenary atop the suit as it began to rise, using its giant sword to prop itself back up. During the dwarf's respite, Schukara dug her blades into the suits hatch, using all her strength to pry it open.

"Wrong target!" the suit called, only to be struck in the leg by another cannonball.

In response, the suit reached over to the cage, ripping off a bar before launching it at Onyx with keen precision, destroying the cannon and its surroundings. "I said, wrong target!"

With its attention drawn, Arlowe sprinted over to the ironsoul suit, spotting the exposed power lines operating the suit's leg; a substance known as xestus mimicked the movements of the pilot, volatile once damaged.

Putting all his strength behind his swing, Arlowe slashed at the lines, causing the leg to shut down, bringing the suit down onto one knee.

Forced into a new position by its damaged leg, Reitgrar could see the prince beneath him, raising up the suit's fist to crush him.

Luckily, as the fist was about to land, Onyx leapt in the way to create a portal similar to when they first met, though the spell only had enough strength to land the fist at their side rather than be completely redirected.

The assassin held out his hand to Arlowe, offering a sphere no bigger than the palm of his hand.

"Your friend looks busy getting Reit out of there, and there's reinforcements on the way. There should be an opening where you damaged the xestus lines. Twist this, throw it in and take cover." Onyx drew a dagger into each hand. "I'll stop the boss's goons from getting close. Be quick."

Onyx lunged toward the encroaching gang members, followed by a dark mist that seemed to unnerve Reitgrar's charging forces.

Though Reitgrar's suit swung its colossal blade at Arlowe, the prince was able to slide underneath the attack, rushing toward the leg with the sphere in hand. Twisting the sphere as instructed, Arlowe threw it up the leg before diving into the dirt.

An explosion rocked the suit, causing the whole mech to shut down. With the suit so heavily damaged, Schukara made one last push, prying the hatch open, suspended by its chains for Schukara to board.

The crime lord was still inside, hooked up to his machine unconscious. "Even with all this power, ya' couldn't win. How's it feel ta' lose?" Schukara scoffed, approaching her target with a blade raised.

"Why don't you tell me, darl?" Reitgrar coughed, using the last of the suits energy to grab the mercenary, throwing Schukara from the cockpit. The dwarf ripped himself free of the machine, jumping out after her.

Their fight had taken its toll on him. His body was covered in blood, courtesy of Onyx's explosive blasting away the flesh from his legs.

"Enough, all of you!" he demanded, freezing the crowds into silence. "The suit should'a made short work of you. It 'ad its chance." A hammer, flung from the crowd, landed in his grasp. "*I* am Reitgrar Omasis! *I* decide when this ends!"

110

Schukara stood right back up, moving towards the dwarf with her blades ready to cut him down. "Why'd ya do it? Why did ya' do what ya' did ta' those poor people?"

Reitgrar began to laugh, filling the silent arena with his amusement. "I did what I did to survive. That's what it's always been about: survival. I wasn't beneath doing what I did, and I'm still not. I'd rather die than go back ta' square one—"

The dwarf raised his hammer in time to block a crossbow bolt aimed at his head. As the bolt dropped to the floor, everyone turned to see Onyx reloading his crossbow.

"Clever," Reitgrar commented. "You got me monologuing to make an easy target outta me. Maybe we're not so different."

Arlowe looked over to Onyx, who he could see visibly twitching at the dwarf's statement.

Reitgrar checked his hammer, noticing the scratch from the crossbow bolt, before flinging it at Onyx, knocking him a tremendous distance across the arena.

"I mentioned survival earlier? I meant it. You didn't think I'd come peacefully, did you?" he taunted. The dwarf performing an elemental dash to close the gap between them, shaking the ground beneath his feet. "Try an' stop me, Parle!"

Before Schukara could react, Reitgrar stole a sword from her before raising the earth beneath her feet, tossing her back. In his haste and fury, however, Reitgrar had forgotten about Arlowe, allowing the prince a chance to strike.

Swinging his blade, Arlowe was able to slice down the dwarf's arm, leaving a bloody wound in its wake.

Reitgrar retaliated, wrapping the arena's stone around the prince's throat. "Arn should never have completed your race, tuupaan!" barked the dwarf, depriving Arlowe of his breath as he slapped the blade from his grasp. "The elves have always been a nuisance, but *your* kind is an infection that spreads across our land, pretending to be more than what you are!"

Arlowe barely evaded the frenzied swing of the crime lord's hammer, his head light and vision blurred. "Coming from the one using an ironsoul suit to fight his battles?" he questioned, able enough to twist the dwarf's wrist to take back Schukara's blade.

"Think fast!" Schukara kicked her opponent back with as much force as she could muster; the magic that strangled the prince had been released.

Reitgrar lifted his hand to cast a spell, only for Arlowe to move in from the side, severing it from its owner. Schukara's sword found its mark, piercing Reitgrar's chest, pinning him to the ground.

"I never asked; Reitgrar? As in Reitgrar tha' Dwarven Exemplar?" Schukara scoffed. "He must be rollin' in his grave, being associated with tha' likes of you."

Reitgrar tried to laugh, though his chuckles turned to coughs; his lungs filled with blood. "I regret nothin', elf. I lived my time well, did what I set out to do. Can you say the same?"

The dwarf spluttered, falling dead before them.

Schukara rose from his body, looking around to find Arlowe. Her companion was a few meters away with his blade regained, tending to the assassin.

As Onyx finally got to his feet, he pushed Arlowe towards the elf. "You can't stay here," he choked. "You need to go before the dwarf's goons become organised enough to swarm you. I'll meet you topside."

"Onyx, we're a team. We can't keep doing this—" Arlowe was cut off by the assassin placing a finger over his lips, motioning his other hand to create the dark mist around himself once more.

"Fancy statue. Don't be late, Your Majesty."

As Onyx ran towards the remaining arena combatants, Arlowe could see Schukara at the arena wall, moving through a damaged portion of it, courtesy of the ironsoul suit.

"What about him?" Schukara asked. "You're leavin' him?"

"I wouldn't leave him if I didn't have faith. Come on, we don't want to be late."

Arlowe and Schukara found their way to fresh air once more, met by the sparkle of the night sky. The city appeared even more beautiful at night, though Arlowe only had one destination in mind, heading to the front gates to find his partner.

*

The two had waited for nearly an hour, with no sign of the assassin. While Schukara shuffled around, unable to keep her feet still, Arlowe stood patiently, looking all around for any sign of his partner.

"Will Onyx be okay?" Xanth asked. "I'm worried about him."

"He'll be here," Arlowe replied, unintentionally saying it out loud.

"He'd better," Schukara grunted, catching the prince's attention. "Tha' lil' thief likely took off with tha' dwarf's hammer. Since I have nothing to turn in, I can't claim tha' bounty from tha' guild."

A whistle sounded from above their heads, attracting their eyes to the top of the nearby statue, revealing Onyx sat at the top.

"Sorry I took so long," he apologised. "Once I got out of the sewers, I tracked down an associate in the area and passed on the news of Reitgrar's demise."

Onyx hopped off the statue, taking a large purse from his backpack, passing it to Arlowe. "Don't spend it all in one place, unless you're throwing it my way."

The assassin's hand then grazed Arlowe's chest, pushing him to one side to inspect the elf that, as of yet, he had not met. "And look what my partner dragged in: my knight in shining armour."

"I wasn't there fer' you," Schukara responded, bluntly.

"Well, you couldn't have been there for Arlowe, since you thought making him a combatant in an illegal underground arena was a good idea."

The elf's fists had begun to clench. "And what were you doin' there?"

The assassin began to toy with her temper. "Do I look equipped to go to a ball?"

"Yeah, ta' murder everyone!"

"And I'm supposed to forget about the dwarf whose life you just cut short?"

"I killed accordin' ta' ma' contract! *You* killed a bunch of his men, at minimum."

"And you didn't? It doesn't matter to me, but I doubt the contract sanctioned the added murder."

Before the two could continue their rabble, Arlowe had lost his temper.

"Enough!" he yelled, stopping the argument dead in its tracks.

Arlowe lowered his head, pressing the bridge of his nose with his fingers. "Onyx, though I've 'hired' you, you're free to leave at any time, I won't stop you."

The assassin looked awestruck. "Arlowe, are you saying—"

"And Schukara, just because you stood by my side at Eyenridge's fall, don't feel as though you're obligated to stand by me now. You're free to go about your business."

The two stood speechless at their ally's statement.

The prince took a deep breath, raising his head to look at them both. "Look, you two, I need your help. I don't expect you to agree with each other on everything, but I think you both know how much of a threat the kharakians are. If you're with me on this, I need you to put these problems behind us. Am I clear?"

As Schukara turned to offer her hand, Onyx held out the head of Reitgrar's hammer, offering it in return. "Here, take it. The dwarf's hammer was one-of-a-kind. My guild had no issues taking the handle, so yours should be golden taking the defining piece."

Schukara gently took the head of the hammer, taken aback by his gift. "Thanks. That

114

was… mighty generous of ya'."

While the two still seemed a little uncomfortable with each other, the tension in the air had cleared, pleasing Arlowe.

Schukara turned to the prince. "You should head up ta' tha' castle. Don't know if it'll be yer' turn, but we were gone a while. Might be good ta' check in."

"What about you two?" Arlowe asked. "Where will I find you?"

Onyx stepped forward. "If Schukara's up for it, we can check out the local watering hole. Defiant tradition states that whoever lands the killing blow gets a drink, courtesy of their colleagues."

"I have ta' turn this thing in first," Schukara stated, referring to the hammer head under her arm. "But I have a counter offer; I'll buy *you* a drink fer' savin' us down there. Couldn't have taken down that ironsoul suit without you and yer' decision ta' take tha' cannon."

Onyx shrugged. "My master always told me never to decline a drink from a lady. After you."

Onyx and Schukara waved, splitting away as they travelled up the hill to the nearest tavern.

Xanth's voice lit up in Arlowe's mind. "They're both so cool."

"Hey," interrupted Arlowe. "What about me?"

"Don't worry, you're still the coolest."

"And you're a terrible liar," Arlowe declared, laughing. "Though I'll admit, they are pretty cool. Come on, the castle awaits."

Chapter Eight:

"Still, we persisted as the dead watched on."

1st Arandbern

Land's Legacy

2084∞ (Current Age)

"Now you're just showing off. My liver's about to commit suicide, and my brain isn't far off. You win."

Schukara finished chugging another tankard of ale, slamming it down onto the table, wiping the drink from her lips. "I can't believe you'd offer drinks when yer' such a lightweight!" she guffawed, sliding her tankard over to join the rest.

Onyx pushed the remainder of his drink away, nearly falling off of his chair. "While I agree that I'm a lightweight, it's more that you have the constitution of a dwarf. We've been kicking these back for the past couple of hours."

The elf beamed with pride at her accomplishment, making it hard for the assassin not to become infected by her cheery personality, laughing alongside her.

Schukara rose to her feet, dropping a fat purse of gold at the bar for their services.

"Well, since I drank ya' under tha' table so soon, I'm gonna head up ta' tha' castle. Hopefully, Arlowe's done by now," she voiced, reaching for the door. "Ya' comin'?"

Onyx struggled to his feet, grasping the table to avoid collapsing. "I think I've got the courage for it, but I'm predicting a heavy hangover coming my way, so I'll probably find somewhere quiet for it to blow over," The assassin stumbled towards the opposite entrance. "I don't think the royal family would be happy to see me in this state anyway."

Schukara followed Onyx out, only for him to disappear into the morning crowd.

"Hope that's not how he treats all his gals," she mused, setting off.

*

Even early in the morning, the protesting had not ceased. Many of the night guards passed by the elf wearily, replaced by their daytime counterparts ready to keep the new day's rabble from the castle's entry hall.

Looking around, Schukara couldn't see any sign of the prince, leading her to believe that his number had been called. To make sure, she approached one of the remaining night guards, packing up his equipment for the journey home.

"S'cuse me, but have ya' seen a young human around?" she asked politely. "Brown hair, green gambeson, prob'ly smells a lil' like sewage?"

The guard peeked up, turning pale at her question. "Y-you must mean Prince Artaven, r-right? He entered the castle recently. I'll escor-escort you to him right now! Follow me!"

Before Schukara could even confirm her friend's name, the elf was being led straight into the castle, bypassing all of the protesters and the guards. *By tha' Angel Thessalia, what did Arlowe do for tha' guard ta' react like that? I didn't even mention his name.*

The guard guided her into the entrance hall, before taking a clumsy bow and leaving.

In the corner of the hall, Schukara could see the royal guest in all his glory. Arlowe was slumped against the wall asleep with his face smushed against it.

"Wake up, sleepyhead. Tha' wakin' world needs ya'," she whispered, giving his nose a light tap.

Arlowe jolted up, readjusting his hair and gambeson, before realising who stood before him. "Schu? What are you doing in here?" His eyes widened. "Did you wait in line? How long have I been asleep?"

"Yer' fine. I don't think you've been in here long. Mind tellin' me what's goin' on?"

"Unfortunately, I didn't get back quick enough. My number had been called, and they moved onto the next." The prince pulled out the sheet, crumpled in his palm. "I approached one of the guards asking him if there was anything I could do. He told me to take a new number." He then partially unsheathed his blade. "Luckily, I had this."

The elf became concerned. "Arlowe, what did ya' do?"

Arlowe laughed, sliding the sword out a little more. "Not what you're thinking. This sword belonged to my father. It was the only thing of his that came back from his battle with the titans. Look at the centre of the cross-guard."

"Tha' crest of Fertral?" Schukara queried.

"Look closer. Anyone could have a sword with the Fertral crest on it, but the members of Fertral's royal family had their initials engraved on the crest," Arlowe clarified. "There, in the middle? G.A."

"Garren Artaven?" Schukara crossed her arms at the revelation. "If it's so important, why didn't ya' use that when ya' got here?"

"At the time, I didn't want to risk having it confiscated. Remember, most think I'm dead. There *were* people crazy enough to go back to Eyenridge. It's not out of the question that someone could've taken this sword from my body."

Arlowe slid his weapon back into place, giving out a sigh. "I got desperate, took a risk. Luckily, it paid off. The guard I brought it up to believed I really was a member of Eyenridge's royal family, and brought me straight in. Poor guy looked frightened half to death."

Schukara giggled, remembering the guard that let her in, realising that the two guards had to have been one and the same.

The doors of the entrance hall creaked open, with a well-dressed middle-aged woman appearing from the halls; her dark hair was delicately woven around a glistening tiara.

"Prince Artaven? My name is Keila Thaedlon, and I will be escorting you to our king," she declared softly, offering her hand. "I am honoured to meet you and offer my most sincere condolences on behalf of Hietruce."

The prince rose, taking her hand before bowing. "Please, call me Arlowe. The honour is mine, and I thank you for your sympathies," he stated. "Is all well in Thaedlon?"

Keila gestured for them to follow, leading both Arlowe and Schukara through the castle's great halls. "Honestly? We've seen better days. Hietruce and Quazin are spread thin trying to contain the kharakians, and the other countries are hesitant to send aid without a plan in place. They don't want to go too long without their armies should the necromancers of Grandgrave plan an attack."

Arlowe rushed forward, halting their progress to the council chambers. "Grandgrave? What are you talking about?"

"The result of tha' Necromancer Rebellions, Arlowe," Schukara mentioned. "Tha' necromancers didn't just disappear when tha' Sixth Invasion began. While Tyreiin's forces helped us fight back against tha' titans, the necromancers took their opportunity and began butcherin' tha' continent. By tha' time tha' invasion ended, most of Tyreiin was under their control. There're rumours that some are still fightin' back, though I think most're just bein' hopeful."

Keila spoke up. "The fight with the kharakians couldn't have come at a worse time, and most don't feel safe. Between the beasts and the necromancers, we're really caught between a golem and a hard place. My father is doing everything he can, but doubt is really starting to spread through our country."

Arlowe stood aside for Keila to proceed, stunned at how bad the situation actually was.

"Ya' didn't know," voiced the elf, spotting the guilt in her partner's eyes. "You were young, you'd never been informed. There was nothin' ya' could've done."

The prince shook his head. "But I always knew that relations between the necromancers and the rest the world was strained," he growled. "If *I* knew, so young, why wasn't this dealt with before it was too late?"

Schukara shrugged. "Once this is over, a reformed Fertral could lead tha' charge?"

"A whole continent has already suffered at minimum." Arlowe gripped the hilt of his blade tight as he followed behind Keila. "If we're to help, I pray our time with the kharakians is fleeting."

The council chamber doors opened, releasing a wave of arguments that flooded the once-quiet halls. Directly across from them sat King Demetrius, clothed in his royal attire, cape and sceptre. His eyes had begun scanning the door to discern a reason for the intrusion, uninterested in the vitriol developing before him.

As his eyes fell upon Keila and her guests, he slowly descended from his throne in disbelief. "It can't be. Arlowe?"

Demetrius marched towards the prince, his audience silenced. The king stopped mere inches from Arlowe; tears formed quickly in his stern old eyes.

"It has been a long time, my boy. The last time I saw you, you were merely a babe in your mother's arms," the king uttered, taking a knee.

As he did, Demetrius took Arlowe's hands, placing his head upon them. "I failed once before by not being able to protect them, and I failed again by not being there to protect you. I have brought great dishonour to the kinship your father and I shared, and I hope that you can find it in your heart to forgive this foolish king."

Arlowe tugged his hands, acquiring the attention of the king. "Guilty or not, I don't want anyone on their knees before me," said Arlowe. "Please, stand and face me."

120

Demetrius rose, regaining his composure as the prince spoke. "I forgive you."

The king smiled, shaking his hands. "Thank you, Arlowe. I'm glad to see you alive."

Keila stepped forward, assisting her father back to his throne. As he climbed the stairs to his seat, the sound of discontent returned. A collection of nobles still filled the chamber, eager for the king's attention.

As the king placed himself into his throne, he made his decision clear. "You may leave."

Arlowe approached the throne, revelling in the sneering of the nobles. He had no kind words; only a smile, which only served to rile them further.

"What makes *him* more important than us, sire?" a dwarven noble to the front called out. "We have been here longer and have much more to offer than this vagabond!"

Keila moved past her father. "Why you—"

Demetrius raised his hand. "Enough Keila. I can handle this," he asserted, returning her to his side. "Do you think me blind, Brufraen? Deaf?" Brufraen didn't respond. "I asked you a question!"

"No, my king," Brufraen murmured; his confidence was shaken by Demetrius' sudden shift in mood.

"No? Are you sure? Then should I ignore all of the reports of you and your group entering the west wing of the castle despite it being restricted solely to the monarchy, guards and staff?"

"No, my king. We're sorry for—"

"No, you're not. You're sorry for getting caught, not for what you did. And what were you here to talk to me about? What were you to offer? Let me guess, you were here to criticize my choices, as usual?"

Brufraen was silent, as were the rest of the nobles.

Demetrius continued. "As a final note, I suggest you change your tone with my guest. That 'vagabond' is Arlowe Artaven of Fertral, and the son of my closest friend; not dead as the tabloids would have you believe. Unless you can offer anything greater than his survival, get out of my sight."

Like the guard before, the nobles went pale at the realisation of who Arlowe was, bowing profusely to him as they exited the chamber. The prince shrank at the attention.

Demetrius turned his attention back to Arlowe. "Give the nobility a few days and their spines will grow back, trust me. Their need for control over my fair city has no bounds." His pleasant demeanour had returned. "Now, I know this seems like an ambiguous question, but is there anything I can do for you?"

"I would ask for your aid," Arlowe responded, "though from what I've heard, I'm assuming that's not so easy."

Demetrius looked to Keila, who shied away at his gaze. "Then you'll be surprised to hear that you *have* my aid."

Arlowe and Schukara looked at each other confused. "Forgive me fer' speakin' out of turn, yer' highness, but is that possible?" Schukara posed. "Is it really that simple?"

"Brace yourself, girl," Demetrius chuckled, flicking a switch under the arm of his throne to raise a circular table between himself and Arlowe. "That was the one piece of good news I can give you."

"Then, what's the bad news?" Arlowe posed.

"The other countries have a luxury: they can choose whether they arm themselves for the kharakians or the necromancers. Hietruce does not have that luxury," Demetrius pronounced, with Keila using a pointer to highlight the locations her father was announcing. "You have our aid fighting the kharakians because we're already fighting back, whereas Vexinth to the northwest is fortuitous to be far from both threats. The northern Calaveil and north-eastern Ryvineon are hesitant to join the fray as the necromancers could strike them at any moment."

"And Quazin is already occupied," Schukara muttered. "What do we do?"

"As much as I want to, the Hietruen and Qualish forces to the south are spread too thin for us to help any further physically. You being alive however, changes things drastically. While I stay here tending to my people, you can act as an envoy between the remaining countries, pledging our aid against the necromancers in exchange for their aid against the kharakians. How you do that will be left to your discretion."

Xanth's voice emerged in Arlowe's head, surprising him that his young friend was even remotely interested in their political talks. "Are there any weaknesses we can exploit? They clearly have magical powers, and they're only getting stronger. Is there any way we could learn more about them?"

Arlowe nodded in agreement with the voice in his head, relaying the information to the king. "The kharakians are adapting. I saw it with my own eyes; they're even beginning to communicate with us. Has anyone been researching them? Is there anywhere where we can learn more about them?"

Keila placed her pointer on Thaedlon. "The kharakians were born of a curse, meaning they count as magical creatures. If anywhere would know more, it'd be our Arcane Guild. You could visit the others as you travel to the capitals too. Two dragons with one spear!"

"I agree," Demetrius voiced. "Remember that their home is suspended in the air too. If you find a magical spell for flying, it may come in handy. My forces don't have wings, and I won't send them out if we have no way of entering Kharaki."

Arlowe moved away from the table, visualising what route he would take through Argestra. "So that's it then? Request the help of the other countries, visit the Arcane

Guilds for information on our enemy and find a way to infiltrate our enemy's home?"

Demetrius flicked the switch on his throne again, returning his table from whence it came. "I apologise once more for being unable to help further. I'd send one of my own with you, though I imagine you have a motley band by your side already?"

Schukara cleared her throat. "I guess you could say that," Arlowe stated.

Demetrius smiled, reminded of his own adventures. "Just like your father. That's good to know. Now, be on your way. I'd offer you comforts, but time is of the essence here. Go and equip yourself under my name, and report to Keila on any developments."

Arlowe and Schukara departed the castle, content with their audience with the king.

As the two entered the courtyard, the prince turned to face his elven friend. "So, where'd you leave Onyx?"

The mercenary crossed her arms, recalling her last encounter with him. "That dang varmint drank himself silly, 'n' then vanished. Why?"

"I want to leave while the sun's still high in the sky, but there's still the Arcane Guild to visit. While I get a head start on their library, do you think you could find him?"

"Fine, but I'm not carryin' him," Schukara remarked, doing so with a smirk on her face. "I've already had to carry ya' through danger twice. My back's killin'."

"I'll remember that when I'm pulling you out of the fire for a change," Arlowe retorted, splitting off from his witty companion to revisit the Guild District.

*

As Arlowe made his way down Thaedlon's extensive street, Xanth appeared in his mind once more, filling his journey with conversation.

"I was wondering," he pondered. "What was your childhood like?"

"What brought you to that question?" Arlowe queried in return.

"Well, you're a prince. Was it weird growing up as one?"

"A little. My parents were very modest people and didn't make much of a barrier between themselves and their people. I had a public education, I wasn't showered with gifts and I often helped out around the city. I got bullied by the noble kids at times for the things I didn't have, but I still believe my parents raised me right. I was grateful for what I had and was thankful for what the day brought."

Since he was passing the bazaar on his way to the guild, Arlowe thought it best to take the king's offer and stop by the smithy to better equip himself.

"Did you get along with your parents?" Xanth asked.

The wall behind the merchant was lined with weapons, each looking deadlier than the last. "My father was... difficult." The prince turned his attention to the shields on the table before him. "And my mother was very protective."

"What do you mean?"

Arlowe had begun trying on the smithy's wares, strapping on cuirasses, pauldrons and cuisses, eagerly strapping the metal to his body in preparation for his next journey.

"When I was younger, my parents argued a lot about my future. My father was told he was too aggressive and my mother was told she was too passive. To be fair, neither were wrong," Arlowe noted, struggling to keep his history child-friendly. "When my mother passed, my father thought it best for me to train constantly, study politics constantly. I understand what he was trying to do, but at the time, I think he forgot I was mourning too. It drove a wedge between us."

"But you still loved him?"

"Of course. He wanted me to be at my best. I don't agree with some of his methods, but I appreciate what he did for me." Arlowe stood, adjusting the gorget around his throat. "I didn't know them long, but I wish them well wherever they are. Hopefully, they're happy with how I turned out. That'd settle a few of their arguments."

As the prince returned to the stall to settle the cost of the armour, his eyes caught a large heater shield, which he took to his left. The shield provided reasonable protection, yet also felt sturdy and required little effort to lift it, proving itself worthy enough to be added to the prince's new ensemble.

Making up for lost time, Arlowe moved from the bazaar into a brisk jog towards the guild, hoping that his allies had not beaten him there. Though he was able to dodge the incoming populace of the city traversing up the street, his perception had failed him as he turned into the Guild District.

Arlowe hit something hard and rebounded towards the floor. Looking up, a bundle of books had begun toppling towards him, unable to be held back by the slender limbs that had been carrying them.

"Watch out!" called a voice from behind the books, though it was already too late. The carrier's legs had given way, dropping the top half of the books onto Arlowe.

As the prince recovered from his slight concussion, he had noticed that the rest of the books had landed on the poor soul that he bumped into, leaping up to clear them away.

"I'm so sorry! I wasn't paying attention!" Arlowe cried out. "Are you okay?"

A pair of ocean-blue eyes hastily scanned over the landslide of books; she was too preoccupied to remember Arlowe's part in the collapse. It was only as he held out his hand to her that she became aware of his presence, dusting off her lab coat with the aid of her long sleeves.

"No, that was my fault," she responded, speaking as gentle as she looked. Some of her blonde hair had escaped its bindings, veiling her eyes. "I need to stop carrying so many books around. Are *you* okay?"

The prince rubbed his head, laughing at his realisation. "Actually, you did me a favour. I forgot my need for a helmet!"

The two began collecting all of the books that he had so carelessly sent flying, though their progress had faltered as the two began to converse.

"*Vekaakrans at the Gate?*" Arlowe read, being familiar with the book. "I really enjoyed this one. Not many works of fiction highlight the plights of the dwarves. Most go the easy way and simply cast them as villains due to their past role in slavery."

"It's interesting to read about the vekaakran demons too," the woman replied. "Most write about the conquerors as they were the first, or about the praisyl or titans as they were a more recent plague of demon, so it's refreshing to read about a different kind."

Arlowe looked up from the book, placing it onto his pile. "I know it must seem obvious by how many books you have here, but you must be an avid reader."

The woman brought a book close to her chest. "Books can act as a way to educate ourselves about the world around us, but also allow us to escape when we learn a little too much." She placed the book on her pile to pick up a different one. "It's an odd sensation being scared of a world you're immersed in without actually being in any danger. I love it."

It was rare for Arlowe to go in depth with his love of literature; his mind raced with all the questions he could ask while he had the chance. "What's your favourite book?" he posed, happy with his choice.

"It's called *'The Sorrow of an Aigahn Maiden'*," the woman replied, continuing to round up her books. "It tells of a young girl, raised within the religion of Aigahki. She leaves the natural boundaries of her home, meeting all manner of people and creatures on her journey in the hopes of bringing her vision of peace to the world."

"Did she succeed?"

"No. The story is bittersweet. While the majority of the novel focuses on her compromising personality and will to do good, she ultimately perishes. You should pick up a copy when you get the chance. I always pick one up whenever I visit an Arcane Guild library."

Arlowe moved over the last of the books, placing them in a neat stack next to his new friend. "I'm being incredibly rude. I never got your name. I'm Arlowe, and you are?"

"Antoinetta," she responded, giving a large bow. "I'm being just as rude. Did you need anything from the Guild District? I hope I haven't impeded you in any way."

"As a matter of fact, you may be able to help me. I was directed to the Arcane Guild to look for information on the kharakians and—"

"You want me to help you?"

Arlowe stumbled over his words. "Y-yes, if you can. If it's an inconvenience to you, I can—"

The prince was cut off by Antoinetta taking hold of his hand. "I'm a member of the Arcane Guild. It's no problem at all, I'd be glad to help. Follow me!"

The prince was pulled a few steps towards the guild before another voice stopped them. "You were gettin' a head start alright, but it wasn't with tha' library!"

The two turned to see Schukara, followed by Onyx clasping his head. "You work fast, Your Highness," he muttered. "Who do we have the pleasure of addressing?"

Arlowe had become flustered, unable to get his words out. "Wait, it's not like that! I made her drop the books, but by accident, so I helped collect them, but then we—"

Schukara simply glanced at Onyx, smirking.

The woman approached the two, offering a bow to the both of them. "You must be Arlowe's friends. My name is Antoinetta, and I'm a member of the Arcane Guild," she declared, receiving a nod from Schukara and a stare from Onyx. "Arlowe accidently bumped into me, though he was kind enough to help me pick all these books up. I was

128

about to escort him to the guild if you would like to join us?"

"Gladly!" Schukara exclaimed; the assassin recoiled from her volume. "If ya' continue to escort Arlowe, Onyx and I'll transport yer' books, right Onyx?"

The assassin simply shot her a look of disdain, while Arlowe glanced at her like a rabbit caught in the searchlights.

Antoinetta nodded, taking Arlowe's hand once more, leading him towards her guild hall. Schukara patted Onyx on the back, taking a majority of the books as a favour to him.

The assassin waited for the two to be out of earshot. "I don't like her," he vocalized. "Too peppy."

"And we're supposed to take tha' word of an infamous assassin? Lighten up," Schukara scolded, nudging the assassin to drop the books that had been so carefully stacked upon him. "It's nice ta' see tha' envoy out of his depth in a *good* way."

Though he was anxious at being dragged around so roughly, Arlowe couldn't help but be excited at the thought of a new library to scour. "Xanth, I hope you'll be keeping an eye out. Hopefully, there'll be a ton of research material to look through!"

"Arl... ...think somet... ...ong... I don... ...ow wh... ...at's ha... ...e y... ...ou t..."

"Xanth?"

"Arlowe?"

Arlowe refocused his attention on his world, realising that he had already been led inside of the guild, introduced to someone by Antoinetta.

"Are you sure you're okay?" she asked.

"Sorry. I was daydreaming," he said, taking in the sights around him to readjust.

"About what, I wonder?" joked Schukara. Antoinetta blushed at her statement.

"Arlowe, I'd like to introduce you to our guild master, Gretchin Ardimauda,"

Antoinetta announced, revealing a plump dwarf hidden behind her coat.

Gretchin was dressed in a lab coat similar in style to Antoinetta's, stepping forward to shake Arlowe's hand.

"It is an honour, Arlowe. May I call you Arlowe?" queried the grey-haired dwarf. "I know that Lucine preferred to be called by her first name. If she had a gold coin purely for every time she asked people to stop calling her 'Your Highness'—"

"You knew my mother?" the prince posed, unintentionally cutting off the guild master.

Gretchin smiled at Arlowe's intrigue. "Oh yes! While she was adventuring with your father, she would always find time to visit the Arcane Guild. Even after she got married, both would visit the Guild District, though your father would always prefer the Warforged Guild. You know what they say; men were born of Arn's divine plan, and women born of a need to preserve it."

Antoinetta tapped Gretchin's shoulder. "Sorry for interrupting you, Miss Ardimauda, but Arlowe came to visit the library?"

Arlowe chimed in. "I need to collect any information we can find on the kharakians. Keila Thaedlon recommended the Arcane Guilds, with this one being a priority before we leave."

Gretchin rubbed her wrinkled chin, recalling the contents of the library. "Hmm, we may have something of use, but I can't say for certain." Unveiling her trusty walking stick, the dwarf proceeded further into the guild, with Antoinetta gesturing for them to follow. "I'm sure our chief librarian will be able to assist us."

The group progressed down a set of stairs towards the library, with Gretchin tapping her walking stick on the front desk to get the attention of the man behind it.

The human sat up from his slump, perturbed at where the knocking noise came from, only to relax once he figured out that his guild master was short enough to be concealed by the desk.

"I see you're reading a book on the theory of invisibility, my dear," Gretchin stated playfully. "Are you enjoying it?"

"I'd enjoy it more if you didn't play little pranks dependent on my choice of reading material," the man muttered, making his way around the desk. "What can I, the great Alaric, do for you today?"

Gretchin motioned for Arlowe to step forward as she taking a step back herself.

"I'm looking for any information on the kharakians," Arlowe answered. "Gretchin brought me to you. Do you know where I could find it?"

"It must be important stuff if the guild master's leading you around," Alaric commented, leaving his post. "I'm warning you, there's not much. The kharakians aren't often researched due to their, uh, explosive temperament. Follow me."

The group were escorted through legions of bookcases, with some nearly reaching the glass roof high above them. Beyond the sound of their footsteps, only the occasional turning of a page or a cough of the library's inhabitants filled the air, leaving it as a silent void ready to suck one into their choice of literature.

Arlowe marvelled at how long it took to reach the back of the library, with the front desk being too far away to even see from where he was.

"Here we are," Alaric declared, awaking the prince from his trance. "This is where we store scraps of research that didn't have enough substance to form a complete research paper. If what you're looking for would be anywhere, it would be here."

Tables were pulled out of the bookcases, allowing the group to start fishing through the folders for any sign of kharakian information. Folders returned to the shelves as quickly as they were taken, though nothing of note had been picked up.

"What the...?" Alaric questioned. "What is this?"

Arlowe perked up at his comment, eager to see what he found. "Did you find the research?"

"No," he responded, holding some kind of bandage in his hand. "This must be some kind of joke. Some punk must've put their dirty bandages in with the research when I wasn't looking. I swear when I—"

As Alaric pulled the remainder of the bandage from the folder, it convulsed, leaning towards him before piercing through his chest with the aptitude of a blade.

Alaric recoiled, with Arlowe, Schukara and Onyx all stepping forward to defend him. More of the bandage began to appear, eventually leading to a frail body stumbling at them from around the corner.

The bandage was a piece of the creature's skin, skin that completely covered its body, its mouth and eye sockets included.

"What is that?" whispered Antoinetta, slinking away to safety only to bump into the bookcase at her back.

The creature's head jerked to face the direction of the noise, creating a split directly down the centre of its body to reveal the skeleton underneath, with the skin acting as paper-like tentacles rooted at the spine.

The beast fired its skin at Antoinetta, though a barrier was cast to protect her, conjured by Gretchin and her walking stick.

As the creature prepared another attack aimed at the guild master, Gretchin placed another barrier, this time to contain it, cutting off the skin as it was mere inches from her face. "I'm not sure how a prenomen found its way into my guild, but I shall make sure that it leaves. Promptly."

The skeletal being let out a ghastly scream, partially muted by the barrier, though still

132

unnerving to all in its presence.

Firing its tentacles into the ground, the prenomen brought them up past the barrier to break Gretchin's staff, knocking her off-guard as it freed itself from its prison.

Surrounded by Arlowe's band, the prenomen used its multiple wrappings to launch itself into the air, turning translucent to avoid detection. The creature leapt from bookcase to bookcase, striking any it passed to confuse its prey.

As Gretchin readied another spell, one of the prenomen's wrappings grabbed her wrist, snapping it before dragging her upwards.

Though Onyx armed himself with his crossbow, firing it with deadly accuracy, the creature was unfazed by the bolt in its skull. Its skin proceeded to engulf Gretchin until she was no longer visible.

Constricted, the guild master screamed out in agony until she could scream no more; her bones continued to snap and crunch long after her demise.

The prenomen's skin reopened, releasing the remnants of Gretchin. Her skull and a few bones that had not finished dissolving dropped to the floor; the air soon filled with the smell of rotten eggs.

Arlowe's band surrounded it once more as the creature dropped to the ground, though with another scream, the creature let out a wave of energy, knocking them back.

Antoinetta stepped forward, gaining the prenomen's attention.

"Don't worry everyone, I can stop this!" she called, casting a spell at the creature. As she closed her eyes to release her spell, however, the light in her hands fizzled out.

In response, the prenomen began to glow, bringing all of its wrappings towards it ribs to prepare a spell of its own. Antoinetta stood frozen as the skeleton grew brighter, its energy emanating strongly enough to be felt by those in its vicinity.

As the prenomen's gathered magic erupted from its chest, Alaric charged forth to knock Antoinetta away, though his deed rewarded him with being sliced in half by the creature's beam. The nearby bookcases toppled from the prenomen's power, filling the room with ominous black flames and a choking smog.

Craving its next meal, the prenomen wasted no time snatching up the top half of Alaric's corpse, pulling it within to regain its strength.

Arlowe marched forward with his shield raised, deflecting the blows from its tentacles, though the creature adapted quickly.

Reaching underneath to swipe at the prince's ankles, the prenomen raised him into the air to create an easy target.

But a plan had already been set into motion, Alaric's death granting them precious seconds to devise. "Now!" Arlowe yelled.

Onyx and Schukara flanked the creature on Arlowe's signal, with the former sliding into the prenomen's ankles to bring it down whilst the latter drew her blades to cut off its skin at the spine. The creature flailed in agony, its weakness exposed.

Though its health had deteriorated upon the loss of its skin, the monster took Onyx's throat into its grasp, flinging a bookcase towards Schukara to trap her against another.

Onyx was lucky that the prenomen had lost most of its strength, as it would've had no issue crushing his windpipe otherwise. However, its grip was still becoming tighter and tighter, with the assassin unable to remove the cold hands from his throat.

Schukara tried to shove the bookcase pinning her aside, though its weight was too much. She was unable to intervene.

As Onyx was about to lose consciousness, the tightening hand ceased, allowing him to breath the air he had so often taken for granted. Arlowe, untangled from the tentacle that bound him, had plunged his blade into the top of the prenomen's spine.

As the prince twisted his sword to one side, the prenomen weakened further, though it still had no intention of releasing its target. In one last motion, the sword rotated ninety degrees, snapping the skeleton's neck.

The creature collapsed to the floor, dissolved to nothing, not unlike what it had done to the late guild master.

Arlowe assisted Schukara with the bookcases, freeing her before turning his attention to Antoinetta.

The girl had been doused in Alaric's blood, left traumatised by her encounter with the undead being. "I wanted to help. I wanted to help. I wanted to help," she repeated over and over, cradling herself.

The prince brought her close, though he couldn't stop her from rocking.

A crowd of footsteps raced towards the group, led by a weedy looking male in a grey jacket. "What happened here?" he demanded; his voice was filled with the sound of infection. "Antoinetta, are you okay?"

Arlowe recounted what had occurred in the library, including the deaths of the guild master and the chief librarian. "We did what we could, but we weren't prepared for something like that. Gretchin called it a prenomen? What is that?"

The man wiped the blood from Antoinetta's face, the woman still immune to all acts of communication. "It's an undead creature. I can only guess that it was a trap. Sure, it was dangerous to you, but I'd bet that its priority was Miss Ardimauda."

"Why do you say that?"

"Someone's targeting the Arcane Guild, specifically the council. There's a mole in the guild, has to be. No one in Grandgrave could have this level of precision, this accuracy, killing our high-ranking members. We've already lost two-thirds of the council as it stands. It's sending the guild into disarray. New members are drying up, and no one wants to take a higher position in the chain. Gretchin was one of the few who dared. Now look at her, or what's left of her at least."

"It's hardly tha' time fer' jokes!" Schukara blurted, held back by the assassin. "Have some decency!"

Calming Antoinetta's breathing, his gaze now rested upon the prince. "You're Arlowe Artaven, right? I'd tread carefully. If the culprit's aware that you're involved with the guild, they may set a trap for you."

"You seem quite informed," Arlowe uttered against the ominous warning.

"I'd be suspicious too, but I have to be. Being the head of the Arcane Guild janitorial staff, I either find out what happened, or I'm somehow involved in it. Nothing I can do about that."

Antoinetta awoke from her unresponsive state, tearing up upon seeing the male. "Caspus?" She jumped into his arms, bawling her eyes out. "I didn't know what to do! I tried to fight back, but my spell failed! They're dead because I did nothing!"

Caspus held her close, escorting her away from the gruesome scene.

Arlowe glanced around at the chaos, saddened that the research he had been looking for had likely been set ablaze by the creature, and that lives were lost looking for it.

"Let's go," Onyx said in comfort, patting the prince on the back. "The guild members have this covered. There's nothing more for us here. Vexinth's calling."

Arlowe nodded, following his companions out of the guild and towards the front gates.

*

The mood in Thaedlon had shifted; it seemed as though the news of the Arcane Guild had already spread. Most of the citizens had retreated indoors, the only indicator of life being the eyes that peered through the windows of their homes and the few individuals that had the confidence to keep to their daily routine.

136

The city was barren, with the loud chatter of the markets now replaced with only hushed mutterings. Arlowe should have felt more comfortable surrounded by less people, though he only felt the contrary.

"Attacked where they should be at their safest," Arlowe spat. "People shouldn't have to live in fear like this."

"From what I've been told by my guildmates, these murders are on a large scale. No Arcane Guild has been unaffected," Onyx commented. "The good news, to me at least, is that the Defiant aren't involved. The elevenths would've found our energy at the crime scenes. The bad news is that they've got no leads and no potential motive beyond killing the guild's council. These are dark times for us all."

The group arrived at the front gate, checking their supplies to make sure they were set for the long journey north. "I think that's everythin'," Schukara confirmed. "Let's—"

"Stop!" a voice cried out. "Wait!"

Searching for the source of the call, the group could see Antoinetta charging towards them, clutching a book within her arms.

As she neared, her feet failed her. Unable to slow her descent from the hill, the woman ended up crashing into Arlowe, knocking them both to the ground.

"I assume that was for earlier?" Arlowe jested in pain, rising back onto his feet.

Antoinetta struggled to make eye contact with the prince, blushing at her mistake. The girl took a book that had fallen to her side, holding it out to him.

"Please, take this with you," she murmured.

Arlowe took the book, scanning its title. "Hm? *'Evret's Fate'*? I didn't know there was a book of this! My father used to tell it to me. Did you find this?"

Antoinetta nodded, still facing the floor.

Arlowe brought her in close, hugging her tightly. "Thank you. I appreciate you finding this for me."

Antoinetta blushed wildly before taking hold of him, nuzzling into his embrace.

As the prince went to release her, the clumsy elf moved up to his ear. "Be careful on your travels. I hope we meet again soon," she whispered, still blushing as she moved away.

Arlowe placed the book in his backpack, waving to her as they started their departure once more.

*

In the hills beyond Thaedlon, the goblin and amalgam watched restlessly as the group left Thaedlon.

"Is it time?" Arrsk asked. "We've been following since tha' village. It should be—"

"Soon, young one," voiced Baxka. "Our power is still growing; our body still fresh from the vault."

"Hmph."

The lights within the amalgam's sockets peered at a hand shaking with anger. The voices spoke as one. "We will continue to watch, and we will continue to wait. The spirits of Kaxrax hunger for Arlowe's demise, and our revenge will be sweet."

With the goblin upon their back, the amalgam moved onwards, once again following the trail of their hunt.

Chapter Nine:

"According to some, revenge is like a small rectangular confectionary."

Though the group had entered Vexinth, their trek north was far from complete. The rich plains that had been by their side had begun to recede, with the ashen gravel of the new country there to greet them.

"You've seen the undead before? I've only ever read of them," Arlowe stated, putting the finishing touches on their camp, leftover from the last adventurer that had used it.

Schukara began the camp's fire, placing herself on a nearby log to remove her heavy boots. "Back when there still was a necromancer division of tha' Arcane Guild, you'd sometimes find tha' undead assistin' guilds like tha' Warforged if they needed magical assistance. Been awhile since it was that way though."

"My master and I killed a few. Even more so once the necromancers went murder-happy," Onyx added in, sharpening one of his blades. "Even took down a lich. Well, my master did anyway. Would've killed me if the old man hadn't stepped in. They're not called the strongest undead for no reason."

Arlowe rested himself on his own log. "Can we change the subject? We've been talking about the undead for days. I've never been a fan of necromancers and their undead arts. They give me the creeps."

As he threw kindling onto their fire, the prince cleared his throat. "I want to thank you two for sticking with me. By now, you must be tempted to move on. We've had a few close encounters already."

Onyx shrugged, looking to his elven ally. "I haven't got anywhere else to be, though I know Schukara's got a reason for sticking around."

Schukara in turn glared at her mask-clad partner. "What do *you* know?"

Onyx placed his dagger into its sheath, retrieving the other to sharpen. "What do you mean? You told me about your own personal journey over drinks," he affirmed, chuckling to himself. "Your body might be tolerant, but your words? Not so much."

Schukara sighed, pressing her fingers into her temples. "Look, Arlowe? I'm not as altruistic as ya' seem ta' think I am. I like helpin' people, I like helpin' in general, but I've been lookin' fer' help in return."

"You've certainly found it here," the prince insisted. "What do you need?"

"I'm tryin' ta' find my sister."

Arlowe cocked his head. "Why didn't you tell us? We could have aided you sooner."

"Because I didn't know if I could trust ya'," she voiced. "No offense, but I'd only known you fer' a short time, and when ya' told me that you'd been workin' with an assassin? That didn't make me feel any better."

"No offence?" Onyx asked.

"Ya' have a good head on yer' shoulders. Both of ya'. I'm sorry that I didn't tell ya', but I think y'all understand why I kept it ta' myself," Schukara continued. "It won't happen again."

Arlowe had started moving around the fire, handing out the rations to his friends. "No, I understand. There's no need to apologise."

Schukara smiled at his response.

"I mean, a little apology for that assassin jab would be nice," Onyx muttered, his mouth filled with bread.

"What's that?" the elf posed, putting a hand to her ear. "All I heard was 'I'm so cool 'cause I resemble what a five-year-old thinks an assassin looks like'."

The group laughed heartily alongside her.

Though the company warmed Arlowe's heart, it still felt empty without the voice in his head. He had tried to regain communication with Xanth, though his mind remained silent. He stood guard most nights and needed rest ready for their next push, so travelling back to the caverns proved to be a difficult task.

The prince held the information from his allies not from a lack of trust but rather because, even to him, the story of how they met sounded more like fiction.

As the group sat around their latest campfire, Arlowe thought it best to reveal his secret, believing that nothing should be held from those involved with him.

"Can I tell you two something?" His companions looked up from their meals. "I haven't been completely honest with you either."

Schukara and Onyx glanced at each other, worried of the words that were to follow.

"Sure," Schukara responded, placing down her ration. "Lay it on us."

"I told you both that a nearby pond saved my life. That... wasn't entirely true."

The assassin leaned back, looking towards the sky. "Hm. Even *if* you broke the water tension before landing, I thought your story was a bit off. How did you survive then? What, did you appear somewhere else?"

Arlowe was unsure of how to respond, mostly due to Onyx's answer being correct. He took a deep breath, realising how absurd his story would sound.

"I woke up on a stone slab believing I was dead. I travelled through hallways that never ended and followed green-eyed people who ran from me. As I reached a central chamber, I was greeted by their kind, welcoming me to their home. These pterravun, they helped me survive, not just by stealing me from our world, but also by tending to my wounds."

The prince's allies were lost for words, as he predicted. Schukara appeared ready to talk more, while Onyx remained deep in thought.

"Are ya' sure ya' weren't seeing a possible afterlife?" questioned the elf, appearing doubtful. "I've been travellin' fer' a while now and I've never heard of those green-eyed creatures. What d'ya call 'em? Pterravun?"

"Schu, you saw me fall from that castle," Arlowe replied. "Others fell from the ballista cables; a closer distance to the ground. If they didn't survive, what chance would I have had?"

"What's the relevance of this story?" Onyx asked, awakening from his thoughts. "Not to be rude, but if you're telling us this, surely there has to be a reason."

The assassin looked deep into his partner's eyes, searching for any hint of a lie, pressuring him to speak.

"There was a boy who I befriended down there," Arlowe answered, maintaining his eye contact with the assassin. "He's been instrumental to our success thus far. Even if we ignore that his kind saved my life, he's been pointing out the weaknesses of my opponents, kept my health at the forefront of his mind and has generally been keeping me sane through some of my darkest moments."

"So, what's the reason?" Onyx asked again.

Looking down, the prince focused his mind, once again devoid of contact. "I can't hear him. I haven't heard from him in days. I'm worried."

"Is there anything you can do from here?"

"Possibly."

"Then do it."

Onyx's gaze had not left him. "I don't know how much I believe. I don't think it matters," noted the assassin. "If that kid's important to you, do what you have to. Our journey's far from over, and we'll need all the help we can get."

Arlowe nodded, reminding himself of Bela's advice. *She closes her eyes and thinks of this place.* He did as the queen instructed, trying to attune his mind to the pterravun caverns.

At first, he felt no different, though this feeling lasted briefly.

*

Arlowe felt a tug, followed by a drastic change in temperature. Opening his eyes, the deep green of the underground filled his sight, proving to him that his attempt had been successful.

Rushing down the staircase to the thrones, Arlowe was halted by the large hand of Conquest blocking his path. "Arlowe! You made it back! It's good to—"

"Where's Xanth? I need to find him," blurted Arlowe, immediately knocking the smile from Conquest's face.

"You go to the hallways. I'll find Bela," he declared, moving himself aside to grant Arlowe passage.

Arlowe rushed through the central chamber. "Xanth? Xanth, where are you?" he called out. "Are you okay?"

Though not visible to the prince, Conquest and Bela must have entered the hallways, as their voices also called for their son, to no avail.

The prince checked room after room, though each one he found to be empty only caused his anxiety to increase further. As he moved on to a different hallway, Bela's voice echoed through to him. "Arlowe, come to my voice. We've found him!"

Arlowe ran towards the queen's voice to be met with his partner. Dropping to his knees, he hugged the boy tight. Xanth was hugging him even tighter.

"Arlowe! You had us scared!" Conquest announced, returning to his jolly self. "Why did you have to find our boy? Did something concern you?"

Arlowe tried to raise himself, though Xanth refused to let go, keeping him crouched. "When I last left, your son created some kind of connection with me. I hadn't heard from him in days," he explained. "I thought something had happened to him."

Bela gave a sigh of relief, happy to see that no harm had come to either of the boys. "Thank you for caring so much about our son, Arlowe. I've never seen him confide in someone like this." Xanth began to release his friend, though his face remained firmly facing downwards. "We'll leave you two to talk."

Xanth waited until his parents were out of sight before speaking. "I'm sorry if I made you angry," he murmured. "If I said something wrong, you should've told me."

"What?" asked Arlowe, confused. "You didn't say anything wrong."

"Then why did you cut our connection?"

"Xanth, I didn't do anything. I don't even know how this connection works."

The boy sat in the sand cross-legged. "We were talking, and after that, I lost contact with you. It took you so long to come back too. I thought something had happened."

Arlowe rustled his charcoal hair. "I thought something had happened to *you*. I couldn't hear you." He sat himself beside the boy. "And I'm sorry that it took me so long to come back. It took me a few tries. I've never been back before, have I?"

Xanth didn't respond to the prince's comment, though he did lean into Arlowe. "I'm glad you're okay," he finally mumbled; his mouth was hidden behind his knees.

The prince smiled, happy that his friend still had trust in him. "Maybe it's an age thing?" he theorized. "You said that other pterravun can look through eyes and speak with their minds too? Maybe you're just not as good at it yet."

Xanth shrugged his shoulders, still facing away from him. "Mm."

"Would you feel better if I told you what happened?"

144

That seemed to be the right question to ask, as Xanth turned wide-eyed, nodding his head strongly as an answer. Arlowe repositioned himself to sit more comfortably, before reeling off what had happened.

"No way!" Xanth exclaimed. "It took out the guild master?"

"And the chief librarian."

"And that whole portion of library?"

"Mm-hm."

Xanth leaned back, feeling defeated. "I'm sorry, Arlowe. I know that the guild was important. It's stupid that people died over a bit of information."

"Well," Arlowe replied, "I do have this. I was hoping you could do me a favour." He reached into his backpack, pulling out the copy of Evret's Fate.

"What do you want me to do?" Xanth queried, looking at the book from all angles.

"You remember that story I told you? The story of Evret and the kharakians? *That's* the book of the story. My father could always tell it me from memory, so I never saw a book. Would you mind reading it in your spare time and let me know if there was anything my father left out? There's probably not, but I want to make sure."

Xanth looked at the book in awe, delicately flicking through its pages. "Where did you find this? I thought you came out of the library empty-handed?"

"I almost did, but Antoinetta handed it to me before I left the city."

"Mm." The pterravun paused before continuing his reading.

"Xanth? What's wrong?" The boy kept on reading, avoiding Arlowe's question. "Did she say something that bothered you?"

"Mm-mm."

"Are you sure?"

Xanth began to puff up, evidently uncomfortable answering the question, with

Arlowe able to see that the boy was gripping the book much tighter than before.

"It's okay Xanth, you don't have to—"

"I was jealous," blurted the boy, curling himself back up next to Arlowe following his statement.

At once, Arlowe understood the issue. "Are you jealous of the others too?"

"Mm-mm," Xanth grunted, shaking his head. "I thought you were ignoring me when you started talking to her. It didn't help that I lost my connection to you."

Though they were friends, Arlowe had to remember that Xanth was still a child, and though intelligent for his age, the boy was also still prone to bouts of jealousy and a lack of understanding.

"I'm not pushing you away, Xanth. I wouldn't do that to you." The pterravun did not move. "Do you want to bind yourself to me once more? It's a lonely world without you by my side," he stated, moving his hair from his forehead.

Xanth tried to keep himself turned away. His finger had intended to touch Arlowe's forehead, though it ended up making contact with his eyebrow, cheek and nostril instead. "Did I get it?"

Arlowe couldn't help but laugh. "Almost. Maybe next time you won't get snot on your finger."

"Ew! Nose juice!" Xanth called out, spinning around as he wiped it onto the walls. "Let me try again." The boy took his other index finger to place upon Arlowe's forehead, blinding him with green like before.

"Can you hear me?" Arlowe voiced using his mind.

"I can," Xanth responded. "I can see me through your eyes too, so it looks like we're connected again."

The prince nodded, picking himself up off of the floor. "Well, now that I know you're safe, I should head back to my camp. I can't imagine what my disappearance looked like to Schu and Onyx."

Xanth walked with Arlowe through the hallways towards the central chamber, though he remained oddly silent. As they reached the chamber, Xanth stayed in the hallways, hiding behind the arch. "Promise me you'll come back when I go silent again?" The boy shuffled his feet in the sand. "I panic when I can't see what's happening."

Arlowe returned to the arch, before kneeling and holding out his fist. "I promise."

With his other hand, he shaped the boy's hand into a fist. Readying his own, he gestured for Xanth to raise his, bumping them together. "Boom."

Xanth looked happy, though confused at what had just happened. "What was that?"

"I don't know. Onyx taught it to me."

"He's so cool."

The prince smiled to himself. Though Xanth clearly wasn't five, he couldn't get Schukara's comment out of his head.

Arlowe travelled through the crowds of pterravun, waving to them as he climbed the staircase towards the portal. As he placed his hand upon it, he turned to see Xanth, giving him a nod before closing his eyes.

*

The bitter cold quickly returned, sending a shiver up Arlowe's spine. He opened his eyes to see Schukara sat where she had previously been, her eyebrows raised at his entrance.

"Wow, er, maybe ya' should've led with that. No way I can't believe ya' now."

"That's the first time I've ever travelled there myself," Arlowe responded. "What did it look like to you?"

"A green aura surrounded ya', and then ya' kinda just faded away. I don't know how ta' explain it better than that."

The camp had one key difference: their resident assassin had disappeared once more.

"I know you're not his babysitter, but where's Onyx gone this time?" Arlowe queried. "I didn't think I'd been gone that long."

Schukara shrugged her shoulders, taking a bite of the ration he had left behind. "He was here ta' witness ya' disappear, but then he heard a noise in tha' bushes over there 'n' ran off. No idea what he heard though. I didn't hear a thing. Tha' man has tha' hearin' of an owl. It borders on scary."

The elf took a small bottle from her pack, uncorking it before consuming some of its contents. She held the bottle out to Arlowe.

"No thanks," he declined, gesturing for her to recork it. "Did Onyx tell you anything about himself? You know, while he was inebriated?"

Schukara shook her head. "Nothin'," she replied. "In ma' eyes, if yer' that drunk 'n' can still hold onto yer' dark secrets, they must be real important."

A finger prodded Arlowe's shoulder, causing him to flinch and fall off the log.

"Nothing to worry about, Your Highness," Onyx sniggered, moving around the log. "Though I thought my ears were burning for a reason."

"Where did you go?" Arlowe questioned, finding himself comfortable where he fell.

Onyx held up a broken piece of wire, casting it aside. "Tip to you guys: when I camp, I surround it with wire. If someone or something puts tension on it, I can hear the twang and prepare myself."

"Like an owl," Schukara mouthed, turning her neck and pecking more like a pigeon.

"Arlowe, mind lending a hand?" Onyx asked. "Schu, could you hold down the fort?"

Schukara stood to attention. "Why me? Am I not good enough ta' join on yer' investigation?"

148

"No. If anything I'd say you're more qualified than our prince here."

"He's not wrong," Arlowe confirmed.

"But this is Arlowe's journey, and we're helping *him* along," Onyx continued. "I know where the disturbance came from, and I want to know how Arlowe would proceed with this. Besides, if I saw you in the camp, I'd run a mile."

Schukara mulled over what Onyx had said, giving a face showing her approval. "You win this one. I'll be here."

The two left the camp, with the assassin leading through a path of carved brambles, cut away by his blades. "So, what are we looking for?" Arlowe questioned. "Do you know what snagged your line?"

"I don't know what caught the wire, but I did find something interesting while I went in search of what did. Thought you might want to see for yourself."

The two dropped down dips in the landscape and pushed back the wild nature of Vexinth blocking their path, ending their small trek by entering into another large expanse of ashen gravel, devoid of features beyond a few lonely stones.

Arlowe was about to ask about the scenery before noticing a figure far in the distance sat upon one of the large rocks. The two were uncertain whether the individual would be useful, let alone know who tripped the wire, though they had nothing to lose by asking. Onyx gestured for him to take the lead.

Though they got closer still, the figure, a red-haired human male, remained motionless. Onyx kept his distance, whistling to get his attention. Once that had failed, the assassin resorted to physical contact, throwing rocks at the man's coat, again, to no success. The prince grabbed his arm, stopping him from throwing more.

Arlowe stood directly in front of the man, his eyes blank as he watched over the horizon. The male must have been in some kind of meditative state, though neither of them could tell for certain.

"Hello?" Arlowe pronounced. "Can you hear me?"

To their surprise, the man responded, though still in his trance. "Hello there," he replied. "I did not expect this, for the spirits to be so calm and communicative."

The partners looked to each other, confused by the man's words. "We're not spirits, answered the prince. "We're living beings stood before you."

"Spirits are sometimes unaware of the fate that has befallen them and as a result are unaware that they now live as spirits. Please, allow me to assist you."

Onyx reached out to the stranger, hoping to wake him. "Look, I don't know where your mind is, but—"

In an instant, the man shot forward, striking Onyx in multiple places. The assassin's body had frozen, unable to stop himself from falling to the floor.

The prince drew his weapon as the stranger arose from the stone, though he seemed uninterested in him. Arlowe had noticed that his hand was filled with dust, and that his eyes were more interested in the gravel swirling around their feet.

"Move!" yelled the stranger, grabbing Onyx's frozen body before dodging back. The gravel had collected above the three and had tried to crush them.

Though uninjured by the bombardment, Arlowe had been launched back by the impact, taking cover behind a nearby boulder.

On the other side of the impact, the stranger placed his hands over the assassin, removing the stiffness from his body.

"I suggest you stay put," warned the man. "Our assailant is not to be trifled with." Onyx nodded in agreement, holding back as the stranger walked out into the open.

Throwing the dust into the air, the stranger exposed the attacker. A spirit was revealed to them with eyes of burning fury, equipped with stone grieves and boots. The gravel

150

that had assaulted them was also the handiwork of the spirit, which formed them into large arms to be utilised as weapons.

The creature lunged forward, swinging once in and once out, with the stranger dodging both attacks. In response, the man placed his hand upon its left arm, breaking away the gravel in one swift motion.

Enraged by the loss of its arm, the creature punched forward into the ground, knocking the stranger away with a powerful shockwave. The impact had kicked up the dust of the land, cloaking the creature from the hunter.

Using the concealment to its advantage, the spirit used its power to grow larger in size. Arlowe was now only tall enough to make eye contact with the spirit's knee. He feared for the stranger's safety, seeing his silhouette slumped upon the ground.

Wasting no time, the creature repeatedly slammed down its arm in an attempt to snuff out the hunter's life, shaking the earth in its outrage.

As the dust cleared, both the spirit and the adventurers looked for any sign of the stranger, expecting his blood to have painted the gravel landscape. Neither, however, had realised that the man still lived, using the dust just as much to his advantage as the creature did.

The stranger was able to evade the majority of the blows, clambering on to the spirit's arm as it let out the last of its uproar. By the time the spirit was aware, the hunter's plan had already succeeded.

Running across the spirit's arm, the stranger then jumped toward its face. As the spirit reached for him, the man had pulled out a small collection of flower petals, thrusting them into the spirit's eye.

The spirit shrieked in pain, wrestling to maintain its size. As the creature struggled to remove the petals, the hunter had already slid down its back, striking at the marking on its back with his mace.

The spirit flickered, immediately returning to its original size. Stumbling away from the fight, the creature surrounded itself with a whirlwind of gravel, disappearing entirely.

Arlowe and Onyx emerged from their cover, approaching the stranger. The man was taking a deep breath with his hands on his knees, falling backwards onto the floor to rest.

"Where's my drink?" he asked himself, feeling over his coat for any sign of a bottle.

"Keeping your senses sharp, old man?" Onyx called out. "I'm still curious as to why you thought we were spirits, and why you paralysed me."

The stranger guzzled the fluid from his bottle, wiping the residue from his beard. He raised a finger to ask for patience, returning the bottle to his inside pocket.

"You're in desolate land, you two. Very far from the standard path connecting the countries. I assume you're travelling *very* directly to save time?"

"Doesn't answer my question," the assassin asserted.

"Yes, it does, my masked friend," the stranger noted. "This is one of the most barren spots in the country. I didn't expect to see anyone else out here."

Arlowe could tell that if any diplomacy was to be made, he had to tag his partner out.

"Onyx, this isn't getting us anywhere. Cool off." The assassin turned his back, raising his hand for the prince to continue with the man. "We're sorry for interfering with you. We only came to ask you a few questions. We didn't mean to get involved."

The stranger smiled, waving away Arlowe's concern. "So long as you don't throw rocks at me too, you can ask as many as you like," he stated, shooting a look at Onyx. "The name's Gill. What's on your mind?"

"It's nice to meet you Gill," Arlowe responded, bowing his head. "What're you doing this far out? My friend noticed you while he was patrolling—"

"Those elevenths you've been hearing about? He's one of them," Onyx mentioned, butting in. "They're hunters of the supernatural and often play the role of detectives when they're not hunting. That's why he's out here."

Arlowe's eyes lit up, with Xanth sounding equally as excited. "I've never heard of elevenths before!" exclaimed the pterravun. "He must be powerful if he could take on that spirit on his own!"

Gill had been tapping up and down his arm, shaking the pins and needles from it. "You're well informed, though I must admit, your attitude leaves something to be desired." He turned his attention back to Arlowe. "I'm just glad neither of you were hurt. As I said, I wasn't expecting anyone but the spirit."

"Why didn't the spirit attack us?" asked Arlowe, curious as to why the spirit only had the eleventh in its sights.

"Because it only hunts females. That's why I paralysed your friend and pulled him to one side. *I* could see you clearly, but with his choice of apparel, I couldn't tell what he was," Gill answered; the two gazed at each other nervously. "Though it has attacked me because I'm hunting it. Because it considers me a threat. Coincidentally, it has—"

"There's an elven female travelling with us," spoke Arlowe, bringing a temporary silence to the area.

"What?" The eleventh rose swiftly to his feet, his jolly tone quashed. "Where?"

"Her name's Schukara. She's guarding our camp," Onyx replied, pointing over his shoulder. "Back the way we came."

The eleventh rushed past the two towards the brambles, using his mace to knock away anything in his path. Arlowe and Onyx tried to remain closely behind, though the man proved to be incredibly agile despite his appearance claiming otherwise.

153

"I though you defeated that spirit back there?" Arlowe questioned, crashing through the rugged nature by the weight of his armour.

"I did," he replied, "though I didn't *sever* it. Younger defiled spirits have a fight or flight instinct not found in those older, since they're considerably weaker and easier to hunt. If they can't win, they retreat. I haven't severed its link to our world. If your friend is here, that's where the spirit will go."

The three reached the camp, staying just beyond its perimeter to scout for the spirit. As Gill expected, the creature had already engaged Schukara, disorientating the elf with the gravel to land powerful blows with its fists.

"Time is against us. The spirit has already found its target" stated Gill. "Your friend doesn't stand a chance on her own. Lend her your aid."

The two readied themselves, though Onyx seemed reluctant. "What about you? You're the expert."

"Yes, I am. Now go, unless you wish to lose your ally."

The campsite was in shambles, courtesy of the spirit. The spirit had advanced on Schukara, increasing the size of its arm to pull the elf and the tree into the same grasp. Her allies were in its peripheral vision, though the spirit cared not for them.

Arlowe rushed forward, charging into the spirit with his shield raised, though its strength allowed it to easily rival the prince. As Onyx dashed forward to assist him, the spirit punched the ground with tremendous force, knocking both of the would-be saviours off-balance.

As the two were still regaining their footing, the tree that Schukara was pinned against was uprooted by the spirit, swung into them. Schukara was released, though all three had been knocked down by the beast's might.

Onyx rose from the impact, twisting one of his spheres. "Let's see your gravel protect

154

you from this!" he roared, lobbing it at the spirit.

To his surprise, the creature caught the bomb, covering it in a gravel shell.

Onyx's stomach dropped as he realised that the spirit wasn't trying to absorb the blast with the gravel; it had been turned his explosive into a shrapnel bomb.

"Find cover!" he yelled, diving behind one of the logs.

The bomb detonated, sending the collected gravel firing in all directions. Though Arlowe had dropped behind one of the other logs in the nick of time, Onyx was unlucky enough to be caught, taking a piece of gravel through his leg.

"Argh, my leg!" he cried. The assassin looked over his cover, still able to warn Arlowe of the encroaching danger. "Watch out! It's almost on top of you!"

The spirit took the prince's cover, throwing it to one side. Arlowe swung his sword upwards, though the spirit took his arm, slamming him back down into the ground.

With no more interference, the spirit took the unconscious Schukara over its shoulder, dragging her away.

As the spirit reached the edge of the camp, it stopped. The beast raised its free arm forward, only for the gravel to disperse; the hand beneath pressed against an invisible surface.

The sound of crunching leaves turned all of their heads, with Gill strolling into camp. "What's wrong? Something in your way?" he goaded, making the spirit twitch in anger at his words.

Reaching into his coat pocket, the eleventh pulled out a small glass vial, smashing it on the floor the release a lingering gas. "Everyone, up!" the eleventh ordered, readjusting his coat. "That should give you enough get up and go to get through this."

True to his word, as the gas passed through the lungs of Gill's allies, a portion of their strength had returned to them.

Arlowe's chest felt lighter and Onyx's leg wound, though still sore, was restored enough to grant him movement. Schukara had also taken in the healing mist, waking from her daze to strike at the spirit's arm, freeing herself.

"What in tarnation is goin' on?" she shouted, repositioning herself by her allies.

"Would you rather we explain it now?" Arlowe queried, turning his next question to the eleventh. The spirit swung its arms in a primal rage. "What did you do to it?"

"It's trapped and knows it. That's why I needed you to out there protecting your friend," the eleventh clarified. "Titan spirits are repulsed by primrose petals. You bought me enough time to surround the camp with them. Not only can it not leave, but it can't alter its size. Stand ready. This isn't over yet."

The spirit approached slowly, aware that it was outnumbered with nowhere to go.

Following this deadly dance, the four took position based on their strengths. Arlowe stood before the spirit baring his shield with Schukara at his side and Onyx taking position at the flank of the creature.

Gill stood back, equipping himself with a staff. "Let's see what you can all do now that the spirit has no more tricks up its sleeve!"

Arlowe bashed his shield for the spirit's attention, struck by an arm fired to allow Schukara an opportunity to strike. One blade collided with the weakened arm, stunning the creature as the other weapon made contact with the weak spot on its back.

Gill ducked in and out of combat, creating openings for the rest of the group to strike. Ripping away the spirit's gravel arms and forcing it to relocate into more favourable locations with a cache of petals, the beast struggled to maintain its offensive stance.

Retaliating, the spirit lunged for the elf only to be met with Arlowe's guarding shield, held back long enough for the assassin to repeatedly stab at the weak spot while the prince held it in place.

The spirit had lost the edge it previously had. It's strongest skill and its ability to flee had been neutered by the petals, and with the eleventh able to remove its manipulation of the gravel, the fight had already been decided.

Though the spirit refused to surrender, the team of four had bested it. The continued assault brought it to its knees.

The group took a step back as the creature dropped to the floor, flickering from all the damage it had taken. Gill walked up to the spirit, which put a weakened arm around his throat.

The eleventh was unfazed, placing his hand upon the arm to break away the collecting gravel. "I'm sorry that this happened to you," he spoke softly. "May you find peace in the great beyond."

Gill took his other hand, placing his palm on the creature's forehead; his action released a blinding light that took Arlowe's group by surprise.

As their eyes opened, they found themselves in a black void, with Gill still holding on to the spirit. "What is this place?" asked Schukara, her voice echoing in the emptiness.

Gill spoke, though he did not move. "When a person dies and is content, they're free to go to the afterlife. The only thing that can stop them is themselves."

The sound of a baby crying pierced the silence, shushed by an unseen mother. Fluid images emerged in the darkness of a young boy working on a farm with his parents. The images changed rapidly, showing the graves of the mother and father, of travellers passing through the farm and the continued work of a young man upon it.

"Sometimes, a spirit stays. Though they were happy, something keeps them from moving on."

Another image of the man appears. He appeared much older, sat in his rocking chair as he watched over his hard work. To his side sat his trusty dog, old and tired. The man's hand graced the dog's head, rustling its fur. The dog panted softly in appreciation.

The image soon changed to the man's grave, with the dog sat by the tombstone as if waiting for someone.

"Spirits may stay to pass on one last message, to travel somewhere one last time, to keep someone company in the last hours of their own life. Sometimes, this happens."

The dog rested its head, closing its eyes.

"Sometimes, it doesn't."

Gill released his palm, causing the spirit to break apart, fading away. The group remained silent, though Xanth's voice emanated in Arlowe's mind.

"We saw that man's whole life," Xanth mumbled. "Gill released him."

The void faded away, with the landscapes of Vexinth soon returning to their view.

"I'm proud of how you handled yourselves out there." Gill praised. "A defiled spirit may be hostile, but there is always someone trapped underneath. You showed respect to your opponent in spite of the danger, and I am grateful for that."

The group relaxed around the camp, torn apart as it was. "If I may ask, how did the spirit become so aggressive?" Arlowe queried. "I thought spirits were peaceful."

"Spirits are," Gill replied, taking a seat on one of the tossed logs. "Demon spirits are the problem. On their own, they're harmless. Just like regular spirits, they can't interact with the world around them. They can, however, forcibly fuse with the spirits native to our world, becoming a defiled spirit."

"The undead have powers depending on how they initially died," Onyx noted. "How do these defiled spirits get their powers?"

"Addin' ta' that, why was it just targetin' women?" Schukara remarked.

Gill took a sip from his flask. "Spirits get their powers based on the demon that

158

merged with them. That one was physically strong and able to change its size, which means that a titan's spirit found him."

The eleventh then turned his attention to Schukara. "As for the motive, it's complicated. The man died without a spouse and there was nothing in his life to suggest that he resented this, though when a demon spirit corrupts the mind, it can amplify negative emotions. The creature's victims were all unmarried women, so unless you're hiding a ring under that gauntlet, you qualify."

The group sat quiet, licking their wounds from the beating they received.

Gill raised himself from his log, cracking his back. "Well, I'd like to thank you for your hospitality and assistance in my contract, but I'd best depart," he uttered. "Until I report back with news of the spirit's passing, people won't rest easy."

"Would you join us?" Arlowe asked, bringing the eyes of his band upon him. "If we hadn't found you, we would have been in serious danger. Schukara could have been killed from our lack of an understanding in the supernatural, and *we* didn't fare much better."

"That's an interesting proposal," Gill mused, "but I may have to decline."

Onyx scoffed, folding his hands. "Figures. No free will, just like the rest of the elevenths under your guild's thumb."

Gill moved back into the camp, standing his ground against Onyx. "Elevenths have two choices once our powers manifest: hunt the supernatural or die. Our actions and sacrifices have saved countless lives even before our guild was founded."

Onyx shrugged off the statement. "What's your point?"

"I've learned a great deal by helping spirits pass on. What have you learned by plunging a dagger into your victim's throats?"

Gill hit a nerve, with Onyx rushing forward into the eleventh's face. "You don't know anything about me. I'm nothing like what you think the Defiant are."

Schukara stood in the way of the two, though she only needed to hold back Onyx, with Gill keeping his cool. "This ain't gonna be a problem, is it?"

The eleventh raised a hand; Schukara retreated upon the realisation that Onyx had stood down.

"You *are* just like them. You have a purpose, but you have no idea what to do," Gill stated, uninterested in the assassin's snarling expression. "You're lost. You could be so much more; a beacon for your fading guild, but you'd rather alienate those around you. You act alone, even when it doesn't favour you."

Gill's gaze burned through the assassin. "Change is in the air, young one. The bridge is burning, and if you don't cross in time, you'll be left behind."

The eleventh held out his hands, dropping Onyx's daggers and ammunition upon the ground before him.

The assassin took a step back, visibly unnerved by the eleventh. Arlowe and Schukara couldn't tell whether this was from Gill's words or the display of nimble fingers.

Onyx returned his belongings to their rightful places, departing form their ravaged campsite without another word uttered.

"Onyx lost fer' words? There's a first," the mercenary commented, happy to have the weight off her arm. "I'm sorry fer' tha' way he spoke ta' ya'."

"I second that," added Arlowe, approaching the two. "Though I've never seen him so riled up. Hopefully that won't stick."

"I'm a figure of authority. He's an assassin. I expected him to be brazen from the first time we spoke." Gill returned to his log. "It doesn't matter. I hold nothing but good tidings for him. It doesn't affect how I feel."

The eleventh took a sip from his flask, continuing. "With that out of the way though, I

160

said I *may* have to decline. You were heading north when I met you. If you're still heading in that direction, I'd be happy to accompany you. I can give you a definite answer once we reach Vexinth's capital."

Arlowe held out his hand. "If it ends up being a no, it has been an honour meeting you. If it turns out to be a yes, I look forward to working with you."

Gill accepted it, returning a calm shake. "The feeling is mutual." The eleventh reached into his coat, pulling out two rectangular items from his pocket. "Here, Arlowe and Schukara, was it? These are for you," he insisted, wiggling the items into their reach.

Schukara ripped the packaging from the item to reveal chocolate hidden within. "I'm certainly not complainin', but why d'ya have these?" she asked, shoving most of it into her mouth.

"Snacks." The eleventh opened up his coat to reveal a line of various confectionaries. "I can be away from civilization for long periods of time. These make it all worth it."

Arlowe began trying to find the centre of the bar, only for Gill to hand him another. "There's no need to split it. Just take another. I always stock up when I reach anywhere that supplies them."

Arlowe slid both into his pack. "What about Onyx?"

"The assassin got his." A joyful smile ran across his face. "Revenge is a snack best served warm."

Chapter Ten:

"When you cry wolf, you feign help. When you cry dredge, you beg for it."

14th Arandbern

Land's Legacy

2084∞ (Current Age)

With the danger of the defiled spirit long behind them, Arlowe and his band made short work of travelling north. Passing by the snow-topped mountains towards Haaroith, it was only as they sat at their bases that they realised the scale of the peaks. Barely visible were the rope bridges, still in use by the orcs occupying the heights like their ancestors of old.

"The Lifesight Mountains," Xanth murmured. "Your father…"

"I'm sure he's watching over all of us," Arlowe answered, smiling to himself.

Though Onyx maintained a stubborn silence, the journey had been made more interesting by learning more of their eleventh ally.

"You're how old?" The prince was astounded at Gill's age. "Four-hundred and thirty? That's insane."

"Is that impressive?" Schukara queried, looking around at the others. "Not meanin' it in a rude way or nothin'. I have a few more centuries before I even think of retirin'."

"It absolutely is, to humans at least," Gill clarified. "Our kind only has a lifespan of around seventy to eighty years. Elevenths have everlasting life, meaning that the only way I'll be passing is by a fatal injury."

"How do ya' even become an eleventh? Could be an interestin' career path."

"Even the oldest living elevenths couldn't tell you that. Our history is our deeds, the spirits we have sent on. We birth, we hunt, we die. The circumstances of our existence, if they ever existed, have been lost to time."

Arlowe had only been alive for twenty-two and had seen so much already. He found it hard to comprehend the things the eleventh had learned in that time, as well as the things he may have seen.

The group stopped at another crossroads. A frigid sign pointed back at Hietruce, left to Haaroith and right towards a place known as Iorverch.

"The left path takes us to the capital, so that's the one we're going with," Gill voiced, turning the group's direction towards it.

"Do you know of Iorverch, Gill?" Arlowe asked. "Does it have anything of note?"

"I doubt you'll need to visit it. Vexinth has some of the most stubborn, but most reliable horses on the continent. Iorverch is where they're broken in. The people there also grow a large variety of fruits and vegetables, should the weather and harsh soil permit. That's about it." Gill shrugged. "The only other thing of note is that I was born there. Lucky you, since you won't find *that* fact in a history book."

"We should visit."

"Why?"

Arlowe paused after being shut down so bluntly. "What about your family?"

Gill sighed. "Arlowe, I'm *four-hundred and thirty*. It's kind of hard to keep a family when they age and you don't."

A sense of sorrow filled Arlowe's heart. "I'm sorry, Gill. I didn't realise."

"Don't cloud your thoughts with it. You have to be very lucky to have someone grow old with you. It's something the guild teaches you *very* early on," Gill stated. "I stayed in contact. Returned for their funerals. I still have some family there, but I'm not close with them. When you're the great, great, great uncle that only turns up for funerals, it gets awkward. Time's passed me by."

Schukara placed her hand on Gill's shoulder. "It don't hafta' be that way, ya' know?"

"I thank you for the sentiment, but it's not necessary." The eleventh took her hand. "I use the gifts I was granted to give closure not only to the spirits who seek the afterlife, but to the families who have those close to them corrupted by demons. In a way, when I help, I feel like I belong. That is what drives me."

Arlowe and Schukara were amazed at how Gill had reacted to talking about himself, able to see that the saddest stories have their silver linings. The eleventh was evidently comfortable with where he fitted in the world, finding purpose where any normal mind would have found despair.

A little while later, Haaroith had come in to view, with the city's totems raising high into the clouds to give away its position to all who sought to find it. One last hill stood between the travellers and the city, the snow becoming ever deeper.

As they reached the halfway mark, Onyx erupted from his silence, causing those other than Gill to flinch from his outburst.

"Alright, enough's enough!" he exploded. "What have you done?"

"What are you talking about?" Gill responded, amused at Onyx's temper.

"My sheath! Ever since you agreed to come with us, I haven't been able to place my dagger into its sheath!" he elaborated, gripping his blade with a forceful grip. "What did you do?"

Gill moved down the hill towards the assassin, motioning his hand forward. Onyx raised his dagger, though the eleventh moved it to one side with his finger.

Gill sprinkled the dust from the previous day into the sheath. With a short flash of light, the eleventh pulled out a skewered packet of chocolate, its contents falling to the floor. Gill caught two, consuming one and offering the other to the man.

"The dust that I used to expose the spirit? It works both ways," he commented.

164

"You're proving my point. Acting alone. Need I say more?"

Once again, Onyx had been rendered mute, shoving his way past Gill. As Arlowe was to call out his partner's name, Gill raised his hand and shook his head. The assassin had once again vanished, to the dismay of the prince.

The remaining three passed the gargantuan totems into Vexinth's capital, immediately met by the blend of tribal and gothic architecture the country was known for. Arlowe had noticed that Haaroith was much more laid back than Thaedlon, mostly due to not being knocked to-and-fro by the populace.

The prince felt a slight tug from his back, with Schukara handing him a small note.

"I wonder who this could be from," she voiced sarcastically, glancing over Arlowe's shoulder to read its contents.

I doubt you need me for your royal visits, so I'm off to see the sights in my own unique way. I'll find you later, it read, with a little extra nearing the bottom. *PS: Don't let Schukara take you into the sewers. I heard there might be dwarves with ironsoul suits down there. Just making you aware.*

The elf rolled her eyes. "That was one time," she mentioned, grasping her dented armour. "I won't be joinin' ya' anyway. People ta' see, sister ta' find."

"You're looking for your sister?" Gill queried. "Is she missing?"

"I am 'n' she is. Why do ya' ask?"

"I'm already heading to the Eleventh Sense Guild. If you would like to accompany me, we could look for information on your sister while I finish the paperwork regarding my contract."

"It's temptin', but my armour's seen better days…"

Gill placed his hand on his chin, thinking of a solution. "We could visit the Warforged to maintain our equipment and then ask around the city for any sign of your sister. Is that acceptable?"

Schukara turned to Arlowe. "Ya' didn't tell me that partnerin' up with ya' gave me perks like this! I gotta ask, do ya' offer severance pay? Maternity leave? Spa days?"

The prince looked unimpressed. "Pfft, fine. Don't ask 'n' ya' don't get." She turned back to Gill. "Lead the way!" she exclaimed, giggling to herself.

"Been a while since it's been just us two," Xanth commented. "Where next?"

Arlowe found his bearings by using the totems behind him. "My father used to tell me plenty of stories of Haaroith. Apparently, the rulers of this city reside at the northernmost point, meaning that we need to go up there." He pointed to the large hill on the opposite side of the city. "Let's hope we won't have to wait long."

*

"Though I understand your urgency, the Bright Blades are in the middle of very delicate talks with council members from the Administration. You'll have to wait."

The shrine priest's words brought Arlowe to falter, leaning himself against the fence post of his hut. "This seems to be a common occurrence," he muttered. "You wouldn't happen to know when the talks will be finished by any chance?"

The priest placed their palms together. "I am unsure. The Bright Blades are closely tied to the Administration. Both have been organising support for those caught in the conflict. It has not been easy." His hands opened, gesturing for Arlowe to do the same; a symbol was now glowing on the inside of his palm. "When the meetings have concluded, that symbol should disappear. Bring yourself to the shrine atop the hill and you shall be granted entry. Give them my regards."

The priest gave a bow before returning to his hut. Arlowe in turn bowed, leaving the premises to pursue his other priorities.

"I don't mean to jinx us, but I hope we fare better with the Arcane Guild. I can't bear to stand outside any longer. I could use my nipples to joust," he jested, scoring a chuckle from his telepathic ally.

Arlowe was unaware of the location of the Arcane Guild; his boots were forced to trudge through Haaroith's snowy streets in search of it. "How're you doing with that book I lent to you? Making any headway?" he asked. "Xanth?"

"Mm? Oh, sorry!" Xanth replied, sounding as though he had only just awoken. "I'm already through the bulk of the book. There's not really much of note though. They were born of a curse, they're explosive, and they have a weakness to water. We may know more than the book does. There's no mention of an alpha anywhere."

"That's a shame. I hoped we could've salvaged something from Thaedlon's library."

"Don't give up yet. I did find something, though it's not good."

"If we can use it, it can't be that bad."

"The book's author interviewed the remnants of the witches that are still around to this day. One in particular notes that *the kharakians were supposed to be beasts with a singular purpose, unable to grow their numbers or evolve like a natural creature due to the magic that creates them, even if they become permanent.*"

Arlowe stopped in the middle of the street, trying to process what he had been told. "The kharakians are only the weapon, not the ones wielding it. They can't evolve on their own," he deduced. "Someone or something has tampered with them and made them this way. The question is, who would? And what would they have to gain?"

"I don't know," responded Xanth. "I'll let you know if I find anything else."

Arlowe arrived at the city's Arcane Guild, locating it in the southwest sector of the city.

The prince pushed the metal gate open. The steel scraped through the snow, letting out a squeal that echoed through the courtyard. As the sound concluded, only his entering footsteps filled the area with sound, keeping Arlowe on his toes.

"Where is everyone? This doesn't feel right," Xanth commented, though Arlowe didn't answer. After what had transpired in Thaedlon, the prince cautiously approached the guild hall with his hand tightly gripping the hilt of his blade.

Like with the gate, Arlowe gave the door a light shove, opening it with ease. As he did, both the sight and the smell from within turned his stomach.

A slaughter had occurred within the halls, with the former guild members used as the interior's decorations. A ghastly stench took hold of Arlowe's senses, forcing him back to retch.

The prince took hold of the door, yanking it shut to ward off the smell. As he descended the stairs to look for the Haaroith Guard, four silhouettes appeared at the courtyard gate, with one waving to him.

"Arlowe? Is that you?" the waving silhouette called, running closer to reveal itself as Antoinetta. The prince put up his hand, warding her away. "Arlowe?"

"Get the guards. Now," he murmured, holding his stomach. Antoinetta seemed frightened by his display, running back towards the gate with great haste.

*

It didn't take long for the guards to arrive on the scene, cordoning off the guild to the general public. Bodies wrapped in sheets were lined in a row to the side of the steps; those who almost got a taste of freedom before being torn asunder.

A large detachment of guards had already entered the guild, leaving the rest to keep the public out and take statements from any potential witnesses, including the prince.

"Thank you for your time, and I thank you on behalf of the city for reporting this incident at your earliest convenience," spoke the guard, returning his notepad to the pocket on his belt. "Is there anything we can do for you?"

168

Arlowe looked up from his perch on the steps, offering the guard a smile of reassurance. "I'll be fine, thank you. I suggest you..." The prince gestured to the ever-growing number of bodies recovered from the guild, being covered by the guard's colleagues. The guard gave a salute, before lending his assistance to the effort.

Antoinetta approached Arlowe cautiously, crouching in front of him with her head and arms rested on her knees. "Are you okay? You've gone pale."

Arlowe nodded, peering over to see Caspus and two others speaking with each other. "What are you doing here? And who are they?"

"Well, you must remember Caspus! He's our—"

"Head of the janitorial staff. I remember. And those two?"

Antoinetta stuttered at being cut off by Arlowe, remembering him as being a much warmer individual. "T-the human is Kellen, a-and the orc is called Ushnar. They transferred here after what had happened at Thaedlon. They didn't feel safe," she explained, regaining her composure. "Students of the Arcane Guild usually get escorted during a transfer, but with the guild's resources spread so thin, Caspus offered to bring them. He regularly visits the guilds to make sure they're kept up to standard anyway."

"That's rough," noted Xanth. "They transferred due to the upset within Thaedlon and walked into this? I don't envy them."

"Don't you think something's off?" asked Arlowe, keeping an eye on his surroundings. "The first two guilds we visit and they've both been attacked? Back-to-back? It's too convenient."

The prince's thoughts concerned the pterravun. "What are you saying?"

"I don't know who the culprit is, but what I do know is they're trying to make me a suspect. I'm one of the few people who was with Thaedlon's guild master and chief librarian before they perished, and I'm apparently the first to stumble across the massacre here? If the guards start thinking I'm the culprit, that'll make it so much more difficult for me to find out who the culprit really is."

"But you only recently left Eyenridge. There's no way you could've committed the older murders."

"And who's to say I wasn't orchestrating the events safely from my castle? I'm next in line for the throne. Politically speaking, I'm more powerful than I want to admit." Arlowe paused. "My main concern is if eyes start focusing on me, that could hinder my rally against the kharakians. That can't happen."

A guard approached Caspus, leading him to one side with his notepad drawn. The two students reconvened with Antoinetta. "Greetings Arlowe, it's a pleasure to meet you," voiced Kellen, drawing Arlowe's attention.

The prince rose to his feet. "How do you know my name?"

"Antoinetta spoke about you *a lot.* Like, I'm pretty sure your name is half of her vocabulary." The mage cleared his throat and began to tap his foot. "And you know what they say: *It's a—"*

"No! No more singing!" Ushnar barked, rubbing his temple. "Do you *ever* shut up?"

"Antoinetta spoke about nothing but Arlowe. Why can't *I* speak?" Kellen demanded. "Sing of what I enjoy?"

"Antoinetta's songs of Arlowe had the charm of an ocean's whisper. Your songs had all the charm of a banshee's wail."

Antoinetta's face turned from a pale white to bright red, reminiscent of strawberries; her coat sleeve was lifted to hide her embarrassment.

Kellen brought his fellow student in close laughing, though all he received from her in return was a jab under his rib, winding him.

170

"I deserved that," he muttered, chuckling as he reeled from her blow.

"Between your singing and the teasing you put her through during our trip north, I personally support your statement," pronounced Ushnar, turning to face the envoy. "Like my associate said: it's an honour to meet you. I hope there's a chance of us working together in the future. You look like a man who can get things done."

Suddenly, two loud bangs came from the doors of the guild. A guard had tackled through, slamming it behind him before dropping to the ground from exhaustion. "I couldn't, I wanted to but, they're in there. I need… want to… Arn's mercy, I failed them! I'm a fucking coward!"

The man continued to rave, clutching the helmet on his head.

The sound drew the nearby guards, as well as the four stood just beyond. The small crowd amassed to see the guard in a pool of his own blood, writhing in pain. Large portions of his armour appeared to have been ripped open with what looked like teeth; a set of three slashes graced the front of his cuirass.

"His armour's melting," Xanth mentioned, pointing out to Arlowe that a corrosive substance was still eating at the man's armour long after the attack.

The commotion also drew the attention of the guard captain, sorrowful at the sight of another potential death. "By the Fragments, take the man away!" he barked. "If there's no-one here who can help him, I suggest you take him to someone who can."

"What do we do about the guild, Captain Oril?" questioned another guard.

"Seal it," Oril ordered. "Whatever's in there, I don't want it getting out. Am I clear?"

Arlowe approached the captain, outraged at his proposal. "You can't do that! There could be survivors in there. We have to look for them!"

The captain faced the prince, struggling to contain his frustration. "Do you think I don't want to look for them? I'm close to my men, but I have to keep a level head," he growled, pacing before Arlowe. "I have a choice: I could use the remainder of my men to search for any survivors. However, not only am I putting their lives at risk, but if we provoke whatever's in there, and it comes out, I'm risking the lives of the people too. Or, I can seal it and wait for support from the guilds. My men stay safe. The people stay safe. What would you have me do?"

Arlowe nodded in agreement with Oril, understanding the feeling of great pressure upon oneself. "Let me in."

The captain raised an eyebrow. "Why would I do that?"

"You have no men to spare. I'm not one of your men."

"They could all be dead. You'd risk your life at the possibility alone?"

"I would."

Oril stared at the prince, turning back to face his men. "I want two men at the door, and the rest of you either securing the perimeter or continuing to cover the bodies. This man here is staring death in the eyes to rescue our comrades. Show him your utmost respect."

The guard captain bowed to Arlowe, returning to his original post.

Like their superior, the rest of the guards dispersed, leaving the prince and the three guild members by his side to devise a plan.

"I'm going in. I'll clear the way and send them down the path I've cleared," Arlowe instructed, departing for the guild's innards. "Tend to the wounded as soon as you can. I doubt there will be many."

Antoinetta took Arlowe's hand, stopping him from entering the guild alone. "If you're going in there, I'm coming with you. The guild is my home. Without it, I'd be on the streets," she argued. "I owe the guild my life. I want to return the favour."

Ushnar stepped forward. "Third time I've transferred now. I keep hoping that the next guild'll be different. I keep running," he voiced. "It's time to stop. If you'll have me, I'll be by your side too."

Arlowe nodded, accepting the offers. Their gazes turned to Kellen, who was looking at them with a worried expression. "What? I'm not going in there! I'm a pacifist!"

"You're joking," remarked the orc.

"You're joking," Kellen mimicked mockingly, including his fingers to replicate Ushnar's protruding teeth. "No, I'm not. I'd be as useless as a chocolate teapot in there. I'll wait outside and stick to the old plan."

"Whatever's taken refuge in there was able to take down the entire guild and a platoon of guards and he wants to sit around and wait for the threat to come to us? He's unbelievable," stated Ushnar, shaking his head in disapproval as he led Arlowe and Antoinetta up the stairs to the guild hall entrance. "We'd best move swiftly. Our chances to come out of this unscathed look slim to none."

The metallic smell of blood filled Arlowe's nostrils once more, accompanied by a vile pungence that attempted to suffocate the group. Though the prince decided to march onwards with his senses being assaulted, Antoinetta opted to place her sleeve over her nose. Ushnar decided that the scarf around his neck could double as a mask to guard him from the repulsive odour, covering his face.

The guards stationed by the door sealed them in with a barricade, the subsequent slam frightening Antoinetta enough for her trembling legs to buckle from the fright.

As her head faced the floor, her eyes made note of a strange print, shaped from the blood of those trapped inside. "What do you think did that?" Ushnar asked, his voice muffled by his scarf.

"They look like paw prints. Did the Arcane Guild have animals?" Xanth questioned.

"Even if they did, I can't think of a natural animal that has paw prints like that,"

Arlowe answered, posing Xanth's question to Antoinetta. "Any idea what could've made those prints?"

Antoinetta crawled further in, taking a closer look at the trail of paw prints. "They're too close together for it to be bipedal. I want to say that it's a wild dire wolf, but I fear I'm being optimistic."

Arlowe took the lead. "And realistically? What could it be?"

"I'd put my gold on dredges," the orc voiced. "I imagine the necromancers are involved with this. If there's paw prints on the grounds of a necromancer attack, a dredge is the only creature that it could be."

"If there are dredges, we must tread *very* carefully." Antoinetta took a breath to still her worry. "From what I've read, they use the darkness to their advantage, and where you find one, you'll find a pack."

While Arlowe and Ushnar pushed forward through the halls and central chamber with their sword and wand drawn respectively, Antoinetta had been lighting the candles as they progressed. While it should have been a blessing to see, the sight of more mutilated corpses had begun to appear; the corpses of both the guild members too far in, and of the guards that had attempted to retrieve them.

"Xanth, you know what to do," Arlowe mentioned.

"Will you be safe?"

"You can listen to what I hear so that we're on the same page," he compromised, "but this is a bit much for your eyes."

"Please don't avoid my questions."

Antoinetta tugged Arlowe's arm, pointing him to an unlit turn. "I heard something from over there."

The prince raised his palm for the two to keep their position, approaching the corner with his shield raised and his blade poised to strike. The sound of deep breathing filled the air, confirming to Arlowe that Antoinetta had not begun hearing things.

The prince swiftly turned the corner, knocked back by a powerful strike upon his shield. Peering over his shield, Arlowe was surprised to see a guard stood before him.

His uniform was shredded and covered with blood. The force of the strike must have come from a surge of adrenaline, as the guard appeared drained, shaking and unable to maintain his stance.

Arlowe signalled for his allies to join him as the guard did the same, revealing an ally from behind each side of the door.

The elven guard was accompanied by one human and one dwarf. "Are y-you here for u-us?" the elf posed, struggling to keep his quaking in check.

"What happened to you? Where're the others?" Ushnar queried.

The elf looked away, no longer able to keep eye contact with the group. The human guard spoke in his stead, though she was just as shaken as her colleague was.

"Twenty-four of us came in to secure the guild and search for survivors. We found only death," she answered, wiping the blood and tears from her face. "The things in here, they rushed us. Once the majority of us had been killed, they prowled around, picking us off one by one. Some were ripped apart; some had their bodies melted like snow in the sun. Karkdugan, Sael and I only found each other recently. We hid. That was the only way we could evade those things."

"If you're all that's left, we'll escort you outside to safety. Oril is waiting for your return," Arlowe pronounced, bringing a small bit of life back into their eyes. "Let's go. Nothing good can come from staying here."

Moving back through the central chamber, Arlowe could immediately tell that something was off. "Antoinetta? The candles on the way through. You lit those, right?"

The mage nodded slowly. The path they had lit on their way in had turned pitch black. Something had followed behind them, luring them further in with a maintained lie of safety.

Luckily, Arlowe could make out a rope near the doorway they had exited, believing this to be the pulley system that operated the curtains high above them. The prince turned to the guard who last spoke. "What's your name, soldier?"

"Kirk, sir."

"Would you mind drawing the curtains, Kirk?"

Kirk gulped. She placed her hands on the rope to begin moving the curtains from the windows. As she did, the dim light divulged what Arlowe had expected since noticing the lack of light.

At first, the room was barren, giving relief to the group. However, a creak from one of the beams above drew their attention upwards, revealing a dozen wolf-like beings. They all stared down at them with the same corrosive fluid Xanth had recognised earlier, dripping from their maws.

Their blank white eyes stared down in unison from the rafters; their jaws were bent into unnatural smiles, heads swivelled to one side. Their flesh barely stretched over their emaciated bodies as their limbs struggled to remain in their sockets. Scrappy fur dotted the flesh, their venom-filled veins able to be seen through their hairless patches.

As Arlowe took a step forward, one of the wolves leapt down, blocking the way to the entrance hall. Ushnar moved the survivors to the prince's flank, calling to him from the back. "These things carved a bloody swathe through the Arcane Guild and the guards that came to protect it! We stand no chance against them!"

The prince raised his shield as the dredge moved into a quadrupedal state, telegraphing its readiness to lunge towards him. "We don't need to win, we need to

176

survive," he responded, keeping his eyes on the beast. "Ushnar, protect the rear. Kirk, take the right and give the left to whichever of your allies is better rested. Antoinetta, if you have any spells at your disposal, now is the time to use them. Keep us safe."

The group moved with Arlowe, following him forward as he charged. Reacting, the dredge guarding the door gave out an ear-piercing howl, signalling for its pack to join the fray.

Arlowe thrust his sword forward, tearing through the dredge's torso. In response, the creature dug the blade further in, slamming itself against the prince's shield whilst reaching around it with its deadly claws.

From the monster's mouth came the sound of retching. Arlowe backed away in the nick of time to avoid the corrosive expulsion. Moving quickly, he yanked the blade free from the dredge, using it to carve into its neck.

The dredge drew breath, still yelping from the strike, retreating for another to takes its place. The supporting beast dropped from the ceiling to surprise its prey, yet Arlowe was able to best the dredge. Using its momentum to strengthen the strike from his shield, he winded it, knocking it away from the door.

Meanwhile, the additional dredges had found what they needed to secure a successful kill: an opening. Two dredges charged into the left, and though Karkdugan had enough strength to repel one, his previous injuries refused his body the chance to repel another.

Eager to keep his comrade alive, Sael moved in to strip the dredge from the dwarf, though another leapt from the ceiling above them, tackling the elf away.

Unable to be stopped, the dredge pinning Karkdugan to the ground dug its claws into his chest before released its corrosive vomit upon the dwarf, melting him into a grotesque pool of melted skin and organs.

The elven guardsman snapped at the sight of another death, throwing his weapon to one side. "No! No, no, no! I surrender! Have mercy!" he screamed, attempting to sprint past the dredges to safety.

Surprising no-one, the dredges had no mercy to give. The wolf closest knocked him to the ground, using its claws to rip him to pieces. "Sana, I knew nothing!" he screamed repeatedly until his throat was torn apart, coerced into silence.

Ushnar had been hit by one of the dredge's swipes, though the orc dissipated. Appearing a short distance away, Ushnar marched forward, his wand shaking with a bright energy.

"Eyes shut, now!" he yelled, raising the wand to cast a burst of bright light.

Heeding the orc's instruction, the party avoided the effects of the spell. The dredges had been blinded, with those on the ground swinging wildly in the hopes of connecting their swings.

The wolves above were not exempt. Unable to maintain their balance on their perches above, they thrashed in pain as they hit the stone floor; there was nothing below to cushion their fall.

"Everyone, this way!" Arlowe exclaimed, gesturing to the group towards the door with one hand whilst pushing away a dredge with his shield in the other.

Kirk shoved the dredge attacking her to one side, rushing into the entrance hall to safety. Antoinetta approached and raised her hands to fire a handful of bright bolts into Arlowe's assailant, giving him freedom once more.

Arlowe moved through the doorway, though the mage did not follow. "What are you doing? We need to go!" Arlowe screamed. The dredges were regaining their sight.

"They're faster than us. We need a decoy if we're to escape," Antoinetta replied, moving her hands as if shaping an item from clay. "I want to help."

The girl pushed her hands forward as if throwing out what she had crafted, spawning

178

a giant dredge from thin air to threaten those in the central chamber.

"What did you do?" Arlowe questioned, stunned at the size of the creature.

"It's an illusion. I'm an illumancer," she voiced, smiling at the prince.

Unfortunately, not all of the dredges had been fooled by Antoinetta's trick. One of the monsters had kept itself stable in the rafters above, able to see the two behind the illusion from its vantage point.

Without a second thought, the creature vaulted from the ceiling, lunging at Antoinetta with an unmatched ferocity. The beast shoved the prince through the doorway, giving itself the chance to feast upon the young woman's flesh.

Unimpeded, the dredge placed its jaws around her arm and its foot upon her chest, pulling and pushing respectively until the arm was ripped away from its owner.

As Antoinetta screamed in anguish, the beast bit into her torso, throwing her to one side in preparation for the charging prince.

Arlowe swung his blade, severing the dredge's hand, blocking a swing from the other. Though it was able to plant its teeth into his shoulder, Arlowe fought through the pain of the acid making contact with his skin, forcing his sword up through the monster's head to bring it the death it truly deserved.

As the dredge dropped limp, Arlowe knew he had a decision to make. Before him laid Antoinetta beneath an illusion ready to fade, injured and alone. Behind him was the exit, safety guaranteed, though Antoinetta had no chance of lasting on her own.

"Ushnar? Are you there?" Arlowe called out, hoping that the orc could solve his dilemma. Alas, the orc had disappeared, with the lack of a response leading him to believe that the burst of light was the last boon he had to offer. He was all Antoinetta had.

Casting aside his doubts, Arlowe sprinted towards the elf, hoping to reach her in time.

The illusion began to flicker, though he was willing to risk facing death once more. He offered his hand to Antoinetta who looked up at him with piteous eyes.

"Arlowe? Are you there?"

*

"Arlowe?" The prince jolted upright, as if waking from a dream. He found himself sat on the steps outside of the Arcane Guild with Gill grasping his shoulder, shaking him from his daze. "Can you hear me?"

"What about me?" Xanth added. "Can you hear me?"

Arlowe nodded, hearing Xanth give out a sigh of relief as he took a few breaths to calm his raging stomach. "Gill? What are you doing here?"

"Word travels fast, especially with senses like mine. How are you feeling?"

Arlowe looked around, panicked. "Where's Antoinetta? Did she get out?"

"Do you not remember?" Gill posed, appearing confused at Arlowe's statement. "You carried her out." Arlowe was silent, unable to remember anything beyond rushing forward to save her. "According to a guard out here, Kirk, I believe her name was, you barged through those doors holding the poor girl. You handed her over to the head of the janitorial staff before sitting as you were on these steps. You were completely unresponsive."

Arlowe began rising to his feet, receiving help from Gill to fully stand. "Thanks. I appreciate it," he muttered, leaving Gill's hold to support himself.

Looking forward, Arlowe could see the janitor approaching him, with a furious sight plastered across his face. "Caspus! How is Antoin—"

Caspus' fist graced Arlowe's face with enough force to knock him back down to the floor, grabbing him by the collar to bring their faces together.

"Arlowe!" the pterravun called out in fear.

"What possessed you into thinking that taking her in there was a good idea?" Caspus barked, his voice echoing through the silent courtyard. "Your foolish actions have scarred her for life!"

"We wanted to help," Arlowe choked. "There were survivors."

"There was a *chance* of survivors!" the janitor corrected. "You couldn't know for certain that they'd still be alive!"

"Reinforcements... wouldn't have arrived in time."

"And what did your victory secure? Hm? One guard?" Caspus' voice was filled with contempt. "I hope it was worth it."

The janitor carelessly dropped Arlowe to the ground, raising his boot to strike him again, though Gill's intervention warded him away.

"If it would please you," the eleventh offered, "I'd be more than happy to investigate this incident on behalf of the Eleventh Sense Guild, sir."

Caspus' face already gave away his answer.

"He's already done enough. I want neither him nor any who stand with him involved in this any further. There's enough to clean up without it being made worse. As soon as you are able, I want you to leave. I suggest you make haste."

"Where is she? I need to know that she's okay," Arlowe loudly insisted, struggling to his feet without Gill's aid. The janitor briefly paused at Arlowe's determination, though he continued his departure, spitefully refusing the prince his answer.

"Arlowe? Arlowe, listen to me," persisted Gill, unable to peel the prince's hateful eyes from the janitor. The eleventh grabbed Arlowe's face, demanding his attention. "I want you to tell me everything you know about the guild, these murders, anything that could be considered useful. Do you understand me?"

Arlowe pulled Gill's hand away, rubbing where he had gripped so harshly. "What does it matter? Caspus told us not to interfere. This area will be covered in security until its scrubbed clean. What's the point?"

Gill scanned the courtyard, keeping his eye on the janitor. "Schukara told me what occurred within Thaedlon's Arcane Guild. Tell me, do you care for these people?"

Arlowe was lost for words. "What? Of course I do."

"And you believe that something more sinister hides behind the guise of these attacks?"

"Gill, stop—"

"Then why are you giving up?"

"I'm not giving up!"

"Then lend me your knowledge, your experiences! Tell me what you know!" Arlowe fell quiet. "Did you give up when your city went up in flames? When your people were butchered in the streets?"

"Is this meant to make me feel better?" Arlowe queried, gritting his teeth. Gill continued to wait for his answer. "No, I didn't."

"Your actions led you to Thaedlon, where you crafted the plan to take the fight to the kharakians. You gave people hope," pronounced the eleventh. "Did you give up at the sight of the prenomen, or did you stand and fight to keep it contained within the library? Did you give up when you faced the defiled spirit, or did you fight not only to save your friend, but to save a damned soul also?"

Arlowe gave a sigh. "What's your point, Gill?"

Gill turned, gesturing for the prince to follow. "My point is that when you chose not to back down, the world around you became that little bit brighter. Guide the people though this fog, lest we all become lost in it. Your allies stand by you readily."

The two reached the gate, with Schukara waiting to greet them.

182

"How ya' doin' bud?" She gave Arlowe's chest a nudge.

The prince simply glanced at Schukara, helping her to understand without uttering a word.

Arlowe looked to his eleventh companion. "You said allies earlier. Plural. Does that include you?"

Gill nodded. "The guild permitted it, so long as I deal with any local situations while I travel. I accepted."

Schukara laughed, drawing the attention of her friends. "I'm sure Onyx will be thrilled with that."

Gill pulled a note from his pocket, handing it to Schukara. "I'm sure he will. Read this."

Schukara unfolded the note to peruse its contents.

Gill, would you kindly meet me in the alley to the side of the live artist's stall? Four tolls of the church bells. I promise I won't stab you, shady as this sounds. It's urgent.

Arlowe and Schukara glanced at each other, surprised that Onyx had asked exclusively for Gill rather than either of them. "Well, at least he clarified that he *wouldn't* stab ya'," noted Schukara, passing back the note.

"Come, I'll lead you to the northern gate. We can speak of the Arcane Guild on our way." The eleventh tucked the note neatly into a pocket. "After that, I'll see what the assassin has in store for me."

Chapter Eleven:

"The pen is neither mightier, nor more intelligent than the sword."

14th Arandbern

Land's Legacy

2084∞ (Current Age)

"And Kellen and Ushnar were the two that came with Caspus?"

Though they neared Haaroith's northern gates, Gill had plenty of questions left to ask. His trusty notepad took every little detail it could, tying any possible connection together with great scrutiny.

"I'll say in advance that I can't promise anything will come from this. Given more time, I'd be able to analyse the situation more thoroughly," he stated, returning his notepad to one of the many pockets on the inside of his coat. "Unfortunately, the kharakians aren't the waiting type. I'll do what I can with what time I have."

Arlowe nodded. "As with our current endeavours, the sooner we deal with this, the more lives that are spared."

Schukara spoke up. "Gill, when're ya' gonna tell us what yer' up to?"

The three reached the gate, with Gill wearing a smirk across his face. "Eleventh's don't always work within the confines of the law. To be on the safe side, I'll be keeping my business to myself, if I may?" He bowed courteously. "I pray that your audience with the Bright Blades bears fruit."

The two waved their eleventh companion off, Schukara taking the lead through the gate only to be stopped by the prince's own hesitation. "What's tha' matter Arlowe? Somethin' caught yer' eye?"

The prince looked to the hut he had visited earlier. The mark placed upon his palm by the priest had disappeared, though the building appeared empty with the shrine priest nowhere in sight. "I guess we can go ahead."

The two ascended the beautiful path before them. Where Haaroith was laden with snow crushed under the fur-covered boots of its people, pristine snow sat entirely untouched all around this path, decorating the trees and surrounding flora with delicate sparkles.

The group had noticed snowfall as they travelled to the northernmost part of the continent, though the temperature hadn't been cold enough for it to settle. Here though, the snow was allowed to collect unimpeded, creating an oddly serene wasteland.

"What is that stuff?" asked Xanth, astounded at the amount all around.

"You mean snow? You don't know what snow is?" Arlowe picked some up to scrunch into a ball.

"Mm-mm. We have a small stream in the central chamber. It's not that interesting though."

Arlowe thought of the caves, so warm by comparison to the frigid climate of Vexinth.

"At least you're nice and toasty in there," he thought, shivering from the cold. "Think of snow as really cold water. This is what it turns into at this temperature, and as I've just demonstrated, it becomes quite malleable—"

"Are ya' communicatin' with him? Yer' friend?" Schukara queried, unintentionally crossing their conversation. "Onyx don't seem that impressed, but I find it fascinatin'. Xanth, wasn't it?"

"You told them about me?" Xanth called out, surprised at his name being spoken by someone other than Arlowe. "Wait, no, hold on! Ooh, this is so exciting! I have an idea! Offer Schukara your finger, like what I asked to do to you! Please? Do you remember how?"

185

The prince stopped, taken aback by the boy's energy. "First Xanth, that was terrible phrasing, and second, you didn't ask, you gave. There's a huge difference." He turned his attention back to the elf, pausing their climb. "An odd request: may I place my index finger upon your forehead? The voice in my head is keen for you to accept. Did any of that make sense to you?"

"Nope," she admitted. "But, these're tha' people that gave ya' a second set of eyes and a second chance of life, so it'd be rude not ta' oblige."

Schukara motioned her head forward, brushing aside her fringe for Arlowe to make contact. As his finger pressed down, her eyes glowed a vivid green, like Xanth's had when the connection was made with him.

"Hoo-wee, whatever ya' did, it makes ya' awfully dizzy," Schukara commented, trying her best to keep her balance. "Hello? Is anyone there?"

Neither Arlowe nor Schukara could hear anything. "Xanth, are you there?" the prince posed.

Though it took a little longer, the pterravun's voice finally emerged in their minds, proving his idea to be a success.

"Hello," he spoke softly, with Arlowe realising that Xanth hadn't expected his plan to work, withdrawing back into his shell similar to how they first met.

"Hey darlin'," the elf voiced quietly; her voice was purposely kept low to avoid spooking the child. "It's nice ta' meet'cha. My name's Schukara. I'm a friend of Arlowe's, as I imagine yer' aware."

The silence persisted, though Xanth eventually drew the courage to speak once more. "You sound funny."

"Yer' not the first ta' notice," she mentioned between snorts of laughter, wiping a tear from her eye. "Oh my, he's adorable Arlowe." The mercenary gestured for the two to continue up the hill. "So, what's Xanth like? What interests does he have?"

Arlowe had no answer. It had only just occurred to him that he knew nothing of his pterravun companion.

Schukara gave the prince's shoulder a nudge. "Really? Ya' encountered a hidden group of telepathic beings 'n' ya' never asked 'em any questions?"

Arlowe was lost for words. "Oh, err…"

The prince's shoulder was nudged a second time. "Realisin' it now, yer' inner scholar must be kickin' itself!"

"In Arlowe's defence, I've been asking him all of the questions," Xanth stated. "Then we lost our connection and—"

"I was jokin', Xanth. Didn't mean nothin' by it," Schukara insisted, calming the boy. "Though I'll admit, it's admirable ta' see ya' come ta' Arlowe's defence like that. Ya' seem like quite tha' noble soul."

The three looked up the path, still a long way off from reaching the top, though the shrine was at least in sight, its silhouette hidden behind the ever-growing blizzard.

Arlowe cleared his throat. "Well Xanth, give us a fact about yourself. It'd be nice to actually know something about you."

Xanth didn't speak, prompting Schukara to. "Shall I start? Would that help?"

"Mm-hmm," agreed Xanth.

"Fair enough. Did ya' know that tha' boys in my village thought I was a boy too? Like, until ma' late teens? I was always tusslin', doin' farmwork, trainin' with tha' guards. Ma always gave me tha' choice ta' be a lady, but I hated tha' laid back lifestyle." A smile came with her reminiscence. "I guess ya' can see why I look tha' way I do with the way I spent ma' childhood. Wouldn't trade it fer' tha' world."

Arlowe nodded to her, thanking her for her input. "You're up next Xanth. Schukara did her part."

"I live in a cave. Is that a sufficient fact?"

"I walked into that one. Something we don't know?"

"I used to work. What about that?"

Arlowe chuckled, hearing a playful tone in Xanth's voice. "Want to be more specific, you cheeky sod?"

"Fine, fine!" Xanth giggled. "I used to clean pipes. It was warm and really noisy but working gave me food and a place to sleep. Some of my friends weren't so lucky."

"Did they not eat, or sleep?"

"No, they did. Some just stopped turning up for work. I did other things too, but I never saw them again."

Arlowe could see that Xanth's answers were bringing a concerned look to Schukara's face. "Xanth, what 'other things' did ya' do?" she queried.

"Hm? Oh, I used to help build tunnels. I carried boom sticks too, though I was never allowed to use them."

The elf seemed shocked. "Y'all were buildin' tunnels? How old are ya'?"

"I'm ten," Xanth replied. "Why?"

Schukara shot a look to Arlowe. "Just wonderin'. It's been a long time since I was ten. A hundred an' eighty-two years have flown by me."

"Wow, you're old."

Arlowe's eyes widened in shock. "Xanth!"

"Did I say something wrong?" the pterravun asked worryingly. "I'm so sorry, Schukara!"

Schukara didn't react, signalling to Arlowe that their connection had been cut.

"I don't think she heard you, but I'll pass on the message," Arlowe rejoined, offering his attention to the mercenary. "Schu, Xanth wants you to know that he's sorry."

The elf smiled. "No harm done, darlin'. It was a pleasure ta' meet'cha," she voiced, bowing her head to the prince for Xanth to see. "Looks like we're nearin' tha' top. Took us long enough."

The three reached the peak of the hill to find an old wooden shrine, damaged by the passage of time. Though the buildings in Haaroith looked to be maintained regularly, this particular structure appeared to have been untouched for years. Scouting around, Arlowe could spot no guards or priests, leaving the building to occupy the howling winds alone.

"Did anyone mention what ya' were meant ta' do?" Schukara posed amidst the building blizzard, examining the front of the building.

Arlowe moved to the front door. "I only know that they're waiting for me." The prince knocked on the door only for it to slide open of its own accord, granting them the entry they sought.

Deeming them sufficiently within, the door behind them slid shut, with the two torches closest to them flickering to life. As if by command, additional torches lit in sets of two, providing a path of light for the guests to follow.

A voice that travelled along the wind. "We foresaw your visit, Arlowe Artaven. Come forth and join us. No harm shall befall you within these walls."

Arlowe gestured for Schukara to join him, following the path of torches further in. The two remained wary of their surroundings, uncomforted by the words on the wind.

The three slowly pushed onwards, keeping their eyes on anything else out of the ordinary. "It's really clean in here," uttered Xanth.

The prince flinched at the abrupt words; Schukara flinched at his reaction. "Arn's mercy! Xanth, are you trying to give me a heart attack?" he questioned out of breath, poking his temple to explain his behaviour to his elven partner. "What do you mean?"

"The outside looked all battered and broken, but in here, well, there's nothing out of place."

"Arlowe, check this out," Schukara spoke, lifting her foot to show the melted snow dripping from her boot. "I assume yer' talkin' 'bout tha' state of this place? Look behind us. Where's our mess?"

Schukara wasn't wrong. The two of them should've been leaving wet footprints through the shrine, though looking back, the floor looked as perfectly polished as it did before them.

"The Bright Blades should recommend who cleans their shrine in return for the Construction Guild's aid," Arlowe mentioned, waving his arm. "Come on, I'd rather not keep our hosts waiting."

The prince and the mercenary reached the end of the long hall, arriving in a room scarce in decoration. The only items of note were a small table sat in the centre of the room and three swords adorning the wall facing them.

"Where do you think Haaroith's rulers are?" Xanth asked. "There's no-one here, but someone named you specifically."

Arlowe walked forward, resting himself against the table, pressing his hands against the wood. "Take a closer look at those weapons on the wall. What's the first thing that comes to mind?"

"They're shiny?"

"You could say they're quite bright."

"Do you mean—"

As Xanth caught on to Arlowe's deduction, the blades upon the wall came to life, floating down from their mounts to greet the visitors. "Woah," the pterravun uttered,

190

astounded at the sight.

"Welcome, Prince Artaven and friend," the central blade announced, floating towards the elf. "May we have your name too, my dear?"

Schukara straightened up. "It's Schukara, ma'am."

"Schukara?"

"Parle. Schukara Parle. It's an honour."

"The honour is with us. It is very nice to meet you, Schukara Parle." The sword floated back, repositioning itself behind the table with a blade to each of its sides.

"Introductions are in order. My name is Bright Blade Artemis the First, to my left is Bright Blade Athena the Second and to my right is Bright Blade Ulysses the Third. Together, we are the Council of Blades, protectors of the people of Vexinth. As stated earlier, we foresaw your visit, Prince Artaven, and though we know not of your reason for being here, we can assume that the news you bring will not be pleasant."

"Did you hear of Eyenridge and Fertral? Of the kharakians?" the prince posed.

"We did. We still do," Artemis spoke. "Not only have we pledged our supplies to their eradication, but we were also the ones who convinced the Administration and the guilds under their wing to divert supplies your way too, despite their ongoing concerns with the necromancers."

"Then I hope I'm not overstepping my boundaries when I ask for you to join us. Physically." The prince lowered his head in embarrassment. "I understand that you have done much for us and I am grateful for that, but what we need is good men and women fighting this—"

"Done," spoke Artemis, simultaneously cutting off the prince and surprising him with their immediate response. "An announcement will go out alerting the city of our involvement with you. So long as you provide us with the relevant information such as where the armies will gather, where they will be accommodated and what resources should be transported, we will assist where we can."

Arlowe and Schukara looked to each other, both stunned at how painless it was to recruit Haaroith into their growing army.

"S'cuse me," Schukara voiced. "Sorry ta' butt in on this, but why're ya' so eager ta' join us? Not complainin' or nothin', just curious."

"What do you mean?" queried Artemis.

"The people of Fertral demand retribution, and the Artavens have a history with the Thaedlons, hence their involvement. I didn't expect others to join us so easily," Arlowe declared. "As my partner said, we're not complaining, but there must be a reason for you to answer so quickly."

Ulysses moved forward. "The economy is a good place to start," he explained. "Eyenridge was one of the largest providers of produce to the Administration, as well as being rich in both iron and oil. Fertral in turn was also a large customer within the Administration, meaning that profits have been lost. Losing your country was quite the complication, and one that must be rectified."

Before Arlowe could speak, Athena swapped places with Ulysses for her turn.

"Secondly, we are in a satisfactory position to aid you," she spoke. "We sit far from the kharakians and sit on the opposite side of the continent from Grandgrave, shielding us from the necromancers. The only reason we haven't assisted you against either before is that we imagine our forces alongside your own would not be enough. With the aid of the other countries, this is no longer so."

Arlowe held his tongue, expecting Artemis to complete the listings of the other blades. She did not disappoint.

"One final point: you forget the debt we owe to Fertral. To your father," she expressed. "Vexinth was already under siege by the titans, slowly advancing towards the capital. His plan was to bring their leader, the Core, towards the Lifesight Mountains. If he had failed, Haaroith would have been destroyed. We trusted him, and he did not fail us. As a gesture of our gratitude, we would be honoured to return your country to you, ridding it of its current occupants in the process."

Arlowe moved back from the table to give a large bow to the blades. "I thank you with every fibre of my being, your graces. I shall send word to Thaedlon at once."

"I wouldn't thank us yet, young Arlowe," voiced Artemis. "The war is far from over, and our victory is not guaranteed. Save your thanks for then, should it come."

The prince nodded, turning himself to leave. As he reached the hallway leading to the exit, he turned back to face the blades. "I forgot to mention; the priest sends his regards." The blades turned to each other, though their voices were silent. Schukara's hand graced the prince's back, escorting him from the room.

The two exited the shrine, with the door once again closing behind them. "I do believe that a bit of retail therapy is in order," declared the elf, stretching her arms above her head.

"How do you figure?" Arlowe asked.

Schukara raised her hand to her ear, signalling for Arlowe to listen to the bells coming from the city.

"Hear that?" Two tolls of the bell emerged from the silhouette of the city. "Onyx 'n' Gill won't be meetin' fer' a lil' while yet. Besides, a few extra supplies fer' tha' road can never be a bad thing."

"Schukara?"

"Yeah?"

"Thanks for being here. I appreciate the company."

Schukara smiled. "Yer' welcome. After recent circumstances, I just wanted ta' make sure you were safe."

The prince agreed, following by her side as they departed from the council's shrine.

The path they had used to reach the shrine had become no less difficult to traverse, though the two appreciated the descent after the uphill climb they so recently had to make. Through a collection of slips and stumbles, the prince and the mercenary reached the bottom, breathing a sigh of relief as the northern gate came into view.

"Wait," spoke the elf, moving her arm in front of Arlowe. "D'ya see that?" The prince had been oblivious to his surroundings due to seeing nothing but white, though Schukara was perceptive enough to spot a shape leaning by the wooden fence nearing the gate. The outline of a blade filled the figures hand, putting the two back into a wary state. "Who goes there?"

The figure moved its head in response, pushing away from the fence to approach them, sword in hand. Schukara drew hers, moving one to her front to strike and one to her side to protect Arlowe.

The figure came close enough to be identified. A young half-elf, his head and face decorated with burgundy alongside his dull red eyes, contrasted against their icy surroundings.

"Interesting talk with the blades, I hope?" he scoffed, swinging a black blade playfully in his hand. "You're a fool to trust them."

Arlowe gently pressed his hand against his companion's blade, now able to pass her. "Who am I speaking to?" He kept his hands visible, hoping to avoid conflict.

"Did the Bright Blades appear honourable? Courteous? It's a lie. They're using you. They don't take part in anything unless it benefits them. Why do you think they're the only rulers that have direct contact with the Administration?" The man moved forward,

194

a few paces from the prince. "Everything comes at a cost. What did they ask for?"

"Fertral is economically valuable, and they're repaying a debt," Arlowe answered. "Their reward is our stability."

"If your stability was at risk, why didn't they help sooner? If the kharakians were such a threat to their precious economy, why didn't they gather the forces way back when?" the man interrogated, smirking confidently at what he'd asked. "The kharakians aren't a new threat. Unless, they were waiting for an opportunity like this."

Arlowe moved forward himself, entering the stranger's personal space. "I need their armies and supplies. I won't make an enemy of them. Don't speak of what you don't understand."

The man cocked his head. "I know more than you think, and I'd be killed for that alone. The Bright Blades are a threat, and by extension, you will be their enabler."

Xanth spoke up. "He isn't telling us everything. I don't trust him."

Noting the pterravun's unease, the prince skirted around the man, continuing to the gate. "Let us take our leave, Schukara. I won't be motioned on speculation alone. I have nothing more to say."

"So you won't hear me?" the stranger questioned.

Arlowe stayed silent, waiting for Schukara to be by his side. As they took steps together, a new voice appeared among them. "Wait."

Schukara spun towards the source of the voice, though Arlowe kept his back turned. "Who was that?" she posed.

The man faced them, though no words left his mouth. Instead, a faint glow appeared from his sword.

"Listen to me," echoed the blade, taking a different approach to their wielder. "I cannot deny the truth my partner speaks. The Bright Blades are not to be trusted, and we seek the aid of any who could put a stop to their acts. Would you reconsider?"

"I'll hear no more." The prince turned his head. "And if your bearer believes that threatening his way around will work, he may find the help you seek, but he won't find it with us."

Finalising their conversation, Arlowe pressed on towards the northern gate, followed by Schukara. Though the prince kept his eyes forward, Schukara looked back to the man and his sword, only to see the path devoid of life once more.

Like Arlowe's patience, the two had vanished.

*

"Schukara, are we actually going to walk around the market?"

"Achoo! Ugh, one more minute? Pleeeeeease?"

Arlowe could understand the elf's hesitance. Highpeak Market was known as the warmest part of the city. With the amount of fires that burned there accompanied by every food stall that offered the warmth of their ovens to the general public, those less accustomed to the cold found it to be a haven.

The prince was also aware that Schukara was acclimatised to a warmer climate, meaning that here, the elf was reduced to huddling next to a brazier in a large blanket she had purchased.

What had she said back in the warmth of Eyenridge? We huddle 'round our fires in this weather. Arlowe smiled at the terrible accent conjured in his head.

"Wanna join me?" the elf offered, lifting an arm.

Arlowe raised a hand. "No, but thanks for thinking of me. Savour your heat."

"Then at least sit. I look weird sat here on ma' own. Help me blend in." The prince sat, crossing his legs. "Tell me 'bout yer' problems, Arlowe. I'd hafta' be blind ta' not see somethin' plaguin' ya'," the mercenary spoke softly, trying to maintain eye contact with her partner.

Arlowe shook his head. "It's nothing."

"Oh, it's somethin'. Haven't seen ya' this quiet since we first met at that tavern." He was silent. "It's about that Antoinetta girl, ain't it?"

"I guess you could say it opened my eyes." His head was hung low. "It made everything else make much more sense."

"It wasn't yer' fault."

"That's beside the point. She could've died because of me and will definitely not be how she was before. It's been the same story since I was forced out of Eyenridge." Arlowe swallowed the lump in his throat, looking Schukara dead in the eyes. "Did I tell you about my run-in with a band of mercenaries? From Quazin?"

The elf shook her head. "Ya' didn't."

"They helped me out of the city. Assisted me against my first encounter with an alpha kharakian. In return, I helped them take back their camp, 'overrun' by goblins. We slaughtered them all."

"I'm sure they attacked ya' first."

"Even if they did, the band killed everyone. Not just the warriors. Women and children. I carried one to the funeral pyre. The fight had nothing to do with her."

Schukara spoke not a word, though her eyes continued to watch the prince.

"Back in Thaedlon, we lost Gretchin and Alaric because we all charged in without thinking of the consequences" the prince raved. "We had no coordination; that's something a leader would've thought of."

"Arlowe."

"Arn, you speak of not leaving me alone? That I won't be safe? Yet what did Onyx and I do on our journey here? We left *you* behind. Alone. Without Gill's intervention you would've been killed and—"

"Arlowe!" The prince raised his head, awoken from his rant. "That's enough. Ya' can stop now."

The prince was unsure of what to say, lowering his head once more. "I'm... sorry."

Schukara sighed, clicking for Arlowe to look at her. "Lotta' ifs and woulds. Ya' can't predict what'll happen, Arlowe. You've made mistakes, but yer' on a just path."

"Am I?"

"Do ya' think I'd join ya' if yer' goal was ta' assist tha' kharakians? Were you tha' one that slaughtered those goblins? Did ya' rip off Antoinetta's arm yerself?" the mercenary posed, refusing to lessen her gaze. "We stand by ya' 'cause we agree with yer' cause. We're a team."

Arlowe shook his head. "I can't even keep you all from fighting."

"You've done what ya' can. Ya' didn't hafta make Onyx and I put aside our differences, nor did ya' hafta accept Gill's choice ta' let tha' assassin storm off on his own," Schukara stated. "Ya' laid tha' groundwork. *We* need to start offerin' olive branches ta' each other."

"You're going to give Onyx a chance?" Arlowe asked. "Never thought I'd see the day."

"Tha' day is still young!" The elf giggled to herself. "Look at it this way: did ya' really think a mercenary, an assassin, an eleventh 'n' a voice in yer' head would all get along? Sounds more like a crappy joke ta' me."

Arlowe cracked a smile, relaxing his posture a little. "You're right. I'm being foolish."

As the two relaxed by the soothing fire, a loud explosion rocked the city, shocking the two to their feet. In the distance, a factory could be seen expelling masses of smoke; its

198

fires raged into a fiery crown.

Schukara glanced at Arlowe, who was watching the factory with as much intensity as the fires that were engulfing it. "We're goin', right?"

The prince looked at her, a spark of life reanimating in his eyes. "You didn't think I'd say no, did you? Let's go see if we can help."

As the two came closer to the factory, the anger of the populace could be heard, with the guards evacuating the building of those with hair singed and clothes blackened.

What remained of them had amassed by the gates to the factory, with Guard Captain Oril offering one hand to escort the survivors out, and another equipped with a blade to ward off others from entering.

"Not all of the survivors are accounted for! Find our families!"

"If we couldn't trust you with the Arcane Guild, why should we trust the guard now?"

"How dare you threaten those that you swore to protect! You're no better than the ones who caused this!"

The guards were fighting a losing battle, struggling against the increasingly irate populace of Haaroith. Though violence had been enacted against them, Oril forced his men to passively hold the line, uninterested in retaliating against those he was sworn to keep safe. The people were acting in fear.

"No-one goes in, and that's final!" bellowed the guard captain, aware that the pot was close to boiling over. "That factory is deteriorating fast, and I can't promise your safety if you got in there! You all need to stay put!"

Arlowe shoved his way through with Schukara in tow, able to reach the guard captain to speak. "Oril!" he called. "Is there anything we can do to help?"

"I'd rather you didn't!" he replied, moving his blade in their direction. "If I let you through now, others will follow. Even if I'm vilified for my actions, letting people in to find their loved ones will only result in more death. I won't be held responsible for that."

A member of the crowd pointed to the factory, drawing their attention to his finding. "There, in the window! It's the Dairgersmire Slaughterer!"

One by one, the crowd looked up, doubling their anger at the sight of the man in the factory window, putting all the more pressure on the guards holding them back.

The blade-wielding man moved from the window once his appearance had sparked interest from the crowd, indicating that this was his intention.

"Arlowe, that was tha' half-elf from earlier! By the gate!" Schukara noted, barely able to speak over the masses. "Kinda hard ta' miss tha' red hair and black blade combo!"

The crowd made another attempt, leaping at the guard captain to move him from the factory gate. Using this to his advantage, Arlowe rushed forward, sprinting by Oril towards the factory.

"Stop!" ordered the captain. "Return immediately, Arlowe! That's unauthorized entry!"

Schukara moved to Oril's aid, standing by him against the masses. "Arlowe knows what he's doin', guard captain! Focus yer' effort on keepin' these lot outta tha' fire! I'm with ya'!"

As Arlowe reached the doors of the factory, a voice called from above.

"Hey you! Down there!" The prince searched to see a handful of workers on a bridge connected to the main building. "We need help! The building we came from is completely engulfed in flames and we can't get this door open. I think something's blocking it on the other side!" called the worker, repeatedly yanking at the door.

"I'll see what I can do from inside! Stay put!" he yelled back, entering into the blaze.

"His eyes were on you," Xanth noted. "He knew you'd come."

Distorted air filled the inside of the factory, boiling the prince as soon as he set foot inside. Though his balance faltered, a moment to focus his mind allowed him to press on.

To his right above him, Arlowe could see a metal bar through the handle of the door, refusing the survivors their escape. Luckily, though some of the factory had collapsed from the damage, the stairs remained intact, granting him access to the upper floor.

However, as he approached them, a familiar sight greeted him from the balcony above.

"I knew if we made enough noise, you'd come. Ever the hero, aren't you, Your Highness?" The stranger leaned over the bars, relaxed despite the circumstances.

"Did you do this?" Arlowe questioned; his sword-arm was ready to engage. "What do you want from me?"

The stranger sniggered, retaining his stance, though his words did not follow. "I find it amusing that we had to cause some kind of destructive act to get your attention. Now that we're a threat, your heroic soul can't refuse to put an end to our actions." The black blade glimmered as it spoke. "Shame about the factory, though. I heard it was quite profitable for the Bright Blades and the Administration."

Arlowe blinked, and the man was gone, reappearing on the opposite balcony.

"You're hostile towards us because *you* don't trust us, and yet, I don't agree with how trusting someone in *your* position is, and you refuse to hear what we have to say." One more blink and the stranger moved again, this time sitting down to Arlowe's right. "We both know there's more to the kharakians than simply being destructive for the sake of it. You're not stupid."

The prince moved towards the stairs, aiming to move the bar from the door to free the workers.

As he got halfway up, the stranger appeared behind him in the centre of the room, the blade continuing from her bearer.

"The Bright Blades have never been interested in the plight of your people, yet they act now that a new player has possibly joined the fray? Surely, you've wondered why?"

Arlowe continued around the balcony, confronted by the man and his blade. "The lady was speaking. What say you?"

With the two in his way, Arlowe drew his own blade, preparing to strike. "I say that I want you out of my way. Those people are innocent!" he ordered, raising his shield.

"Then come and save them, hero." taunted the blade, leading Arlowe to bring his sword down upon them.

The swords clashed, with the stranger quickly charging forward to tackle Arlowe back, winding him. Without a moment to spare, the stranger had appeared by Arlowe's side to strike, blocked by his shield in the nick of time.

Though the prince was able to match the stranger blow for blow, he couldn't avoid being pushed back without compromising his position, unable to keep up with the man's impressive swordsmanship.

"You're interested in me just as much as the Bright Blades are. Why?" Arlowe posed, forced further down the balcony. "What do you have to gain?"

The stranger lowered his weapon, relaxing his posture. "I fight for my freedom," declared the blade. "My existence alone deems me a perfect candidate for execution, though they'll never admit why publicly. Those I have bonded with, including the man you see before you, mean nothing to the Bright Blades. There will be no-one to mourn their deaths as they hunt for me."

The man moved the blade back into position. "Strike me down, if you can. I didn't ask for this, and I doubt I'll be the last in their little witch hunt."

As the stranger lunged forward, Arlowe found his opening and swung, though the stranger moved his hand forward, knocking the prince off of the balcony with an unseen force.

As the prince picked himself up from the floor, the stranger appeared in front of him, sat on the stairs leading up to the blocked door. "If you don't trust us, then don't. We won't stop you," he declared.

"But don't trust the Bright Blades," the blade furthered. "Use their men and supplies for all we care but keep your involvement with them to a minimum. You may think the Bright Blades in the right and we in the wrong, though if you opened your eyes you would see that the world is nothing but grey. The power enhancing the kharakians could change our world as we know it, and the Bright Blades are using you to get it."

The man pulled the metal bar from behind his back, with the workers trapped outside running past Arlowe to safety.

The blade continued. "You appear as the hero that saved their lives, we passed on our message to you and a source of income has gone up in smoke for the Bright Blades. Everyone wins in my eyes."

"Unless you still wish to stop us?" posed the man. "What's your moral compass telling you?"

Arlowe was still reeling from his drop, though his blade still rested in his palm. As he struggled to his feet, the stranger and his blade were surprised to see him return it to its sheath.

"Go. Get out of here," he asserted. "I'll keep my eye on the Bright Blades, but understand that if we meet again under these circumstances, I won't hesitate."

The stranger sheathed his own blade, bowing to the prince.

"We will meet again, Arlowe. Hopefully, it will be under cooler circumstances," he uttered, moving backwards into the smoke and out of sight.

The factory squealed in pain, with one of the ceiling beams falling mere inches from Arlowe's feet. The building cracked under the weight it could no longer hold, with Xanth fully aware of the danger. "Arlowe, get out of there!"

A hand gripped the prince's arm. One of the workers from the bridge had hold of him, pulling him towards the factory entrance.

"You can't stay here, sir! It's too dangerous! Come on!"

Arlowe ran through the doors, held open by more of the workers eager to evacuate the prince. He and the workers collapsed to the ground as they exited the inferno, watching as the factory crumbled from its injuries, leaving only a scorched husk behind.

Once the thrill of escaping the building had settled, the workers collected around Arlowe, helping him to his feet.

"We didn't think anyone was coming!" voiced the worker who had pulled him from the factory. "You saved our lives. We won't forget what you've done for us."

Arlowe thought back to the stranger's words, and though he avoided revealing who had actually saved them, he couldn't bring himself to name himself as their saviour.

"There's no debt to be paid. You saved my life too," Arlowe announced, wiping the soot from his suit. "Go. Be with your families. You have my thanks, all of you."

As the workers scurried off towards the crowds beyond the gate, they stumbled across the guard captain, who they bowed to as they passed. Oril continued to Arlowe with Schukara by his side, wearing a look of disapproval upon his face.

"According to the law, I should have you arrested," pronounced the guard captain, offering his hand. "That won't be happening. Between Kirk's life and the lives of those workers, I see no reason to imprison you. My superiors can go to Erethys if they think otherwise."

"Thank you, guard captain," Arlowe replied, gratefully taking his hand. "I'm sorry for my interference in the matters of your city."

Oril shook his head. "You've been a nuisance, sure, but you put the people of Haaroith before yourself. Twice. You're alright in my book."

Schukara moved forward, taking hold of Arlowe's shoulder. "Everythin' alright? Ya' look a lil' well done," she jested, dusting off his cuirass.

"A little?" Arlowe turned his attention back to the guard captain. "The Dairgersmire Slaughterer. What do you know about him?" He peered over at the ruins of the factory; his mind was curious as to the whereabouts of the stranger and his blade.

"Terrorist, plain and simple," Oril spat, clearly against the man's methods. "Valerius Pridesworn. Half-elf. Orphan of Ainsley and Kelrora. Lovely people, unlike their son. Used to be an alright sort until he came across that damned sword of his. Been a plague on this country ever since. There's a bounty on his head, but no-one's been able to collect it."

The guard captain handed Arlowe a slip of paper. "Nothing more I can say. He's not the type that enjoys sitting down for a chat. Safe travels, to you and yours."

Schukara waited for the guard captain to leave before speaking her mind. "That wasn't everythin', was it?" she queried. "What happened in there?"

Arlowe leaned against a nearby post, reading the contents of the note. "Valerius and his blade made a possible connection between the kharakians and the Bright Blades, and based on what I already know, their theory is convincing to say the least."

Schukara folded her arms. "Please tell me yer' not trustin' terrorists."

"I don't trust them, but every terrorist has an end goal. What do they achieve by going against the Bright Blades? Anarchy? I doubt it." Arlowe shook his head free of the thought, leading Schukara from the factory's vicinity. "The blades aren't my enemies, but I do agree with Valerius and his blade that their involvement is questionable. I'll stay neutral for now and see what else I can find before I pick a side in their quarrel."

Schukara shrugged her shoulders. "Ya' enjoy tha' company of an assassin, why not a terrorist too?" The two cracked up at her comment. "Anyway, shall we actually pick up tha' supplies we need from tha' market? I imagine Onyx and Gill will be ready ta' meet soon."

"Actually..." Arlowe took a deep breath. "Could you do me a *huge* favour?"

The mercenary's curiosity was piqued. "Hm? What is it?"

"Could you pick up what we need without me?" He shook the note in his hand. "We're strapped for time, and there's someone I'd like to visit before we leave."

Though Arlowe didn't make it easy by flapping it around, Schukara was able to make out the contents of the note, beaming with happiness.

"Sure. I'll meet you by tha' totems."

The prince bowed to the mercenary, leaving in a hurry.

Bed 7, Schukara thought. *I wonder what that's all about.*

Chapter Twelve:

"Where are you?"

14th Arandbern
Land's Legacy
2084∞ (Current Age)

As instructed, Gill followed the note from Onyx to the letter, entering the alley to find it suspiciously empty. Keeping his ear ready for the four tolls of the bell, the eleventh took a bar of chocolate from his coat pocket, relaxing himself against the wall to enjoy its contents.

As if by clockwork, as soon as the bell tolled, a corpse fell before him, coating the grey walls with the blood of the unlucky soul. Shortly after, the assassin climbed down from the top of the building, taking a closer look at his victim.

"Thanks for coming," he voiced, rising from his analysis of the splattered man. "I half- expected you not to come. We haven't been on the best of terms."

"I could sense you, so the surprise factor was wasted," Gill commented, seeing now that his treat contained portions of the assassin's victim, dropping it to the floor. "And if I may correct, *you* haven't been on the best of terms with *me*. I'd rather you weren't at my throat. It makes working together difficult."

Onyx crossed his arms. "Well, help me with this, and I may take more of a liking to you."

"And what am I helping you with? The note didn't mention anything, and you're being rather coy."

The assassin refused to answer the eleventh, motioning for him to follow. "I imagine you'll find out soon enough. Come on, we're wasting time and I'd rather not have the

Royal Highness and his noble protector on my case."

Gill was quick to note that Onyx was leading him solely through alleyways, though he was unsure whether this was because of the bounty on his head or due to his elusive plans. Unsurprisingly, the alleyways were quiet, though the eleventh could feel eyes upon him; a lack of soul energy in the area forced him to admit they were alone.

Breaking the silence, Gill thought it best to converse with Onyx, hoping to understand both him and his motives. "So, that man back there. Friend of yours?"

"Totally. Used to play sacred law with him all the time. I'm not a fan of losing."

"I'll call your bluff."

Onyx chuckled at the eleventh's call out. "The Eleventh Sense Guild must be missing a detective of your calibre."

"I suppose."

"As I imagine you're aware, the Defiant aren't too keen on freelance assassins. Most perform sloppy work and he was no exception. Tried to kill a noble and ended up trying to kill the entire family to cover his tracks. Unfortunately for him, the eldest son escaped and called for his head. We were only too happy to oblige."

"Your guild is on the decline and you're still taking contracts?" Gill queried, curious of the Defiant's activities.

"Some are, some aren't."

"And what about you? You're still operating."

Onyx stopped, in turn stopping his ally. "You're asking a lot of questions. Mind if I ask one?"

"Of course," Gill answered. "What do you want to know?"

"I didn't ask you to come immediately. What were you doing between receiving that note and coming to aid me?" Gill bit his tongue, unsure of what to say. "Interesting.

Ask me a whole host of questions and I'm supposed to answer, but you're allowed to keep it zipped? Put up or shut up."

Onyx carried on down the alleyway, though Gill did not follow.

"Onyx," voiced the eleventh; his voice halted the man at a potential bite.

Gill moved to the assassin, keeping his voice down. "I'll give you your answer on two conditions."

"And what are these conditions?"

"The information I hold could be dangerous in the wrong hands, as I imagine yours is too," Gill whispered. "Not only do we trade secret for secret, but we keep them to ourselves. Do you understand?"

Onyx was silent, keeping a firm eye contact on the eleventh, aware that the man was deadly serious. "Where were you?"

Gill gestured for them to walk, keeping close to the assassin. "Did you hear about the Arcane Guild?"

"It was attacked. Arlowe went in and saved a few guards. What of it?"

"I slipped into the courtyard while no-one was looking and investigated."

Onyx glanced at Gill, who was keeping his eyes watching all around. "That area has been sealed off by the guards. You broke in?" he questioned, intrigued at Gill's criminal activities. "I'm impressed."

Gill looked back. "I'm not sure why you're all so surprised. Though I am with the Administration, if there's information I need that they won't give, occasionally the law must be... unaware of me. A case must be solved by any means." The eleventh took a breath. "Swear to me that this information goes nowhere unless stated otherwise."

Onyx rolled his eyes. "Yeah sure, whatever."

Gill grabbed the shoulder of the assassin to spin him around, his face embellished with a serious expression. "Swear to me."

Though it crossed Onyx's mind to rip Gill's hand away with a smart remark, this didn't feel like the time. "I swear." With an agreement in place, he removed the eleventh's hand from his shoulder. "What did you find that has you so on edge?"

Gill took a breath to calm himself, continuing their walk. "Two things: firstly, Arlowe made me aware of two Arcane Guild students that he met after reporting the massacre, a human named Kellen and an orc named Ushnar. I couldn't find them."

Onyx's brow furrowed. "What do you mean you couldn't find them?"

"Apparently, Kellen waited outside to assist any survivors that escaped. Not only was he not there when I arrived, but based on the description Arlowe gave me, no-one's seen him."

"And Ushnar?"

"I can't say for certain. The dredges had vanished by the time I got there, though not all of the bodies had been evacuated. I whistled one of the guards over and bribed him, asking him if any orcs known as Ushnar had been recovered. He didn't recognise the name and the Haaroith Arcane Guild had no records of any orc guild members, meaning that he should've been the only orc body. He hasn't turned up."

"Wait, the dredges vanished?" Onyx questioned. "They could be on the loose!"

"Not possible," Gill replied. "Their trails ended inside the guild, meaning that a necromancer was responsible. No other kind of magic can summon the undead."

The two reached a blocked off area of the city, with a sign hanging from the wall reading, *No entry. Haaroith guards only. Trespassers will be prosecuted.*

Onyx turned to Gill. "So, you can't find the two students, one of which may still be in the guild halls." The assassin wiggled a finger in the air. "You said two things. Unless I missed something, that was one."

The eleventh paused, uneasy at his own words. "Arlowe was there."

Where Gill wore his serious look, Onyx wore one of confusion. "We *know* he was there. That's where he said he was going."

"Allow me to clarify. I can sense *when* people have been somewhere. Postcognition. I could sense Arlowe's soul energy when he supposedly first arrived at the scene of the crime, but I also sensed his presence earlier than that."

"Are you sure your powers aren't lessening in your age?" Onyx questioned, unable to even get a smirk from the eleventh. "He should've been to see Haaroith's leaders earlier in the day, or at the least planning a meeting for later."

"Yet I found his energy within the guild alongside many other sources of soul energy, indicating that he was there before the bloodshed began."

"How is that possible?" Onyx posed. "Is that possible?"

"I don't know."

The two stood by the wall, unsure of what to say. Both of them knew what Gill's senses meant, though neither were sure of how to proceed.

Rather than speak, Onyx began to act, climbing the wall to reach the other side. Shaking his head of worry, the assassin spoke to Gill as he reached the top. "Arlowe's alright. We'll keep an eye on him, but I don't think he'd be involved in these guild murders."

"Is that a hint of trust I hear?"

"Sure, why not?" Onyx replied. "Is it that hard to believe?"

Gill finally showed a smile, clambering up and past the wall with ease. "Your turn. What's swirling around in that mysterious little head of yours?"

"We're not far now. It makes more sense to explain when we get there."

The alleys were ill-lit, illuminated only by the angle of the sun travelling across the sky to the west. Without the masses of Haaroith making use of them, the alleyways had become the perfect nesting ground for rats, stealing the crumbs from the populated streets for their mischief back home.

Onyx and Gill finally arrived at an inky dead end. "Here we are!" the assassin declared, raising his arms in a display as if introducing the eleventh to a luxurious home.

"Here we are…? Where? I see nothing of value here," Gill stated, inspecting the dingy corner. "I'm sure that note contained the phrase *I promise I won't stab you.* I hope your word is true."

Onyx chuckled, showing his sheaths to be filled. "This is what I needed you for. That postcognition that you mentioned earlier? Use it here."

"My postcognition? I'll assume this is regarding someone who's no longer with us?" Gill queried. "Just to make you aware, the longer they've been deceased, the harder it'll be to use my powers. Doubly so if there's nothing to focus my energy on."

The assassin drifted further in, pulling a pallet away to reveal a small amount of dried blood underneath it. "I came earlier to make sure it was still here. Luckily, your guild documented the scene and found no culprit. No one came to bring down the walls, so no one's been to clean it up. This should do, right?"

Gill nodded, approaching the stain. Placing his hand upon it, the eleventh focused his mind, looking out for any remnant of soul energy in the surrounding area. At first, his powers found nothing, leading him to believe that the crime scene was too old, though his persistence eventually rewarded him.

"Have you found anything?" Onyx asked, concerned with the eleventh's lack of movement.

"No, not yet. I can't seem to… Wait, hold on. I may have something," Gill conveyed, rising back up to his feet. His eyes were opened wide, with the assassin able to see that they were different whilst under the effects of his unique powers. The eleventh's pupils had gone as white as snow, almost blending in to the rest of the eye if not for the black outlines and a deep red mark travelling down the centre of the irises.

"What do you see?" Onyx questioned, keen to know more of his partner's vision.

"I see some kind of conflict," Gill answered, making sure to note every occurrence within his postcognitive state. "Whoever fought here was heavily equipped, using all the weapons in their arsenal. Based on what I know, I'd take a guess at him being a member of the Defiant. However…"

The eleventh closed his eyes, reopening them with his eyes back to their usual colour. "Something wasn't right," he continued. "I couldn't—"

"See the attacker? Their soul energy?"

Gill turned his head to face the assassin. "You knew what we'd find here. How?"

"You already figured out that this was important to me. Did you really think I wouldn't hire other elevenths to help me?"

"You never told me your secret. If there was ever a good time for you to inform me, it would be now."

Onyx placed himself on a nearby barrel, preparing to sharpen his blades as he spoke. "People have theorised what's been sending the Defiant into extinction. Some have guessed a new assassin guild forming, whilst others have wagered on a lack of faith, with most of us leaving the fold. They're wrong."

"Whatever it was that I couldn't see…"

"Is the thing that's picking us off one by one."

Gill leaned against the wall opposite Onyx, crossing his arms. "Did you know this assassin personally?"

"You could say that. He was my master."

"I'm sorry for your loss."

"Master Hollow deserved better than being cornered in an alleyway like a rabid dog. The guild was adamant that we had nothing to fear, but my master was having none of it. Even I tried to convince him, but he wouldn't see reason. We were only separated for a few moments, and in that time, they found him."

"Surely the Defiant were aware of a threat once the man hunting it had been killed?" Gill queried. "You said other elevenths have looked into this? They would've seen the same thing I did."

"You'd think so, but no." Onyx looked up. "They've banned anyone from looking further into it. They're essentially saying that if we don't even acknowledge its existence, it'll leave us alone."

"And has it?"

"There's another site I wanted you to use your powers on. Fresher site than this. Figure it out."

Onyx disembarked from the barrel, returning his blade to its place at his side. Gill wanted to say something to ease the assassin's mind, though nothing he could say would make the situation any easier.

The lack of answers was evidently getting under the assassin's skin. Though peering into his past and current situation was helping Gill to understand his lack of trust for the authorities and his own guild, Onyx was becoming all the more distant. Desperate.

The two climbed over another wall, with Gill able to hear the bustle of the crowds once more. Directly in front was a chalk outline of a body. Only tape cordoned off the populace of the city instead of a full-blown wall. Chalk numbers lined the floors and walls, indicating to the eleventh that the murderer had been just as brutal with this assassin as they had been with Onyx's master.

"I didn't realise it was this fresh," Gill observed, analysing the new surroundings. Among the crime scene sat a card from the Eleventh Sense Guild, which he remembered was usually left to identify which member had been there with the guards.

Signed, Siegfried Durwood, it read. "Of course, it was Siegfried," he muttered under his breath. "Anything for a bit of fame, old friend?"

"What was that?" Onyx asked, putting a hand to his ear.

"An old guild acquaintance. Haven't seen him in years," Gill replied, sating the assassin's curiosity. "Where are the guards? There's no one here but us."

Onyx shrugged his shoulders. "There were a lot of casualties at the Arcane Guild, but I'm not sure why there's no one here now. *I* didn't pull any strings."

As Gill swept through the alley for any additional clues to assist the case, Onyx glanced at the crowd beyond. "Everyone looks skittish, like they're expecting something bad to happen at any moment."

"Can you blame them? The entire Arcane Guild dead, people murdered in their alleys? It was only recently that the war with the titans ended and now we're dealing with a war not only with the kharakians but with the necromancers too." Gill stated; his eyes remained glued to the crime scene. "I don't envy the common citizen walking the street. These are dangerous times."

His focus unwavering, the assassin never took his eyes from the passing men and women. "Does it bother you?"

"Does what bother me?"

"The state of it all right now. I'm sure the world was never this crazy."

"My job is to make things less crazy. You're living *in* my world."

Onyx gave out a short laugh. "At least you have your senses. All us every day folk have are our wits. You're lucky you have them at your disposal."

"Walk yourself into a defiled spirit's nest with half the equipment you need to put it down and tell me I'm lucky as I move on to the next."

"Touc—"

Onyx froze, acquiring Gill's attention. "Onyx? What is it?"

Peering down the alleyway, Gill could make out a well-equipped man passing by. The eleventh recognised him from his postcognitive state, though it was the assassin that confirmed what he saw.

"Master," Onyx mumbled, moving towards the crowd. "It can't be."

Gill intercepted Onyx; a sense of foreboding filled the eleventh's mind as he approached. "No, it can't. We've both seen his corpse, you in that alley and I through my visions. Why would he be wandering the same streets that he was hunted in?"

Onyx's eyes were filled with uncertainty, though they refused to meet his partner's. Moving away from the eleventh, the assassin rushed towards the streets and around the corner to begin his own investigation.

"I'll be right back," he called, disappearing from view. "Let me know what you find."

Lost for words, Gill merely turned his attention back to his work, eager to put the case to bed. He returned to the chalk outline, placing his hand upon the dried fluids to assist him in his postcognitive state once more.

His vision proved largely uninformative, only reaffirming what he was already aware of. Though the assassin appeared to give her all for a chance at survival, her murderer gave no such opportunity.

Inflicting clean and effective wounds to the woman, the attacker left her body for the authorities to find; his vision showed no signs of theft or desecration. Without an autopsy report on hand, Gill could only assume motives, frustrating him.

"Gill? Is that you?"

Footsteps brought his attention to where Onyx had departed. Arlowe and Schukara made their way into the alley, pausing as they became aware of the crime scene. "We didn't expect to see you," the prince spoke. "Is this Onyx's little errand?"

Though this was a nice surprise, Gill refused to let it distract him from his work.

"What are you two doing here? I find it hard to believe you searched the city for me." He kept to finding any clues that he may have missed. "We planned to meet once our affairs were done with."

Arlowe strolled through the crime scene, moving his face closer to anything of interest. "I could ask you the same. What are you doing in this alley?"

"That's for Onyx to divulge, not I. How did you find us?"

Schukara chimed in. "Our meetin' with tha' blades was done and dusted ages ago."

"And?"

"And they're in, so we thought we'd take in tha' sights while we waited. Saw ya' on our way past 'n' thought we'd check in."

Gill returned from his postcognitive state, putting a larger focus on his allies. "Good, good. What does Xanth think of the city?" he queried. "What of the baked goods of Highpeak Market or the vekaakran statues lining the Arythol cathedral?"

Both Arlowe and Schukara froze, looking to each other, though the prince eventually decided he would speak. "He enjoyed them. Why do you ask?"

"Haaroith is rich in culture. It wouldn't be fair for the boy to be missing out on it," he responded, turning his attention upon Onyx returning from the streets, arriving out of breath. "Did you find him?"

The assassin looked up, shaking his head. "No. It's like he just vanished." He stood by Schukara's side. "I climbed the nearby rooftops for a good vantage point, but I couldn't find a trace."

"Of Master, what was his name? Halo? Hallowed?"

Like the others, Onyx paused before answering. "You mean Hollow?"

Gill wasn't a fool. Ignoring who they were, he was blocked in and surrounded. One of his 'allies' prowled behind him, blocking the way he had entered while the other two stood side-by-side at the only other way out.

Arlowe and Schukara's explanation on finding him was weak at best, and the pause from his question regarding Xanth only reinforced his suspicion.

The final nail in the coffin came with Onyx's response. The assassin held his master in very high regard and would've rudely corrected him for a mistake like that. Instead, he struggled to give his master's name as an answer.

"Who are you?" Gill posed, addressing the three.

Silence filled the air. "What do you mean, Gill? We're—"

Arlowe was cut off by the eleventh aiming his crossbow with lightning reflexes, firing it at the assassin. In that same time, Schukara stood forward, stealing the bolt out of the air, saving her partner's life.

"Shall I ask again? If *I* don't have the ability to pluck my ammunition from the air, neither should you," he continued. "You're not my allies, but you're not natural either. What *are* you?"

All three dropped their acts, unveiling weapons from thin air not used by their respective owners, with Arlowe drawing a katana, Schukara a pair of bladed tonfas and Onyx with a pair of magical staffs.

"You're perceptive. It's a shame that your abilities have been used for a task so fruitless," uttered Arlowe, taking in the voice of a young woman. "Our quarrel is with the Defiant, and our objective is to locate Onyx. You may walk away."

218

Gill reloaded his crossbow, swapping it for the staff resting on his back. "You're supernatural beings butchering individuals with no explanation for your actions. I can't let you walk away."

The fake Arlowe shook his head. "Disappointing. Think of the lives you could save by leaving us to our mission, yet your code forbids you from such an act." A metallic twang came from every word. "How many people can a broken eleventh truly save?"

Predicting the oncoming attack, a second Onyx emerged from behind the fake Schukara and Onyx, slashing their throats as he blinked by them at unnatural speeds. "Here I am."

"Is that you?" Gill questioned, examining the wounded Onyx; his throat had healed to an uncut state. "If you say that you can do that, I'll call your bluff again."

"You know, I wish I could," the assassin retorted. "They drew their weapons on you. It made sense to strike first. That, and I wanted to prove that I'm me."

The fake Arlowe stood calmly to their flank. "You are the assassin Onyx, member of the Defiant. We have watched you." His katana lowered. "Why do you pursue us?"

"You killed my master," Onyx answered. "He was the only thing I held dear in this world and you cut him down without a second thought."

"It was necessary."

"Why? What did he do?"

"Did he not tell you?"

Onyx fell quiet. The eleventh spoke in his place. "Is there any way this can end peacefully? Onyx has done nothing wrong here. He was a victim. Help us understand."

The fake Arlowe paused a moment, making its decision. "We will cease our hunt if Onyx ceases his. He was a victim and was not meant to be involved, but if he continues, we will have no choice but to persist."

"You think I'll just let this go?" the assassin yelled, flustered by the words of the fraud. "I will never surrender, and if I have to die to bring honour to my master's name, so be it."

Gill held back his partner, keeping his voice low. "Onyx, this won't end well. There may be a time to fight but now isn't the time."

"My decision is final," Onyx hissed, throwing Gill's hand aside to draw his blades.

"The time for compromise has clearly ended," declared the fake Arlowe, gesturing for the frauds to spread out for the oncoming attack. "Eleventh, will you side with the assassin? Or will you walk away? We leave that choice in your hands."

Gill sighed a breath of frustration, readying himself. "I'm not abandoning you, kid, but we're going to have a *long* talk once this is over."

Predicting an obvious lunge forward, the fake Arlowe had already planned where the assassin's dagger would land. The fraud ducked under Onyx's jab to strike at his upper torso with the hilt of his blade, though as the attack was about to connect, a small barrier formed between the two points; the blow was deflected.

After summoning the barrier, the eleventh faced the fraud at his back, taking the brunt of a fireball flung by the fake Onyx. Thinking fast, the eleventh casted a spell in return, transferring the flames covering him back to the caster.

As his spell ended, the fake Schukara entered the fray. The fraud dug the blades of her tonfas into Gill's back, throwing him to one side, separating him from Onyx.

Escaping a swing from the fake Arlowe, Onyx moved close to stab him with a flurry of blows, though the fraud's punctures were recovering as quickly as they had been inflicted. The fraud did not flinch, nor show any indication of pain.

A swift kick stumbled the assassin back into a suitable range for the katana to be effective again. Though Onyx had tried to parry one of Arlowe's swift swings, the bearer's force knocked him off-balance, sliding one of his daggers across the alley.

Though he fought admirably with only one blade, the fraud swung under to force the assassin into the air, plucking him from it to throw him into the nearby wall; the crack produced from his shoulder echoed through the alleys.

Meanwhile, Gill had been left fighting against both the fake Schukara and fake Onyx, isolated from keeping his partner safe. In the corner of his eye, he was able to catch the fake Onyx using one staff to prepare another fireball, whilst using the other to shield himself from any returning fire.

Thinking fast, Gill made an evident move for Schukara to block, kicking her away before utilizing his own magic to dispel the fake Onyx's attack.

To his surprise, his spell did much more than cancel out the fireball. The Onyx before him dropped onto his knee, convulsing from the dispel. Whatever magic was disguising the fraud was being partially removed.

Though the creature was clearly trying its best to remain under control, it couldn't stop the occasional reveal of snow-white skin and black markings underneath.

While the fake Onyx had temporarily been dealt with, the fake Schukara was still a problem. Nimbly moving back into the fight, the fraud fought with elegance, dancing around the eleventh with ease.

Somehow, as their brawl had initiated, the frauds had found a way to hide their soul energy. Gill's powers were useless against them. The only edge he had was in the use of his precognition, and without soul energy to enable it, the ability was useless.

The fake Schukara moved in and out of combat with little difficulty, unrelenting as she slowly cut the eleventh to pieces. As the wounds racked up, Gill found himself moving slower, his reflexes becoming sluggish. Even if he could see her soul energy, the fraud was a powerful opponent that could've easily gone toe-to-toe with his powers fully at his disposal.

Feinting a hit, Schukara followed up with a punch, connecting not only her fist with his face, but the back of Gill's head with the nearby wall, sending his senses reeling.

Taking advantage of his weakened state, the fake Schukara stepped to one side, allowing the fake Onyx to fire a shockwave at him, slamming him back into the wall with great force, taking him out of the fight.

Though beaten and bloody, unable to interact with the world around him, Gill could still witness what the frauds had in store for Onyx.

The two that had fought him positioned themselves behind the assassin, one to each side. The fake Arlowe had gestured for them to leave him be, smacking him down every time he had the audacity to lash out at him.

Though they were speaking, the eleventh couldn't make out what they were saying, hearing only muffles.

"I won't beg," Onyx snarled, wiping the blood from his lip. "Kill me. I won't cease."

"Never say that you had no choice," Arlowe replied, lunging at the assassin.

Without any time to react, the assassin was hit with enough force to throw him into the air. The fake Arlowe swung his blade. The assassin's elbow had been cut clean; his body collapsed in a heap.

"Even with his death, you are devoted to your master. We are devoted to ours. We were not sent to kill, though we were sent to warn." The Arlowe imposter gracefully returned the katana to its ornate sheath. "Your path does not involve us, lest it come to an early end. Your hand is the offering, though you may still be the sacrifice."

The three turned to leave, exiting the alleyway; their mission was complete.

As they joined the crowd, masking their soul energy among the citizens, Gill crawled over to Onyx's body, feeling it for a pulse. He found none.

222

"Not like this," he growled through the pain, rolling the assassin onto his back. The eleventh took a syringe from the pocket on his leg, plunging it into Onyx's chest, following it up with a handful of healing magic. "Come on… Come on!"

The assassin spluttered, coughing up a mouthful of blood, gasping for air.

"Gill," he struggled. "Is that you? What's happening?"

"I'm here," Gill replied, trying to keep him calm. "I'm here. I need you to stay still."

"What… about you? You're in… a bad spot… too."

"Stay still. I've got you."

The assassin fell unconscious, unable to keep his mind afloat.

*

Onyx was surprised that he was awaking. His surroundings were a blur, the light drifting through the alleyways blinding him.

He looked down to see a bandaged stump where his arm used to be. He could see the missing limb across the alley from him, even though he could still feel twitches from his arm, as if it was still connected to him.

Peering up, he could see Gill, still injured from their fight with those disguised as their allies. The eleventh appeared to be using healing magic on himself, though his light was constantly going out. Amongst everything else that had happened, this was one more thing he was accountable for.

"Gill?" The eleventh looked to him; his face was unemotive. "Thank you."

"I don't want your thanks. Keep it to yourself."

"I… don't understand. What do you mean?"

Gill struggled to his feet, coming closer to Onyx. He then lowered himself to the assassin's level, resting his arms over his knees.

"Those things. Do you not know what they are?" he demanded. "Or are you still keeping secrets?"

Onyx weakly shook his head. "I don't know what they are. I swear."

"You know, I thought highly of you, regardless of how you treated me," Gill spoke low, his voice barely concealing a boiling anger. "Everyone else had a reason for travelling with Arlowe, myself included. All except you."

He rose, pacing back and forth across the crime scene as he proceeded. "Because of your actions, you've not only made yourself a target. You've made a target of anyone who travels with you, and if Arlowe falls before facing the kharakians, that may seal Argestra's fate."

Onyx arose from his slump, clasping his arm. "What would you have me do?" His voice could hardly be raised, pitifully breaking at the slightest increase. "What could I do?"

"Not drag your supposed allies to the fucking slaughter!" Gill's declaration froze the assassin stiff, keeping his tongue still and his eyes low. As the echoes of the eleventh settled, so did Onyx, falling back to the wall in shame.

Gill scanned his surrounding, making sure that none were drawn to them by his outburst. "You will heed their advice," he growled, unable to look the assassin in the eye. "And if I even suspect that you're compromising our safety, I will have no qualms sending you on your way."

The eleventh began his own departure of the alley, using his staff as a makeshift walking stick.

Realising he was being left behind, Onyx used the wall as a standing aid to follow Gill out, only to be gestured not to.

"Where are you going?" Onyx questioned. "We're a team."

"Are we?" Onyx had nothing to say. "I want to look over my notes of this case in private. Head to the totems to meet Arlowe and Schukara," Gill instructed. "Let them know I'll be late."

As Gill moved from the alley entrance, the light pouring in revealed a glimmer to the assassin's left. He reached for the dagger, though his stump only push it further away. Falling back into his own blood, Onyx gave up, defeated.

As Onyx looked up to the darkening skies, an odd sensation flowed through him. A shiver shot through his spine, jolting him upright. His eyes were drawn to the rooftop above him, and for a brief moment, saw a silhouette watching down over him.

The figure appeared unremarkable, except for one large eye covering the length of its face, from the peak of its head to its chin.

As soon as Onyx had blinked, the figure was gone, yet he couldn't shake the image of the eye from his mind. The assassin struggled to his feet, taking the fallen blade into his one well hand before leaving the crime scene as quickly as his legs could carry him.

*

As the day neared its end, Gill arrived at the totems feeling better than he had before. His wounds had been cleansed and bandaged to avoid infection and his magical powers had returned to their former strength, allowing him to passively heal himself as he roamed Haaroith's streets.

Though Arlowe was nowhere to be seen, Schukara and Onyx had arrived at the specified location, with the elf seemingly having a one-sided conversation with the assassin. Gill stood nearby, curious of what Schukara had to say.

"Onyx please, talk ta' me," she begged, though Onyx would not budge regarding his silence. "I don't know if yer' aware, or if ya' even care, but I'm worried about ya'. Please say somethin'."

Gill approached the two, bringing much needed relief to the mercenary. "Gill! I'm so glad yer' okay. After seein' Onyx like that, I was worried somethin' had happened ta' you too." Schukara signalled with her head for Gill to follow, leading him far enough away that Onyx wouldn't hear them. "What happened while we were gone? Tha' boy hasn't spoken a lick since I found him here."

"He was lucky *I* found him," Gill answered. "Shortly after meeting, we were ambushed. I had no idea who they were, but they knew Onyx. Despite being outnumbered, he thought it best to engage them. You can tell how well that went."

Schukara cocked her head, sceptical at Gill's words. "That's… vague."

"I only know what I saw, which wasn't much. I just stepped in to defend Onyx the best I could. I imagine he knows a great deal more than I do."

"What about tha' guards? Can they do anythin'?"

Gill shrugged, looking for any nearby guards. "Even if a decent number survived the attack on the Arcane Guild and weren't caught up in this terror attack I keep hearing about, we were in a restricted area. They won't support us."

Schukara shook her head. "So, there's nothing we can do?"

"Maybe one day, but for now we need to learn from our losses and move forward." Gill looked over to the assassin, already aware that he was listening in. Onyx continued to gaze over for a moment, though his head eventually returned to where it was facing. "Speaking of moving, where is Arlowe? Shouldn't he be here by now?"

Schukara looked off into the sunset, warmed by the thought of Arlowe's actions. "He took a lil' detour. Our royal envoy is showin' his heart of gold again."

*

"Hey, it's me. I hope I'm not intruding. I just wanted to make sure you were okay."

Arlowe leaned forward, resting his arms on his legs. The room was almost entirely soundless, filled only by the almost silent breaths of its occupant.

226

The prince had his hands together, praying for Antoinetta to open her eyes, though Arn must have been punishing him for causing this trauma in the first place, as her eyes remained shut.

"*Castral 3:11-12. Not all I do may be right, my son. I do not claim to be omniscient. However, my punishments are just. Think on them, and you will understand them to be rightful and true. Retribution makes no mistakes,*" he quoted, opening his eyes. "I've never known what to think of that passage. Is *my* punishment *your* suffering? Or is it still yet to come?"

Arlowe placed his hand upon the girl's arm, oddly cold yet warm enough to not arouse concern. "The sanamancers are telling me that you've been immune to most of their healing spells, though luckily you've been making a recovery regardless. It's just my luck that you wouldn't be awake before I left."

The prince sat up, stretching the cramps from his back. "Get well soon Antoinetta, and thank you for everything you've done for me. I hope that one day you could forgive me for what I've done." Arlowe put his hand on the bed, rising to his feet. As he did, Antoinetta's hand lightly grasped his, keeping him by her side. "I'll take that as a sign?" A light smile could be seen upon her delicate face.

The door to the room opened, with Caspus stood within its frame. Arlowe lightly pulled his hand from the girl's grasp, leaving the room with a bow for the janitor. The door was shut behind him, and he was ready to leave the city knowing that Antoinetta had been left in the hands of those that could keep her safe.

"Will we see her again?" Xanth asked, sounding teary.

"Fate cannot be manipulated, but it knows what it's doing," Arlowe answered. "If we hope, we may."

Chapter Thirteen:

"Prejudice is a veil used by both the innocent and the guilty."

19th Arandbern
Land's Legacy
2084∞ (Current Age)

Once Arlowe re-joined his band, informed on what had happened in his absence, the group travelled southeast on a road that would lead them towards the border connecting Vexinth to Calaveil.

As they came closer to the border, the five could see the vibrant hills of Calaveil, much easier on the eyes than the harsh greys of Vexinth. A constant breeze roamed the lands, and though the temperature could not match the deathly wail of Vexinth's air, the cold still burdened the group's elf, bundling herself beneath her trusty blanket.

The mercenary sneezed, giving a brief shiver before continuing her march forward. "Anyone else freezin' their undergarments off?" she asked. "Nowhere should be so cold that I can sneeze an' create disposable daggers."

"I'm noticing a change in the temperature. It's starting to feel like the Land's Death in Fertral," Arlowe replied.

"Land's Death? The leaves are still turnin' here! It's only gonna get colder!" Schukara began rubbing her hands together, breathing on them to gather as much heat as possible. "Forgive me fer' sayin', but tha' kharakians would be a welcome sight. Could use one of 'em as a portable campfire."

She turned to the assassin. "What d'ya think Onyx? That sound good?"

Onyx was in another world to the others, not even registering what had been said to him. Instead, he merely pressed onwards with his stump resting in his hand.

Schukara turned back around. "The wind really is outta his sails," she muttered. "He looks so lost."

"I think you're reading him wrong," Gill interjected. "He doesn't look lost to me. Look at those eyes. I feel he's more focused now than he's ever been."

Onyx shot a quick look to Gill; only the eleventh spotted the brief break in his daydreaming.

"So, Arlowe," Xanth spoke. "Who do we have left to call upon? We have the support of Hietruce and Vexinth. Who's next?"

Arlowe raised his hand, addressing his allies. "I'm answering Xanth, but I'm making you all aware. Our next destination is Calaveil, where I'm at a bit of a disadvantage. I imagine there'll always be a Thaedlon on the throne and the Bright Blades are, well, the Bright Blades, but Calaveil's rulers work on a voting system where they can serve a maximum of ten years, with the populace voting every two." The prince held his head in concentration. "Last time I checked, an elf known as Elaith… Origauilor ruled Wicilil, though I'm pretty sure she was serving her final term? My point is, I'm not sure who we'll find there. Hopefully, they'll be co-operative."

"Will we have the support of Ryvineon?" Gill posed. "With Vexinth and Calaveil joining Hietruce and Quazin who are already holding the line, Ryvineon will be the only country uninvolved."

"I'm not sure if we'll even have time," Arlowe answered. "On my way to visit Antoinetta, I sent one letter to Thaedlon detailing our dealings with Vexinth and another to Ryvineon. I asked if they could possibly send someone to Calaveil to discuss their inclusion in our war effort. Hopefully, I'll hear something soon."

As the group pushed on, Schukara increased her pace to reach Arlowe at the front.

"Hey, I have somethin' for ya'," she whispered, handing him a musty old book.

"Thanks, Schu," uttered the prince, gratefully taking it. "What is it?"

"It's a book I picked up from tha' market. I thought of you. I'm sure you'll find it ta' be an… interestin' read."

With nothing more to say, the mercenary dipped back into the pack, leaving Arlowe and Xanth with the book.

The prince took a closer look at his gift. *What's this? The Submission of the Humans?*

He turned the book over to read the synopsis. Apparently, the book was a historical piece looking back at human slavery at the hands of the elves and dwarves. *Don't get me wrong, I finished my copy of the Pursuits of an Argestran Knight, so a new book is welcomed, but why this one in particular?*

Arlowe flipped the book open, noticing that one of the pages had been folded to act as a bookmark for those without one. Hurt at seeing the book slightly damaged, he flicked over to unfold the page only for the words within to catch his eye. Portions of the page read, *…dwarves refused… …turning their numbers against… …went missing… …never found…*

As he readied himself to delve further into the specifics of the book, Gill acquired the attention of the group through his whistle, silencing them. "Do you hear that?"

"I bet Onyx can," Schukara commented, kept quiet by the eleventh hushing her.

Gill signalled for the group to follow, speaking as he led them. "I can hear something in the distance. Sounds aggressive."

"If it's aggressive, shouldn't we be avoiding it?" Arlowe queried. "We found you out in the middle of nowhere and got involved with a defiled spirit. Is this wise?"

Gill shook his head. "I thought I heard someone mention necromancy. If there are necromancers around here, we need to put an end to their activities. They may get involved with our war effort and not in a good way."

Hiding behind the local wilderness, the group could make out two guards and a small collective of what appeared to be mages. Though some of the group were unable to hear exactly what was being spoken, it was obvious that neither the guards nor the mages were particularly keen on each other.

"For the last time, we're not necromancers!" yelled the mage leading his pack.

One of the guards moved forward, sizing up to the young mage. "Then why weren't you taking the main road when we found you? You tried to hide from us when we hailed you."

"You had your weapons drawn!"

The other guard stepped forward, aiding her colleague. "We have to be wary. Anyone travelling east could be moving towards Grandgrave. Your actions thus far haven't eased our suspicions."

A young man continued to argue, outraged at his treatment. "The way you're acting is one of the reasons why the necromancers rebelled in the first place!"

The two guards looked at each other with eyebrows raised. The first took hold of the man's wrist, bringing him close. "Nor has that," he snarled.

Gill quickly cleared his throat before rising from his hiding spot, moving down the hill to defuse the situation before him. "Excuse me? Greetings. Sorry to interrupt you. We were passing through and heard a commotion on our way by. Is there anything we can do to help?"

The male guard let go of the mage as he turned his attention to the disturbance, though he kept the mages in his peripheral. "This situation is under control," he declared, appearing incredibly aggressive. "You have no business being here."

Gill reached into his pocket, handing a card to the guard. "Gill Wiksend, eleventh of the Eleventh Sense Guild," he introduced, taking back his card. "If this was just a simple scuffle, you wouldn't have even seen me. However, I overheard you conversing about necromancy. What more can you tell me about what's going on here."

The guards looked past Gill, with the second pointing out Arlowe, Schukara and Onyx. "Who're they?" the woman asked.

"They're my travelling companions. My guild has allowed me to travel with them and solve any issues I may come across in the process."

The female guard sighed. "Apologies, eleventh. It isn't often you see one of your kind. Less so travelling with others," she continued. "The name's Leslie, and this is my partner Hendorff. We're part of the border patrol."

"What seems ta' be tha' problem here?" Schukara asked, glancing over the guards and mages.

An old man stepped forward, with both Arlowe's band and the border patrol believing him to be the elder of the mages. "These guards believe us to be necromancers passing through on our way to Grandgrave! Can you believe it?"

"Well, are you?" Onyx questioned, finally breaking his silence.

The old man's face turned sour. "No! When I heard that the Arcane Guilds to the west had been attacked, I gathered my pupils and brought them east," explained the elder. "Hopefully, we'll be able to outrun whatever's on the loose!"

Leslie performed a loud cough, reacquiring the attention of the mages and their elder. "Then you won't mind holding on for a member of the Arcane Guild to come and assess your abilities? I don't believe they've ever been wrong regarding what schools an individual dabbles in."

The young mage swapped places with the elder, moving into Leslie's personal space to intimidate her. "What? You can't do that! That could take hours! Days, even! We've done nothing wrong!"

Leslie placed her palm on the young man's chest, shoving him back; the guards were barely fazed by his lacklustre attempt at intimidation. "Don't worry, we'll take good care of you."

As the young mage regained his balance, he readied himself to leap at the guards, only for Arlowe to stand between the two with his arms out.

"Hold on! I understand that they could be dangerous, but don't you think you're being harsh?" the prince directed to the guards. "You're guards, people that the general populace can trust. How can you expect this group to show you respect when you're showing none to them?"

Leslie had nothing to say, though Hendorff was quick to respond to the prince. "If I had my way, every necromancer would be buried deep underground to starve and suffocate for years like the days of old."

His statement enraged the majority of the mages, with the prince's allies having to join him in holding both sides back.

"Woah, that's extreme," Schukara commented. "I'll be blunt, I ain't fond of necromancers, but yer' on a whole 'nother level."

"My family stood proudly as one of the few to survive from the First Invasion through to the current day, still ready to fight any who passed through those accursed gates," Hendorff replied, looking to the mages with ferocity in his eyes. "A group of necromancers cut them down before fleeing during their little rebellion. Of my entire family, only I saw the dawn of the titans. There couldn't be a greater form of dishonour to my family than that."

"That's irrelevant," Gill noted, gaining the ire of the grieving guard. "Even if this group *were* necromancers, *they* didn't kill your family. You can't blame the entire collective for what a fraction did."

Hendorff spat at the eleventh's feet. "While I continue to hear reports of their 'deeds', eleventh, my thoughts on them shall not change."

Whilst Gill focused his attention on the guards, Arlowe turned his to the mages, hoping to pry any information he could from them. After their treatment at the hands of Hendorff, even the prince's worst approach would seem delicate by comparison.

Arlowe proceeded towards the young mage and the elder, aware of their cautious eyes. "What can we do for you?" blurted the young mage. "Have the guards decided they've done enough? Sent *you* to deal with us instead?"

The prince raised his hands, moving no closer as to not rile the young man further. "I have no quarrel with you. I'm just curious."

"About?"

"You travelled east to escape? Does that mean you came from the west?"

"Shocking, I know. What about it?"

Arlowe cocked his head. "While I don't agree with Hendorff's beliefs, he is in his rights to stop you," he voiced. "If you came from the west, you could've been involved in the Arcane Guild murders."

The elder snapped, raving like a madman. "Do you assume that every traveller on the road performs massacres on a regular basis? We're innocent, yet you treat us as criminals despite having no proof! This is absurd!"

"Look, I didn't accuse you of anything," Arlowe replied, defending himself. "You could be a suspect. There's no need—"

"It's always the same! Mages accused of everything in this world! There used to be a time where magic was treasured! Now it's used more as an excuse to kill!" the elder ranted, involving the guards once more.

Hendorff and Leslie placed their hands around their hilts, advancing on the mages.

234

"Keep him under control or else," warned Leslie. "We are authorised to use deadly force if need be."

"Please, we're innocent," a young girl from the mages quietly called, appearing as though she scraped all of her courage into that one sentence.

Hendorff pointed to the girl, silencing her. "Shut it! You're detained until we can—"

"Hey!" called out the young mage, interrupting the guard. "There's no need to be rude to her, y-you shit-eating brute!"

Hendorff went silent for a moment. "What did you say?" he spoke, quiet but menacing. "Are you insulting a member of the Vexin Guard?"

"N-no," the young mage replied timidly. "I'm *describing* a member of the Vexin Guard. Y-you ass!"

Hendorff's brow quivered, his teeth gnashing in anger. "This farce has gone on long enough. I'll bring you in myself!" The guard gripped the axe within his hands tightly, charging at the young mage. "I'll pressure out those necrotic powers! I know what you are! No need to call upon the Arcane Guild!"

As the guard came close enough to slash his target, a bolt of ice hit his hand, connecting the axe to the ground behind him. Looking forward, Hendorff found that the elder was the one responsible for the intervention.

"We've had enough," the elder spoke, appearing much calmer than he had been a few moments ago. "You wanted a necromancer? You wanted to bury and starve one? I would like to see you try."

"Oscar, what's Master Quelthen saying?" asked the girl, holding on to the young mage. "You said no one would get hurt."

Before anyone could react, the elder released a shockwave knocking back ally and foe alike, even breaking the ice restraining Hendorff, shattering his axe and fingers in the process.

Though Gill drew and fired his crossbow before another spell could be cast, the bolt penetrating the heart of the elder was not enough to stop him. Master Quelthen ripped the bolt from his breast, with a simple throw burying it into the ground as if firing it himself.

A glow of light emanated in the elder's hand, firing it into the floor to create a circle of peculiar runes, opening it up for a ghastly creature to enter the world.

The summoned being hovered into Katosus wearing a stained mask decorated with what appeared to be a paper talisman. Its arms were forced forward and its legs bound, with additional ghostly hands orbiting the creature's marked body.

The elder stood by his summoned creature, drawing a wand from his sleeve. "I was innocent. Followed every rule. It appears as though a necromancer will be punished no matter what they do." He removed his hood; a purple light seeped from his eyes. "I may as well live up to the fear you've generated. At least that way I have a good chance at getting to safety."

Hendorff held no fear in his heart, rising up to swing at the creature with his intact hand, though it was to no avail. One of the creature's disembodied hands stole the axe he had spare before its main hands took hold of his arms, ripping them apart with a bloody fervour.

Claiming the spoils of its victory, the creature placed its hands within the body of the guard, siphoning the blood from him to leave only a drained corpse behind.

Arlowe and his allies took cover behind a group of nearby boulders, drawing their weapons. "Gill, what is that thing?" requested the prince.

"Traveller. Undead creature," he answered. "When they engage in combat, they can teleport and as you just saw, they're deadly when in close proximity. Keep creating

236

space between you and it, stay on your toes and do *not* touch the mask. Doing so will only enrage it."

"Then how do we stop it?" Schukara posed. "What's tha' plan?"

Gill peeked over the boulders, aware that both the elder and the traveller were searching the area. "We need that Master Quelthen weakened or dead. Only then can we send the traveller back to the Vault of Undeath."

"And how do we do that?" Arlowe queried.

"Given time, I could send the traveller back from whence it came. However, it doesn't look like we have time. We need a true spellcaster to send it back," the eleventh uttered, looking over their cover again to spot the traveller hunting the mages.

"Luckily, I don't think the elder wants any witnesses. As long as those mages aren't loyal, one of them could perform the spell to send it back," Gill continued, formulating a plan in his mind. "We just have to make sure they don't all die."

Arlowe positioned himself, preparing to rush out of their cover. "Gill, keep the traveller busy for as long as you can. Schukara, get that guard to safety and then assist Gill. If Leslie wants to help, let her. We need all the help we can get."

"Onyx, I need you to…" His eyes fell upon the stump. "…to round up those mages and then aid me against Master Quelthen. *If* you're able."

"Don't concern yourself with me. I'll do as instructed," Onyx growled. "Let's go."

The eleventh got to work immediately, keeping his own advice to hold his distance, and his precognition to avoid the traveller's grasp.

Taking every opportunity he could get, Gill fired bolts laced with various herbs from his crossbow into the traveller's rotten body, though the creature showed no signs of slowing down.

Using where they were stood before the shockwave as a marker, Schukara's search took her to a small hill to the east, locating Leslie's crumpled body lying at the bottom. The elf rushed to the base of the hill, removing the guard's helmet only to have it leak blood onto the soil beneath it.

Schukara grasped Leslie's body, leaning it against the same rock that she impacted against. "Leslie? Can ya' hear me?" the mercenary asked slowly, spotting dilated pupils. "Ugh, I know tha' basics, but a medic I ain't."

Though dazed, Leslie was able to respond to Schukara. "Help me... up. I... can fight. Hendorff's always ru... running into trouble," she slurred, struggling to keep her head stable.

"Hendorff's gone Leslie," Schukara regretfully answered. "He fought bravely. Ya' should be proud."

Leslie paused for a moment, unable to get her words out. "I have t... to avenge him. He wasn't per... perfect, not by a long... shot, but he was a... good man. He deserved better."

"You stay put. Keep yerself awake. Ya' need medical aid, not more fightin'. We'll come get you once this monster's been put ta' bed. Yer' safe now."

Schukara rushed up the hill to aid her companions, leaving the lone guard to reflect on her pain and sorrow.

Meanwhile, Arlowe had engaged the elder, keeping him from the mages whilst also acting as a distraction for Onyx to get there first. A distraction was all he could be, as Quelthen had him bested in every conceivable way. "Old age can never shackle the true potential of a necromancer, boy!"

Quelthen forced his hand forward, penetrating Arlowe's shield before flinging it from his grip, electrocuting him once his defences had been removed. The prince dropped to his knees shaking from the impact, knocked down by another bolt summoned from the necromancer's wand.

"Be a good boy and stay put," the elder uttered, turning his back on the prince. "I can't imagine *him* fleeing. Too headstrong. Those who were accompanying me, however; now they are a different story. If I'm exposed before reaching Grandgrave, I'll never be free."

Quelthen departed, following the trail of mage corpses south.

Onyx had made good progress by avoiding the fighting entirely. Using the local wilderness to the west where they had previously hidden, the assassin reached the mages in good time.

"You've got to be kidding me," he groaned, spotting the two surviving mages out in the open with a barrier up. "They think that'll protect them? They don't stand a chance out there."

The assassin scanned for the most direct route between his concealment and the mages, unable to find any more cover to utilise. "I don't have a choice. If there's a chance I can get to them before their elder does, I have to take it."

Onyx sprinted for the mages, reaching them in good time. "Both of you need to come with me," he insisted, taking hold of Oscar's sleeve.

The young man snatched his coat sleeve back, scowling at the assassin. "We're not going anywhere. Not without—"

A bolt of electricity slammed into the barrier, shattering it instantly. Though Onyx was quick enough to move out of the way, multiple bolts of electricity zoomed towards them, burning Oscar and killing his colleague.

"You're right. You're not going anywhere," Quelthen affirmed to the mage, appearing from atop the hill readying another bolt. "A shame, Oscar. You would've made a fine necromancer, given time of course."

"Arlowe! Now!" Onyx called, signalling for the prince to strike. A blade sliced through Quelthen's wand with a keen precision, cutting it in two before piercing the elder through the chest.

A swift kick was placed upon the necromancer's chest to knock him down, before Arlowe slid down the hill to join his companion.

Weaponless, the elder fired another bolt from his hand, and though Arlowe was able to block it with his retrieved shield, this resulted in its final defensive manoeuvre. The shield shattered to pieces.

The elder rose from the dirt, his arms fizzling with electrical energy. "You insolent worms! Do you have any idea who you're dealing with? I will scorch the earth, and you all along with it!" Quelthen roared, crackling with power as he charged his magic within his hands. "Die!" he screamed, though his attack never came.

Arlowe and Onyx looked up to see Quelthen missing an arm; his collection of power was gone. Schukara had arrived at the opportune moment, kicking him down to plunge one blade into his hand and one into his elbow, pinning him to the ground.

Unable to defend himself from the assault, Quelthen was powerless to stop Schukara's fists striking his face continually, ending with an armoured headbutt producing a horrific crack as it landed.

"Traveller!" Quelthen shouted despite his broken jaw and missing teeth, still conscious from his beating. "Help me!"

By his command, the traveller materialised behind Schukara, throwing her from the elder down to her allies below, leaving her without her trusty weapons.

Schukara reached the bottom, battered from her armour, though surprisingly she stood, able to go on. "This needs ta' end. We can't keep this up forever," she pronounced. "Where's that Oscar feller?"

240

The two looked around, realising that the apprentice had fled. "I didn't see him when you came down the hill. The old man must've scared him off," Xanth voiced. "What do we do now?"

"The girl from earlier. Has anyone seen *her*," Onyx stated, leaving Arlowe and Schukara puzzled. "Black hair? Frail build? Clung to that Oscar? I didn't see her body—" Onyx paused, turning his head slightly. "Do you hear that? Crying."

The assassin scanned his surroundings, making out where the noise was coming from.

"It's coming from that direction," he commented, pointing out a tree in the distance. "Nothing else over there to hide behind. That has to be her."

"I'll go find her. Keep Quelthen down and watch out for the traveller," Arlowe conveyed, placing a hand upon each of his allies' shoulders. "I'll be back soon."

The traveller aided its decrepit master to his feet, allowing him to watch the direction that the prince had hurried off in. "I'll deal with the elf and the assassin," Quelthen directed, forcing his jaw back into position. "That tree seems important. Find out what it is and bring me the boy's head while you're there. "

Arlowe reached the tree, finding the dark-haired girl hidden behind it. Though her blue tunic had been damaged by the outraged strikes of her master and his summoned beast, her white skirt dirtied and torn, the girl was nonetheless unharmed.

Discovered, the girl turned to run, only to trip up on one of the tree roots. "Please," she whimpered, tears rolling down her cheeks. "Leave me be. I'll only hinder you."

The prince spotted a burn on the girl's leg, reaching into his pack for his water and some bandages. "Here, let me help you," he offered, receiving no refusal from the mage. "This may sting a bit."

The girl winced at the pain, though it didn't take long for Arlowe to apply the bandage. "You shouldn't be here," she muttered, curling up with her back to the tree.

"Leave me here. Be safe."

"Listen to me. You're not facing this alone," Arlowe spoke gently, waking the girl from her downcast state. "I know you're scared, Erethys, I am too, but I don't plan on dying out here and I won't let you."

"But… you don't even know me."

"What's your name?"

The girl paused. "Daria."

"I wish the circumstances were different, but it's nice to meet you Daria." Arlowe offered his hand to her. "May I save you now?"

Daria was mesmerised by the prince, taking his hand to lift herself up, answering his question without a single word.

The moment between the two was fleeting, as the traveller had found Arlowe, and by extension, her.

Wasting no time, the traveller obeyed the commands of the one who summoned it, lunging at Arlowe with the aim of tearing his head from his shoulders. Missing its swing, the creature tried again, though this time all it accomplished were four deep slices down the front of Arlowe's cuirass.

In the distance, unknown to both Arlowe and the traveller, Gill had his crossbow locked and ready to fire, though the tree provided adequate cover to the beast. "Come on, Arlowe," Gill murmured. "Remember what I said. Keep. Creating. Space."

Arlowe proceeded to fight back the traveller's many hands, though for every one he swatted away, another would replace it. Overwhelmed, he retreated backwards, keeping Daria close behind him.

Spotting the weakness, the monster disappeared, rematerialising behind them with the prince unable to stop it.

"Time to take your medicine," Gill quipped, firing a bolt that dug into the traveller's skin. The creature lost control of itself, teleporting wildly around Arlowe and Daria whilst clawing at the bolt in its neck.

The eleventh summoned a brief ball of light, signalling to the prince and the mage. "Over here!"

Arlowe and Gill regrouped, joined by the only mage still with them. "What took you so long?" Arlowe jested.

"This," the eleventh responded, presenting a bolt topped with a plant to the prince.

The prince was wide-eyed. "You were going to cook the traveller?"

Gill placed the bolt into his crossbow. "Some herbs have healing properties. Most healing herbs are damaging to lesser undead creatures, though the more powerful ones are only weak to a small handful and it differs for each one. This one doesn't seem fond of goldenrod."

"Will it kill it?" Arlowe questioned, watching the frenzied undead.

"You can't kill what is summoned from the Vault of Undeath," Gill answered. "However, so long as you keep on top of the creature's weakness, you can keep them powerless until you have the means of sending them back." Gill fired another bolt, staggering the traveller. "Go deal with Quelthen. Cut his connection to the traveller."

The eleventh turned his attention to the girl. "I apologise for imposing, but may I ask a favour?"

Daria took a step back. "W-what could I do?" she queried near-silent, struggling with Gill's outgoing personality.

"How good are you at casting spells under duress?"

Arlowe darted to where he last saw Quelthen, able to see from a distance that Schukara and Onyx were struggling with him. The elf dived to retrieve her weapons, though the elder was precise, blasting her away with his partially regenerated arm.

"You're not that intimidating when I can see you, girl," he gloated.

Onyx crept up in his blind spot, burying a blade within the elder's side, though all he could accomplish was attracting Quelthen's attention.

"And you were never intimidating to begin with," he barked, a backhand sending the assassin down into the dirt. The elder ripped the dagger from his abdomen, lazily throwing it back to him. "Try again."

Arlowe marched into view, though his blade remained by his side. "Call off your traveller! I won't ask you again."

Quelthen moved forward, delighted to see a new opponent. "And why would I do that? Your companions are starting to tire while I grow bored, and now you stand before me ready to be humiliated."

"Do you expect me to believe that?" Arlowe goaded. "Kill us and move on to Grandgrave if you're so sure."

"An excellent idea. I may even gather your bodies to—" A surprise to them both, Onyx had reappeared, taking hold of the elder's shoulder, forcing him to turn. "Did you not learn your lesson last—"

The assassin buried his dagger deep within the elder's eye socket, slashing it through to the other socket to blind him.

As Quelthen reached out to grab the assassin, Onyx began unnaturally flitting around the elder, slicing at his muscles with the accuracy of a surgeon, immobilizing him.

"Once feeling returns to my limbs, assassin, I will—"

Onyx refused to let him continue, repeatedly stomping down on the elder's head with great force. Every time he saw twitching from one of his limbs, he would slice them again, uninterested in the necromancer's mobility.

244

"Good work Onyx!" Schukara called out. "He should be weak enough fer'—" Onyx continued to stomp and continued to cut, eventually reducing Quelthen's face to a gurgling mush. "Onyx, ya' can stop now."

"Stop," Quelthen choked, barely audible from the injuries he'd received. "Please, stop…"

"Xanth, close your eyes," Arlowe ordered.

"But—"

"Close them."

Schukara stepped forward, intending to restrain the assassin. "Onyx, I said stop!"

Onyx pointed his dagger at her, ceasing her advance. Though Quelthen's new arm had regenerated enough to grasp the assassin's leg, it was too weak to stop one last blow. The arm turned limp, motionless along with its owner.

"The elder is no more," Gill confirmed to Daria, firing another bolt at the traveller. "His soul energy has dissipated. We need to hurry."

"Hurry with what?" Daria replied worryingly.

Gill searched his satchel of herbs, finding only three more pieces. "Can you dispel magic?"

"Y-yes. It's one of the basic spells you learn."

"Indeed. I need you to cast it continuously as opposed to as a single spell. That's why I needed you. I don't have those kinds of reserves. I'm only partially trained in magic."

Daria looked at her hands. "I don't even know if I can."

Gill placed a hand on her shoulder, offering a smile to brighten her cold demeanour. "I'll be here the whole time. If it starts advancing, some goldenrod should stop it for a time." Gill took another bolt from the quiver on his coat. "You know what I think?"

"Mm?"

"I don't think you're as bad at spellcasting as you think you are."

"I... don't know."

"Do your best. I can expect nothing more."

Daria readied the spell carefully within her hand, placing the dispel upon the stunned traveller. "I've got it."

"Now hold it," Gill responded, reloading his crossbow. "Put all your energy into it. Don't let go."

The traveller felt the dispel ripple within itself, screeching as it pushed its body to its limits, teleporting small distances despite the tainted bolts sprouting from its body.

The traveller's scream broke the girl's concentration, cancelling out her hold upon it. "I can't," she professed, falling to her knees.

"You can," Gill argued. "Again."

Daria stood back up, casting the dispel upon her target.

The traveller's movements had only become more erratic, aware of what would happen if it failed. It swiftly materialised before Daria, though Gill fired his second-to-last bolt, sapping the energy from it.

Unfortunately, the young mage had lost control of her spell once more, frightened by her proximity to the necrotic beast. "I can't! There has to be another way!" she wept, inching away.

"Once more!" Gill called as he loaded his last bolt. "Give it everything you've got! I won't let it hurt you!"

Daria connected the dispel one more time, feeling the energy that the traveller was exuding just to crawl towards her. Though terrified and ready to give in, the young mage had seen enough death for today, pouring all her strength into the dispel.

The traveller shared the girl's thought, using every last shred of its own strength to

246

teleport one more time, close enough to bring its arm down on her, claws and all.

Daria kept her eyes open, waiting for the monster to reach her, though Gill stood in the way, taking the blow in her place.

The traveller's claws pierced the eleventh's shoulder, though the beast had no more strength to take back its arm. In response, Gill wrapped his fingers around the traveller's throat, lifting it into the air with his crossbow pressed against its chest, pulling the trigger.

The monster had gone limp, unable to muster the energy to go on. "Now," Gill voiced, signalling for Daria to finish her spell.

With one last push, the traveller disintegrated, leaving nothing but a small pile of dust within the eleventh's hand. Only now had Daria realised what she had done, placing her hands over her mouth in shock.

Gill allowed the dust in his hand to leave, spreading it through the air as he turned to her. "That last dispel? That was you at your best," he commented, breathless as he applauded. "Thank you for aiding me."

Arlowe and Schukara returned from their struggle with Quelthen, with Onyx following in tow. "Is it over?" the prince asked, kneeling by Daria's side.

The mage tried her best to answer, though only sobs came out.

"It is," Gill answered in her place. "The group of us succeeded against *one* skilled necromancer. Let that sink in."

Arlowe was stunned that a lone necromancer could cause so much damage, though for the time being, his attention was elsewhere. "Are you okay?" he asked Daria, offering a handkerchief from his backpack. "Here, take this."

The mage ignored the handkerchief, wrapping her arms around him before finally letting her sadness run free. Tears trickled down Arlowe's armour, though he kept himself still, offering Daria the comfort she sought.

"Could… someone give me a… hand?" a voice asked, with Schukara recognising it as the surviving border guard.

The elf took Leslie's arm, lifting her up the hill and onto her shoulder for support. "I told ya' ta' rest," scolded Schukara. "I wasn't gonna leave ya' down there."

The guard raised her hand, gesturing for the mercenary not to worry. The group all had their eyes focused on her, and in turn, Leslie let out a chuckle, grasping her rib in pain.

"I know what you're all thinking; no, I'm not arresting her," she stated. "Has that Quelthen fellow been dealt with?"

Arlowe stepped forward, leaving Daria with the handkerchief. "He's dead."

"Then justice has been served and Hendorff has been avenged. The elder was the aggressor and murderer, not these poor souls," she continued, standing on her own. "Nor her. She was a victim in this. I won't have her arrested."

"You have our thanks," Gill replied, bowing to her. "Do you need an escort? We're heading to Calaveil if you wish to come along?"

Leslie shook her head. "I appreciate the offer, but I'll have to turn it down," she spoke. "The border patrol has an outpost nearby that's visited often. If you could escort me there, I'd be thankful. My legs still aren't stable. If you need somewhere to stay until the next morning, I'm sure we could accommodate you."

"Any objections?" the prince queried, neither seeing nor hearing any protests from his allies. A sympathetic gaze fell to the mage. "Would you like to come with us? You'll be safe there." Daria delicately nodded, meaning that Arlowe was in agreement with every ally. "Lead the way. We've got your back."

*

Within the hour, the group arrived at the border patrol outpost, seen in the distance as a tall stone tower decorated one side with the flag of Vexinth and the other with the flag of Calaveil. Though the tower was the only structure of note at the outpost, multiple camps surrounded it with only a handful occupied.

"Pick a camp and rest up," Leslie offered, stretching out her back. "I'm grateful for what you did back there. If there's anything we can do, the commander of this post resides in the tower. I assume you won't need any directions?"

"I'm not sure. Spare a hint?" Arlowe voiced, joining in with Leslie's jests. "Thank you for this."

"It's the least we can do. Take care of yourselves." The guard gave a salute to the group before departing to the tower.

It didn't take long for the group to settle, sat on the logs acting as benches, warmed by the campfire in the centre.

Arlowe had his back rested against the tree next to his seating with Daria sat close to him. Schukara, as expected, sat on the floor nearest to the campfire, as Gill stood opposite, placing the finishing touches on their soup for the night.

As Schukara was about to doze off from the warmth, the counting of her allies stirred her. "Someone's missing," she mumbled, rubbing her head. "Where's Onyx? I don't see him."

"He went to collect more wood from the outpost stores," Gill replied. "I'll go find him. I imagine he's tried pushing himself too hard again." The eleventh sprinkled a little seasoning into the pot, completing the dish. "The food's ready, dig in."

"Gill, yer' a star," the elf praised, rabidly grabbing the bowls and ladle ready to serve.

The eleventh entered the cellar of the tower, lit by a single torch. In the centre stood Onyx, surprising Gill that he had no tricks planned for someone's arrival.

"You wanted to speak to me?" Onyx posed to him.

"What makes you think I have anything of note to ask?" Gill asked in return.

"When something's on your mind, you make a face." The assassin waved a hand across his mask. "It's as obvious as water being wet."

Gill began picking up firewood, handing them to Onyx. "I saw what happened to Quelthen. How'd you do it?"

"How'd you know to ask the fraud about Xanth?"

"Arlowe informed me of him on the way to Haaroith's northern gate. There, answer for an answer. Don't avoid my question."

The assassin took the firewood a piece at a time, placing them under his arm. "I stopped him from using his limbs. Not much of a secret. I'm sure you have the reflexes to—"

"You appeared from nowhere to strike at him. Your speed was near blinding. You stunted his regenerative capabilities," Gill listed. "Would you have me believe that any of your guild can do that?"

Onyx rejected any further aid from the eleventh, collecting the firewood himself. "I struck a deal."

"With?"

"The Altane."

Gill froze, unnerved by the words that Onyx had spoken. "If you're lying—"

"I'm not lying."

The eleventh looked into the assassin's eyes, seeing no deception. "No, you're not."

"I'm sure you have questions," Onyx replied. "Speak them."

"Few people know of the Altane, fewer ever speak to them. 'They who see all.' How did you find them?"

"They found me."

Both men placed down their firewood, sitting on the piles around them.

"Shortly after my master perished, I wandered without aim. I wanted his killers dead, but even with the aid of your guild, I couldn't find anything." Onyx took a breath, not keen on his recounting. "At my lowest, an... entity appeared before me offering great power and a promise that the culprits would be found."

"Did you find them?"

"No. Frustrated that our deal wasn't being kept, I cut them off. It ripped its blessing from me and left me for dead. From there I reconnected with the Defiant and worked to find any scraps of information I could, which eventually led me to Arlowe."

Footsteps from outside caught Gill's attention, though they passed quickly, returning him to a relaxed state. "That doesn't explain what you did back there. How?"

"From time to time, I've been able to tap into what remains of that power, though it only occurs when I need it most. I don't decide," Onyx answered. "I'm still trying to figure if the deal was ever truly cut. I still occasionally have access to the powers and I *did* find Master Hollow's killers. Maybe this was part of their plans."

"Maybe," Gill responded, picking up the firewood he dropped. "Thank you."

Onyx glanced at his partner in confusion. "What for?"

"I still don't trust you. Not entirely. It's to be expected," the eleventh divulged. "You're unsure, frustrated. Acting on impulse."

Onyx rolled his eyes, bracing for the oncoming rant. "But," Gill proceeded. "you're a good kid. You care about those close to you, doing what you can for them regardless of the outcome. You joined Arlowe to save yourself. Now you're staying because you can help. You never knew how to do that before."

"I still want justice."

"Every journey begins with a single step. Learn to trust, and that justice you can see a hundred miles away? It might not be as far as you think."

*

Onyx and Gill returned to the camp, dropping the wood to sit by their friends.

"You two might want to dig in," Arlowe called, passing them a bowl each. "If Schu had her way, the whole meal would be hers!"

Both men gratefully took the offer, pouring the last few mouthfuls of the cooking pot into their bowls, devouring their meals.

As Gill tackled his last few slurps, he peered over to see Daria shivering. "You didn't eat, did you?"

The camp turned their attention to her, only making her feel more uncomfortable.

"You told me you served yourself up some food," Arlowe claimed, becoming concerned. The prince looked into the cooking pot for any remaining soup, though the pot laid bare. "There's none left."

Schukara perked up, reaching into her pack. "Not ta' worry! I bought extra provisions from tha' market in Haaroith. We'll just cook up another meal! Tha' pot's still warm."

Daria began to sob. "No," she quietly mumbled, disagreeing. "I don't want to be a burden to your group. You'll have no rations."

"You won't be," Arlowe argued, beginning the preparations for another meal. "I'm a light eater, but I'm sure Onyx and Gill are still hungry."

"Ahem! Yer' favourite mercenary could go fer' another dish too. I promise I won't eat yers' darlin'," Schukara joked, handing Daria two slices of bread. "And here, eat 'em 'fore I do!"

Gill reached into his coat pocket. "Arlowe, catch!" A bag of chocolates landed in his hand. "For our guest. I don't think I've ever been her size, bless her," he chuckled, stirring the soup.

Handed a fresh bowl, the young mage became overwhelmed by the group's kindness, sipping at the soup seasoned by her falling tears.

"While I'm cleaning this up, it might be best for you all to nestle up ready to sleep," Gill noted. "There's still some ground to cover between here and Wicilil. I'll bring you your meals."

"Who's taking first watch?" Onyx queried, assisting Gill with the bowls. "I don't mind."

Arlowe raised his hand. "You don't have to worry about that, Onyx. Eleventh's can meditate to rest whilst keeping their senses aware of their surroundings," he informed. "Maybe if you ask nicely?"

The prince's comment brought a smile to Gill's face. "No need for that. I was planning on doing so anyway, though if any of you remain awake, well, company *is* good for the soul."

As Schukara reached for her blanket she could see Daria leaned against Arlowe, both giving a pitying expression. The young mage had fallen into a deep sleep, resting upon the prince's armoured shoulder.

"She must've been exhausted," she noted, beginning to giggle. "She's got chocolate all 'round her mouth."

Gill took the bowl and placed a blanket of his over the girl, being careful not to nudge her. "Anything I can do for you, Arlowe?" he offered, smiling at his predicament. "Looks like you might be there a while."

"Yes, could you get my book out for me please?" he asked. "I can read like this. Probably won't get much sleep though."

The eleventh took the book from his backpack, handing it to him before returning to the cooking pot. Arlowe flicked open the book, turning its pages to continue where he left off.

"Everything looks so warm and cosy," Xanth spoke. "Are you going to stay like that all night?"

"I think so," Arlowe replied, keeping their conversation within his mind. "I'd rather not wake her."

"Do you think she's okay?"

"She'll be fine. Rest will do her—"

Arlowe found the page he read earlier.

When the dwarves refused to free their captives as the elves had done, a mass of human slaves revolted, turning their numbers against the dwarven slavers.

While most were returned to their pens, a large number had simply gone missing. Though to this day some of the underground walls are still adorned with the Dwarvish phrase 'Kaldaren ordein', historians have found no trace of the elusive humans.

Some have claimed to see green-eyed creatures skulking the dwarven underground, though these reports have been written as forgotten demon sightings.

"Xanth? Do you mind if I have my mind to myself for tonight?"

Chapter Fourteen:

"Utava."

20th Arandbern

Land's Legacy

2084∞ (Current Age)

Pat pat pat.

With his eyes still closed, Arlowe weakly attempted to swat away whoever was trying

to interrupt his dreams. "Mm, you're lucky I'm a merciful monarch," he mumbled; a

smile reached across his shattered face. "Still, if you continue—"

Pat pat pat. Pat pat pat pat pat pat pat pat pa—

The prince opened his eyes to see Schukara; another slap was prepared in the angle of

her wrist. "Good morning, Schu. Lovely day to try and pat someone to death." Arlowe

stretched as best he could, his movement restricted by the sleeping mage.

As he did so, his foot clunked against something hard. Upon further inspection, the

item appeared to be a crudely crafted shield, with a lick of paint resembling his

country's runic crest. "A shield? Where did that come from?"

Schukara picked it up from the floor, leaning it back up against the nearby tree. "It's a

gift from us." The elf beamed with pride. "Gill gathered tha' wood, I carved it and

Onyx found some leftovers from tha' tower ta' help piece it together. It's not much ta'

look at, but it does its job."

The prince was lost for words, stunned at receiving such a thoughtful gift. "Thank

you, and pass on my regards to the others. I love it."

The mercenary chuckled to herself. "Don't thank us yet. It's yer' job ta' wake up tha'

sleepin' beauty."

Peeking over, Daria was still rested upon him, drool trickling from her mouth. "Still out cold, huh?"

Schukara nodded. "We've been up fer' a good hour now. Haven't heard so much as a peep."

"You've been up for an hour? Why didn't you wake me?"

The elf shrugged. "She looked like she needed a lil' longer, 'n' movin' you would've woken her up." Schukara took the book from Arlowe's lap, placing it in his backpack. "Besides, Gill technically doesn't sleep, I'm an early riser 'n' Onyx... Well, Onyx is mopin' around. Hopefully tha' real Onyx'll come back soon. I miss him."

Arlowe could see their assassin at the edge of the camp collecting his things. "Yeah, me too." He reached over to Daria, nudging her awake. "Hey, Daria? Rise and shine."

The mage opened her eyes, rubbing the sleep from her face; the imprint of the envoy's armoured shoulder was pressed into her cheek.

"Where am—" At once, she leapt up, fearfully looking around to verify where she was. "I'm so sorry," she mumbled, keeping her head down. "It won't happen again."

Before the prince could say anything to calm her worries, the girl had already fled from their conversation, leaving Arlowe and Schukara to question what had just occurred.

*

Over the next two days, the group covered an astounding amount of ground, trekking through Calaveil in good time. It wasn't long until Arlowe's band stumbled across the famed Titanic Canyon: the landmass ripped in two with the arrival of the Titan Core.

"Arlowe, could I ask you something?" Xanth queried, too preoccupied to notice the view before him.

The prince answered through their telepathy. "What's on your mind?"

Xanth hesitated, though his trust in Arlowe brought his question to light. "Is Onyx okay? I'm worried about him."

"I am too. I think we all are."

"Could you talk to him?"

"He doesn't seem too keen on talking right now, Xanth. I don't want to push him."

"Please? It doesn't seem right leaving him to his thoughts right now."

Arlowe sighed, relenting as he saw Onyx staring across the canyon alone. "This looks like a better time than ever," he commented. "Wish me luck."

The prince stood by the assassin's side, staring over the jagged rocks and crashing waves beneath them. Arlowe shifted a stone towards the edge with his foot, allowing it to drop to the watery depths below.

"Can we talk?" The assassin said nothing. "We haven't really had the chance."

"There's nothing to talk about," he responded, skirting the edge of the canyon.

"Onyx, stop."

The assassin turned his body, slowly approaching the prince with purpose in his step. "Don't presume to give me orders, Your Highness. I still see no coin of yours in *my* pocket to make it so."

Arlowe was hardly phased by the attempt of intimidation. "I don't want this Onyx."

"I told you that there was nothing to talk about. Leave it."

"Why are you being so hostile with me? I want to help you."

"I didn't ask."

"You shouldn't have to." This time, Onyx had no answer. "Do you expect me to believe that someone as capable as you, allied with an eleventh, had their arm taken by common thugs? And should I believe that the chats you and Gill are having are nothing more than idle chitchat? You're helping me, whether for coin or not, and I want to help you in return, but I can't if you're still keeping secrets from me."

"I can't Arlowe," Onyx voiced, unable to look the prince in the eyes. "Call it cliché, but I'm expendable. You're not. I can't involve you in my affairs. I swear in Aros' name, I didn't want Gill to become as integral to my search as he's become."

"Then stop what you're doing, for now," Arlowe proposed. "You're my friend. You're not expendable to me. If you can, put a pin in it. We'll gather our strength, defeat the kharakians and take on your task together. Being alone is your choice and I respect that, but I'd rather be by your side."

Onyx thought on the words of the fraud. *Your path does not involve us, lest it come to an early end.* The assassin shivered at the words, his stump shaking from the memory.

A huff of frustration was all Arlowe received, with Onyx continuing his stroll by the edge of the canyon.

"Thank you," Xanth voiced. "Some reassurance from those he cares about must be a huge weight off of his chest."

As the rest of his allies passed him, Gill patted Arlowe's back, giving him a smile and a nod as he strolled onwards. "We're here for him. All of us." Arlowe replied, allowing Daria to catch up to someone.

"By the way, why are we speaking solely in your mind again?" Xanth asked. "Is something wrong?"

The mage walked at the prince's side, though she kept to herself. "Nothing's wrong Xanth, don't worry," Arlowe explained, trying to comfort his concerns. "It's just, Schukara and Onyx already know about you and I think Gill's getting there. Talking to thin air doesn't seem wise when she already seems so jumpy."

"Oh, okay. Thanks for helping me understand."

"Don't mention it."

Peering over, the prince could see that Daria had stopped to stare at the water inhabiting the canyon, and by extension, the ocean far in the distance.

"Beautiful, isn't it?" he uttered, testing his charisma to begin a conversation. "It would be more beautiful to me if I could swim. Drowning terrifies me."

Xanth sputtered at the statement. "Was that meant to be reassuring?"

"If it wasn't for your intervention, I'd probably be out there right now," Daria responded. Her voice was as light as Calaveil's breeze, easing the prince's concerns with every word.

Arlowe regained his composure. "Did you want to go?"

"To Grandgrave? No."

"They were forcing you." Arlowe recoiled at his statement. "I'm sorry. The first proper talk we've had and we're speaking about this."

Daria shook her head, gesturing for them to walk. "Don't apologise. It feels nice to know that you care." The girl looked to Arlowe with a pair of sparkling doe-eyes, grey in colour. "As the Necromancer Rebellions moved into full swing, I was taken from Caermyythen, my village. Quelthen never spoke of his intentions to us, though as the years went by, our group felt... different. Maybe he was silently converting us whilst we were being guided? I don't know."

"I know it's rude to ask, but how old are you?"

"I'm twenty. Why?"

Arlowe was stunned at her answer. "Wait. That means you were nine when they took you," he deduced. "You survived out there during the Sixth Invasion? At that age?"

Daria looked to the ground. "The group was a lot bigger back then. I'm lucky to have survived."

"The Necromancer Rebellions began years ago," Arlowe noted. "How come you were still being guided to Grandgrave now?"

"I tried to be as awkward as possible," Daria replied. "That mage arguing with the guards? Oscar? He was leading us. He wouldn't leave me behind."

"You were awkward for a *long* time."

"I didn't want to go."

"You said you were from, where? Car... mythan?" Arlowe shook his head at butchering the name of her home. "We're not acting as your new captors. We could find you an escort home."

"It's been a long time. It's not my home anymore," Daria answered, trying to suppress her sadness. "Gill spoke to me earlier. It was more of a one-way conversation but I didn't mind. He asked me if I'd consider joining you."

"He did? Have you made a decision?"

"I think so." Her answer piqued the prince's interest. "You all seem wonderful, helping me without even knowing who I am. Having you all as a kind of pseudo-family? That would make me very happy."

Arlowe smiled at the mage's kind words, though Xanth's voice re-emerged, questioning Arlowe once more. "Could she be one?" he queried. "A necromancer, I mean. We don't really know anything about her."

The thought had already crossed Arlowe's mind, though a way to ask about her magical capabilities he did not yet possess.

"That'll be Gill's logic coming into play. Beyond his solid comprehension of sanamancy and Onyx's illumancy, we lack a true mage," the prince admitted. "Though I hope you don't take that the wrong way. We'd be happy to have you all the same."

Daria veiled a smile. "You sound almost as apologetic as I do," she giggled.

Arlowe grinned at her words; she wasn't wrong.

"In all seriousness, I do understand," she continued. "Schukara informed me of your business with the kharakians. How you're raising an army and that the people you've assembled here are the best of the best. I wouldn't want to weaken what you've created here."

Arlowe rolled his eyes as he heard Schukara's boasts, though he had to admit that the group's morale would've been a lot lower without her presence. "What can you do?"

"Well, I'm mostly adept with spells not classified under a single school. Basic ones such as magical detection, dispels and magic missiles, though I've also practiced in the schools of sanamancy, conjurmancy and illumancy, though barely."

"And you're not a…"

Daria looked to Arlowe confused for a moment. "I'm not a…?" The mage clicked almost immediately afterwards. "A necromancer?" She lifted her sleeve. "My eyes aren't purple and my veins aren't showing black. Hopefully that's enough proof for you? I can't think of any other way to show you."

Arlowe waved the statement away. "We'll leave it for now. You're clearly not doing any of us any harm." His tone lowered. "Just, promise me that you'll let the Calaveon Arcane Guild assess you. After Quelthen, I'd rather not take any chances. None of us are particularly keen on the necrotic arts."

"I promise," Daria agreed, finally revealing to him her pleasant smile.

"Eed-mod yed…"

Arlowe stopped, looking around for the origin of the strange noise. "Xanth, did you say something?" he questioned, hastily searching his surroundings.

"No, I'm reading," replied the pterravun. "What did you hear?"

"Stye, elnolev-iroh…"

Daria stood before the prince, hoping to calm him. "Arlowe, are you feeling alright?" She too surveyed their surroundings. "What has your attention?"

Arlowe turned to the mage, his eyes bright blue. "Analaise sunaadra," he pronounced, surprising both the mage and the pterravun.

"What was that?"

"Arlowe? Arlowe, can you hear me?"

The prince shook his head, opening his eyes to reveal the natural brown that Daria remembered. "Ugh, my head is ringing. What's going on?"

The voice spoke again. "Utava…"

Though Daria and Xanth were still unable to hear the voices, Arlowe turned his attention to the cliff's edge. "That sound, it's coming from over there," he insisted, making his way over.

Unable to keep his attention, Daria thought it best to involve the rest of their band. "Everyone! Something isn't right with Arlowe!" she called, bringing them over in a hurry.

"Arlowe, come back from the edge!" Gill shouted, connecting some wire to one of his crossbow bolts.

As the prince reached the edge, his mind went temporarily silent, unable to hear the strange language that had tried to communicate with him. As he glanced over at the waters below, the voice reappeared behind him. "You can help."

Arlowe spun to find the owner of the peculiar voice, though in its place he instead found what he believed to be a wolf lunging for him, forcing him back from solid ground.

As his body slipped over the edge, Gill had just enough time to fire a bolt laced with wire, piercing his shield to keep him from the deathly fall.

262

"Of all the things that could kill you now, another great fall would just be embarrassing!" Gill roared, gritting his teeth as he tugged against the line.

The eleventh heaved with all his might, unable to stop the momentum slamming Arlowe into the side of the cliff.

Unable to feel the tug of Arlowe's weight, Gill rushed over to the edge of the cliff with the rest of the group in tow, spotting only the wire dangling over the water.

For a moment, Arlowe was forced to remain still, his senses still recovering from his impact with the cliff. However, as he came to, his body panicked, his eyes filled with the sight of water.

As he threw himself back in fear, he came to the realisation that he had not fallen down the length of the canyon. Rather, he had somehow smashed through the cliff, hiding out of sight below his allies.

"Arlowe! We can't see ya'! Are ya' down there?"

"Arlowe? Arlowe?"

"Arlowe, can you hear us! Call up if you can!"

The voices of Schukara, Onyx and Gill became clearer as his senses returned to him.

"I'm down here!" he called, holding his chest in pain. "I'm… in some kind of cave?"

"There's no way for us to get to you safely," Gill replied. "We'll try and find another way in. Hold tight!"

Arlowe collapsed against the nearby wall, taking deep breaths after the latest series of events. He thought back to the voice he had heard. *Everyone had been looking my way yet no one warned me of an attack? The beast had leapt for me yet the only mark that my armour has is from the traveller?* Something wasn't right.

"Arlowe, are you alright? Can you hear me yet?" Xanth gasped, sounding out of breath himself.

"Xanth, calm down. I can hear you. I'm alive. I'm… I'm okay."

A sigh of relief from Xanth flew through his mind. "It was like I was locked away. Like I was muted behind glass."

"What do you mean?"

"I could see everything that was happening, but you weren't answering me."

Arlowe paused, trying his best to make sense of his situation. "Xanth, did you see a wolf? Did you hear anything?"

"No," he replied. "I heard you speak in a tongue I've never heard before, but all I saw was you retreating backwards off the cliff as though you *were* being attacked."

The prince glanced at the hole he had made, spotting the wire dangling just out of reach with the new shield upon his arm still retaining the eleventh's bolt, wedged tightly within the wood. "Good thing Daria made everyone aware. Falling into the water from that height would've been like hitting solid rock," Arlowe mused. "If Arn wanted me to fly he should've had one of the Arisen join us."

Unable to grow his own set of wings and fly atop the clouds, the prince turned his attention to the cliff chamber he inhabited. The cavern looked to be carved, covered in an old language he didn't recognise.

The text on the walls lit the chamber in a dim white, barely allowing the prince his sight to navigate his way through it. Though a few pieces of parchment and the occasional trinket could be found littering the halls as he explored, they found no trace of what used to occupy the cold cavern.

"What is this place? It's incredible." Arlowe's voice echoed, ricocheting his wonder through the empty stone halls. "Other than my graceful entrance, this place has been preserved perfectly."

"What makes this place so special?" Xanth posed, unable to comprehend Arlowe's enthusiasm. "Could you explain your excitement?"

"In all my reading, I've never seen any of the races write in symbols," he explained, scanning for everything of note. "There's always been a set structure of letters. The races that go back further in recorded history like the dragons and dwarves had a letter system for their languages. Even the demons wrote in a letter-based structure."

"But whatever resided here had a language based in symbols?"

"Exactly! That means that we've either found the lost history of a race or…"

"Or?"

Arlowe collected his thoughts for a moment. "Or, it means we've found the remains of a race that preceded every other."

Xanth began to laugh with joy. "That's amazing! Is that even possible—"

The pterravun's voice ended abruptly. "Xanth?" Arlowe's enthusiasm faded fast as his mind remained silent. "Xanth? Can you hear me?"

"Foltava…"

In his excitement, he had forgotten about the voices that had led him into the chamber in the first place. All alone, the prince held the hilt of his blade ready to defend himself, though he felt no comfort trapped within the halls.

To his right, Arlowe spotted movement, positive that some kind of quadrupedal creature had slinked out of sight. "What the—"

"Ulow…"

As the voice spoke again, the letters adorning the walls began pulsing, creating a synchronised wave travelling through the hallways; these waves were creating a path for him to follow. His breath was held, following the trail and whatever had created it, hoping that the glowing path would lead him back to his allies and not into a trap.

Arlowe took turn after turn, occasionally spotting concentrations of light around the next, though they were never there as he reached them.

"Xanth? Are you still there?" The prince questioned, hearing nothing from his mind nor the cavern. "Isolating me from my friends is one thing, but severing my connection to Xanth? That's not a coincidence."

After the prolonged traipsing through the halls, Arlowe eventually found himself in some kind of underground amphitheatre, decorated with stone seats, pillars and stage. The glowing symbols that had led him to this room had begun pulsing upwards as opposed to forwards. This was where he was meant to be.

Arlowe slowly descended the stairs, stopping at one of the benches half way down. Upon it laid what appeared to be some form of script, though like everything else he had found, the document was written in symbols that he had no way of translating, though this would not stop him from trying.

"How many of your masterpieces have been lost to the annals of history?" Arlowe asked the theatre. "A shame to be sure."

"Nedril reiltas-ein. Olielle lunaala, quess tu logren."

A blinding light emerged at the central point of the stage, exuding a force powerful enough to stagger the prince, forced to take hold of the bench by his side.

As the light slowly faded, becoming dim enough for Arlowe to see, the wolf-like creature he had previously seen was stood before him, ghostly in form. The symbols lining the theatre's walls now remained active, no longer necessary in guiding the prince.

"Do you wish me harm?" Arlowe posed to the being, still dazed by the fading light. The creature looked his way. It shook its head at his question.

"May I come forward?" This time, the creature gave a slight nod, allowing Arlowe to continue his descent. "Do you have questions for me?"

"Possibly."

"You speak Bridge? You speak in my language?" the prince queried, stunned at receiving an answer. The wolf nodded. "What are you?"

"I speak for Species Eighteen. I am Vence."

"Species Eighteen? Vence? What does that mean?"

The creature moved forward, noble in its appearance. "Irrelevant. I am here to deliver a message and my time is short. The Untainted Lands are collapsing and there is no escape unless there is intervention."

"What can I do?" Arlowe questioned, struggling to comprehend the 'Vence'. "I can barely understand you. Where are the Untainted Lands?"

"The traitor is the key. Break his chains to break ours."

The wolf began to fade, unable to maintain its form. "What does that mean?" Arlowe insisted on a more precise message. "Don't go!"

The blinding light returned, knocking the prince back, blinding him once more. As the light faded to a bearable level, Arlowe was alone once more.

With the wolf's departure, even the energy embodying the symbols had vanished, turning the chamber into a murky collection of featureless tunnels.

Arlowe slowly rose to his feet; the fall only added to his pain. "Xanth? The creature's gone. Can you hear me?" he asked, climbing onto the edge of the stage. "Xanth?"

"Mm Hmre. Mrmowe?"

"Xanth?"

"I'm here. Can you hear me, Arlowe?"

"There you are." He shook the ache from his head. "It looks like whatever I was communicating with can meddle with my mind. Block out others and keep itself hidden."

Xanth paused. "Is that possible? What was it?"

"I don't know." The prince reminded himself of what he was told. "'The traitor is the key. Break his chains to break ours'. That's what it told me before it vanished. Do you have any idea of what that means?"

"No, sorry," the pterravun replied. "Did it say anything else?"

"Species Eighteen? Vence? Untainted Lands? Does that mean anything to you?"

"I don't think so."

The sound of moving stone caught Arlowe's attention, with an orange glow beginning to fill the empty halls. "Arlowe? Are ya' in here?" called a familiar voice.

"That's Schukara!" Xanth excitedly responded. "How did she get down here?"

Arlowe listened closely, hearing multiple footsteps exploring the chamber. "They found a way in." He gathered his energy, calling out to them. "Everyone! I'm in here!"

One by one, his allies arrived in the amphitheatre, each seeming relieved to find the prince in one piece.

However, though Arlowe expected four, a fifth figure stood in the doorway, blade in hand. "Nice to see you again," a female spoke, the blade glowing alongside the voice.

"Yeah, what she said," continued the figure, coming forth from the shadows to reveal Valerius and his black blade.

Arlowe clumsily dropped from the stage, drawing his blade from its sheath to prepare for the terrorist. "What are you doing here?" he demanded, trying his best to keep his stance. "I told you I wouldn't hesitate."

Schukara approached him, pulling his sword-arm down. "Arlowe, he was tha' one who got us in here," she vouched, looking over at the man. "I was suspicious too, but he said he needed ta' find ya'. He got us in. It's urgent."

The prince returned his blade back to his side, ascending the stairs to meet his supposed ally. "So, I have you to thank for getting me out of here." After a brief moment of tension, Arlowe held out his hand, offering it to Valerius. "Schukara said it's urgent. I at least owe you a chance to speak."

The terrorist gestured for Arlowe to lower his hand. He instead took a seat upon the stone benches. "You found it, didn't you," he voiced.

Arlowe was stunned. "You know about—"

"Species Eighteen. How do you think I found you?" Valerius held up his blade, drawing attention to it. "With Adrestia's assistance, I can follow the trail of the fae. That same trail led me to you."

Gill perked up at Valerius' words. "The fae?"

"Do you know of them?" Adrestia asked, carried over Valerius' shoulder.

"Not much," the eleventh admitted. "There are old ruins dotted all around Katosus. They weren't crafted by any living race in this age, nor by any of the demons, pre-invasion or otherwise. The structure we're standing in right now is proof of that. That word you used, fae, is the name given to a possible race that came before the dragons."

"They *did* come before the dragons," the blade informed. "It isn't 'possible'. It's fact."

"Excuse me," Daria asked, shrinking as attention turned to her. "How would you know something like that? About something that pre-dates us?"

Valerius scanned the room before looking to his blade. "Can *we* trust *them*?"

"We don't have a choice, Valerie. We're out of time," the blade answered, turning Valerius' expression sour. "We blades are very old. Ancient, you might say. Every time one of our partners passes on from this world, our hilts are passed on to a new one, with their consent. Once a blade has become experienced enough, powerful enough, they have the choice to become a Bright Blade. That choice has been taken from me."

"Why?" Arlowe questioned. "You must have done something for them to make that decision."

"As far as I can tell, I was the first to find one of those messages from 'Species Eighteen', though Bright Blade Artemis was not far behind," she continued. "Artemis made it clear that those messages and what they led to belonged to her. Realising that she was not the only one who found the message from Species Eighteen, she killed my partner at the time, sending me back into the void with the intent on killing anyone who held me to keep me out of her affairs."

"Ever since I was bound to her, Adrestia and I have been tracking the messages sent by Species Eighteen, getting in, accessing them and getting out before the Bright Blades can do anything about it," Valerius added. "When we're not tracking Species Eighteen, we're striking at the Bright Blades where it hurts."

"Wait, wait, wait!" Schukara blurted, waving her hands. "Arlowe and I saw y'all 'striking at them' first-hand. You may be inconveniencin' tha' Bright Blades, but yer' also leaving people without employment. Can't work if everythin' is burnt ta' tha' ground."

"Rebuilding what was destroyed requires work, and the Bright Blades offer emergency funding to those that can't take work in that specific field, paying them until their job has been restored or replaced," Adrestia shook, though of anger or regret, none could tell. "They're our people too. If we didn't care, we *could* have left those workers in the fire. We *could* have let them all burn."

"We're veering off-topic," Arlowe called, raising his hand to silence those in the room. "What does this have to do with the kharakians? In that factory you made a connection between them and the Bright Blades. I assume you have the answer?"

270

"Indeed," Adrestia responded. "Small flickers of energy draw myself and others to these messages, though there is one we cannot ignore."

"Which is?"

"At Kharaki. A huge surge of energy spiked there over a month ago."

"That was around when Eyenridge was attacked!" Schukara announced.

"Precisely." Adrestia began to glow brighter. "Ever since that spike, there has also been a huge influx of messages; too many for Valerius and I to keep away from Artemis and the other Bright Blades. That's why they agreed to help you. Of everyone, you would be the most likely to enter Kharaki, finding that power source in the process."

"Hold on. I can't sense these flickers and surges, and yet, I was able to find that message left by Species Eighteen?" Arlowe argued. "How is that possible? I don't wield a black blade."

"I don't know," Valerius replied, circling to examine the peculiar envoy. "Maybe you're the chosen one? Wouldn't that be something?"

"What about Xanth?" Onyx queried. "You know? The voice in your head?"

"Yeah! Xanth!" Schukara agreed. "His ability ta' connect with ya' from wherever he is must've had some kind of effect on ya'!"

"Xanth?" asked Daria, confused at the strange word. "What's a Xanth?"

"What's going on?" Xanth spoke, stirred by his name. "Why is everyone talking about me?"

"Xanth is part of an underground community that saved my life. He uses his telepathic abilities to see through my eyes as we travel. I'll explain in more detail later," Arlowe divulged. His attention was then brought to the pterravun. "Is it possible that our connection made me more susceptible to the fae?"

"Possibly?" Xanth replied, sounding unsure. "The outside world was alien to us until recently, so all of this is new to me."

"Then it's a possibility," Arlowe communicated back to those within the amphitheatre. "Thank you, Xanth."

"So, what do you say?" Adrestia questioned. "What's your plan going forward?"

The prince looked over his allies, each curious to hear how the revelation of the fae had altered his end goal. "My plan hasn't changed."

Valerius cocked his head. "Even with all you know?"

Arlowe paced the theatre. "The kharakians are a threat to everyone, regardless of what's causing it. My plan is as it was: gather as many of the armies of Argestra as I can muster, march on Kharaki and finally put an end to their madness."

"And the surge of energy?"

"Outside of the increase in messages from Species Eighteen and its connection with the kharakian assault, we don't know what it is or what it's truly capable of. I'm not fond of playing things by ear, but we won't know what that surge is until we stand upon Kharaki, so I can't let it influence our plans. The kharakians fall first."

Valerius rose from the bench. "Well, then I believe that our usefulness for now is at an end." The bearer swapped Adrestia to his free hand, stretching his arm. "Good luck to you all. We wish you well."

"Will you not join us?" Arlowe voiced, noticing the disapproval in Schukara's face. "I can't express enough how useful your knowledge of the fae could be."

"Even if Valerie here wasn't the brooding, lone wolf type, we can't," Adrestia mocked. Valerius didn't bite. "You're allied with the Bright Blades. Travelling with us would make that arrangement very complicated. That, and I'd rather not lose another partner if I can help it. We like to be on the move. Staying in towns and cities for days at a time wouldn't be a great idea for us."

"Thought you didn't trust us anyway," Valerius added. "We're terrorists. Not a good image for you."

"I'm a prince who frequently speaks with the voice in his head and has an assassin by his side. At such a difficult time, do you think it's my image that I'm worried about?" the prince retorted, becoming still. "I trust you, but only because of what I've seen today. I don't agree with your methods, you said it yourself, you're terrorists. But these messages? Species Eighteen? It's too important to put to one side. If you won't join us, will you contact me if anything changes?"

"We will," Adrestia agreed, speaking in Valerius' place. "Valerie's hard to warm to, but he's a good man. Hopefully our actions will speak loudly when it matters."

"I hope so too. Safe travels."

With Arlowe's blessing, the two exited the theatre. Their steps echoed as they departed the cavern.

Schukara approached, bringing Arlowe in for a big hug. "I'm glad that yer' okay," she spoke, detaching herself. "Really need to get'cha flyin' lessons, huh?"

"Where to now?" Onyx interjected. "I assume we'll be continuing towards Wicilil?"

"If we continue how we have been, Wicilil should only be a few days away," Gill answered. "Hopefully there'll be no more interrupt—"

The group went on edge as soon as Gill's comment ended abruptly. Schukara walked up to the eleventh, patting his shoulder. "What's tha' matter? Headache or—"

"A huge concentration of soul energy is moving this way," he warned as his body shuddered. "That energy is giving me a bad feeling."

The sound of a conflict echoed through the halls of the chamber, ending with a crack that echoed even louder.

Undeterred, Arlowe crept to the entrance of the theatre, all eyes on him.

"Whatever it is, Valerius may need our help," he rallied, drawing his blade. "Keep your weapons drawn but lowered. I'd prefer to avoid a fight if we can help it."

"I'll go ahead," Gill offered. "If what lies beyond turns out to be hostile, I can hold their attention."

Onyx stepped forward. "Any of us could, but would it help?" He looked to Arlowe. "We keep separating. Where's it gotten us? We're stronger together."

"I agree," Schukara added, smiling at Onyx words. "No offence to yer' plan, Gill."

"None taken. His words are wise." The eleventh stood at the theatre's exit patiently. "What's the plan, Arlowe? I'll wait on your orders."

The prince nodded. "Lead me to the entrance. I'm not exactly sure where Valerius opened this place up from. Once we're there, make sure our surroundings are clear before we leave. With you here, there's no excuse for being ambushed as soon as we're out the door."

Gill bowed. "Understood. Everyone, on me."

As his band travelled back through the dark passages, Arlowe noticed their new addition grasping onto her staff tightly, walking slower than the rest. "Daria?"

"Hm? Yes, Arlowe?"

"Everything will be okay. Nothing's stopping us from reaching Wicilil," he expressed. "I promise."

With difficulty, the mage's eyes eventually reached the prince's. "I promise too. I'll try my best to keep you safe."

Gill took cover by the side of the entrance, looking all around for any signs of soul energy. "I sense three, though I imagine that two of them are Valerius and Adrestia based on the two sizes side by side."

"And the third?" Arlowe queried.

"It's bigger than the black blade but smaller than the terrorist. Maybe that large amount of soul energy I sensed dropped it off?" The eleventh dismissed his claim, looking up. "Regardless, I believe it safe."

Arlowe moved into the doorway. Valerius was laid upon the ground beaten, with Adrestia buried in the dirt by his side.

A goblin rested upon his back.

Upon noticing the prince, the goblin rose with a large grin decorating its face. "I'm glad you're 'ere," he spoke, appearing in a jolly mood. "I spotted this man, all tense an' tha' like, 'n' thought a massage was in order. Friend of yours?"

"Who are you?" Arlowe questioned, remaining within the structure. "We're not interested in a fight. That man there, could you let him go?"

"Let 'im go? Why would I do that? He was very rude. VERY rude."

"Could you *please* let him go? I apologise if he caused offence."

"If *he* caused offence? Naw. Not 'im. You."

Arlowe's eyes glanced over his allies; all were unsure of what the goblin meant.

"Arlowe, I don't think yer' askin' tha' right questions," Schukara voiced, peeking around the doorway. "How did one goblin take down a black blade? Props if he actually did, but I ain't sure if it's that simple."

"Come on out," offered the goblin. "Arrsk is curious ta' meet ya', Arlowe."

Unease set in for the prince. "How do you know my name? How did you know I was here?" he demanded. "Who are you?"

Though Gill shook his head in disapproval, Arlowe moved out into the open, catching his ankle against a piece of string. As he did, small explosions set off around his feet, forcing out all but Daria from the structure.

"Arlowe! Are you—" Gill scanned the ground, noticing the remains of the explosives. "What are these? Some kind of firecracker?"

"Nice trap!" Schukara uttered, mocking the goblin. "Got any others?"

The goblin began chuckling before erupting into laughter, unable to contain his howling. "Why is he laughing?" Xanth questioned. "You outnumber him."

Arrsk wiped a tear from his eye, stood comfortably atop Valerius. "They weren't meant ta' hurt you!"

"Then what were they meant to do?" Onyx pressed. "Answer us!"

"We knew ya' had an eleventh with ya'. We knew you'd look fer' our soul energy!" he explained in-between breaks of giggling. "Ya' can only look so far."

As Arlowe advanced, an impact on the hill above the doorway rocked the surrounding area, kicking up dust for a brief moment.

As the group swiped the dust away, they turned to see a monstrous skeletal being unravel itself from the impact, slamming its gigantic hands over the side of the hill.

Arlowe and his band could only look in horror as the fusion of bones looked over each one of them before keeping its gaze upon the envoy.

"That's what I sensed," Gill voiced. "What's an amalgam doing here?"

"An amalgam?" Arrsk questioned, still in awe of his partner. "Nah, Kaxrax has a much better ring to it, don't you think, Kaxrax?"

The amalgam grew tense, crushing the earth held in their palm as hundreds of voices spoke at once; there were too many for the group to understand.

At once, the voices stopped, with the beast slamming their fists against the ground before letting out a tremendous roar in unison. "Arlowe!"

Chapter Fifteen:

"The dangers of one's past hunt without remorse."

20th Arandbern

Land's Legacy

2084∞ (Current Age)

Kaxrax recklessly fired their vessel from the hillside, crashing into Arlowe's party, sweeping them all away with their clawed hands to isolate the prince from his allies. Once they had been cleared, the amalgam took Arlowe into their cold grip, slamming him into the ground to cease his struggling.

"We found you!" Rilit exclaimed, bringing Arlowe face-to-face with the behemoth. "Hmm, all of you? You have friends! Good. An audience for your execution!"

As the amalgam's grip tightened, a crossbow bolt struck their ghastly arm, forcing them to release their recent capture. Turning their head, the monster found Gill reloading his crossbow with a herb-laced bolt, swapping it out for his staff.

"Focus, Rilit!" the beggar Kivyx hissed. "Though Arlowe *is* our priority, they too must be punished. Accomplices of the murderer."

Gill charged forward, striking away the swings of the amalgam as Onyx retrieved the prince, dragging him back to the cover of a nearby hill to catch his breath. "It knows you?" the assassin asked. "Do you know it?"

Arlowe pulled a broken piece of his cuirass away, able to once again breath properly. "Trust me, I'd know if I'd met something like *that*."

As the battle with the amalgam raged, Schukara had approached the creature's ally. Arrsk had been trying to drag both Valerius and Adrestia away, though their difference in size had made for a monumental task.

"I'll ask nicely: put him down," Schukara declared, though Arrsk continued to drag the man and his blade. "Ya' deaf, goblin?"

"Soz sweetheart, but I have no interest in payin' ya' any attention," he answered. "I am talkin' to a woman, right? I once read that women have tits on their armour. A woman wit' no tits ain't no woman."

Biting her tongue, Schukara marched forward, only to be halted as her feet stuck to the ground. "What tha'?"

The goblin had been successful. Luring her towards him with his taunting, Arrsk had caught her in one of his traps, continuing to drag the man and blade with a gleeful skip in his step. "I suggest ya' go no further," she warned.

The goblin dropped Valerius' arm in awe of her audacity.

"And what're ya' gonna do?" Arrsk revealed a bottle from his pocket, sticking his foot to the floor with his magic only to unstick it with the contents of the bottle. "Yer' over there, ya' dumb bitch, 'n' I'm over 'ere! I've trapped ya'! Yer' threats don't—"

As Arrsk carried on, Schukara abruptly threw one of her blades at the goblin. Bracing for injury, he lowered his arms to find himself no worse for wear, seeing the sword to his side. "Ha! Ya' missed!"

"Did I?"

Arrsk looked down, noticing that the blade had penetrated his boot, pinning him to the spot. "Bollocks. Look, we're both stuck now, so, er, why don't we make a deal?"

"We're *both* stuck? Ya' sure about that?"

Arrsk looked down again, seeing the elf step out of her boots, placing her bare feet upon the blades of grass before her. Schukara stepped forward, careful of any more traps as she reached the shaking goblin.

"Here's tha' deal," she bartered, crouching to his height. "You give me that solution so I can get ma' boots, 'n' I'll take ma' sword back. Dare ya' ta' say no."

278

Arrsk trembled, rushing to find the solution. Locating it, he sheepishly handed it over, watching as the mercenary returned her boots back to their rightful place.

Once done, the elf returned, pulling her sword from his boot and back to her side.

"So… I'm, er, free ta' go?" Arrsk asked with a nervous smile. "No 'ard feelins'?"

Without warning, Schukara kicked Arrsk in a style reminiscent of a ball, launching him far from Valerius. "Pleasure doin' business with ya'," she mused, approaching the goblin's body at the edge of the canyon.

Onyx weaved through the battle-torn environment, finding himself out of sight behind the amalgam. Using his position to his advantage, the assassin aimed his dagger between the bones of Kaxrax, though the blade bent at being pressed against the condensed souls holding the body together.

"A riddle!" he called, retreating. "How can one kill what cannot be stabbed?"

Knowing full well that they held the advantage in their fight, the amalgam refused to humour the assassin and eleventh a moment longer, turning their attention to Arlowe's cover.

Lacking subtlety, Kaxrax leapt from their previous conflict, landing behind the hill ready to pounce. "Come out, come out, Arlowe," Amizi sung before vaulting over the hill and lunging, surprised at catching nothing. "What? Where did he go?"

Aware he was the amalgam's primary focus, Arlowe shifted to a nearby rock for shelter, waiting for them to be drawn to his last known location.

Once there, Arlowe took the spare bar of chocolate Gill had given him from his pack, opening its contents before climbing to the top of the hill.

Jumping onto Kaxrax's back, he rubbed the melted chocolate into the eye sockets of the behemoth. "No!" Rilit screeched in fear. "I can't see!"

The amalgam viciously convulsed, unable to remove the obstruction from their eyes.

"Calm down, you fools!" Baxka hollered, hoping to stabilize the body. "We have vision from the eye sockets all over this form!"

"I don't want to return to the darkness, Baxka! It was so cold!" Amizi cried, forgetting the capabilities of her new body.

As the amalgam scratched their sockets clean, Arlowe regrouped with his allies hoping to find a winning strategy.

"Gill, you know the drill by now," the prince voiced. "What do we need to know about this amalgam? Kaxrax?"

"One of the most powerful forms of undead. Unnaturally strong, unnaturally heavy, extremely resilient to damage," uttered the eleventh, shaking his head. "We were taken by surprise and our resources are dwindling. Our best outcome is to force it away. Killing it is not an option."

"And how are we going to drive it away?" Onyx questioned, throwing his bent dagger to one side. "I doubt Schukara's carrying a crate worth of undead repellent."

"What about explosives?" Xanth queried, jogging Arlowe's memory. "One explosive was enough to heavily damage Reitgrar's ironsoul suit. Is Onyx carrying any?"

Arlowe relayed the message. "Xanth's idea; are you carrying any explosives?"

The assassin checked through his equipment. "Three bombs. Why?"

Arlowe then turned his attention to Gill. "Would three bombs be enough?"

"Possibly," Gill replied. "I don't think we have an alternative. They'll have to do."

Onyx took a sphere into his hand. "Better make them count," he uttered. "Looks like the fight's back on."

The amalgam had finally clawed the last of the chocolate from their sockets, turning all attention to the three. "Clever trick," Kweez praised, slowly advancing on them. "Fool us once, tear you apart twice. Come here and do it again."

280

Retreating backwards, Onyx pressed the sphere against his chest, twisting it.

"What are you doing?" Gill whispered, grasping the assassin's wrist. "I think the amalgam trying to kill us is enough of a problem."

"Not the same sphere, Gill. I can try to kill you with a smoke bomb if you'd like?" Onyx retorted, taking back his wrist with a smirk. "Definitely harder, but not impossible."

Dropping it to the floor, Onyx and those around him had become engulfed in a thick smoke. "Here's a trick for you, you freak," the assassin taunted. "A game too. If you can find us, you win a prize. Good luck!"

Shaking with rage, Kaxrax blindly charged into the smokescreen, flailing their arms wildly in the hopes of making contact with one of their enemies. "You're all outmatched!" Kweez called into the smoke. "Surrender, and I'll make your deaths quick! That includes you, Arlowe!"

The amalgam's surroundings were oddly silent, unable to hear the scurrying of their prey. A butterfly fluttered past their face, quickly taking Kaxrax's attention.

"That's a mourning cloak!" Amizi excitedly mentioned, urging their vessel to face it. "They're a butterfly that can survive in cold climates. You can tell based on its velvety appearance and ochre adornments."

"You're joking, right?" Rilit complained. "We shouldn't let our guard down!"

"They're Arrsk's favourite," added Kivyx. "He'd always show me one that he netted along with passing me a gold piece. Whenever I saw one, they reminded me of him."

The amalgam raised their hand, allowing the butterfly to land on the tip of their finger. The voices resonated with positivity, with only a few shifting to disapproval.

"Are you there?" Onyx called out, snapping Kaxrax back to reality. "This smoke is just buying us time. We're outmatched. We can't win this."

"An amalgam is too much for us," Gill added, sounding defeated. "We're wasting our time here."

"We surrender," Arlowe's voice filled Kaxrax with a wave of relief. "We're done hiding. We're over here."

The amalgam slowly knuckle-walked to the voices, tightly clenching their gargantuan fist as they ended the search atop their prey. "Reveal yourself, lest we retract our bargain," Baxka spoke.

"What do you mean? You're stood over us," Onyx uttered, bringing the amalgam's gaze down to spot a metallic sphere rolling beneath them. "Enjoy your prize."

From a safe distance beyond the smoke, the three watched as what smoke lingered was flung by the detonation of the explosive, leaving a stunned Kaxrax reeling from the blast.

The behemoth shook their head, regaining their senses as they remembered the butterfly. Kaxrax searched around desperately, spotting the crumpled insect dead upon the ground. Their anger had been stoked like a grand fireplace.

"No," voiced the goblins under their breath, bringing their body to set free a horrendous scream, charging at the three with renewed aggression. "No!"

Meanwhile, Schukara had cornered Arrsk at the edge of the canyon, leaving the goblin pathetically raising his dagger in self-defence. "Call off that beast," she threatened. "This could be resolved peacefully, ya' know? There's no need fer' this!"

"There's every need!" Arrsk yelled, lowering his weapon. "Goblins could 'ave a place in this world, but 'cause our ancestors made a mistake, we all suffer! Ya' won't treat us fairly, 'cause no one else has! Do yer' worst, whore!"

The elf advanced on the goblin, both raising their weapons. Schukara made the first move, bringing her blade down upon Arrsk, though he was swift.

282

The goblin evaded to one side, thrusting his own blade forward, slicing a piece of the mercenary's hair free as she dodged.

To his dismay, this left him exposed. Schukara snatched the goblin's wrist out of the air, disarming him of his blade before striking back with her own.

The bloody impact flung Arrsk's frail body; his eyes opened to the sight of the canyon's edge.

Schukara stood over the goblin, who was bleeding heavily. Arrsk had regenerated quickly from his injuries, though he still lacked the energy to stand, unable to look higher than the elf's knees.

"That's it, that's it. I'm through. I can't contend with you," he spat, speaking through gritted teeth. "Come grab me. I'm clearly not goin' anywhere."

The mercenary took a step forward to collect the goblin, though as she did, she soon realised that she couldn't stop, losing her footing. The goblin had spawned another trick, greasing her path, aiming to escape by making her fall to her death.

Failing to grab hold of anything, the elf went over the edge, bringing the goblin to tears of laughter.

"Nra's nutsack, how many times could I 'ave outwitted her? Maybe she was a woman. As bright as an eclipse," he ridiculed, strolling over to the edge. "I wonder how she landed?"

A voice emerged from the descent. "Why don'cha tell me?"

A hand took hold of the goblin's leg. He was now over the edge himself. Dangling above the waters far below, he realised that the elf never fell. Instead, as she went over, she had managed to stab one of her swords into a narrow crevice, preventing her fall.

"Well, the view's nice, but I'd best get back ta' my partner. Partners? Ah, who cares," rambled the goblin, struggling out of Schukara's grasp, climbing over her back up to safety. "Good luck getting back up! I've heard armour is pretty heavy!"

The goblin wasn't lying. Schukara wasn't weak by any means, but trying to lift her own weight with the added weight of the armour was proving to be more than she could handle. Repeated attempts were made to reach higher or dig her feet in, though no opportunity came.

The mercenary let out a sigh, giving up on the idea of making it back alive. "Good job, Parle," she sarcastically praised. "Ma always said ya' never learnt from yer' mistakes. I can't count how many times she's proved me right without bein' here."

The sound of Arrsk screaming in pain broke through Schukara's reflection. Peering up, the mercenary could see a familiar figure looking down at her.

"Remove your blade from the crevice." A battered Valerius held out his hand. "I can catch you when you—"

"Yer' nowhere near!"

"What other choice have you got? Let go."

"Ma always told me not ta' trust strangers," the elf mumbled, shrugging her thought away. "She also told me not to jump from high places, so what can ya' do?"

Taking a deep breath, Schukara pressed her foot against the side of the cliff, retrieving her sword from the stone.

Though she prepared herself to fall, her body instead ascended the cliff. Valerius had taken her into his grasp, using Adrestia's powers as his own to lift her to safety.

As Schukara was placed back onto solid ground, Valerius collapsed from exhaustion, not yet recovered from Kaxrax's assault.

Behind him, Schukara found Arrsk with Adrestia pierced through his arm, keeping him from fleeing, though the goblin continued to tug against the sword regardless.

"I'm not done yet. Help me up," Valerius muttered, struggling to his knees.

284

Schukara took his arm, assisting him in rising back to his feet. "Stay here. Ya' need ta' rest," she insisted. "I'll deal with tha' goblin."

The man snatched his arm back. "I'm not one of your band. I don't take orders from you."

"I'm tryin' ta' help! Why're ya' bein' so stubborn!"

"I'm doing what I think is best. Aid me or get out of my way!"

"Excuse me!" Adrestia called, breaking up the two's feud. "Not meaning to come between a married couple and their argument, but I don't feel comfortable being near this rabid goblin."

While Schukara and Valerius had been arguing, Arrsk had been tugging and rubbing against the black blade, and with one final heave, tore his arm from his torso, granting himself his freedom.

Reacting quickly, the goblin then casted another spell, transforming into a mouse to hide amongst the grass, escaping his pursuers.

Valerius stumbled over to Adrestia, pulling her from the ground and wiping her of Arrsk's blood. "You owe me," the blade voiced, evidently disgusted. "That was foul."

"You've been through worse," Valerius noted, turning to Schukara. "Got any ideas of where that wretch has gone now?"

Schukara could hear the sound of her group's conflict with Kaxrax, taking the lead. "Tha' safest place for him is by tha' amalgam's side. That's where he'll be. We need to catch up ta' him before he makes things worse."

Kaxrax kept their onslaught up, though Arlowe, Onyx and Gill had so far been lucky enough to avoid being crushed under the amalgam's immense blows.

Maintaining the offensive, the amalgam refused to allow their foes a chance to breathe, stunting any would-be plan.

"Gill, any ideas?" Arlowe questioned, keeping to a safe distance.

"I can remove one of my senses alongside a target of my choice," Gill replied, visibly struggling to ward off the amalgam's strikes. "I can try to blind it, but if it decides to go on a rampage, we're in trouble."

"I can help with that!" Xanth announced. "Arlowe, I need you to get close to that amalgam."

"I'll need *you* to elaborate," Arlowe voiced, concerned that his pterravun ally had gone mad. "I'd rather not get closer if I can help it."

"I can enter the creature's mind like I did with Schukara. If Gill blinds it, you can make contact for me to enter its mind and distract it."

Though cobbled together, no other plan had been brought forward, forcing them to charge towards the beast. "Gill, do it!" the prince ordered, diving out of the way of another powerful slam.

The eleventh focused his energy; his eyes became white as he tapped into his supernatural abilities.

In response, the light shining from within Kaxrax's many sockets had gone dark. The behemoth took a hold of their skull, cracking it under the force generated by their frustration and fear.

"Enough of this!" Kweez shouted, proceeding to swing their fists wildly. "We know your games. We refuse to be paralysed twice!"

Though Arlowe came close, a stray swipe from Kaxrax connected, sending him crashing into a nearby boulder.

"Sorry Xanth. I did what I could," Arlowe struggled, incapable of moving.

"No, that was perfect! Your hand made contact!" Xanth exclaimed. "It's about time I did something to help!"

286

"We gave you a chance, Arlowe!" Kivyx yelled, accompanying the body's rampage. "You chose this path!"

"We'll mash you into paste!" Rilit continued. "You deserve much less than we're offering, scum!"

"In Arn's name and my own, I suggest you cease your attack. Hearken to the words of the gods," a voice announced, silencing every voice within the beast.

Arlowe was privy to this voice; Xanth was posing as another in an attempt to fool the behemoth.

"What sorcery is this?" Kweez screeched, the body frantically searching for the source of the voice despite the loss of their sight. "Speak!"

"I am Aros, son of Arn. I cannot idly stand by whilst you tamper with the envoy. His journey is not yet over."

"This is nonsense. Clearly another trick—"

"Silence!" The amalgam went still. "Another word and your quest for vengeance shall be the least of your concerns!"

Arlowe raised his head, signalling to Onyx. "Throw it!"

The voices of the amalgam bickered for a moment, undecipherable to those listening, though one voice spoke out with their consensus.

"You lie," Baxka answered, followed by the anger of the other residents within the body. "Where were you during our injustice? When we became what you see? We reject you, as you rejected us. Your precious 'envoy' will die by our hands."

The voice of Aros did not answer, replaced by a clatter between the amalgam's feet. Kaxrax's vision returned just in time to find another of Onyx's bombs, unable to defend themselves from the blast.

"I can't do any more," Xanth voiced, sounding exhausted from his commune with the amalgam. "So many voices. I think I need to lie down for a moment."

"Onyx!" Gill pronounced, using his healing magic against the monster to keep them in place. "My sanamancy won't hold! This is all I have left! Throw the bomb!"

"Release us!" the amalgam bellowed in unison, wrestling against the magic scorching them. "We demand it!"

Onyx took the final bomb from behind his cloak, arming it against his shoulder.

As the assassin prepared to lob the explosive, Arrsk appeared by his side, snatching it from his grasp. "No! You can't!"

"Yoink! Looks like I can!" he shouted as he climbed, leaping from Onyx's shoulders to throw the bomb in a different direction; it was headed for the approaching Schukara and Valerius. "Oops! My hand slipped! Ha ha ha!"

Spotting the incoming projectile, Valerius thrust his telekinesis forward in an attempt to rid themselves of the bomb, though he knew the timer neared its end.

The terrorist stood between Schukara and the imminent explosion, taking the brunt of the explosive force, their bodies thrown back from the detonation.

Waking from her daze, Schukara rushed to a motionless Valerius expecting the worst. Luckily, the man had survived, though he was heavily wounded; his armour was ripped apart with the wounds visible within.

The terrorist opened his eyes, irritated at the elf's concern. "Go," he sputtered, weakly pushing her away. "The fight isn't over."

"I told you... to let... us... go!" Kaxrax roared, breaking free of Gill's magic. Taking advantage of his weakened state, the amalgam charged forward, delivering a full-force punch that knocked Gill down into the dirt, removing another inconvenience from their warpath.

"Kaxrax! Could use a hand!" Arrsk requested, chased by Onyx and Schukara.

288

Wasting no time, the amalgam rushed towards Arrsk's pursuers, grabbing onto Schukara's leg to use her as a makeshift weapon, slamming her against the assassin to take them both out.

"Pathetic," Amizi voiced, looking down upon the defeated souls. "You should know when to quit."

Arrsk sprinted over to the downed Arlowe, using every ounce of his remaining strength to lift the prince's arm for Kaxrax. The amalgam took him by his arms, reminiscent to a child and their doll as Arrsk took his place upon their shoulder.

The behemoth then gripped onto Arlowe's other arm, bringing him close. "There's no one left to save you, Arlowe," Baxka uttered, tightening their hold upon him. "History will forget you as it forgot us, and your legacy will turn to ash in the hands gifted to us by the sick gods that made them a reality. But first, we'll cherish this moment. Savour every last drop of your anguish."

As Kaxrax began to pull, drawing out the screams of their victim, Daria sat shivering within the fae chambers, unable to bring herself to act. "What can I do? What can I do? My powers are no match for that amalgam. There's nothing I can do."

She placed her hands over her ears as Arlowe's screams worsened, tears filling her eyes. "Stop it! Stop it, Daria! You're the only one left who can do anything! Even if it means—"

Arlowe's screams grew louder still, urging the mage to her feet. Her mind was made up. "They may not understand, but they'll be safe. I owe them that."

Kaxrax continued to pull, adding a building pressure on Arlowe's arms, enjoying the tune of his pained song and the accompaniments of every crack. "More, Kaxrax! I wanna see how many octaves our new instrument has—"

From his vantage, the goblin could see Daria approaching them, nudging Kaxrax's head to warn them. "Er, 'ello?" he greeted, calling down. "Ya' lost? Have a name?"

"Let him go," Daria mumbled; her legs were ready to buckle in fear.

Arrsk and Kaxrax looked to each other before bursting out into laughter.

"That's a funny name, human," Arrsk replied, making his dagger visible, "but we're a little busy here, so if you could just—"

"I'm warning you. Put him down."

Still holding an arm in each hand, Kaxrax lowered the prince to better see the mage.

"It was funny the first time, girl, but now your joke's gone stale," Rilit spoke, shaking their shoulder for the goblin to dismount. "Arrsk, deal with our guest. I have other matters to attend to."

"Daria." Arlowe weakly lifted his head. "Save yourself. Try to wake the others and get to—" Continuing the torture, Kaxrax once again yanked the prince's arms.

"Enough!" called the mage, letting out a huge wave of energy, enveloping herself within the purple mist that had been expelled by her magic. "I won't stand by while you torture him! This ends here!"

The burst of energy blew Arrsk back, forcing him to hold onto the amalgam to ground himself. "What's going on?" he yelled, squinting to get a better look through the mist. "Who is she?"

"Irrelevant," uttered the voices of Kaxrax, speaking as one. "Arlowe dies. Nothing else matters." However, try as they might, the amalgam could not pull Arlowe's arms any further, as if a force was holding them back.

"Kaxrax? What's wrong?" the goblin questioned, turning back to the mist. "What did you do to them?"

A pair of glowing purple eyes stood out through the mist, followed by their owner. Daria had transformed; her robe had become armour as skeletal wings sprouted from her back. Her hand, covered in black veins, was held out, gripping onto something seemingly invisible.

"I told you to let him go," she spoke, her voice warped by the power she had unleashed.

Whipping her hand to the side, Kaxrax's right arm exploded into pieces, dropping Arlowe in the process. A blast of healing was fired at the amalgam for good measure, stunting their recovery. "Leave," she demanded.

Refusing the mage's order, Kaxrax charged with their remaining arm, leaping into the air to bring it down on her.

Unfortunately for the souls, Daria was far too fast. She evaded to the side as she knocked their arm away, forcing the beast to collide into the ground with a tremendous crash.

The mage made short work of the creature's retaliation, parrying their powerful blows with ease, counterattacking by slamming her staff down upon their skull before knocking them back with a barrage of magical missiles.

Kaxrax let out a pitiful squeal, dropping to the ground from the impact of the darts.

"This... is impossible!" Kivyx spat.

"We need to retreat," Baxka voiced; the whole body writhed in disapproval. "We have to. If we stay, we won't get another chance."

Arrsk ran up to the amalgam, giving his all to help them to their feet. "We can't give up! We're so close!"

"There's nothing we can do, my sweet," Amizi expressed.

"Unless you can match that level of power, you fool," Rilit spat.

Arrsk had no answer, allowing himself to be taken by the amalgam.

"This isn't over," Kweez threatened, raising the body to its feet. "Surrender is not an option. Your shadow has died, Arlowe, replaced by us. Our return is inevitable and with it, so too is your demise."

Ending their speech, the amalgam turned, launching their body into the air and far from the chaos they had wrought.

Content with the goblin and amalgam's retreat, Daria returned back to her familiar form, breathing a sigh of relief.

"I made a promise," she spoke under her breath. "Nothing will stop us from—"

The mage heard footsteps coming from behind her, though to her surprise, all she found was her loss of her consciousness.

*

"You're too soft! She's one of them! We've come too far to be sabotaged now!"

"Yer' outta line! She saved us, or does that mean nothin' ta' ya'?

"Having my life saved doesn't mean anything if I'm only going to lose it later on down the line!"

Daria awoke from her unconscious state, feeling the tight embrace of rope around her wrists keeping her mobility from her. Opening her left eye, she could see Onyx to one side of Arlowe with Schukara on the other, figuring them to be the source of the argument.

Gill was crouched to her side, holding a cloth to her right eye. The eleventh could clearly tell that she had stirred, though for some reason he kept it to himself, continuing to tend to her injury.

"So what're ya' suggestin'? That we kill her?" Schukara questioned, struggling to control her temper.

"I never suggested. I stated." Onyx's voice was cold; his remaining dagger was gripped tightly in his hand. "Put the pieces together. We found her travelling from the west with, at minimum one other necromancer whilst the Necromancer Rebellions persist and the Arcane Guild Murders are at an all-time high? Even if she's not connected, she still lied about her abilities, maybe more."

"Are ya' also gonna accuse the thousands of people that've fled north 'n' east due ta' tha' kharakians? Many of which I imagine *were* necromancers?" the mercenary replied, crossing her arms. "They're not all bad, contrary ta' what ya' believe."

"The current state of necromancers doesn't concern me. What does is that she handled that amalgam without breaking a sweat; something we couldn't do between the five of us, if you count Xanth. She was able to attain that transformation, her 'wraithic form', with minimal duress. That's something rarely seen amongst necromancers."

The assassin then pointed the dagger toward the mage. "To make matters worse, her wraithic form is that of a lich, the strongest wraithic form one can have. If she turns on us, we wouldn't stand a chance."

The elf spat at the assassin's feet. "Try ta' make it sound as noble as ya' want. Yer' not just killin' tha' one that saved ya', yer' puttin' out her life on speculation and fear alone."

"Maybe, but I'm willing to take that risk. We have enough to deal with. If she goes rogue, we're done." Onyx spotted Schukara's eyes wander, noticing that Daria had awoken. "Maybe I could make her talk."

The assassin began his approach towards her. "The guilt won't weigh on *me* at least."

Schukara wrapped her hand around Onyx's throat, partially lifting him into the air. "If you touch a single hair on that girl's head, I will slice what fingers ya' have left, one by one."

"That's enough!" Arlowe announced, bringing his allies in line. Schukara placed

Onyx back on the ground, with Onyx returning his dagger back to his sheath. "I've heard all I need to."

"Arlowe, listen—" A finger across the lips was all it took to quiet the assassin, with Arlowe moving past him towards the mage.

Daria kept her head down, unable to look the prince in the eyes. "Daria?" The only response Arlowe received was the girl struggling to hold back her tears, failing to hide them as they fell onto her lap.

The prince drew his blade, with only the sharp sound of its retrieval filling the air. "Arlowe, think about this," Gill uttered, taking his pained rib into his hand. "Are you sure it's wise to—"

"My decision is made." Gill was silenced, taking a step back from his friend. Arlowe stepped forward with his weapon loosely held in his hand. "I'm ready."

Daria lowered her head, preparing for Arlowe's judgment, though even after she heard the drop of his sword, she felt no pain.

Looking up, she found that he had instead cut her binds, returning the blade back to his sheath. The mage was lost for words. "Why...?"

Arlowe looked to her. "We've wasted enough time here," he voiced. "I want you and Gill to continue east. The last thing we want is to be out here if that amalgam returns. The closer we get to Wicilil, the better." The prince shifted his attention to the eleventh. "Can you do that?"

Gill nodded, aiding Daria to her feet before walking by her side, helping her shake off the stillness in her legs that being stationary had brought.

"Did you know?" Onyx posed.

"Xanth and I were suspicious," Arlowe responded, his back still turned.

"So you did know." The prince remained quiet. "Arlowe, she's a threat. She can't be

294

trusted."

"So, when are you going to stab *me*?"

"What?"

Arlowe faced his allies that had stayed behind. "I didn't know you were an assassin when we first met. I later found out that you lied to me. You knew I was uncomfortable with that. Due to our circumstances, and later our friendship, I wanted you to stay.

"She *knew* that I was uncomfortable about necromancers and she promised me that when we reached Wicilil that she'd be assessed by the Arcane Guild *knowing* that what she was would be revealed to me. She promised that we'd make it there safely. She kept us alive out there.

"I *know* that she's dangerous and I'm aware that you're not fond of necromancers either, more so than the rest of us, but that girl is *not* your enemy. Based on her age, she is clearly *not* one of the necromancers that fought you and your master and she is *not* someone to abuse due to *your* bad blood with them.

"Your points are justified, but I won't tolerate abuse to any of our own because of *your* beliefs."

Arlowe took a deep breath; the outburst was uncharacteristic of him. Onyx and Schukara stood silent, awaiting his next orders. "We need to catch up to Gill and Daria. There's still a lot of ground to cover and none of us are feeling particularly healthy."

The two said not a word, following closely behind him.

*

It didn't take long for Arlowe's band caught up with Gill and Daria, continuing east towards Wicilil. Though their trek was commendable given their circumstances, the skies were darkening, making travel much more dangerous.

"We should stop soon," Schukara called. "We've done well. I think we all need somethin' ta' eat 'n' a place ta' rest up."

"There's a mostly-concealed patch of land over there. High enough for a vantage point whilst giving us ample cover," Gill added, testing his sanamancy to find his hand glowing. "My magic seems to have recovered too. Once we're settled, everyone get in line. You all look terrible."

The camp came along in good time, even with tiredness and injuries plaguing the group. Across the camp, Arlowe could spot Gill asking Daria to sit and rest, though the mage would do no such thing, assisting with the construction of the camp despite his insistence.

"Stay still," Gill grumbled, treating the large bruise across Onyx's stomach. "It's going to hurt. You were slapped by a girl in armour."

"Not the first time," Onyx replied, winking.

"As a weapon." The eleventh slapped his injury. The assassin winced, though he chuckled through the pain. "Stay. Still."

"Could ya' hurry up?" Schukara mumbled, fixing up the group's meal. "Gill's our cook, but since yer' such a whiner, I have ta' step in."

Onyx whistled for Gill's attention. "Yeah, you'd better get back to cooking. Our specialty is killing things. The food is no exception."

As the rest of his group bantered though the night, Arlowe found himself further out, checking up on the mage that had isolated herself. Leaned against a tree, Daria was staring up at the stars and the three moons with her pack rested across her legs.

"You don't have to be here," she voiced, noticing Arlowe's arrival. "You have questions, don't you?"

Arlowe looked up to the sky for a moment, admiring the sight. "How truthful were you with me? When we met?"

296

"I was born in Caermyythen. I studied a lot. I didn't have many friends. My parents fought a lot. They tried to hide it to keep me happy, keep the image of a happy family, but I was always aware.

"Some of the other kids in my village took to bullying me. I never fought back. They'd heard of what happens to people that perform the necromancer ritual. They wanted me to be their subject and I was too much of a coward to fight back. Some of the others did the ritual too. Oscar was one of them.

"When the Necromancer Rebellions began, they all ran. I was too scared to tell my parents what I'd done, of what repercussions awaited me, and so I ran too."

Arlowe nodded to himself, noting the similarities. "And you survived out there? Like you told me?"

"I watched so many people die. Demons, guards, those that I *thought* were my friends. I didn't kill any of them, but I didn't do anything to change their fates either. I just watched. I'm a monster."

"You're not a monster," Arlowe stated gently, taking her attention from the night sky. "That's what they made you to be. Did you ever choose?"

"Choose what?"

"Choose anything? In your life?" Daria looked away. "After tonight, we'll be continuing on to Wicilil. I want you to come with us. Once you're there, you have a choice. You can either stay with us or you can leave us. If you decide to leave, we can visit the Arcane Guild and talk about your abilities. They harbour no ill will for necromancers who turn themselves over willingly. I knew one in—"

"I'm not going," Daria bluntly spoke. "I made a promise."

"You *promised* that we'd make it to Wicilil," Arlowe uttered, confused by her words. "We'll make it there."

"I also promised that I'd keep you safe."

"What do you get out of this?" Arlowe posed. "By aiding us?"

"I get to be by the side of those willing to stand up and make a difference." Daria paced the outskirts in frustration. "Not all necromancers want to be murderous conquerors."

"From what I've been told, peaceful necromancers are few and far between."

"And who told you that? Town criers and newspapers?" Daria queried, agitated at his assumption. "What about the necromancers working with the Arcane Guild? Working to bring peace? And what of those who are a part of the school yet detached from the conflict? Crypt keepers? Librarians? Even some priests are necrotic."

The prince held up his hands. "That's my fault. I'm sorry. I didn't know."

"I didn't know until I became one," the mage replied. "But now I do, and I don't want the lives of the necromancers who were killed for rallying peacefully to have died in vain. For the necromancers who were forced to torture criminals only to have it turned on them, to have died in vain. For the necromancers being murdered in the streets, who have abstained from combat against Grandgrave, to have died in vain. This rebellion has to end, but so too does the centuries-long discrimination."

"You may be damaged and broken, feeling alone," voiced the prince. "But, so do the stars. You burn bright for what you believe in. Don't lose that."

Daria blushed at Arlowe's kind words, hiding her face. "I'd like to be alone, if you don't mind?"

"Of course. Promise me you'll join us when you're ready?"

"I promise."

Arlowe gave a slight bow, leaving Daria's presence to re-join the camp and his group. As he got halfway there, three taps on wood drew his attention to Onyx, perched within the nearby tree.

"How long have you been there?" the prince queried.

"Long enough," uttered the assassin. "Just be glad you weren't here when I was trying to climb this thing." He waved his stump, hopping down from the tree.

"Are you against my decision?"

"It doesn't matter what I think." Onyx walked by Arlowe's side towards the camp. "Look, Arlowe, I'm sorry. For everything, recent and otherwise. I won't apologise to Daria for what I did; I still don't trust her. However, I feel as though I've let you all down. You, Schukara, Gill, Xanth. You trusted me even though you were probably right not to. I didn't return the trust."

"It's okay."

"No, it's not." He stopped, holding a book out to the prince. "Gill knows what I'm about and I've made Schukara aware too. Everything you need to know is in this journal. Take it."

Arlowe took hold of the book, though he kept it in the assassin's grasp. "Are you sure?"

Onyx shrugged. "Not really, but it feels right." The journal was urged into the prince's hand. "Just don't go looking for my real name. It's not in there. Being mysterious suits me just fine."

"Do I look five to you? Because you sounded *so* cool just then," Arlowe jested, nudging the assassin's arm. "You go ahead. I'll be back soon."

"Don't be late," Onyx warned. "If you miss supper, Schukara won't."

Arlowe nodded to him, watching the assassin follow his nose towards the welcoming scent of food.

Alone, the prince decided to flick through the journal, aided by the light of the moon.

Introduction to the Defiant, details on his late master, past contracts. "Pretty standard, for Onyx at least," he noted to himself.

As Arlowe continued to read, a familiar voice could be heard within his head. "Mm, Arlowe?"

"Good evening Xanth," he welcomed. "You were out for a while. How are you feeling?"

"My head hurts," the pterravun answered, sighing deeply. "There were so many voices."

"I know. I heard them too."

"What happened? Did we win?"

Arlowe paused for a moment. "No, we didn't. Daria fended the amalgam off. We'd all be dead without her."

"Huh? Daria did?" Xanth questioned. "How?"

"She's a necromancer, Xanth. She used her powers to keep us safe."

"I thought necromancers were bad?"

"Some are. I believe she's one of the good ones."

"I think I understand," Xanth spoke, still sounding unsure despite his words. "What's that?"

"Oh, this?" Arlowe brought the book closer to his face. "Onyx gave this to me. It's his journal. He wants to be more open with everyone. It's very detailed. We'll have to—"

Arlowe stopped, scanning the journal in more detail.

"What is it?" the pterravun asked.

"There are notes in here referring to the hunting of the Defiant. I didn't see this section. Some look written by Onyx, but others look older, possibly the writings of his master?" Arlowe read. His eyes were glued to the pages. "I've been seeing the word 'Altane' throughout the book, though it's most concentrated here. Does this Altane sound familiar to you?"

"I've never heard of it."

"Hmm, something to query Onyx about then."

The prince placed the book back into his backpack.

"So, are you done for the night?" Xanth let out a mighty yawn. "I imagine you could use the rest after today."

"Not yet," Arlowe replied, taking another book out to replace Onyx's journal. "I'd like to come visit you. I need to talk to your parents."

"Am I in trouble?"

"No, but it only occurred to me recently that I never asked about the history of your people." *The Submission of the Humans* rested in the prince's hands. "I have questions. I'll see you soon."

Chapter Sixteen:

"The most heartfelt moment can be all the more bittersweet."

24th Arandbern

Land's Legacy

2084∞ (Current Age)

"Interesting findings, young Arlowe. Tell us more of what you've found."

Conquest was leaning forward in his throne, sat between an equally interested Bela and Kaat; their subjects lined the sides of the chamber. Xanth stood closely by Arlowe's side, who was briskly leafing through his book, finding every corner that had been pinched.

"How old are you all, if you don't mind me asking?" Arlowe queried, looking towards the three monarchs.

"Fifty-three," Conquest answered.

"Isn't it rude to ask a lady her age?" Bela posed. "I'm thirty-three."

Kaat didn't respond, though the words eventually left her lips from the pressure of watching eyes. "Sixteen."

With barely a moment to spare, Arlowe replied to their ages. "Miner. Kitchen wench. Serving—"

"Stop!" Kaat questioned. Her lisp brought a smile to a few faces. "Our roles. H-how did you know our roles? I've never told a soul beyond mother and father!"

"I am curious also," Bela continued, standing from her seat. "How are you so informed? Surely a book doesn't have the answers that we can't provide."

"Not long ago, Xanth connected my mind with a friend of ours," the prince stated.

"Her name's Schukara," Xanth added, smiling at Arlowe.

"Right. Xanth spoke about himself, mentioning that he used to clean pipes and carry 'boom sticks'. Schukara caught on quicker than I did and passed this book to me. It contains documentation on the history of dwarven slavers and their slaves. Certain sections started to add up and your responses have only solidified that."

Conquest leaned back into his throne, pressing his hand to his chin. "I apologise, Arlowe but where are you going with this? We're aware of our enslaved origins. You could've just asked us. The soreness of the subject has long since passed."

"How long ago did you escape?"

Conquest thought to himself for a moment. "We escaped the dwarves three years ago."

Arlowe shook his head. "I thought something wasn't right."

"What do you mean?" Bela questioned.

Arlowe flicked to another page in his book, placing his finger upon the exact excerpt he needed. "There's a section here documenting a small collection of humans over a century before the disdogen accords were written up to ban slavery. They went missing shortly after their escape and were never found. That was over two millennia ago."

The chamber went silent. The pterravun people had no words. Conquest remained sat, staring to the ground, with Kaat leaving the room altogether.

"I-impossible," Bela muttered, looking at her hand. "That's *not* possible. It can't be. We escaped three years ago. I've counted the days."

"And you have no recollection of arriving at this place?" Arlowe posed, sensing the rising tension within the hall. "Of ever leaving?"

"Between the never-ending hallways and inactive portal, we've always been stuck here."

"But *how* did you get trapped here? What happened between you escaping and ending up in this cave system?"

"I... don't remember."

The voices of the pterravun people had risen throughout the chamber, filled with panicked questions and resignation of hope. Xanth held onto the bottom of Arlowe's gambeson, glancing around the hall with worry in his eyes.

"Everyone!" Conquest called, reining in his panicked people. "Please, lend me your ears!"

The pterravun calmed, though the anxiety in the room remained.

"Husband?" Bela queried.

Conquest placed his hands on the arms of his throne, lifting himself to his feet. The king took a few steps forward, his head raised to address the masses.

"I don't know what the gods have in store for us, or if they're even aware of our existence, but it is evident that we have a purpose!" declared the king with a sparkle in his eyes. "Through our unknowing intervention, we saved Prince Artaven, allowing him to strike back against those who stole his home and murdered his countrymen! We have been blessed to save those unfortunate in the past and stand ready to aid those who find themselves here in the future!"

Bela stepped forward. "Conquest is right! The lives we save, even unaware as we are, are creating a brighter tomorrow for those beyond us! Should we not continue that legacy until the end of time?" The crowd cheered once. "Should we not stand strong during their time of need?" The crowd cheered twice.

"And should we not party given the opportunity? Until our bodies give out?" Conquest yelled, bringing the crowd to a third cheer.

The chamber erupted with celebration.

Arlowe approached the thrones with Xanth, warmed by the positivity of the pterravun people. "I'm sorry that I broke the news to you all," he voiced, barely audible over the

304

sound of renewed partying. "Maybe it wasn't my place."

"No! There's no need for apologies, Arlowe!" Conquest bellowed, joining in with the festivities. "Who else would've told us? We knew naught, and while he knows much more than we do, Xanth was very much in the dark until you came along. You have our gratitude, not our disapproval!"

Xanth tugged at the prince's arm, acquiring his attention. "I'm still tired," the boy spoke, rubbing his eyes. "I'm gonna go rest. Don't go too far without me. I worry."

Arlowe rustled the boy's hair, kneeling to his level. "Don't worry, I need to rest too," he mentioned, letting out a yawn that infected the young pterravun. "Get plenty of sleep. I'll need everyone at their best."

Xanth nodded, waving as he strolled towards the hallways.

"Take care of yourself, Arlowe," Bela uttered, placing a hand upon his shoulder. "We'll be waiting for your return."

Arlowe paused for a moment, only turning once Xanth was out of sight. "Bela, can I ask a favour?"

"What is it?"

"Ending the kharakian curse won't be an easy task. I don't know if…"

"You're worried you may not come back."

"I know you're his mother, which is why this sounds so stupid, but if I don't come back, take care of him for me? He's quite fond of that room of his."

Arlowe advanced up the stairway towards the portal, focusing his mind. "He seems certain you'll defeat the kharakians," Bela called.

"I will defeat them," Arlowe answered, "but at what cost?"

*

Arlowe woke up the following morning leant against one of the few trees by their camp; his armour and book were rested nearby. Taking his time to stretch out the stiffness, the prince slowly re-equipped his armour, clipping every piece back into its rightful place.

Peering around as he dressed himself, the prince could see what remained of their camp from the previous night. Schukara and Gill had mostly packed everything up while Daria stayed out of their way, still appearing awkward from the events of the previous day.

Once he was ready, Arlowe made his way to the mage. His ears pricked up as he came closer.

"Are you humming?" he queried, concluding that the tune was coming from her.

Answering his suspicions, as soon as Daria was asked, the tune stopped. Her eyes falling back to the floor as they usually were.

"S-sorry," she murmured. "If I do it again, just let me know. I don't want to bother anyone."

"You don't have to stop. I liked it," Arlowe voiced, trying to meet his eyes with hers. "You must be in a better mood if you're humming? Especially a tune like that."

Daria lightly shrugged. "I like music."

"Were you humming a specific piece of music?"

"No, I'm just making up little lyrics in my head. Though my humming may sound reminiscent of..." Daria suddenly turned away. "I-it doesn't matter. I'm babbling."

"Daria, you're not boring me," Arlowe insisted. "Go on, speak your mind."

The mage finally brought her eyes up, appearing slightly more confident than before. "It may sound reminiscent of the works of Josef, the famed composer and conductor of the Ryvineon orchestra. I'm very fond of the aautgal's work. One particular favourite of mine is Josef's Symphony No. 4"

"I'm more partial to Josef's Wrejorick Minuet, followed closely by Symphony No. 2."

Daria seemed stunned. "You have an interest in…"

Arlowe smiled at her amazement. "It got me out of my shell."

"Hey, you two!" Schukara called, waving her hand. "Get over here!"

The two approached, surprised at the cleanliness of the camp.

"Morning to you both," Gill greeted, handing the elf her filled pack. "I hope you slept well. This should be our last push to Wicilil, especially with that amalgam still out there."

"Where's Onyx?" Arlowe questioned, looking around. "And where did Valerius go? I haven't seen him since the stalkers fled."

"Onyx is out scouting. Said he had a bad feeling," stated the eleventh. "Could just be paranoia, but I don't blame him."

"And Valerius departed just before tha' argument yesterday," Schukara added. "Healed himself up 'n' went on his way. Said there was no point in stickin' 'round where it didn't concern him."

The eleventh turned his attention to Daria. "How's the bruise? It's definitely faded," he examined, though Daria retreated at the attention.

"It's fine. It doesn't hurt anymore," she timidly spoke.

The eleventh reached into his pocket, pulling out an item Daria was all too familiar with. "Take this. You look starved." Gill urged the chocolate forward. "No offence."

Daria took the chocolate, placing it into her pocket. "Thanks. I'm not as hungry as I was, but I appreciate it all the same."

Gill spun his head, prompting the others to look in the same direction.

The eleventh caught the flailing of their assassin, waving his intact arm in the air. "I need you all up here! Preferably now!"

Gill turned back to Arlowe, tilting his head towards Onyx. "Arlowe, could you and Schukara see what all the commotion's about?" he posed. "Daria, would you mind helping me? I'm almost done."

The mage nodded. "I'll do what I can." She then spun to face Arlowe and Schukara. "We'll be right behind you."

The prince and the mercenary left the campsite, beginning their ascent of the large hill before them. Seeing their trek as a long one, Schukara felt it a suitable time to say what was on her mind.

"Hey, Arlowe?" she asked, preparing her words. "I... saw tha' book by yer' side earlier. Did you...?"

"I did."

"Sorry if I'm buttin' in, but I gotta know; was ma' hunch right?"

"I believe so. Their ages and job roles synced up to the content of the book, though there was a huge time difference between their accounts and the documents."

"How so?" Schukara queried. "A decade? Two?"

"Not decades," Arlowe corrected, "nor centuries."

The mercenary's eyes widened. "A millennium?" The prince gestured his thumb for her to continue climbing. "Two!"

Arlowe nodded. "They believed they escaped three years ago."

"I can't imagine."

"Neither can they."

Schukara shrugged. "As long as they took it well." Arlowe looked away. "They *did* take it well, right?"

"Not at first, but their king straightened everything out."

"Then what's botherin' ya?"

Once again, Schukara had seen right through him.

"Xanth? Are you awake yet?" The prince's mind remained quiet. "Most of my questions were answered. I didn't go in with many to begin with."

Schukara cocked her head. "What didn't ya' ask?"

Arlowe let out a frustrated sigh. "The book notes that green-eyed creatures have been seen in the dwarven undergrounds, yet when I asked if they'd found a way to escape, their queen said that they hadn't."

"And ya' don't believe her?"

"No, I do, but something doesn't add up. None of them remember what happened between escaping their captors and ending up where they are now. Furthermore, no one knows why they've seemingly been trapped in time and I don't even understand how they're alive down there. There are gaps in all of their memories and something about that, I don't know, it makes me uncomfortable."

"They saved ya', nursed ya', gifted ya' a friend in Xanth. Is it somethin' that *has* ta' weigh on yer' mind?" Schukara lightly punched the prince's arm, knocking him from his thoughtful state. "Whatever was found underground wasn't necessarily pterravun in origin. There're still demons trapped down there from tha' First Invasion. Their eyes come in all kinds of colours."

"And if it wasn't a rogue demon?"

The elf chuckled to herself. "Accordin' ta' Ma, Ava had dull green eyes. Ya' never know, maybe they found my sister squattin' with tha' dwarves."

Before their conversation could go any further, Onyx approached them, stopping them from proceeding to the top of the hill. "Arlowe..." he muttered, seeming concerned.

"Onyx?" Arlowe addressed. "Are you okay?"

"Y-yeah, I am," he voiced, struggling to look him in the eyes. "Look, I'd brace yourself. Both of you."

Without another word, the assassin returned back up the hill, leading the two to the top. It was only as they reached its peak that the prince understood why Onyx had warned them. "No…"

From the hill, Arlowe could make out a battlefield of corpses and craters, limbs laid strewn across the scorched lands missing their owners. Hilts were buried in the dirt, pushed much harder than by any brute force; the smell of melting flesh was still fresh.

Arlowe began to panic, for a moment remembering the war-torn streets of Eyenridge and what they had left in their wake. The kharakians had made it past the borders.

"By tha' Angels…" Schukara muttered. "How? They were contained…"

"They must've broken through somewhere," Onyx answered, looking over the torched horizon. "Just because they're here doesn't mean the whole border has fallen. It could've reformed."

"I thought we had more time…" Arlowe mumbled, bringing his breathing into check.

"Arlowe? It's not over," the elf assured.

The prince took a deep breath, regaining his composure. "Unless they contact me, Ryvineon is no longer an option," he declared, standing before his two companions. "We aid Wicilil in whatever way we can and then return to Thaedlon. Even if the border gains additional defences. The kharakians won't let up. All this time that we've been gathering aid, they've been growing stronger too. We can't give them any more of an advantage. They've come too far already."

"We're with you," Onyx voiced, readjusting his mask.

"Let's get this done," Schukara added. "Argestra's hurtin'. Let's pop this kharakian pimple."

Behind them, Gill and Daria had climbed the hill, looking out in horror over the eviscerated landscape. "We heard you on our way up," Gill commented. "Let us make haste."

Arlowe and his companions travelled into the midst of the destruction, seeing up close the damage of the kharakians, though they did not linger. Wicilil was in sight, though still far into the distance, urging them to a brisk pace.

Their surroundings were ominously quiet considering the recent conflict. The winds whistled through the barren battlefield, accompanied only by the sound of the group's footsteps.

"I didn't ask," Schukara noted, catching up to Arlowe. "How's Xanth? Is he feelin' alright? He didn't answer when we were speakin' earlier."

Arlowe shook his head. "Aiding us against Kaxrax exhausted him," he replied. "I got to see him briefly when I spoke with the pterravun, but he returned to his rest immediately afterwards."

"He'll be fine. Prob'ly just overexerted himself—" Schukara was cut off by an ear-piercing roar, filling the void of their surroundings with its displeasure. "What was that?"

"I can sense it. The amalgam has returned," the eleventh warned. "Run!"

The group paid heed to Gill's instruction, beginning the sprint across the charred field. This was not to last, however, as their adversaries had no intention of letting them escape again.

In the corner of his eye, Onyx was able to make out an object coming towards them, growing larger with each passing second. "Incoming!" he yelled, hoping to warn his allies in time.

Though the boulder made no direct contact with any of the group, some were still flung by the force of the impact, forcing them to recover before proceeding.

In that time, the hunter made its move, advancing upon them with a powerful leap.

Kaxrax landed with Arrsk upon their back; a plan was already in their mind. The monster found Daria, taking her into their grasp.

"Necromancer, what you did before," voiced Baxka. "Do it again. Strike us down."

Daria struggled, crushed within the grip of the amalgam. "I... can't," she mumbled, unable to free herself.

"Good," Arrsk noted, looking straight at his target. "No more interruptions then. Arlowe dies today."

The amalgam held up the mage, squeezing her ever so slightly tighter. "Let's cut to the chase," Rilit spoke, holding out their left arm. "We want you. Surrender to us and we'll let her go."

"Arlowe, I can't..." Daria strained. "If I stay, you'll get there safe..."

"What's it going to be?" Arrsk asked with a smug grin across his face. "We're gonna catch ya' anyway. Why not make it simple?"

Arlowe stepped forward, making his decision clear. "Let her go."

"Arlowe..." Daria muttered.

"Our plan hasn't changed. We're getting to Wicilil safe and sound."

Without a chance to brace, a huge burst of light erupted from their sides, blinding all parties. "Another ally, Arlowe?" Amizi questioned. "It matters not. Another plaything to rip apart!"

"That's not one of my allies!" the prince called. "Everyone, get down!"

A fireball emerged from the light, making contact with Kaxrax's arm.

312

Daria was released, though her right arm had been badly burnt from the fireball's detonation, clutching it in agony as she was dropped to the ground.

The light faded, revealing a new presence on the field. An alpha kharakian stood before them, materialising a molten spear into its hands.

"It was only a matter of time," announced the monster; the group raised their weapons as it summoned its own spear. "Face oblivion."

The alpha lunged, thrusting its spear forward. Arlowe blocked a strike intended for Daria, carving its spear-arm off with one deft blow.

Focusing as hard as she could given her circumstances, Daria fired one magic missile at the alpha, sending it through its other arm. Schukara charged against the defenceless kharakian to land the finishing blow, cleaving its head from its shoulders.

While Onyx and Gill were holding off the goblin and the amalgam, another flash of light appeared, with one of the injured kharakian bodies becoming another alpha.

In their blind spot, the alpha doused Kaxrax in flames, knocked down by one of the beast's powerful swings.

"Your quarrel does not concern us, cursed one!" Kweez yelled.

The alpha paid no attention, plunging its spear into the monster's torso. "All will burn," the alpha replied, materialising another spear to attack with. "That is our fate."

"We refuse your fire," Kivyx spat, stomping down and crushing the kharakian's lower half, before grabbing and ripping away its top half. "We refuse your fate."

With the previous alpha dead, another flash of light erupted nearby. The latest of the alphas charged directly for Arlowe, sending a fresh spear ahead.

"They're not dead!" Arlowe screamed, deflecting the projectile. "The bodies were dormant! Any can become an alpha!"

Blocking the beast's attack, the prince pierced its torso. "Onyx, Schukara, go on to

Wicilil and kill any kharakians still alive so we can—"

Kaxrax tackled into Arlowe and the alpha, knocking them both to the ground. "Is that all you know how to do?" Arrsk mocked from atop his monstrous ally. "Flee?"

Spotting the convulsing alpha, the prince leapt out of the way, watching the kharakian detonate in Kaxrax's face.

Arlowe turned to face his assassin and mercenary. "Go!"

Onyx and Schukara ran ahead, leaving Arlowe, Daria and Gill to hold off the amalgam and the unending alphas.

Another alpha approached from a nearby flash of light, creating a triangle of conflict.

"Aid us, cursed one," Baxka proposed, acquiring the attention of the glowing kharakian. "Arlowe is at his weakest. No equipment, fewer allies, a necromancer that refuses to fight and—"

The amalgam stopped. Every light in every socket peered down to see an injured kharakian grabbing at their leg. "What is the meaning of this?"

"You are a hindrance," the alpha stated, slamming its spear upon the ground. "Their fire will consume all. None are exempt."

A torn-apart kharakian tumbled down a nearby slope, dragging itself towards Kaxrax. Another had appeared by its other leg, latching on.

The goblin and amalgam looked around, seeing hordes of damaged kharakians dragging and crawling towards them, eager to take hold.

In response, the amalgam lifted its leg, crushing the head of the first that had grabbed them. "We reject," the voices called together.

"You have no choice. None do," answered the alpha, turning from them as the two became surrounded by kharakians, steeling themselves for the oncoming explosions.

The alpha faced the prince and his remaining allies. "We're glad you survived

314

Eyenridge, Arlowe Artaven."

Striking a nerve, Arlowe charged at the creature, evading its spear to cut it down with two well-placed swings. "I'm saddened that you did too."

The creature became nothing but dust, though as they had come to expect, another burst of light appeared, birthing a new alpha. "Follow us, Arlowe. Come into the fire."

Gill stood at the prince's side. "Go with Daria. Head towards the city," he insisted. "Fighting this alpha is pointless and Daria's arm is bad. The closer we can get to Wicilil, the better. I'll cover you."

Arlowe took the mage's good arm, begrudgingly leaving his fight against the alpha.

"You'll get your chance," Daria assured him, trying her best to ease his mind.

Gill ran closely behind the two, using his staff and removal of senses to ward off the advances of the alpha, only killing it when absolutely necessary.

The creature refused to back down, re-emerging from every angle, though the eleventh's senses and equipment had him one step ahead of their aggressor.

Another crash impacted before Arlowe and Daria, ceasing any further progress. Kaxrax arose from its jump scorched and damaged, though still able to throw its weight around.

"This ends, here and now!" their voices screamed, snatching Arlowe up into its hand before throwing him at the ground with a great deal of force. The voices screamed in excitement, conversing so much that their words were incomprehensible.

As Kaxrax raised its arm to deliver the lethal blow, an arrow hit Arrsk through the chest, knocking him from the amalgam's shoulder.

"Arrsk!" cried the monster, its body shuddering as the personalities within its bodies argued over their next move.

"Kill! Kill Arlowe!" screamed Rilit.

"But Arrsk!" Amizi cried.

"Arlowe's death will release us!" Kweez argued.

"But Arrsk won't survive!" countered Kivyx.

Fighting amongst themselves for too long, Arrsk had been grabbed by an injured kharakian, unable to wrestle free. "Kaxrax! Kaxrax! Help me! Please!" he whimpered. The kharakian began to convulse. "Kaxrax!"

The amalgam dived towards the goblin, taking him within their melded hands to shield him from the blast. Another kharakian took hold, followed by more and more, all ignited ready to blow.

"We do this together," the villagers collectively spoke, keeping Arrsk close as the explosions began, "or not at all."

A thundering choir of hooves sounded from the city, the group able to see Calaveil's banner coming closer. Riders from Wicilil had been dispatched, likely drawn by the explosions of the kharakians.

One of the horses came close to Arlowe, with Onyx dropping down by his side.

"Come on, up you get," he said with haste, lifting the prince to his feet and onto the horse. "Go! Get him to the city! Schukara, help me with the alpha!"

The assassin and mercenary held off the alpha's assault as Gill and Daria mounted the horses sent to escort, carrying them to the city's guarding embrace.

Shortly after, they too mounted the last of the horses, escaping the battlefield and the threats that had hunted them this far.

The alpha simply stood and watched as Arlowe and his allies made their getaway. "Soon," it pronounced, turning to dust as its previous bodies had done before.

The horses galloped swiftly across the fields and through the front gates, closed at once by the guards stood nearby. While some of the group dismounted by themselves,

316

others, such as Arlowe and Daria, were aided down by their riders, still recovering from their injuries.

"Thank you," Arlowe praised, assisted to the ground by the one who rode for him. "You have my gratitude."

"You're lucky we found you," the rider replied. "If you hadn't sent that letter, we wouldn't have known anyone was on those roads. Most see kharakian craters and turn the other way."

"Meriwa's right," called a monotonal voice from the stairs leading to the city. "I knew you wouldn't turn away. I had my soldiers keep an eye out. Good thing they kept an ear out too."

The group looked up, seeing an aautgal carrying a phenomenally large claymore across its back, clad in royal green attire.

"*Your* soldiers?" Arlowe posed. "May I have your name, my lord?"

"You can drop the formalities, Arlowe," the aautgal answered. "I worked as a simple enchanter in Seeleijae before gaining my position as 'Ass on Throne'. Call me David, or Dave, or, I don't know, that one aautgal everyone mistook for a statue during the royal meeting."

Arlowe looked to his companions, relieved that he wasn't the only one taken by surprise by David's less-than-royal attitude.

"I like him. Them. It?" Onyx commented, shrugging as everyone turned to face him. "The aautgal has charisma, what can I say?"

"Shall we walk?" David asked, leading the group through its city.

Though Wicilil was a sight to behold, the band's sights were set lower. The casualties of the city were evident, with many of its soldiers slumped along the steps and roads.

Occasionally, a medic could be seen bustling around, the men and women eager to ease the pain of their beaten and broken.

One soldier in particular, his armour scorched and shredded, had been banging on the door of a house the whole time; his strained voice and hard knocks on the wood echoed through the bloodied streets.

Feeling pity, Arlowe approached the man. "Sir, can I help you?" he offered, holding out his hand.

The man spun, grabbing the prince's arm tight, pulling him in close. "You're a traitor!" he screamed, shaking with rage. "You're just like them! Traitor! Traitor!"

Arlowe pulled his arm free, retreating from the crazed soldier. Like an actor who had finished their performance, the man returned from his rambling to the door, slamming at it begging to be let back in.

"Your intentions are good, Artaven, but there's no point," David conveyed. "His mind is gone, taken by the kharakians. He screams throughout the day, only stopping once his throat has given out."

"Surely there's something we can do," Arlowe insisted.

"That's his own house. His own door. Try explaining that to him."

"Go ahead without me," Gill voiced. "This is your business, Arlowe, not mine. I can be of better use tending to the wounded."

"If you'll have me, so can I," Daria replied. "I still have one good hand. I can help these people."

Arlowe gestured for them to go, following David further into the city.

"Sure would be *handy* if we had healin' powers too," Schukara commented, looking over at their assassin.

"I get you. I feel helpless walking past all these casualties," Onyx agreed. "Also, you said that on purpose."

318

"I assume you have a plan for the kharakians, and for us due to your appearance?" David questioned, breaking up the chitchat; its eyes were focused straight ahead.

"As my letter stated, we have the aid of Hietruce, Vexinth and the Administration, as well as having Quazin's aid across the border to halt their advance," Arlowe explained. "We didn't realise how bad the situation was. Once our negotiations are complete, we'll be returning to Thaedlon to begin the assault. Ryvineon's assistance is no longer an option."

"It wouldn't be anyway," David replied.

"What d'ya mean?" Schukara queried. "What's happened?"

"That's the problem," answered the stone king. "We don't know. Ryvineon's gone silent. Letters haven't been returned, public or otherwise, and the last time we sent a messenger, they didn't return. We would've investigated further if not for these pests at our walls."

"That's why I've heard nothing back," Arlowe deduced.

Climbing another flight of stairs, a loud crash sounded further ahead, quickening their pace to the top.

"The kharakians found another way into the city?" David shouted. "Impossible!"

Onyx listened to the chaos ahead. "Something tells me that's not the kharakians." The assassin nodded to his own suspicions. "Oddly enough, I believe there's something out there even *more* persistent."

The group reached the central point of the city, halted by a rush of citizens escaping past them. "Go! Flee! Our concerns lie not with any of you!" a goblin screeched over the masses.

"We want Arlowe!" a collective called, revealing a damaged amalgam at the city's stone centrepiece, now a pile of rubble. "No city wall will stop our march! The ends of

Äkin mean nothing to us!"

Spotting its prey, Kaxrax readied itself to leap. Schukara and Onyx reached for their weapons in response, though Arlowe stepped forward with his weapon comfortably in its sheath.

"Stop!" he called, pausing the creature for a moment. "Just, stop this!"

"Arlowe, what're ya' doin'?" Schukara barked. "That thing wants yer' head. Ya' ain't persuadin' it!"

The prince's weapon remained untouched. "You know my name! You've said it before!" Arlowe claimed.

"Arlowe…" Kaxrax growled.

"How do you know me?" he questioned. "You've known my name since our first encounter. Who are you?"

Gill and Daria appeared from behind them, drawn like the others. "How can that thing still stand?" Daria questioned. "First at the ruins and now here?"

"We're missing a piece of the puzzle. This has gone far beyond simply stepping foot in the wrong territory," Gill replied. "I imagine an answer will grace us shortly."

"You ran from our village, you ran from those ruins and you ran when we found you here," the chorus of goblins growled. For a moment, Arlowe was oblivious, though all at once the prince was reminded of his past, evident by the shaken look on his face. "That look. Now you remember."

"I do," Arlowe admitted.

Schukara came forward. "What happened? Why are these two huntin' ya'?"

"I told you before that I was rescued from Eyenridge by a band of Quazin mercenaries?" The elf nodded, reminded of the tale told in Haaroith. "I aided them in taking their camp back."

"Except that it was our home!" Arrsk called, drawing his blade. "They lied to you."

"You didn't question their motives?" Onyx asked.

Arlowe shook his head. "Not until it was too late."

"How many did you kill?" Daria queried, partially hidden behind Gill.

"One," he answered, struggling to keep his eyes from the monster before him. "Once I realised what had happened, I cut all connections with them. I placed a young goblin girl that I'd tried to save upon the funeral pyre. I refused their blood money."

"Touching, but pointless," Kivyx spat. "It must be a terrible feeling, being alive."

"Get off your high horse, Arlowe," Amizi added. "You were their enabler. You were just as instrumental as they were."

"You think that this admittance excuses you? Frees you of your sins?" Baxka questioned, appearing much calmer than the other voices.

"No," Arlowe uttered, moving closer still, his hands open to remove the possibility of another concealed attack. "My life is yours. I can't undo what I've done, but I can release you from your torment."

For a moment, the amalgam argued amongst itself, unsure of how to proceed following this odd proposal.

"We... don't understand," it replied after a momentary pause.

"There's a catch somewhere," Arrsk voiced, sceptical of the prince's words. "Spill yer' guts. What're ya' sayin'?"

"I think we can both agree that the kharakians still need to be stopped." Arlowe aimed his explanation at the goblin. "If I die, the amalgam will pass on. When that happens, *you'll* be all alone. Nowhere on this continent will be safe from them and I doubt that any dock would grant a goblin passage, especially if it gets out that you were the accomplice in the murder of a monarch."

"Then what do you suggest?" snarled Kweez. "That we wait?"

"For now. Let me make things right and I'll come to you without question."

"Kaxrax…" Arrsk mumbled, suddenly unsure of what to do.

The amalgam turned its gaze to Arlowe, forcing its hand into him with amazing speed, crushing him into the stone pavement. "We may never get this chance again," contended the voices. "We were never given a choice. Yours can rot as we have!"

Charging from the group, David lunged forward in an attempt to save Arlowe's life.

"Kaxrax, aautgal front!" Arrsk warned, granting the amalgam time to wind up a strike, directly hitting the king.

However, David stood strong, unmoved by Kaxrax's swing. "His offer is noble, beast! He knew not of you and lives with his regret!"

Taking advantage of the amalgam's surprise, David unlatched the claymore from the bindings on its back, bringing it down upon a weak point in the arm to sever it from the beast.

Kaxrax shrieked at the loss of its arm, freeing Arlowe only to lunge forward, swinging again at David, this time knocking the king down. "He also looked noble when he watched us die! His word means nothing!" Rilit howled.

Though Arlowe was able to get to his feet, aiming to reach David, Arrsk had watched his escape. The goblin tackled him back down to the ground with his dagger raised.

"Yer' not getting' away this time!" he yelled, stopped only by the prince holding back his wrist. "As long as you die, tha' villagers of Kaxrax pass on! You owe them that!"

Arlowe's allies prepared themselves to enter the fray, though David held them back, even as Kaxrax advanced upon him. "Now!" called the aautgal, signalling to the city.

Waves of Arcane Guild members had appeared from out of sight, lining the nearby balconies with spells prepared. All at once, the mages fired their healing magic at the amalgam, pinning it down with the powers of restoration harmful to the undead.

"No!" Kaxrax screamed, unable to drag itself any closer to its target. "No!"

A crossbow bolt struck Arrsk's dagger, disarming him. Another pierced his rib, knocking him down by Arlowe's side.

Though the goblin ripped out the bolt, already beginning to regenerate, Schukara had come to her companion's aid, aiding Arlowe to his feet whilst keeping her boot firmly upon the goblin's arm.

"Fuck you! Fuck you, fuck you, fuck you! You're gonna die, Arlowe! Nothing else matters!" Arrsk raved, struggling to free himself. "Nothing else matters!"

*

Once all had calmed, a caravan of golems had arrived to collect the defeated amalgam, with an additional golem equipped as a mobile prison to collect the goblin.

"Your collective ego faltered when it believed it could take on an entire city," David stated as it passed by them. "Take them away."

"Wait," Baxka mumbled, weakened by the magic of the mages. "Arlowe…"

Arlowe looked in their direction, though he did not speak. "We will never stop…"

"When all is said and done, I'll find you," he promised. "If you still see it fit, the debt *will* be paid."

As Arlowe concluded, the golems proceeded in taking the criminals away. Arrsk's eyes remained glued to Arlowe, only breaking away once the corner had been turned.

"Where will they go?" Gill asked as David joined them.

"While we do have a standard prison, that is used more for your run-of-the-mill criminals like the goblin," the aautgal responded. "The other one, or how many you wish to count, is headed towards our high-security prison. Each cell caters to each specific prisoner. That amalgam, for example, will be in a cell flooded with sanamancy on the regular."

"I apologise for bringing those two with us," Arlowe voiced. "I didn't think that they'd follow us this far out until I realised who they were."

"Well, they weren't too destructive, if we're comparing them to the kharakians at least." The king faced the broken centrepiece. "Still, I can't help but feel bad for that statue. Feels like I just lost a cousin or something," David jested, though its face betrayed no instance of humour.

"Guess tha' phrase 'face like an aautgal' is true," Schukara commented. "What now?"

"Now? Now we negotiate," David stated, holding its hand to the side. One of Wicilil's soldiers came forth, passing over a scroll for the aautgal to read. "Hm, this isn't good."

"Is there anything we can do?" the prince asked.

"Unless you have the ability to bring back the souls that the kharakians have taken from our city, no, there is naught you can do." David lowered the scroll. "I can't give you my whole army. Too many lie injured or dead. Our city would be vulnerable should the border fall again."

"A portion of your army would suffice," Arlowe bartered, folding his arms as he spoke. "If Kharaki falls, your city has one less threat to worry about and the Administration could regain lost profits caused by the kharakians, which can be used to aid your people and repair your city. Furthermore, the inclusion of your army would be respected by the other monarchs involved, making them more likely to move their border protection east towards Grandgrave."

Slowly nodding at Arlowe's proposition, David held out its hand again. The aautgal took a quill, scribing into the scroll before handing it back.

"I can't promise you how many Calaveon soldiers you'll have, though I assure you

324

that every one of our soldiers equates to three of any other," the stone king boasted. "Calaveil stands by you. Maybe the other countries will acknowledge me now. We need to come together more often, for everyone's sake."

"Thank you, David," Arlowe voiced, beginning to bow before remembering who he was speaking to. "We won't be departing yet. We still need to visit the Arcane Guild for more information on our enemy, though hopefully everything will be wrapped up within the afternoon."

David brought its claymore back into its bindings. "I was about to mention the guilds. I understand that you're already allied with Vexinth, which means that the Administration will be involved somewhere in all this, but I'd suggest asking for any additional aid in person. At this time, I imagine any extra hands wouldn't go amiss."

"That's a good point," Gill added. "I can speak with the Calaveon branch of the Eleventh Sense Guild. See if any of my colleagues would consider lending a hand knowing I'm involved."

"I can check up with tha' Warforged too," voiced Schukara. "I know I said I left a while ago, but a few of ma' old friends may be this way."

The group peered at Onyx. "Yeah, yeah, I'll check on my end," muttered the assassin, raising his stump. "Who knows, maybe I'll get sympathy aid?"

"I'll send word when I've gathered my men," David pronounced. "Don't keep us waiting. My wife says I'm very impatient. I'd rather you not prove her right."

The aautgal saluted, strolling towards the city's castle alongside its men.

"He's... It's... married?" Onyx questioned, baffled at David's statement.

"Face like an aautgal," Gill noted, shrugging. "No wonder it's illegal for them to gamble."

"They say size ain't everythin', but... wow. Lucky gal?" Schukara whispered, holding back her giggles.

Arlowe took a few steps up the stairs, elevated above his companions. "Let's get to work, everyone!" he declared. "We're low on time. Schukara, Onyx, Gill, meet up with your respective guilds, do what you need to and then reconvene by the Arcane Guild gates. Daria and I will meet you there."

"We'll try not to be too long," the elf replied, winking at Arlowe. "I don't wanna miss tha' magic."

"Hey!" Daria softly voiced, blushing as the group made her the focus of their conversation. "We were... going to the Arcane Guild anyway..."

"Go on, get to it!" Arlowe called, sending off his allies.

Onyx passed by Daria without a word, Gill patted her shoulder and Schukara, though still chuckling to herself, gave the mage a comforting squeeze on the arm.

"Sorry about that," Arlowe expressed, returning from the stairway.

"No, there's no need," the mage communicated, still recovering from her panic. "I can tell you're all close. I guess I'm just not accustomed to a group's banter."

"Well, if you decide to stick around, I'm sure it's something you'll get used to."

"Arlowe, could I...?" Daria moved forward, pressing her lips against the prince's before retreating backwards. The two stared at each other, both caught in the moment, both by surprise. "I want to stay. That's my choice."

Arlowe held out his hand, offering it to her. He was astounded by the glimmer of her purple eyes, the beauty of her full smile and the zest in her determination. "Stay a little longer?"

The mage accepted his hand, pulled into a tight embrace, warmed by their kiss. Foreheads touching, Daria pulled away slightly to look into Arlowe's eyes. "You know what I am," she whispered.

326

"I do. You're honest, you're kind and you're inspiring."

"That's not what I meant... Can we..."

"You've chosen to stay despite knowing how dangerous this is. You saved my life," Arlowe stated, taking a moment. "I trust you. My title means nothing if I can't have you by my side."

The couple kissed once more, remaining close to one another; their heartbeats played as one against their united chests.

"We saved each other," Daria corrected, speaking into Arlowe's ear.

"I guess, but you weren't the one nearly ripped in half. You almost had two of me," Arlowe joked, bringing them both to laughter. "That humming? From earlier?"

Daria cocked her head. "What about it?"

"Promise that you'll sing for me?"

"We're making a lot of promises."

"Promise!"

The heavens suddenly opened up around them, soaking the city and those stood within. Arlowe raised his shield arm, protecting Daria from the rainfall, though this came at the cost of being struck by it himself.

"On one condition," Daria voiced, her face changing to one of worry, placing her arms around the prince's waist. "Once this is all over, with the kharakians and the visions. Come back safe and I'll sing for you."

All Arlowe could offer in return was a smile of reassurance, taking her hand to escort the mage to the Arcane Guild, fully aware of the severity of their situation.

Chapter Seventeen:

"Lies can work as well as any illusion.
A chosen few can weave any to their liking."

24th Arandbern

Land's Legacy

2084∞ (Current Age)

Finding shelter from the pouring rain, Arlowe hid himself beneath an empty market stand awaiting the return of his necrotic partner. "Is this rain ever going to stop?" Arlowe posed to the clouded skies. "Really makes me realise that I took Fertral's weather for granted."

Taking him by surprise, the sky responded to his comment, speaking in an echoed, ghostly tone. "Youuu could buy an umbrellaaa. A shiiield with a hole isn't a good substituuute…"

The prince rolled his eyes. "You can't fool me like you did the amalgam, Xanth. I know you too well," he retorted, chuckling at the boy's attempt to fool him. "I assume you're well rested. You seem in good spirits."

"I feel much better. No more headaches," he answered, sounding as though he was stretching away the tiredness of his body. "How much trouble did you get into while I was gone?"

"What makes you think we got into trouble?"

"Because things always go wrong when I'm not around. I'm like a, uh, a good luck charm!"

Arlowe sat himself upon the stall, preparing his words. "Do you want the good news or the bad news?"

"Good first," Xanth replied. "I want to know that you're all okay."

"Alright. Arrsk and Kaxrax found us again."

"The goblin and the amalgam?"

"Correct. Luckily, with the aid of Wicilil and their leader David, the two have been isolated and locked away."

Xanth didn't answer for a moment. "That's good news. Why don't you sound happier about that?"

"Because… Do you remember that camp?" Arlowe posed. "We accompanied Vernard's men to take it back?"

"What about it?"

"Those goblins and that amalgam are one in the same."

"No…" Arlowe was waiting for more questions, which inevitably came from the curious child. "I guess… I guess it does make sense. Is there anything you can do for them?"

Uninterested in lying to his partner, the prince came clean, against his better judgment. "I promised them my life."

"What?"

"Their hatred is what binds them. Sacrificing my life means that theirs can be free. The only condition is that I need to make sure that Argestra is safe before I go. I won't leave it endangered."

"You were barely involved! They can't blame you for that!" Xanth exclaimed, outraged at his friend's statement. "That's not fair!"

"But they do, and though I can tell they're trying to keep their collateral damage to a minimum, their goal is still putting lives at risk, including the lives of my friends," Arlowe explained, trying to calm the boy. "Life doesn't have to be fair."

"And that was the good news?" Xanth huffed, frustrated at being unable to change the prince's mind. "What's the bad news?"

"The kharakians were here. We crossed a scorched battlefield to reach the city."

"They've broken through?"

"Apparently so. As a result, the king is currently in talks of how his armies will be split and then we're returning to Thaedlon. We're out of time."

"How is everyone?" Xanth asked, trying to change the tone. "Is everyone safe?"

"Onyx and Schukara seem a little shaken but appear to be holding up fine, Gill only came out with a few scrapes and though my back is killing me, I can't complain." Arlowe counted each ally on his fingers. "Daria's arm was burnt by one of the alphas. She's currently having it treated."

"Will she be okay?"

"Necromancers can regenerate and heal, though those same powers don't deal with anything superficial. I expect that—"

Whilst speaking of the mage, Daria had crept up on Arlowe, surprising him with her arrival.

"Hey, where did you go?" she queried, appearing confused. "You said you'd wait."

"I'm sorry. The rain got worse," the prince apologised, noticing the altered colour of her eyes. "Did they treat your eyes too? They're grey again."

Daria looked to the side, revealing their true purple colour for a moment. "If they knew what I was, they wouldn't help me," she mentioned, glancing back at the market. "The rainfall has lessened. Do you want to depart?"

Arlowe nodded, following her out onto the market, strolling along by her side. It didn't take the prince long to see the bandage, green in colour, covering the length of her forearm. "How is it?" he queried, gesturing his head towards the injury.

"Being undead has its perks. It makes it incredibly unlikely that I'd contract an infection, though I brought extra bandages to keep it clean," Daria replied. "I guess we should be lucky that the fireball hit *me*. My regeneration is speeding up the recovery."

"I'm sorry that—"

"Don't say it. There's no need. I made my choice."

Arlowe felt the weak touch of her hand upon his, gently taking a hold of it. "I like the colour you chose," he commented, bringing it close to a portion of his gambeson.

"Oh no, you caught me," she sarcastically remarked. "I was hoping you wouldn't notice. Looks like I'll need to hide my arm and the bandage."

"You don't have to hide anything."

"Arlowe, people don't need to see my scars."

"Shall I just cover my face then?"

Daria froze, remembering the scars resting upon Arlowe's face. "I-I'm really, really s—"

"Don't say it Daria, there's no need," the prince mimicked, revelling in the mage's muddle of words.

"B-but... I didn't mean... Are you—"

Arlowe stopped, halting Daria in place too. "Daria, relax. I was just teasing. It doesn't bother me."

The mage came closer, lifting her arm to move the prince's hair from his cheek. "How did it happen?"

Arlowe took her hand, helping her place it upon the scars. "A huge wave of kharakians pushed into the city once when I was younger. Escaping back to the castle, a kharakian ambushed me, though my mother fought it back. They wounded each other and the kharakian ignited. Being the fool I am, I rushed up to save her, though my father pulled me back. I survived, burnt, but she was gone."

"Do you hate them?" Daria asked. "After everything they've done?"

"I *did*. Not now though." Arlowe took a deep breath. "Now, I hate what my ancestors did. If they weren't so greedy, so power hungry, then their descendants wouldn't be suffering hundreds of years later. The kharakians are just enacting our punishment."

"Does your scar hurt? After all this time?"

"It does, and I hope it continues to. That pain reminds me of what we've yet to lose. It pushes me," Arlowe said with a smile. "In a way, it's why I'm here."

Daria pulled her hand away, placing it behind her back. "And you say I'm inspirational," she praised, motioning for them to continue. "And I know there's no need, but I'm sorry about taking your teasing the wrong way. I'm not used to being treated like this."

"Apology accepted," Arlowe voiced, waving away the awkwardness in the air. "Speaking of: how *has* the group been treating you? Well, I hope."

"Gill has been kind, even more so after finding out about my necromancy. I get the feeling that he's seen a great deal in his time, so I can understand meeting a necromancer wouldn't be so out of the ordinary for him." Her tone changed to one of appreciation. "Plus, the man has the right idea carrying extra treats in his pockets. More people should adopt that."

"What about Schukara and Onyx?"

"I really like Schukara, though I've noticed that she keeps her distance unless she has a reason to come close and then she retreats again," Daria noted, pondering for a moment. "It's understandable though. I hid something from her. She doesn't seem keen on those that keep secrets. She acts similarly around Onyx."

"And *as* for Onyx," she continued, "I don't know. It's evident that he doesn't like me. He won't talk or even look at me."

"Onyx and his master were constantly hunting and hunted by necromancers during the early years of the Necromancer Rebellions *and* the Sixth Invasion," Arlowe clarified. "That, and I think he knows not to pick a fight with you, especially after the power you displayed against Kaxrax."

"And what about me?" Xanth questioned. "I was one of our founding members, yet I remain forgotten."

"Xanth, you and Daria have never spoken," the prince answered. "Also, founding member? What?"

Daria stared into Arlowe's eyes, curious. "Ah, you're communicating with Xanth." She leaned in closer, mumbling to herself. "I imagine there has to be *some* kind of telepathic link. Is there any way we could extend that link to another person?"

Arlowe wiggled his finger in the air. "Xanth already figured that one out, first with Schu and then with Kaxrax. I can make contact to include you in the link, temporarily." He motioned his finger forward. "May I?"

Daria nodded. "You have my consent."

The prince lightly pressed the tip of his finger against her forehead. The mage let out a groan, covering her eyes as the connection was being established.

"Don't worry, the green will pass," he reassured; remembering the first time Xanth had connected with him. "It *is* disorientating at first."

Daria moved her hand away, revealing to Arlowe that the inclusion was a success, evident by the momentary shimmer of green from her eyes.

"Xanth? Can you hear me?" she asked, scanning their surroundings as if she was expecting him to appear from nowhere.

"Hello," he responded, seeming shy as usual. "You're Daria?"

"I am. I appreciate you connecting with me. I wanted to thank you for helping us with the amalgam. You were very brave to add your consciousness to theirs."

"I-I just did what I thought was best," Xanth stammered. "You're the brave one! You saved everyone from the amalgam! You were way more brave than me."

"It's not a contest, Xanth," Arlowe spoke, joining in. "You were both brave. You should both be proud."

"I'm glad you're with us, Xanth, and not just because of your contributions," Daria noted, covering a smile. "But because it also means Arlowe isn't completely insane."

The two began to giggle, struggling to keep them contained.

"I don't know," Xanth added. "Sometimes I wonder."

The mage and the pterravun burst into laughter, leaving Arlowe to visibly scoff, grinning at their jabs as they reached the gates of the Arcane Guild.

"Have you seen who we're allied with?" he posed to them, shaking his head. "I'll have you know that I'm probably the most normal person in our group."

"You're a prince!" Daria stated, still chuckling to herself.

"Ah, yes. All hail Prince Artaven, Lord of the Rubble."

"A title's a title, *Your Majesty.*"

Arlowe gave a bow, shoved through the gates by a giggling Daria.

Filling the visitors with relief, the city's Arcane Guild appeared relatively normal; it was a courtyard bustling with activity and progress. Researchers rushed to-and-fro whilst the students casually strolled to their next lecture, all watched over by the guild's vigilant battlemages.

Arlowe and Daria weaved through the busy courtyard avoiding the waves of members; all appeared too preoccupied to even notice them. Passing into the tunnel that would lead them up to the guild hall, the two were greeted by the battlemages, saluting them on their way up.

334

The two eventually reached the entrance to the guild hall, amazed at how high up it was from the courtyard. The entire city could be seen through the tunnel of glass, the citizens comparable to tiny ants.

"After that, I think I understand what David was saying," Arlowe spoke through gasps of breath. "If Eyenridge had stairways leading everywhere, I'd be three times the man I am too."

Daria sat at the top, waiting for Arlowe to finish the last few steps. "You may just be out of shape," she mocked.

"Or maybe you're… just incredibly healthy…"

"Would you say the undead are healthy?"

"Touché."

Entering through the archway to the reception desk, the two were saluted once more by another pair of battlemages, stalwart in their watch. Considering how high up they were, Arlowe was unsurprised to see that the guild hall consisted mainly of glass, offering a spectacular view to the other areas of the guild.

A set of training grounds sat at a lower elevation to each side of the reception; one with cover and one without, while the guild council chambers stood directly ahead of them, sat at the highest point.

"I'll only be a moment. Take in the sights," Arlowe voiced, sending Daria to see the views that the guild hall had to offer. "I'm sure Xanth would appreciate them over a reception desk too."

"We won't be far," Daria spoke.

"If anything comes up, let us know," Xanth added.

The prince moved his way up to the desk, waving to the desk attendant that, so far, had paid him no attention.

"Excuse me? I was wondering if you could help me?" The attendant said nothing, continuing to scribble away in her notepad. "Uh, I'm looking for the library. Do you know where it's located?" Like before, the attendant ignored him, refusing to take her gaze away from her notes. "Fine, uh, thanks anyway. Good luck with... whatever you're working on."

Keeping his eye on the receptionist, Arlowe returned to Daria who had been waiting on the opposite side of the room. "Are you two ready to go on?"

The mage cocked in head, baffled. "Go? Go where? What's wrong?" she questioned, looking over his shoulder at the reception desk.

"She wouldn't speak to me. Maybe because we're not a part of the guild? Still, very rude of her." Arlowe shook his head in frustration, leading them further in. "Looks like we're finding the library on our own."

The two traversed the campus, finding themselves in the central lobby, dining areas and living quarters before eventually finding the library.

Arlowe stepped inside, his eyes as large as dinner plates. "Oh my," he gasped, wandering further in for a better view. "How could I forget where we were? What we were headed towards?"

It was only as he stood within the library that Arlowe realised where he was. Floors upon floors of bookcases, all filled to the brim with tomes and documents of anything one could ask about, rested before him.

Both the height and length of the library seemed to go on unending; a jungle of knowledge to be explored. Arlowe was inside the Calaveon Grand Library, the nexus of all information from Argestra and beyond.

"I've always dreamed of coming here," he mumbled, overwhelmed by the gargantuan scale of the library. "I begged my father to let me live here when I was younger. I would call it the naivety of youth, but truthfully, my thoughts on the matter never changed."

"You didn't have anything like this?" Daria queried, as much in awe as Arlowe was. "Back in Eyenridge?"

The prince shook his head. "Looking at this, it makes me realise how underdeveloped my country really was. I wonder how far we could have really gone if the kharakians never existed. If the other countries had united sooner to end them."

Arlowe took a book from the nearest shelf, calmed by the familiar feel of its cover upon his hands. "My father knew how important learning was to me. He spent days building me a little hideaway, with lockers that I could secure my imported books in to keep them safe from kharakian attacks." He scoffed at his own words. "The other countries depriving us of their knowledge. Keeping books in metal lockers. What a mess."

"But at least you know its faults. You know what needs to change," Xanth expressed. "No one else has to go through what you did. What your country did."

Daria stepped forward. "And as for the other countries, you're uniting them *now*. This can't happen again. The tale of the prince, the envoy who brought his kingdom back from the brink of destruction, will double as a tale of celebration and of the dangers of disunion."

The mage took the book from the prince's grasp, returning it to its place on the shelf. "Come on," she urged. "We have a lot of library to explore."

Arlowe nodded in agreement, warmed by the support of his allies.

While the two searched for anything that could narrow their literary hunt, Xanth was able to catch a glimpse of an official looking desk to the left of the entrance. "What about that thing over there?" he questioned, making his companions aware of it.

"*That* looks to be the information desk. Thanks, Xanth," expressed the prince, turning to Daria. "Could you go and see if the library has some kind of catalogue?"

"I can do that," she replied, heading for the desk. "How will I find you?"

"Communicate with me through Xanth. Failing that, look down the aisles. I doubt I'll be far. For now, at least."

Leaving Arlowe to scour the aisles, Daria made her way to the desk in search of a possible index. Though she initially believed the information desk to be unmanned, the mage could make out a person in Arcane Guild uniform reading near the back wall.

"Excuse me. I was looking for a—"

The librarian shushed the girl, rudely cutting her off before pointing to a lofty book sat upon the desk in the far corner. Answering her request, the man then returned to his book, having no more time for idle chatter.

Daria's brow furrowed, now understanding Arlowe's comment on the rudeness of the guild's inhabitants. However, though a complaint wobbled on the end of her tongue, she held it, too uncomfortable with confrontation to make an issue of it.

"Arlowe, am I still connected with you and Xanth?" the mage asked, flicking over the pages of the immense book.

"I'm here," Arlowe replied. "Did you find the index? I'm having no luck searching on my end."

"Give me a second. If I'm reading this right, books on the kharakians should be on… library floor three, bookcase five."

"Could you also give me the location of books regarding dragons and sorvanc tribes?"

"Library floor one, bookcases four-hundred and fifty-three to sixty-one. Any reason?"

"Extra reading material. Meet me there?"

"I'm on my way."

338

Daria closed the index, shooting a look at the librarian before entering the pillars of literature and research.

"How long do you think it'd take someone to read all of these books?" she pondered, speaking out loud.

"Surely you wouldn't read all of them," voiced Xanth, causing the mage to flinch. "What's wrong?"

The mage took a breath, composing herself. "It's not your fault. I'm still getting used to having a voice in my head. I wasn't expecting you to answer my question. I was posing it to myself."

"Oh."

Daria felt as though her words had come out wrong, not intending to hurt the pterravun's feelings. "I can pose one to you though! What's your favourite kind of book?"

Xanth thought for a moment. "Outside of a few medical books down here, the only book I've read is one that Arlowe gave me. It was about the kharakians."

"Okay then, what books would you read if you had the choice?"

"When I first met Arlowe, he drew a map in the sand," Xanth recollected, sounding enthused at the memory. "I enjoyed learning of your world."

"You'd like geography books then. Bestiary and botany books may also be—"

"Daria, look ahead!"

Waking from their conversation, an orc in guild uniform was bolting towards her, with the mage barely able to evade out of his way.

"Hey!" Daria exclaimed, slamming her shoulder into the wooden bookcase, receiving no apology for his lack of warning.

Shortly afterwards, Arlowe had turned the corner, hastily looking around before spotting Daria, rushing up to her.

"Are you okay?" he questioned, knelt by her side.

"I'm fine, don't worry about me," Daria answered, rubbing away the pain of her injury.

"Did you see which way he went?"

"He carried on towards the library entrance."

"He looked familiar…" Xanth voiced.

Arlowe nodded at his statement. "There was an orc at Haaroith's guild hall. Ushnar. He ran when I saw him. I need to speak with him."

"He couldn't have gotten farther than the central lobby," declared the mage, leading the prince into the connecting hallway. "Why would he run?"

"I thought he perished back in Haaroith at the hands of the dredges that were unleashed there, yet he's here alive and well," Arlowe replied, kicking open the doors to the lobby. "If he's alive, he's a suspect."

The two looked over the multiple floors, with Xanth catching sight of Ushnar higher up. "He's there, on the next floor up!"

"Someone, grab that man!" he exclaimed, though his declaration was seemingly ignored by all.

The guild members continued to saunter through the lobby. Xanth's voice emerged in their mind. "Why are they not reacting?"

"We don't have time for this. Daria, head up here and follow him. I'll cut across the lobby and see if I can get ahead," the prince instructed. "He's important to the Arcane Guild murders. We need him alive!"

Daria took the stairway to the upper floors, hot on the orc's heels. "Stop!" she called. "You're important to the investigation!"

"The investigation can stew in Erethys for all I care!" yelled the orc, winded in his speech. "I applied for a transfer for my own safety, almost perished for lending a hand and now I'm being labelled as the Arcane Guild Murderer? They'll leave me to rot in a cell until proven otherwise! I just want to be left alone!"

Ushnar took a left turn, heading up the stairway towards the council chambers, though Daria turned the corner to find the orc stopped dead in his tracks with Arlowe waiting atop them.

"I knew you'd come this way. There's nowhere for you to go," he declared, slowly descending. "If you're not the murderer, help me find them."

The orc clenched his fist, sprinting forward. "How do I know that *you're* not the murderer?" he howled, thrusting his fist forward.

Reacting to his aggression, Arlowe dodged back before going to grab him, only for Ushnar to dissipate, replaced by another behind him. "Get away from me! Let me go!"

Arlowe and Daria ran into the chambers to see Ushnar stepping onto one of the open windows. "He's going to jump!" Xanth called. "Stop him!"

"Ushnar, wait! It doesn't have to be like this," the prince pleaded, holding out his hand as he slowly advanced to the window. "You're not alone. I've been wrongly accused too. We can get through this together."

The orc shook his head. "No, we can't," Ushnar uttered; tears filled his eyes. "I believed that I could make a difference, show my name in a new light. All I've accomplished is that I've dragged my name further into the mud."

"And you can't change that if you jump. Let us help you."

Ushnar looked away for a moment, only to shake his head in disapproval.

"It's apparent that I'll be a threat wherever I go, there's no changing that. I just wanted to make my family proud. To make my damn kid proud." The orc's fingers loosened their grip. "I only wanted to belong."

Though Arlowe rushed forward, his hand fell short. Time slowed for the prince, seeing the same resignation in Ushnar's eyes that he had only a few weeks prior. The orc continued to fall away from his reach, uninterested in retracting his suicide, falling from sight to the ground far below.

Arlowe closed his eyes, grasping his forehead whilst letting his frustration out in one pent-up scream.

"You did everything you could," Xanth spoke, trying to comfort his friend.

The pessimist on Arlowe's shoulder had a thousand things to say, though the prince turned to his other for the boy's sake. "He'll be remembered. Maybe not by many, but by us. Wherever he is, I hope they take him in with open arms."

"Arlowe…" Daria whimpered, stood by one of the Arcane Guild Councillors. "Look…"

Daria moved her hand from left to right, moving through the Councillor's body with no complication. The mage then cast a spell, revealing blood along the walls and corpses slumped around the room.

"They were hidden," Xanth deduced, looking over the bodies. "Is the whole guild covered in an illusion?"

"Xanth, eyes shut until I knock on the doorframe," Arlowe uttered, walking towards the entryway. "We need to alert the Calaveon guard of what has happened here."

Daria remained in the hall, still looking over the unfortunate victims. "Shouldn't we do something?"

"It's out of our hands," Arlowe spoke, sounding disappointed. "We did what we could. The guards will take over. The spell will be removed, and the families will be notified of their losses. Come on."

342

The two slowly made their way back to the reception. A slither of discomfort travelled down their spines from the awareness that they had been surrounded by the murderer's handiwork at every given moment.

"Why do this?" Daria murmured, traipsing through the guild hall. "Is peace not an option?"

"As much as I wish it was, it's not that simple," Arlowe replied, holding the door to the reception open for the mage. "I once read, *the freedom of thought is as much a blessing as it is a curse, both from which we'll never be free. As long as that remains, there'll never be peace.*"

"Who said that?" the mage asked.

"Bromley Artaven, the first Artaven of Eyenridge."

The two re-entered the reception, hearing commotion from the other side. "Who's here?" Xanth queried, watching as his friends grew closer. "Is that…?"

In the distance, Arlowe could make out Caspus, stood alongside a handful of guards and two more members of the Arcane Guild. One of the guards was walking back and forth, bringing the battlemages they had met earlier to repeatedly salute.

"Pre-programmed illusions," Caspus examined, signalling to one of the mages. "I thought something was off. Remove it."

Following orders, the mage waved their hand, removing not only the battlemage illusions, but also the illusion of the whole room, unveiling the corpses hidden within.

Barring the janitor, those within the room recoiled, stunned at what was uncovered.

Caspus turned to the stairway, spotting Arlowe and Daria at the top. "Arlowe? Why are you here?" he questioned. "You appear to be leaving, and with another no less? Interesting."

The prince came before the janitor, followed closely behind by his necrotic ally.

343

"Daria, this is Caspus, the head janitor of the Arcane Guild. Caspus, this is Daria, one of my travelling companions."

"Greetings," he pronounced, offering a slight bow. "I did recall there being more of you."

"They're off dealing with their own tasks."

"And what are *you* doing *here*?"

"Following my meeting with David, I came here with Daria to find information on the kharakians," Arlowe stated, taking note of the janitor's untrusting gaze. "While in the library, I came across Ushnar who ran once I had noticed him. The chase took us to the guild's council chambers, where the orc jumped from one of the windows, evading capture."

"And then you decided to leave?" Caspus posed, crossing his arms.

"And *then* we decided to contact the guard once we realised what had happened," the prince argued, trying to counter Caspus' accusations.

The captain of the guards marched forward. "We'll have to ask you and your partner to stay put until we've done a sweep of the grounds, sir. If you're here, you're involved," he stated, sending his men and one of the mages up the stairway towards the central lobby. "I'm sure you can understand this being a delicate matter."

"When did *you* get here?" Arlowe posed to Caspus. "And why do you have an entourage of guards with you? Were you expecting something to happen?"

Caspus showed a brief smirk, scoffing at Arlowe's questions. "I got here yesterday afternoon, where I took refuge in a nearby guest house," he answered, his face returning to its more aggressive look. "As for the guards, their patrol brought them this way, so I asked them to accompany me. I'm glad I did."

"Did you know Ushnar was alive?"

"Ushnar? The orc that transferred to Haaroith?"

"Yes."

"How would I have known of his wellbeing?" Caspus spat. "I got him to the guild as I was asked, nothing more. I'm a janitor, I don't hold a register of every member."

Before Arlowe could go on, two of the guards returned to the reception escorting a traumatised member of the Arcane Guild.

"We've swept the guild council chambers. Councillor Einluthor was the only one we found alive," one of the guards announced, gently lowering the Councillor onto a chair in the corner of the room. "Apparently, the Councillor heard a scream from the chambers and hid inside one of the laboratories until we found him. He estimates that he's been in there for a few hours."

"Did he see the murderer?" Caspus questioned.

Einluthor shook his head, sobbing into his hands. The other guard knelt by the Councillor's side, taking his shoulder.

"He did not," continued the guard. "The Councillor did hear the screams of what he believed to be banshees. That would explain how so many lost their lives here."

"Banshees," Caspus pondered. "There seems to be little environmental damage minus the windows. Banshees would make sense."

"So this was another necromancer attack?" Daria queried, acquiring the attention of those around her.

"Yes, I believe it was," uttered the janitor, turning to one of the mages beside him. "You. I require your aid again."

The mage stepped forward, placing a spell upon Arlowe.

"What is this?" the prince demanded, feeling no ill effects from the spell. "What do you think you're doing?"

"Narrowing our search," Caspus growled, gesturing for the mage to continue, moving on to the prince's companion. "Now, to her."

Daria looked to Arlowe fearfully, realising too late what spell was being cast upon her. "Wait, don't—"

Casting the dispel, Daria's illusion had been broken, revealing her purple eyes and black veins to those within the room.

"I thought so. Guards, seize her," Caspus ordered, giving Arlowe a look of disgust. "Even if the prince is involved, he'll gain impunity until his crusade against the kharakians is complete. The same cannot be said for the girl."

"You've been at every crime scene too!" Arlowe yelled, stood between the approaching guards and Daria. "*And* you have a connection with Ushnar, who conveniently disappeared during the massacre of the Haaroith Arcane Guild!"

Caspus rolled his eyes, droll in his tone as he repeated the same alibi. "As I've mentioned in the past, I'm the head janitor. I must travel between the guilds. It's my job."

Arlowe gritted his teeth; he was losing his ground. "And what of the orc?"

"What of him? He may be involved, but he doesn't stand here now. You two do. Your necromancer ally can be kept in custody until we know for certain that she is not involved whilst you stand in the middle of the continent's combined armies with a few thousand eyes on you, at minimum," Caspus explained. "Now stand aside!"

One of the guards barged his way past the prince, aiming to take Daria's arm. She held him back with her necrotic strength, though it wasn't the pleading of innocence that was to spill from her lips.

"Hold on!" she contended, forcing herself forward with her arm outstretched. "You didn't narrow your search enough!"

Though Caspus had come forward to aid the guards, the spell that Daria was pressured to cast had caused an adverse effect on the janitor, bringing him to the ground at once.

"What did you do?" questioned the nearing guard, ripping her wrist out of the air. "Assault and resisting arrest are crimes that—"

"Yoskolo, wait," uttered the other guard stood by Arlowe. "What's happening to the guild halls?"

Examining his surroundings, it didn't take Arlowe long to spot the guard's observations. Though the guild beyond the entrance hall appeared clean, with not a single item out of place, a fading illusion revealed an entire guild fallen into disrepair; the bodies of the guild's members filled the macabre scene.

The collection of guards returned from their patrol, bursting through the door. "What is going on?" the arriving mage expelled in anger. "I was removing the illusions piece-by-piece for the guards when it all came down at once."

"Daria, what did you do?" Xanth asked, though he found the mage unaware of his question. "Is it possible that Caspus and the illusions were linked?"

"What did you do to him?" Arlowe posed to Daria, still looking over Caspus' lifeless body.

The mage took her arm back from the guard, rubbing away the pain of his grip.

"I only used a dispel on him. I don't understand why he—" Another layer of illusion faded. Caspus now carried a scythe across his back with black veins adorning his hands. "Is he…"

The guard nearest to Arlowe knelt down, turning the janitor over, lifting his sleeves and opening his eyelids, nodding at his discovery.

"He is," the guard stated; disapproval filled his tone. "The Arcane Guild's head janitor is a necromancer and we've been letting him in and out of investigations, back and forth across Argestra."

"Let's not get ahead of ourselves now," Yoskolo spoke, standing by his partner's side. "Just because he *is* one doesn't mean he's the one—

A small gurgle brought their attentions to the examining guard, now propped up by a scythe penetrating his throat. Caspus' weapon was swiftly removed, allowing the body to fall down face-first into its own blood.

"Qimmiq, no!" cried his partner, drawing his axe and shield. Caspus lazily turned to the guard, unfazed by Yoskolo's grief. "Your life is forfeit, you undead bastard!"

Yoskolo charged forward, rallying the guards and mages by his side to attack Caspus in honour of his fallen friend.

"No witnesses," mumbled Caspus, sluggishly poising himself to cast a spell.

Before the guards could swarm the head janitor, their way had been blocked by a prenomen; its wrappings writhed in excitement for a new hunt.

"Nearest guards, hold the line with me!" Yoskolo declared, defending his allies from the beast's assault. "Back line and mages, focus on the janitor and—"

Cutting off the guard's orders, Caspus' scythe cut through his beast, digging itself into Yoskolo's skull, ending his life.

"Pointless," Caspus uttered, walking by the prenomen. One of the wrappings pulled his scythe from the guard's corpse, returning it to its master. "Kill them all."

Arlowe rushed into the mayhem with his weapon drawn, only to be stopped by Caspus as the prenomen leapt into the midst of the guards, dissolving their ranks to pick them off one by one.

With blinding speed, the janitor hit the prince's hand with the metal of the scythe's handle, stealing his sword to throw it to one side before forcing him back with the

348

scythe's edge.

Daria fired a magic missile at Caspus, though in another feat of speed, the janitor cleaved the dart in two, shocking them both.

"This is a waste of time," Caspus slurred, backed up by his prenomen who had finished with the guards, absorbing their energy.

"Why are you doing this?" Arlowe questioned, returning to his feet. "What do you stand to gain from this?"

"Why would I tell you?" the janitor replied, appearing ready to doze off. "You'll all be dead soon anyway."

One of the mages by Daria had a hand filled with ice behind his back, launching it at Caspus only for the prenomen to block it, flash-freezing the tentacles.

Using one of its remaining pieces of flesh, the prenomen whipped the skin around the mage's throat, crushing his skull into the ground.

Thinking fast, Daria fired a wave of healing towards the prenomen, stunting the recovery of its limbs.

"Finish them off," Caspus instructed, sending the near-fleshless prenomen to deal with Daria and the last surviving guild mage.

"Call it off!" Arlowe demanded, barely avoiding the janitor's swings.

The prenomen grabbed the mages with a tentacle each, bringing its arms to its torso.

"It's releasing its energy!" cried the remaining mage, struggling to free herself from the undead's hold. "We're trapped!"

Daria used her sanamancy to burn away the wrappings, though the stunting of the prenomen's regeneration had ended. The creature took them in with a new ensemble of tentacles. Its power was becoming visible, felt by those within the room.

Daria fired another wave of healing at the prenomen, burning away the tentacles before stealing away the frightened mage. "We need to retreat back! We need to help—"

The prenomen rushed forward, taking one mage in each hand, slamming them into the wall. Though Daria released every bit of sanamancy she could, visibly burning the creature, the prenomen refused to budge, so close to unleashing its energy.

"Agh, get off!" she screamed, unable to move.

Caspus prepared his frail body to strike again, though in his pause, Councillor Einluthor leapt across his back in a futile attempt to restrain the janitor.

"Stop this unnecessary bloodshed!" he shouted, though the councillor's plea had fallen on deaf ears.

Caspus broke free of his hold, elbowing Einluthor in the nose with enough force to incapacitate the poor man.

His sacrifice wouldn't be for nothing; Arlowe found a much-needed distraction. The prince placed his boot onto the janitor's knee, breaking his leg with a well-placed kick.

Surprisingly, Caspus showed no sign of pain, clambering onto his good leg. "This is disappointing," Caspus moaned, letting out a sigh.

Darting forward, Arlowe judged the length of Caspus' swing, dodging backwards to avoid it before advancing further.

Deflecting a blow with his shield, Arlowe took the scythe from the janitor's weak grip before delivering a powerful uppercut, knocking Caspus down.

Running out of time, the prince moved the blade of Caspus' scythe around the prenomen's right leg, severing the foot to topple it.

The prince then pulled the mages to one side before gripping the creature's neck, directing the body and its energy away from them. "It's over now, you—"

His hand reached for his own weapon; his sheath was empty. He had no means of ending the beast's life. "Daria, my blade—"

Using the last of its strength, the prenomen pulled Arlowe under its skin, turning its sights on the now-revealed councillor.

"No! Stay away!" yelled the Councillor, backing himself up to the wall.

With not a moment to spare, Daria took the staff that had rested over her back, lobbing it at the prenomen with as much force as she could muster.

The creature was unperturbed by the girl's attack, plucking the staff out of the air and away from her grasp. It was only as a surge of healing magic flowed through the stolen weapon that the prenomen realised the trap it had fallen prey to.

The prenomen screamed in pain, dropping to its knees from the searing agony. Disrupting its skin, a steaming Arlowe dropped out of the thrashing tentacles, coughing as he weakly lifted himself from the ground.

"Arlowe, the axe!" Xanth called, spotting Yoskolo's weapon by his side. "Get it!"

The prince took the axe, slicing away a stray tentacle before plunging the weapon through the prenomen's neck, watching as the beast dissolved back to the vault.

At last, there was peace. The janitor was beaten, his summoned undead dispatched.

Daria inspected the fallen Caspus, comparing her injuries to his. "Your leg is still broken?" she questioned, unable to see any of his wounds closing or healing. "Why are you regenerating so slow?"

"That was close," Xanth commented, watching through Arlowe's eyes to see more guards arrive at the guild hall reception, barring the entrance. "Tell Daria to illusion up before the guards see her."

The prince nudged his necrotic companion, gesturing to his eyes and arm. Daria nodded, casting a spell upon herself before joining Arlowe and the guards around Caspus.

"Well, look at that boys. Survivors," announced the guard at the front; her helmet was decorated in fur trims denoting of a higher rank. "Bringing trouble with you, Arlowe? It's barely been twenty-four hours."

"I'm sorry, I don't think we've met," Arlowe replied, offering his hand.

The guard removed her helmet, revealing the rider who had saved him earlier that day. "Like David said, you can drop the formalities. It's Meriwa."

Meriwa sat herself upon the reception desk, taking a small cylindrical item from her pocket. The object was lit with her finger before putting it to her lips. A puff of smoke blew into the air.

The small wrapping was then offered forward. "Snaps?"

Arlowe waved away the offer. "No thanks. I'd rather live longer than thirty."

Meriwa chuckled, taking another drag from the root. "I'm a guard living in a world filled with demons, necromancers and whatever else Arn thought was funny to include. If I die from a pack of snaipzroots, I'll have lived a good life," she commented, letting out another breath of smoke. "Enough about me; what's going on here?"

Arlowe recounted the events that lead them to the injured janitor, who was propped up against one of the benches remaining perfectly still and silent. "You arrived not long after," he finished, tying up his tale. "I believe that's everything."

"Really? So, we have the Arcane Guild Murderer at last!" Meriwa celebrated, pressing the snap against her chest plate to put out its flame. "Anyone got anything to add?"

Arlowe tensed up, keeping Daria's magical capabilities out of his account. The prince looked over at Daria and the one surviving mage, both shaking their heads at Meriwa's question, with Daria shooting a look of concern over to him.

"I have a request, if you would hear it," came a voice from the corner of the room,

352

turning everyone's attention to Councillor Einluthor, finally approaching the rest of the group.

"And what does the surviving egghead have to say?" Meriwa posed, hopping off the desk.

The councillor wiped the blood from his now-crooked nose, nabbing a handkerchief from his front pocket. "Reports have reached the guild claiming that Eyenridge's monarch has been under a hefty amount of scrutiny since his forced departure."

"What's your point? You're ascending the hills to reach the capital."

"Most of the reports against Arlowe were signed by Caspus Molvo. Clearly the janitor was trying to turn the investigation elsewhere whilst he butchered most of the council and half of the guild as a whole."

The councillor cleared his throat as he looked out over the desecrated guild. "My point, if I may be so bold, is that I personally vouch for the innocence of Arlowe and his company and wish to offer him a formal apology on behalf of the guild."

"You know that your vouch doesn't remove them as suspects, right?" Meriwa explained. "The courts clear everything, not us."

"I don't expect it to."

Meriwa shrugged, patting one of her guards on the shoulder. "Right, well, we'll escort the murderous janitor to the lock-up and then begin the clean-up," she stated, turning to Arlowe. "Good luck with the kharakians. You'll need it. Maybe I'll see you in Thaedlon."

Arlowe nodded, watching Meriwa and her guards funnel out of the guild, leaving only Daria, Einluthor and himself.

"Thank you," Daria expressed, showing a smile for the Councillor. "Why did you—"

"Just go," Einluthor muttered, cutting off the mage's words. His eyes were still pointed towards the horizon. "I... have nothing else to say to you."

Daria fumbled, her smile dropping from her face. "I... don't understand."

The Councillor spun; rage filled his eyes. "The only thing that is stopping me from reporting you to the authorities is that you brought down another of your kind, tarveins," he asserted, cursing her through his hushed teeth. "Life has never been kind but having your mockery of it walking the same streets is unacceptable. Even uninvolved, death follows you all."

"Now you listen here—" Arlowe spat as he came to Daria's defence, though her hand halted him, allowing the Councillor to storm off. "Daria?"

"It's okay. He's right," she mumbled. "Do you remember what I told you?"

"You're not all conquerors."

"Until I can prove him otherwise, what is there to say?" she sighed, defeated. "I'll meet you at the bottom. Don't forget your sword."

"Daria, I..." Arlowe watched helplessly as the mage began her descent to the courtyard, unable to find the words to stop her. "Great job, Arlowe. That was the perfect time for your mouth to go dry," he hissed, criticizing himself.

"Your sword is over near the window, to the left," Xanth mentioned, keeping his voice quiet. "Do you want me to go for a bit?"

Arlowe shook his head. "No, you're okay. There's no need to go," he communicated, rubbing his temple. "It's just, sometimes I can be such an idiot. Daria needed me then and I buckled."

"When my sister gets upset, I give her some space first. Then I ask her how she feels later."

"I thought you didn't like your sister?"

"I don't like her, but I don't hate her. She's my sister," Xanth stated. "Sometimes people just need some time to think. Maybe Daria does too."

Arlowe sighed, nodding along to Xanth's words. "You are wise and kind far beyond your years, Xanth. Maybe some of it will rub off on me." The prince glanced around, unable to locate his missing weapon. "You said left, right?"

"No, left," Xanth giggled.

"Very funny. I see it." Arlowe found his blade amongst the shattered glass of the windows, noticing a peculiar detail of his sword. "What the…"

"What is it—" Like Arlowe, Xanth had paused upon realising what had been seen. "Where did that come from?"

Upon Arlowe's blade rested a coating of blood, stained onto the metal.

"I don't know." Arlowe scanned the floor where his blade had been resting. "There's no blood here and I know *I* didn't use it."

"Are you sure?"

"I'm positive," Arlowe replied, feeling down the cold edge. "It's dry."

"Hmm." Xanth had no answer. "When was the last time your sword was exposed? Other than when Caspus disarmed you?"

"The alpha kharakian, but kharakians don't have blood. In the past, my blade has only ever been coated in ash."

"Maybe the alpha is different?"

Arlowe didn't feel too sure about the boy's theory, unnerved at the sight of the unknown blood.

"I… don't know," mumbled the prince, returning the blade to his sheath, uncomfortable with looking at the blood for another moment. "I hope the others have fared better than we have…"

Chapter Eighteen:

"W̶E̶ ̶S̶E̶E̶ ̶Y̶O̶U̶ ̶A̶S̶S̶A̶S̶S̶I̶N̶.̶ ̶Y̶O̶U̶R̶ ̶P̶R̶E̶S̶E̶N̶C̶E̶ ̶W̶A̶S̶ ̶N̶E̶V̶E̶R̶ ̶F̶O̶R̶G̶O̶T̶T̶E̶N̶.̶"

24th Arandbern
Land's Legacy
2084∞ (Current Age)

Onyx, it's good to hear from you. It's been too long. As expected, you knew who to

contact considering so few of us even acknowledge your existence anymore. Not like

the good old days when—

"Get to the point, my friend. I'm not getting any younger."

I'm sorry for exposing our connection, but I brought up our correspondence to the

guild. Of course, they already knew of our exchanges; of the contracts you had

completed, the men you had saved, Erethys, even of your exploits alongside Prince

Artaven of Eyenridge. Though they have no intention of thanking you, spoken or

otherwise, they have an offer. Accompanying this note is a contract for the death of

someone within Wicilil. Complete the contract, and the Defiant will not only send a

portion of their supplies to the war effort in Thaedlon, but will also keep a watchful eye

over the Calaveon forces travelling west.

Onyx noticed a second sheet of paper behind the note, ignoring it for the moment.

One more thing before I send this: please, let go of Master Hollow. I know how much

you cared about him, I still do too. But what you're doing is unhealthy. I've heard that

you've been wounded out there. Come back to us before it's too—

The assassin crumpled up the sheet of paper, tossing it aside. "I won't turn a blind eye

Archie," Onyx noted, taking the second sheet into his grasp. "That was my problem

with the guild in the first place."

*

As day turned to night, the assassin prowled the rooftops, hunting for his prey.

Looking down a murky alleyway beneath him, Onyx found his target, linking her to the picture on the contract.

"They never learn," he tutted, departing the rooftops for the dark alley below.

Unseen by his target, Onyx crept up on the unknowing victim. Covering her mouth, the assassin dug a blade fixed on the heel of his boot into her ankle, smothering her screams from the public a short distance away.

The assassin threw her to the ground, placing his dagger on her throat at the precise moment that she was about to let out a scream. "Don't complicate things," he instructed, returning the blade back into its sheath, replacing it with the paper contract.

"What do you want with me?" muttered the target, gripping her ankle in pain. "What have I done?"

Onyx cleared his throat, reading the contract properly. "Let's find out together," he stated. "Selma Velechinski, wanted for… littering? Not really something you call an assassin on. Hold on. Excessive noise, dangerous operation of a wagon? What?"

"Please let me go…"

Selma tried to move, though Onyx showed her the blade on his boot.

"Ah, here we go. Robbery, arson, forgery. Huh, you're an operation expert. I can respect that—"

Onyx paused for a moment as he reached the bottom of the contract. "Sale of dangerous goods, sexual assault, child trafficking…"

The two stared at each other. Onyx's blade could have cut the tension in the air, though he chose another target to aim his disgust at instead. "Well, would you look at that? My empathy's gone," he uttered, returning the contract to his pocket.

"Wait!" Selma called, wriggling away, futile in her effort. "We can make a deal! I can pay you!"

"I *have* a deal," Onyx answered, drawing his dagger. "You're shit out of luck."

A dagger appeared from the rooftops, piercing through the target's throat, though the blade belonged not to the assassin. "Target located, Sulpaec'Sra!" a goblin screeched, taking a new dagger from her pack.

"Well done," asserted a voice from behind him.

A city guard stood at Onyx's flank, though the disguise quickly fell. A human female with long chestnut hair bound into a ponytail approached; a pair of glasses hung loosely from her face, reflecting the glimmer of a katana that rested in her hand.

Though the assassin did not recognise the woman's appearance, her voice and weapon of choice made her identity apparent.

"It's you," he stated, moving back in fear. "Why are you here?"

The woman continued to advance, calling out in her cold, metallic voice. "Your hand was the offering. You have made yourself the sacrifice."

*

"Huh, don't think I've ever been ta' one of these before," Schukara commented, entering into the courtyard of the Eleventh Sense Guild.

Though the yard was well furnished, with decorative plants and benches leading up to the large stone building at the yards centre, there didn't seem to be anyone around to enjoy the tidy surroundings.

"Gill must be in there," the elf figured, climbing the stairs to a firm oak door.

The knocks of the mercenary echoed over the courtyard, accompanied by the clunk of an eyepiece opening from the other side, scanning the visitor.

With another swift clunk the eyepiece closed, followed by a symphony of locks turning, informing Schukara of the guild's cautious nature.

358

The door finally cracked open with a hand pulling it aside. Gill stood in the doorway, nodding to the elf.

"Ah, it's you Schukara," the eleventh voiced; regret filled his tone. "If you're here, then my negotiations have taken longer than I expected. Come, everything is being finalised now."

The elf took a step forward, toying with one of the many locks. "Bit excessive, don'cha think?"

A smile graced Gill's face, tilting his head as a sign for her to enter. "A humorous statement, posing that question to an eleventh," he remarked as he closed the door, allowing all of the locks a moment to rearm. "Why do you think the mark of our guild is that of the eyepiece and door? *Ever vigilant, ever staunch, ever sensing.*"

Gill gestured for Schukara to follow, leading her through the enormous halls of the elevenths, though they were not as the mercenary expected.

The Warforged Guild adorned their halls in trophies and past contracts. The Eleventh Sense Guild was clearly a lot more modest, leaving only notes of the supernatural beings yet to be hunted along the empty shelves.

"So, where is everyone?" the mercenary queried; her eyes caught on the biographies lining the walls, not of the elevenths, but of the defiled spirits removed from their world. "Yer' tha' only person I've seen so far."

"Most elevenths stay in the field. The only time they come back to a guild hall is to use it as a rest stop. Gather intel from any other elevenths in the area."

"So, ya' weren't successful in recruitin' anyone then?"

"I didn't say that."

The two entered what appeared to be the main hall, with Gill tapping on the doorway, acquiring the attention of the two individuals on the opposite side of the room.

"Sieg, Gor, I'd like you to meet Schukara Parle," Gill announced, calling the human and hobgoblin to him. "Schukara's a friend I made through our mutual goal of aiding Prince Artaven. She's also a well-trained swords—"

"No. Way." Schukara rushed past her eleventh companion, looking the other two elevenths up and down to confirm her suspicions, turning back to Gill in amazement. "Ya' know these two?"

Gill shrugged. "Gor? Yes. Siegfried? Eh, it's a long story and I…"

"Why'd ya' never say?" she questioned, stunned at Gill's lack of interest. "Gill, this is Gor Peneh, hobgoblin eleventh and tha' one and only Hunter of tha' Eleventh Sense Guild. *The* eleventh hunter."

She then gestured to her right. "And meh? You're meh-ing *the* Siegfried Durwood? Victor over the Hundred-Year Spectre? He's one of tha' most recognisable members of tha' Eleventh Sense Guild!"

The elf spun to face them, bowing in respect. "It's an honour ta' make yer' acquaintance. I'm a huge fan."

"There's no need for the bowing, Ms. Parle," Gor insisted. The dark-skinned hobgoblin stood her up straight. "Fame goes. Our senses stay."

"Speak for yourself, Gor," argued Siegfried, taking Schukara's hand to shake it. "It's always good to meet one of my fans. A pleasure to meet you, Skuchara."

"Uh, Schukara," the elf corrected.

The human smiled, giving a confused look. "Bless you."

Gill rolled his eyes at Siegfried's smug attitude. "Don't feed his ego too much, Schukara," he voiced, evidently unamused. "A cocky eleventh is a dead eleventh."

Siegfried nudged the mercenary's shoulder to gain her attention. "Yet, here I am," the human jested, putting his hand to his mouth with a playful smile on his face. "I'd watch him, elf. Ol' Gill's just bitter that I'm famous and he could've been. We used to be partners, once upon a time."

"I didn't want that life," Gill growled. "The elevenths exist to aid Argestra against supernatural threats. Profiting from fame is a gross misuse of our powers."

"Funny. Those profits go into my equipment, which in turn aids the people."

"And yet you've never exceeded my contract completion count, have a higher failure rate and have never beaten me one-on-one, and I'm not even one of the guild's best. That fame has made you soft."

The hall had gone deathly silent. The two elevenths stared each other down in disgust.

"Gill, don'cha think yer' bein' a lil'—" Schukara's plea was halted by the sight of Gor raising her hand. Her head shook in disapproval.

Siegfried marched towards Gill, coming face-to-face with his old partner. "What happened to you, Gill? You changed."

Gill maintained eye contact, unflinching. "So did you, and not for the better."

Appearing hurt for a moment, Siegfried stormed from Gill's presence, knocking him aside as he left the guild's main hall.

"Well, at a minimum, you have my support," Gor pronounced, strolling over to the vexed eleventh. "I'll have words with Siegfried. He can't be famous in a world that the kharakians destroy. He'll see reason."

"Don't hold your breath," Gill debated, still looking to the doorway. "Knowing that I'm involved, you won't be speaking with him. You'll be speaking with his pride."

The eleventh readjusted his coat, turning towards the entrance. "Enjoy yourself out there, Gor. I hope you haven't gone soft too."

"Don't fret for me," she mentioned, revealing a fanged smile. "Few of us have a one-hundred percent success rate. That won't be changing." The hobgoblin nodded to

Schukara. "Keep him safe."

The elf nodded in agreement, waving goodbye as she departed by the side of her companion.

As the two entered the guild courtyard, Gill reached into his coat pocket, handing Schukara a stack of posters. The elf took a closer look at them, spotting her sister's name and details printed upon them.

"Ya' didn't forget," she spoke, slightly choked up at another remembering her search.

"I know, I'm a saint," Gill responded, placing one of his posters onto a nearby notice board. "You look like you have something on your mind."

Schukara wasn't aware that she was that obvious, though after so much happening in such a short space of time, she couldn't blame herself for her curiosity.

"So, you 'n' tha' great Siegfried Durwood were partners?" she asked.

The two departed, moving back onto Wicilil's streets with the bustling crowds.

"Just call him Siegfried. The whole title just reminds me of his banners that I see everywhere," Gill muttered, handing posters to passing members of the public. "We used to be. We made a good team too. Sieg was born with a silver spoon in his mouth, though by the time he was fully involved with the guild, it seemed that he had grown out of his bratty entitled phase. He was talented, but also kind and respectful to those we met."

"What happened?"

"Elevenths are often revered, as you demonstrated back at the hall. Most heroes in the old fictional tales are at minimum loosely based on elevenths. Adding to that, our guild is one of the few to have a consistently good reputation and due to our busy lifestyles, you could potentially go your whole life never meeting one."

In veiled anger, one of the posters had been crushed in his palm. "Following *our* confrontation with the Hundred-Year Spectre," Gill made sure to clarify, "Siegfried found himself in the spotlight and revelled in it."

"And ya' were against that?"

Gill attempted to fix the crumpled poster, though the damage had already been done.

"Not necessarily. Though they are few, a handful of elevenths in history have been icons in the public eye, though most have kept up their training and have continued to serve the people.

"According to reports, Siegfried is rarely out in the field, and when he is, his natural talent gets him out by the skin of his teeth. Now, he squanders his powers to play the role of an entertainer.

"To cut a long story short: he wanted me to join him. As you can see, I declined. Ever since, conversations between the two of us have been... awkward at best."

Unable to do anything more, the balled poster was dropped into the puddle by his boot; the dark ink of the print turned the waters to a deep black.

Schukara faced Gill, showing a look of pity. "If he ever left that life, would you have him back?"

"Without a shadow of a doubt," he replied, giving a sigh of disappointment. "That, however, will never happen. As far as I can tell, the Siegfried I knew is long gone. What you saw in that guild hall was a stranger holding his name. Nothing more."

Gill took a closer look at the fresh poster in his hand, finally making eye contact with the mercenary. "Now that you have your answer, may I ask you a question in return?"

"Go ahead." The elf was caught off-guard by the eleventh's request. "What is it?"

"Your sister? Ava?" he posed, taking another look over her portrait. "She's been missing for a long time, hasn't she?"

"How could ya' tell?"

"You're young. I estimate you to be less than two hundred years old, yet you're quite experienced in combat. Your accent gives away Southern Ryvineon, yet I can't think of any trained swordsmen of note in that area that fight in your particular style. You're self-taught," Gill deduced. "Early training and street smarts? I believe that you left your home young. If you left there to travel, finding Ava would be your reason."

"No wonder yer' guild's called upon fer' detective work," Schukara declared, wide-eyed at Gill's analysis. "I need ta' find her. There're wrongs ta' set right."

"Do you have faith that she'll be found?" Gill asked. "Why did she leave?"

Schukara paused for a second, unsure of how to answer his questions. "I… have faith. If I didn't, I wouldn't be here," she answered, swapping her awkward stance for one of confidence. "I'll be lookin' fer' her 'til tha' day I die."

"Well, if things don't go to plan with the kharakians and we fall, come find me," Gill offered, turning his back to put up a poster. "We'll search together. We'll cover the entire afterlife in posters if we have to."

Schukara found it hard not to smile at Gill's honest concern, handing out the posters content with knowing one as genuine as he.

"Excuse me," Gill stated, snapping Schukara from her thoughts. "Can I help you?"

Looking around, the elf could see her companion calling out to a dwarf in the crowd; his eyes were harshly focused on the eleventh. As Gill took a step forward, the dwarf retreated into an alley. The man had vanished from sight.

"That was strange," Schukara uttered, noticing Gill continue to scan his surroundings.

"He wasn't an anomaly," he voiced, bringing her attention to the huge mass of people around them. "There are more. Near that potion stand, for example."

The elf looked over and, as told, an aautgal was watching them, and like the dwarf before retreated back, swallowed by the crowd back into hiding.

"What's goin' on Gill?" the mercenary questioned, perturbed by the eyes upon her. "Surely yer' senses ain't pickin' up eyesight."

"Onyx informed you of those that hunt him, yes?"

"The ones that took his hand?"

"They're toying with me. Turning their soul energy on and off knowing that my senses would pick up on it," he explained, turning to the elf. "I know of no other creature with that kind of ability."

"Are they wardin' us away, or threatenin' us to not to go on?"

Gill closed his eyes, focusing his senses to stretch as far as physically possible. "It matters not," he stated, opening them with a clear plan in mind. "Onyx needs us."

*

Onyx narrowly avoided the wide swing of his attacker, propping himself up against the alley wall with his trembling stump raised in surrender.

"Why are you here?" he questioned, still retreating backwards.

"We warned you not to seek us further. That warning was broken," the shapeshifter claimed, readying another swipe. "No further words will be exchanged."

"I've broken nothing! You have the wrong—"

With blinding speed, Onyx was once again able to shift from the swing of the shapeshifter's blade, though he knew that his time was limited. Without that ability to communicate with the stalker and the inability to damage her, the assassin had only his reflexes to rely on, praying for any kind of intervention.

Throwing a smoke bomb to the floor in an attempt to mask his escape, Onyx turned tail only to have his calf sliced, collapsing to the ground in pain.

"Warning!" called the goblin from the rooftop. "Two targets incoming!"

The shapeshifter raised her katana, though the ensuing strike had been halted.

Turning the corner into the alleyway, Gill pointed a loaded crossbow at his partner's assailant.

"Get away from him!" he yelled, firing the crossbow directly into the shapeshifter's face. She retreated, though her soul energy purposely flickered in the eleventh's mind to remind him of her presence.

Gill held out his hand, lifting the assassin back onto his feet.

"Thanks Gill," Onyx muttered, struggling to stand. "Where's Schu?"

The clash of blades sounded from the opposite side of the alley, with the two able to see their elven ally holding off a dozen goblins identical to the rooftop scout.

"Take care of her, Gill!" she exclaimed. "These goblins ain't nothin'!"

Wrapping her hand around the bolt buried in her eye socket, the shapeshifter ripped the bolt from her skull, tossing it to one side.

"You were warned, eleventh," stated the stalker, watching with eyes regenerated. "Any who stand with Onyx will perish by our hand."

Drawing his mace, Gill evaded the shapeshifter's steel, striking his weapon into her arm before kicking her back, placing himself between the two.

"Tell me you had nothing to do with this," Gill demanded from the assassin, watching the stalker's arm crack back into place.

"No, I was hunting a— Watch out!"

Swiftly casting a spell, Gill's feet had been frozen, with the shapeshifter rushing forward to strike at him.

Acting fast, Gill released a chemical from his pocket, defrosting one of his feet. With partial freedom, this allowed him enough flexibility to duck under her swing, breaking free his other foot before breaking her arm with the mace once more.

Rotating out his mace for his staff, Gill pushed forward, moving in and out of combat with ease despite having no soul energy to take advantage of.

Rather than wound the shapeshifter, the eleventh instead kept her away with the length of his staff, making her unable to close in on him and deliver a lethal blow.

"Stop this!" Gill yelled, lobbing a glass sphere at his opponent, exploding on contact.

The shapeshifter rushed from the dust, repeatedly swinging at the eleventh.

"Get him," she ordered, summoning an aautgal from behind Onyx. The stone giant took the assassin's throat, pinning him to the wall.

Gill propelled his staff forward, knocking the shapeshifter down before turning his attention to Onyx. He rushed to stop the aautgal, though the goblin watching from her vantage point had other plans for him.

Jumping from the rooftops, the goblin landed upon the eleventh, digging her blade into his back; the force of her landing dropped them both to the floor.

"Oops!" mocked the goblin. "Sorry about the rough landing—"

Gill grabbed the goblin, gripping her head before forcing her face into the nearby wall, rendering her unconscious. A trail of white blood leaked down the wall as the goblin slumped to the ground.

"Get out of my way," he growled, leaving her as a heap upon the ground.

The goblin must have been the source of the additional enemies, as the aautgal and duplicate goblins dissipated from the area upon her defeat. One threat still remained.

The shapeshifter had returned. Her katana pierced through the eleventh's chest, finally sated from the foreplay of combat.

"Gill!" Schukara shrieked, bringing the stalker's throat between her two blades, cleaving her head from her shoulders in a bout of rage.

Onyx carried himself over to his injured ally, still struggling with his sliced calf.

"This isn't how it was supposed to be," he mumbled, stumbling to him with the aid of the wall to guide him. "I kept my promise, Gill. I did as you asked."

Without warning, the headless shapeshifter struck Schukara across the chest, launching her back down the alley before hurling a fireball at the assassin.

Though he was able to dive away from the projectile, the explosive energy of the spell slung him into the wall, his senses reeling as his head connected with the solid stone wall, knocking him out cold.

*

As the assassin regained consciousness, his eyes caught a glint of danger. He threw himself back at the sight of the shapeshifter's blade inches from his face, though no attack came.

On closer inspection, Onyx could see that his attacker was frozen in mid-air, with the rest of the alleyway as still as she was. The dagger from Gill's back had been flung by the creature, the weapon motionless in the air. It had been aimed at the mercenary's head, who had charged forward to avenge the fallen eleventh.

Though the injury remained visible on Onyx's leg, this didn't stop him shuffling out from under the blade, back to his feet. The injury made no impact on his movement.

"What's going on?" he questioned, hearing his voice echo through the still alley.

Looking behind him to Wicilil's streets, the crowds had become stuck in time just as the birds had above him, paralysed in the air. "This isn't right. Why has everything stopped?"

The sound of another's breathing caught Onyx's attention, bringing his eyes to a set of nearby pipes with another familiar sight crouched upon them.

"I've seen you before," Onyx claimed, remembering the eye-masked being from the last time he was hunted, though this time the figure stayed, watching him from above.

"Who are you?" he asked, receiving no answer. "Did you do this?"

368

The masked being simply cocked its head, as if trying to understand the assassin. The figure looked over Onyx's shoulder, with the assassin suddenly hearing the sound of a baby's cry from behind him. "What the—"

Spinning to find the source of the noise, Onyx found himself in a lavish bedchamber, occupied by a doctor and a woman holding her crying child; the intensity of the sun through the window forced him to shield his eyes.

"There, there," the woman gently spoke, calming the child. "It's so good to finally meet you, little one."

Onyx moved over to the left-most portion of the bedchamber, uneasy at what he was witnessing. The doctor moved to his equipment, removing his mask.

"If I may be so bold to ask, do you have a name for the boy?" he queried, washing his hands. "I understand if you're a little preoccupied."

"Don't cry, my baby. You'll make your mother cry too," the mother whispered to her child, wiping a tear from her cheek. "His name will be Konrad, Doctor."

The assassin's heart sank. "A fine name," the doctor praised, taking a closer look at the child. "I wish you the best of luck in our wild world, Konrad. You'll need it."

"Too bad you've only ever encountered the bad."

Onyx's attention broke off from the touching moment, viciously searching for the source of the voice. "Who said that?"

A knock on the door resonated within the room, with a voice bellowing through it.

"Zaara! Zaara, are you in there? Are you okay?" called the man, unusually distorted. "I wish to see my child!"

Looking back, the eyes of the doctor and the mother were focused not on the door, but on him, sending shivers through his body.

"Would you open the door please?" the doctor kindly asked, with the assassin obliging, uncomfortable as he was. "Quickly now."

Onyx gripped the handle, slowly turning it to open the door.

Strangely, the assassin found only darkness behind the door, looking back only to realise that his location had changed once more.

"Enough with these games!" he yelled, entering into the darkness. "Show yourself!"

Ahead, Onyx could make out what looked to be a collection of barrels and storage units. Beyond them, a dim light could be seen alongside the sound of rustling, bringing him to draw a dagger as he snuck forward.

Peering around his cover, the assassin could make out a young child, looking to be of seven or eight years of age. Wrappers of various foods littered the floor, with the light source coming from an ornate candelabrum.

A creak by Onyx's side alerted him to the presence of another, finding a masked man sat on a barrel behind the child, seemingly appearing from the darkness just as his location had. "Is that... Master?" he questioned, retaining his cover.

The child turned, hard-boiled sweets in hand, dropping them in fear at the sight of the man sat before him. "W-who are y-you?" the boy stuttered, backing away as far as he could.

"I've heard much about you, Konrad," replied the stranger. "You need not worry yourself. I come as a friend."

"I have lots of friends. I don't remember you."

"Then allow me to introduce myself. My name is Hollow."

"That's a stupid name. How can you be hollow?"

The man chuckled. "I have no idea," he replied, leaning forward. "Tell me of your troubles, young one."

The boy crossed his arms, sour-faced. "I have no troubles," he answered, looking away. "You don't know me. Don't pretend you do."

"Should I recall the time you came across a mugging, cutting the ropes that secured heavy equipment to crush the criminal, saving the victim?" the man asked, straightening his posture. "Or perhaps the time you saved the baker and his wife from that arsonist, locking him in the mess he started? You hid your identity with a simple blanket, the eyeholes cut out. I do enjoy that one."

The boy was astonished, aware that his past deeds had not only been discovered, but that he had been watched the whole time. "Please, don't tell my mother or father," he mumbled, nearly weeping.

"Why did you do it?"

"To make a difference. To do what's right."

"Would your family agree with your decisions?"

The boy lifted his head, agitated by the stranger's statement. "I don't get to make decisions. I do what I'm told," he responded, his fist tensing. "I'm safe, they say. They keep me locked away as a sign of love."

"And that's why you lash out at them? Why you steal? Why you flee?"

"Maybe if they let go, stop *loving* me, then maybe I can do what I really want."

"And what *do* you want?"

"I've seen beyond our home. Too many slip through our laws whilst those who need it are left outside to rot. It doesn't work as it should," the boy recited. "I want to be the gatekeeper. The judge and jury to a broken system."

"That sounds rehearsed, though no less honest." The stranger slid from his seat, approaching the boy. "What would you say if I told you I had the answer to your problem?" he posed, seeing the sparkle in the child's eye.

"I'd say you were lying."

"Are you so sure?" The boy didn't respond; his bluff called. "Come with me."

The boy seemed baffled. "Where would we go?"

The stranger knelt, face-to-face with the boy. "Wherever we're needed," he voiced, offering his hand. "The choice is yours."

Hesitant, the boy slowly reached out, eventually taking the stranger's hand.

"And you took the offer with no thoughts of the consequences," whispered the voice from the darkness. A singular wooden desk emerged in the distance; his surroundings returned to black. "It wouldn't be the last time either…"

Upon the desk sat one lone poster, with Onyx noticing the boy's face sketched onto it. 'MISSING' was printed in bold characters with his description following.

Echoing in the darkness, the assassin could make out the distorted voices of the mother and father searching for their son, to no avail.

"Son! Son, where are you? Your mother and I are worried sick!"

"Have you seen my boy? He hasn't been seen in days! We're desperate!"

The voice emerged once more. "Despite your insistence to aid others, it's interesting to see you thinking only of yourself. Is that not sweet hypocrisy?"

Throwing aside the poster, the table now contained various documents, which Onyx immediately recognised as the floorplan of an old mansion.

"My first mission…" he stated, seeing not a single word out of place.

"Where it all started to go wrong."

Out of nowhere, Onyx's arm was grabbed, forcibly spinning him around before slapping the dagger from his hand, lifting him by his throat.

"Big fuckin' mistake comin' for me, assassin!" a dwarf screamed, slamming him through the table, shattering it in half. "I'm gonna enjoy beatin' you to a bloody pulp!"

Returning the air to his lungs, Onyx briskly looked around to find himself in what

372

appeared to be a display room, filled with all manner of items from high-grade weapons and armours to old, dusty pieces of mining history, brought together by fine linens and the taxidermy of once-proud beasts.

The firm hands of the dwarf returned around Onyx's throat, ready to crush the windpipe of the assassin.

Using the blade fitted into his boot, Onyx began stabbing it into the dwarf's ankle, though wounded as he was; the dwarf had no intention of releasing his grip.

"Enjoy the afterlife, killer!" he yelled through gritted teeth. "This'll feel like a warm-up compared to what I'll do when I get there!"

As his vision faded, Onyx could see a metal goblet just out of reach, fallen from the broken table. Taking it in hand with his adrenaline peaking, Onyx slugged the dwarf in the face, knocking him down as he choked, stealing back his sought-after breath.

Clumsily rushing back to his feet, Onyx threw the goblet to one side, taking the dagger still in its sheath.

The dwarf slumped against one of his display cabinets, a large black bruise gracing his face. "Wait! Wait, wait, wait! Stop!" he called, holding up a shaking hand as the assassin neared; his uncovered eye welled up with tears. "I'm just defending my home! My livelihood! I don't want to die! You came here hunting me! I don't want this!"

Onyx lowered his weapon, unaware of the dwarf's façade.

The assassin's nerves suddenly spasmed with the pain of electrocution, unable to prevent a powerful blow to the face courtesy of the dwarf's calloused knuckles.

"Imbecile," mocked the dwarf, waving his hand free of his spell. He smashed one of the display case to his back, retrieving a colossal warhammer from its innards. "As if I'd beg. Now, back to your execution—"

The warhammer clattered to the floor, with Hollow by the dwarf's side. His blade penetrated into the thug's neck, allowing the corpse to fall by its precious weapon.

"You let your guard down," Hollow voiced, strolling by his pupil. "For all intents and purposes, you should be dead. I expected far better from you."

"You were weak," the voice breathed.

Hollow moved over to his student, offering his aid. "Take your failure in your stride and learn from it."

"You never did," it echoed once more.

Onyx took his master's hand, rising to his feet, only to be greeted by the masked creature, blinding him as he stood.

The assassin recoiled back, feeling a chill across his neck as his sight returned, now stood before his master's corpse in the alleys of Haaroith. "No…"

"You failed him," the voice reverberated through his mind, riding along the winds of the connected alleyways. "You needed us. You couldn't have avenged him on your own, Konrad."

Onyx bolted out of the alleyway, rushing to the masses of people passing him by. "I need help! Can someone help me!" he pleaded, receiving no answer. Frustrated, he took the arm of a passer-by, pulling her close. "Please help me. My master was—"

The woman's head turned almost one-hundred and eighty degrees, the face replaced with one sideways eye stretched from forehead to chin. "What? What's going—"

At once, the wave of citizens stopped dead, all turning to Onyx, all with an eye replacing their faces, all watching.

With the sense of dread snatching away what composure had left, Onyx scarpered back to the alley, only for his master to grapple with him. His face too had been replaced by the sideways eye, twitching as it focused on him.

"Let me go!" Onyx yelped; his arms were taken by the encroaching public. "Don't do this master! Listen to me!"

With Onyx restrained, the turned Hollow simply watched as the crowd swallowed him up, pulling and tearing at his clothing and flesh, breaking his bones and ripping his muscles apart. The assassin screamed as his body came apart before his eyes.

"Stop! Gah! No! Help me! Arrgh!"

With one resounding click, the pain ended. Onyx reluctantly opened his eyes, lying flat against the ground within a black void, infinitely stretching beyond his perception.

"Where... am I...?" he asked, echoing through the nothingness.

The assassin turned to see the masked figure only a few steps away, its hand still in the shape to perform a click. "S-stop this. What d-do you want?" he questioned. "Why are you doing this?"

The masked figure lowered its arm. "The Altane has shown me who you really are," it whispered, sounding as though its voice was originating from inside his head.

"You make it sound like you sought out the Altane."

"I did."

"Why?"

"To find you again."

"Again?"

With another click of its fingers, the masked figure vanished into the void. In a blink, Onyx no longer found himself within the emptiness.

Instead, the familiar setting of Thaedlon surrounded him. The streets seemed darker and were ominously deserted, with strange cracks covering the buildings and roads, as well as the sky far above.

"You're a disgrace," declared a voice from behind, with Onyx glancing over his shoulder to see himself, though with his arm still intact. "Hollow? The Defiant? How do they help you now? The Altane gave me a taste of their power and now I can become that same gatekeeper that you craved so much."

"Even in death, I am loyal to my master," Onyx replied, unsheathing his blade.

As he spoke, the skies rumbled, darkening further. The sound of lightening cracked through the air, making visible tentacles that crept through the openings in the sky.

On the ground, the cracks had torn themselves apart to reveal thousands of curious eyes of varied shapes and sizes, all focused on the assassin.

"He taught me how to attain that title," he continued, staring down the copy. "Even with all their powers, the Altane couldn't bring him back, nor did they aid my search!"

Onyx charged towards his doppelganger, initiating combat via a plethora of swift thrusts from his dagger. In turn, the fake Onyx drew his own blades, deflecting every blow put against him.

"This is laughable," he mocked, untouched by the assassin's strikes. "Would you like me to tie an arm behind my back?"

Catching him off-guard, Onyx called on a familiar power that had been welling up within his chest, appearing by his enemy in an instant.

More whirlwind than human, Onyx buried his blade into the doppelganger's wrist before breaking his other arm, immediately following up with his throat, torso and legs, sliced to pieces.

The assassin kicked his duplicate back with phenomenal force only to materialise behind him, holding up the fake with a blade through his neck.

Pulling the dagger away, Onyx's doppelganger dropped to the floor, though the creature still drew breath. "You... shun the Altane... yet you con... tinue to use their powers..." it gurgled through the blood filling its lungs and throat.

"What's your point?" questioned the assassin; his blade craved more.

376

"A murderer, a... liar and a hypo... crite," it listed, convulsing.

At once, tentacles erupted from the wounds Onyx had created, all aimed at him.

One wrapped itself around his throat whilst two took his arms and two took his legs, snapping them all at once, with Onyx letting out only gasps of pain as the tentacle grew tighter.

"I thought I knew you. Knowing that is no longer the case, makes this much easier."

One of the tentacles reached to the floor, retrieving Onyx's blade, placing it in the doppelganger's hand before winding itself around the assassin's waist, restricting every last bit of his movement.

"Do... it. Kill... me," he stated, savouring every word he could muster through the constriction of his throat. "The Fragments... will... judge me... appro... priately..."

The fake Onyx plunged his blade into the assassin's chest, stabbing him over and over again. The blade tore through nerve and organ, its work briefly shown upon its steel before being reinserted.

His soul was ready to depart, yet every time, a sick energy allowed the brutal surgery to continue.

Though his muffled screams worsened, the skewering continued, twisting the dagger with every puncture. "The fragments aren't here," the fake replied, relishing in his suffering. "Remember, only They listen."

For a moment, the torture ceased. Onyx opened his eyes, hazy from the pain, seeing not the doppelganger, but the masked figure in his place, wiping the blood and tissue from the dagger across its shoulder.

The tentacle around his throat loosened, with the figure coming closer. "Who are you?" he coughed, gasping for breath.

The figure cocked its head once more; the eye upon its mask blinked as it spoke, still echoing in his mind.

"I can't kill you from where I am. Your own powers conflict against mine. But, I will find you. I promise you, Konrad," he declared, confident in his words. He tightened his grip around the daggers handle. "For now, the Sparrow wishes for your waking."

As the doppelganger slowly pushed the tip of the blade into the assassin's eye socket, soaking in his struggle and fear, Onyx felt the weight upon him release.

Onyx's body hit the floor, jolting back to a wall for safety as he landed. The assassin ripped open his tunic at once, finding scars of the stab wounds he had just received.

"Is this… real?" he questioned, spotting a loose sheet of paper to his side.

Looking over the sheet, Onyx immediately recognised it as the contract sent by the Defiant, lifting himself to his feet to see the target hurrying down the alleyway, turning the corner out of sight.

Onyx slid back down to the ground, removing his mask to wipe the blood leaking from his eye. "Was that nothing but a dream?"

The blood dripping upon the ground told the contrary. "Looks like I'll need to write an apology to Archie," he muttered, closing up his tunic. "After all, the Altane are nothing but hearsay, right?"

"Debatable," answered a metallic voice, this time not within his head, accompanied by the head of Selma Velechinski rolling towards him. "Take this, as an apology for our presence."

Onyx had so far been looking down. His hood covered his face whilst his mask rested in his hand, though he knew who stood before him: the shapeshifter.

"I'd pretend to be more shocked, but I'm not going to," he voiced, re-equipping his mask. "Why are you here?"

"In our previous encounter, we warned you not to interfere with us further. We believed you had continued and planned to eliminate you."

"Is that still the case?"

The shapeshifter paused for a moment. "Negative. Our analysis was incorrect," she uttered. "At first, we believed that it was your soul energy searching for us, though on closer inspection, there were discrepancies between their soul energy and your own."

Taking a small sack from his backpack, Onyx delicately placed the severed head of his target inside, keeping his eye on the mysterious hunter.

"Well, thanks I guess," he spoke, expressing his gratitude despite the circumstances. "Because of your aid, the war effort has a little more fuel to burn on."

The shapeshifter shrugged. "The head was a gesture to you. What you do with it matters not to us," she replied, stepping to the edge of the rooftop. "My kind have no interest in the political matters of your world."

"Wait," the assassin ordered, pausing her departure. "Your kind? What are you?"

"What does it matter?"

"At one time, I believed you to be a part of the Altane. But, if you were, then why did they have to manipulate you into hunting me with that pseudo soul energy. It doesn't add up."

The shapeshifter turned, responding only with a slight bow before leaping to the streets below, leaving Onyx alone upon the rooftops.

"And you only add to this mystery." Onyx peered over his shoulder. "I know you're there. That Sulpaec'Sra made it quite clear when she looked past me."

The sound of a slight breeze resonated in the assassin's mind, though he saw naught but the dark mist that rested where the masked figure had been. *The Sparrow?* Onyx picked up the bloodied sack. *Looks like I have a few more letters to write.*

Chapter Nineteen:

"A curse is like a parasite, stealing away what one holds dear."

25th Arandbern

Land's Legacy

2084∞ (Current Age)

"So, you had no luck?"

"Yeah, it was pretty uneventful fer' us. Some Warforged support here, a few posters there. Did I forget somethin'?" Schukara was acting nonchalant, though it was clear that her energy was bubbling beneath her calm act. "Oh yeah, 'n' Gill acquirin' tha' aid of Gor Peneh *and* Siegfried Durwood! Can ya' believe it?"

The elf was practically bouncing around the pavilion where the group had met, shocking some of the public passing through as she vented her excitement.

"You're kidding," the prince replied, taken aback by the mercenary's enkindled delight, making sure not to be knocked into the fountain he was perched upon. "I've never been that interested in Siegfried's exploits, but to get him *and* the Hunter of the Eleventh Sense Guild on our side? I'm impressed. I didn't think they'd take part."

"Finally, someone else who doesn't worship the ground Sieg walks on," Gill grumbled, slipping a piece of chocolate from his pocket into his mouth. "As for Gor, she may be the Hunter, but she remains an eleventh like the rest of us. As long as she survives this, it opens doors for her. She knows what she's doing."

Schukara stopped on the spot, clenching her fists and letting out a long breath before turning to the prince, once again lowering her energy to a more appropriate level.

"So, what about you two?" she posed with a devious grin, looking back and forth between the prince and his necrotic companion. "I hope there were no... shenanigans?"

As Arlowe failed to answer, the jovial tone within the pavilion started to shift. The prince glanced at Daria; she was solely focused on the flowers, unaware of their conversation. He couldn't blame her after what they had just been through.

The prince went through step-by-step what had happened, leaving nothing out of his account. "The remaining councillor will be heading back to Thaedlon alongside what forces David can muster. I imagine the surviving guild members will stay by his side. To keep him safe."

The group sat in awe of Arlowe's statement with only the ambience of the night-time city to replace their words. Schukara seemed lost, appearing to be formulating her words whilst Gill had kept his eyes trained on the prince, unmoving.

"I—" Schukara stopped herself, trying again. "What… What about tha' murderer?" she questioned. "He was caught, right? He's in custody?"

"Caspus Molvo has been arrested by Wicilil's guardsmen and is currently awaiting his trial," Arlowe responded, rubbing the bruise on his wrist. "He's been framing us every step of the way."

The elf thought to herself for a moment. "I can't believe he did all this."

"He knew we'd visit the Arcane Guild seeking their research materials, so he carved his way through the guild only to come back later with a handful of guards to frame Daria. When his plan backfired, Caspus sought to kill us all. No witnesses."

Schukara swallowed a lump in her throat. "Was he…?"

Arlowe nodded. "Purple eyes, black veins. Irrefutable."

"And he can summon? From tha' vault?"

"That's what he used to 'clean up' the guilds he visited."

Schukara leant against the post to her back, shaking her head in disbelief.

Gill stood himself up, taking his turn. "Is the threat contained?"

Arlowe shrugged his shoulders. "Caspus has been taken to the same prison that

Kaxrax calls home."

"What about the other suspects?"

"Daria has been by my side the whole time we've been together, Kellen hasn't been accounted for since Haaroith's attack and Ushnar—" Arlowe paused, raising the eleventh's curiosity. "Ushnar is dead."

Keeping eye contact with the prince, Gill could make out Onyx in his peripheral, sat upon the rooftop above with his finger to his mouth.

"I understand," he voiced, dropping his questions.

"We're not all accounted for," Xanth stated, feeling comfortable enough to join them. "Where's Onyx?"

Arlowe pointed to his forehead. "Xanth's makes a good point: Where *is* Onyx?"

The eleventh peered up at the rooftop, noting the assassin's disappearance.

"That old chestnut," he uttered, consuming another of his treats. "One could make a drinking game on the frequency of that question, but I fear the alcohol required would topple the hardiest of dwarves."

"I didn't realise I was in such high demand!" exclaimed a voice from the nearby doorway, with the assassin emerging from its cover. "I haven't been gone *that* long."

Daria stifled a tear from the shock. Arlowe took notice of her whimpers, though the mage dismissed him with a shake of her head.

"And I think you're underestimating an ally, Gill," Onyx continued, lowering his voice at the sight of a shaking Daria. "Schukara's been known to drink dwarves under the table."

"I'm often told I have veins filled with whisky, a heart filled with rum 'n' looks given by an Angel on absinthe," the mercenary jested, cheekily sticking out her tongue.

"No wonder you're single. Anyone who tells you that is either a bartender or someone six-feet under from alcohol poisoning."

"Scathin'. If yer' skills were half as sharp as yer' wit, you'd be twice tha' assassin," she claimed, winking. "Speakin' of, ya' find yer' elusive club?"

"The guild offered me a contract. It was a success."

"How many dead this time?"

"You wouldn't have defended her. We'll leave it at—"

Arlowe had been staring at Onyx with a worried expression, finally pushing the assassin to question him. "Something on my face, Your Majesty?"

"Onyx," uttered the prince, coming a step closer. "You're bleeding. It's coming from your mask, down your nose."

The assassin took a step back to maintain his distance, wiping away what could be seen. "It's nothing. Don't worry about it."

"Were you injured—"

"Arlowe, don't—"

The prince's concerns were cut short by the blast of a deafening horn filling the streets of the city, with the afeared populace rushing from the direction of the walls.

Arlowe turned his gaze to Schukara, who already had her eyes fixed on him. "Is that…?"

"Tha' evacuation horn…" the elf affirmed, keeping her hands close to the weapons on her waist. "What's our next move?"

Before Arlowe could answer, a young soldier stumbled to his side, clunking up to him in ill-fitting armour.

"Prince, hah, Artaven of Eyenridge?" the soldier queried, struggling to catch his breath. "King David, hah, sent me to find you. They asked that I-I find you and escort you to the southern ramparts."

"Have a moment, soldier," Arlowe instructed, taking the young man's shoulder. "What's your name?"

The soldier did as he was told, taking a few deep breaths before continuing. "It's Declan. Declan Hardcastle."

"Are you capable of escorting us now?"

"I-I think so, sir."

"Everyone, on Declan!" he ordered to his allies, turning back to the young soldier. "Lead the way. We're right behind you."

Making haste, the band bundled behind the young solder, making their way through the frightened crowds crashing against them on their way to safety.

"What prompted tha' use of tha' horn?" Schukara called over the panicked streets. "Surely there ain't another attack? It's barely been a day!"

"I've heard from some of the other guards that another wave of kharakians has arrived," Declan responded, forming a crude path for the prince and his companions to follow. "There have also been rumours of a unique-looking kharakian leading them."

"That sounds like the alpha," Xanth voiced, fearful in his tone. "It's back?"

"From what we saw on our way here, I assume that whatever the alpha is, it can take control of any kharakian's body," Arlowe answered through their link. "As long as they continue to spread, the alpha can be anywhere it wishes."

"Here we are."

Snapped from their conversation, the prince found himself at the base of the main wall with his allies already ascending to the top.

"King David is at the top," Declan spoke, stepping to one side. "Um, excuse me, my liege? A word, if I may speak freely?"

Arlowe gestured for his allies to go ahead, returning to the soldier's side.

384

"I'd have you speak no other way," the prince insisted. "You can drop the formalities, Declan. We're equals on the battlefield. Call me Arlowe."

"Arlowe, o-our numbers are dwindling by the day an-and the enemy just keeps coming. The attacks are becoming more frequent. I've lost a lot of friends."

Arlowe took the young soldier's shoulder. "Declan, breathe."

Declan was too panicked to heed the instruction. "I know I'm just a face in the crowd here, but please, is this a battle we can win?"

"Declan."

"Can we, sir?"

"I don't know."

Declan's eyes fell to the ground. "I hate this. All this war and death," he muttered, already defeated. "I shouldn't be here. I'm not the one who should have made it."

Arlowe sat down on a step, waving to get the soldier's attention. "You're not alone in feeling that way. There are those that feel the same way that aren't even armed." The prince leaned back on the stairs. "Do you know why I do this? Why *I'm* here?"

"To bring peace?"

"I spent a long time in my castle, hiding away from the world's problems. Believing they would go away." The prince pointed to the fleeing civilians. "I stand here to bring hope to those who stand by my side and to those who rely on us for their safety. Without that hope, we have nothing."

"And what if I lose my will to fight? To protect them?"

Arlowe stood from the step, stretching out his arms. "Then they may as well give in to that same despair," he stated, coming a couple of steps closer to the young soldier. "We can't hide forever. Our problems won't just go away. They'll just take advantage of our inaction. There's nothing in Äkin we can't solve if we rise to action together."

Declan remained still for a moment, though he eventually turned with his arm outstretched; a determined expression replaced his look of uncertainty.

"G-Good luck out there, Prince—" He cleared his throat. "Good luck, Arlowe."

"Good luck to you too." Arlowe took his hand tight. "I'll see you on the other side."

Declan nodded, giving a quick bow before departing back into the flustered streets.

The prince returned to the stairs, climbing halfway up before needing to stop.

"Arlowe?" The pterravun could sense the tension in his friend's mind. "Take a second and breathe. I can't remember the last time you gave yourself the chance."

Arlowe let out a brief sigh, pushing himself to the top of the wall.

"Not until this is over, Xanth."

"That creature leading them. It looks different to the last time it was here," declared David as its eyes scanning over the alpha's unique appearance from the top of the wall.

"It seems much stronger than when it was hunting us here," Gill added, gazing through his spyglass.

"That's the alpha kharakian," voiced the prince, re-joining his allies. "I first met one during my escape from Eyenridge. From what I can tell, a connection is formed with one of the standard kharakians and something, unknown to us, possesses it. Depending on how many kharakians it absorbs during the transformation determines how powerful the alpha becomes."

"I see. So that's why we were able to hold it off on our way here. It wasn't absorbing anything," the eleventh deduced, offering his spyglass around. "Do we have a plan?"

"The kharakians have a much smaller army than last time, but they seem much more organised due to that alpha," commented the aautgal, pointing towards the entrance to Wicilil. "The majority of their numbers will have to come through the tunnel. It's the only way in. In case of climbers, I have archers positioned on the walls to keep the

386

cursed ones out."

"Arlowe? Are you okay?" Daria asked, tugging on his wrist. "Arlowe?"

The prince's eyes were focused on the incoming monsters, though with another tug the mage was able to regain his focus.

"I am, and I'm ready," he insisted, looking to David. "Your plan? May I add to it?"

"You're the expert." The king gestured for him to continue. "Go on."

"Do you know of any rune experts?"

"You're looking at one. That was my job before taking charge here."

"I need you to round up any spare materials you have. Chains, straps, ammunition, as long as they attach or dig in, they're fair game," he explained, pacing over the wall. "Take everything you find and hand it over to the Runic Guild. Calming runes need to be placed on *all* of them."

"This is a waste of time," Onyx argued, crossing his arms. "The kharakians are on our doorstep and you want to go on a charity run?"

"I managed to find scraps of research on the kharakians within the Arcane Guild library that could prove crucial not only here, but during the final assault in Fertral," Arlowe divulged, retrieving the papers from his pack. "It's common knowledge that individuals who regularly come into contact with kharakians learn enrage spells to detonate them at a distance, but the opposite spell works on them too."

"Calming spells?" Gill queried, appearing sceptical. "That's not possible, Arlowe. Calming spells don't last long enough to be effective on the kharakians. They wear off too soon to be viable."

"The spells, yes, but not enchanted items." The prince took a quiver at his feet, holding them up as an example. "Once worn or embedded into a target, the enchanted effect doesn't wear off..."

"...shutting them off on a continuous basis until the item is taken or removed." Gill nodded in agreement, passing his spyglass to the prince. "What about the alpha? Are there any weaknesses we can exploit there?"

For the first time, Arlowe was able to analyse the creature from a safe distance.

"Back in Eyenridge, the group I was with was able to bring down a water tower on it. It didn't die from the impact, but its abilities were severely hampered," he responded, lowering the tool as the alpha looked back at him. "As for the calming effect, there's no historical documentation on an 'alpha kharakian', so I have no idea how the spells and enchantments will react."

"We should mobilize," David pronounced, departing the wall as it removed the bindings holding the claymore upon its back. "I'm trusting you with the care of this city. I'll gather up the members of the Runic Guild and have them deliver any items we enchant. The kharakians will learn not to back Calaveil into a corner."

With David's exit, Arlowe handed back the spyglass, looking over his allies.

"This won't be like Eyenridge. Today, Wicilil stands against the kharakians, and when the time comes, so will Fertral!" he announced, escorting his team to the courtyard. "Onyx, Gill, remain on the walls and aid the archers up here. Onyx, you know illusion magic. If any reach the top, calm and incapacitate."

"Could I create a connection with Onyx?" Xanth posed.

The prince signalled for the assassin to stay put. "Onyx, could you hold on a moment?" he asked, focusing inwards. "Xanth, why would you want to do that?"

"Not only can I provide a link between you and Onyx, but whenever he looks into the city I'll have a vantage point, so I can relay what I see to you!"

Arlowe glanced over the wall. The kharakians were nearly in breathing distance of the tunnel entrance. "Onyx, can Xanth connect with you?"

The assassin recoiled. "What? Why?"

"Communication, vantage point, why are you arguing with me? We don't have time."

"Look, I…" Seeing the kharakians so close, Onyx bit his tongue, stepping towards the prince. "Fine, do what you have to."

Arlowe placed a finger on the assassin's forehead, watching as he adjusted to the connection; his eyes shimmered with green for a moment.

"Is it done?" the prince posed through the telepathy. "Can you both hear me?"

"Yeah, I can hear you," Onyx answered, his mouth unmoving. "I suggest you go. The alpha won't wait."

The prince nodded, motioning for Schukara and Daria to follow.

Xanth could sense the tension oozing from the assassin, though he thought it best to dispel it. "Thank you, Onyx, I won't—"

"I want silence unless it's about the matter at hand," Onyx ordered; his eyes were fixed over the walls. "My mind should be my own. It hasn't been for a long time, and you're just making it… complicated."

"Daria, I need you to gather what remains of the Arcane Guild, then return to me," Arlowe ordered, hastening for the tunnel exit. "When the kharakians enter the city, I'll signal for their aid. Can you do that?"

"Will they listen to me?" she questioned, expressing her concern. "I-I'm not a member of their guild, I'm not—"

Arlowe stopped in his tracks, turning to face the mage. "This goes beyond whether they'll follow you Daria," the prince asserted. "Tell them you speak on my behalf, on the king's behalf, Erethys, on the behalf of the people you're protecting. We stand united or we won't be standing at all."

Daria nodded to the prince's instructions. "Remember what we promised. Come back safe," she uttered, hurrying back into the streets.

With only one ally left, the prince and the mercenary made their way into the entrance tunnel, watching as some of the tunnel's steps raised to create cover for the soldiers stood within. "Where d'ya want me?" Schukara asked, catching up to the prince.

"You're with me," the prince replied, with each of them taking a bow and quiver on the way down. "The soldiers are being positioned by David and unlike the Arcane Guild, the other guilds still have their structure. That, and I appreciate having someone at my back. Doubly so that it's you."

"This is bringin' back some awful memories," the elf noted, moving her helmet from her waist to her head.

"This won't be like Eyenridge."

"Yeah, yer' wearing clothes this time!"

The splintering noise of the wooden gate cracked through the entirety of the tunnel, silencing its inhabitants. "You ready Schu?" Arlowe spoke, notching an arrow.

The elf clenched the shaft of her bow. "Ready? I was ready tha' day Eyenridge fell."

Another crack echoed, the gate struggling to hold back the might of the invaders.

"Into cover, everyone!" Arlowe ordered, watching as the gate exploded open, releasing the horde into the tunnel. "Here they come!"

"Start raising the blockades!" yelled the guard captain, slashing at one of the kharakians. "Cut off the first wave of invaders from the rest!"

On his order, a section of the tunnel began to raise, with the kharakians clambering over the rising wall.

Though he had been accurate with his shots, a lone kharakian had slipped past, striking Arlowe at his side.

Given no time to prepare, the prince raised his bow in defence, though it mattered not.

390

The kharakian was frozen in place. "How did…"

A magic missile flew past the prince's face, piercing straight through another kharakian's head. Daria at the top of the stairway carrying a filled bag.

"Place this on it!" she called out, throwing a single handcuff to Arlowe.

With the calming spell wearing off, Arlowe quickly tossed his bow to one side, placing the cuff around the kharakians wrist, watching as the beast fell into inactivity.

"The calming enchantments work!" he announced, waving to Daria. "Throw some more down! The soldiers can use these to avoid the detonations!"

Another explosion sounded down the tunnel; the alpha emerged from the decimated blockade. "Activate the next!" commanded the captain, though the alpha was aware of the order, flickering next to the soldier. "Wha— No! No, stop!"

Ignoring his pleas, the alpha took the captain in hand, forcing his body into the gaps of the defensive wall, jamming the mechanisms inside.

The sound of the captain's screams and crunching bones horrified those defending the tunnel, with some of the soldiers dropping their weapons, fleeing back up to the safety of the city.

Another kharakian stood from one freshly murdered to charge at Arlowe, a molten spear in hand, though the creature was easily dispatched by the prince.

His father's sword pierced through the kharakian, though still holding on, the beast ignited itself for detonation.

Spotting the struggle, Schukara swapped her bow for an enchanted chain at her feet, swinging it around the beast's wrist to cancel the ignition and deactivate the monster.

Suddenly, three molten spears landed by the inactive kharakian, glowing ever brighter. Realizing what this meant, Arlowe and Schukara dived to the safety of the risen cover, barely escaping the volatile explosions.

The prince looked back at the crater, making out the alpha just beyond it. The creature had a Calaveon soldier ripped in two within its grasp, throwing the pieces to one side.

"All this chaos, all this destruction," spoke the alpha, turning its gaze upon him. "It has to end."

"At least we can agree on that," Arlowe muttered to himself, drawing his blade. "Everyone, to the courtyard! There's nothing more we can do here!"

He kept at their flank, defending them from the advancing kharakians.

Teleporting to his side, the alpha kharakian thrusted its spear towards the prince, though Arlowe was ready for the attack.

The spear was allowed to go through the hole in his shield, twisting it out of the alpha's hand before throwing it aside as it began to ignite.

Pushing the offensive, the alpha pushed its palm forward, unleashing a blast of flames to engulf the prince.

In the nick of time, Daria was able to place a barrier between the two, powerful enough to absorb the damaging effect, yet unable to cancel out the momentum that the blast created, shooting Arlowe to the top of the tunnel.

Rising from the rubble, Arlowe was aided up to his feet by his elven companion, calling up to the guards at the top. "We're the last ones out! Raise tha' blockades!"

"Which one?" a soldier called back.

Schukara watched in horror as the kharakians flooded into the tunnel. "All of them!"

The cacophony of gears and stone soon grated through the tunnel. The prince and mercenary made quick their escape to the courtyard.

Though the alpha kharakian was quick enough to flicker past two of the blockades, and had enough strength to push a third back down into the ground, another set had risen up before it, separating the beast and its kind from the rest of the city.

Nearing the top, Arlowe looked back to see a building light glowing through the tempered glass of the blockades. "Take cover!" Arlowe screamed as he tackled Schukara to the ground, covering his head as an eruption of fire poured from the tunnel, sending the debris hurtling across the city.

Standing from the smoke and debris, Arlowe was slammed back into the ground. The alpha stood over him with a spear brought over his head, narrowly missing its mark as the prince rolled to safety.

More kharakians surfaced from the ruined tunnel, holding off Schukara and Daria from aiding their royal companion.

"A-Arcane Guild mages!" the mage directed, barely heard over the battlefield. She looked to Schukara in concern. "I'm not... loud enough!"

The elf smiled at the admission. "You organised them! Leave tha' rest ta' me!" Two more kharakians were cut down as she cleared her throat. "Arcane Guild mages, stand in formation!" Schukara instructed.

Uninterested in letting him escape, the alpha melted its hand through Arlowe's cuirass to lift him, grabbing his left wrist with the other as the prince prepared to penetrate its fiery chest with his blade.

"Now!" Arlowe ordered, yelling through the agony of his melting flesh. "Water!"

From the next level of the city, the mages let loose torrents of water focused on the alpha. The beast, forced to drop the prince, created a blazing barrier that doubled as both a shield for its protection and a blinding wave of steam for its armies to advance.

The mocking tone of the alpha pierced through the misty cloak. "Do you think the curse so simple?"

"What's going on down there?" Onyx questioned from atop the wall, sending another kharakian climber down to its demise. "Where's Arlowe?"

"Arlowe's in trouble!" cried the pterravun. "You have to do something!"

Gill focused his senses, able to see the movement of soul energy through the steam. "The alpha kharakian is closing in on—" His tongue was caught. A series of lights darted towards them. "To the ground!"

A collection of glowing spears collided with the wall, shaking the structure to its very foundations; the archers beside them were blown to pieces like the portions of wall they stood upon.

The two rose to their feet, wiping away the rubble that coated them.

"Get down there!" the eleventh coughed, allowing a kharakian to reach the peak of the wall before swiftly placing a bangle around the creature's wrist. "I can handle the situation up here!"

Arlowe retreated further into the steam, his weapon in hand. The kharakian forces rushed through the vapor veil, surrounding him as more of their kind used the steam to conceal their rapid approach.

A silhouette formed before him, glowing brighter with every passing moment. "It is not too late," spoke the voice of the alpha kharakian, advancing forward with another spear materialising by its side. "Finish this."

"Gladly," came the voice of the assassin, firing a bolt at the outline of the glowing spear, shutting it off.

Pulling Arlowe away from the lunge of a new spear, Onyx withdrew his crossbow for a dagger, blinking by the creature's side to pierce its wrist, temporarily disarming it.

Though unable to wield its spear, the alpha was still able to cast its magic, blasting the troublesome assassin out of sight.

"Arlowe," it beckoned through the steam. "I am what you seek."

Reaching the creature's blind spot, Arlowe flung an enchanted chain over the alpha

394

kharakian's head, pulling it back as it reached the beast's neck. "I've got you—"

The alpha turned to face him, holding the chain away from its molten flesh with no physical contact. "What? How?"

The beast snatched its free hand closer, stealing the chain from Arlowe's grasp, dangling it within the air. "Their power amplifies us, makes us stronger." Obeying its master, the chain flung itself at the prince, wrapping itself around his ankle. "I am powerless to stop this massacre."

Before Arlowe could react, the chain pulled against his weight, lifting him up into the air before swinging him back down into the ground, smashing his body against the remainder of his suit.

The familiar voice gave an order that stole the alpha's attention. "Ready! Aim! Fire!"

Daria had crafted another barrier, shielding Arlowe as a volley of arrows flew over his head, deactivating any kharakians that were hit by the volley.

The alpha continued past the bodies of its inferior brethren, burning away the arrows that had managed to pierce its incandescent skin.

"This isn't working," Onyx noted as he picked himself up, sensing the futility of fighting the creature. "It shrugs off conventional weaponry, can't be calmed and has a defensive strategy against water. Not to be the bearer of bad news, but this thing may not have a weakness."

"That's exactly what was said during the Demon Invasions," Arlowe uttered through their telepathy. "It has to have a weakness!"

"Maybe it has a weakness we can't see," Xanth vocalized, silencing those in the link. "Arlowe, I need you to trust me."

Beyond their conversation, the ground shook. David braced itself against the incredible force of the alpha kharakian as it stood before the prince.

"If you have a strategy, I suggest you take it!" bellowed the aautgal, retaining its defensive stance against another blow, sending deep cracks down its arms. "Now!"

Arlowe shook his head. "Xanth, we don't know what could happen."

"I'm willing to take that risk," uttered the pterravun. "Are you?"

Noticing a deactivated kharakian at his side, Arlowe sheathed his weapon, shifting over to the creature's body.

"Arlowe, are you sure about this?" Onyx questioned, watching his ally take the creature's head into his hands. "We still don't know how Xanth's magic works and—"

"Give me an alternative," the prince answered, dropping to the ground unconscious.

From his own perspective, Arlowe felt his body suddenly shift to a new location, evident by the lack of conflict and sweltering temperature.

As the green in his eyes dissipated, the prince stood, placed within what appeared to be a tremendous, crimson cavern.

Arlowe wiped away the immense sweat that was collecting upon his brow. "Xanth? Onyx? Can either of you hear me?" he asked, hesitant of where he was.

"I can hear you," the pterravun replied. "Though I can't hear Onyx. Whatever I did must have broken our connection." Arlowe inspected his immediate vicinity, allowing Xanth to do the same. "Where are we?"

"Wherever you've brought us, we won't be staying long." Arlowe knelt to the ground, getting a feel for the material that made up the charred cavern.

"We can't be in Kharaki. This substance looks more like what the kharakians are made of than the red stone that makes up the cursed city," he examined, easily breaking up the malleable, clay-like material. "Do you think being here would freak out a kharakian?"

"What do you mean?" Xanth posed.

"Well, wouldn't you be unnerved if you found yourself in a cavern made of flesh?"

Arlowe rose to his feet, inspecting the cavern further. Behind him laid a dead end, with pod-like structures lining each side.

"What are those?" posed the pterravun. "They look like giant eggs."

"If they're like eggs, they may have something in them," Arlowe guessed, moving towards one. "If they do, it may give us an answer as to what this place is."

"Or give us more questions."

The prince moved his face close to one of the pods, making out the shape of something humanoid within. "There *is* something in there," he stated, accidentally wiping his hand across the pod only to find a slim layer of film covering the egg. "Oh, so I can pull this away and..."

Upon seeing the pod's contents, Arlowe took a step back, unsettled by the sight. "That's not a kharakian."

Bundled within the egg-like container laid a human, positioned like a babe in its mother's womb. Small portions of their exposed bodies appeared to be replaced with kharakian parts, though for the most part they remained wholly untouched. It was a soldier, adorned with a Fertren crest.

Arlowe moved over to the next few pods, pulling back the film that covered them.

"T-there's not just soldiers here," muttered Xanth, stumbling over his words in shock. "There are civilians in some of these pods. What are they doing here?"

Before Arlowe could answer, a pearl of light rose above the pods. The inhabitants convulsed, settling as the pieces of light shot off to the other side of the cavern, out of view.

"I don't know," responded the prince, leaving the pod to follow the light sources. "What I do know, is that we may have found the weakness we're looking for."

Claymore clashed against spear as David parried the strikes of the alpha kharakian, holding its ground with the aid of his city as the adventurers gathered their strength.

Recognising the injuries within the group, Daria swapped from an offensive stance to one of support, letting out a spell that doused the area in restorative energy.

"This should ease the pain," the mage declared, reanimating some of the nearby kharakians to their side, only for the alpha to take them back under its control. "We can't hold the walls anymore. Where's Gill?"

"Arlowe, we need to fall back," Onyx ordered, receiving no reply. "Arlowe, are you there? Xanth?"

"What d'ya mean 'are you there'?" Schukara posed, fending off the never-ending horde. "What happened to them?"

"Xanth connected his mind to one of the unconscious kharakians, and Arlowe fell shortly after," he explained. "But something's wrong. It's like my connection to Xanth has been cut."

The elf sheathed one of her blades, turning to those by her side. "I haven't seen Gill, but I haven't seen any kharakians coming from tha' wall either," she voiced, lifting the visor of her helmet. "Onyx, keep 'em back. I'm gonna fetch our eleventh." The elf looked over to Daria. "If things get hairy, could ya' throw in some cover fire?"

The mage nodded to her. "I'll do what I can."

"I suggest making it snappy!" David announced; a chunk of its torso crumbled to the ground. "I won't be able to hold back our guest for long!"

Hurried by the king's words, Schukara rushed onto the shattered wall, praying to the Angels for Gill's safety.

It didn't take long for the mercenary to locate her fallen ally. A bronze duster jacket was laid upon the ground surrounded by ardent red bodies.

"There ya' are!" she exclaimed, identifying a gash on Gill's leg as she came closer. "What happened ta' ya'?"

The eleventh pointed to his broken vials scattered over the ruined wall, aided to his feet by his elven partner. His staff doubled as his walking stick.

"I'm the last one here," he replied. "I've kept the wall clear, but I've exhausted most of my resources in the process."

"Ya' should've called fer' help, or not sent down Onyx in tha' first place."

"You needed the extra hand and I could manage—"

"Yer' death means somethin' ta' us, ya' fool! We're a team!"

Powerful impacts against stone drew her attention up. Without Onyx and the archers manning Wicilil's walls, the kharakians were able to bide their time stuck to the sides, now unimpeded with the eleventh unable to stop their collective threat.

Realising that they were outnumbered, Schukara hastily searched for anything of use, only for Gill to reveal one of Onyx's spheres, twisting it.

"Let's hope this isn't filled with confetti or something," he choked, throwing it in the direction of the assembling kharakians, detonating as the timer reached its end.

Schukara picked up her companion, placing his arm over her shoulder and escaping back to their struggling allies.

"What happened to Arlowe?" Gill huffed, straining as his leg pressed against the steps.

"That's a good question," the mercenary responded. "Ya' can ask him when he gets back."

*

399

"That looks important," Xanth deduced, pointing out a giant tank-like structure at the far-end of the cavern. The machine collected the light from the kharakian pods, humming loudly to announce its activity. "What do you think it does?"

Though Xanth was unaffected, Arlowe had only grown weaker as he reached the large chamber. The heat was slowly sapping his energy.

"It doesn't matter what it does," he asserted, unsheathing his blade. "If its kharakian in origin, it's better off destroyed."

Readying his weapon, Arlowe brought his blade into the odd glass-like material, prizing it back to see the damage he inflicted repairing itself.

"Great," he grumbled. "Looks like I'll need something with—"

In the reflection of the tank, the prince could make out the distorted image of a kharakian behind him. Ducking under its spear, he plunged his steel into its throat.

"Where did that come from?" shrieked Xanth, watching as more kharakians materialised from the cavern, proceeding towards them. "What do we do?"

"I don't know how long I can hold them off for," Arlowe stated, slicing up more of the kharakians despite his exhaustion. "If there's nothing we can do here, pull us out!"

"Hold on! Just give me a minute!"

"Xanth!" A spear grazed Arlowe's sword-arm, knocking his balance. "We don't have a minute!"

The prince kicked away one kharakian as he pierced the stomach of another, preparing for another wave as the approaching creatures all turned to dust, fading from his sight.

"What did you do?" questioned the prince, looking over to the kharakian he had cut down; its eyes were a bright green.

"I don't know." Xanth sounded both excited and shaken. "I just tried to communicate with one, like I did with Kaxrax."

Another voice appeared in the prince's mind. "Arl... ...anth? Are y... ...there?"

The two both recognised the voice. "Onyx?"

"Arlowe? Xanth? Are you there? I heard something! Where are you?"

Back in the courtyard, the alpha had gone cold, deactivated right before the eyes of its victims. Though the standard kharakians continued to attack, with the weight of the alpha lifted from their shoulders, the city was finally able to defend itself from the invaders, holding them back to great success.

Wasting no time, Onyx rushed forward, cutting down the inactive alpha, watching it turn to dust as its body collapsed to the floor.

"What happened?" David queried, resting its weight upon its claymore; the aautgal's body was beaten and broken.

"Wherever they are, Arlowe and Xanth must be doing something to the kharakians," Onyx relayed, stumbling over to the king. "Sorry for stealing your thunder."

The king raised its hand, standing up straight. "I have no interest in glory. This battle rests in all our hands."

"We unintentionally drew the attention of the kharakians here," the prince enlightened, still speaking through their mental link. "Xanth, could you elaborate?"

"The alpha kharakian has to make a connection with one of its kind to join them," Xanth added, sounding amazed at the benefits of his actions. "I didn't realise connecting to them would have any effect!"

One lone kharakian emerged from the remnants of the tunnel, though it did not charge at them. Instead, the injured creature raised its remaining arm, letting out a weak beam of light before transforming into a new alpha, halting the surviving beasts.

"That isn't the same alpha we fought," Gill stated, positioning himself in front of their unconscious companion.

"Arlowe, the alpha's back. Whatever Xanth did was temporary," the assassin warned. "Get out."

"Clearly, we haven't pressured you enough," uttered the alpha, slurring its words. "We will accelerate your arrival."

Schukara took a step towards the beast; her weapon was poised to strike. "What're ya' talkin' about? 'Accelerate our arrival'?"

"There is no more time," wheezed the beast, lumbering closer. "Your annihilation comes ever closer."

Unable to contain herself, the elf lunged forward, skewering the alpha. "We're coming for ya'."

"I await you, as does he."

The statement of the alpha turned Onyx's stomach. "Xanth, get out. Now."

"But this could turn the tide in our favour!" the pterravun argued. "This could make a difference!"

The alpha upon Schukara's blades toppled to the ground lifeless, doubling his protests. "Xanth, get—"

"Onyx? Are you there?" Arlowe called, to no avail. "Xanth, get us out of here."

The silence in his mind lingered, bringing his sight upon the emerald-eyed kharakian.

A great flash burned Arlowe's eyes, blinding him before a sharp pain lingered in his lower abdomen, holding him in place.

As his eyesight returned, the prince found himself face-to-face with the alpha kharakian, now present before him.

"We find ourselves wondering how you found your way here, though it no longer matters now," the creature pronounced, ripping its spear out of the human. "I have

402

what I need."

Arlowe's attention was brought to a green globe floating above the alpha's shoulder, dancing down its arm. "No…" he spat. "You couldn't have…"

"Arlowe! I can't see anything!" screamed the globe, answering the prince's fears. "Help me—"

The alpha kharakian brought the globe into its hand, smashing it to pieces. The energy collected coursed down the creature's arm.

"Did you believe *that* to be the extent of our forces? That we would have no control over our minds?" demanded the alpha, sneering down its nose. "Our assault on this city was at a minimal scale. Your resistance was—"

"Give him back," interrupted the prince, struggling back to his feet. "Give him back!"

Barrelling forward, Arlowe viciously slashed at the alpha, putting every ounce of strength into his swings, though his efforts were wasted.

The alpha had what it wanted, knocking away every swipe before landing an explosive kick to the prince's chest, advancing on its victim. "I'm not done."

"Remarkable," the alpha praised, sending its spear away. "Even when faced with insurmountable odds, you would still stand against me."

Arlowe tried to stand, keeping a hand on the ground to hold his balance. "We deserved you. I never even blamed your kind when you killed my mother. But the moment you grew beyond your curse and started infecting the entire continent with your destruction? *That* was the moment you went too far."

"You misunderstand; the curse wants this. I do not."

"And where did *you* come from? The dreaded alpha? The kharakians were always a collective. Why have we never seen *you* before?"

"We have… ascended, though not of our own volition. I used the power just as the curse did—"

"Enough!" Arlowe continued his assault against the creature. "When your curse stayed its course, I could pity it. That pity left the moment Eyenridge burned!" the prince roared, burying the blade through the monster's chest. "Give Xanth back to me! Take my mind but leave his alone!"

"The final hour will soon be at hand. You both shall meet again," asserted the alpha, holding the prince within the air. "Leave this place. Find the traitor. Break the chains."

A harsh pain took hold of Arlowe's mind. His body turned numb; his vision faded.

"Xanth!" he screamed out, though the screeching within his head made it hard to hear even himself. "I won't let you go, Xanth! I—"

Gasping for air, the prince's mind had reunited with his body. Both were back in Wicilil.

Dropping his blade, Arlowe charged to the remains of the alpha, only for the creature to turn to dust within his grasp. "No, you can't! You…"

Struggling to stay conscious, the prince readied his head to hit the ground, only for the hands of his allies to take him, lifting him up with pride.

"Arlowe, ya' did it!" exclaimed Schukara, holding the bulk of his weight. "It was tough, but in tha' end, we found tha' alpha's weakness! Now they don't stand a chance!"

A lack of response from Arlowe quickly altered the faces of his companions, with only Onyx retaining a solemn face. "Arlowe?"

"Arlowe? The kharakians are gone," Daria spoke softly, taking his hand. "What happened? Why were you calling for Xanth?"

In the time that his friends came to his aid, Arlowe's eyes never left the horizon; a bitter sensation fed on the bruises of his soul. "He's gone," the prince mumbled, shaking his head in disbelief. "I couldn't stop the alpha from taking him."

"We'll find him, and when we do—"

"Arlowe, we don't have time for this woe is me bullshit," Onyx contended, cutting off the mage's kind words with his own harsher tone. "That alpha just tore the front half of this city to shreds, and the only thing that made any difference has just been taken from your mind. If the kharakians are that powerful with a small force that slipped through the border, we need to—"

"Ya' think now's tha' time?" Schukara barked, exploding at the assassin. "Yer' incredible sometimes, ya' know that?"

"No," Arlowe coughed, breaking off their argument before it could begin. "No, he's right. I appreciate you protecting me, Schu, but our time is shorter than ever." Daria aided the prince in rising to his feet, allowing her to heal the various wounds that laid across his body. "We need to move against Kharaki before it's too late."

*

After clearing the obstacle that was the ruined entrance tunnel, Arlowe and his allies stood upon the scorched battlefield. Once prepared for their next journey, they were approached by the aautgal king and a band of its own.

"Greetings, Arlowe," David addressed, with Meriwa and the soldiers following, all saluting at once. "These men will be joining you back to Thaedlon, led by Meriwa. They're the best this country has, with the best equipment I can offer."

"There's one problem with that, David," Arlowe uttered, focused more on the cleaning of his pack than of their discussion. "We're travelling south, not west."

All who surrounded the prince looked to him in confusion, questioning his words. "I don't understand," Schukara stated, resting her hand upon the helmet strapped to her waist. "You said yerself that we need ta' move. Why're we taking a longer way back?"

Removing a book from his pack, Arlowe rose, handing the publication over to the elf.

"I was tasked with three objectives: seek the aid of the other countries, locate more information on our enemies and find a way to enter Kharaki," Arlowe clarified, placing his finger upon the tome. "With Xanth's aid, I figured out the last one."

"You want to call upon the dragons," Daria remembered, apprehensive to receive the answer. "The dragons and the sorvanc are a proud kind. Why would they help us?"

"Not all of them, no. The sorvanc tribes are too scattered for that." The prince flicked the book open, directing their attention to a map of Argestra. "However, the kharakians came from the south, through a territory in which one of their shrines is located. If the kharakians made it through, they fought the dragons and their followers and won."

"And if you're wrong?" David queried; a rabble formed within its ranks. "Then?"

"Then we're doomed to fail. We need their flight on our side. Name me another who can provide the same boon. You said it yourself, we need to come together, for everyone's sake."

"And who are *they*?" questioned Meriwa, flicking a snap in the direction of a band of hooded men, knelt upon the hills to the west.

"That's not ominous at all," a soldier commented back, though the two were hushed by the gaze of their king.

"Arlowe, would you mind explaining?" David asked.

"They're with me," Onyx revealed, speaking in Arlowe's place. "Do you really believe Arlowe would be in league with shady individuals? You think he's the type?"

"Explain," David asked again, firmer this time. "Why are they here?"

"I did what I was asked. The favour? They'll escort your men safely to Thaedlon."

"They don't really strike me as safe," Meriwa noted, silenced once again by her king, this time with the clearing of its throat.

406

"Well, I guess that's it then," spoke the aautgal, offering its hand to the prince. "Without you and those that stand by you, the entire city would've gone up in flames. Your friend saved Wicilil."

Arlowe hesitated before taking the king's stone hand, looking to him with a fire in his eyes. "I'll get him back, whatever it takes," he stated, attempting to take his hand back only for it to be stuck within the aautgal's grasp. "What are you—"

"Patience instead of haste, hope over revenge," David recited. The aautgal took his father's sword from Meriwa, handing it back to him. "Would this Xanth tolerate these negative emotions? I presume not."

Releasing his hand, David turned to its men, leaving Arlowe to his.

"I-I need to see Xanth," the prince stumbled, struggling to get his words out right. "His mind may be… it may be gone, but his body…"

"Go," Daria urged, halting the prince's verbal avalanche.

Arlowe nodded, sending himself to the pterravun's home.

*

The hour was late. Arlowe's appearance had caught the attention of the inhabitants within, and by extension their queen, standing from her throne.

"Arlowe, welcome back," Bela greeted, gesturing for Conquest to join her. "What can we do for you?"

The prince descended the staircase, uttering not a single word. As he reached the bottom, he impelled his eyes up to meet theirs.

"I need you to come with me," he requested, setting free a breath of air at last.

Chapter Twenty:

"Though the dragons may soar, shattered wings will bring their fall."

30th Arandbern

Land's Legacy

2084∞ (Current Age)

The road ahead was not kind to the weary adventurers, with every step reminding them of the rising danger. Their travels took them south, following the destructive trail left by the kharakian hordes. They passed charred forests and levelled villages, all left with the corpses of those who fought, the roads filled with those who tried to flee.

Due to travelling along one of the kharakians many warpaths, camping proved incredibly dangerous. Even with their eleventh's ability to sense soul energy from afar, the group couldn't stay in any one place for too long, lest a new horde catch them unprepared, ending their quest short.

On the night before their estimated arrival, Daria slipped away from the makeshift camp, finding the prince at the outskirts. Reading through the notes on the kharakians, the moon bathed Arlowe in its light, offering what it could to him.

"I'm sure this is normally the other way around," Daria spoke, keeping her voice low to match the tranquil night. "May I join you?"

"Of course. You're always welcome by my side," the prince replied, his eyes fixed on the research notes. "I'm sure any of the others would've been better company though. I'm just reading through these scraps."

"How many times have you read through them now?"

"Too many." Arlowe dropped the notes to his side, letting out a breath of tension. "If there's even the most minute detail that I'm missing, I need to know about it. I want to make sure that this doesn't—"

Cutting off the prince's worries, the mage knelt down, pushing his fallen hand aside to tuck herself beneath his arm.

"You've brought countries together, guarded those who couldn't protect themselves and had the eyes of death upon you on multiple occasions, only to stare back each time," she whispered, gripping ever tighter. "No matter what happens, Argestra stood ready due to *your* actions."

"Some still believe me dead."

"I've heard rumours of a spectral envoy, and of those loyal or crazy enough to follow."

Arlowe chuckled to himself. "I've pegged most of the others. Which are you?"

"Me?" Daria asked, pressing her lips against his. "Call me crazy. I fell in love with a dead man."

Arlowe smiled, wrapping his arm around the woman's waist. "And I with a dead woman. If Arn lives on, it has a curious sense of humour."

*

"Are we there yet?" Schukara's question drew groans from her travelling companions. "How many times have I asked that now?" she asked, withdrawing a little.

"Too many to count," Onyx mumbled, rolling the stiffness out of his shoulders. "Why don't you go climb a tree or something? Elves like to do that, yeah?"

"Nah, you'd chop it down along with tha' rest of tha' forest. Humans like to do that, yeah?"

"Well, it's not slander if it's true."

"We should be close," uttered Gill, keeping an eye on his surroundings. "You sound eager, Schu."

Gill's observation seemingly brought life back into the elf, with Schukara unable to contain her energy. "Standin' by Arlowe's side, I was one of tha' first ta' witness an alpha! I've met royalty and celebrities, and now dragons? You bet I'm eager!"

"Prepare to be disappointed then," Onyx commented. "They're probably dead. We're re-treading the steps of the horde from Wicilil. There's no way the dragons would've just let them waltz through."

The mercenary ignored the assassin's pessimistic attitude, savouring her excitement.

"How much do you know of the dragons, Schukara?" the eleventh posed, taking her attention. "Have you ever met a sorvanc before?"

"I'd know if I did," the elf admitted, pondering. "I know *of* tha' dragons and I know *of* tha' dragon followers, but nothin' more than that."

"Have you heard of the Ascension Wars? Of—"

"The Logritrian dragon Ban-Gauon, the Tyrenian dragon Hso-Dyeiih and the Argestran dragon Sei-Yau."

Looking up, Daria found the three all looking to her in amazement. "W-what? Did I say something wrong?" she murmured, lowering her head to Gill. "I apologise. I didn't mean to interrupt you."

"No, it's fine," voiced the eleventh, calming her worries.

"You can't blame us for being surprised," Onyx added, focusing on her. "You've barely said a word since we departed from Wicilil, though that's hardly anything new."

Gill cleared his throat, staving off the assassin's hostility to return to his conversation with the necromancer. "I'm quite familiar with the Draconity and its history, but if you're just as familiar I urge you to come forward and speak," he offered, rubbing his throat. "A rest from exposition would do me good."

"The Draconity?" Schukara queried. "Now yer' losin' me."

Daria took a moment to build up the courage to speak, taking a deep breath before proceeding. "The Draconity is a religion formed by those who first served the dragons. Their belief is that the dragons within our world are not creations like us, but the children of Arn itself. Furthermore, it is also believed by the Draconity that Arn's true form is more draconic than humanoid, seeing the images beyond their faith as false."

"That don't sound like a very popular religion," argued the elf, absorbed in the tale.

"In actuality, the religion was practically non-existent until after the Ascension Wars. The dragons are a proud race, but none have been arrogant enough to believe themselves better than any of their own kind. Their followers placed them on that metaphorical pedestal."

"What changed with tha' Ascension Wars? Oh, 'n' those dragons ya' said, Bon-Goron, So-Yay 'n' S—"

"A word of warning: remember their names," Gill intervened, holding up his hand to pause the elf's words. "It is wise to be respectful towards any dragon, but learn the names of the Great Dragon Unifiers. Without them, the dragons wouldn't be as organised and peaceful as they are today."

"It doesn't do the tale justice, but in short, Ban-Gauon wanted to enslave all life on Katosus," Daria continued. "Another, the Shikithian dragon Dis-Utemhi, opposed the rival dragon's vision of slavery. The two rallied those loyal to their causes and warred, without thought for those they were fighting over.

"Ban-Gauon was later assassinated and Hso-Dyeiih, an imaagen at the time, ascended to the form of a dragon to take the place of its late master.

"As the war proceeded, a dragon known as Sei-Yau watched over the bloodshed of its kind, and in response, infused others created by Arn with its own draconic blood.

411

Using these newly dubbed sorvanc, Sei-Yau brought an end to both sides, ending the war with a promise of protection to the races they initially intended to control."

"Imaagen? Sorvanc?" Onyx questioned. "Could you clarify?"

The mage took note of the assassin's polite curiosity, more than happy to do so. "An imaagen is a juvenile dragon, more or less." Onyx nodded for her to continue. "And as I mentioned before, the sorvanc are anyone who has become infused with draconic blood. They become faster and stronger, sprouting wings to grant them flight."

Onyx's gave a devious smile. "Could *I* become one?"

"Not easily. In modern times, to become a sorvanc, one must first become a soreiku. Also known as a disciple of the dragons, you must train for many years. Only then may you be granted the honour of taking the ascension ritual."

"Yer mighty keen on this," Schukara noted, nudging the assassin's shoulder.

"Any information is good information," Onyx countered, bowing to Daria. "Do you know the full tale? I'd be interested to know more of the unifiers."

The mage shrugged. "Only if you say please."

"Don't push your luck."

Daria simply giggled in response. "Fine, fine. Aware of a disturbance in Argestra, Ban-Gauon..."

Impressed with the respectful discussion on show, Gill raised his pace slightly, catching up to the prince who, up to this point, had said not a single word.

"Enjoying the history lesson Arlowe?" the eleventh queried, forced to pat the prince's shoulder to break his focus. "Arlowe?"

"Hm?" Arlowe shook his head, waking from his daze. "Yeah, the Ascension Wars. Ban-Gauon, Hso-Dyeiih and Sei-Yau? Xanth would've enjoyed that one."

"Still nothing?"

412

"Not a word. I'm still connected with the pterravun, but Xanth is unresponsive."

Gill paused a moment. "Is he…?"

"No," Arlowe answered. "He's breathing, but unable to wake."

"What about his family? The people?"

"The people don't know. After the revelation of their actual age, Conquest made sure not to replicate that panic." Arlowe paused himself, readying his next statement. "The response from his family was varied. His sister, Kaat, didn't seem keen on me to begin with. Now she won't come anywhere near me."

"And the parents?"

"His mother Bela was trying to be as supportive to me as possible, though I could tell she was struggling. Conquest, on the other hand, didn't leave his son's side. He refuses to eat or sleep and hasn't said a word to anyone since his son fell ill."

Gill put his arm ahead of Arlowe, stopping him and the others in their tracks. "Trying to create a connection with Xanth won't work. You know it won't. The only way he's coming back is if you find him, and for that, you need to focus on what's ahead."

"You didn't stop us to up my spirits."

"That's a start." The eleventh turned to the forested area at their side. "I know you're there. Please, reveal yourself. We mean no harm."

In the undergrowth, golden eyes pierced through the darkness. "Remain where you are," demanded a voice; its owner emerged from the bushes to reveal a dwarf equipped with a halberd and plate-mail armour. He had been watching them from a safe distance. "You stand in the territory of Mao-Yr. Identify yourselves."

Recognising the tell of Onyx readying a sarcastic remark, Gill cut in to answer the dwarf's request. "Soreiku, we come on behalf of Arlowe Artaven, Prince of Fertral and Envoy of Argestra. He is joined by Schukara Parle, Gill Wiksend, Daria Elsforth…"

The eleventh hesitated, unsure of how to introduce Onyx only for the assassin to attempt himself. "And Onyx, ass—"

Onyx's words faltered as Gill's hand connected with his throat, dropping the man to his knees. "*Assistant* to the prince, sworn under oath to speak only when spoken—"

"Leave," interrupted the dwarf, unfazed by the choking 'assistant'. "There's nothing here, for you or I. The draconic shrine has been overrun; the inhabitants slain. It's not safe here."

With his warning issued, the dwarf left the adventurers, continuing through the undergrowth, much to Arlowe's surprise.

"Wait," called the prince, pursuing the soreiku. "Where are you going?" The dwarf didn't answer. "We need your help."

"Find it elsewhere."

"The dragon shrine has been overrun? It was the kharakians, wasn't it?"

The dwarf stopped, though he remained facing away. "You knew?" he asked; his voice was overtaken by an angered tone.

Before Arlowe could answer, the soreiku swung his halberd to steal the prince's balance, tackling him into the ground.

Arlowe rose back to his feet, joined by his companions. "Everyone, into position," he ordered, drawing his blade. "Don't make us do this."

Defying the prince's request, the soreiku charged at Arlowe only for Gill to intercept him. Adapting to his new opponent, the dwarf released a powerful swing, impressively cleaving a tree in two with ease, though missing his intended target.

Swinging once more, Gill temporarily removed the dwarf's sense of touch, moving to one side as the soreiku unintentionally launched the halberd into another innocent tree, toppling it.

414

Regaining his lost sense, the dragon-blooded dwarf immediately continued his assault on Gill, with the eleventh retreating from their brawl.

Attempting a retrieval of his halberd, the soreiku was met by the mercenary inspecting his weapon. "Haven't used one a' these things in a very long time," Schukara remarked, pointing it towards her opponent. "Pretty sure these're fer' stabbin', not swingin'."

Unable to close the gap, the dwarf instead chose to unleash a wave of frost upon her, only to watch the ice freeze in mid-air, stopped from a barrier Daria had projected.

Marching forward, the soreiku aimed the beam of ice at the mage, clashing against another of her barriers. The dwarf's magic was powerful, quickly breaking through, though Daria was confident that her magic would last long enough, persevering through his assault.

The soreiku felt a swipe from behind him. The burlap sack attached to his back had been severed by a bolt, fired by the eleventh.

Suddenly panicked, the dwarf cancelled out his spell, rushing to the sack only for the prince's assistant to blink in, stealing it before blinking back out.

"That's enough," Arlowe stated, taking the sack delivered by Onyx, placing it onto the ground with his weapon pointed towards it. "This fighting isn't getting us anywhere. Let us speak."

"You knew of our enemy. How?" questioned the dwarf, speaking through gritted teeth.

"The kharakians that struck here continued north, launching an assault on Calaveil's capital city. We barely stopped them there. Taking note of the path they took to get here, I realised that they must've fought their way through you."

"And you're here to do what? Scavenge what remains?"

"We came to aid you, in the hopes that you could aid us in return."

The dwarf scoffed at the prince's words, gesturing for them to follow. "Let me show you something, Your Majesty."

Following his trail back through the undergrowth, Arlowe and his band found themselves stood upon a cliff edge; the familiar scent of the kharakians led their eyes to a smouldering shrine.

Smoked ivory struggled to gleam through the damage it had sustained, the surrounding crops decimated. The statues of the three dragon unifiers had been toppled, their heads melted and shattered, unrecognisable to even the most devout of the Draconity.

"The Dragon Shrine of the East, now a monument to our failures," stated the soreiku, turning to face the prince. "I suggest you journey to one of the other shrines. If you seek our aid, you won't find it here."

"That's not an option," Schukara voiced, acquiring the dwarf's ire. "We're running outta what little time we have."

"And what would you have me do? Have me ascend? Sprout wings and carry you?" the soreiku posed, snatching back his halberd from the elf. "A dragon is what you seek, a sorvanc at minimum. I am a simple soreiku. There's nothing I can do."

"Is there not?" Gill asked, his eyes focused on the dwarf. "Tell me, soreiku, what do you plan to do now that your shrine has been captured and you stand alone beyond the walls of your home? Where were you headed?"

"Don't treat me for a fool, eleventh. I know what you are. You can see what the others cannot."

"What can you see, Gill?" Arlowe queried, reaching for the contents of the bag. "What's with the question—"

To Arlowe's amazement, in his hand rested an azure-coloured egg, opening the eyes of all but Gill.

"Your eleventh friend can sense soul energy, which means he could sense two energy sources coming from me," the soreiku revealed, fixed to the spot. "From the moment we met, he knew I wasn't alone."

"Is that... a dragon egg?" Daria quizzed, enamoured by its contents.

"The last; a lone survivor from the attack," the dwarf replied, watching the egg return to the sack. "Once it was known that I held the final egg, I was tasked with retreating, keeping it safe until it could be safely returned. When the invaders had moved on."

"I hate to break it to you, but with the way the wind is blowing, that time won't exist," the assassin conveyed, using a spyglass borrowed to take a closer look at the shrine. "But don't listen to me. I am just a humble servant."

Tying up the burlap sack, Arlowe approached the dwarf, handing back the egg. "My assistant is right," voiced Arlowe; in his peripheral he spotted the assassin shaking his head with a smirk lining his face. "The destruction of the kharakians has travelled far. One last stand against them is being made to the west. If we fail, the revival of your shrine means nothing. If you're going to do it, it needs to be done now. Take it."

The soreiku glanced at the prince, gently taking back the egg. "Entering the shrine is suicide. My home is doomed. What should I do?"

"That's simple. We stand by you ready."

The dwarf thought to himself for a moment, looking over his disfigured home one more time. "My master, Mao-Yr, fought to rid our kind of its isolationist ways all those years ago. If I turned you away during my hour of need, it would prove that I have learned nothing," he expressed, pulling his halberd from the ground with renewed zeal. "Let us make haste for the shrine, lest our efforts be for naught."

"May I have your name?" Arlowe queried to the soreiku, watching as the dwarf had already began descending from their vantage point. "I'd rather not be disrespectful."

"Is now the time?" the dwarf questioned back, focused on his home. "If we perish, the kinsmen awaiting me already know my name. If we succeed, this one offers his name to you as ally."

Meeting minimal resistance on his approach of the shrine, the soreiku made short work of the few kharakians patrolling the outer perimeter, allowing Arlowe's band to simply follow in tow.

"He could save some for us," Onyx mentioned, watching the dwarf rip the beasts apart one by one. "I'm pretty sure it's Arlowe's destiny to rid the world of them."

"It is," Schukara replied, marking a kharakian for him to fire at, the assassin dropping it. "Don't mean we can't cull a few. Makes *me* feel a tad better."

The soreiku let out a wide swing, tearing down two more kharakians before ramming his halberds spike into a third, bracing for a detonation only for the creature to dim, slumping to the floor with barely a flicker.

The dwarf peered over his shoulder, spotting the prince nodding to his magical partner, presuming her to be the reason for the absent bang. "Your skills are as impressive as I've heard," Arlowe praised, standing by his new ally.

"Do you think it wise to mock me so quickly?" the dwarf asked in return.

"I'm not mocking you. If the egg wasn't involved, I imagine our conflict would have ended much differently."

"Maybe, though I have no intention of letting my anger get the better of me again," the soreiku stated; his body appeared much more relaxed than before. "You spoke of our skills. We are not a vocal kind. Where did you hear of them?"

"My father fought by the side of your kind for a brief time. He even wore a suit and shield made of sorvein metal."

"Nonsense," the dwarf dismissed, revealing a doubtful look. "Sorvein metal can only be worked by a dragon master and a chosen sorvanc armourer, rarely given to those outside of the soreiku that take the ascension ritual."

"I understand your suspicion. In your shoes, I wouldn't believe me either," Arlowe admitted, reaching for his weapon. "The only thing I have of his is this sword."

"If that's *his* blade, then surely that proves your tale false," the dwarf argued, scanning his eyes over the steel with great scrutiny. "Those gifted by the dragons fully equip those chosen. Where is his sorvein blade?"

"Where I'm from, each new leader follows a tradition that when they come into power, a weapon of their choice is made for them, to be carried until their final day." The prince shrugged his shoulders. "Though I'm sure he was thankful, knowing my father, he would've denied the blade to keep his own by his side."

"Not many would turn down the offer of a dragon."

"My father was not a fearful man. People often asked how he marched over Argestra with his cast-iron balls."

"Is that all of them?" Daria asked, breaking up their conversation. "I can't see any more of them."

"Doubtful," Gill spoke; his eyes were closed, mind focused. "Stay vigilant. I sense many ahead."

The group climbed the tall staircase, entering the innards of the shrine, surrounded once again by the bodies of innocents and beasts. Two more kharakians rushed from the shadows, though the soreiku cut them down in mere moments, the beasts calmed to hide the band's infiltration.

To their surprise, one of the cursed creatures survived; the calming spell upon it had worn off. Rather than fight them in its sorry state, the kharakian began dragging itself away.

The beast seemed to be drawn to the grating sound of kharakian groans echoing further into the halls. Though Arlowe and the soreiku both aimed to slay it, Gill held up his hand for them to wait, allowing the beast to re-join its kind.

"What are you doing?" the dwarf questioned, watching the kharakian leave his sight.

"We must tread carefully," Gill whispered, surveying the shrine. "The horde remains. I can sense their concentration, travelling through the halls. We should follow our new friend. Learn more."

Keeping close, the adventurers and their dragon-blooded companion shadowed the broken kharakian; the groans of the horde grew ever harsher.

As the beast dragged itself around one more corner, the eleventh called for the group to halt, peeking around to see waves of broken kharakians all carrying themselves in the same direction.

"Where're they goin'?" Schukara queried, too curious not to look.

"I have to know," Gill muttered, moving from his cover towards the molten collective.

"Gill, what are you—" Though Arlowe was unable to stop the eleventh in time, this worked in Gill's favour, proving his theory correct.

"They're not attacking you," the prince observed, watching the kharakians move around the eleventh as if he was just another obstacle to avoid. "Why?"

"The kharakians we've been fighting have a different function to these broken ones," Gill divulged, remaining still. "That just begs the question: what *is* that function?"

One by one, the group stepped into the mass of kharakians, following them further down into the charred shrine.

420

"You know, for some reason, my instincts are telling me it isn't safe to walk among exploding beasts," Onyx complained, gracefully waddling through the kharakians. "If I may speak further, Your Highness, does anyone know how far down these things are planning to go?"

"There seems to be a point further down where they—" Before he could finish, Gill's careful steps turned into a sprint. The eleventh rushed to a nearby opening with his mace in hand. "You need to get that egg where it needs to go."

"What do you mean? We're—" Arlowe peered through the opening. His heart sunk in dread. "They're not..."

Collapsing through the openings, the broken kharakians had gathered at the base of the shrine, letting out a rhythmic glow as they surrounded the structures foundations.

"They're going to bring down the whole shrine!" Daria gasped.

"They can't do this!" yelled the dwarf, held back by the mercenary.

"Y'all heard Gill!" Schukara declared to Arlowe and the soreiku, drawing her blades. "We'll stay here and do what we can! You two need ta' get this mess sorted before this whole place comes down on us!"

Begrudgingly accepting the elf's words, the dwarf stormed back up the path they had taken, crushing any broken kharakians that found themselves underneath his heel.

Arlowe turned back to face his allies; only the assassin had not yet departed.

"It sucks that Xanth couldn't be with us. He would've loved today." Onyx took a bolt from one of his pockets, reloading his crossbow before returning it back behind his cape. "Once this is over with, we'll get him back. You'll have another story to tell him," he reassured, leaving the prince to his task as he dived from the opening.

Though the soreiku had scaled the shrine at an astounding rate, the prince was easily able to follow his trail, guided by executed kharakians and the deafening war cries that

421

invited more to their deaths.

"Hold on!" Arlowe called up, finally catching sight of the dwarf. "How will the egg help here? I doubt your plan is to play this as it comes!"

"The pedestal atop the shrine is a powerful artefact capable of accelerating the growth of those still within the confines of their shell! In the event that there are none to replace the late master of the shrine!" the soreiku bellowed back, tearing another kharakian apart. "If we're to save this shrine, the egg must be hatched!"

"And what if the pedestal no longer—"

At once, a tremendous roar blasted through the halls. The two braced as the shrine was violently shaken, transforming the loosened architecture above into a deadly bombardment.

The prince dived to safety, though in his evasion he lost sight of the dwarf. "Are you okay? Soreiku?"

Leaving his cover, Arlowe nimbly clambered over the fallen stone to the aid of his dragon-blooded ally, eager to find him unharmed.

To his relief, the soreiku wasn't far from where he last saw him, unscathed. "My master is alive?" uttered the dwarf, brushing his hand over a piece of the debris.

"Is that possible?" Arlowe asked, only now aware of his newly-frosted surroundings as the dust cleared from his vision. "I thought you were all that was—"

"I know what I said," the soreiku interrupted, mounting the last of the stairs. "I was forced to abandon my master once. I won't do it again."

As the two stepped onto the bloodied peak, all that was there to greet them was death. The corpses of the dragons that had chosen to stay were all around them.

Powerless, the prince and the soreiku could only watch as a kharakians spear flew towards the last dragon, piercing its hide and propelling it into the wall behind it with a potent detonation.

Charging a spell in one palm with the axe of a dead sorvanc in the other, the dwarf blasted one of the kharakians, flash-freezing the creature before throwing the axe, shattering it to pieces.

"Did I get your attention?" the soreiku barked, returning his halberd into both hands. "I'm taking back my home, then, I'm coming for yours!"

The kharakians before them all turned to attention. An alpha emerged from their crowd, its spear glowing in anticipation.

"This is my last stop before coming home," Arlowe declared, acquiring the alpha's gaze. "Any last words to speak through your puppets?"

Choosing to speak with actions instead of words, the prince was nonetheless stunned. A great light engulfed the peak, dimming to reveal a second alpha standing beside the first, glowing just as intensely.

"How could you—" Arlowe muttered, stuttering in disbelief. "That should be impossible."

"*That* is a challenge!" the dwarf roared, charging straight at the two alphas.

Eerily silent, the alpha kharakians immediately separated from one another, focusing on one attacker each.

Finding only one target upon his advance, the soreiku swung his halberd, digging his weapon deep into the rib of his alpha, before lifting it into the air, bringing it back down with tremendous force.

Attempting to follow up on his attack, the dwarf brought his armoured foot down on the alpha's head only for it to flicker away, reappearing behind him with a spear in hand. The beast disarmed the soreiku, knocking him down with a quick blast from its hand.

Meanwhile, the second alpha had flickered forward, promptly engaging Arlowe with a swing of its own spear before materialising a new set, blasting away at the ground behind him to deny him any kind of retreat.

Realising what his alpha was attempting, the prince sprinted forward, closing the gap between the two before slicing away the creature's arm, piercing his blade through its torso to snuff it out.

Unfortunately, the alpha was far more resilient than Arlowe had anticipated, summoning a new arm to hold the sword within itself.

The creature superheated its body to heat up the blade, the new temperature pressuring the prince to let go. The alpha then landed a powerful kick on its disarmed target, knocking him closer to the deathly drop it had created for him.

An explosion had sounded from below them; the stones of the shrine shifted and cracked as the structure began to lean. Arlowe and the soreiku adjusted their balance accordingly, well aware of the battle raging below.

*

"I need focus on the eastern foundation!" Daria cried, summoning down a storm of magic missiles upon the pressured stone column. "I promise I won't hit you!"

Rushing from her assigned foundation, Schukara engaged the broken kharakians on Daria's, understanding what the mage meant as the mystical darts continued to hail down, targeting only the horde.

In the corner of her eye, the elf could make out a small spherical object approaching the stone before exploding, clearing any kharakians around its blast radius.

"Schu, your foundation is being overrun!" Onyx yelled, dicing apart any that came close to him. "You need to clear them!"

"Are ya' insane?" contested the mercenary, forced back into position. "You could've just started a chain reaction!"

"If the kharakians were that volatile, we'd all be dead by now! We need to hold this area for as long as possible. These risks are buying us valuable seconds!"

"Focus!" Gill demanded; his senses overwhelmed. "They know what we're doing, both above and below! Prepare yourselves!"

As if answering to the eleventh's warning, a huge wave of broken kharakians began pouring through the openings to the cavern. The beasts dragged themselves with much greater force, using their numbers to keep the intruders out of their way.

Temporarily halting her magic missiles, Daria instead turned to her illusion magic. Conjuring forth a new foundation, the mage diverted some of the horde's attention to a false fifth.

"I can't hold up an illusion like this for long!" she informed, still throwing out an occasional dart to deal with her own foundation. "This plan needs to work!"

"We'll know soon enough!" shouted Onyx, blinking back and forth through the crowds of broken monsters, pushing his powers to their limits. "Arlowe'll pull through. He always has!"

*

"Arlowe! I need you to get up!" beckoned the soreiku, pinned by his alpha. "Arlowe, the egg!"

Rising against his aggressor, Arlowe searched frantically for the egg's bright blue shell, still shaken from the blast of his own alpha.

Evading another of the beast's blows, the prince could see the sack that the egg was kept in, with the egg itself free of its carrier, picking up speed down the incline of the shrine.

With only one chance to catch it, Arlowe sprinted towards his alpha, dodging another swing before diving at the egg, fully aware that he was wide open for an attack.

Shoving the egg into his pack, Arlowe could only retreat as another explosive spear flew towards him. The blast sent the prince hurtling down the leaning peak, his body struggling to hold traction.

Arlowe remained still for a moment, finally stationary from the abrasion of his fall. As he lifted his head, he found the halberd of his draconic ally guarding him with the soreiku stood between him and the two alphas.

Poised, the dwarf's weapon was thrust forward and then down into the ground, immobilizing the alpha on his left before ripping the blade out of the alpha on the right, throwing it down by the prince's side.

Flickering, the restrained alpha quickly escaped from the halberds pin, though the soreiku was prepared. Ducking under a flung spear, he took his weapon back into hand, cutting their chests wide open in one clean sweep.

"We can't keep this up. I don't have a damn choice," stated the dwarf, breathless. "Master Mao-Yr! I call upon you! Cast your judgment upon these abominations!"

The peak shook, though this was not the doing of the kharakians far below.

At the top of the peaks incline, the navy-blue dragon sluggishly moved its limbs into place, using what strength still resided in its arms and wings to lift its immense weight.

"Soreiku…" Mao-Yr spoke, its voice low. The ancient creature struggled to hold onto its own words; a scorched tongue was visible through its mutilated face. "You came back… against my wishes…"

"They need us, Master."

"We made a promise to them. I was there." The dragon peered down at the alpha kharakians. "The soreiku that left my side those few days ago exists no longer. In his place, stands a future sorvanc with the shrine's best interests at heart."

426

Readying its breath, the alphas prepared spells of their own against the dragon. Arlowe recognised it as the spell that projected a fiery barrier, protecting them against the water of their enemies a few days prior.

Taking his sword back into his grasp, the prince rushed back up the incline.

He targeted the alpha on his right with a well-place slash before immediately diving behind an upturned stone, narrowly avoided the icy blast from the maw of the soreiku's master.

As the chilling breath faded, the prince and the soreiku left their cover at the sound of a quaking collapse. The dragon stood no longer; the last of its power given to offer the two the boon.

"Mao-Yr…" muttered the soreiku, grieving over the loss of his master.

Facing the alphas, Arlowe found that while one of them had come out of the dragon's attack unscathed, the alpha he had struck had lost its hand, cancelling out its spell. As a result, the alpha had come out brittle, wrestling with its body to move.

Refusing to let it recover, he charged towards the alpha, kicking its leg into pieces before forcing his blade through the beast's throat. The body faded to a frosty dust.

With the bag still gripped tightly in his hand, the prince turned to the soreiku below him, throwing down his pack.

"Take the egg up to the pedestal," he urged, focusing his attention on the last alpha standing. "I'll hold it off."

"Can you stand up to such a beast alone?" the soreiku questioned, placing the pack over his shoulder. "My master only cleared one, and that was due to you."

"If that egg doesn't hatch, we're all done for," he responded, slowly closing the gap on the alpha. "I'll hold it here."

Attempting to disengage from the creature, the alpha materialised a new batch of molten spears for the dwarf.

Intercepting, Arlowe came into close proximity, stealing away the beast's attention to buy the soreiku and the egg the time they needed.

The alpha kharakian brought one of the spears into its hand, slamming it into the ground to detonate the floor beneath it. The beast flickered onto solid ground as Arlowe dived away, taking the high ground over its opponent.

"Why aren't you speaking?" the prince posed as he parried the swings of the alpha, kept on his toes by its constant flickering around their battlefield. "Hmph, I never thought I would have wanted you to speak again."

The soreiku climbed to the top of the pedestal, watching down as his ally clashed against the alpha kharakian. With every moment that passed, more of the floor began to disappear. Their battlefield was shrinking, and so too were their chances of success.

Another explosion sounded from the shrine's base. The dwarf had to ground himself as the shrine tipped ever closer towards its breaking point. Leaning so far, the soreiku could see movement from his master's body, the dragon slipping from where it lay.

Taking the egg from the pack, the soreiku moved it towards the glowing light of the pedestal, only to stop as he came so close.

"What are you doing?" Arlowe called up; his feet struggled against the combination of the missing stones and the slanting peak. "Place the egg!"

"Not with that alpha still standing! I can't risk it turning on the hatchling!" the soreiku roared, holding back their victory. "Keep it with you!"

"I don't know how much longer I can last! Double for the shrine! Place the egg!"

"Just a little more!"

As the dwarf had predicted, one more explosion sounded from the shrine's foundations, dangerously balancing the structure between life and death. The corpse of

428

his master shifted, beginning its descent down the peaks slope, sending it hurtling towards the prince and the alpha.

Understanding what his dragon-blooded ally had planned, Arlowe rushed to avoid the oncoming body, rabidly pursued by the surviving alpha.

Firing another of its spears, the floor before the prince crumbled away, giving him no choice but to slide further down to continue his evasion.

Racing across the lowest point of the crippled tower's peak, Arlowe kept his eyes up. The sight of another lethal fall turned his stomach.

Flickering closely behind, the alpha sent its spears ahead, blasting apart more of the stone floor to deter the prince from making one final bound to safety.

Aware that it had failed to stop him, watching its target escape to one of the last sections of stable ground, the monster sent out one last spear before bracing itself, struck by the body of its last hunt.

Though Arlowe was confident in his leap, catapulting himself over the breach, he had failed to account for the alpha's interference. The spear had only grazed his lower abdomen, though that was enough to send the prince off his chosen course.

Reaching out, his hand barely grasped the jutting stones, dangling over the many floors far beneath him.

Looking over his shoulder, the dragon's remains had toppled over the edge, yet the alpha stood upon it, using its explosive powers to cast itself back to safety.

Swinging with all the force he could muster with one hand as he clung to the remnants of the tower's peak with the other, the prince was able to decapitate the beast with its own momentum, turning it to dust upon the high winds.

The alpha proved to be a hindrance still, as even in death its actions continued to haunt Arlowe. Halting his climb to execute the beast, the prince had left himself little time to climb back up to the base of the pedestal.

He watched the stone floor fall apart as he desperately tried to take hold of it; the blood of the felled dragon coated what remained of any stable ground.

"Soreiku! Are you there?" Arlowe yelled, losing his grip from one of the stones. The same hand let go of his father's sword, unable to catch it without letting go entirely. "Soreiku!"

Unable to clutch the stone any longer, the prince felt the pull of gravity as his hand released. His eyes darted for anything of use, only to stop suddenly within the air. A chill quickly reached his leg.

Arlowe glanced back up to see it surrounded in ice, attached to the stones he had been desperately holding on to.

"Soreiku?" Arlowe queried in wonder, attempting to pull himself up to no avail. "Soreiku, was that—"

As the prince returned to his upended position, a serpentine profile faced him, rendering him mute. The serpent watched him for a moment before bowing its head.

"Greetings," spoke the serpent. "You must be this Arlowe I have been told about. A pleasure to meet you."

Arlowe remained wide-eyed, sure that this was some kind of dream, yet he proceeded to be polite despite his circumstances. "A pleasure to meet you too. Er, do you know where my friend is? We were separated."

The serpent lifted its arm. The dwarf clambered onto it, nearing Arlowe. "I'm here prince," he announced, offering his hand. "We stand, or hang, in the presence of an imaagen, but the infection within the shrine still needs to be purged. We need to act lest this all be for nothing."

"I'm a little disarmed," Arlowe replied. The ice was broken by the imaagen, dropping

430

him to the soreiku's side. "How are we supposed to fight them all?"

The dwarf scoffed, finally seeming at ease. "You came to us in our time of need, against the odds. Now, we return the favour."

*

"I'm falterin' here!" Schukara declared, cutting back wave upon wave of broken kharakians. "Onyx, got any more of those bombs?"

"I don't know! What if I start a chain reaction?" he shouted. A vexed expression took over the elf's face. "I'm low on everything! Don't tell me you had planned on this happening today!"

"Keep your focus! I sense a powerful soul above us!" Gill beckoned, seeking to up the morale of his allies.

"I... can't..." Daria muttered, incapable of holding up the illusion any longer. Pulling herself up to higher ground, the mage collapsed, gasping for air. "There's... nothing more... we can do..."

As if tempting fate, a blast of ice coated the base of the shrine following Daria's words. Arlowe emerged from its icy origin, rushing towards them.

"Everyone! Reconvene at Daria's position!" he commanded, sprinting there himself. "Double time! Go!"

As the prince and his companions evacuated to safer ground, the soreiku entered into the base of the shrine mounted atop the imaagen, marking targets for the serpent to blast with its chilling breath.

"The foundations first! Keep our home standing!" the dwarf bellowed, thrusting out his halberd.

With the glow of the kharakians filling its sight, the imaagen exhaled upon the foundations, encasing both the climbing invaders and the crumbling stone in a thick layer of ice.

"Go back from whence you came, like the one that led you here," the serpent preached to the last of the kharakians, freezing them in place. With a sweep of its tail, the invaders had turned to dust like the alpha before them. "Ashes to ashes, dust to dust."

*

With the threat contained and the shrine recovered, Arlowe and his band dropped down from their safe zone, aiding the imaagen in cleaning up any kharakian stragglers.

"You were right, Onyx," Schukara spoke, digging her blade into another kharakian. "Arlowe did pull through."

Arlowe had Daria's arm across his shoulder, watching the assassin fire off the last of his bolts from their vantage point. "Were you worried about me Onyx?" he voiced in a babying tone.

Onyx gave him a middle finger and a smile in return. "Not the response I expected from my assistant!"

"That looks to be all of them," Gill stated, approaching them alongside the imaagen.

Daria left the aid of the prince to stand on her own. "You have your home back, you and the soreiku." She looked over the shrine and its icy repairs. "I hope nothing like this happens again."

"Speakin' of, where's yer' dragon-blooded buddy?" Schukara posed to Arlowe, scanning the area. "I don't see him."

"I... am aware of his location," the imaagen said softly, its head held down. "However, I am unsure of whether he would want to be disturbed."

Beyond the shrine, the serpent guided the group to a nearby hill that overlooked its entrance, and by extension, the soreiku and the fallen dragon.

432

The soreiku's words were carried upon the winds, his eyes focused on Mao-Yr's unmoving form.

"Nez vji xopf g'mux apfis zus xopht epf dessz zua, nez vji xevist uug jiewip xetj zuas jepft d'mie, nez zua ivis xojuav foggodamz, nez zua niiv xju zua jewi mutv, epf nez zua ci haoif vu xipitt epf teivz."

"Excuse me," Daria mumbled, gaining the attention of the sombre imaagen. "I beg your forgiveness, but I don't believe any of us speak your draconic tongue. What is he saying?"

"Ah, I apologise. I wasn't aware," the imaagen answered. "What you're hearing are the last words, spoken for a dragon after their passing. If you listen, I shall repeat."

"Et zua jewi etipfif, etipf upi-nusie."

"As you have ascended, ascend once more."

"Vji f'sedupov, uug vji leno, tuswepd epf gimm'x lopf."

"The Draconity, of the Kami, sorvanc and fellow kind."

"Nez vjiz xevdj uwis zua. Nez vjiz xevdj uwis at emm."

"May they watch over you. May they watch over us all."

Completing his eulogy, the soreiku raised his arm to signal the group over, his head unturned. One by one, the dwarf had his new companions by his side, stood in silence to respect the deceased.

"I want to thank you all for being here. It was good of you all to give me this moment" he solemnly spoke, placing his hand over the dragon's cold chest. "If you have any questions, you may ask them. That's the least I owe you for your service."

Arlowe's eyes were drawn to the wounds covering the dragon's body, from front legs to stomach, wings to tail, though he kept his observations to himself, returning to the matter at hand. "What happens now?"

"You mentioned a last stand against those things. That you sought our aid?"

"Is that possible?"

"That question is out of my hands," the dwarf answered as he turned to the imaagen; its eyes focused intensely on the dragon it was never permitted to meet. "Will you ascend? Take Mao-Yr's place as master of our shrine?"

The serpent stood silent for a moment, glancing over those that had made its survival possible. "I will."

Tucking in its wings and limbs, the imaagen's body started to solidify; the skin turning a milky white as it began to glow, blinding those in its presence. As the light grew brighter, bringing with it a wave of heat, a new set of powerful wings burst free from the imaagen, slamming down into the ground before slowly straightening out.

The shattering of the imaagen's pale skin ceased the blinding light; its metamorphosis from serpent to dragon was complete. Its azure skin was much deeper, sporting a more muscular frame and frosty mane, finalized with an icy faceplate.

"It is done. What you seek now stands before you," the soreiku stated, offering a bow to the dragon. "How do you feel, Master?"

"It is hard to describe." The dragon moved to Mao-Yr. "A short while ago, I was nothing but a thought within shell, hearing the words of a parent, learning before my birth. Now, I am all that remains of our shrine, dragon in form."

"*We* are all that remains. You're not alone."

"Yer' transformation," voiced the mesmerized elf. "How is that possible? That kinda energy 'n' mass…"

"It is hard to explain the method in Arn's madness, is it not?" the dragon replied, resting itself. "Every imaagen carries a flicker of energy deep within every cell of their body that grows stronger with every passing day. Though the time differs from

434

imaagen to imaagen, eventually that power becomes too much to bear, metamorphosising our bodies into what you call dragons."

"Yet you were able to transform with less than a few hours of energy?" questioned the eleventh. "How so?"

"That, I do not know. All I can tell you is that, for a reason unknown to any of my kind, a shrine must always have one with the mantle of master. That need accelerates the metamorphosis, though I must admit I am exhausted from it. My own energy was added to aid my ascension."

"Your name. Do you have one?" Daria queried; her voice was a mixture of fright and awe.

"Mao-Yr spoke before I was born, and though I answered, it could not hear me. I heard a name intended for the first of its children: Ota-Rnshi."

"And you're taking it?"

"Mao-Yr gave its life for mine. To take the name gifted for their child would be a great honour."

"Master Ota-Rnshi," the soreiku expressed, meeting eyes with the dragon. "Forgive me for my interruption, but those that attacked us are amassing to the west with the intent of overrunning the continent. If we're to involve ourselves, we must act now."

"You speak truly." Ota-Rnshi returned to the steps of the shrine. "Come. My frailty forbids me from taking off at once. The height of the shrine should be sufficient."

"Arlowe." The prince was halted by the dwarf's words, curious as to the reason. "Could we speak?"

Arlowe looked up to the Onyx, nodding for him to go on. "I'll be with you shortly." The assassin nodded back, continuing on.

"You required a word?" Arlowe asked, returning to the base of the steps to meet with the dwarf.

"You saw them, didn't you?"

The prince's eyes were drawn to the late dragon's wounds once more. "I did, as I'm sure some of my allies did too." The soreiku remained quiet. "*Those* wounds predate the attack. The kharakians didn't inflict those."

"No, they didn't."

Arlowe folded his arms. "Do you know who could have?"

The soreiku placed his hand over the older wounds. "For years, the shrines have been trying to reach out, prove to those beyond the Draconity that the Ascension Wars are a thing of the past," he explained. "Some have appreciated our outreach, communicating and even trading with us. Others have expressed a desire for us to stay away, which we are more than happy to oblige."

"I doubt everyone reacted that way."

"There are those that we have encountered that have spurned our attempted negotiations, aggressive enough to strike at our shrines when our backs our turned. Most of us turned the other cheek to them."

Arlowe cocked his head. "Most?"

"Some of the soreiku, myself included," the soreiku said in shame, "were outraged that Master Mao-Yr did nothing to stop those that meant to harm us, however minor their risk. I heard rumours of the soreiku banding together, led by a sorvanc, to oust our master from the shrine with deadly force. I did nothing to stop them."

"And then the kharakians struck."

"Indeed."

Arlowe moved to the dragon himself, inspecting the wounds alongside the dwarf. "Why tell me this?"

"You kept your word to aid us. I believe you can keep your word here. If what occurred here becomes common knowledge, it could be the catalyst required to start a new war; a war neither wanted nor needed. If the death of Mao-Yr was meant to wrongly implicate the outsiders, if my brothers and sisters were actually responsible for this, we would war amongst ourselves. It would pull all Draconity support away from Arn's creations, and—"

"If the outsiders *were* responsible, it could turn us all against each other."

The soreiku released a sigh of frustration, turning his gaze to the prince. "Do you understand what I'm saying?"

Arlowe nodded, looking back to the crippled shrine and his companions upon it. "If this information were to find itself in the wrong hands, it could doom us all."

"I understand that I'm asking much of you. I apologise for that, but I just want to bury the hatchet," the soreiku expressed, moving to one side to reveal Garren's blade, dug into the ground. "Would you keep this from the world? Accept this burden alongside me?"

Arlowe walked over to his sword, firmly gripping the hilt before returning it to his grasp and sheath. "On one condition: you never told me your name," he bartered, offering his hand.

Gracing him with a smile at last, the dwarf took his hand, returning one shake and one bow. "My name is Kardus Holrakai, and I stood with your Pa against the titans."

Chapter Twenty-One:

"Treat the day as your last, until you walk upon the familiar ground of tomorrow."

31ˢᵗ Arandbern

Land's Legacy

2084∞ (Current Age)

As the sun dipped to its slumber, ushering in the radiant oranges and purples that brought the night, the dragon glided swiftly through its vibrant performance, making short work of the journey Arlowe had taken to find them.

"Master, don't overexert yourself," Kardus requested, stood upon the dragon's neck. "Your strength is needed for the kharakians. Using it all now only denies it later."

"We've been in the air awhile now. I'll stay grounded once we reach Thaedlon," Ota-Rnshi replied, turning its head slightly to see the others upon its back. "Go. I'm sure the prince has his questions, and the company would do you good."

Giving a reluctant nod, Kardus slowly departed from his master's neck, joining the group further back.

"Are we there yet?" the assassin spoke in a mocking accent, reaching into his pack. "I think I'm gonna rustle up some grub, y'all want anything?"

The soreiku glanced over to Onyx's target, noticing that the elf had her focus elsewhere; her skin was much paler than normal.

"You look green at the gills," Kardus stated. "Do you need us to land?"

"No! Don't do—" Schukara held her hand across her mouth, holding back her sickness. "Don't stop on my account. It'll pass."

Kardus grinned at the mercenary's misfortune, patting her shoulder. "I threw up three times on my first flight. *On* the dragon. You're doing great."

438

Approaching Arlowe and the rest of his companions, a wrapped provision was tenderly placed into the soreiku's hand, with the sneaky mage returning to her spot on the dragon.

"No, it's okay. I don't need this," he voiced, trying to offer it back to Daria.

"We insist," Gill spoke, taking a spot with his own ration. "We made good time on your shrine, so we have plenty to spare. That, and you fought alongside us, so it's only fair that you eat too."

"That's not even mentioning Ota-Rnshi taking us back to Thaedlon," Arlowe added, wiping his mouth clean. "It's just a shame we don't have anything to offer as thanks."

"For now, I am sated knowing that my home is safe," the dragon answered, focused on its flight. "However, should we come out of this battle alive, I'm sure some of your livestock could be spared."

"I'm sure we can arrange something."

"So, Arlowe," Kardus said with hesitation, taking his own place among the group. "I questioned you at the shrine. I guess it's your turn to do the same with me."

Arlowe thought to himself, figuring out which of his many questions to ask. "I guess we should start with a straightforward question," he decided, crossing his arms. "You and my father fought in the Sixth Invasion. You must have been close."

"Did Garren ever talk to you about the dwarves?"

"A little. He spoke of fighting the dwarves shortly after becoming king."

Kardus sighed, shaking his head. "Modest bastard." The soreiku reached for a pouch on his belt, taking a swig before showing a smile. "You know of the Naturalists and the Golemites?"

"Two sides of the war below," Arlowe answered correctly. "The Naturalists want to focus Arn's gifts on their golems and machinery, whereas the Golemites wish to augment their bodies with golem parts, sacrificing them in the process."

"There were warning signs, but the conflict didn't truly begin until, what, twenty fifty-seven? Fifty-eight?" Gill queried. "I remember as if it were yesterday. Nasty stuff."

"I remember too," Schukara expressed, weakly lifting her arm. "I don't go near tha' underground fer' that reason."

Kardus cleared his throat. "Twenty fifty-eight, I was with my Naturalist allies coming up from the underground when we were ambushed by one of the largest groups of Golemites I had ever seen. Ironsoul suits, explosives *and* they had us outnumbered."

"And Garren?" Gill asked.

"Well, apparently our little disagreement spooked the nearby city. You can guess who we caught the attention of." The dwarf moved his vision solely onto Arlowe. "Despite the circumstances, I wish you could've been there to see it. Your father walked straight into the fire with only a few men at his side and ordered our immediate surrenders. We all laughed. We all stopped when he single-handedly took down one of the suits. He lost two men during the fight, but he got his surrender."

"Is that a big deal?" Onyx questioned, appearing bored. "We took down a suit."

"Yeah, a scrapped one," Arlowe argued. "And it took three of us. My father took down a fresh suit on his own."

Daria raised her hand for Kardus' attention. "Did that peace last? With the dwarves?"

"Where do you think he got the suits to fight the titans?" Kardus began to pace, deep in his reminiscence. "After that, how could I not admire the man? I was the first by his side, the first to accept every damn suicide mission he put us through and…" His pacing stopped. "The first to find him after his sacrifice. Fitting, I suppose."

"I never saw his body," Arlowe spoke, his eyes closed as he thought back to the

440

moment a knock had sounded upon his door. "One of his other companions came to break the news to me. Oxbig, I believe."

"There was hardly anything left, kid. He detonated the suit's core," Kardus explained as softly as he could manage. "As for informing you, yes, it was Oxbig that did so. Oxbig being the man-child he is, you two were very close. He wanted to speak to you personally, so it fell to me to transport what remained of our friend."

Though silence fell over Ota-Rnshi's back for a moment, Arlowe was quick to break it, posing further questions to the groups surprise. "Why didn't you tell me sooner?"

"About your father?"

"About *you*. When we met, you fought us. You heard my name. Why initiate?"

"Partially because I didn't want you to know who I was and get sentimental on me, do something rash that would jeopardise your safety. Partially because you were travelling with an assassin."

Onyx looked to Arlowe, and Arlowe to him in return. "Don't look surprised," Kardus scoffed. "You think I've never met an assassin before? If there was anything Garren didn't teach me, another in our group did. Assistant? Really?"

"And what of the questions?" the prince posed. "You acted convincing for someone who already knew the answers."

"Actually, that isn't entirely true."

"But, the sorvein armaments?"

"Garren was tight-lipped about a lot of the things he did. I never knew why he didn't take the sorvein blade, and I was by his side when the dragons offered us their services. I was asking you because I was genuinely curious. Because he never told us."

"I'm ready to descend. Everyone brace for the landing!" Ota-Rnshi called, allowing the group a moment to grip tightly to its back. "Let us hope they are not eager shots!"

"Arlowe!" Kardus bellowed, loud enough to be heard over the beat of his master's wings. "If I have offended you, I offer my apologies!"

"Don't mistake my lack of grief for anger, Kardus! I've grieved!" Arlowe yelled back. "My father wouldn't want me wasting my time when there's so much at stake! I'm just glad you're alive, and that you remember him fondly!"

Below them, the prince could make out the citizens of Thaedlon clustering together in the streets below; the lights of their torches decorated the streets as each one hurried forward to see the azure dragon in the skies above them.

"Over there," Onyx instructed, pointing the dragon to the castle courtyard. "That looks like the best place to land, if you're keen on keeping your feet clean anyway."

As it closed in on the landing zone, lifting up the dust around him, Ota-Rnshi reared its wings to land only to collapse as it came so close, dropping a wing to its side to stop those rested upon from falling to the slabbed floor beneath them.

Kardus vaulted over the dragon's wing. His armour clattered as he landed, rushing to Ota-Rnshi's front.

"Master! Have you sustained injuries?" he questioned, checking for any breakages.

"I remain well. I… am merely exhausted," the dragon replied, moving onto all fours to steady those on its back. "I suggest that those upon me depart. I have no intention of inflicting injuries due to my stumbling form."

"Kardus, give me a hand?" Arlowe called down, aided back to solid ground. "Could you do me a favour? I imagine our entrance has garnered a lot of attention."

"You want me to get your friends down?"

The prince peered up to see the mercenary flopped over the dragon's wing, groaning. "Maybe aid Schukara down first."

"Greetings, dragon," came a voice opposite Ota-Rnshi, obscured by its mass. "What

442

brings you to Thaedlon's capital?"

The prince rounded the dragon's leg, met by the welcoming sight of King Demetrius and the Bright Blades, as well as those dressed in the garbs signifying their attachments to the Administration or the varying guilds.

"I am merely here at the behest of another," Ota-Rnshi declared. "I believe the envoy is who you wish to speak to."

"Arlowe! I'm glad you made it back!" Demetrius announced, followed by Keila and another, whom the prince recognised as Donovan, one of his many sons. "Assist them, my children. I must speak with Arlowe at once."

Following their father's instructions, Keila and Donovan slowly neared the dragon. Their lack of experience with the creature's kind made the two fearful.

"There is no need for your apprehension," uttered the dragon master, bowing to them. "I have no quarrel with your kind."

Demetrius' children bowed in return, proceeding to aid those atop its back.

"And how've things been here?" Schukara posed to the gathered council, her health quickly returning.

"Our combined forces have been doing a remarkable job holding back the kharakian savages," voiced Artemis, speaking to Arlowe through a magical projection. "There *have* been casualties, but for now, Argestra continues to stand."

"Barely," argued the prince, cutting the commotion from those gathered.

"I'm sorry?"

"A small group of kharakians must've broken through somewhere. Ota-Rnshi is the last of the eastern dragon shrine, and Wicilil stands in ruins. It would've been like Eyenridge all over again if we weren't there."

Artemis turned her back. "An isolated incident."

Demetrius placed himself between the two rulers. "I think that's enough—"

"'Isolated incident'?" Arlowe had stepped forward, moving Demetrius aside. "Would the same be said if Haaroith had been attacked? Razed to the ground?"

"Careful, Arlowe," Ulysses warned. "Our forces can be pulled back just as easily as they were deployed. I'd choose my next words wisely, if I were you."

"When you threaten me, you threaten your neighbours," Arlowe answered, watching as the commotion around them began to pick back up. "If Vexin forces are pulled back, our chances of success plummet. If we succeed against the kharakians without you, I imagine the other countries will be less inclined to pledge their aid to you in return. If we fail, you stand against the kharakians alone."

Ulysses' metaphorical tongue had been caught. "Those are the words I have chosen."

"This is disappointing, Arlowe," Athena continued in place of her brother, looming over the prince. "We gave our support unconditionally, and as a token of gratitude that we could never repay to your father. You dishonour his name with every criticism you send our way."

"I'm sure he's disappointed at me looking at this from every possible angle," the prince retorted; the face of Demetrius became one of perplexity. "Why didn't you tell me of the fae energy upon Kharaki? Or was that not important enough to share?"

The crowd grew louder, questioning the word that had left Arlowe's lips.

"How did you...?" Artemis cut herself off, already aware of the answer. "Supporting terrorists, are we Arlowe?"

"A terrorist you made?"

"It's a shame that you have sunken so low."

"It's a shame that this information was never vital enough to reach the ears of the other rulers, let alone the ears of the one who would stand on Kharaki in your place."

444

"This conversation is over." Athena faded from the crowd's view first followed by Ulysses, leaving only Artemis left within the projection. "Our forces will remain until the kharakians have been dealt with, wherein they will then return to us. Haaroith will remember this, Artaven."

Discomfort was evident, plastered on the faces of Keila, Donovan and the lingering guild leaders. Demetrius had been left speechless, unable to stop the departure of the blades.

"Guess I'll say it," Gill voiced, the eleventh and the mage reassembling with them. "What now?"

"F-for now, I guess our plan remains as it was. We wait on the kharakians," Demetrius stuttered, spinning to face those beside him. "I think that's a good time for us to break off. Everyone, take a moment and then meet me back inside."

As the courtyard cleared of its occupants, Arlowe proceeded towards Demetrius; a question burned in his mind. "We *wait* on the kharakians?"

"The Bright Blades didn't make that part clear. Allow me to clarify," the king expressed, keeping his voice low. "We took your advice about calming the kharakians. Instead of killing them, I devoted a portion of my army to capturing them so that they couldn't return to Kharaki. However, their numbers have dropped off. Significantly."

"So, where've they gone?" the elf posed, having the same thought as her companions. "The cursed city's still clearly over yonder."

"We don't know. We've had no reports of the monsters breaking through our ranks, nor had any reports of any further attacks beyond us. The only place they could be is on Kharaki itself."

"So, we wait?" Daria asked.

"I assume you have something in mind for if this waiting goes wrong?" Gill added.

"They won't wait forever, and neither should we."

"For now, we have no choice," Demetrius uttered, his attention now upon the dragon. "We need boots on Kharaki. Until your new ally can reliably fly you up there, there's nothing more we can do."

"Ready your forces," Ota-Rnshi stated, aware of its involvement in their discussion. "A night's rest should be all I need. Tomorrow, I can fly to the accursed city."

"If you require somewhere to sleep, the castle gardens should suit you." The king's hand was pointed to one side of the castle. "They are private to all but a select few."

The dragon bowed at his offer. "I thank you for your generosity."

"I'd be wary of him master. I don't remember King Demetrius being so charitable." Kardus joined the prince's band within the courtyard. "It has been a long time, D."

Demetrius squinted, processing the voice before turning pale, realising who stood before him in such a confrontational manner. "Kardus? You're alive?"

"You both knew my father. You travelled together?" Arlowe queried, sensing the hostility between the two.

"Another fight?" Keila grumbled, shaking her head. "I'm surprised we're all working together at this point."

Kardus peered over, recognising the children. "All grown up, hopefully ready to right their father's wrongs." The dwarf moved to the prince's side; his face clearly unimpressed. "Found the missing ones?"

Keila and Donovan looked away. Their father began to shake. "How did you know?"

"You think Oxbig only speaks to you?"

"I think I'll be having words with him."

"You wouldn't dare. The man's soft, but at least he has a spine, unlike you."

Arlowe nodded to his allies, preparing them for the oncoming collision; his hand was

446

placed before Kardus. "Whatever's going on here, we can—"

Demetrius cut off the prince's words, yelling out his own. "While you've been off gallivanting, I've been prioritising the safety of this continent! My spine is firmly at my back!"

"Gallivanting?" Kardus threw Arlowe's arm aside, advancing further upon his old partner. "I joined the Draconity. Losing my closest friend made any other choice minimal by comparison!"

"He was my friend too! I—"

"Don't lie to me! To us all! You abandoned us when we needed you, just so you could live your life of luxury!"

Demetrius drew a blade from his sleeve as Kardus retrieved his halberd only for Arlowe to stand between them with Garren's blade drawn, attracting their eyes to the familiar steel.

"Weapons down, now!" he ordered; his allies readied their own weapons.

"This doesn't concern you, Arlowe!" Kardus barked, poised to strike.

"It does now." Arlowe peered up at Ota-Rnshi, aware of the dragon's support. "Stand down, both of you."

"Kardus," spoke the dragon; its icy breath leaked from its mouth in anticipation. "Heed his instructions."

The prince then realigned the sword to face Demetrius, staring his steely gaze.

"It is an offence to threaten a monarch, Arlowe," the king warned.

"Arrest me then," the prince replied, unmoving.

Silence hit the courtyard, with any movement likely to result in retaliation. The soreiku and the king kept their eyes trained over one another, though it was Kardus who lowered his weapon first.

"I ask for forgiveness, Master," uttered the dwarf, kneeling to the dragon with his halberd placed upon the ground. "I was rash, searching for combat. I apologise that you had to involve yourself."

The dragon relieved its maw of frost, nudging the soreiku to rise. "Atone for your mistakes today and learn so that you may not repeat them tomorrow," Ota-Rnshi encouraged, beginning its stride towards the castle gardens. "Let us leave."

Following his master, Kardus came to Demetrius' side. The king still held his dagger openly. "I'm doing this for Arlowe and Garren, not for you."

The king lowered his weapon, returning it to its sheath. "I am too, Kardus."

"No you're not, D. You're doing this to ease your conscience and redeem yourself, nothing more."

While Demetrius' children rushed to their father to calm him, Arlowe turned to his companions, drawing them together.

"It's been a long few days," he said wearily, offering the group a smile of reassurance. "Go and get yourselves some rest. You've definitely earned it."

Keila came to the prince's side, waving at the band for their attention. "If you would like to follow us!" she announced, joined by her brother. "We've prepared rooms for you all to stay in. We can escort you there."

"Do ya' have enough rooms prepped?" Schukara queried, rolling the tension from her shoulders. "Last time we were here, ya' only knew of Arlowe 'n' I."

"My father had a feeling that Arlowe would end up bringing back more people than before. If anything, we have too many rooms, especially if any of you are more comfortable sharing!"

All eyes of the group focused on Daria, much to her dismay. "Lead the way, please," the red-cheeked mage mumbled, making the first move toward the castle.

One by one, those by Arlowe's side departed, to the king's knowledge leaving only him and the prince, though Arlowe could make out the assassin on a distant rooftop, spectating over them both.

"Can we talk?" the prince asked, aware of the king's discomfort.

"I shall do my best to answer," Demetrius replied, perching himself upon one of the courtyard ornaments.

Arlowe did the same, easing into what felt more like an interrogation than a 'talk'. "What Kardus said, about you abandoning your allies? I want to hear your side."

Demetrius nodded, letting loose a sigh. "The war with the titans had only been on for six years, but it felt like a lifetime. We were struggling, badly I may add. I had been by your father's side over the whole six years of that invasion, but when he put his plan on the table to set off the cores of the ironsoul suits, to end the Titan Core's life, well, that was where I backed down."

"Why?"

"My own father passed away during the Sixth Invasion, and though he died peacefully in his sleep, Aros rest his soul, I was then just as much king as I was Garren's ally. Right then, I had a choice to make: do I die following your father against the titans and their core, or do I return home to tend to the people that now look entirely to me for their survival?"

"My father was a king *and* led the charge."

"And he was braver than I could ever be, but I had no faith in your father and his plan. If it failed, we would have had no chance at stopping the titans then."

Arlowe stood, passing the king with a gesture for him to follow. "Why didn't you tell me this?"

Demetrius trailed behind, his eyes still facing the floor. "If you knew of what I did, I

449

feared you wouldn't have aided us. If I was there, maybe your father…"

"I would have aided regardless. My father's death has nothing to do with the kharakians."

"Arlowe, I'm—"

The prince reached the top of the steps to the castle entrance, raising a hand to cut off the king's words; his gaze returned to Demetrius.

"I understand why you backed down. You were right to take direct control of your country on the chance that my father's plan didn't work. The titans would've left much more destruction in their wake than they already had. I don't fault you for that.

"What I take a problem with was your lack of faith in him. He told me stories of you. Of all of you. Kardus, Oxbig, my mother and you. He told me that even during the toughest times he held his trust in you, even at times where he shouldn't have. For you to lose faith in him at such a crucial moment is a disservice to the bond you shared with him. I don't blame Kardus for the way he feels.

"I'm not interested in apologies anymore. Apologies won't fight our enemies for us. If Kardus is correct, and you want to make right your wrongs, I need you on my side. I need to trust that you won't lose faith in *me* when it counts. But only you can tell when that time comes."

Having nothing more to say, the prince faced away from his father's old ally, leaving the speechless king to rest himself for the curse's final day.

*

With the light of the morn seeping through the crack in the silk curtains, Arlowe was roused from his slumber, reaching over to feel the emptiness of the beds opposite side. "Daria?"

His hand held only the sheets that had been delicately left to keep him within his

450

dreams; her staff the only other bit of proof that she had been with him. The prince had been left to wallow in the bed alone.

"Arlowe?"

His eyes shot open, lifting himself from the soft pillows; his senses searched desperately for the call.

"Arlowe? I'm at the door."

Arlowe followed the instructions, spotting Tibor, another of Demetrius' children, stood in the doorway. "Sorry, I thought you were someone else," the prince noted, rolling from the bed with the sheet covering his lap.

"Are you feeling okay? You look spooked."

Arlowe spun his finger to the son, signalling for him to turn as he began dressing himself. "No, I'm fine. I'm just not used to rest like that."

"With the lady?"

Arlowe coughed, caught off-guard. "No, not like that. I mean, in a bed like this," he chuckled, throwing on his shirt. "How did you know I was with someone last night anyway?"

Tibor shrugged. "I don't sleep much. I saw her leave your room on my wanders."

Fully dressed, Arlowe tapped on the bedframe for Tibor to spin back around. "Do you know how to get a man into his armour?"

The boy rushed in, eager to help. "You've come to the right place! Let's get your stuff!"

As Arlowe had the various pieces of armour attached to him, the thought of his companions came to mind. "Hey, Tibor. You said you were up early. Did you see where any of my friends went?"

Tibor had his tongue sticking out as he tightened the straps on the prince's armour.

"Hmm, I'm not sure," he mumbled, clearly focusing too hard. "I saw your girlfriend leave. She smiled at me. She's pretty."

"What about Schukara? Gill?"

"I saw a knight leave really early. Shiny, ponytail, pretty."

Arlowe shook his head. "Was Gill pretty too?"

The boy chose to ignore him. "I didn't see him. He must've been up *really* early."

Without thinking, the prince continued down his list. "Onyx?"

"Who?"

"Never mind."

The prince stood, every piece of his armour exactly where it needed to be. Tibor made his way out of the room only to stop at the doorway.

"I heard from my brother that your eleventh friend was headed in the direction of the guild district. Maybe you'll find him there?"

"Thank you, Tibor. For my armour and the tip," Arlowe praised, taking Daria's staff with him. "Tell your siblings I said hi, and keep yourself safe."

*

The morning sun beamed across the city, drenching its inhabitants in a scorching heat. An ideal day for most before the storm preferred by none.

To Arlowe's surprise, there was a buzz around Thaedlon that he hadn't expected. Despite the kharakian threat looming over them, the people seemed calm, ready to face whatever the day brought. The districts were hectic with celebration, and though the prince felt out of his element within the crowds, it filled him with delight to see happiness on every face he passed.

Though the city as a whole was filled with elation, one street in particular drew the prince's attention. Unique-looking stalls had been erected, with soldiers and civilians

452

alike guided into participation by the elven priests that attended them. Silaasan, Arlowe figured, pleased to see the religion tending to its flock.

As the prince was about to move on, the familiar accent of his own elven ally drew his attention, making out Schukara among the bustling street. The mercenary spotted him only a moment later.

"Arlowe? What're ya' doin' here?" Schukara called, hailing him over.

"I thought I'd check up on my favourite elf," he answered. She rolled her eyes at the compliment. "You were up early."

"*I* got up on good time. *You* slept through."

"Schu, the sun's only just risen."

"I know what I said." Schukara took a piece of paper from her pack, sticking it to the wall. *Avangeline Parle.* "Ya' joinin' in on tha' festivities?"

Arlowe peeled his eyes from the poster. "Festivities?"

"I'll show ya'." She gestured for him to follow her. "Due to tha' kharakians, there're many that practice Silaasan within tha' city that may never get ta' take their pilgrimage ta' tha' Shrine of tha' Angels. I've been there twice, but others ain't as lucky ta' be a wanderer like me," she explained, dodging through the oncoming children. "So, I got up early, started workin' on these lil' stalls. Over time, others started getting involved 'n' before we knew it, our own lil' shrine was done."

"And you wanted to, what? Simulate the activities of an actual Silaan shrine?"

"Exactly! I know it's not much, but I just wanted ta' calm tha' folk 'round here, Silaans 'n' non-Silaans alike. In truth, I never expected it ta' get this busy!"

Arlowe looked over one of the nearby activities. A priest was playing a simple board game with one of the guards, shaking hands and showing their gratitude to each other, urging the prince to shed his anxious shell. "May I join in?"

"Really?" Schukara questioned, exploding with happiness. "Of course ya' can! Tha' more, tha' merrier!"

"How do I take part?" Arlowe posed. "What are these trials?"

"Allow me ta' explain," the elf declared, pointing him to the varying stalls. "There're ten Angels, includin' tha' Archangel Silaas. Each Angel has a trial ta' take part in, though only Silaas' is compulsory. Every other trial is completely optional, dependin' on what support ya' feel ya' need. Understand?"

Before he knew it, Arlowe was guided deep into the Silaan culture, escorted around each of the trials by his elven ally.

"This is Velethuil's trial, one of return," Schukara voiced. "Ya' take a piece of fruit or two, tear it open to retrieve the seeds, 'n' then ya' plant 'em, allowin' a whole new plant ta' grow."

Schukara glanced over, seeing one of the raspberries Arlowe had taken missing from his hand. "To be fair, I haven't eaten yet."

"Ta' be fair, I didn't say tha' fruit was fresh."

The prince looked down at the remaining raspberry, finding it shrivelled, darker than normal. The foul taste of the berry slammed into his taste buds, forcing him to retch it into a nearby bucket. "You'd be surprised how often people've been doin' that today," Schukara remarked.

"Okay, what about this one?" Arlowe posed, still recovering from his last trial. He pointed to a stall littered with books. "I don't have to eat any of these, do I?"

"Only if ya' want to," Schukara replied, picking one up. "This trial is Sana's, tha' Angel of Knowledge. It's pretty simple. Ya' quietly look through until ya' find a book that looks interestin' 'n' then return it when yer' done."

"When I'm done?" Arlowe asked, spotting the vagueness of her statement. "I could

454

be back tomorrow, I could be back in a few years. Won't they miss the book?"

"Tha' point is that you've learned somethin'. That yer' willin' ta' pass on what ya' know to who ya' meet. Eventually, you'll return it fer' others ta' discover."

Arlowe rustled through the store of books, amazed at the variety brought to the stall. It didn't take long for one of the books to catch his eye, attracting him with its golden spine. "An encyclopaedia of the Katosian Religions," mumbled the prince, wiping the dust from its cover. *We'll read again, Xanth. I promise.*

After a time, the prince and the mercenary stood at the centre of the street, looking over the remaining stalls.

"What about Thessalia's trial?" Schukara offered, pointing it out. "It's tha' trial of regret. Tha' priests burn ya' with magical energy whilst ya' remind yourself of yer' regrets."

"Burning?" Arlowe uttered, feeling a twinge of pain from his melted wrist and a tingle from his face. "I'll pass. What about that one from earlier? The priest and the board game?"

"Rysanthir's trial?" Schukara could see the line for the stall, going so far as to move those waiting back onto the main street. "The trial is meant ta' improve, but I feel tha' only thing I'll be improving is ma' patience."

"And that one?" Arlowe pointed to a more colourful event. "Is that a trial? Over there, where they're throwing paint?"

The elf seemed to squirm at Arlowe's mentioning of the trial. "I've… never done that one."

Arlowe cocked his head. "Well, could you at least tell me what it is? Why they're covering in paint?"

The elf sighed. "That's Khiiral's trial, one of humility," she answered. "Ya' strip ta' yer' essentials 'n' then tha' paint, symbolising yer' embarrassments, is thrown until yer' covered, where ya' then wash it all away."

"That sounds... fun! Why haven't you taken part?"

"Oh, Lorelei's trial seems low on numbers!" Schukara voiced, switching back to a peppier personality as she pulled the prince to the trial. "This one's much more up our alley!"

Though Schukara's assertive change in conversation raised concern in Arlowe's mind, he felt that now was not the best time to pry, leaving her to enjoy what time they had left.

Before them stood two powerful men, each carrying their own grand longswords, swinging and dodging each other's blows. "This is it!" the elf exclaimed. "Tha' trial of honour! A personal favourite of mine!"

One of the men's weapons made contact; a loud squeak echoed over the street. Tears of held laughter filled Arlowe's eyes, struggling to keep his own noises to himself.

"What was that?" he sputtered, struggling to stay calm.

Schukara picked up one of the battle axes by her side, whacking the prince with it to produce the same noise. "Ya' have a choice of whether ta' use lethal or non-lethal weapons," the mercenary demonstated, returning the faux axe to its barrel.

"Why not use a staff, or one of many other weapons that won't kill?"

"They're mainly here fer' tha' kids, though some, like these gentlemen use 'em ta' avoid injury entirely when a war is closin' in."

The two men lowered their weapons, patting each other on their greased muscles as they exited the ring; the man closest to Schukara gave her a seductive wink.

"Angel Dain, make me forget that," she commented, shuddering at what she was forced to witness. "Let's get in there."

456

Arlowe reached for a fake weapon only for Schukara to draw one of her blades, placing it over his wrist.

"What are you doing?" the prince questioned, freezing in place.

"Ya' think tha' kharakians are gonna be usin' fakes?" she asked him, raising her weapon. "Our skills need ta' be sharp. There ain't second chances."

Understanding her, Arlowe drew his father's blade before positioning himself, ready to intercept the elf's style of combat.

Schukara took the first move, bringing down one of her blades before bringing up another, blocked by the prince's own swings.

"I can't think of a better time to ask," Arlowe called, continuing to defend against the mercenary's strikes. "After the kharakians, where do you plan to go?"

"Neither can I," the elf giggled, circling her opponent in preparation for another assault. "Ava's out there, Arlowe. You know that. I know that. It's just a matter of findin' her."

The two rushed each other, trading dodged blow after parried strike, both giving their all.

"It could take years to find her. Decades. Your search could easily outlive *me*."

"If that's what it takes, then that's what I'll hafta do."

"You could stay by my side. We could search together."

A well-timed swing of Schukara's sword slammed into Arlowe's armoured rib, forcing him to step back and regain his balance.

"As soon as Fertral's back on its feet, the people'll crown ya' as its king," she stated, checking over her blade. "From there, there's only so much ya' can do for me. Once yer' in that throne, tha' search for my sister'll be tha' least of yer' worries."

Arlowe stood up straight, approaching the elf with weapon raised once more, re-engaging. "So, you're going to go alone?" he questioned, getting back into the rhythm of their sparring match. "I assume you haven't asked the others for their opinion?"

"They have their own concerns." The elf caught the prince's blade between her two. "I'll be fine. Go ahead 'n' keep savin' the world. It's a good look for ya'."

"What if we want to help? Ignore our duties?"

"Well now yer' just bein' foolish!" Taking a wide swipe, Schukara opened herself up to Arlowe, allowing the prince to relieve her of a blade. "You've all done more than enough fer' me."

As the elf readied one last strike, the prince retreated his blade back into its sheath.

"You're a skilled warrior," he commended, bowing whilst she still held her weapon above him. "I hope it helps you find Ava."

Schukara lowered her weapon, watching Arlowe leave the ring; her stress wavered from his kind words.

"Arlowe," she hollered, his attention brought upon a shield that rested in her hands. "Think fast!"

The shield was tossed over to him, gracing his hands with its superb feel. The material felt superior to that of any other shield he had known.

"Where did you get this?" he queried, strapping it to his arm, testing its weight. "Surely you didn't expect me precisely at this moment in time?"

"I had it hidden with my pack. C'mere." The elf pushed her fingers into the shield, tearing away a layer that, unbeknown to Arlowe, was rested over the top.

Taken away, the prince could make out an intense green, rotating the shield to see Fertral's sigil decorating it; the tree-like runic symbol was instantly recognisable to him.

Arlowe gawked at the craftsmanship and attention to detail of his country's mark,

458

looking to Schukara in disbelief. "How?"

The elf gave a shrug. "When I travel, tha' money I save stays with the town or city, 'n' I head on ta' tha' next ta' make my money. Rinse 'n' repeat." She traced her finger around the linework of the sigil. "I had a feelin' I'd be travelling with ya' fer' a while, so once I'd tended ta' those less fortunate than I, I went ta' see my old Warforged buddies here. I knew we'd be back here, so I had this waitin' for us."

Amazed by her generosity, Arlowe went to offer another bow, only for Schukara to stop him, bowing in his place.

"You've guarded all of us, not just from physical threats, but of hits to our morale too. Whatever comes next, whether I'm with ya' or not," she avowed, "well, I wanted ta' make sure ya' could keep doing it, 'n' do it well."

The two returned to the festive street, just as lively as it was when Arlowe began his tour. "I'd best move on," he stated, staring at the sun. "I have a few non-elven favourites I still need to meet."

"Before ya' go, would ya' join me in a prayer?" Schukara asked, taking her holy book into hand.

"Of course. We never did Silaas's trial."

Schukara smiled, opening up her book of faith. "Are there any verses ya' wish ta' speak? From the Uanun?"

Arlowe shook his head, resting on a nearby stool. "The only holy text I'm familiar with is the Castral. Arytholity's all I know in that regard."

"I'll translate to tha' common tongue," spoke the elf, clearing her throat.

"Alaila, Creation, Chapter forty-nine, verses one ta' seven.

"As Arn's light dimmed, taken from a world both grateful 'n' warm, detestable 'n' hatin', tha' Archangel rose ta' fill tha' void left behind, raisin' those worthy ta' his

side.

"Silaas called ta' his brothers 'n' sisters, "Come forth unto tha' light, not of death,
but of renewal.

"Come forth Velethuil, Estelar 'n' Rysanthir, those that judged fairly under duress.

"Come forth Thessalia, Lorelei 'n' Khiiral, who gave their mercy in times most
difficult.

"Come forth Dain, Sana 'n' Castien, that guarded all against tha' temptations of evil.

"Angels, High Angels and Archangel, as elven risen, ascend ta' aid those of Arn's
creation bound in their mortality, 'n' be restless in yer' aid of their suffering.

"As custodians of our fallen lord's mantle 'n' heaven, tha' weight we bear means all
ta' those in desperation. Be tha' example for those who wish ta' follow. Teach them ta'
comfort and ta' guide each other as Arn taught us, 'n' test them, not ta' criticize their
failings, but ta' maintain tha' dimmin' light in our absence, and in his."

Ending her prayer, Schukara offered one last bow to her trusted companion, with the
prince offering one in return. "You do the Angels proud," Arlowe noted, standing up
straight. "You follow their qualities to the letter."

"Everyone's hurtin'," Schukara responded, leading the prince back to the street's
entrance. "I'm not just out here fer' Ava. I'm here fer' Eyenridge. I'm here fer' Gill 'n'
Daria. You 'n' Xanth. Heck, even Onyx. I'm here to bring tha' light."

Arlowe glanced at his side, noticing a stall with a single priest and no line.

"Excuse me," he posed to the elven man. "Is this a trial?"

"It is, my son. This is Estelar's trial, one of generosity," he spoke, pushing forward a
small worn box. "A most simple trial: a donation is all that is required."

The prince took a tightly clasped purse from his pack, dropping a handful of gold
pieces into the box. "Well, one more trial for the road."

460

"Where'd ya' get tha' money from?" Schukara queried, reminded of Arlowe's penniless claims.

"I've been saving it. Skipping meals, travelling ill-equipped and the like," he replied, playfully throwing the purse into the air. "My turn: do you know where I can find our roguish friend?"

*

Contrasting the lively streets that Schukara had immersed herself in, the elf's directions had led Arlowe to a deserted part of the city; every footstep echoed as the prince's boot touched the ground.

Placing a careful eye over his surroundings, Arlowe could see no stone out of place nor house vandalised, yet the lack of civilians still brought him to tread cautiously, musing on whether his assassin was partially the reason for it.

To his right, a bucket had fallen onto its side, bringing his gaze over a bearded orc partially hidden beside it.

"Excuse me," Arlowe called. The orc retreated behind a nearby barrel. "Could you help me?"

The orc peeked back out, looking the prince up and down before using the barrel as an aid to stand. "Could you stay there? For now, at least?" Arlowe nodded. "You got any food?"

"I have some spare rations in my pack. I'm more than willing to pass a couple over."

"I'd be happy to do what I can in return."

Arlowe reached into his pack, taking out a couple of wrapped provisions before tossing them to the orc.

Realising that the stranger had been true to his word, the orc waved for the prince to come closer as he tore open the wrapping, devouring the contents.

"Is that better?" Arlowe asked, happy to see him fed. The orc appeared to be homeless; the assumption was drawn from his rough attire and a tremendous odour of urine.

"Much," the orc replied, already finished with his meal. "Thank you, kind sir. Not everyone is so charitable. I can't count how many times I've been promised food for my help only to be lied to."

"I'm looking for the library. I'm meeting an ally of mine there."

The orc froze, retreating back slightly. "You don't want to go there."

"Why wouldn't I?"

The orc gulped. His eyes flitted around, clearly looking out for someone. "There was someone here earlier today. They were headed for the library too. Offered me food only to renege on our deal and threaten my life."

Arlowe shook his head. "Dark skin? Midnight blue outfit? Metal mask?"

The orc seemed stunned. "How do you know of him?"

"He's the ally I mentioned," the prince begrudgingly answered. "Do you know where the library is?"

"At least one of you has manners," the orc spat. "Go down this street, then take your first left. The library should be directly ahead. You can't miss it."

Arlowe thanked the orc for his aid, passing him another ration before following the directions given.

The orc beggar wasn't wrong. As soon as he turned the corner, the prince was greeted with a building of a much grander scale than those that stood beside it. Stained glass windows decorated the front, with statues of the conqueror demons atop like the cherry on the metaphorical cake.

If there isn't an elaborate trap here waiting for me, I'll be very disappointed. Arlowe rapped his hands across the door only for it to open at the lightest pressure. *Here we go.*

The prince moved the wooden door aside, taking in a whiff of the library's air as he stepped in. As it was outside, the library was devoid of anyone Arlowe could see, though the musty smell of the tomes within eased his mind.

Taking a lantern from the nearest table, Arlowe closed the door behind him before exploring the building; its interior as well kept as its exterior. Every chair was set in place, with every book in the correct category and alphabetical order, though he had to pull his attention away, reminding himself of why he was here.

"Thaedlon Guard. Is anyone there?" he shouted with authority, hoping to provoke a reaction. "We got reports of a local man being attacked by a masked thug. We're looking for witnesses."

Finding no success on the ground floor, Arlowe ascended the staircase to the next. As he did, a click could be heard on the balcony to his right. The prince shone his lantern over Onyx, bathing him in its light. "There you are."

Realising who stood before him, the assassin returned the crossbow back behind his cape before returning to the murky depths of the upper library, leaving without the utterance of a single word.

"Nice to see you too," Arlowe announced, reaching the next floor. "What's the matter with you? Attacking beggars? And what was that? I was playing the role of a curious guard and your first instinct was to shoot?"

The assassin spoke not a word, heightening Arlowe's curiosity. The prince spotted a source of light in the direction that Onyx had withdrawn, heading towards it. "And don't get me started on your eavesdropping on my conversation with King—"

As Arlowe rounded the corner, what awaited him cancelled out what he had to say.

Two illusions, crafted by Onyx, stood side by side. To the left was a woman dressed in tight casual clothing with glasses rested upon the bridge of her nose. The only unique feature about her was the katana that rested in her hand.

On the right, however, was something *far* different. While the body of the creature appeared humanoid, everything else about it seemed very wrong. Its skin was a chalk white with eyes of the same colour, making it appear more as a mannequin than anything else; black scorch marks adorned its head, chest and limbs.

"Your journal mentioned a shapeshifter with a katana. She disguised herself as me on your first encounter," Arlowe remembered, taking a closer look at the left-most illusion. "I always knew I'd look good as a woman."

The prince's humour had no effect on the assassin, whose arm quivered at the illusions. "That's just one of them. I assume this is her preferred form," Onyx spoke at last, gripping his stump. "As for the other, that's what I believe they look like. Underneath their façade."

"Is this really what you want to be doing with the time you have left?" Onyx didn't answer. "Don't."

"He deserved better."

Arlowe placed his hand softly on Onyx's shoulder. "*You* deserve better."

The assassin shrugged off the arm, moving away from him. "If they murdered someone you held close, would you hunt them down? What if it was one of us? What if it was Daria?" he posed, back turned. "Just making sure we're on the same page."

"That's not a fair comparison and you know it," Arlowe answered, preparing himself for the anger that was sure to follow from his words. "Those shapeshifters have no interest unless you seek them out. Whatever your master did to be hunted by them has nothing to do with you."

"Don't you dare."

"Tell me what you know about them. How many of *them* are there? Do you have a way to consistently hunt them? Their fighting styles, languages, favoured forms? Do you even know *what* they are?" Arlowe approached, wary of the assassin's next action. "Please Onyx, don't do this."

"I don't have a choice!" yelled the assassin, flinging a dagger in frustration that missed Arlowe's face by mere inches. The illusions flickered from sight. "They're near impossible to find *now*. If they disappear, my master's honour is tainted forever. I need to get to them first."

Their eyes finally met. "I can't convince you otherwise, can I?"

Onyx shook his head. "I don't think you can."

Accepting his decision, Arlowe took the purse from his pack, hanging it upon the dagger fixed into the library's wood.

"What is that?" the assassin posed, coming closer.

"You already know."

"I don't want it."

"I'm fulfilling our deal."

"I'm not interested in the deal anymore. Keep it."

Arlowe turned to face him, confused. "Why?"

Onyx wrenched his dagger free of the wall, pointing it towards Arlowe. The hilt faced him with the purse offered. "Pessimistic thought of the day: If I die out there, there's a good chance Katosus remains unchanged. My guild cares not for me and my master has already passed on. If *you* die, I know that our world will change, and not for the better. That's why I want you to take the money. It's wasted on me."

Obliging, the prince took the money back into his grasp. "I never expected to part on good terms with an assassin," Arlowe mused, offering Onyx a handshake with the other. "I'd be lying if I said I wouldn't miss your company."

The assassin looked down at the outstretched hand, smirking. "I swear it's as natural to you as breathing."

"Testing your patience?"

"Handshakes! You're always offering people handshakes! How have you not noticed? The frequency of them, it would drive any normal man mad!"

"I never noticed," Arlowe commented, re-offering his hand. "I can't back down now. I've already offered to shake your hand."

"And now you'll wince every time you offer one." Onyx took the prince's hand, shaking it. "You're welcome."

"If you get into trouble, ever, come and find me."

"You're a good man, Arlowe," Onyx murmured, "though I don't think you needed me to figure that one out."

*

Arlowe pushed open the gates to the Eleventh Sense Guild, barged past by one wearing the guild's mark.

"Pardon me," Arlowe spoke, forced aside to let the woman through.

"You don't want to go in there," she replied, seeming eager to leave. "I wish I hadn't."

Before Arlowe could have pressed the woman for more answers, the sound of vicious yelling burst forth from the guild hall; the skittish eleventh fled to safety.

Investigating the source of the rage, the prince found the door to the guild ajar, able to see Gill inside with what could be made out as a red-faced Siegfried.

"Not again," Arlowe grumbled, sympathising for his eleventh companion.

466

"You're throwing your life away, you fool!" Siegfried bellowed, pacing angrily back and forth. "Can you not see that this is futile? Or are you blind to all this?"

Gill hadn't moved an inch, merely watching his old partner tire himself out. "It's our duty."

"Our duty?" Siegfried broke from his anger to scoff at Gill, snapping free of his ranting and pacing with a calmer, sorrowful expression upon his face. "Gill, I'm begging you. Following these people will only lead to your death. This isn't your fight. Stand by my side again as partners—"

Gill raised his hand. "No."

Siegfried was stunned at Gill's blunt refusal, flaring up once again. "No?"

"The kharakians are one victory away from becoming a catastrophe we can't recover from. In such an event, all of the guilds are inclined to aid in ending their threat, including us," Gill scolded, crossing his arms in defiance of Siegfried's selfish desire. "If you have no interest in Argestra's safety, it proves that the only thing left of your eleventh status is the title you carry."

"I am the hero that these people look up to!"

"You can't have the ground you walk on worshipped if everyone lies dead upon it."

Pushed to his breaking point, Siegfried unsheathed one of the blades, pointing it at Gill before pulling a trigger located on its hilt.

Narrowly avoiding the blast, Gill kicked down one of the tables to use as cover, shaking his head at Arlowe for him not to intervene.

Siegfried advanced on his old partner firing two more rounds, though Gill was prepared for the brazen assault. using the table as both cover and a battering ram.

Siegfried evaded over it, though before he could pull the trigger again, Gill slammed his staff into the blade's firing cylinder, making it unable to unload its used rounds.

Drawing his other blade, Siegfried rushed to make another shot, though Gill took advantage of the weapon's weight, leaping over the round before drawing his mace to block a second.

Not dissuaded by his old partner countering every move he made, Siegfried persisted in his attempt to beat him, removing their abilities to see.

"Let's see how skilled you really are!" blurted the rival, charging forth.

In tune with his lost senses and what remained, Gill used the same power himself, cancelling out their sense of touch before landing a kick on Siegfried's wrist, forcing him to release the functioning gun blade.

Both regaining their senses, Siegfried advanced once more, hoping to achieve any kind of victory. Alas, this was not to be.

With only one damaged gun blade left in his hand, Gill swapped to his staff, knocking him down to the ground with a well-placed strike.

Struggling to stand, Siegfried pounded the ground with his fist, gasping for breath. "I'm going to survive this damn war and I'm going to bring down Aracaria! Not you!" he screamed, piquing both Arlowe and Gill's interests.

"Aracaria was always my goal, never yours," Gill uttered, kneeling to Siegfried's level. "I feel ready for the kharakians. I've never felt ready for her. She'll rip you to pieces as an off-hand gesture."

Taking him by the collar, Gill forcefully pulled Siegfried to his feet, though his old partner pushed back as soon as he was stable. "I am the superior eleventh! I'll prove it with her demise!"

Gill crouched to reach the broken gun blade by his side, examining the weapon. "If that's the case, take a reliable weapon over one used purely for your image."

Too flustered to return another response to the repeated jabbing of his ego, Siegfried took his still-functioning gun blade to the guild hall's exterior, pointing it at Arlowe as soon as he turned the corner.

"This is all your fault!" he yelled; his finger quivered over the trigger. "If you hadn't interfered, we could have—"

Before the round could be fired, a bolt cut off the rabid eleventh's accusations, breaking the firing mechanism of his weapon.

The assaulter and victim both peered in, able to see Gill loading another bolt into his crossbow, staring his old partner down.

At last accepting defeat, Siegfried scurried off at the sight of the loaded crossbow, leaving the remains of his iconic weapons behind.

Relieved to not have a hole through his skull, Arlowe entered into the guild hall, making sure that the door was firmly secured behind him. Gill had his back turned, looking out through the room's main window.

"I apologise for my partner's behaviour," the eleventh voiced wearily, sounding to Arlowe as though their argument had lasted far longer than his exposure to it.

"There's no need," Arlowe replied, standing by the side of his supernatural companion. "If that were the case, I'd be begging for your forgiveness over Onyx."

The two chuckled to themselves; the air of tension left by Siegfried lifted with each passing moment.

With a smile still on his face, Gill took an overturned stool a few steps away, rotating it back to its natural state before gesturing for Arlowe to do the same. "I assume you came to see us all off. A noble thing to do."

"A mandatory one. Who knows where you'll all scatter to? You especially," Arlowe stated, placing himself upon his own stool. "What got Siegfried whipped up into that frenzy in the first place?"

"Asking me to abandon you. He clearly doesn't know me like he used to," Gill muttered, shaking his head. "I say he's dead to me, and yet here we are, still encountering one another. Losing himself further with every passing day."

"He mentioned an Aracaria?"

Gill took a moment, processing the word spoken to him. "It occurs to me that we've never spoken about my time as an eleventh. Do you remember when we first met?"

"You were hunting a corrupted spirit," Arlowe recollected. "Is that what Aracaria is?"

"Calling Aracaria a corrupted spirit is like comparing a meteor to a fireball. Aracaria is... so much more."

"How so?"

Gill stood from his chair, relying heavily on his hands as he proceeded to explain.

"When a corrupted spirit is first formed, the creatures are weak and easy to eliminate. On occasion, the corrupted spirit is cunning, able to elude those that seek it. Left to prosper in our world, a corrupted spirit can become much stronger."

"Like the one you were hunting when we met you."

"Aracaria is what happens when a corrupted spirit remains in our world for generations."

Arlowe gulped at the statement. "And you were hunting something like that?"

Gill nodded, returning to his seat. "Aracaria is a legend within the Eleventh Sense Guild. She has survived for centuries, leaving thousands of young corpses in the wake of her arrivals. Many old friends of mine have perished hunting her. I may be the one to stop her, or I may be another on her long list of victims. It bothers me not."

Arlowe sunk slightly; his conscience weighed him down. "Gill, if that's the case, I need to apologise for keeping you by my side. You never mentioned this to me. To any of us."

Gill waved away Arlowe's concern, offering him smile to calm his worries. "You don't have to apologise for anything. I have to look at this rationally, Arlowe. If Aracaria gets her way, many more will die, but if our mutual enemy gets their way? We lose everyone. What I want has its time and place, and that isn't now."

"I hope we've offered half of what hunting Aracaria could," Arlowe mumbled.

"More so than you think. Between the kharakian attacks, the Arcane Guild Murders, Schukara's missing sister, Onyx's shapeshifter problem and my own run-ins with Sieg, well, I've been content being so busy whilst in good company," Gill insisted. "You've kept my senses sharp and a grin on my face. I appreciate it."

Gill rose one more time from his stool, motioning his head to the entrance. He led Arlowe back through the entrance hall, kicking away the remnants of Siegfried's gun blade out of their way.

Arlowe followed behind, watching as the door closed behind him. "Hey, Gill?"

The eleventh stopped in his tracks. "Hm?"

"Stay in contact, would you?"

"Any particular reason?"

"I'll be easy to find, restoring Eyenridge to its former glory. I want you to have someone there to tell your stories to. I want to hear of your success against Aracaria."

Gill thought to himself, approaching Arlowe as he did. "I often don't bother with staying in touch. Haven't for a while," Gill uttered, seeming to reach his conclusion by the smile resting upon his face. "You've been good to me. I think I shall."

Arlowe offered his hand to the eleventh, only to wince at the sight of it. "He was right…"

"He made you aware, didn't he?"

Arlowe looked up, staring at Gill in disbelief. "You knew?" he gasped, seeing the elevenths kind smile slowly turn into a playful smirk.

"We betted over it," Gill replied with a hint of shame. "He didn't think he'd have to point it out until the end of the road. That means he owes me."

"I expect nothing less from Onyx. I expected better from you."

"An eleventh's job is to keep one on their toes regardless of circumstance."

Taking another moment to laugh at Arlowe's expense, the two resumed their stroll to the courtyard gate.

"You know, Onyx refused to accept my payment," the prince divulged, acquiring a raised eyebrow from the eleventh. "It's a crazy world we live in."

"Indeed it is," Gill replied as he opened the gate, gesturing for Arlowe to exit first. "If you still hold the coin, I'd suggest putting it to good use."

"Are you not interested in the money?"

"You have to understand, we made that bet a long time ago. If he was using the money on anything other than his equipment, I'd be tempted, but that is not the case, is it?"

Closing the gate behind himself, Gill turned to Arlowe; the prince's face was filled with uncertainty. "Do you require an escort to the meeting point?" the eleventh offered, though Arlowe simply shook his head, declining his aid.

"I'll meet you there. There's one more person I have to check in on before I'm done."

*

Journeying to the farthest reaches of Thaedlon, the prince found himself on a street far removed from the city's modern décor. The smooth floor beneath his heel shifted to that of a cobbled texture; much of the old dwarven architecture was still present among the ancient houses.

Towards the end of the street, Arlowe could make out what looked to be an old school house. Though in a rough state, it was clear that the surrounding residents had continued to tend to the structure long after the end of its original purpose. The building was surrounded by various tools, paints and flowers.

Surveying the archaic structure in search of an entrance, the prince turned the corner to find the school's only entry way surrounded by a group of silent strangers. Each one looked him up and down before returning to their focus on the door, unnerving him.

"Can I help—" Arlowe was cut off by a chorus of hushes as the group once again turned back to the door. "What are you—"

The collective mutterings of the group collected in harmony, with an elderly woman leaving the pack to meet with him. "Could you please be quiet?" she asked, forceful in her tone and in her shunting of the prince. "We're trying to listen."

It was rare for Arlowe to be spoken to in such a way, even less so by someone of this woman's age, though he eventually brought himself to respond.

"Excuse me," he whispered. The woman nodded in approval. "What's going on here? Why are you all stood outside of this building?"

"We're listening to the music."

"Music?"

"Listen," the woman ordered, bluntly putting her finger to her ear.

Arlowe did as he was told, surprised to find music on the air with a delicate voice accompanying it, only for both to abruptly end and restart. "What a marvellous musician."

Though Arlowe was unfamiliar with what he could hear of the instrument being played, the voice singing alongside it was too familiar to ignore. He made his way past the woman only to have his wrist grabbed, halting him.

"Mabel, let him go."

The unrecognised voice clearly had influence, as the woman let go as quickly as she had latched on. The crowd separated to reveal a wizened elf, slowly coming closer with the assistance of one younger. "I apologise for my friend's behaviour. You're not the first to join us, and some have been quite disruptive. What brings you to this corner of Thaedlon, sir?"

"I'm looking for a friend of mine," Arlowe answered, bowing his head to the elf. "I believe I've found her."

"Have you?" the elf asked, relaxing onto his cane. "And where might that friend be?"

"Right through those doors."

"Am I right in presuming you plan to take her away?"

"I'm not taking her anywhere. She's joining me of her own accord."

"I see," the elf replied, tittering at the prince's words. "It's a shame to see such talent face the fires of war."

"She made that choice so that others don't have to," the prince voiced, slowly guided to the entrance by the elf. "I'm proud to call her my ally, and prouder still to call her the woman I adore."

As they reached the building's entrance, the elf loosened his grip of Arlowe, allowing him to leave his presence. "Cherish her, my boy. She seems to be a unique soul."

"I will."

The elf gave a bow as Arlowe departed.

Arlowe glanced back at the crowd as he entered the school. The old elven man had vanished from the crowd, with those same people seemingly unaware that he was ever there to begin with.

"Ugh, no, that sounds awful. Again." The frustrated tone of Daria's voice echoed through the building, giving the prince a chance to slip into the main hall undetected. "I will get this right."

The mage stood centre stage. Arlowe entered at the top of a steep set of stairs, looking out over the entirety of the hall. The space was theatrically decorated; a historic blend of old dwarven theatre mixed with modern furnishings such as the refurbished circles and stage curtains.

As the prince made his way closer to the stage, channelling his inner Onyx to make it there as stealthily as possible, the violin positioned in Daria's hand began to play. After completing a simple introduction, the mage took a visible breath before singing to the room with accompanying melody.

"Never saw the world until I stopped running,

"It's changed so much since I stopped breathing,

"Tell me my place, for all my wondering,

"What you saw in me, my heart unwavering.

"Find me, I'm forever lost,

"So cold and broken,

"Hold me through the frost,

"My dreams awoken,

"The misfortune laid on you,

"Yet your warm smile, still breaking through,

"O fiba sie, O muwi zua,

"O rigei ciuu, la voila croix,

"I..."

Arlowe had stepped up onto the stage, though a creak gave away his presence. The violin screeched, as Daria was made aware, almost dropped from her shock.

"It's okay! It's only me!" the prince spoke, hurrying to comfort the mage. "Please, continue."

"You weren't supposed to hear that," Daria choked, her hair covering her embarrassment. "It's... not ready yet."

"I-if it's any consolation, I've only just arrived. We could say you gave me a sampling?" Daria didn't answer, prompting Arlowe to approach her, attempting to see through her cloak of hair. "Daria, that was incredible. You composed that yourself?"

She nodded, making eye contact with him. "I wanted to make something for you."

The sound of applause and cheering made its way through the window, drawing Daria's attention to it. "What's that?" she asked, moving closer to the cheering.

"You have quite the following outside."

Daria spun in horror; withdrawing back into the shell she had only just emerged from. "Other people were listening? No. No no no no no no!"

Arlowe took her arm, stopping her nervous pacing with a comforting smile. "Hey, it's okay. There's no need to panic."

As he let go, Daria took a deep breath, sitting herself upon the edge of the stage. "Intentional or not, your music has been easing the people of this city. I'd say that's a glowing recommendation."

Acquiring no response from the mage, Arlowe took the spot by her side, looking over the empty audience across from them. "To say I've never seen you with an instrument, you played that violin with the precision of an expert. How come?"

"I had one, years ago," Daria mumbled, her posture slowly relaxing. "My half-size eldoraichi. My parents got it me for my birthday. It was closer to me than any friend."

"What happened to it?"

"It didn't survive the long journey to Grandgrave."

"Demons?"

476

"Worse, critics."

The two laughed, with Daria taking Arlowe's hand into her own.

"So, where did this one come from?" Arlowe queried, looking over the violin. "That looks like an eldoraichi."

"It is. Other than being a full-size violin, it looks nearly identical to my Janine."

Arlowe turned to Daria confused. "Janine?"

"Janine was my violin," she answered, delicately handing the instrument to Arlowe. "I don't know where the name came from. It just felt like the right name for her."

A moment of clarity came to Arlowe's face in the form of concern, looking over the eldoraichi. "Daria, where did you get *this* violin from?"

"I saw the violin through the window."

"So, you broke in?"

"No, I was able to lift the wind…" Arlowe pointed out the broken latch hanging from the window she had used to enter, tapping his bicep to remind Daria of her necrotic strength. "Oh, I… I didn't mean to… Sometimes I forget how strong I…"

"Don't worry about it. I think the city has more to worry about than a broken window," he remarked, returning the eldoraichi on its stand. "We'd best leave this here. I doubt the kharakians have any interest in music. If that were the case, we would've had a band marching against them, not an army."

Daria rose to her feet, ready to descend from the stage. "Are we ready to meet the others?"

"Not yet," Arlowe stated, with Daria holding off on her exit. "I've spoken to everyone else. I need to talk to you."

Her head tilted. "What's on your mind?"

"After the kharakians, what do you plan to do? Where will you go?" Arlowe posed to her. "That is, if we even make it through this."

"You have to. You promised." Daria took a step forward, though oddly she maintained her distance. "I want to... I want to come with you, if you would have me. Not just because of what we have together, but because I have nowhere else to go."

"What about your parents? You could always return to Caermyythen?"

"I haven't seen them in years," Daria expressed, beginning to fidget. "Those that I left with attacked the town as we fled. I don't know if I could."

"I don't have to go back to Eyenridge immediately," he proposed. Daria was unsure of where his words led. "I could accompany you to Caermyythen, help you set your story straight. Everyone deserves a family."

"I don't... I..." Though Arlowe was ready to comfort her, already taking the first step, Daria rushed towards him, leaping into his arms before pressing her lips against his; her tears uncontrollable as they wetted Arlowe's skin.

"I couldn't do that to you. Regardless of my intentions, they'll see me for what I am!" she argued, shaking her head. "They'll vilify me. They'll vilify *you*."

"Then let them," he debated, confident in his choice. "If you were anything like you think you are, do you think I'd still be here?"

Daria stroked the prince's face, wiping him clean of her teardrops. "Is there anything I can do for you? To thank you for everything you've done?"

Arlowe looked deep into her eyes, nodding at her proposal. "I want you to let go of your illusion. I want you to be who you truly are," he gently spoke, noting the fear in those same eyes.

"I..." Daria closed her eyes. Her eyelids fluttered open to reveal the transition back from grey to the deep purple he had grown so close to; her black veins were visible once more. "What do you think?"

"I think that you're finally at peace with yourself. I love you."

Unable to speak, Daria simply embraced her prince once more, both enthralled in the warmness of their breaths and the proximity of their bodies as their lips pushed harshly against one another; a battle of worship for one another raged on.

As Daria finally retreated, the two reassured in each other's grasp, the door to the hall drew their attention with a loud crash. Their attention was drawn to their elven ally stood breathless in the doorway.

"Schukara? What are you doing here?" Arlowe posed, dropping Daria to her feet.

"Yer' not easy ta' find!" she blurted, shaking her head to refocus. "Not tha' point! You need ta' get outside! Now!"

"Why? What's happening?"

"There's someone here ya' need ta' see!"

Before Arlowe could inquire further, his elven companion had rushed out as fast as she had rushed in. Moved by Schukara's urgency, the prince and the mage did the same.

"Who do you think it is?" Daria questioned, following closely behind Arlowe as they pushed through the hallway.

"I don't know. Kardus? Valerius? One of Demetrius', what, eighteen kids?" Arlowe racked for his brain over who it could be. "Let's just hope it's not one of our adversaries. Now isn't the time."

As the prince crashed through the school doors, his eyes flitted back and forth around the school's outskirts, spotting only Schukara leaned near the cobbled street. "Who were you talking about? I don't—"

"Back in my day, you'd be ridiculed for diddlin' a ginger. You've definitely raised the bar diddlin' the dead."

Stepping out from the street's cover, a man in ash-stained clothing appeared tapping a tune with his pipe upon the stonework. "It's been a while, kid."

Daria had picked up on Arlowe's hesitance, nudging him. "Arlowe? What's wrong?"

"Cael." Arlowe's heart swelled, moving slowly before sprinting at his old mentor. The tears in his eyes built, taken into the old man's arms. "I thought I lost you."

"And I the same." The two looked up, both able to see the glow of Kharaki in the distance. "I'd say we need to catch up, but I doubt we're gonna have the time. Gimme the short version."

Chapter Twenty-Two:

"Being able to see a world that may cease to be…"

1ˢᵗ Nofabelos

Land's Legacy

2084∞ (Current Age)

Cael poured himself another glass of wine, downing it like the many that came before. "If it were me, I would'a had that amalgam shakin' in fear. Mavis demands respect!" the tutor bragged, stopping himself from taking another glass as he noticed his lack of balance. Wisely, he returned the named dagger to his boot.

Arlowe chuckled at Cael's teetering, pleased to take his mind away from the oncoming battle.

Demetrius had led the prince's band and the last of those willing into Fertral himself, guiding them to the camp located closest to Kharaki. The king had offered the tent to the two, aware of their past bond and eagerness to inform each other of their adventures.

"Who knew being a hero was such hard work?" Cael posed, already aware of the answer, planting himself beside his former pupil. "No offence, but I'm glad I'm not standing where you are right now."

"You make it sound like I chose to be the royal envoy," Arlowe replied, taken under Cael's shoulder. "You also forget that I have the pterravun to thank for my life."

"Don't. I'm still trying to wrap my head around that one." The tutor took his trusty pipe from his pocket, taking a few puffs as he relaxed further back. "Who knew you'd accomplish so much without me? Brings a tear to my eye."

"Who knew you were capable of fighting, old man? Searching for me *and* evacuating the country? I thought your old tales were just that. Proved me wrong."

Cael took a few more puffs from his pipe, revelling in Arlowe's praise before returning the pipe from whence it came, wiping the ash down his front as the prince had always remembered.

Arlowe smirked at the mess. "Old habits, eh?"

"I'm aware that I haven't changed a bit. You, however," Cael commented, looking his former pupil from head to toe. "If I may speak so boldly, kid, I remember you once stating that the guilds were nothing short of self-serving; that assassins were disturbed monsters and that necromancers were meant for Erethys and not the Vault."

Arlowe admired the crest of his shield that was propped up by the tent door; through the doorway, a ruined Eyenridge rested in the horizon. "I'm aware of how I felt.

"I'm also aware that my earlier self hadn't been dragged into a war beside them. That opened my eyes. I was young, naive. I only went by what I read and what I was told. Now I know that we're too complicated to be explained by mere words. They fail us. We're all just trying to get by.

"The world was so beautiful from the top of those ivory towers. It's a weakness I've taken great pleasure in shedding away at last."

Cael downed one last glass. "They're an odd ensemble."

"You're not the first to say."

"And I doubt I'll be the last."

As if on cue, a hand pulled the fabric of the tent away. Onyx stood in the doorway.

"Arlowe? You're wanted at the war tent," he spoke, scanning Cael with suspicion before leaving the same way he had entered.

Acknowledging the call, Arlowe strapped the shield to his arm, departing the tent alongside his tutor. "Will you be joining us? Against the kharakians?" the prince posed to him, anxious of the response.

482

Cael shook his head. "It's not my place to be up there," he said; the disappointment showed on his student's face. "My time is over, Arlowe. I'm not as young as I used to be. I'd be a hinderance to you. I'm better off down here making sure that the forces you've gathered aren't overwhelmed. We only get one shot at this."

Arlowe nodded, accepting Cael's reasoning. "Where will I find you? Once this nightmare is ended?"

"At home."

Hugging it out one more time, the two went their separate ways, this time on their own terms.

As the prince closed in on the war tent, a whistle brought his attention back to Cael, calling up to him.

"I can't speak for those who follow you. I can't speak for the dead either. I can only speak for myself, and I want you to know that you've done me proud many times over. Your father's blade suits you so much so that I almost mistook you for him."

Waving to him as he turned, all Arlowe could offer was a wave back, watching the man that had sought him for so long leave him once more. He knew that they would meet again, in this life or the next.

"Goodbye, Cael. I'll see you soon."

Entering into the tent, Arlowe found his allies on one side of the war table, with Demetrius and Kardus stood opposite. All within greeted the prince as he joined the meeting.

"Thank you for coming," Demetrius welcomed, bowing his head as the prince's gaze was placed upon him.

Arlowe approached the table, leaning over it. "Who knows how long we have. What's the plan?"

"Well, with you here, we can discuss those potential strategies."

"Potential?" Arlowe questioned, noticing that the table's decorations were all to one side. The map was bare. "There is a plan in place, right?"

"The orders devised for the armies gathered have not changed," Demetrius explained, moving a Thaedlon-crested piece in place. "Those placed in designated capture squads are to calm and capture any kharakians on sight, whilst everyone else is to act as a blockade, halting the kharakians from advancing any further."

"And us?"

Kardus placed a Kharaki-shaped piece onto the board, adding Fertral and Draconity symbols alongside it. "Ota-Rnshi will fly you up to Kharaki where you will find the source of the problem and end it," he declared, returning back to Demetrius' side. "I understand your hesitance. I'm not keen on this either."

"This plan is as bare bones as it gets," Onyx spoke, voicing his displeasure at the 'plan'. "If the enemy makes any move, we'll have to adapt. Heavily."

"Have your scouts noticed anything out of the ordinary?" Gill questioned.

Demetrius shook his head. "We've had our scouts close to the crater beneath the city. The silence of the opposing army is the only anomaly we've had."

"Without tha' enemy, what more can we do?" Schukara expressed to her allies, staring at the near-empty table. "Worst-case scenario, they rush us all at once. In that regard, we know what ta' do. We stick ta' tha' plan."

"Precisely," Kardus agreed, placing six flag pieces in a hexagonal ring around Kharaki. "There will be flare checkpoints at these locations. The command post will give orders to the northern-most checkpoint, firing off the appropriate flare, which the others will then replicate to give orders on masse."

Taking a mental note of the positions, Arlowe nodded to his band to gauge their readiness, acquiring a nod in return from all. "Anything else we need to know?"

"Stay safe out there," Demetrius added, taking the Fertral piece into hand. "I don't mean to understate my appreciation for those gathered here, but you are the ones that will end Kharaki's curse. I don't think I have to explain how crucial this is."

"Is that everything then?" Onyx posed, itching to leave the tent.

"I have something to say," Arlowe uttered, moving to the tent's entrance with everyone in sight. "When I was thrown from my castle, I never expected to have my life given back to me. To find myself on this path.

"I never expected to fight so closely alongside those who favour the guilds, I never expected myself to fight alongside those who gladly hunt for sport and I certainly didn't expect to find myself fighting alongside a member of the undead.

"From the scorched lands that the kharakians have conquered to the bloodied halls of the Arcane Guilds, from the goblins that have hunted us to the fae that found us. I am honoured to be standing beside each of you here, as well as those not present that aided us in getting this far.

"I don't know what exactly we'll find at Kharaki's centre. I don't know if we'll get Xanth back. I don't know if we'll make it. What I do know is that each of your actions made this possible, and because of that, you have my undying gratitude. Believe me when I say that regardless of whether you trust me or not, my trust will forever be placed in all of you.

"We're almost there. Fertral's freedom awaits us, and it's long been overdue."

*

It didn't take long for Arlowe's band to reach the blockade. The scorched fields were desolate, dotted with the corpses of the unfortunate few who fell too soon, never seeing the fires of combat. Trebuchets lined the hills, with military ironsoul suits stationed on the front lines ready to take any pressure from those by their sides.

Not even a whisper echoed from the surrounding troops, stood patiently with the cursed city in their sights, watching for any development with bated breath.

Ota-Rnshi followed the group to the blockade, noting the comforted looks of those present. "The looks of solace," it spoke, bowing back to the soldiers. "It comforts me to know that I offer hope to these men."

"It's almost like not having you here would be detrimental," Onyx commented. "Collecting the armies and researching is optional, but flying to the city? We weren't blessed enough to receive wings."

Schukara groaned at Onyx's words, flaring up. "Is now really tha' time ta' be so negative?"

"Negative, no. Realistic, yeah."

"What's tha' difference?"

"If I was being negative, I'd say that if we fall, Katosus is doomed."

"And realistically?"

"If we fall, the necromancers in Grandgrave will go from one army to two against the kharakians. The beasts can't win either way."

"That's enough, you two," Arlowe voiced, cutting the chatter. "The necromancers won't have to come and collect us. When the time's right, we'll be heading there of our own accord."

A nudge from Daria took his attention, following where the mage was pointing. "Arlowe, is that—"

"Long time, no see," uttered Valerius, sat on a boulder looking to Kharaki; Adrestia rested over his shoulder. "You all look well."

"We thought you'd be travelling from the north," the blade added, glowing as it

486

spoke. "It's good to see you all again."

"So this is who the Bright Blades were referencing," Kardus announced, looking over Valerius; the wielder was now poised to defend himself. "Is it right to trust him?"

Valerius felt resistance from his blade, Adrestia shaking in his hand. "Valerius, stand down," she scolded, bringing him to lower her. "I have faith in your abilities. Not enough to take down a soreiku and his master, however."

"He didn't have to give me the information on the fae, nor inform me on Species Eighteen. He's been more helpful than most," Arlowe answered, watching both parties relax themselves. "If he was to backstab me, he couldn't have picked a worse time."

"You mentioned the Bright Blades. They know of our alliance?" Valerius queried, returning Adrestia to his shoulder.

"They found out when I mentioned the energy spike on Kharaki."

"Makes sense, I guess."

"You're not angry?"

Valerius shrugged, with the black blade continuing for him. "They can't hunt us any more than they already are without drawing attention to themselves. Occasionally, we are able to convince those that hunt us to shed their single-minded ways. Besides, it doesn't change what's happening right now. That energy is our priority."

"It's good ta' have ya' here," Schukara said with a smile.

"Don't get used to it. Once this mess has been dealt with, I imagine I'll be back on the road," Valerius replied, turning his attention to Arlowe. "Have you heard anything else from Species—"

A low rumble shook through the ground, silencing any word, any movement.

Arlowe felt something small graze his hand, lifting it to see a spec of black resting upon it. One by one, the group too felt the flakes of soot fall onto them, only to see their fall becoming stronger, dousing them in a downpour of darkness.

As the floor around them began to change in colour, another rumble came from the floating city; its molten contents flowed into the crater below.

A flicker began to appear before Arlowe, blinking back and forth, erratic in its behaviour. "Valerius, are you…?"

"Species Eighteen," he voiced, confirming the prince's suspicions. "Something's not right."

Growing ever faster, the flickering continued to dart back and forth, unable to control itself. Both Arlowe and Valerius became overwhelmed, with both uttering the same word. "Utava."

As the word was spoken, Kharaki exploded with rage. Horror was visible in the eyes of all as the kharakians emerged from the city, overflowing from all sides, descending to the battlefield below.

"Green flare!" yelled one of the captains, drawing attention to the lime-coloured signal beaming through the powdery sky. "Everyone, brace yourselves! They're coming all at once!"

As the kharakians drew ever closer, the calming spells of the awaiting mages and the calm-infused arrows of the notched archers had already begun to fire, toppling the leading kharakians with keen precision.

Unfazed by their deactivated brethren, the kharakians closed the gap in mere moments, crashing into the front lines without restraint, willing to sacrifice themselves for the slightest advantage.

Though the kharakians were being felled at an astounding rate, so too were the armies gathered to stop them. A handful of ironsoul suits had already become defunct from the assault.

488

"Into position!" Arlowe commanded, scattering his own band to aid those he had called upon. "Give the calming squads time to cull their numbers!"

"I'm with you, Arlowe," Valerius called, bringing Adrestia into both hands.

"As am I," Kardus spoke, facing the dragon. "Master, lay waste to them at their drop zones! Avoid their spears!"

With his orders given, Ota-Rnshi took to the skies, blasting the regenerated kharakians with waves of ice, keeping them from ever entering the fray.

In the time it took Arlowe to reach the front lines, the bodies of his allies had already begun to pile high. The kharakians were now clambering over the corpse wall to reach their targets.

"Fall back! They have the high ground!" Arlowe bellowed; the kharakians flooded down the bodies to reach their prey.

Onyx dived head first into the oncoming hordes, blinking back and forth as he carved them to pieces.

"This can't be maintained! Their regeneration bolsters their numbers!" he shouted, feigning his capture only to blink away from his detonating captor, destroying the surrounding kharakians in the process. "What's next?"

A soldier's life taken by a monster's spear, the prince and the mercenary took the man's body, moving him back, ordering a replacement by their side. "Can't we just head up there now?" Schukara called out, cutting down more of the creatures.

"Not yet!" Arlowe responded, watching an illusion of Daria's creation hold off a larger wave of kharakians. "We need to hold them off until we've deactivated enough of them to make a difference! I'm not leaving until the troops have no reason to fall back further!"

"Mages, to the left! Archers, hold!" Gill instructed, directing the calming spells at swathes of the battlefield to impede the latest wave of the kharakian horde, aiming to steady the concentrated tides. "Archers, fire left!"

As the archers let loose their arrows, downing another cluster, the eleventh could make out a prepared spear in one of the kharakians hands.

He swiftly fired a bolt at the creature only for it to hit too late, watching the weapon leave its hand at the last moment.

He could predict the trajectory. He knew where it would land. "Arlowe!"

The prince peered up at the abrupt warning, able to see the spear yet unable to avoid it nor raise his shield in time.

As the spear neared his face, the projectile turned to dust before him, striking him with a coughing fit rather than taking his head.

"Agh, what happened?" he choked, looking to Gill. "Could that be..."

Gill glanced at the aggressor, who momentarily stood from his injury only to mysteriously turn to dust. A glimmer of green temporarily encompassed its body as it fell.

"Arlowe!" Schukara screamed, rushing towards him. "Arlowe, ya' need ta' move—"

An explosion knocked him off his feet, now barely able to see; His hearing was limited to only a whistle.

Someone was yanking at his arm. "Arlowe! Arlowe, can ya' hear me?"

"What happened?" Arlowe weakly asked the blur, who he now recognised as Schukara, lifted back onto his feet by both her and the assassin.

His senses quickly returning, the prince looked up to see Kharaki violently shaking to expel balls of light, dropping them onto the battlefield with devastating effect.

"They're bombin' us!" Schukara exclaimed, ready to avoid another strike.

"I don't think so," Onyx argued, looking over the locations that were being bombarded. "The kharakians are blowing themselves up."

"Why would they do somethin' so hinderin' ta' themselves?"

"They're doing the opposite, Schu. They're regaining those calmed," Arlowe noted, looking to the creatures falling from their city. "Once they're deactivated, whatever's controlling them can't use them anymore, but if they're released via death…"

"Then they can return ta' be reborn," Schukara growled.

Among the chaos, the group peered up to see the soot-filled skies glistening with a crimson red; the other colours of the flares passed over to reveal the severity of their situation.

Unleashing a blast of ice upon the advancing kharakians, Ota-Rnshi dropped to the side of Arlowe, already carrying Gill and Daria upon its back.

"Arlowe, we must make haste for the city!" it called to him, lowering its wing for them to mount. "The horde's numbers are increasing! Our only chance now is to end the threat before too many of our own perish!"

Wasting no time, Arlowe, Onyx and Schukara ascended onto the dragon's back, looking down to see Kardus and Valerius still fighting off the horde.

"Come on, we need to go!" Arlowe ordered, offering out his hand.

"Leave us!" Valerius roared, forcing the molten aggressors back with a thrust of his hand. "Adrestia and I will stay here! It's gonna get worse before it gets better!"

"Don't worry about us!" Adrestia added, dug into one of the creatures. "I'll keep the brooding one and I alive!"

Ota-Rnshi gazed at Kardus, who let out a sigh as he cleaved apart those before him. "You said it yourself, Master! Their numbers are getting out of control! I'll give you as much time as I can muster!" he yelled, pointing his halberd to the city. "Our retribution is at hand!"

As the dragon readied itself to fly, Arlowe caught a glimpse of Cael holding back the horde. Though overwhelmed, the tutor had enough time to spot the prince, giving a firm nod of approval to his former pupil as he took to the skies in search of Kharaki's end.

The dragon ascended hard, making haste for the city, rising too high for the spears to reach it.

"This is it," Arlowe uttered; his eyes were focused on the city that no longer held fear over his heart. "Last-minute checks. Is everyone ready?"

"I've been ready fer' too long," Schukara said with gusto. "It's time those vermin met their maker!"

"One more threat purged from our world. I'm glad to be a part of it," Gill answered.

"Whatever happens, I'm glad to have been beside you all. I'm as ready as I'll ever be," Daria expressed.

Being the only one not to speak, all eyes were on Onyx. His own were on the prince.

"I guess I'll be the one to ask," voiced the assassin, acquiring Arlowe's attention. "I can see it in your eyes. What has you so rattled?"

The prince thought to himself for a moment, looking back at Kharaki. "Where were the alphas?"

Aware of the ever-growing cascade of kharakians all around, the dragon chose to circle the city, evading the city's artillery in search of a safe drop point.

"There," Ota-Rnshi uttered, swooping towards a jutting rock devoid of enemies.

Still in flight, the dragon master brought himself to the side of the cooled stone, coming close enough for the riders to leap onto the enemy territory without compromising its own safety.

"Ota-Rnshi, re-join Kardus and aid those down below!" Arlowe assisted his allies

492

onto the city, offering his hand. "That blockade needs to be held!"

"How will I know when to retrieve you?" the dragon questioned, only for Gill to pre-emptively turn with his crossbow raised. The kharakian army were aware of their presence.

"Go!" Arlowe yelled, sending the dragon back as he drew his blade to hold off the assailants.

Spears flew through the air, and while Ota-Rnshi was nimble enough to avoid them, the floating city had other ways of dealing with the pest.

Aware of the infiltration, the city had materialised a vortex of accretion disks. Spinning the debris rapidly in an act to separate, the dragon master was forced to disengage and resume its fight down below.

"We knew it was likely ta' be a one-way trip," Schukara declared as the band positioned themselves to strike at the mass of kharakians charging wildly towards them. "Here they come!"

"Weapons down!" Arlowe commanded, aware of the concerned looks of his allies.

"You're insane!" Onyx called, refusing the order.

"Trust me!" The prince lowered his sword. "I wouldn't order it unless I was certain."

As instructed, the group lowered their weapons, their breaths held as the small horde passed by them entirely, leaping down after Ota-Rnshi.

"A higher priority?" Daria posed, baffled as much as the others. "It was like we didn't exist to them."

"This way," Arlowe spoke, heading towards the main stream of kharakians. "I think I know."

"Why aren't they attacking us?" Onyx questioned. "They've never had a problem attacking us before."

Arlowe moved into the crowds of kharakians. The monsters rushed by him, heading directly for the battlefield. One by one, the prince gestured for his companions to join his side, and like him, the kharakians rushed around them, unaware of their existence.

"Look at their eyes," Arlowe uttered, guiding his band through the beasts to the central point of the city.

"There are glimmers of green," Gill answered, drawing their attention to them. "It's not the first time I've seen green either. He's still alive."

Bar the prince, the group looked to the eleventh in awe. "He's alive?" Schukara exclaimed, a smile beaming across her face. "He's alive!"

Arlowe passed under a stone portcullis, seeing no sign of danger ahead. Signalling the all-clear, the band headed deeper within. "We just have to find him."

The roars of the kharakian savages were suspiciously replaced with an ominous silence, unnerving the group second only to the rhythmic sound of a heartbeat further in.

Contrasting to Kharaki's outskirts, the inner sectors of the city were barren, devoid of the monsters, alive or dead. The ground they walked upon seemed clean in a sense, with not a pebble out of place. Even the burning scent of the beasts had receded, as if this was a purer area than the rest.

Pure. Arlowe scoffed at the thought. *As if the kharakians were capable of such a thing.*

Unimpeded by the city's inhabitants, the prince marched to the highest point in Kharaki, the peak dead ahead. It was poetic to Arlowe considering that this journey had started at the highest point of his own home.

"Gill, can ya' sense anythin'?" Schukara posed, unable to adapt back to the lack of action. "This ain't makin' any sense ta' me."

494

"I can only hear what you can. That heartbeat," he responded, scanning his eyes over all he could see. "I sense no ambush, nor any spirits."

"Nothin'?"

"All I know is that Arlowe is listening to something, and that something is guiding him. Species Eighteen, I assume."

Gill's assumption wasn't far from actuality. Species Eighteen was with them, flickering to and from the central point of the city, though the prince had no need for its guidance. He only had need of what the vence was trying to tell him.

Listening in, the fae's messages were crackled and broken, with 'traitor' being one of the few he could understand. *The traitor is the key*, he repeated over and over in his mind, setting foot into a large chamber. *Break his chains to break ours.*

The chamber was empty. Nothing rested on the floor. No kharakians, alpha or otherwise stood ready to challenge them. A louder heartbeat was all that the chamber contained, scattering the group across the room in search of anything of note.

"This is anticlimactic. There's... nothing here?" Onyx questioned, rushing over to one of the opposing archways to find a path simply leading them down to the other side of the city. "This is the big curse? An empty city?"

"What do we do now, Arlowe?" Daria queried, struggling with the lack of answers. "There has to be something here. This can't all be for naught."

Gill cleared his throat to gain the attention of his allies. "I think your sights are a little too low."

Immediately aware of what was implied, the group slowly raised their heads to the origin point of the curse.

A pulsing orb floated above them, suspended in mid-air by an unknown power The glowing energy was synchronised with the heartbeat that echoed in their minds.

Below it was a singular kharakian, limp and lifeless as it hung from a vine-like tentacle that was tightly gripped around its neck. Like the orb, the body pulsed with energy, yet no response came from it.

Onyx aimed his crossbow at the restrained creature. "Let's end this."

"It's not that simple," Arlowe warned, gesturing for the assassin to hold. "Aim for the torso."

"What? Arlowe, we need to—"

"Aim for the torso."

Begrudgingly acknowledging the command, Onyx lowered his arm, hitting the creature directly in the chest.

Unnerving all but the prince, the kharakian let out a wailing scream as its body dangled above them. One of its hands pulled at the bolt whilst the other weakly tugged against that which choked it so.

"Please, stop! Croix'ra hara," the creature uttered, seeming to swap back and forth between two personalities. "You have to stop this madness! Croixr sx'ffarlanu shevv ba atarnev. Stop! E coinixast las aeslaar wlath broikan moireva."

"It's speakin' in Bridge and in Elvish," Schukara noted, seeming confused. "Haven't we been hearin' it exclusively in Bridge?"

"Bring it down," Arlowe ordered.

Onyx loaded another bolt, glancing at the prince with concern. "Through the head?"

"Cut what holds it."

Gazing over his other companions, each as unsure as he, Onyx pulled the trigger to fire the bolt.

Piercing through the tentacle that held the kharakian, the beast dropped to the ground. The kharakian crashed onto the ground before them. Its molten blood spilled from its

496

limbs broken.

"No more! No more! Have mercy!" the monster cried, its body regenerating as it spoke. "Tha and las n'lauh!"

Arlowe stood before the body, blade in hand. "That's enough, Evret."

The mutterings of his allies came to a halt with the uttering of the creature's name. "That's a bold accusation, Arlowe," Gill voiced, standing beside him. "*This* is Evret Rainerus? How so?"

"Look around you. Focus on our surroundings. What do you see?"

"It's just a bunch of stupid rocks," Onyx scoffed. "What are you getting at?"

Schukara's eyes widened, stunned at the revelation. "No, look, on tha' walls, tha' ground. It's shaped."

The group followed her descriptions, now seeing the intentional shapes of Kharaki. The details of windows and doors upon the walls alongside oddly specific architecture decorating the buildings, with the path they had just walked covered in unique gaps; the whole city too close in image of another to ignore.

"Kharaki's shape mirrors Thaedlon," Onyx muttered.

"Evret started his bloody campaign *from* Thaedlon. It makes sense that the curse would form around his own memories," Arlowe explained, his eyes fixed upon the kharakian. "Species Eighteen told me to find the traitor. The alpha said the same thing itself. If we're connecting this to the kharakians, I can't think of any greater traitor than the one that tainted our lands with the curse to begin with."

Transforming into a form more reminiscent of an alpha, the newly discovered Evret quickly rose to strike at Arlowe.

The prince avoided his lunge, breaking his leg with a powerful kick before stabbing the man through his shoulder, knocking him back down to the ground.

"His words gave him away too. Telling us to *come into the fire*? *Accelerate our arrival*? He wasn't threatening us, he was pushing us to end this," Arlowe continued, circling the human-kharakian hybrid with his weapon raised. "As for the Elvish, that was the language spoken by those that cursed him. It speaks in their tongue."

"As I died, a light swallowed me whole. Slavanka! The molten curse wrapping around my sinful soul. Croixr soix'v bavoinus toi tha c'xrsa!"

Once more the general rose, and once more was he struck down, wrestling with his injuries and with himself. "I have been at the forefront of every kill, every massacre, forced to watch what I had wrought. Intertwined, every kharakian death killed me by extension, only for the curse to bring me back over and over until it was finally sated."

"But it never was," Daria deduced, giving the man a pitying look.

"Whet las woirsa then en atarney nlauhtmera?"

"What is worse than an eternal nightmare?" the elf translated, unable to take her eyes from him.

Glowing ever brighter, Evret forced himself back onto his feet, materialising a spear into his hands. Though his allies were prepared, Arlowe held out his hand in protest, taking on the disgraced general alone.

The monster charged forward, grazing the prince's side only to be struck in the back by his shield, knocking him down.

Refusing to be beaten, Evret rose with his spear, landing strike after strike upon Arlowe, though every hit bounced from his shield allowing the prince enough time to find an opening, slicing into his legs to keep him from rising again.

"That surge of energy Valerius and Adrestia referenced?" Arlowe mentioned, whipping the molten blood from his blade. "It changed him. It altered the curse."

"Make it stop! Braek tha chelans!" Evret screamed, writhing in pain. "The curse…"

498

"The curse has been supercharged by the fae energy. That's why their numbers have gotten to unstable levels. That's why we've never had sightings of alphas before. Only now has the curse had the power to create them all."

"We're runnin' outta time!" the elf informed, approaching Arlowe and Evret. "Enough toyin' with him. Put him outta his misery."

The prince kept his gaze over the fallen general. "You of all people should understand I want nothing more, but we can't."

Schukara looked to the prince stunned. "Why not?"

Arlowe held out his hand, gesturing to Evret. "End his life. You'll understand."

"I…" The mercenary was hesitant, though she nodded at the offer, poising herself as would an executioner. "This is fer' Eyenridge, ya' bastard."

Though the general muttered, appearing to weep, Schukara's judgment was swift, taking his head from his shoulders in a single moment.

The head let out a pained sigh as it turned to dust, followed by the limp body, only for the dust to collect above them, recreating Evret in the same hanged position above them.

"No more! No more!" Evret cried out, sobbing as he pulled against the vine. "Ha dasarlas noithlanu vass."

"What?" Schukara questioned, lowering her weapons, confounded by the sight. "Why did he…"

"Onyx, Daria, on me," Arlowe ordered, turning to Schukara with a pained expression. "Do you see now? We can't kill him. We have to break the chains."

The two joined him, one on each side. "And how do we do that?" Gill posed; his own crossbow was readied for another volatile reaction. "How do we break them?"

Arlowe peered to each side. "Calm him."

The assassin and the mage glanced at each other aware of the effect the spell had on standard kharakians and the lack of effect it had upon the alphas, though the look of rage upon Arlowe's face was enough for them to heed the command without question.

Defying their expectations, Evret neither deactivated nor ignored the united calming spells. Screaming in agony, the general began to convulse, glowing brighter with every passing moment.

"Arlowe, he looks ready to detonate," Onyx argued, relaxing his casting hand.

"Don't let up," the prince responded; his hand shielded his eyes from the growing light.

"This is inhumane, even by my standards. We need to stop."

"Evret isn't the one we're torturing."

As Evret's body continued to reject the spells, his body thrown into severe convulsions. The light soon engulfed the man's body, with the temperature of the chamber rapidly approaching unsafe levels.

"That's it!" Arlowe called, covering his eyes. "Daria, cast a barrier!"

As the light faded, still blinding the prince and his companions, something heavy landed before them, echoing through the empty kharakian streets.

"I sense two life signs ahead," Gill stated, warning the band.

"What has Evret done?" Schukara spat, recovering from the daze.

Now able, Arlowe opened his eyes to what stood before them. "That wasn't Evret."

Whimpering and weary, Evret's throat rested in the grip of another.

"La em fraa," pronounced the beast; a hulking kharakian twice the size of any other upon the city; its body pulsed to the beat of the orb. The kharakian wore armour as black as obsidian, with a frame within that would put any at peak physical condition to shame. The creature burned with the volcanic heat of its people. The mark of

Eyenridge branded onto its chest.

Evret attempted to release himself, straining to prise himself free, though the kharakian that held him only gripped tighter; the general's mutterings were near silent.

"Give... him... back..."

Weakly placing his hand upon the monster's chest plate, Evret's arm began to glow brighter. Though the monstrous kharakian had taken notice, crushing the general's neck, a hint of green glimmered within its eyes. The beast was frozen in place.

"Xanth," Arlowe gasped, the doubts giving way to the hope of the young pterravun's safety.

Using the glimmer to his advantage, Evret unleashed a powerful explosion to force his release, knocking the kharakian curse down as he fired himself into the ground, collapsed before the intruders with his arm blown to pieces.

"Arlowe..." uttered the hybrid general, holding out his intact hand, a green energy sheltered within. "He has returned..."

Hope overriding his caution, Arlowe leapt for the energy, his sight turning a familiar green. "Arlowe?"

"Xanth!" Arlowe called out with delight, the anger within slowly going dormant. "I'm so sorry for putting you in danger like—"

"We don't have time for apologies!" Xanth replied, focusing his friend. "We need to stop The Lancerneta!"

"Tha' Incarnate," Schukara translated, looking to Arlowe. "We can hear him too."

The Incarnate rose from its injuries, materialising a gigantic spear into its hand.

"I'll explain later. The chains are broken, but the curse still stands," Xanth expressed. A glimmer appeared in Evret's eyes. "Evret, can you fight?"

The disgraced general rose to his feet, even with his injuries still healing.

"I can do much more than that," he uttered, a molten energy enveloping his hand. "Tapping into the network."

As the energy dispersed, an explosion sounded above the heads of those gathered, with a handful of kharakians landing by the side of their summoner.

Both sides awaited the first move. The Incarnate staring down those that dared to stand before it, patient as it paced.

"What do we strike? The Incarnate or the orb?" Daria posed, speaking through the shared telepathy of the pterravun.

"The Incarnate is the curse's last line of defence," Evret choked.

Then no matter what happens, that orb is of the highest priority," Arlowe declared.

His father's blade was gripped tightly in hand as he swapped from telepathy to spoken word. "We've gathered our armies, we know their weaknesses, we found the traitor and we broke his chains. Today, Kharaki finally falls!"

Chapter Twenty-Three:

"...is a vile affliction,
second only to an inability to stop it."

1st Nofabelos

Land's Legacy

2084∞ (Current Age)

"Vat tha flaras t'xrn croixrs soix'vs toi esh!" the Incarnate bellowed, unleashing a salvo of volatile spears at the oncoming charge, readying its explosive energy in one hand with its personal spear poised to strike in the other.

"I can handle that!" Evret yelled, firing his own wave of spears towards the Incarnate, intercepting most of the airborne projectiles with his own as his kharakian soldiers used their bodies to protect Arlowe's advance. "I'll summon more! Focus on the Incarnate!"

"Xanth, any idea on how to bring this monster down?" Arlowe questioned, swinging his blade at the Incarnate only for a stray spear to strike at his side, knocking him back.

"I don't think we can," answered the pterravun, noticing the orb in the collective vision of his companions. "While I wasn't able to access that orb during my time in the network, I was able to learn about it."

"Keep it brief, Xanth!" Onyx called as his weapons and ammunitions bounced from the Incarnate's rigid armour.

"Not only does the orb distribute bursts of the fae energy to enable the alphas, it's also an inhibitor. The artefact makes sure to feed the curse whilst making sure not to gorge it, but if we could damage it enough..."

"We could overload the curse," Arlowe deduced, turning to their mage. "Daria, strike the orb! Bring it down!"

"No, Arlowe, wait!"

Though Xanth had attempted to intervene, the spell had already been cast. A volley of magic missiles targeted the orb, only for a protective barrier to encase it, reflecting the darts back at the caster.

Given a fiery charge, the missiles sailed back over the heads of the mage's allies, crashing at her feet before erupting in unison.

"Daria!" the prince exclaimed, unable to see her through the risen dust. "Daria, are you there?"

"Stay calm, I'm fine!" the mage replied, lowering a barrier of her own. "What now?"

"I'm not sure how much help I can be now that the Incarnate is in full control." Xanth peered through Arlowe's eyes; an idea emerged as his own fell upon Evret. "I can't access the network, but I know someone who can."

"Absolutely not." Those who were able looked to Arlowe. The prince had no interest in gazing upon the general. "We can't trust him, especially in the network."

The Incarnate swung its spear up, compromising the assassin's defences. The beast materialised another spear to impale him, though Evret was quick to detonate it.

As the Incarnate focused its attention upon the general, Evret flung himself back, summoning another wave of kharakians to join the fray, replacing the fallen.

"Arlowe, I can help," the general pleaded. "Allow me this."

"We don't have the time not to trust him," Gill voiced, throwing a healing vial at the assassin as he parried one of the Incarnate's strikes.

Schukara lunged forward, her strikes blocked by the beast. "I assume there won't be any more kharakians whilst yer' in there?"

"The elf is correct," Evret replied, summoning one more wave of kharakians to bolster the last, fending off the Incarnate. "My aid will not persist until my mind

504

returns to its body. We must not dally."

Arlowe looked upon the fight raging before them. His allies were struggling even with the continued pressure of Evret's beasts.

"Fine," he muttered, moving to the mage's side. "Daria, cast a barrier over us. We won't be long."

As Daria's magic formed around them, Evret held his palm forward, positioning it before the prince. "Are you comfortable for me to proceed?"

"Just get us in."

Taking the general's hand in his, Arlowe felt his surroundings shift. Losing control to Evret, his consciousness faded.

As his vision returned, the prince came to see the hybrid general stood above him. His blade was brought back to hand in preparation for Evret's ambush.

Though the steel neared his face, Evret remained unfazed, making his move on the network's core. "The connection is complete. This way, Arlowe."

Following closely behind, the prince kept his wits about him, refusing to admit that Evret had nothing in store for him. People could change, of that the prince was certain. *But Evret Rainerus? The remorseless general that had his men cut through thousands of innocents for personal gain? Doubtful.*

"Due to the curse, I have seen life for far longer than the average human," Evret spoke, still leading them towards the core. "Fertral has changed so much, as has Argestra as a whole. I can still remember setting foot beyond my country for the first time. It was… exhilarating."

Arlowe didn't answer, leaving Evret to waste his breath; his mind was focused on the mission.

"I remember the early days. I served the Garrick family, the first of the families to lead Eyenridge. From you being here, it is clear that that was not meant to be."

"I can't blame you for the Garricks, as they fell to the Second Invasion," Arlowe replied, taking Evret's notice. "That doesn't exempt you from the Winthrops, who you killed before the Fourth."

"You know your history."

"Mainly human, though I am trying to branch out. The downside to that is that I know a great deal about your kind," Arlowe asserted, taking a kind of pleasure in knocking the general's confidence. "Five sixty, nine ninety-nine, fourteen sixteen and sixteen eighty-nine. Those years mark your most prominent massacres. And then there was twenty sixty-nine. It came alongside the Necromancer Rebellions, and just before the Sixth Invasion. You almost had us."

"I…" Evret was stunned, in awe of the prince's knowledge. "I look forward to walking upon the land with my own free will once more. To put right my mistakes—"

"You can't put them right. Why do you think *we're* here?" Once more, Evret went silent. "Do you think people would even want your help? After everything you did?"

"I am still remembered?"

"Even before their outbreak, the kharakians were a blight upon the land. As long as they still exist, the memories remain fresh in our minds. Your actions still haunt us to this day."

Though Arlowe proceeded, Evret stopped in his tracks, deep in thought. "I saw what happened to her. To Lucine." The prince halted too; his back was turned to the general. "I was forced to—"

At once, Arlowe swung himself around, pointing his father's sword directly at Evret's throat, silencing him in an instant. The general was frozen in place by the furious look in the man's eyes.

506

"Utter my mother's name again and once you've served your purpose, I'll take you apart myself," he threatened, his voice low as the words forced themselves through his gritted teeth. "Don't even attempt to deceive me into believing you've changed."

"Hundreds of years of torture can change a man."

"You're no man, merely a kharakian attempting to mimic one." Arlowe lowered his blade, continuing to the core. "It's a shame that it took those few hundred years for you to grow a conscience."

Following the trail of lights that led him before, the prince and the general found themselves before the network's core. Arlowe recognised the central tank that neither he nor Xanth could access.

"I remember this thing. I tried to break it open on the chance that it would lend us an advantage," he stated, placing his hand upon where he had struck it last. "It regenerates faster than it can be broken."

"If we can make the tiniest opening, I can access the core and shut down that barrier," Evret explained, tensing his fist. "Ready your blade."

Arlowe positioned his weapon to his side, striking at the tank with all his might.

"Again!" Evret called, with the prince digging his blade back into the barbaric incision.

"Again!" The sword hit its mark again; the tank's consistency turned from hard glass into a warm goo.

"Again!" Once more, Arlowe's blade landed, with a huge crack forming down the length of the tank.

Evret, taking the opportunity to strike into it, engulfed his hand into the structure's wound. As quickly as it had been damaged, the structure regenerated itself, shearing the general's hand from its body.

"Are you okay?" Arlowe asked of him, flicking the residue from his weapon.

Evret focused his molten energy, replacing the hand that he had lost. "It is done. Momentarily, we should hear from your allies."

On cue, a voice lit up in the prince's mind. "Arlowe, are you there?" Xanth questioned, his voice frantic. "If you can hear me, the barrier is down!"

"I'm here, Xanth. We're coming out." Xanth didn't respond. "Can he hear me?"

"My priority was getting the barrier down. From there, I then tried to grant some level of communication. It seems I could only enable it one way," Evret answered. "It doesn't matter now. Let us leave this—"

"Soi pradlactebva, uanarav," came the familiar Elvish of the Incarnate. A pulsing spear was telekinetically lifted to its side, pointed at the two. "Wa hela noi f'xrthar x'sa foir thlas."

The spear was launched, though the intruders were not its intended target. Whistling past them both, the spear jammed itself into the restored tank, screaming as it grew brighter.

Before he could react, Arlowe felt an unseen force push against him, slamming his back into the side of the chamber to avoid the detonation.

Though still reeling from the blow, the prince could see the fragments of the tank around him, squirming as they failed to piece back together. Only the base of the core remained.

"Evret?" Arlowe coughed, using the pod by his side to aid him back to his feet. "Evret, are you there?"

Emerging from the smoke, the Incarnate approached the prince, propelling a spear into his arm to remove any chance of his escape.

"You won't win," Arlowe hissed through the pain. "My allies will bring you down in

508

my stead. Do your worst."

The Incarnate slowly lowered a new spear towards his chest. The metal of his cuirass began to melt away.

"Why do you think... I... would... merely... kill... you. You're no... kharakian," the creature spoke, stunning Arlowe with its use of Bridge, hearing his voice among its own. "I'll take you apart myself."

Ready to dissect its subject, the spear the beast held disintegrated as it was thrust towards the prince, turning its attention to the one responsible.

Evret had appeared at the Incarnate's back, clenching a light within his fist.

"I'll see you back at Kharaki!" the general called, with Arlowe seeing only the watchful eye of the Incarnate as Evret faded from sight.

His own vision darkened as the connection was severed.

As his sight returned, Arlowe woke to his body and Evret's behind a shield of Daria's creation; the two had been guarded by her whilst she cast in support to those fighting the Incarnate.

The general's kharakians had been crushed, with Gill taking a wounding blow in place of Onyx, leaving only the assassin and the mercenary to hold back the great monster.

Taking his father's blade back into hand, Arlowe rushed into the Incarnate, taking some of the strain from his allies.

"Gill, fall back to the shield," he ordered through the telepathy, knocked down onto his knee as a strike from the creature's spear collided with his shield. "Onyx, strike at the orb before the curse regains its barrier! We may not get another chance!"

Blinking through one of the Incarnate's sweeps, Onyx reappeared atop the pulsing artefact. The assassin sliced his dagger through the tentacles holding the orb above them, swinging down from one as the kharakian artefact fell from the sky.

As the orb crashed to the ground, Onyx blinked back by Arlowe and Schukara's side, grasping a much smaller sphere within his palm as he re-joined the struggle. "I think we may need someone with a little more strength in their swing. Any takers?"

"Gill, d'ya think you've got it in ya'?" the mercenary questioned, parrying the Incarnate's assault. "Arlowe 'n' I can hold the beast off!"

"With pleasure," the eleventh pronounced, his hand gripped upon the hilt of his mace.

The elf then moved her attention to the general. "Evret, ya' got any more troops on tha' way?"

"Make them last," the general declared, weakly lifting a burning hand into the air. His kharakians landed amid the chaos of his allies and the curse's protector.

"That's it then! Onyx, do yer' thing!"

On Schukara's mark, the assassin released the sphere, dousing their surroundings in a blinding cloud of smoke. Enabled, the eleventh sprinted forward without the Incarnate's interference, aiming directly for the orb.

Aware of the smoke's intention, the Incarnate lashed out in Gill's direction, blind. Making contact with a body, the beast returned its spear only to find one of Evret's soldiers fixed upon it, convulsing wildly.

As the ground rocked behind him, Gill leapt into the air, bringing down his mace upon the orb with everything he had, breaking it open to release the pent-up energy within.

*

Down below, upon the scorched Fertral battlefield, Valerius and Kardus continued to fight against the unending horde, refusing to tire at the ever-replenishing numbers.

Valerius released Adrestia into the crowds, cutting down a line of the monsters before

510

digging his blade into one of his choice, telekinetically pulling her back into his grasp as the creature ignited to take out entire areas at a safe distance.

As he released Adrestia again, a spear knocked the black blade off-course, driven into the dirt out of the hands of her wielder.

Unable to call his blade back and incapable of holding off the horde with his magic alone, Valerius was blind-sided, knocked down by a blast of explosive energy. Dazed, the wielder was clambered upon by a group of kharakians, all initiating their suicidal detonations.

As the screeching of the ignited bodies reached their crescendo, a long weapon came between Valerius and the kharakians. Kardus hurled the monsters back into the masses, helping his ally back to his feet.

"Is your goal to lay down and die, or is to stand up and fight for what you believe in?" Kardus queried, tearing apart another wave with his halberd.

Valerius held out his hand, calling back Adrestia through the nearing kharakians.

"Why do I get the feeling you haven't learned your lesson?" she quipped, used to carve up those that approached. "I'm ready to proceed, thank you for—"

Suddenly, Valerius, Kardus and those gathered nearby were rendered blind.

"What is that?" Valerius questioned, sensing the energy of what stood before them.

Kardus squinted through the dimming light, ready to engage the alpha that had answered the call. "It's about time you showed up."

*

With the orb struggling to inhibit the power it fed to the curse, the Incarnate used its now-enhanced telekinesis to grip those surrounding it, throwing the intruders back as it matched its pulsing with the artefact. The orb surrounded itself in coat of white energy, guarded by the beast and its own aura.

"The creature is pulsing brighter," Gill observed, able to see the Incarnate's power grow through its soul energy.

"It's consuming more of the fae energy," Evret announced, lifting his hand into the air. "If we keep this up, the overload will be unavoidable."

As the burning energy collected in the general's hand, the Incarnate held out its own, turning Evret's flame from red to white.

"Tha cxrsa ulalas, tha cxrsa tekas ewecr," recited the beast. The kharakians called upon by the general landed instead by the Incarnate, opposing the summoner.

"Evret, what's going on?" Arlowe questioned, watching the row of monsters grow brighter.

The general held his wrist in pain. "I-I have lost control of the network."

Using its immense energy to exceed its past limits, the Incarnate took what was stolen, replacing Evret's kharakians with its own alphas, loyal not to the general, but to the curse.

"Evret... blight... ed... by... the network. Noi oina las sefa froim x's." The Incarnate pointed directly at Arlowe. "Your... turn... Xanth."

"What does that mean? What do you mean?" Arlowe demanded, a panic setting in. "Xanth? Xanth!"

Xanth snapped back to his own vision as the screams of his people echoed through the hallways. Sudden detonations shook the underground, turning his home into a cave-in at any moment.

The young pterravun rushed from his room, beelining straight for the central chamber, sure to find his parents and an explanation there.

As soon as the boy entered in through the archway, his eyes widened in dread. Kharakians had flooded through the inactive portal, with an alpha stood on the highest

512

point, looking out proudly over the carnage.

"Arlowe, they're here!" Xanth cried through their telepathy, able to see his sister cowering behind a toppled pillar, bolting over to comfort her. "What do we do?"

"Xanth, stay where you are, I'm coming in!"

"You can't! They're coming through the portal!"

Arlowe growled in anger, forced to accept there was nothing he could do. "Just... stay safe! Don't do anything heroic. We need you if we're going to end this threat!"

"My warriors, into formation!" Bela commanded, forming a line of pterravun soldiers against the gathering horde. "Conquest, gather the others into the hallways! Hurry!"

Xanth could see a figure moving towards them, guarding Kaat only to relax at the sight of his father. The giant of a man pulled both children to their feet.

"We have to move, my dears!" he voiced, out of breath. His body shook as he spoke. "We can't stay here!"

As Xanth was dragged to safety, he glanced up at the alpha again. Searching through the chaos from its vantage point, the creature found the boy as he left the cover of the pillar. "Father, the alpha!"

The alpha soon leapt into the fray only for Bela to predict its movements, standing between the alpha and her family, goading it into focusing on her. "What's the matter? Are the pterravun elite not good enough for you?"

"Take an alpha each!" Arlowe ordered, watching Evret take on the Incarnate. "Xanth, is there anything you can do on your end?"

"You still haven't made contact with the Incarnate," Xanth explained, gasping as he ran. "It's likely it knows what you're trying to do and what I'm capable of. I can't do any more until you make that connection."

"Can't any of us make contact with the Incarnate?" Daria posed, firing a barrage of magic missiles at her alpha. "You're connected to us all now."

"Arlowe is my primary connection to your world. It has to be him."

Though engaging his own alpha, the prince kept his eyes over the battlefield. Every command he made was an attempt at keeping his allies alive a few moments longer.

"Xanth, stun Schukara's alpha to give her some breathing room! Gill, fire a bolt to knock my alpha off-balance! Onyx, can you blink over to the orb?"

"I can't. That energy field is nullifying my magic whenever I try to get close. I can't leave myself so exposed."

"Daria, can you—"

Looking to the cries of desperation, Arlowe could see the necromancer struggling with her alpha. Only able to block so much of the beast's assault, the creature's explosive magic was enough to blow through her barrier, striking her down with a powerful thrust of its spear.

As the alpha placed its foot upon the mage, aiming its spear down upon her head, the assassin blinked from his own alpha to tackle into Daria's. With moments to spare, he aided her back to her feet.

"Quickly, cast a barrier!" he called, defended as both of their alphas focused their unified might upon the two. "You need to transform!"

"I need to be under great duress!" protested the mage, struggling to stand as she maintained the barriers.

"How is this not great duress?"

"We can win this, Onyx! I know we can!"

As both alphas brought down a combined explosion, the assassin threw down another smoke bomb, blinking them both from the attack. "I wish I shared your optimism," he muttered, their magic wearing them both down.

Giving as much back as he could take, Evret and the Incarnate traded vicious blows with one another, quickly recovering from the injuries dealt to each other.

"The curse's time is over," Evret announced, stabbing his spear through his previous captor. "We've outlived our purpose. Now we're nothing but an infection Katosus can't shake off."

The Incarnate shoved its palm into the general's torso, using the fae's energy to throw him back, disintegrating Evret's spear to reform it in its own hands. "Croix hela noi exthoirlat'cr hara," the beast returned, holding its palm out once more.

This time Evret was fixed in place. The spear he was constructing had been dispelled by the Incarnate's superior power, leaving him disarmed.

"Release me! You've shackled me for too long!"

"As you command... general."

Pulsing the spear to the orb's beat, the Incarnate released the awaiting spear into Evret's body, shattering him into pieces.

"Evret!" Xanth cried, able to see what had occurred through the band's collective eyes. "No!"

Onyx created a window to redirect an attack back at his alpha, noting the late general's body scattered over the battleground. "What just happened? Why didn't he fight back?"

"The Incarnate knew we'd try to exploit the network to our advantage again." The young pterravun tried to suppress his tears, though his sadness bled through into his words. "That's how the kharakians have found my people. That's how it had complete control over Evret. We had access to it, and now it has access to us."

Arlowe searched around. The Incarnate summoned a bombardment of spears, watching over the work of its minions. "Schukara, Gill, to me!"

The mercenary and the eleventh moved into formation at the prince's side.

"What're we doin' Arlowe?" Schukara queried in hesitance, backing away from the united beasts. "This is becomin' too much of a burden ta' bear."

"You're right. If we leave this any longer, we'll run out of options," Arlowe noted, forming a makeshift plan in his mind. "Xanth, is there anything you can do? Xanth?"

Shepherding his children into one of the hallway's many rooms, Conquest brought his arm across both of his children. The father held them back, shielding them both against the oncoming forces.

"Close your eyes, little ones," he comforted, holding them tight. "This will all be over soon."

Though Kaat closed her eyes, sinking into his anxious embrace, Xanth's eyes remained open. The boy could see through his father's courageous act. He noticed the shaking limb that held him.

The clashing of weapons drew the young pterravun's attention to the doorway; all three were able to see Bela as she fought off the alpha only for the monster to find an opening. Gazing over her shoulder to her family, her attention waned long enough for the beast to impale her leg with its spear.

The alpha held her tight, using its explosive energy to fire the helpless pterravun queen into the wall of her family's room. Bela had been rendered unconscious; she could do no more.

The alpha entered into the room of Conquest and his children, stepping over the motionless mother in search of the irksome boy.

"No you d-don't," mumbled Conquest, stirring up the courage as he stood from his children. "Take another step, and... and I'll be forced t-to deal with you."

Opposing the king, the alpha took one more step, materialising a spear into its hand as

516

it led more of its kind into the room.

Answering appropriately, Conquest stormed forward, side-stepping the beast's spear to tackle it into the wall. Taking advantage of its disorientation, the king took the beast's ankles, swinging it as an improvised weapon against the reinforcements.

Seeing another spear appearing in the alpha's hand, Conquest slammed the creature into the floor before forcing its throat to the wall. "I feel I must make this clear!" the man announced, balling his hand into a fist. "You! Don't! Touch! My! Family!"

Conquest's fist crashed into the alpha's face repeatedly, ending with a knee crushing its head against the wall.

Victorious, the king let out a sigh, stuttering to his children as he attended to his wife. "Kaat, Xanth, I… I'm so sorry that you, uh, had to witness that brutality. I-I was just trying to protect—"

Unaware of the alpha's recovery, a spear pierced through the king's chest. The spear faded as the beast gave its last breath, though Conquest's body had already collapsed to the ground.

Tears formed in the face of the man that had failed his progeny. A smile was all he could offer to calm them, though his eyes betrayed a mind worried for their safety in his absence.

The children screamed in horror, tugging at their father's withering body. "Father!"

"Here's the plan," Arlowe informed, retreating from the encroaching alphas. "We can't take on these alphas. There's too many and we don't have the time. We need to make it past at least two, with at least one of us holding off the third."

"I can blind one of them whilst still advancing," Gill offered, dodging one of the alpha's spears. "And I'll hold off the third. I've had my moment of respite. Schukara should take the orb."

"What about tha' second? And tha' Incarnate?" posed the elf.

"I'll deal with those," Arlowe replied, taking in a deep breath. "This is all we have left. Are you both ready?"

Schukara and Gill nodded, charging forward alongside the prince towards the alphas.

"Gill, now!" Arlowe ordered, with the eleventh activating his unique ability, watching the first alpha stumble as its sight was stolen.

"First alpha's a goner!" Schukara celebrated. "We're comin' up on tha' second!"

"Xanth, I know you're in danger, I know you're scared, but we need you, now more than ever," the prince pleaded, swiftly advancing into the second alpha's range. "I know you can do it, my friend."

Without a word, the second alpha froze in place. "Good job, Xanth," Gill praised, placing his hand over his staff. "The second alpha has been passed! The third approaches!"

Taking the initiative, the third alpha charged into the three, though the eleventh was one step ahead. "Dive, one to each side!"

Doing as instructed, Arlowe and Schukara dived out of the way, watching as Gill used his senses to predict where the alpha would appear, knocking down both the beast and its readied spear.

"Go. I'll hold these three off, though I doubt I'll be able to keep them from you for long. I'm not what they're after," warned the eleventh, swapping to his mace as he turned back to the regrouping alphas. "Hungry, fellas? Come get some!"

As Arlowe and Schukara pushed towards the Incarnate, the beast unleashed another salvo of spears. The prince brought the mercenary to his flank, slowly pushing closer with his shield at his front.

"Knew that thing'd come in handy!" the elf commented, the praise for herself audible

518

in her voice. "We need ta' make a move on that Incarnate! We're sittin' ducks here!"

"I know! We just need—" Arlowe peered over the shield, spotting the familiar flicker of the white wolf. "There's our opening. We just need to hold out a little longer."

Jarred by his abrupt change in confidence, Schukara was able to briefly catch a glimpse of the prince's eyes turn a bright blue. She was aware that at that moment, her partner wasn't there.

"Be ready on Arlowe's signal," came a voice from the envoy's lips that was not his own. "I'll draw the molten beast's attention."

An astounded Schukara nodded her head, watching as Arlowe's eyes returned to their brownish hue. "Follow me," he instructed, his disposition calm and collected as he rose from his defensive position, his blade poised to make contact.

Though the elf was unable to see as Arlowe did, Species Eighteen became ever clearer to the prince as it rushed towards the Incarnate's flank. The wolf's white fur danced through the non-existent wind; its blue markings overflowed with magical properties, all aimed at their final hurdle.

The Incarnate continued its hail of spears, with Arlowe's charge lagging, forced to deflect and cut away at the unending assault. His advance became slower and slower.

One of the alphas had bypassed the eleventh, launching a spear at Schukara as a tiny barrier appeared to block its impact. The protection disappeared as soon as it had arrived, with Daria dropping to her knee from exhaustion.

Onyx took her weight onto his shoulder, conjuring an illusion in their place to evade another attack. "Arlowe, do something!"

The prince could see what the Incarnate intended, watching it flicker in anticipation for his strike. "Focus on staying alive! This may be our only chance!"

"We're running out of options!"

Arlowe's eye stayed locked on the Incarnate, with the wolf closing in in his peripheral. "Almost there," he mumbled, counting down the seconds. "Dropping... the shield... now!"

The wolf leapt into the Incarnate's back, stumbling it just enough for Arlowe's blade to scrape across its armour. "Xanth, stun it!" he yelled, pointing Schukara to the pulsing artefact. "Go! Get the orb!"

Xanth's powers could only do so much, with the prince fired into the ground, unable to stop the Incarnate's explosive power. "Argh!"

Struggling against Xanth's interference, the Incarnate flung a spear at the mercenary only for the spear to disintegrate within the air in a flash of green light. Its body had become sluggish and burdened.

"This is for my father," the pterravun whispered to the beast. The boy kept the Incarnate still as the prince rose to hold off the incoming alpha. "This ends today."

With nothing in her way, Schukara brought her swords to her sides, leaping into the air to bring them down upon the orb, near-splitting the artefact in two.

Waking from her blacked-out state, Bela choked at the sight of her bloodied husband, though she kept her emotions in check as she saw the same alpha stood over her Kaat and Xanth.

Taking back her blade, the grieving queen cut down the monster, becoming the wall between her children and the incoming kharakians.

"Mother, father isn't moving!" Kaat wailed, huddled into the corner.

Xanth took one of his father's arms as his tearful sister took another, peering over with concern as Bela said not a word. The two dragged their father's body to the back of the room, shaking him for a response.

Scaring them both, Conquest sputtered back to life; a large portion of his blood flowed down his tunic. "It's... it's okay. I'm... okay, I... just need a minute..."

As Kaat rushed into her father's sight, Xanth rose to face his mother, agitated by her lack of consoling only to be as apprehensive as she. "They're not moving," Bela spoke, examining the kharakian in the doorway, stood, yet seemingly inactive.

"Be careful, mother," Xanth warned, seeing more dormant kharakians filling the hallway. "Arlowe, what's going on? Can anyone hear me?"

At last, Xanth was able to tap into the vision of his allies, shook at the sight of the orb. "Arlowe, what—"

"Xanth!" Arlowe called, sounding as though this wasn't his first attempt at communication. "Destroy as many as you can! Turn them to dust! The curse hasn't overloaded yet!"

"Mother, this isn't over!" Xanth yelled; his trepidation turned to terror. "Strike them down! Hurry!"

Bela put her sword to the dormant kharakian, cutting through it into the hallway only to find the other monsters lighting up one by one, all transforming at once.

*

"Boom, there goes another one!" Cael screamed, enraging the centre of another wave as he held off the masses. The forces by his side dwindled rapidly, his magic only barely keeping the tide of monsters at bay. "I can hold these pests off for now, but I need reinforcements!"

"We have no more soldiers in reserve! We're waiting on those discharged from the infirmaries!" a commanding officer roared, holding off the kharakians by Cael's side. "A caravan of golems is estimated to be here in ten minutes!"

"We need more than cripples and pebbles! Is further retreat an option?"

"We're spread too thin! Any further and we'll leave openings in our ranks! We have injured holding out behind us!"

Though pressured by the swelling number of the kharakians, one in particular caught Cael's attention. The beast was beginning to glow, yet it had no injuries nor came close enough to kill any but its own with its detonation. "Guess I'll put you out of your—"

As Cael was ready to cast an enraging spell upon the monster, the kharakian engulfed the area in a burst of light. The aged tutor had no choice but to cast a personal barrier upon himself, shielded as his vision returned.

With the light dimming, Cael found himself face-to-face with an alpha. "Take whatever form ya' wish. One more for the slaughter, as my father would have—"

Another burst of light appeared upon the battlefield. One by one the kharakians transformed, a minefield of luminescence as an army of alphas came forth.

Cael kept his gaze upon the alpha that stood before him. "I have faith, beast! Can you say the same?"

The monster began its approach, joined by its empowered kin. "Tha cxrsa shevv urent croix e marc'cr, ax'tlanux'lashlanu croix'r vlafa bafoira croix cen baer w'latnass toi croix'r dafaet!"

Cael brought Mavis into hand, unfamiliar with the language. "I doubt that was a plea for surrender."

*

Pulling together a body being ripped apart by unbridled power, the Incarnate wrapped its invisible magic around each of the intruders, pulling them all to a central point before it.

"Thlas ands hara!" it roared, absorbing its alphas to enhance its already overflowing power, its hands now a searing white. "Burn!"

Pre-empting danger, Daria casted a barrier, shielding all from the Incarnate's molten

522

stream.

To their dismay, the fires had already begun to melt through, breaking down what little protection the mage had left to offer. "My magic… isn't holding!"

"My senses aren't working either," Gill noted, looking to Arlowe. "And I can't hear Xanth."

The prince shook his head. "Neither can I."

A purple mist formed around the group, swirling faster and faster, with Daria shrouded from the sight of her allies. Skeletal wings sprouted from the mage's silhouette.

The Incarnate could still feel his grasp upon the intruders, though all it could see were the eyes of the grave staring back.

"The Incarnate is sapping our magic," announced the lich; her body continued to buckle under the immense pressure. "Even in my current state, I can't hold this barrier forever."

"Can't ya' pull tha' Incarnate apart? Like ya' did with Kaxrax?" Schukara questioned.

"As long as the fae energy is flowing through the Incarnate, it will simply regenerate through my attacks." A crack formed in the mage's renewed barrier, the fury of the fire unabating. "Besides, with my magic being depleted at such a rate, I need to use what I have left to keep you all safe."

As the barrier gradually melted away, leaving less and less for the group to take cover behind, Arlowe became aware that one of them had not been trapped by the Incarnate.

A barely-regenerated Evret had dragged his unresponsive body to the orb, slowly materialising a spear as he grew closer.

Alas, as the general attempted to shatter the curse, weakly thrusting his spear into the artefact, the aura surrounding the orb turned his spear to ash. His attempts were futile.

As the barrier grew smaller still, Evret climbed onto the orb as fast as his split fingers could lift him. The magic within his palms fizzled from the fae aura and his strength was hardly enough to break the orb in two.

"This won't work," Evret mumbled, looking down at the same hands that were attempting to pry the artefact apart. "No one said this curse couldn't double as a gift."

Igniting his body, the general glanced at his new allies. Arlowe's eyes rested upon him. "Maybe I was wrong about you!" the prince called, smiling to the general.

"Say goodbye to Xanth for me!" Evret called back, his own vision growing brighter. "And thank you, for breaking my chains at last."

Aware of Daria's state, weakened too much to concern it further, the Incarnate relieved the intruders of its burning wrath, though it's decision to turn its attention towards Evret had been made far too late.

Evret's body exploded upon the orb, blowing the artefact to pieces. His sacrifice sent out a shockwave throughout Kharaki and beyond.

"H'las radamptlaoin? H'las secr'laflaca? Lat woin't sela croix." The Incarnate faded from view; Arlowe and his companions were released from its cursed grip.

"Arlowe? Arlowe, can you hear me?" Xanth cried, watching as his mother barely held back the alpha kharakians entering into the room; his father barely clung to life.

Knocked down by their combined power, Bela braced herself for the end, only to find herself no worse for wear. The spears aimed at her had turned to dust, floating on the winds of the pterravun caves alongside the alphas that had faded too, unable to act without the curse's connection.

"I knew he could do it," Conquest choked with a grin gracing his hairy face.

"Xanth, are you there?" Arlowe asked through their telepathy, no longer silenced by the fae energy. "Xanth, what's happening down there?"

"They're gone Arlowe." The boy dropped to the floor from exhaustion. "We've done it."

*

As the shockwave flew over the decimated battlefield below, the dusted alphas scattered to the winds in a glistening display. The kharakians that remained disintegrated their spears, raising their arms to show their surrender at last.

Kardus, Valerius and Adrestia watched amazed, all content in their victory.

"Do you hear that?" posed the blade. "There is someone nearby. They are in great pain."

The three searched their surroundings, locating a man being handled by a kharakian. To their surprise, as they reached for their weapons, the injured man held out his arm. The kharakian was there to help.

Valerius approached, dismissing the beast with a bow for its deed.

"You're injured," he addressed, tending to a great wound upon the man's shoulder. "My sanamancy isn't great, but it should settle you until we can find you some help."

Cael began to smile, then chuckle before bellowing with laughter, with tears rolling down his face. "I never thought I'd see the day where a kharakian wasn't trying ta' kill me!" The tutor was incapable of drawing his eyes from the kharakian. "He did it. He really did it."

Cael pulled the pipe from his pocket, motioning the kharakians finger under his pipe, choking on the few puffs he had as he wiped his eyes. "'Course, he had to. *I* was his tutor, after all."

Chapter Twenty-Four:

"Though my God is fallible, we shall rise."

1ˢᵗ Nofabelos
Land's Legacy
2084∞ (Current Age)

"It's over," Schukara gasped, looking to her allies in shared disbelief. "We won!"

At once, a resounding snap echoed through the air, with the ground beneath their feet beginning to part. The accretion disks intended to defend Kharaki had become unstable without the curse to guide them, crashing into the floating city.

"Kharaki is falling apart around us!" Gill declared, acquiring Arlowe's attention. "Are there any escape options we may have missed?"

The prince looked to the way they came; the path they had travelled held strong. "It's a long shot, but there may still be a way off if we—"

"Croix thoixuht lat woix'vd ba soi slampva?"

A blast of energy made contact with Arlowe and Onyx, hitting them with enough force to throw them to the other side of the chamber.

The Incarnate, barely held together by the overcharged curse, raised walls of fire upon every exit, trapping them all within the collapsing city. "You thought... it would be... so simple?"

The enraged beast rushed wildly at those still standing, ripping Daria's barrier apart with ease before bringing his spear down upon the mage, breaking the arm of the eleventh who had rushed in to guard her.

Schukara dived into combat, using everything she had left to hold the mighty beast back.

"Xanth, Arlowe already made contact," she yelled, barely avoiding the Incarnate's swings. "Turn it off, stun it, anythin'!"

"I have something else in mind," the pterravun uttered, pausing for a moment. "Get back! Now!"

A figure swooped down from the blackened skies, enveloping the Incarnate in a gale of frost. The molten beast was soon quelled within the summoned ice.

"How?" Daria asked, amazed at the sight of the dragon. "How is Ota-Rnshi here?"

"Due to Arlowe's previous contact with the dragon, I was able to connect our minds to speak," Xanth explained as the dragon landed at their side. "I called for its aid and guided it through the debris. With what little control I still had over the network, I helped clear a path for it to find us."

Ota-Rnshi lowered a wing, assisting Arlowe's companions onto its back. "Climb on. We're leaving."

"Why did you protect me from the Incarnate?" Daria posed to Gill, helping the eleventh up. "The injury would mean far less to me."

"Two arms to cast will always be better than one," Gill replied, returning the favour by lifting the mage on to the dragon alongside him. "We may still need that magic."

As the prince and the assassin arose from the blast, a series of deafening cracks sounded over Kharaki. One of the misaligned accretion disks sheared through the city, splitting it into two.

"It can never be easy, can it?" Arlowe groaned, struggling to his feet.

Though the others had mounted the dragon, Schukara remained on unsteady ground, watching helplessly as her companions drifted further away. "I'm not leavin' until—"

"Get on!" Onyx demanded, signalling for her to go. "Standing on unstable ground is foolish when you have wings by your side!"

Begrudgingly seeing sense in the assassin's words, the elf began to climb the dragon's wing, whistling to Ota-Rnshi for its attention.

"Let's take ta' tha' skies!" she devised, joining the others. "Get ta' tha' other side before we lose 'em!"

Ota-Rnshi shook its head. "The ground beneath them is growing ever more precarious. I can't land by them on the possibility that I destabilize their footing further. I won't jeopardizing their safety."

Arlowe held up a finger, pointing Onyx to the other side. "Go."

The assassin recoiled at the order. "What? No, not without you."

"Onyx, I want you on the other side. Best-case scenario is that you catch me. Worst-case, you're safe."

"You're full of faith, asking the guy with one arm to catch you."

Doing as instructed, the assassin blinked through the debris field, narrowly landing upon the other side. "I did my part! Now it's your turn!" he called, watching Arlowe's focus move from the widening gap. "Arlowe!"

The prince's eyes fell to his side, making out a piece of kharakian slowly regenerating from the smallest shard. "Evret. He's alive."

Onyx's voice called out in desperation. "Arlowe, we need to go!"

"Not without him!"

Sacrificing an already onerous jump, the prince rushed to the shard's side, hastily scooping the piece into his pack.

"We've got him!" Xanth exclaimed, following Arlowe's eyes to Kharaki's ever-growing divide. "Go, go, go!"

Moving as fast as his legs could carry his aching body, Arlowe charged headlong at the city's edge, making the jump as the ground crumbled from beneath his feet.

Though the leap was admirable, the accretion disk Onyx scarcely avoided had no interest in missing twice, with one of the stones bashing into the prince's side.

Thrown back into the air, Arlowe was no longer able to keep his tossing body under control. His only chance at survival was to hold out his arms and pray to Arn that his fingers found solid ground.

Diving to his ally, Onyx snatched his partner's wrist from the air. His rib was crushed against the ground as he anchored himself; his boot blade fit perfectly around the upturned earth.

Shaking the disorientation from his mind, Arlowe found himself suspended, taking the closest graspable protrusion he could find to lift himself up.

"I didn't think almost falling to your death could be turned into a talent!" Onyx gasped, clutching his chest once Arlowe had been lifted to safety.

"We're getting out of here," Arlowe voiced, taking the assassin under his arm and towards their awaiting allies.

With everyone now accounted for, with the brazen duo briskly pulled onto the dragon's back, Ota-Rnshi wasted no time in diving away from the disintegrating city.

Together, Xanth and Daria cleared both the accretion debris and the pieces of falling city from its path, granting them their escape.

As their freedom neared, debris released from the accretion disks collected before them. An unseen force had shifted the cluster to match the dragon's flight path.

"I can do no more," Ota-Rnshi roared, still evading the city's dying fury.

"Xanth? The network?" Arlowe posed as he and his allies dropped to the dragon's back to avoid the gritty hail.

"I-I can't," the pterravun stuttered, fluttering as he attempted again. "There's no network to access. It's gone!"

Daria glanced to Gill. The eleventh nodded for her to proceed. "I can do it," she mumbled, casting a personal barrier forth as she stood against the gathered stone.

"Looks like I've still got it," Gill uttered proudly. "Take us home, Daria."

With one last burst of necrotic magic, Ota-Rnshi and those atop pushed through Kharaki's remnants, greeted by the clear skies, free of the curse's choking smog.

Ota-Rnshi swung its body around, taking a moment to breath as those it carried took in the sight of the city tearing itself apart, collapsing down into the molten crater below.

"Tha' kharakians have been a problem fer' so long. It's hard ta' believe it's finally over," Schukara commented, looking over to her allies with a fatigued smile.

"It's surreal," Daria added, casting her magic over Gill's arm. "It's almost like—"

Pulling them all from their moment of relief, their sight was taken from them in a flash of light. Ota-Rnshi screamed out in pain.

"Gill, what can you see?" Arlowe questioned, already sure of the answer.

"There's only one creature I can think of with such a presence of soul energy," Gill responded, rising to his feet. "The Incarnate returns once more!"

The Incarnate, compelling its body to remain as one, had materialised upon the dragon's back, holding the bases of Ota-Rnshi's wings in an attempt to end their lives with gravity as its weapon of choice.

Joining the eleventh, Arlowe and Schukara rose to fight for the release of their draconic ally, wounding the Incarnate with every bit of strength they had left.

"It's over, you've lost," Arlowe insisted, bringing his blade down over the beast's arm. "Accept your fate! The world doesn't need you anymore!"

The Incarnate was unfazed by their attempts to oust it from the dragon's back; its eyes glowed with an energy not of its own.

"Do you curse the venom, or the being that utilised it? I act as the curse commands."

530

Its voice reverberated as its power knocked the attackers down without so much as a twitch. "When you reach your gods, damn them for making our existence a reality."

Powerless to stop the Incarnate, Arlowe braced himself for the dragon's collision with the battlefield. A spell gleamed in Daria's hand.

The impact came; a loss of consciousness came soon after.

*

His body jolting up in fear of his time unconscious, Arlowe immediately took his head into his hands to ease his disorientation, fighting back the nausea that came with it. His vision was blurred; the prince struggled to centre his weight. His body returned back to the floor with each of his attempts to stand.

As he made yet another attempt to shift himself, a small burst of light exploded before him, bringing his attention to his surroundings. "Where…"

A white void surrounded the prince on all sides, with seemingly no end in sight. The burst of light that roused his senses appeared as small bursts of lightning, dropping sporadically from above him.

"Xanth? Onyx? Anyone?" Arlowe called out. No answer came. "Is *this* the afterlife?"

"I pray not, lest *I* be in a very curious predicament."

Appearing within the void, he soon found the white wolf by his side. "Species Eighteen?"

The wolf nodded. "A true meeting has been long overdue."

"Where are we?"

"We are communicating within your mind."

"So this isn't my physical body?" The wolf shook its head at the prince's question. "Where is it?"

"You are beyond this. Your allies are making an attempt to wake you."

"We survived." The thought of their conflict soon engulfed his mind. "And the Incarnate?"

"Pulling itself back together. Your conflict is not yet over."

Arlowe began to panic, looking to every angle of the void for an escape. "Let me out," he demanded. "I need to be beside them."

"You think I hold you here?" asked the wolf, calming the prince. "Your mind is recovering from the trauma. Be thankful that you're even alive. When it has recovered enough, your mind and body will meet once more."

"And until then?"

The wolf turned, walking further into the void. "Come, let us speak."

The two departed into the void, with Arlowe stumbling through the lightning. His eyes were drawn to flickers created by the sparks, forming shadows that seemed so familiar to him.

"So, this is my mind?" he posed, taking in its vastness. "Is it supposed to be so… empty? I feel like this is a veiled insult."

"That was a joke, yes?" Arlowe nodded, unsure of whether the wolf actually enjoyed it or not. "Amusing."

"Yes, quite."

The silence crawled into the prince's mind, pushing him to use his voice to fill it. "When we last spoke, you mentioned a few words I didn't understand."

"Vence? The Untainted Lands?"

"All I know is the word 'fae', and even then, the meaning of that word eludes me."

"I remember your world."

As Species Eighteen spoke, images appeared in the void for seconds at a time. The shadows produced from the lightning formed an image of Argestra's landmass, watched over by the shapes of its people.

"I remember your kind, as I do those that enslaved them. I remember the draconic ones, the demonic ones and I remember the evil magic that crept in alongside them."

For a moment, a flicker formed by Arlowe's side. An armoured Schukara stood her ground against a masked opponent. A purple light seeped from the elf's visor.

"Are you referring to necromancy?" the prince queried.

"Necromancy is not an evil school of magic, regardless of who wields it," the wolf answered. Arlowe's focus was reacquired as the flicker disappeared from sight. "There is magic out there beyond our comprehension. Pray you never find it."

Arlowe shook his head. "You say you know us, yet hardly anyone remembers you. Where did you come from?"

"We were there before any other."

A new image replaced the last. The shadows formed to create a variety of figures Arlowe didn't recognise surrounding a kind of gateway.

"Our government, the Faegareskh, searched through the realms beyond our own Äkin to escape the warring of our home, to flee the coming invasions and start anew, on our own terms.

"Eventually the Faegareskh found what they referred to as the 'Untainted Lands', free of Arn's other races, free of the demon's destructive cycle. The fae cheered, though they knew not of what the Faegareskh intended. Whoever controlled the Untainted Lands controlled the soul energy of those within. They planned to trap their own kind within the new world, enslaving them with no chance of rebellion, lest those that oppose them have their souls pulled apart.

"The rebels, the Faeurai, found out what the Faegareskh intended, quickly putting a plan in place. Knowing that they wouldn't convince the masses to abandon their 'paradise', the Faeurai instead planned to leave some of their own operatives behind in Äkin. We would show them the sins of their government first-hand, re-opening the portal to bring them back, leaving the Faegareskh trapped in the Untainted Lands forever."

Another flicker appeared to Arlowe, showing Onyx stood against an eye-masked creature. Silhouettes stood by his side, an arm in place of the one he had lost. "You never came back."

"The rescue never came," voice the vence in shame, their head lowered. "Without release, my kind enslaved one another, and without restraint, our government only grew more powerful. Even united, we stood no chance against them. The Faegareskh had won, and we were to be locked in with them for eternity."

The shadows reformed themselves once more, showing a growing darkness absorbing the fae. The wolf was unable to keep his gaze upon the images.

"A corruption came. Slow at first, the Faegareskh looked down upon us, their ravaged slaves, with not a shred of pity. Over time, the corruption spread to the realm itself. The Untainted Lands began taking soul energy as it pleased, unshackled from the whims of its previous masters.

"The Faegareskh tried everything, but nothing worked. They tried to fight it, but the corruption was too strong. They tried to cleanse it, but the corruption had no interest in being cured. They tried to outsmart it, but the corruption was always one step ahead. In no time at all, this corruption had brought us all to our knees.

"Those that survived banded together. The Faegareskh, the Faeurei, it didn't matter. We combined our energy to send a portal back to Äkin; something we were not able to do whilst the Faegareskh kept us as prisoners. We sent messages to aid our cause. But that energy has been stolen. Without it, all hope is lost."

534

One more flicker appeared to the prince, showing Gill stood against a grotesque creature far larger in size than he. The image disappeared as suddenly as it appeared.

"And in the end, your message found me," Arlowe stated, watching the shadows disperse before them both.

"Those messages led us to a governing body known as the Bright Blades, it led us to a blade known as Adrestia and eventually, it led us to you," the wolf answered. "You are our last chance. Our last hope."

"But do you deserve it?"

Species Eighteen turned to face the prince, cocking its head in concern. "Your mind is conflicted."

"You abandoned us," Arlowe argued, pacing back and forth within the void. "You could've aided in putting an end to the Ascension Wars, the Demon Invasions, even the kharakian threat that we face now."

"The races of Äkin were extremely hostile to us," the wolf fired back, manipulating the shadows to form new images. "The elves and dwarves attacked us on a near-constant basis in an attempt to claim our power for their own. I was surprised to see the dragons of your world so peaceful, considering that they too were keen on waging war with us. The fae saw no reason to protect those that seemingly despised us."

"You could've prevented the enslavement of the humans. Your race still existed in Äkin at that time."

"And what would you have had us do? Ask them politely to stop their highly profitable exploitation of your kind? Or would enacting slavery and genocide upon them have taught them a lesson?" The prince's tongue was caught. "Even if we *did* halt the slave trade of your ancestors, the Faegareskh forbade us from interfering with the other races. That was one of the few decisions I believe they chose correctly."

"And the kharakians?"

"You're referring to our energy fuelling them?"

"We made them. The curse falls squarely on our laps." Arlowe glanced at the images. The Incarnate stared back at him. "But the destruction that has been wrought over the last few weeks? The lives that have been taken? That blood is on your hands. You can't deny that."

"No, I cannot," accepted the wolf, facing the Incarnate. "I grieve for those lost, Arlowe, I really do. But you have to understand that if we had not attempted to send that portal, my entire race would have been doomed. We sent that energy out of desperation, to survive."

"Did you know of the kharakians?" Species Eighteen looked at Arlowe, uttering not a word. "Did you know?"

"Does it matter?" the wolf responded.

"It does to me."

Species Eighteen nodded, accepting its choice of words. "On the rare occasion that we could glimpse back into Äkin, we saw them."

"So you did know."

"We didn't know that they would abduct our power."

A third voice cut into the dispute, drawing their attention up. "Arlowe, I repeat, if you can hear me, according to Gill, the Incarnate's energy is dropping rapidly!" an excited Xanth exclaimed, sniffling between his cheers. "Our mission is a success! It's over now! For good!"

"It looks like my injuries are stabilizing," Arlowe stated, watching the void darken in the distance. "Come with me. You're free now."

"Am I?"

536

Doubt began to fill Arlowe's thoughts. "You're free. We won. The Incarnate's energy is petering out."

The wolf shook its head. "What do you think is still holding the Incarnate together?"

"The portal," Arlowe murmured, realising his folly. The murky edges of the void were closing in. "As the Incarnate fades, so does the portal!"

"If the Incarnate is left to burn out, the portal *will* fall. The fae will be trapped forever."

As the prince awaited the approaching darkness, Species Eighteen sat by his side, facing it alongside him. "There is nothing more we can do. You know of us. You know what we've done. All I ask is that you judge us fairly."

The void swallowing them whole, Arlowe gasped back to life, back within the waking world.

*

Before him, his allies laid battered and broken, taking cover behind a cracked barrier of Daria's making.

"This is it, Arlowe!" Onyx called out, resting his back upon a nearby boulder. "Gill said we've won. I need a drink."

"We're not celebrating yet," Arlowe choked, wrestling with his beaten body to return to his feet. "The fae are still trapped. The energy for their portal resides within the Incarnate. We need to get them out."

"There's nothing more we can do," Gill debated, feeling returning to his arm. "The Incarnate has placed a barrier between us and our forces. Even Ota-Rnshi stands on the opposite side."

"We're pushed ta' our limits, Arlowe," Schukara added. "We don't have it in us ta' kill that monster."

Arlowe looked over his allies, blade in hand. "I don't plan on *killing* it. Daria, move the barrier forward."

The Incarnate continued to pound the mage's barrier, using its overwhelming power to break it down. "Laf la favv, soi doi croix!" the beast screeched, doubling its efforts as the prince neared.

"Arlowe, I can't hold it," Daria strained, slipping onto one knee. "Hurry…"

"Just a little longer, Daria," Arlowe pleaded. "We're so close."

The Incarnate materialised a great spear, thrusting it through the barrier.

Predicting his protection to fall, Arlowe evaded to the side, pushing his blade up into the exposed torso of the creature, using every ounce of strength he had left to pierce it through.

"A futile effort," the Incarnate spat, grasping the prince's shoulders. "I'll savour your death most of all."

The beast forced the remainder of the curse's energy through Arlowe's body, though the prince refused to yield, accepting the pain as his sword moved ever deeper into the final kharakian.

For a moment, the pain dulled. The Incarnate turned his head to its flank, seeing the assassin upon it. A dagger was stabbed into its back.

"You don't have the energy to negate my powers anymore. A shame when one can't keep it up," he mocked, peering over at Arlowe. "I'm diverting the damage to us all. We bear the weight together!"

Arlowe's brow furrowed. *Together?*

To the Incarnate's left, Gill buried his mace into the Incarnate's knee, bringing it down for Schukara to plunge her blade into the beast's rib. Both shared the pain of the curse. "We're finishin' this together!" the mercenary called out.

"It's the whole point of a team, right?" the eleventh continued.

Joining their stand, Daria recalled her broken barrier to cast her healing magic upon them all, further hindering the Incarnate's murderous intentions.

"Our song will be sung," the mage uttered.

Recognising that his power could not outlast their efforts, the Incarnate turned to igniting itself, using the fae energy to keep the band's feet firmly in place. The beast's grip upon Arlowe grew even tighter.

The Incarnate's eyes flickered with green; the group aware of the pterravun's involvement. "Arlowe, whatever you're going to do, do it!" Xanth cried out, locked into a battle of wills with the monster. "I can't hold its detonation! Let's finish this, Arlowe! Once and for all!"

Twisting and retracting his blade from the Incarnate, Arlowe reached into his pack with his off-hand to take the shard of Evret, shoving it into the wound his sword had retracted from.

The Incarnate let out a pitiful squeal as the pulsing of its body ended, blasting those gathered aside.

As the group returned to their feet, they found the Incarnate on its knees, slumped over. The glow of its body had dimmed, the barrier around them dispelled.

"Arlowe, what just happened?" Daria posed, joining her allies as they advanced upon the monstrous body. "What did you do to it?"

"Evret?" Arlowe asked, placing his hand over what remained of the beast's armour. "Evret, set them free."

The Incarnate rose its head. The glow of its body had returned, the beat now absent.

"By your order, Prince Artaven," came the voice of the general.

Raising his arm, Evret gathered the fae energy within his hand, crushing it to set off a wide detonation erupting over the battlefield and beyond.

The kharakians that had survived had been turned to ash. Their essence was added to the spell Evret had cast, summoning synchronized flashes over the land.

Taking into account the fallen ruins of the cursed city and Arlowe's survival, a nearby officer took a flare in hand, firing it into the skies. The survivors watched as the remaining flare checkpoints did the same, turning the sky a shimmering gold.

The prince's name was chanted amongst the cheering and singing of the gathered armies, though Arlowe's mind was set on something else.

"Arlowe, are you okay?" Onyx queried, limping to his side. "You should be celebrating. They're calling your name."

"How do we know it worked?" Arlowe questioned, directing his question to Evret. "Are the fae free? Did we save them?"

A voice, familiar to Arlowe, spoke to him not of mind, but physically. "I think I can answer that."

Now in clear view, the band was able to get a better look at the vence's appearance as it stood before them.

The being appeared to be a union of wolf and dragon, with the prince remembering the burning blue markings that shone upon it. Draconic scales decorated its paws and tail, running the length of its back, accompanied by a small set of wings clasped tightly to its body. Tough claws and fangs completed the look, with a pair of burning blue eyes peering up to those it was communing with.

A smile graced Arlowe's face, with those nearby stood amazed, staring in awe of the strange creature.

"My kind have returned to Äkin, though they will be scattered," the wolf clarified, bowing to the prince's companions. "I apologise if any of you believed Arlowe was

540

mad whilst he was under my brief influence."

"Arlowe? Mad? Never!" the assassin said sarcastically. "Isn't that right, Xanth?"

"Look, it's not my fault that Arlowe is a terrible liar," the boy responded.

"How's that porphyria, Your Highness?"

Arlowe rolled his eyes at that particular memory, choosing instead to focus on Species Eighteen.

"How are you feeling?" he posed to the wolf. "A lot has changed since you've been gone."

"I feel good. The darkness within the Untainted Lands doesn't seem to have followed," the wolf replied, taking in its surroundings. "I doubt reintegration will be so simple, but in saying that, I question what is. Thank you for saving as many as you could."

"How many made it through?"

"Nearly a third, though somehow the energy was found to keep the portal open for a few moments longer. We knew the risk."

The prince rested his gaze over Evret, remembering the absorption of the last surviving kharakians, bowing to him. The general bowed in return.

As the celebrations proceeded, Demetrius descended onto the battlefield, joined by Valerius and Adrestia. "The entirety of Argestra, nay Katosus, is in your debt Arlowe!" the king declared, patting the prince's back with glee.

The black blade and wielder looked over the wolf, with Valerius kneeling to their old friend. "A pleasure, Species Eighteen," Adrestia greeted, glowing upon her wielder's shoulder. "We have much to discuss."

"Thank you for passing on the relevant information," the wolf replied.

"Was it worth it?" Valerius posed, rising back to his feet. "Bringing them back?"

"Every race has made mistakes somewhere down the line. The fae are no exception to that," Gill pronounced, glancing over the ravaged lands. "But, as it always is, we must rebuild. A new age awaits."

"Well said, eleventh," Demetrius praised, whistling to his men. The king's elite guard surrounding the band. "However, I regret to inform you all that there is one more thing that needs to be taken care of."

"What's going on?" Daria queried, anxious of the looming soldiers.

Onyx and Schukara drew their weapons, standing between Arlowe and Demetrius' men. "What are you doing?" Onyx questioned, halting their advance. "Arlowe just saved every last one of you!"

"Weapons down," Arlowe ordered, standing before his allies. "What are you doing, Demetrius?"

"It is with a heavy heart when I say: Arlowe Artaven of Eyenridge, you are under arrest."

"On what charges?"

"Caspus Molvo's arrest had no effect. You're being charged with the murder of the Arcane Guild High Council."

Epilogue:

"Stagnating air is common foreshadowing that something terrible is about to happen."

1st Nofabelos

Land's Legacy

2084∞ (Current Age)

"Everybody, in!"

Hurrying those collected into the Arcane Guild library, Demetrius swiftly turned his key, locking them all inside.

Sitting himself at one of the desks, Arlowe locked eyes with the king; the prince had yet to figure out what Demetrius intended.

"Why are we here?" Onyx questioned, blinking on top of one of the bookcases, remembering this to be the first crime scene Arlowe had been involved with.

Demetrius sat on the steps, grasping the bridge of his nose in distress. "I need to talk with you all. Marching Arlowe to the cells would have only aroused suspicion from the citizens," he explained, placing his arms over his knees. "It's hard to make sense of a situation when the local populace is rallying for the freedom of *the* Hero of the Kharakian War."

Pulling the cloth away that concealed Arlowe's handcuffs, Schukara's temper had reached its peak, lashing out at the king. "They'd be right to! This is nonsense! Ya' need ta' release—"

"Do you think it wise to demand from a king?" The library went silent. Not a page stirred, as Demetrius' own temper simmered. "I'm sorry, but I'm taking every precaution here. Einluthor is the last surviving member of the Arcane Guild Council. This is a delicate situation."

543

Daria sat in the chair at Arlowe's side, with the prince noticing her wrists chain-free.

"Why has Daria not been seized?" Arlowe posed. "I assume she's just as much a suspect as I?"

"I've made the mistake of apprehending a necromancer in my youth, Arlowe. Their unnatural strength makes the deed pointless," Demetrius answered, regaining his energy enough to descend his perch. "Besides, I know you and your companions are close. If you came, so would she."

"Would you like me in handcuffs?" Daria asked, offering a weak smile to the prince. "For formalities sake."

Arlowe smirked at her innocence, though he shook his head to decline the offer. "No, it's fine, but thank you for the consideration."

"I don't mean to cast bias, but I don't believe that Arlowe is involved with the murders," Demetrius admitted, addressing the prince's allies. "I need any leads you can dig up, no matter how minute you may think they are."

"Hold on, you believe Arlowe is innocent?" Gill inquired, cocking his head in intrigue. "If that's so, why not fight in our corner? Profess his innocence?"

"I'm putting my neck on the line just by being here. If I'm wrong, and Arlowe is involved somehow, I could be named a rebellion sympathiser; my family could be ousted and killed. I can't afford for that to happen." Demetrius held back his emotions, composing himself. "Now, back to the matter at hand. Leads."

"Let's start with the obvious," Arlowe announced, firmly sat in place. "Daria and I were both at Kharaki when the most recent murders took place. We can't be in two locations at once."

"That's not good enough. Not only are you on record as opposing the guilds—"

"In my youth!"

"But there was nothing stopping you from co-ordinating with others who share that same anti-guild sentiment! The only thing that the janitorial head has told us thus far is that he isn't the brains on this! We don't know how many are out there in plain sight!"

"This is absurd," Onyx stated, drawing their attention to the heights of the bookcase. "Arlowe has nothing to do with this. The people are grasping at straws."

"They can't be blamed for that," Demetrius argued. "Naturally they will look for someone to blame. Their family, their friends, their neighbours, all perished."

The king's declaration turned the assassin mute.

Demetrius proceeded undisturbed. "The murders continued despite Caspus' arrest. Arlowe has been to the last few crime scenes. The rumours of a necromancer in his midst haven't helped. To call it all a coincidence would be an understatement."

"At least with the kharakians, the families of those involved have had closure," Arlowe noted, his eyes gazing downwards. "The families of the mages have had no such thing. Considering the circumstances, it's understandable as to why I'm being accused, Onyx."

Demetrius pulled their attention back once more. "So, I ask again: do any of you have any leads? At all?"

"Have there been any survivors of the attacks?" Daria offered, glancing at Arlowe.

The prince nodded his head. "Kirk."

"Kirk? Who is that?" Demetrius questioned.

"A guard back in Vexinth, the sole survivor of the dredge attack on Haaroith's guild hall."

Demetrius accepted his response, moving to the library's exit. "I'll have one of my men look into this. I'll be back momentarily."

As the king departed, Arlowe peered over his allies; a troubled smile attempted to reassure them. "Be honest with me, guys. How innocent am I looking right now?"

His companions were silent, knocking his confidence. "Well, don't speak all at once."

"Gill," Onyx addressed, his arms folded. "Everything should be on the table."

Arlowe faced the eleventh. "You were investigating the murders. Did you find something?"

Gill begrudgingly nodded. "I did, though it doesn't support you so much as it does implicate you further."

Gauging the tension of those in the room, the eleventh slowly pulled his trusty notepad from his coat pocket, flicking to the relevant pages.

"There have been two accounts of you disappearing with no alibi," he uttered. "In Thaedlon before being found by Onyx and Schukara, and in Wicilil before Daria found you huddled under an empty stall."

"I was turned away by a shrine priest in Thaedlon. The Bright Blades were in talks with the Administration upon my arrival," Arlowe protested, shifting his vision between his allies. "And as for Wicilil, I took a stroll. Daria's treatment wasn't going to last just a few moments and it was raining."

"Two problems with that," Gill stated, abruptly ending the prince's confession. "I investigated both the Thaedlon and Wicilil guild halls despite having to break the law to do so. Your soul energy was there both before and after the massacres."

"And the second?"

"Your story don't make a lick of sense," Schukara continued, softening her tone. "Shrine priests haven't operated fer' tha' Bright Blades fer' over a hundred years. There's no way one could've turned ya' away."

"I can't speak for the soul energy, but I know what I saw! I saw a shrine priest!" Arlowe let out a sigh of frustration, though in a moment a new answer reached his mind. "What about Xanth? He was with me the whole time!"

"Yeah, I could vouch for Arlowe," Xanth added.

"Yeah, no. That won't work," Onyx interrupted, hopping down from his vantage point. "I know you can connect Xanth to others now, but I don't think the supportive voice in your head will hold up in a court of law, unless you're pleading insanity."

"There are also memory lapses to account for," Gill resumed, closing his notepad. "In addition to the shrine priest, you were also unable to recall how you escaped the dredges in Haaroith. I found you outside with no understanding of how you made it out."

As the prince attempted to reason with the facts, Demetrius returned. His solemn appearance set off warning bells in his head.

"I return. Do you want the good news or the bad news?" the king queried, seeming at odds with himself.

"I think we need some good news," Daria voiced, hoping to relight their morale.

"I found some Vexin guardsmen who recognised the name you gave me. They were about ready to ship back to Haaroith, though I caught them just in time."

The group looked around, concerned at the information they had received.

"That's it?" Onyx questioned.

"That's it."

The assassin rotated his hand for more. "And the bad news?"

"She came here, joining her fellow guardsmen despite her physical and mental condition. She went missing before their departure for Kharaki."

"What about Ushnar?" Daria hastily asked. "And… and Arlowe mentioned there was another. K—"

"Kellen?" Demetrius' sudden answer stopped the mage cold. "Gill already passed

547

their names on to me. Considering their races, the new archivist for the guild looked through the last sixty to eighty years of human and orc recruitments and more for good measure and found none fitting their description. If they were a part of the guild, they've both covered their tracks well."

Arlowe had been defeated. His optimism shattered, dumbstruck at his inability to remember the recent past.

"We could go on the run," Onyx noted, standing at the prince's back. "Arlowe just wants to help people. He didn't have his precious kingdom to accomplish what he has."

"We're not goin' on the run," Schukara fired back. "Yer' Highness, is there nothin' we can do?"

"He can't do anything," Onyx spat. "Or won't. Who knows?"

"I have connections. I could shorten the sentence. His new title may aid in avoiding an execution," Demetrius proposed. "Is there any way we can shuffle the soul energy findings under the rug?"

Gill shook his head. "Even if I did, another would eventually find what I already have."

As the debates raged, questioning every tiny detail of the seemingly inevitable trial, Arlowe wracked his brain for any detail he may have missed, looking through the memories that were still crystal clear in his mind. *Was there anything I left behind? Something said that made more sense with context? Anything?*

The eleventh looked to the mage, who had until this point in their debates not said a word. "And what of Daria?"

"I'm through running. I won't apologise for what I am anymore," she spoke, stunning them all with her newfound confidence. "If I'm to be put on trial, there will be no games. I'll do this by the book."

With Daria's statement floating through his mind, Arlowe stood at the revelation her words had brought, silencing those before him. "That's it."

As the prince made his way over to the library's main desk, the king followed closely in protest. "Arlowe, you need to stay put, or else I'll have to—"

"Demetrius, I need you on my side."

Demetrius faltered at his words. "Arlowe, t-that isn't fair."

"I know, but right now, I need you to trust me."

The king bit his tongue, taking a deep breath. "What do you need?"

Arlowe escorted the king towards the library index, gesturing his head to it. "I need you to turn the pages of the index for me. My restraints make doing it myself a little... difficult." Demetrius pulled the obscenely large book to his front, opening the front cover. His fingers awaited instruction. "Go to T."

The king flung the pages across, allowing the prince time to scan the pages. "That's everything in T," Demetrius replied. "Did you find what you were looking for?"

"No," said the prince. "Go back to S."

The delicate pages were thrown ever further, with Arlowe's gaze catching sight of what he sought. "That's it! There should be one copy in this library." The prince peered across the desk to find the check-out log, motioning the king towards it. "In that book, go to the most recent entries."

Demetrius brought the book to Arlowe's face, flicking the pages aside for him. The prince shook his head at his findings.

"Move over to the previous month?" As the pages turned over and over, one in particular caught his attention, raising his arms to stop the king from proceeding further. "Historical!" he exclaimed, the library echoing his statement.

"What?" queried Schukara, looking as baffled as the others. "Historical?"

"The historical section! There's a book there I'm looking for!"

"Over here," Gill called out, with Arlowe rushing to his location. "What are you looking for?"

"S, s, s, s," Arlowe repeated. His repetition halted as he found a gap in the row of books. "It's not here. It's been taken out without permission. Stolen."

"Aros' shattered patience, what is going on?" Demetrius yelled, reaching the end of his tether. "What does one missing book have to do with anything?"

Arlowe rose from his knee, moving to his lover's side. "Daria, break them."

The king attempted to intervene. "No, wait—"

As instructed, Daria took a hold of the chains, crushing them in her grasp to free Arlowe against the king's wishes.

"Where is Einluthor?" Arlowe questioned, challenging Demetrius' temper further.

The king's anger boiled over at last. "Arlowe, I can't tell you that!"

"The murderer is somewhere in this city! Einluthor is all the Arcane Guild has left and he could be being slaughtered at this very moment! I need to know his location!"

"He's surrounded by my elite guard! You're a suspect, they'll kill you on sight!"

"But at least I know he'll be safe!" Demetrius buckled at Arlowe's words, unable to gain traction. "Your 'elite guard' needs to be alive to protect him, which I don't hold much faith in. The murderer has taken down countless Arcane Guild members. What are a few guards to them?"

Demetrius looked upon the expectant faces of Arlowe and his allies; his own face gave off a nervous aura. "At the castle gardens, shake the hand of the statue in the centre. Doing so will open a hatch that will lead you underground."

"And what will we find?"

"Cells, designed to hold those who offer us an advantage in certain... situations."

Arlowe slowly nodded at his honesty, turning to his companions. "We'll talk about this later. Schukara, take Demetrius to safety. Onyx, Gill, Daria, you're with me."

"But I want ta' fight!" Schukara protested, drawing a blade.

"And you will, but Demetrius' safety is paramount. If he perishes, everything could fall into disarray. Can I trust you with his life?"

Schukara stubbornly nodded, taking the king's wrist only for him to stay put.

"How will I know when this is over?" Demetrius asked. "That I made the right choice?"

Arlowe held his breath for a moment. "I guess we're about to find out."

As Schukara escorted the king away, Gill and Daria came forth, both appearing anxious. "We need to go," the eleventh stated, drawing Arlowe's attention to their haste. "Onyx is gone."

The prince looked around, only able to see two of his three companions. "He's going to get himself killed."

*

The three raced up the main street with not a moment to spare, barely evading those gathered in the streets. The castle came closer with every step, though even now, so far out, the speed of the gods couldn't carry them fast enough.

Time refused to freeze even at such a crucial time.

"How did you figure out it was her?" Daria questioned, her undead stamina aiding her through the busy streets. "How did that book help?"

"When we first met, she told me of that book, 'The Sorrow of the Aigahn Maiden'," Arlowe clarified, winded, yet resolute in his charge to the gardens. "She told me she picks one up whenever she visits the different guild halls. The book was missing but wasn't checked out."

"Was that accidental, or was it done on purpose to lure you to her?" Gill posed.

"Does it matter now?"

Arlowe tackled into the garden's gates, still rushing to the central statue. "Regardless, how far can she get? She's going against Demetrius's best—"

The prince stopped at once, stunned at the sight before him. The hand of the statue had been pried off, the gardens decorated in the blood of the unfortunate guards torn limb from limb.

The hatch to the underground had been ripped open, with more of the deceased guards lining the insides.

"No, stop!" yelled a familiar voice from inside; the pleas were made in between bouts of pained screams.

"Einluthor's still alive!" Arlowe called, drawing his weapon. "Gill, senses up. Everyone, on me."

Arlowe's band descended into the bowels of the hidden prison, guided by a magical light that Daria had crafted for them.

"Come on, come on!" the prince repeated, kicking open empty cell after empty cell. "Where is he?"

A scream of agony came a short distance away, unnerving the group as one of the metal doors slammed shut.

"I sense two life signs from over there, one fading fast!" Gill declared, directing Arlowe to the sealed cell.

Placing his boot firmly upon the door, Arlowe breached through into the cell, lowering his weapon as he saw his failure directly in front. "It's you."

With the copy of The Sorrow of the Aigahn Maiden floating before her and a twitching Einluthor hanging from an ornate scythe, Antoinetta stood before them; a sickening smile was draped across her face.

"I was wondering how long it would take you to find me," she announced, gazing over Arlowe with a playful lust. "I just can't seem to let this book go. Sorry that I stole your opportunity to read it."

"Why?" Arlowe asked, unable to comprehend the woman's actions. His blood boiled at her child-like attitude at the situation.

The book was closed; Einluthor was dropped to the ground. The illusion that surrounded Antoinetta was lowered to reveal her purple eyes and black veins. Her ears turned to a rounded shape; her appearance was more akin to human than elven.

Sending away her weapon, her free hand released the bind from her hair and the coat from her body. Her hair dropped to show it crudely hand-cut to match the tattered white dress that barely fit her physique. There was a wild beauty to her, though her malicious intent still bled through.

"Why what?" she queried, pretending to be oblivious to the corpse at her side. "Tell me more."

"The guards, the mages, the council," Gill listed. "*You're* the Arcane Guild Murderer."

"Oh, that." Antoinetta waved the accusation away, making what she had done seem so light. Her body fell into crippling laughter, tears filling her eyes. "Yeah, that was me. Pretty good, right? The looks on your faces this whole time!"

"This is funny to you?" Daria posed, disgusted at her reaction. "How is this funny at all?"

"How is it not funny? Come on, we may as well laugh." Her disposition changed, her tone shifting to something darker. "The realms are just one big joke anyway; our self-awareness is the punch line."

"This bloodshed, what was the point in it?" Arlowe demanded, though Antoinetta remained unfazed.

The woman cleared her throat, putting her hands behind her back, bringing them forth to reveal a top hat and monocle. "The wars of Argestra, of Katosus, of Äkin, started on greed and hatred, of ignorance and sin. Even the gods are not opposed to their transcendent disputes!" Antoinetta spoke in that of a gentleman's tone, returning the props to her back out of sight. "But, if we were all united under one banner, brought together in death as one family, there would be no strife, no hatred. Rape and war, famine and illness; all would cease to be once we offer ourselves to undeath!"

"This is madness," Arlowe argued, raising his blade once more. "The 'free will' of your new world is oddly absent. We're not your thralls."

"The Demon Invasions will never end. Without unification, the demons will one day secure victory over us, taking this world as their own, and if not them, then..."

Antoinetta lowered to her knees, pleading with her guests. "Slavery or death will be your only options. I offer you something more. The chance to live out your lives eternally, free and peaceful, ready to save us from those that lie beyond. I would care for you as my own."

"Your words are hollow," Gill voiced, uninterested in the necromancer's pitch. "Is your plan not hypocritical considering those you've murdered? Were they your family too, or were they simply not worthy of your new world?"

Antoinetta placed a hand around the late councillor's throat, taking a pendant of Arytholity into her grasp; her tone had become tranquil. "I only turn to violence when faced with those that would endanger our kind."

554

Crushing the pendant, the woman looked to Arlowe with a devious grin. "Besides, I'm not the only one with blood on my hands. Did you savour the slaughter, Puppy?"

*

"Where are we going?" Demetrius cried, struggling with his breath as Schukara pulled him through the city. "Why are we not returning to the castle?"

"Yer' castle ain't safe! The murderer could be as close as yer' back garden!" the mercenary answered. "Best place to go is tha' outskirts of tha' city! Tha' camps of Arlowe's gathered forces should still be there! They'd be crazy ta' attack ya' there!"

Transitioning from alleyway to alleyway, the king and his elven bodyguard escaped to the lower levels of the city, only to be stopped as they neared the bottom.

A familiar outline stood in their way, scythe in hand.

Caspus entered into the alley, dragging his scythe behind him. "So, ya' were a part of this after all," Schukara spoke, positioning herself between the janitor and the king.

The necromancer sighed, advancing upon them. "Does it really matter?" he queried, lazily slumping forward. "It's all in the past."

"How did ya' escape?"

"Ugh, a goblin and an amalgam aided me, if you must know."

Schukara drew her blades. "And what're ya' gonna' do ta' us?"

"I'm done talking. Why don't we find out?"

*

"I slipped a suggestion into your mind the first time we met, taking you as an ally with a snap of my fingers," Antoinetta divulged, staring at the prince. The murderer was enraptured by his fearful bearing. "Though it wasn't easy, I'll have you know. Having someone in your head already makes it difficult to go undetected."

"She knows about me," Xanth mumbled. "That's why our connection was broken."

555

"So I…" Arlowe wrestled with his own conscience, aware of what Antoinetta implied. "I killed them."

"You activated my trap in Haaroith, releasing my dredges into the guild hall, just as you terminated most of the council members at Wicilil, giving my little brother time to summon the banshees, killing every witness." Antoinetta put her hand to her mouth, leaning in to whisper. "There were a lot of witnesses."

"And what of your aids? Of Kellen and Ushnar?" Gill questioned, growing colder by the minute. "The shrine priest? The false memories?"

"Drumroll please! Babababababababa—" Antoinetta placed a series of slaps across her knees to build up her audience, the three remained unamused.

Gill fired a crossbow bolt, though the necromancer caught it, ending her performance.

"You're no fun," she hissed, clearing her throat. "The truth is, they were all illusions! Fabrications of my own design! Kellen wasn't much of a stand-out character, though I know Ushnar had a good send off!"

"What's your name? Truthfully?" Arlowe asked, barely able to contain his emotions.

"Miss Antoinetta Unecrosse, Lady of the Unecrosse Estate, though you, my dear Arlowe, may call me your little dove."

"*Lady* Antoinetta Unecrosse, you're under arrest for the murder of the Arcane Guild Council and of all the lives that were unfortunate enough to be in your way."

The necromancer rolled her eyes, examining the bolt in her hand. "Do you really think I led you here so I would be trapped?" Movement from behind stirred her, taking a tight grip of the ammunition in her hand. "All you had to do was let me go. Now I have to break all your toys."

Onyx emerged from the shadows leaping at his prey, though while he was fast, she was faster.

Spinning to face him at speeds unseen, the crossbow bolt was forced into his torso. Taking him, Antoinetta then threw him over her head, directly towards the cold floor.

Though Onyx blinked out of her clutches, the necromancer was not yet through with him. *"The assassin, so brave, so cunning, so brash,"* the necromancer sung. *"You, like your attitude, goes down in a flash!"*

Somehow aware of where he would be, Antoinetta slammed her scythe down upon Onyx, flinging him up before batting him to his allies.

"Next?" the necromancer taunted.

Arlowe and Gill both moved up, with Daria supporting them at Onyx's side.

Antoinetta danced through the assault, shattering the magic missiles targeting her as she parried every strike of the attackers.

Then, pulling him in with an unseen force, she pirouetted Arlowe before kicking him aside, toppling both him and the bookcase he was knocked into.

Reflecting the new wave of darts back at Daria, Antoinetta then turned her attention upon the lone Gill, aware of the powers his enhanced senses provided.

Using her speed to her advantage, the necromancer flung herself at him repeatedly, landing weak hits to tax his precognition. *"The eleventh, supernatural, a sight to be feared,"* she continued, landing a powerful blow upon him. *"But those senses won't stop me, I'll soon be revered!"*

Using her momentum, Antoinetta threw herself into the air, bringing down her scythe upon Gill only to have her lethal blow blocked by a barrier.

Finding the caster, the necromancer swung her scythe through the barrier to incapacitate the eleventh before spinning to face Daria.

"Your gifts are all wasted, temptations never tasted. A shame," Antoinetta re-joined, wildly charging at the mage.

Daria recalled her barrier, repositioning it between them both, though the crazed

necromancer had no time for her games. Her scythe slammed down repeatedly over the

protective shell, providing the beat to her song. *"Vie to purify, this necrotic lullaby,*

now comply to my wish that you'll fall down and—"

The steel of Arlowe's blade pierced through Antoinetta's torso. Her heavy scythe

clattered upon the floor as she stumbled to one side, collapsing to the ground alongside

it with a hand over her wound.

The necromancer splayed herself across the flooring. Her torn white dress soaked up

her black blood. "And then there's you," she mumbled.

"I wish our circumstance were different, but my deeds, too abhorrent." Her song took

a melancholy tone, despair filling her every word as she choked on her blood. *"One*

day I hope that I impress, you the prince, to be your princess."

Arlowe came forth; his allies were still reeling. "Is this a game to you?" he

questioned, watching her head limply face the blood-soaked floor.

Antoinetta's light sobs slowly transformed into giggling, with the necromancer

abruptly raising her arm, firing the prince into the wall, pinning him. The sword within

her was ripped out by her own hand, tossed aside as she closed in on him.

"Oh, my love. My Puppy," she whispered, caressing his cheek. Her scythe was lifted

into the air telekinetically, scraping over his cuirass. "It's hardly a game when one has

already won, no?"

Aware of Arlowe's companions coming to his rescue, Antoinetta used the wall to

propel herself back into the air, crashing down with her scythe to send out a

shockwave, knocking them all back.

"And scene!" the necromancer announced, bowing to her adversaries, pouting at the

lack of a response. "Well, I suppose if I'm not wanted."

"You're not… going anywhere," Onyx struggled, forcing his body back onto its feet.

"Ugh, you're all just as clingy as my pet!" Giving out a whistle, Antoinetta patted her knees, speaking up to the roof above her. "Here boy! Your master awaits!"

The underground prison began to shake. The cell doors clattered against their frames as the hanging torches swung back and forth. Though the structure held strong, a set of razor-sharp claws penetrated through from above, he ceiling torn away by a dominating figure.

"It can't be," Gill said in fear, watching as a black-veined dragon reached in, stealing Antoinetta from them.

"Good boy, Mao-Yr!" praised the necromancer, stroking the ridged head of the undead dragon. "Now, have a word with these fools about how to treat a woman!"

"Mao-Yr, don't!" Arlowe pleaded, though his words fell on deaf ears.

The dragon built up its breath, releasing a blast of ice upon the band. The prince braced himself as his vision was filled with nothing but the chilling breath filling the cell, though his body remained warm.

"I'm not feeling anything," Onyx stated through the telepathy. "What's happening?"

"The cold isn't affecting me either," Gill added. "Arlowe? Daria?"

"I'm here," Arlowe answered. "Daria? Daria!"

As the dragon's assault came to an end, its movements could be heard leaving the prison; Antoinetta's laughter dissipated as they left.

Arlowe attempted to move forward only to find himself unable to. Before him, a barrier had been cast, realising what had been done.

"Daria, lower the barrier! It's over!" he called, watching the barrier fade away. In the corner of the cell, his beloved struggled to move, frozen from the blast.

The three rushed to Daria's side. Onyx blinked to catch her as her body became limp.

"She casted a barrier, but due to Antoinetta separating us she could only cast it so far," the eleventh deduced, examining the frost-free lines upon the floor. "She chose us."

Arlowe took the mage into his arms. Her eyes met with his. "Everyone out, now," he ordered, carrying Daria to the door. "She isn't getting away."

Rushing to the guild's entryway, the four came to find the door encased in ice, likely by the dragon under Antoinetta's control.

"I'm out of bombs," the assassin stated, checking over his body for anything else of use only for his attention to be pulled to a clicking sound. "What's that noise?"

It didn't take long for them to realise that the sound was coming from the eleventh. His palm was filled with his own sphere, which appeared to be made of glass.

"Stand back," he declared, throwing the gadget to the base of the door.

"What is that, Gill?" Arlowe questioned, retreating with Daria to cover.

"It's called an antithetical grenade, or anti-nade for short," he explained, awaiting the timer. "When someone is healed, their wounding energy is released from the body. Most let it disperse. I utilise it."

With a brief muting of noise, the grenade detonated, knocking the frozen doors from their hinges with ease.

"A grenade that charges on pain? I wish I had something like that," Onyx remarked. Gill took his shoulder. "The five-year olds think you're cool enough."

Exiting the guild, the band could see Antoinetta dropping to the courtyard, her dragon on standby far above. Arlowe carefully placed Daria onto the ground, wiping the chilled hair from her cheek before turning to face the necromancer below.

"Antoinetta, stand down!" he ordered. "I refuse to let you leave this city!"

"Hear ye, hear ye," announced the necromancer, ringing a bell produced from her back. "There are those that may think differently, Puppy! Come one, come all!"

From behind the pillar, Caspus arrived dragging Schukara and Demetrius, listlessly dropping them to the ground.

"Let them go!" Arlowe yelled, enraged at their capture.

"Oh, Arlowe! You have much more important things to be dealing with," the necromancer responded, swinging the bell wildly. "Play nice!"

On her signal, the courtyard began to fill with lurchers, bursting forth from the houses and gutters. The screams of the city made it clear that the sudden arrival of the undead horde was not solely with them.

"How did she…" Onyx questioned, too confounded to continue.

"What do you think became of those from the guild? From the underground cistern?" Antoinetta posed. "Waste not, want not!"

As Arlowe attempted to advance, an undead Vexin guard stood before him. Her face quickly reminded him of her identity.

"Kirk," he said with sorrow, raising his blade. "Forgive me for what I'm about to do."

As the undead swarmed the city, keeping those that sought her busy, Antoinetta knelt down to the beaten body of Schukara, lifting her head by the chin.

"I've had my eye on you for a while now," she spoke; her voice was almost calming. "You're so talented, so pretty. You should be my best friend! We could—"

"I'd like ta' see things from yer' point of view, but I can't get ma' head that far up ma' ass," Schukara muttered, cutting in. "I *ain't* yer' friend."

"Don't be silly! Of course you are."

A purple light emanating in her hand, Antoinetta's magic flowed into the elf, making her eyes as vibrant as the necromancer's own. Tightening her grip around Schukara's face in excitement, Antoinetta then let her go, dropping the mercenary's face back down onto the stone floor.

Arlowe's sword clashed with the undead Kirk's as his allies held back the rising tide of the summoned dead. "Someone needs to end this!" Onyx yelled, dashing back and forth through the thralls. "I'm putting a stop to this right now!"

"Onyx, wait!"

Arlowe held out his hand, though his attempt to halt the assassin was futile.

Waiting not a moment longer, Onyx leapt into the crowd, blinking out of sight. At once, the assassin reappeared by Antoinetta's side only to be knocked back by a powerful strike not of the trickster's own. "No, wait…"

Schukara was knelt with a defending arm outstretched, uttering not a word. "Caspus, deal with the pest," Antoinetta ordered, holding onto the mercenary's other arm as she rose to her feet.

"What about Demetrius?" Caspus queried, sat cross-legged at her side.

"Best Friend and I have that covered!"

"Get away from him!" Arlowe screamed, severing Kirk's weapon hand before tackling her down the stairs. "Demetrius, I'm coming! Hold on!"

As Caspus kept the assassin at bay, Antoinetta placed her foot under the king, rolling him onto his back. "Best Friend, ready your weapon."

The prince cut through swathes of the lesser undead, moving as fast as his opposition would let him. "Antoinetta, don't you lay a finger on him!"

"Kill."

"Demetrius!"

The king limply rolled his head to face Arlowe. "I put my trust in you. It was well placed. Thank you for—"

With no intervention, Schukara's blade came down upon Demetrius' neck, decapitating him in full view of those gathered. The undead held Arlowe back, forcing him to watch as the grisly execution reached its conclusion. "No!"

Antoinetta took the head into her grasp, examining the king in closer detail. "Don't weep for him. He awaits you in the new world," she reminded, rolling the head over her shoulders before spinning it on her finger.

Losing interest, the necromancer flicked the head aside, looking to the sky. "It looks to me like today was a great success! Mao-Yr, time to—"

"Master, stop this madness!" Ota-Rnshi had emerged from the castle gardens, aiming straight for its late master.

Alerted by its soul energy, Gill used his senses to remove Mao-Yr's sight, aiding the young dragon in its charge as it ripped its master from the air.

Entangled, both dragons crashed into the side of Thaedlon's castle, headed on a collision course for the courtyard.

As the dust cleared from their impact, Ota-Rnshi's face was being dragged through the stone paving by its master, flung back at the castle before being blown back with a wave of frost.

Mao-Yr fired its breath at Ota-Rnshi repeatedly, blasting its descendant again and again until the stone wall at its back yielded. Still crippled from the kharakians, the young dragon was incapable of keeping up with his undead predecessor, collapsing within the castle defeated.

As Mao-Yr raised its arm to end its successor's life, Antoinetta ceased its attack with a quick whistle. Heeding her command, the dragon remained still.

"Come now Mao-Yr, that child is hardly worth our time," she goaded, clicking her pet to her side. "Ota-Rnshi will understand when its older."

The undead dragon lowered its wing. The collection of Antoinetta, Caspus and

Schukara mounted upon it.

"Antoinetta, stop!" Arlowe yelled, coming so close only to be knocked down by Demetrius' headless body.

Mao-Yr raised its wings, ascending above the chaos of the ravaged city. "The unseen hand of Corruption waits for no one, Puppy!" Antoinetta announced, controlling the body of the king like a puppet, toying with the prince. "We'll meet again, Arlowe! I know you can't resist."

Arlowe kicked the reanimated body away, taking his blade to pierce it through the torso, pinning it to the ground. His eyes looked up in horror, his mission failed, a friend taken. "Schukara!"

*

Without their instigator, the undead fell quickly, though this wasn't without more death and tragedy.

Corpses filled the morning streets. Families killed by their own, pets turning against their masters, the beggars turning on those that had moved their eyes from them. A rotten scent filled the city, constantly reminding those left alive of their losses and of what was still to come.

Arlowe was stood over Demetrius. His body no longer squirmed to be freed. To his disgrace, the king's children had left the safety of the damaged castle, gathered to see the deceased sight of their father. The prince had no words; his blade was still dug deep into the late king's chest.

Of them all, Keila stood by Arlowe's side, kneeling to close the eyes of her father. "I know it's an odd thing to say, but he seems more relaxed than he ever has been," she voiced gently, stroking the cheek of her father, bringing the body and head back together. "The night you spoke to him, he felt like a completely different person. He only spoke about his fears whilst drunk, but we all knew. He cared very much about how you and your father saw him.

"At first, he seemed disappointed in himself, not trusting in your father, though the more he thought on your words, the happier he was. He was proud that you had given him that second chance and he was glad to act on it.

"Thank you for making my father happy in the end."

"What happens now?" Arlowe posed to her, offering a hand for the daughter to rise.

"It will take time for the country to readjust."

"I meant in regards to your family."

"So do I." Keila looked to her brothers and sisters, all there to support her. "As per tradition, when the Monarch of Hietruce passes on, the title is passed down to the eldest child, which our mother and my siblings take no issue in."

"But others will?"

"Though none have succeeded, that hasn't stopped relatives from attempting to break tradition to take the throne as their own. It will only get more complicated considering that our eldest brother, Chidike, considers himself too ill to rule. If he turns down the coronation, I am next in line."

The woman struggled to compose herself. "You're concerned that you'll disappoint him," Arlowe noted, taking her shoulder.

"I promised him I'd find our missing family. I failed."

"You haven't failed. You never stopped."

Keila nodded, taking the sword's hilt, gesturing for Arlowe to do the same. "We'll do our fathers proud," she expressed. Both gently pulled the sword from Demetrius, with the blade moving to Arlowe's hand. "Put a stop to that girl's madness. End her ravings of unifications and unseen horrors so that none may suffer the loss that I have."

Keila released her grip on the blade, offering a bow to the prince as she departed from the courtyard.

As Arlowe entered into the death-laden main street, he found Evret assisting with the heavy carts, hauling them for the exhausted and mourning people.

"Ah, Arlowe," the general greeted, clumsily lowering the cart. "I understand if you wish me to vacate."

"Why?" Arlowe queried, looking at how quickly their immediate area had been cleared. "You're doing good work, and I wanted to speak to you anyway."

"Shall we walk?"

The two walked side by side down the main street, Evret pulling the cart behind him.

"What do you plan to do now?" Arlowe found it intriguing that he be stood next to the man he had blamed for so long. "I pray you won't be hunting us any longer?"

"The Incarnate is but a distant memory," the general insisted, waving a hand of dismissal. "While I was the focus of the curse's attention, the men that followed me down that dark path were afflicted too, becoming the kharakians you became so accustomed to. I assume you... saw them in the pods."

"And now? Do you intend to pursue your goals for peace?"

"I do. Released, we will rebuild." Evret's gaze fell upon the blood red symbol of Eyenridge glowing upon his chest. "I will transform the kharakians into a symbol of hope, not fear, traversing the lands as protectors of the realm."

As they reached the city's entrance, Arlowe could make out Daria waving to him; his companions were gathered beside her. "Arlowe," uttered the general. "You didn't have to keep me alive. Why did you?"

The prince faced away, watching his loyal companions. "I saw good in you. I'm glad to see I was right."

566

"And if that changes? If the urges of the Incarnate re-emerge?"

"Fool me twice, Evret. Fool me twice."

Leaving the company of the general, Arlowe made his way over to his awaiting allies, confused as to the gathering. Kardus and Species Eighteen were among them.

"What are you all doing here?" he queried. "Are you…"

"We're getting Schukara back," Onyx answered, receiving nods from the others. "Antoinetta's going to pay for what she's done."

"And while we're at it, we'll strike at the heart of the Necromancer Rebellion," Gill added.

"Will you be joining us Kardus?" Arlowe posed, though a shake of the head gave him his answer.

"My priority is my master," he responded, motioning his head to the injured dragon across the way. "Once its injuries have settled, we intend to travel to the other dragon shrines in the hopes that neither the kharakians nor the necromancers have slaughtered our kin, though I fully intend to support you once our business has been concluded."

"And you, Species Eighteen? What are your intentions now that you have returned to Äkin?"

The wolf stepped forward, offering a bow to the prince. "While my kind reacclimatize themselves to our old world, I understand that the other races don't have the luxury of time at their disposal. I request that I stay by your side, to learn more of the world we left behind and to end this menace that threatens us all."

"Valerius and Adrestia believed that leaving the Bright Blades to their devices was a recipe for disaster," Arlowe debated. "You would rather stand by *my* side?"

"It is better for us to cover separate ground. The wielder and blade are a competent duo. If I recall, it was I who needed them." The wolf gazed upon the destruction wrought, its attention returned to Arlowe. "Meanwhile, you intend to walk from one war to another? You will not be alone."

"If you're going to be travelling with us, we need a name for you," Daria noted. "Species Eighteen feels a little too…

"Cold? Mechanical?" the assassin blurted. Daria's eyes seared into him. "There I go, reading minds again."

"I am Species Eighteen," the wolf spoke.

"That's the name of your, well, species, correct?" Kardus questioned. "I believe Daria was thinking something more personal."

"I am Species Eighteen," the wolf repeated.

"But surely you're more than that?"

"I apologise. Species Eighteen is part of my classification," the wolf explained. "When being documented, each individual species of the fae is given five identifiers: time of day at birth, belief of the afterlife, season of birth, species name and identification number. It is, for us, how it has always been."

"Well, what are those identifiers, in order?" Arlowe quizzed.

"Morn, astral, Wyntr, vence, eighteen."

"Mawve," Gill voiced; the wolf's head cocked in confusion. "It's a name taken from the first letters of your identifiers. May we use that name?"

"Mawve?" he wondered, seeming to nod in approval. "You may refer to me as such. A pleasure."

"Not meaning to break up this beautiful union, but we're missing someone important," Onyx voiced, reminding them all of the trials ahead. "We've got the collective of necromancers, an undead legion, necrotic dragon, that Antoinetta psychopath and now Schukara to deal with. The sooner we leave, the better."

Arlowe's brow was raised. "I thought you were leaving to find your master's killers?"

"Schukara was kind to me despite our differences, and we had some good times together. We didn't always see eye to eye, but she always had my back. If the roles were reversed, I know she'd come for me." Onyx shrugged his shoulders, turning away. "Besides, I doubt we've seen the last of my assailants. Two targets, one shot."

"And you, Gill?" Arlowe asked, redirecting his question to the eleventh. "What about Aracaria?"

"The guild is stretched thin dealing with the reintegration of the fae, making sure all is well," he explained, nodding to Mawve. "Prior to that, our directive was to aid against Grandgrave. It's like I said before: if the enemy gets their way, we lose everything. I won't risk that just to fuel my own ego."

"Looks like its settled," Kardus declared, shaking their hands one by one. "I wish you well on your journey. I doubt it'll be an easy feat to set this right."

Arlowe's hand was the last he took, offering a firm shake. "When is it ever?"

The soreiku returned to his master. Daria moved underneath Thaedlon's gateways, spinning to face her companions. "It's a long road ahead," the mage voiced. "Are you all ready to go?"

One by one, Arlowe's band moved up.

Onyx was the first. The assassin blinked to the mage's side, with Gill and Mawve following closely behind. "I believe we are," the wolf stated.

"Arlowe, could you come and see me?" Xanth voice was delicate, more so than usual. "Please?"

The prince nodded to himself, aware that the young pterravun had been uncharacteristically quiet since their escape from Kharaki.

"Xanth needs me," Arlowe expressed, gesturing to the path before them. "Go on, I'll catch up."

Daria shook her head. The mage and those alongside her presented him with a row of smiles, reassuring him. "Go to him. We'll be here when you get back."

*

Even the breeze of the underground was wise to tread carefully as the pterravun populace gathered to pay their respects to their fallen king. Conquest laid within a divine stone coffin. Every hair was brushed into place, his royal attire fastened and clean. His appearance was worthy enough to put even the gods to shame.

Bela took to the raised altar, hands behind her back, speaking clearly and fluently to all that had gathered. "From the escape of our dwarven captors to the construction of our home. From the taking in of lost souls to the rescue of our kind from the molten intruders, I think I speak for all when I say that I look back at our king with nothing but pride and respect.

"Though his temper was unmatched, his voice deafening and his mind often preoccupied with celebrations, Conquest had nothing but the best of intentions for his people. Never turning down the opportunity to aid those who needed him regardless of what his power could have made him. His title was given to him not by tradition, but by our unanimous love for him, and he for us.

"I've never been good at speeches. That was always where *he* excelled, though I can say this with confidence: he was a husband like no other, an incredible father to the children not initially his own and a leader that we can all learn from even during his final days."

The queen wiped a singular tear from her cheek, composing herself. "I'll miss you Conquest. We will all miss you. The underground, the life you made for us, it will never be the same as long as you are not in it. Guide those who have fallen here today towards a better life. Kaldaren ordein."

As the choir began to sing for their fallen king, Bela, Kaat and Xanth all approached his rested body, all saying their goodbyes. As it came for the young boy to say his, he waved his hand to the prince, asking for his company.

"I don't know what to say," Xanth murmured, unable to face his father. "Could you say something?"

Arlowe cleared his throat, taking the pterravun under his arm, pulling him close. "Conquest, without you I wouldn't be stood here right now, successful against the kharakians. Without you I wouldn't have met those that I have grown so close to, and without your sacrifice, I would've lost a dear friend." The prince's hand rested over the cold stone, his head bowed in respect. "Rest well. Arn awaits your kind soul."

As the lid closed over Conquest's coffin, Xanth tugged on Arlowe's arm. The prince knelt down at the boy's request, taking him into his arms as he let his emotions flow. "It's going to be okay."

As the wake proceeded, Arlowe and Xanth sat under the stone archway, watching from beyond. Xanth hadn't said a single word; his eyes were fixed upon his father's empty throne.

"Xanth," Arlowe spoke, attempting to pry his attention away. "He'd be proud of you."

"It's my fault," he answered, his eyes unmoving. "I killed him."

"Xanth, you just lost a father. I know how you must feel, but—"

"I could've taken my time with the network, but I was too stubborn to back down." Tears began to fill the boy's eyes, soaking the sand he sat upon. "It's my fault that I got captured, it's my fault that the kharakians found us and it's my fault that he's dead."

"Xanth..."

Noticing her son's state, Bela approached them both, gesturing for the service to continue without her.

"Bela, I…" Arlowe struggled to focus his words. "I wanted to apologise—"

The queen raised a hand, silencing the prince then and there. "Xanth, that isn't the whole truth, is it my son?" she spoke, able to steal his gaze from the throne to her eyes. Her attention shifted to Arlowe. "The day Conquest knew of the lives beyond our own that he could help, he did so to the farthest extent he could, regardless of the detriment to himself."

Arlowe's tongue was caught for a moment, stirring further questions. "He knew? About the dangers?"

"Xanth came to us whenever the odds were against you asking to help, and Conquest always obliged." Bela took Xanth's cheek, wiping a fresh tear from it. "Our son was willing to help you to the bitter end. Even when we lost him, my husband never gave up faith, praying that he would wake to continue the work he and yourself had worked so hard for. I saw a new side of Conquest, and he of Xanth."

The words awaking something within him, Arlowe rose to his feet, drawing the blade from his sheath. "Xanth, would you kneel before me?"

"W-why?" Xanth questioned, concerned of what was to follow.

"Just do it, please? I have something to say."

Xanth moved into place, hesitantly awaiting Arlowe's next decision.

"Prince Xan'El'Th, Son of King Conquest and Queen Be'Ail'La, Hero of the Kharakian War," Arlowe announced, drawing the attention of the pterravun people. "Will you honour your father's memory by joining me once more, ridding the world of those who intend to harm it, even to the risk of your own life?"

Xanth finally gave a smile. "I will keep you safe," he affirmed. "I will keep you all safe."

The prince motioned his father's blade to the boy's left shoulder, then right and finally to the centre of his chest before returning it to his side, offering his hand for Xanth to rise. "Then it is by my authority that I name you Knight Prince Xanth. Right-hand to the throne of Eyenridge, the eyes of the realm. My brother."

"Let's get moving," the newly-knighted pterravun stated, his confidence returned. "It's time we got Schukara back."

Arlowe balled his hand into a fist, bumping it with Xanth. "Letting her go was never an option."

As the prince marched through the applauding crowd, departing to the top of the staircase, Xanth spoke to him once more, this time through his telepathy. "Hey, Arlowe?"

"Yes, Xanth?"

"Safe travels."

Arlowe smiled, comforted that the boy remembered. As he stepped towards the portal, returning to his allies through the emerald light, he opened his mind to answer the kind gesture. The envoy prepared to face his next journey.

"Safe travels, Xanth. I'll see you soon."

Glossary

Characters: (Main & supporting characters. Name and pronunciation respectively)

- Arlowe Artaven - (Ar·low Ar·tar·ven)
- Daria Elsforth - (Dar·ia Els·forth)
- Gill Wiksend - (Gill Wiks·end)
- Onyx - (On·ix)
- Schukara Parle - (Shoe·kara Parle)
- Xanth/Xan'El'Th - (Zan·th/Zan·El·Th)

- Adrestia - (Ad·rest·ia)
- Alaric - (A·lar·ic)
- Amizi - (A·meet·zee)
- Antoinetta Unecrosse - (An·tw·o·net·ta Oon·cross)
- Arkle - (Ark·el)
- Arrsk - (Arr·sk)
- Artemis - (Ar·tem·is)
- Athena - (Ath·ee·na)
- Avangeline Parle - (Av·an·gel·ine Parle)
- Baxka - (Backs·ka)
- Bela/Be'Ail'La - (Be·la/Be·Ail·La)
- Bromley Artaven - (Brom·ley Art·ta·ven)
- Brufraen - (Brew·fray·en)
- Cael - (Kale)
- Calidius - (Ca·lid·e·us)
- Caspus Molvo - (Cas·puss Mol·vo)
- Chidike - (Chi·dee·kay)
- Corla - (Core·la)
- Demetrius Thaedlon - (Dem·ee·tree·us Th·aid·lon)
- Einluthor - (Eye·n·loo·thor)
- Elaith Origauilor - (E·lay·th Oar·i·gway·lor)

- Evret Rainerus - (Ev·ret Rain·air·us)

- Garren Artaven - (Ga·ren Ar·tar·ven)

- Gor Peneh - (Gore Pe·neh)

- Gretchin Ardimauda - (Gret·chin Ar·di·maw·da)

- Kaat/Ka'Orl'At - (Ka·at/Ka·Orel·At)

- Kardus Holrakai - (Car·dus Hol·ra·kai)

- Karkdugan - (Car·k·due·gan)

- Kaxrax - (Kax·rax)

- Keila Thaedlon - (Key·la Th·aid·lon)

- Kellen - (Kel·len)

- Kivyx - (Kiv·ix)

- Kweez - (Qu·eez)

- Levanim - (Lev·a·neem)

- Lucine Artaven - (Lu·seen Ar·ta·ven)

- Lyra - (Lie·ra)

- Mao-Yr - (Ma·ow Ee·r)

- Mawve - (Maw·vay)

- Meriwa - (Me·ri·wah)

- Oril - (Oar·il)

- Ota-Rnshi - (Oat·a Rin·shi)

- Oxbig - (Ox·big)

- Qimmiq - (Kim·mik)

- Quelthen - (Quell·th·en)

- Reitgrar Omasis - (Reet·grar O·ma·sis)

- Rilit - (Ril·eet)

- Sael - (Sail)

- Seigfried Durwood - (See·g·free·d Dur·wood)

- Selma Velechinski - (Sell·ma Vel·e·chin·ski)

- Sulpaec'Sra - (Sool·pay·ec S·ra)

- Tibor - (Tee·bor)

- Ulysses - (You·li·sees)

- Umisdaec - (Oo·miss·day·ec)

- Ushnar - (Ush·nar)
- Valerius Pridesworn - (Va·lair·i·us Pride·sworn)
- Vernard - (Ver·nard)
- Yoskolo - (Yos·col·o)
- Zaara - (Zar·a)

Locations: (Name, pronunciation and information respectively)

- Aauwen - (Ow·oo·wen) - The central country of Argestra, inhabited only by Arn's grave.

- Äkin - (Ay·kin) - The realm of Arn, where the god spent their time creating the planet Katosus.

- Argestra - (Ar·guess·tra) - Central continent, where this book takes place.

- Caermyythen - (Kay·er·my·th·en) - A small village on the border between Calaveil and Aauwen.

- Calaveil - (Ca·la·veil) - The northern country of Argestra.

- Castle of Aalkeitirei Tuupaank - (All·kay·tear·eye Two·pah·n·k) - The royal castle of Thaedlon.

- Dairgersmire - (Dare·gers·mire) - A small village on the border between Hietruce and Vexinth.

- Erethys - (Er·e·th·is) - The realm where Nra and their demon hordes supposedly reside.

- Eyenridge - (Ay·en·ridge) - The capital city of Fertral

- Fertral - (Fer·tral) - The south-western country of Argestra.

- Haaroith - (Haa·roy·th) - The capital city of Vexinth.

- Hietruce - (High·truce) - The western country of Argestra.

- Imikuin - (Im·i·ku·een) - The northern continent.

- Iorverch - (E·your·ver·ch) - A village south of Haaroith, known for its hardy horses.

- Katosus - (Cat·o·suss) - The planet of which the continents reside.

- Kaxrax Village - (Kax·rax) - A village shielding a community of goblins from the kharakian's wrath.

- Kharaki - (Car·ra·ki) - The floating home of the kharakians.

- Logritrias - (Log·grit·ri·as) - The western continent.

- Quazin - (Qua·zin) - The south-eastern country of Argestra.

- Ryvineon - (Riv·in·eon) - The eastern country of Argestra.

- Seeleijae - (See·lie·z·yay) - A town at Calaveil's northern-most point.

- Shikith - (Shi·keith) - The southern continent.

- Stelgaren - (Stel·gar·en) - The capital city of Quazin.

- Templen - (Tem·plen) - The capital city of Ryvineon.

- Thaedlon - (Th·aid·lon) - The capital city of Hietruce.

- Tyreiin - (Tie·rain) - The eastern continent, known in modern times as 'Grandgrave'.

- Vexinth - (Vex·in·th) - The north-western country of Argestra.

- Wicilil - (Whis·i·lil) - The capital city of Calaveil.

- Wrejorick - (Ray·your·ick) - A territory of the dwarves, located underground to the mid-west.

Races: (Name, pronunciation and information respectively)

- Aautgal - (Out·gall) - Stone men, often described as humanoid golems.

- Fae - (Fay) - A mysterious race whose only documentation comes from the ruins they left behind.

   *Faegareskh - (Fay·gar·es·k) - The dominant fae government.

   *Faeurei - (Fay·your·eye) - Rebels against the Faegareskh.

- Graikhurst - (Grey·k·hurst) - The old name for goblins, cursed into their modern-day forms.

- Imaagen - (Im·aah·gen) - A serpentine creature, also known as a juvenile dragon.

- Kharakian - (Car·rak·i·an) - A race of cursed molten soldiers plaguing Eyenridge.

- Praisyl - (Pray·sil) - The demons of the Fifth Invasion.

- Pterravun - (Ter·ra·vun) - An underground collective, spending their days aiding lost souls.

   *Kaldaren ordein – (Cal·dar·en Or·day·n)

- Soreiku - (Sore·ay·ku) - A name given to those that train with dragons that have not yet ascended.

- Sorvanc - (Sore·van·k) - A name given to those infused with dragon blood through a draconic ritual.

- Vekaakran - (Vek·aak·ran) - The demons of the Third Invasion.

Creatures: (Name, pronunciation and information respectively)

- Amalgam - (A·mal·gam) - A necrotic beast made up of multiple corpses and their minds.

- Aracaria - (Ar·a·car·i·a) - An old corrupted spirit, infamous for her long trail of murders.

- Dredge - (Dread·ge) - A necrotic beast on all-fours, equipped with a corrosive venom.

- Lich - (Lit·ch) - A necrotic beast wielding magics alongside the mages that summoned them.

- Lurcher - (Lurch·er) - The most basic form of undead, often seen as risen corpses

- Prenomen - (Pren·o·men) - A necrotic beast wrapped in writhing bandages.

Schools of magic: (Name, pronunciation and information respectively)

- Conjurmancy - (Con·jur·man·sea) - The school of magic that focuses on summoning beasts and weapons.

- Daimancy - (Die·man·sea) - The school of magic used by demons, enhancing their natural abilities.

- Elemancy - (El·e·man·sea) - The school of magic utilizing the elements into forceful blasts of nature.

- Illumancy - (Ill·u·man·sea) - The school of magic that focuses on illusions and trickery.

- Incormancy - (In·cor·man·sea) - A forgotten school, supposed use of the magics of the mind.

- Necromancy - (Neck·ro·man·sea) - The school of magic that focuses on death magic.

- Sanamancy - (Sar·na·men·sea) - The school of magic that focuses on healing and protective barriers.

Religion: (Name, pronunciation and information respectively)

- Aigahki - (Ay·gah·ki) - A belief that Arn is the nature and life force that surrounds all.

- Arytholity - (Ar·i·thol·i·tea) - A belief that Arn is reborn, awaiting all in the afterlife.

- Castral - (Cas·tral) - The Holy Book of Arytholity and Riakhism.

- Draconity - (Dra·con·i·tea) - A belief that the dragons are the children of Arn, willing to guide them.

    *Ban-Gauon - (Baa·n Gau·on) - The Logritrian Dragon.

    *Hso-Dyeiih - (So Die·yay) - The Tyrenian Dragon.

    *Sei-Yau - (Say Yow) - The Argestran Dragon.

    *Dis-Utemhi - (Diss You·tem·he) - The Shikithian Dragon.

- Neo-Riakhism - (Ne·o Ree·ak·ism) - A belief that Aros' Fragments, each individual, watch over all.

- Orythosism - (Or·ith·os·ism) - A belief that Nra is Äkin's true ruler.

- Percial - (Per·sea·al) - The Holy Book of Neo-Riakhism.

- Riakhism - (Ree·ak·ism) - A belief that Aros, whole again, watches over all in their late father's place.

- Silaasan - (Sigh·las·ahn) - A belief that the elves, raised as Angels by Arn, watch over all in their place.

    *Silaas - (Sigh·las) - The Archangel.

    *Velethuil - (Ve·le·thoo·il) - The Angel of Return.

    *Estelar - (Es·te·lar) - The Angel of Generosity.

    *Rysanthir - (Ry·san·th·ir) - The Angel of Improvement.

    *Thessalia - (Th·ess·ah·lia) - The Angel of Regret.

*Lorelei - (Lore·eh·lie) - The Angel of Honour.

*Khiiral - (K·hear·all) - The Angel of Humility.

*Dain - (Dane) - The Angel of Remembrance.

*Sana - (Sah·na) - The Angel of Knowledge.

*Castien - (Cas·tea·en) - The Angel of Debt.

- The Altane - (Al·tane) - A mysterious cult, known by few, met by fewer, their motives known by none.

- Tsaraithi - (Sar·rai·thee) - A lesser-known branch of Aigahki, who's believers shun modern society.

- Uanun - (Oo·ah·nun) - The Holy Book of Silaasan.

Miscellaneous: (Name, pronunciation and information respectively)

- Antithetical Grenade - (An·ti·th·eh·ti·cal) - A bomb fuelled by the negative energy drawn from healing.

- Eldoraichi - (El·door·eye·chi) - A brand of violin.

- Snaipzroot - (Snipe·z·root) - A drug overtaking the popularity of the pipe, rolled and smoked.

The Äkin Calendar
And the comparisons between the world of Katosus and our own.

Timeline:
E.E.A (Early Existence Age)
-2355EEA to 0EEA
(2355 years of recorded history)

C.A (Conqueror's Age)
-1CA to 177CA
(Beginning of collected history/Demon Invasion began 164CA, ended 177CA)

S.A (Siren's Age)
178SA to 749SA
(Demon Invasion began 715SA, ended 749SA)

V.A (Vekaakran's Age)
750VA to 1064VA
(Demon Invasion began 1050VA, ended 1064VA)

A.A (Abomination's Age)
1065AA to 1353AA
(Demon Invasion began 1349AA, ended 1353AA)

P.A (Praisyl's Age)
1354PA to 1643PA
(Demon Invasion began 1632PA, ended 1643PA)

T.A (Titan's Age)
1644TA to 2078TA
(Demon Invasion began 2072TA, ended 2078TA)

8.A (Current Age)
2079∞ to Current Day

Seasons:

Spring: Land's Renewal (LR)

Summer: Land's Fertility (LF)

Autumn: Land's Legacy (LL)

Winter: Land's Death (LD)

Days:
(Based on the dwarven cities and 'Xaac', the dwarven word for 'Day')

Corxaac: Corsorc/Monday (Core·zak)

Osexaac: Osehin/Tuesday (Oh·s·zak)

Wrejorxaac: Wrejorick/Wednesday (Ray·your·zak)

Gexaac: Gexeth/Thursday (Geck·zak)

Revixaac: Revilom/Friday (Rev·i·zak)

Ysxaac: Ysangrir/Saturday (Ee·s·zak)

Nurxaac: Nuracke/Sunday (Nur·zak)

<u>Months:</u>
(Based on the Dwarven Exemplars)

Umisdae: January/Umisdaec, the first recorded dwarven leader and the inventor of dwarven politics.

Welenbern: February/Weldrana, the architect of the dwarven tunnel systems and the creator of the dwarven city schematics.

Reitres: March/Reitgrar, the first true smith, creating reliable weapons and tools for his race.

Strodres: April/Strodrec, the first true inventor, crafting the first railways, heavy machinery and other creations.

Grozres: May/Grozaes, the first golem engineer, creating the first golem and teaching others how to use their gift from Arn.

Sarsaebern: June/Sarsaebela Tyliege, the leading expert in magic, giving a greater understanding in the power of magic and its application.

Dolgalos: July/Dolgrin Audeucann, the champion of the Third Invasion, destroying the Vekaakran Tyrant.

Yalmolos: August/Yalmolim Tolenspech, the diplomat that secured peace and a new economy with the surface.

Thuvalos: September/Thuvin Omek, the creator of the Administration and all the guilds as a result.

Arandbern: October/Arandraek Malvoliis, the leading official on medicine and surgery, and the first to successfully attach a golem limb to a patient with no complications.

Nofabelos: November/Nofabelyn Kitgrous, the first amalgamation engineer, fusing great creations from different races to create machines superior in all ways to the parts that made it.

Unnamed Cycle 12: -/December

Printed in Great Britain
by Amazon

27813057R00335